"YOU WANT ME LIKE HELL, DON'T YOU?" CADE ASKED, HIS DARK EYES HOLDING HERS.

"Cade . . . don't do this to me," Bess whispered shakily as his fingers moved to her mouth.

"What am I doing to you?" he asked deeply, not quite in control anymore.

"I can't help what I feel," she whispered brokenly. She wanted his hard mouth with a passion that was already white-hot, and he'd barely touched her.

He was bending toward her, her breath mingling with his, her body taut in an arch that almost begged to feel his arms, to be held by him. And then he felt the weight of responsibility fall on him. Bess wanted him, but that was all it was. "You're too young and too green for me, Bess," he said coolly, forcing the words out. "Go home to Mama."

QUANTITY SALES

INDIVIDUAL SALES

Denim
and
Lace

Diana Blayne

A DELL BOOK

Published by
Dell Publishing
a division of
Bantam Doubleday Dell Publishing Group, Inc.
666 Fifth Avenue
New York, New York 10103

ISBN: 0-440-20627-8

Printed in the United States of America

Published simultaneously in Canada

May 1990

10 9 8 7 6 5 4 3 2 1

RAD

Denim
and
Lace

Chapter 1

The morning coffee was well under way, and the bride-to-be looked as if she'd stepped from the pages of *Vogue*. But at least one of the guests was trying her best not to look bored to death as she stood amid the muted noises of conversation and coffee being served. These were familiar sounds to Elizabeth Ann Samson; the rattle of delicate rose-patterned china cups in their elegant thin saucers, the rustle of linen napkins, the whisper of skin against silk and wool. She smiled a little, thinking how quickly she'd trade those luxurious sounds for the hiss of coffee boiling over on a campfire and being poured into a cracked white mug. But there was no use hoping for that kind of miracle. Cowboys and debutantes didn't mix. Everyone said so, especially her mother, Gussie. And it didn't make a bit of difference that Cade Hollister had somehow scraped up ten thousand dollars in cash to invest in her father's newest real estate deal. That wouldn't admit him to the elegant drawing room or to any party at the Samson mansion that Bess might invite him to. Bess was too shy to invite him, in the first place. And in the second, he had no use for her. He'd made that very clear three years ago, in a way that still made her faintly nervous around him. But love was inexplicable. It seemed to thrive on rejection. Hers must, she mused silently, because nothing Cade said or did stopped her from wanting him. . . .

"Are you going to Bermuda with us in the spring, Bess?" Nita Cain interrupted her thoughts with a smile. "We thought we might rent a villa and get in some deep-sea fishing."

"I don't know," Bess said as she balanced her cup of black coffee in its saucer. "Mother hasn't mentioned what she wants to do yet."

"Can't you go on vacation without her, just once?" Nita coaxed. "There are several well-placed businessmen on our stretch of beach, and you look sensational in a bikini."

Bess knew exactly what Nita was saying. The older girl had affairs with elegance and ease, and she was beautiful enough to attract any man she liked. She thought Bess was missing out on life, and she wanted to help her out of her rut. But it wouldn't work. Bess didn't have affairs, because the only man she'd ever wanted or ever would want was Cade. Anyone else would be just a poor substitute. Besides, she thought, she'd never match Nita for beauty, even if she tried to be a swinger.

Nita was dark and sultry and outgoing. Bess was tall and lanky and shy. She had shoulder-length brown hair with delicate blond highlights, and it waved toward her face and down her back with delightful fullness. She had soft brown eyes and a complexion that any model would have killed for, but her shyness kept men from looking at her too hard. She didn't have spirit or grace, because Gussie had those things and didn't like competition from her only child. So Bess stayed in the background, as she'd been trained to do, speaking when spoken to and learning French and etiquette and how to plan a banquet, when she'd much rather have been riding alongside Cade when he was rounding up calves at Lariat, the Hollisters' moderately successful cow-calf operation. It was a big ranch, but not modern. It was pretty much the same as it had been over a hundred years ago when one of Cade's ancestors came to Texas looking for trouble and found longhorn cattle instead.

"I can't go without Mother," Bess said, bringing herself back from the dreams again. "She'd be lonely."

"She could go, too, and take your father with her."

Bess laughed softly. "My father doesn't take vacations. He's much too busy. Anyway, he's been in something of a bind just lately. We're all hoping his new real estate project will go over well and take the worry lines out of his face. How was Rio?"

Nita spent the next ten minutes raving over the Italian count she'd met in that fabled city and discussing the delights of nude bathing in the count's private pool. Bess sighed without meaning to. She'd never gone bathing in the nude, or had an affair, or done any of the modern things that with-it young women did.

She was as sheltered as a nun. Gussie led and she followed. Sometimes she wondered why, but she always did it. That seemed to irritate Cade more than anything, that Gussie got her own way and Bess never argued. But Cade didn't want Bess. He'd made that clear three years ago, when Bess had turned twenty, and in a way, it was just as well. Gussie had bigger fish than Cade in mind for her daughter. She disliked Cade and made no secret of it, although Bess had never found out why. Probably it was because the Hollisters lived in an old house with worn carpets and linoleum and drove used cars and never seemed to get ahead. Cade dressed in worn denim and leather boots, and he always smelled of calf and tobacco. The men Bess was allowed to date smelled of Pierre Cardin cologne and brandy and imported cigars. She sighed. She'd have traded them all for one hour in Cade's arms.

She turned, idly scanning the crowded room. This coffee was for a newly engaged socialite. It was one of a round of coffees Bess had been to lately, and they were as boring as her life. Drinking coffee from old china stirred with silver spoons, aimlessly passing the time talking about holiday resorts and investments and the latest styles. And outside those immaculately clean windows, real life in the south Texas brush country was passing them all by. Real people lived in that world, which Bess had only caught a glimpse of. Real people who worked for a living, challenged the land and the weather, wore old clothes and drove old trucks and went to church on Sunday.

Bess glanced at Nita and wondered if she'd ever been inside a church except during the ceremony of one of her three failed marriages. Bess had gone once or twice, but she never seemed to find a place where she felt comfortable. The Hollisters were Baptist. They went to the same church where Cade's grandfather had been a deacon, and everyone knew and respected the family. They might not be rich, but they were well thought of. Sometimes, Bess thought, that might be worth a lot more than a big bankbook.

Several minutes later she escaped out the door and climbed behind the wheel of her silver Jaguar XJ-S, sinking into the leather seat with a long breath of relief. At least here she felt at home, out in the country with no one to tell her what to do. It was a nice change from the house.

She headed home, but as she passed the dirt road that led to the Hollister homeplace, she saw three calves wandering free of the cattle grid. Her brown eyes narrowed as she noticed a break in the fence. She scouted the horizon, but there was no horseman in sight. Turning onto the dirt road, she told herself that it was a necessary trip, not just an excuse to see Cade. It wouldn't do for the Hollisters to lose even one calf with the cattle market down so far because of the continuing drought. Hay had been precious and still was, and the calf crop was dropping early, because it was February and a month before Cade's cows usually dropped their calves. These little ones were obviously the product of cows who'd ignored Cade's rigid breeding program. She smiled to herself, thinking how brave those cows were, to defy him for love.

She was getting silly, she told herself as she wheeled into the yard, where chickens scurried to get out of her way. Her eyes moved lovingly over the big two-story clapboard house with its long porch. A weathered porch swing and two rocking chairs rested there, but only Elise Hollister, Cade's mother, ever had time to sit in them. Cade and Robert, his youngest brother, were always out on the ranch somewhere working. Gary, the middle brother, kept the books for the outfit, and Elise took in sewing to augment the money Cade won at rodeos. He was a top hand with a rope, and he'd made a lot of money on the rodeo circuit in calf roping and team roping. He was good at bareback bronc riding and steer riding as well. Bess worried about him. Last time, at the National Finals Rodeo in Las Vegas in December, he'd pulled a tendon in his leg and it had been weeks before he could walk without a limp. He had scars all over his arms and chest from the falls he'd taken, and a couple of mended bones as well. But without that extra money, they'd never have made their mortgage payments. Cade was a keen businessman, and since his father's death years ago he'd had the bulk of the responsibility for the ranch. It had aged him. He was only thirty-four, but he seemed mature and very adult, even hard to Bess. Not that it affected her feelings for him. Nothing, ever, seemed to change that sad fact.

She got out of the Jaguar, pausing to pet Laddie, the black-and-white border collie that helped the men work the cattle. Cade would get angry if he saw her, because Laddie was a cattle dog, not a petting dog. He didn't like her showing affection to anything on his land, least of all to him. But she thought he might like to know about the wayward calves.

Elise Hollister was in the kitchen. She called for Bess to come in, and Bess opened the screen door, careful not to bang it, because the spring had come loose and there was a small hole in the screening. The linoleum floors were cracked and faded. Compared with the big Samson house the Hollisters' home was a shack, but it was always clean and neat as a pin, because Elise kept it that way. Bess always felt at home on Lariat, and the lack of luxury didn't bother her one bit. It bothered Cade. He never snapped at her more than when she came here, which was rarely. She hadn't really had a good excuse since her father had persuaded Cade three years ago to give her riding lessons, and that hadn't lasted long. Gussie had managed to stop them just after they started, and Cade had seemed relieved. Of course it had been just after his successful attempt to get Bess to stop chasing him, and it had been something of a relief, even to her. Cade's callous behavior had upset her. She often wondered if he regretted it. She did, because it had left her slightly afraid of him. But her stubborn heart had never found another man to fasten itself on. Despite everything, it was still Cade.

He only came to the house to see her father, and that had been a very recent development. His attitude was somehow different. Gussie's hauteur bounced off him these days, for the most part, but the way he looked at Bess was new and a little unsettling. It was as if he was looking for something in her.

But he didn't like her on Lariat. She wondered if it might be because he disliked having her see how he lived, comparing his life-style with hers. But why would that matter to him when he wanted no part of her? She couldn't quite figure Cade out. She was in good company there. He was a mystery even to his mother.

Elise Hollister had gray hair, but she was elegant in

her way, tall and slender and sharp-featured, with kind, dark eyes and a ready smile. She was wearing a cotton print shirtwaist dress, and her eyes twinkled as she moved away from the sink to wipe her hands on a dishcloth.

"Hello, Bess," she said, welcoming the younger woman like a long-lost daughter. "What brings you here?"

"Cade's got some calves out on the highway," she said. "The fence is down, and I thought I'd better tell somebody." She blushed, thinking how transparent she must seem to this warm, quiet woman.

Elise smiled. "That's very kind of you. You look pretty this morning."

"Thank you. I've been to a coffee," Bess said with a kind of sophisticated cynicism. "The daughter of one of Mama's friends is getting married, so I had to make an appearance." She grimaced. "I wanted to go riding, but Mama says I'll fall off the horse and break something vital."

"You ride very well," Elise said. Coming from her it was a compliment because she could ride every bit as well as the cowboys on Lariat.

"You're sweet, but I'll never be in your class." Bess sighed, looking around the neat, clean kitchen. "I envy you, being able to cook. I can't boil water. Every time I sneak into the kitchen and try to learn from Maude, Mama explodes."

"I love to cook," Elise said hesitantly, reluctant to offend Bess by making any remarks about Gussie. "Of course, I've always had to. And around here, food is more important than anything—at least, to my sons," she laughed. "I'm lucky to get a chicken bone at meal-times."

Bess laughed too. "I guess I'd better go."

Elise studied the quiet young face with eyes that saw deep. "Cade's out with some of the boys, checking on the heifers we bred last fall. Some of them are dropping early. I feel rather sorry for whoever let the bulls in with them too early."

Bess knew what she meant. "I hope he can get work somewhere else," she added. "It's some of the new calves that are out on the highway."

Elise nodded. "I'll send Robbie out to get Cade," she said. "Thanks again for stopping by. You wouldn't like some cake and coffee?"

"I would," Bess replied. "But I have to check in by noon, or Mama will send out the Texas Rangers to find me. Thanks anyway."

She climbed back into the Jaguar and pulled back onto the farm road that led to the highway. Her eyes restlessly searched the horizon for Cade, but she knew she wouldn't see him. She spent altogether too much time looking for him. Not that it would do her any good to catch him. Even if he had a wild, secret passion for her—a really laughable thought, she mused—he had too much responsibility on Lariat to marry anyone. He had his mother and two brothers and a respectable amount of land and cattle to oversee. It wasn't realistic to think that such a responsible man would chuck it all for the sake of any woman.

She darted a glance at the calves as she drove past them on her way home. Well, at least they were standing beside the road, not in it, and Robbie, Cade's youngest brother, would find him and tell him about them.

But it would have been so nice if Cade had been at the house. She smiled, indulging yet another daydream that ended with herself in Cade's arms, with his dark eyes full of love as they looked down at her. Always the same dream, she thought. Always the same hopeless reality. She really would have to grow up, she decided. If only she could manage a way to do it without stuffing her overprotective mother into a croker sack and hiding her in the attic.

She smiled at the thought just as her eyes caught a movement in the grass beside the road. She slowed the Jaguar and stopped. A calf was lying there. It might be hurt. She couldn't just leave it there. She pulled over onto the side of the road and cut the engine. Now what was she going to do? she wondered as she got out of the car.

Chapter 2

The long stretch of Texas horizon looked lonely in winter. The man sitting quietly astride the big bay gelding understood loneliness. It had been his constant companion for some years, with only occasional and unsatisfying interludes to numb the ache he could never ease. His dark eyes narrowed on the sleek silver Jaguar paused at the road where his calves were straying, and he wondered if it had just come from the house. Probably it had. Gussie Samson wouldn't have bothered to tell him his calves were out, but her daughter would. Despite all his efforts to drive her away, and his attacks of conscience because of the method he'd once used, Bess kept coming back for more. He wondered sometimes why he didn't just give in and stop tormenting them both. But that was

madness. He was poor and she was rich, and all he
could ever offer her was a brief affair. That wouldn't
do for Bess. It wouldn't do for him either. He had too
many principles and too much moral fiber to compromise her for his own satisfaction. He wanted her hon-
orably or not at all. Besides all that, she was no match
for his passionate temperament, and that was the one
thing that stopped him from letting her get close. He'd
break her gentle spirit in no time. The thought made
him sad, made him even lonelier as he turned it over
in his mind. Bess was all heart, the gentlest creature
he'd ever known except for his own mother.

Bess was made for a palatial house with elegant
white columns, surrounded by white fences and stables and a neat red barn. Someday she'd find a man
who fit into her elegant world, who had the money
and power to keep her in diamonds and furs and spoil
her rotten. He could only give her a life of hard work,
and she wasn't suited for that. She never would be.

Cade Hollister leaned over the pommel of his saddle, his black eyes thoughtful as he watched her get
out of the car and move toward a calf that was down.
That wouldn't do. Not only would she ruin that pretty
and probably expensive green dress she was wearing,
but the mama cow might take exception to her interference and charge her. He urged the horse into motion. The leather creaked softly against his weight and
he winced a little from the lingering soreness in his left
leg. He'd taken top money at the Las Vegas National
Finals Rodeo, but he'd pulled a tendon in the bareback
bronc riding. Now he was hoping he could get back in
peak condition before the San Antonio rodeo. A lot
was riding on his skill with cattle and horses. Too

much. His mother and two brothers were depending on him to keep Lariat solvent, which was not an easy task even at the best of times. His father had died ten years before, but his debts hadn't. Cade was still trying to pay off his father's ruined dream of turning Lariat into an empire.

As he approached Bess, he could see her worried face. She looked the way she did when something was eating at her. Usually she walked when she was upset, and usually it was her mother, Gussie, who caused those long hikes in the Texas brush country south of San Antonio. Gussie was a selfish, careless woman who used her only daughter in much the way a plantation mistress would make use of a slave woman. Cade had watched it for years with emotions ranging from disgust to contempt. What made it so much worse was that Bess didn't seem to realize what a hold her possessive mother had on her, and she made no effort to break it. Bess was twenty-three now, but she had the reserve and shyness of a young girl. Her mother captured the spotlight as her due, wherever they went. Bess was a frail shadow of the elegant, beautiful Gussie, and she was never allowed to forget that she fell short of the mark as far as her mother was concerned.

She was kneeling beside the calf now, and Cade urged his mount into a gallop, attracting her attention. She got up when she spotted him, looking lost and alone and a little frightened. Her long light brown hair was loose for a change, and she had no makeup on. Bess had soulful brown eyes and a complexion like honied cream. Her face was a full oval, soft with tenderness and compassion, and she had a figure that had once driven Cade to drink. She didn't flaunt it, but any man with eyes could see how perfect her full breasts were, rising above a small waist and gently flaring hips to long, alluring legs. But her mother never encouraged her to make the most of her assets. Very likely Gussie didn't want the competition, or to have a daughter who looked like an attractive twenty-three-year-old woman, which would remind Gussie of her own age.

As Cade neared her, the contrast between them was much more noticeable than at a distance. Bess was a lady, and Cade had been raised rough and without the social graces. She was a society girl and he was part Comanche, a cowboy who was expected to come to the back door when Frank Samson had hired him three years ago to teach Bess how to ride. He still bristled with anger remembering how those riding lessons had ended so abruptly, and for what reason. That, too, had been Gussie's fault. Most of the resentments in his adult life could be laid at her door, and foremost of them was the untimely death of his father. He wondered if Bess knew about it. He couldn't imagine that Gussie had ever told her, and Bess would have been too young to remember. Cade, who was thirty-four to Bess's twenty-three, remembered all too well.

Bess Samson saw Cade coming toward her, and all her dreams seemed to merge in him. Her heart jumped up like a startled thing, and she had to clench her teeth to control her scattered emotions. Even though she'd hoped that she might see him at the house, it was a shock to have him actually appear. The calf was hurt or sick, and Cade cared about little lost things, even if he didn't care about her.

Whatever Cade felt, he kept to himself. Except for

one devastating lapse when he'd become a cold, mocking, threatening stranger, he'd kept Bess at a cold distance and treated her with something bordering contempt. She knew that he didn't have much time for rich society girls, but his contempt even extended to her mother, who, God knew, was harmless enough.

She couldn't quite meet those cold black eyes under the wide brim of Cade's Stetson when he reined up in front of her. He wasn't a handsome man. He had strong features, but his face was too angular and broad, his eyebrows too heavy, his nose too formidable and his mouth too thin and cruel. His only saving grace was his exquisite physique. He had the most perfect body Bess had ever seen in her life, broad-shouldered, narrow-hipped, long-legged, and powerful. He looked lithe and slim until he moved into action, and then he was all muscle and masculinity. But Bess tried not to notice those things. It was too embarrassing to remember what had happened between them in the past, and the contempt he still held for her, along with a barely hidden anger.

"I . . . went to the house to tell someone that the calves were out," she stammered. He made her feel like a schoolgirl. "But then when I came back, I saw this little one lying down. . . ."

Cade swung out of the saddle gracefully, although he still favored the leg with the pulled tendon a little when he went to kneel beside the little red-and-white-coated calf. "It's dangerous to go near a downed calf when his mama's close by," he informed her without looking up. His lean, sure hands went over the calf while he checked for injury or disease. "I don't run polled cattle here. Mine have horns, and they use them."

"I know that," she said gently. "Is she all right?"

"She's a he, and no, he's not all right. It looks very much like scours." He stood up, lifting the calf gently in his arms. "I'll take him back with me." He spared her a glance. "Thanks for stopping."

She walked after him. "Can I . . . hold him for you while you get on the horse?" she offered unsteadily.

He stopped at the bay and turned, his eyes twinkling for an instant with surprise. "In that dress?" he asked, letting his eyes run down her slender figure with blatant appreciation. "Silk, isn't it? You'd go home smelling of calf and worse, and the dress would most likely be ruined. His plumbing's torn up," he added dryly, putting it discreetly.

But she only smiled. "I wouldn't mind," she said. "I like little things."

His jaw tautened. "Little things, sick things, stray animals," he added to her list. "Go home, Bess. You don't belong out in the sticks or on a ranch. You were meant for better things."

He laid the calf gently in front of the pommel and swung easily up behind it, positioning it as his hand caught the reins. Bess watched him, her eyes faintly hungry, helpless. He looked down at her and saw that look, and his own eyes began to narrow and darken.

"Go home," he repeated, much more roughly than he meant to, because the sight of her disturbed him so.

She sighed softly. "All right, Cade." She turned and went back to her car, her head lowered.

Cade watched her with an expression that would have spoken volumes, even to an innocent like Bess.

Without another word he turned his horse and headed back toward Lariat.

Bess wanted to watch him ride away, but she'd already given away too much. She loved him so. Why couldn't she stop? Heaven knew, he didn't want her, but she kept flinging herself against the stone wall of his heart.

She climbed back into the car, feeling weary and numb. She wished she could fight him. Maybe if she were spirited, he'd notice her, but she loved him far too much to go against him in any way. She wondered sometimes if that wasn't the problem. He was worse when she knuckled under. She had spirit, it was just that she'd been trained from her childhood not to express it. It was neither dignified nor ladylike to brawl, as Gussie often put it.

Bess pulled the car out into the road, feeling depressed. She was decorative and well-mannered, and her life was as dead as a rattlesnake lying flattened in the middle of the highway. Her life had no adventure, no spark. She was nothing except an extension of Gussie. And not a very attractive extension at that, she realized bitterly.

Her father was home when she got there, and he looked twice his age.

"I thought you were going to be in Dallas until tomorrow," she said as she hugged him warmly. He was only a little taller than she was, dark-eyed with salt-and-pepper hair and a live-wire personality.

"I was," he returned, "but something came up. No, I won't tell you, so stop snooping," he added when she opened her mouth to speak. "It will work out. It's got to."

"Business, I suppose," she murmured.

"Isn't it always?" He loosened his tie and looked around at the black-and-white marble floor leading to a carpeted staircase. There was a Waterford crystal chandelier in the foyer and elegantly furnished rooms off both sides of the hall. "My God, it gets worse every day. No matter how hard I work, I just go backward. Sometimes, Bess, I'd like to chuck it all and go to Africa. I could live in a hut somewhere in the jungle and ride an elephant."

"Africa is in turmoil, most of the jungle has been eaten by the elephants, and some of the little ones are even being transplanted to other countries in an experiment to see if they can repopulate in areas with sufficient vegetation," Bess informed him.

"You and your damned *National Geographic* Specials," he muttered. "Never mind. I'll sign aboard *Moulin à Vent* and help Jacques Cousteau and his son explore what's left of the seas."

"They have a new windship now. Its name is—"

"I'll tell your mother you didn't go to the coffee," he threatened.

She laughed. "Okay, I'll stop. Where is Mama?"

"Upstairs primping. I told her I'd take her to San Antonio for lunch." He checked his watch. "If she gets finished in time."

"She's still beautiful," she reminded her father. "You can't rush beauty."

"I've been trying for twenty-four years," he said. "Next year we celebrate our silver anniversary. They've been good years, despite your mother's hairbrained spending. I hope I can keep enough in the coffers to support her diamond habit," he chuckled, but his eyes didn't laugh. "It's getting to be an ordeal. I've just taken one of the biggest gambles of my financial career, and if it doesn't pay off, I really don't know what we'll do."

Bess frowned because he sounded worried. "Daddy, can I help?"

"Bless you, darling, no. But thank you for caring."

"Mama cares too," she said hesitantly.

"In her own way," he agreed. "I hoped in the beginning that it was really love on her part and not just an attraction to the good life. Then I settled for friendship. We haven't had the best of marriages, but I promise you I've loved her enough for both of us. I still do," he said, smiling.

Her big brown eyes searched his face. "Nita wants me to go down to the Caribbean with her."

"Your mother will have a fit."

"Yes, I know. I don't really want to go anyway."

Frank Samson grimaced. "Yes, you do. You're entitled to a life of your own. It's just that your mother doesn't realize how possessive she is. She leads you around like a puppy, and you let her," he said, pointing a lean finger her way. "You're a big girl now. Stop letting her run over you."

"She means well," Bess began hesitantly.

"Don't wait too long," he added. "Parents can do a lot of damage without realizing it."

"I'm not damaged," she protested, although in a sense she was. She wanted Cade, and her mother would fight her tooth and nail if she knew how badly.

"Where in the world have you been?" Gussie Samson muttered angrily as she came down the staircase in a delicately woven white-and-cream wool suit with pink accessories. Her tinted blond hair was elegantly coiffed and her makeup was perfect. In her younger days Gussie Granger Samson had had a brief career on the stage. Her roles had been supporting ones, not leading ones, but she still acted as if she'd been a full-fledged star, right down to the elegance of her carriage.

"I stopped by Lariat to tell Elise some of their calves got out of the fence," Bess said.

Gussie glared at her with angry green eyes. "I suppose Cade was at the house?"

"No, Cade wasn't at the house," Bess replied quietly.

Gussie sighed angrily. "I don't want you near that man. He's a common cowboy. . . ."

"He's an able and intelligent man with great potential," Frank argued, putting an arm around his wife. "Stop riding him. All that is in the past, remember? And better forgotten."

Gussie flushed, darting a glance at Bess. "Never mind the past," she told Frank quickly. "Shall we go?"

Bess was more in the dark than ever after that statement. She wondered if she knew her parents at all, especially Gussie. But she wasn't one to pry into people's secrets, so she smiled and waved good-bye to her parents and went upstairs to change.

That night she overheard an argument between her parents over money, and although they made up quickly, she couldn't forget it. The next evening a man came to see her father.

"Who is he?" Bess asked Gussie curiously.

"I don't know, darling," Gussie said nervously. "Your father's been in a terrible mood for two days. He snaps and snarls and his color is bad. I don't know what's wrong, but something is."

"Can't you ask him?"

"I did. He only stared at me. There's a party tomorrow night at the River Grill. Want to come with your father and me?" she coaxed. "The Merrills will be there, and their son, Grayson, is going to be with them."

"Gray's very nice, but I don't want to be thrown at him, if you don't mind," she said softly. "I'm not in the market for a rich husband."

"You'll enjoy yourself," Gussie assured her, smiling. "Now, no more arguments. You know you love seafood, and Gray is just back from a month in Europe; he'll be full of stories. You can wear your new gray crepe dress and that pretty fox cape I bought you for Christmas."

"But, Mother . . ."

"Let's have some coffee. Ask Maude to fix a tray, dear, and perhaps your father and his guest will join us, there's a good girl," Gussie added, patting Bess's hand absently.

Bess gave up. It was easier than trying to fight Gussie, but she knew that someday she was going to have to stand up to her. Giving in was a dead end. Her father was right. Odd, she thought, that her father should have made such a statement, when it was usually Cade who disliked Gussie's overbearing maternity. She knew that Cade and her father talked a good deal when they had business meetings about the new real estate investment. But surely Cade wouldn't have talked to her father about so personal a subject. Would he?

She came back from the kitchen still pondering, when Gussie came running toward her, wild-eyed and breathless.

"Your father's guest left, and now Frank's locked the study door and I can't make him answer me!" she cried. "Bess, something is terribly wrong!"

"But, what could—"

They heard the chilling, loud report of a pistol and they both froze in place. Then Bess turned and ran down the hall to the study, trying the door with both hands, banging on it, kicking.

"Daddy!" she screamed. She turned to Gussie. "Call the police!"

"The police?" Gussie just stood in place, white and shaking.

Bess ran to the phone, ignoring her shocked mother, and her hands shook as she searched frantically for the number, dialed it, and gave her sketchy information to the man who answered the phone.

Minutes later sirens wailed toward the house, and the nightmare began. The door to the study was finally forced open. Bess got a brief and all too good look at her father's body, where it was sprawled on the carpet in a pool of blood. She shuddered and had to run into the guest bathroom as her stomach emptied itself. Gussie had gone upstairs even before the police came, in shock, and Bess phoned the doctor when she came out of the bathroom.

The rest of the night went by in a blur of pain, grief, and numb shock. She answered questions until she wanted to scream, vaguely aware that Cade was suddenly there.

He fielded the police, lifted Bess in his hard, strong

arms, and carried her up the staircase into her room. She was barely coherent and shaking all over with mingled horror and fear. "The police . . . !" she whispered huskily.

"I'll cope with everything," he said firmly, easing her down onto the bed. He removed her shoes and gently covered her quivering body with a sheet. "Try to sleep. The doctor is with your mother, but I'll send him along when he's finished."

"He killed himself," she said, choking.

"Lie still. Everything will be all right," he promised. His dark eyes scanned her white face. "If you need me, just yell. I'll be around for a while. At least until you're asleep."

Her eyes searched his hard face and she reached up with a numb hand to touch it while tears escaped her eyes. "Thank you."

He clasped her hand for an instant and then laid it beside her on the coverlet. "I'll be back in a few minutes."

The doctor came and gave her a sedative, murmuring comforting things. She was aware of Cade's concerned gaze once or twice, but then the sedative took effect and she slept. When she woke, the house was empty, and the pain began.

Gussie was no help at all. She wailed and moaned and had hysterics every two hours, and took sedatives by the handful. As the day wore on, Bess began to realize just what a headache she'd inherited. If this was any indication of what was to come, her life was going to be hell.

Cade hadn't come back. She found that curious, since she knew he'd been there the night before, but apparently he'd made all the arrangements and had felt that Gussie wouldn't welcome his presence.

"I'm so glad you're strong, Bess," Gussie sniffed as they sat in the living room. "I couldn't have coped."

"I didn't. Cade did," Bess said quietly. "He carried me upstairs and got the doctor. I caved in too."

"You mean that man was in my house all night?" Gussie raged. "I won't have him here, I won't!"

"This is no time for hysterics, Mama," Bess said in a soothing tone. "I couldn't attend to details, but Cade did. Whatever you think of him, Daddy liked him, they were friends." She shuddered to think of Cade having to see what she'd seen through that opened door. He'd liked her father. "Why did he do it?" she asked huskily. "Why? I don't understand what's happened. Daddy was rational and strong. . . ."

"We'll know soon enough," Gussie said. "Now, do get me some coffee, darling, please. We'll sit and talk."

Their attorney, Donald Hughes, came to the house just after lunch to tell them what was going on prior to the reading of the will, which would be the next day, after the funeral. Cade had arranged the funeral, too, thank God, with Donald's help.

Bess listened to Donald's quiet voice with a feeling of utter shock, and Gussie's face went from white to red to paste.

"We're what?" Gussie faltered.

"You're bankrupt," Donald replied gently. "The investment scheme your husband involved himself in was a fake. The perpetrators are already out of the country and can't be extradicted. Frank invested everything he had. That's gone, along with Cade's ten thousand dollars. And unfortunately Frank guaranteed Cade's money back to the penny. I'm sorry. It's all legal. There's nothing you can do, I'm afraid."

There was one thing Gussie could do, and she did it. She fainted.

Bess sat there with her eyes glued to the lawyer's face, not moving, not speaking as she tried to absorb what Donald had said. Her father had been involved in an illegal operation, and it had failed. He'd lost everything and sold out his friends, and that was why he'd killed himself.

That was understandable, in a way. But now Gussie and Bess were left with his debts and they were going to lose everything. Worst of all, they were going to lose the house. It would mean having to move and being poor, and having to start again from scratch. Bess looked down at her mother, absently thinking that Gussie even looked beautiful when she was unconscious. Bess wished she could faint, too, and wake up to find that it was all just a bad dream. But Donald was very real and so was her mother. It was all real. And her problems were only just beginning.

Chapter 3

Bess was a little calmer by nightfall. Except that Gussie was wearing on her nerves. She wondered how she was going to cope with everything. When the shock finally wore off, it would be much worse, she knew.

It had started to snow. The silent feathering of it in the darkness was almost reverent, but Bess only half-noticed the white blanket covering the ground. A pickup truck, an old familiar one, pulled into the driveway, its headlights blinding her for an instant before it stopped and the engine was cut off. Cade. She relaxed, just a little. Somehow she'd known that he would come back.

"Who's that outside, Bess?" Gussie asked, pausing on the landing upstairs to look down at her daughter.

"It's Cade," Bess replied and waited for the inevitable explosion.

"Again?" Gussie said wearily. "He'll want his money of course."

"You know very well he didn't come for that," Bess said gently. "He's come to see about us. Can't you be a little grateful for all he's done already? Neither of us was able to cope with the funeral arrangements, and that's a fact."

Gussie backed down. "Yes, I'm grateful," she said, wiping away more tears. "But it's hard to be grateful to Cade. He's made things so difficult over the years, Bess. Elise and I were once friends, did you know? It's because of Cade that we aren't anymore. No matter," she said when Bess tried to question her. "It's all over now. I'm going upstairs, darling. I can't talk to him. Not now."

She watched her mother move tiredly back into her bedroom with a sinking feeling that her life was going to be unbearable from now on. Her father's unexpected suicide had shocked the small Texas community almost as much as it had astounded Frank Samson's family. None of the scandal had been his fault. He'd been an innocent pawn in the fraud. Cade wouldn't blame him, though, or his family. Cade had too much sense of family himself to do that.

She peeked out the lace curtain, her soft brown eyes hungry for just the sight of the man outside. She pushed the long honey-brown hair from her shoulders, idly tugging it into a ponytail that abruptly fell apart. Cade had that effect on her. He made her nervous, he excited her, he colored her life. She was twenty-three, but still a sheltered innocent, because her father had been unusually strict. Maybe that was why Cade wouldn't have anything to do with her. He'd been raised strictly, too, and his family was staunchly Baptist. Seducing innocents would be unthinkable to such a man, so it hadn't been surprising that Cade acted as if she didn't even exist most of the time.

Of course he had a lot on his mind. But he was nothing like his younger brothers, Robert and Gary, whom she adored. Cade never flirted with her or asked her out. He probably never would, she wasn't his type, as he'd told her once. She could still blush about that, remembering her shy worship of him the summer he'd taught her to ride and what he'd done about it.

Bess knew that he'd lost far more than he could spare because of her father, and she wondered how in the world she and her flighty, spendthrift mother were ever going to settle the debts. *Oh, Dad,* she thought with a bitter smile, *what a mess you've landed us all in.* She spared a thought for that poor, tortured man who hadn't been able to bear the disgrace he'd brought on his family. She'd loved him, despite his weakness. It was hard giving him up this way.

Outside, the wind blew up, but it didn't slow Cade's quick, hard stride. She knew that a hurricane wouldn't, once he set his mind on something. Bess shivered a little as she saw him heading toward the front door, his worn, dark raincoat brushing the high grass as he walked through it, snow melting as it fell against the brim of his gray Stetson. He walked as he did everything else, relentlessly, with strides that would have made two of hers. As he came into the light from the porch, she got a glimpse of cold dark eyes and a deeply tanned face.

He had very masculine features, a jutting brow and a straight nose and a mouth like a Greek statue's. His cheekbones were high and his eyes were very nearly black. His hair, too, was very nearly black, and thick and straight, always neatly cut, very conventionally, and neatly combed. He was tall and lean and sensuous, with powerful long legs and big feet. Bess adored the very sight of him—worn clothes, battered Stetson, and all. His lack of wealth had never bothered her. Her mother's frank dislike of him was the major stumbling block. That, and Cade's cold indifference. She thought sometimes that she'd never live down that long-ago confrontation with him, that he'd never forget she'd thrown herself at him. Looking back, her own audacity shocked her. She wasn't a flirt, but Cade would never believe it now.

He was at the door before she realized it, towering over her as she stood in the doorway to greet him. He stared at her narrowly. She was wearing a pale green silk dress, and her big brown eyes were full of sadness.

The grief in her eyes disturbed him. "Open the door, Bess," he said quietly.

She did, immediately. His voice had a deep, drawling authority despite the fact that he rarely raised it. He could make his toughest cowhands jump when he spoke in that quiet tone. He was a hard man, because his life had made him into one. Old Coleman Hollister hadn't spared Cade, though he'd been indulgent enough with his younger sons. Cade had been the firstborn, and Old Man Hollister had groomed him carefully to take over the ranch when the time came.

Apparently he'd done a good job of it. Cade had a great track record with the money he made on the rodeo circuit.

He strode into the hall without taking off his hat. He had the knack of hiding his strongest feelings, with the exception of his bad temper, so Cade looked down at her without showing any emotion. Bess looked tired, he thought, and Gussie had probably been giving her hell. Her soft oval face was flushed, but it only made her lovelier, right down to that straight nose over a sweet bow of a mouth. He didn't want to take it out on Bess, but the sight of her caused its usual physical response and made him uncomfortable. There were a hundred reasons why he couldn't have Bess, no matter how badly he wanted her.

"Where's your mother?" he asked.

"Lying down." She'd already chewed the lipstick off her lower lip. Now she started on the upper one. He made her feel much younger than her twenty-three years.

"How are you?" He was watching her still, with that dark appraisal that disturbed her so.

"I'll do. Thank you for all you've done," she said. "Mother was grateful too."

"Was she? My mother and some of the other neighbors are bringing dinner and supper over for you tomorrow," he added. "No arguments. It's the way things are done. The fact that you've got money doesn't set you that far apart."

"But we don't have money," she said, smiling ruefully. "Not anymore."

"Yes, I know."

She looked up, defeated. "I guess you know, too,

that we're going to lose everything we have. I only hope we'll have enough money to repay you and the other investors."

"I didn't come here to talk business," he said quietly. "I came to see if I could do anything else to help."

She had to fight tears. "No," she said. "Heaven knows, you've already done more than your share, Cade."

"You look tired," he said, his dark eyes sweeping over her creamy skin now pale with fatigue. She had big brown eyes, a peaches-and-cream complexion, and a body that made him ache every time he looked at it. She wasn't pretty. Without makeup she was fairly plain. But Cade saw her with eyes that had known her most of her life, and they found her lovely. She didn't know that. He'd made sure she didn't know it. He had to.

He removed his hat, unloading snow onto the faded Oriental rug, onto his worn boots. "Mother and the boys send their condolences too," he added, and his eyes darkened as he looked down at her.

Bess misunderstood that dark appraisal. He looked at her as if he despised her. Probably he did, too, she thought miserably. She was her father's daughter, and her father's risky venture might have cost him his ranch. She knew he'd had to borrow heavily to scrape up the money to invest in her father's venture. Why had he done it? she wondered. But, then, who could ever figure Cade?

"That's very kind of them, considering what my father cost you all," she replied.

A corner of his mouth curled up, and it wasn't a kind smile. "We lost our shirts," he said. He reached into his pocket for a cigarette and without bothering to ask if she minded, lit it. He let out a thick cloud of smoke, his eyes taking in her thinness, the unhealthy whiteness of her face. "But you know that already. Your mother is going to have hell adjusting."

That was true. "She isn't strong," she said absently, lowering her eyes to his broad chest. Muscles rippled there when he breathed. He was powerfully built, for all his slimness. She'd seen him without a shirt, working in the fields in the summer, and the memory of it made her feel warm all over. With his shirt off, he was devastating. Bronzed muscle, covered with a thick, sexy wedge of hair that ran from his chest down to his lean stomach, into the belt at his jeans. . . .

"She smothers you," he returned, cutting into her shocking thoughts. "She always has. You're twenty-three, but you act sixteen. She'll never let you grow up. She needs somebody to lean on. Now that your father's gone, you'll be her prop. She'll wear you down and bring you down, just as she did him."

Her dark eyes flinched. "What do you know about my mother?" she demanded. "You hate her, God knows why . . ."

"Yes, I do," he said without hesitation, and his black eyes pierced hers, glittering like flaming coals. "And God does know why. You don't know what she really is, but you'll find out someday. But it will be too late."

"What can I do, Cade, walk out on her?" she cried. "How could I, when she's just lost everything! I'm all she's got."

"And she's all you'll ever have," he returned coldly. "Cold comfort in your old age. She's a selfish, cruel little opportunist with an eye to the main chance and her own comfort. Given a choice between you and a luxurious life-style, she'd dump you like yesterday's garbage."

She wanted to hit him. He aroused the most violent sensations in her. He always had. She hated that cold look on his face, the devastating masculinity of him that put her back up even at a distance. But she kept her feelings to herself, especially her temper. "You don't know either of us," she said.

He moved a little closer, threatening her now with just the warmth of his body, his superior height. He looked down at her with an expression in his eyes that made her toes curl inside her shoes.

"I know what I need to know," he said. He studied her face in the silence of the hall. "You're very pale, little one," he said then, his voice so soft that it didn't even sound like Cade's. "I'm sorry about your father. He was a good man. Just misguided and gullible. He didn't force any of us to invest, you know. He was as badly fooled by the deal as we were."

"Thank you," she said huskily, fighting tears. "That's a very tolerant attitude to take." Her eyes searched his. "But it won't save Lariat," she said sadly, remembering Cade's dreams for his family ranch. "Will it?"

"I'll save Lariat," he said, and at that moment he looked as if he could do anything. One eye narrowed as he studied her. "Don't let Gussie own you," he said suddenly. "You're a woman, not her little girl. Start acting your age."

Her eyebrows shot up. "How?"

"My God," he said heavily. "Don't you even know?"

His eyes dropped to her soft mouth. He stared at it intently, and he was standing so close to her that she could smell the leather of his vest, feel the warmth of him as his finger gently caressed her parted lips. The acrid smoke from his cigarette drifted past her nostrils, but it didn't even register. His dark eyes were on hers, and she'd never seen them so close. He had lashes as thick as her own, and tiny lines beside his eyes. His nose had a small crook in it that was only visible this close, as if it had been broken. His mouth . . . oh, his mouth! she thought achingly, looking at its chiseled lines, already feeling the hardness of it. She'd wondered for years how it would feel to kiss him, to be close to him. But Cade was like the moon. This was the closest he'd ever come to her, except for that one time when he'd only meant to frighten her, and she didn't even move for fear that he might move away. He might kiss her . . . !

But a tiny sigh worked its way out of her tight throat, and it seemed to break the spell. His head lifted, and there wasn't a trace of expression on his dark face. He moved away from her, without a word. But he kept his back to her for a long moment, quietly smoking his cigarette. That long, intense scrutiny had his heart turning cartwheels, and it would never do to let Bess see how vulnerable she made him.

"We'll pay you back somehow," she said after a minute.

He turned, as if the statement made him angry. "Will you? How?"

"I'll find a way. I'm not helpless, even if I am a mere woman in your eyes," she added with a faint smile.

He looked as formidable as a cold marble statue. "Challenging me?" he asked in a softly dangerous tone. His dark eyes mocked her. "That's been tried before, but go ahead if you feel lucky."

She almost did. But those nearly black eyes had made men back down, and she was just a grieving shadow of a woman.

"Please thank your mother for her concern," she said quietly. "I'm sure you have better things to do than bother with us."

"Your father was my friend," he said shortly. "I valued him, regardless of what happened."

He turned toward the door without glancing at her.

"I'll be in touch," he said as he reached for the doorknob and pulled open the big front door with its huge silver knocker. "Don't worry. We'll work out something."

Her eyes closed. She was sick all over. Just last week she'd been planning parties and helping her mother choose flowers for a coming-out party. And now their world was in shreds. Their wealth was gone, their friends had deserted them. They were at the mercy of the courts. Miss Samson of Spanish House was now just plain Bess.

"It's a long way to fall," Cade was saying. "From debutante to poverty. But sometimes it takes a fall to get us out of a rut. It can be a challenge and an opportunity, or it can be a disaster. That depends on you. Try to remember that it's not life but our reactions to it that shape us."

For Cade it was a long speech. She stared at him hungrily, wishing she had the right to cry in his arms. She needed someone to hold her until the pain stopped. Gussie hadn't noticed that her own daughter was grieving, but Cade had. He noticed things about her that no one else on earth seemed to, but he was ice cold when he was around her, as if he felt supremely indifferent toward her most of the time.

She smiled faintly, thinking how uncannily he could read her mind. Sleet was mixing with the snow, making a hissing sound.

"Thanks for the wise words. But I think I can live without money," she said after a minute.

"Maybe you can," he replied. "But can your mother?"

"She'll cope," she returned.

"Like hell she'll cope." He tugged the hat closer over his forehead and spared her one last sweeping appraisal. God, she looked tired! He could only imagine the demands Gussie was already making on her, and she was showing the pressure. "Get some rest. You look like a walking corpse."

He was gone then, without another word. As if he cared if she became a corpse, she thought hysterically. She'd lived for years on the vague hope that he might look at her one day and see someone he could love. That was the biggest joke of all. If there was any love in Cade, it was for Lariat, the Braided *L*, which had been founded by a Hollister fresh from the Civil War. There was a lot of history in Lariat. In a way the Hollisters were more a founding family of Texas than the Samsons. The Samson fortune was only two generations old, and it had been a matter of chance, not brains, that old man Barker Samson from back East had bought telephone stock in the early days of that newfangled invention. But the Hollisters were still poor.

She went upstairs to see about Gussie. It was an

unusual nickname for a woman named Geraldine, but her father had always called her mother that.

Gussie was stretched out on the elegant pink ruffled coverlet of her bed with a tissue under her equally pink nose. Thanks to face-lifts, annual visits to an exclusive health spa and meticulous dieting, and a platinum-blonde rinse, Gussie looked more like Bess's sister than her mother. She had always been a beauty, but age had lent her a maturity that gave her elegance as well. She'd removed the satin robe, and underneath it she was wearing a frothy white negligee ensemble that made her huge dark eyes look even darker and her delicate skin paler.

"There you are, darling," she said with a sob. "Has he gone?"

"Yes, he's gone," Bess said quietly.

Her mother's face actually blanched. She averted her eyes. "He's blamed me for years," she murmured, still half in shock, "and it wasn't even my fault, but he'd never believe me even if I told him the truth. I suppose we should be grateful that he hasn't raided the stables to get his money back in kind. The horses will bring something. . . ."

Here we go again, Bess thought. "You know he wouldn't do that. He said we'll work something out, after the funeral."

"No one held a gun on him and made him invest a penny," Gussie said savagely. "I hope he does lose everything! Maybe he'll be less arrogant!"

"Cade would be arrogant in rags, and you know it," Bess said softly. "We'll have to sell the house, Mama."

Gussie looked horrified. She sat straight up, her

careful coiffure unwinding in a long bleached tangle. "Sell my house? Never!"

"It's the only way. We'll still owe more than we have," she said, staring out the window at the driving sleet. "But I have that journalism degree. I might get a job on a newspaper."

"We'd starve. No, thank you. You can find something with an advertising agency. That pays much better."

Bess turned, staring at her. "Mama, I can't take the pressure of an advertising agency."

"Well, darling, we certainly can't survive on newspaper pay," her mother said, laughing mirthlessly.

Bess's eyes lifted. "I wasn't aware that you were going to expect me to support both of us."

"You don't expect me to offer to get a job?" Gussie exclaimed. "Heavens, child, I can't do anything! I've never had to work!"

Bess sat down on the end of the bed, viewing her mother's renewed weeping with cynicism. Cade had said that her mother wouldn't be able to cope. Perhaps he knew her after all.

"Crying won't help."

"I've just lost my husband," Gussie wailed into her tissue. "And I adored him!"

That might have been true, but it seemed to Bess that all the affection was on her father's side. Frank Samson had worshiped Gussie, and Bess imagined that Gussie's demands for bigger and better status symbols had led her desperate father to one last gamble. But it had failed. She shook her head. Her poor mother. Gussie was a butterfly. She should have married a stronger man than her father, a man who could have controlled her wild spending.

"How could he do this to us?" Gussie asked tearfully. "How could he destroy us?"

"I'm sure he didn't mean to."

"Silly, stupid man," came the harsh reply, and the veneer of suffering was eclipsed for a second by sheer, cruel rage. "We had friends and social standing. And now we're disgraced because he lost his head over a bad investment! He didn't have to kill himself!"

Bess stared at her mother. "Probably he wasn't thinking clearly. He knew he'd lost everything, and so had the other investors."

"I'll never believe that your father would do anything dishonest, even to make more money," Gussie said haughtily.

"He didn't do it on purpose," Bess said, feeling the pain of losing her father all over again, just by having to discuss what had caused his suicide. "He was taken in, just like the others. What made it so much worse was that he talked most of the investors into going along with him." She stared at her tearful mother. "You didn't know that it was a bogus company, did you?"

Gussie stared at her curiously. "No. Of course not." She started weeping again. "I simply must have the doctor. Do call him for me, darling."

"Mother, you've had the doctor. He can't do anything else."

"Well, then, get me those tranquillizers, darling. I'll take another."

"You've had three already."

"I'll take another," Gussie said firmly. "Fetch them."

Just for an instant Bess thought of saying no, or telling her mother to fetch them herself. But her tender heart wouldn't let her. She couldn't be that cruel to a stranger, much less her own grieving mother. But as she rose to do what she was asked, she could see that she was going to end up an unpaid servant if she didn't do something quick. But what? How could she walk out on Gussie now? She didn't have a brother or a sister, there was only herself to handle things. She couldn't remember a time in her life when she'd felt so alone. Her poor father—at least he was out of it. She only wished she didn't feel so numb. She'd loved him, in her way. But she couldn't even cry for him. Gussie was doing enough of that for both of them anyway.

She went to bed much later, but she didn't sleep. The past couple of days had been nightmarish. If it hadn't been for Cade, she didn't know how she and Gussie would have managed at all. And there was still the funeral to get through tomorrow.

Her thoughts drifted back through layers of time to the last day Cade had been teaching her how to ride. He'd grown impatient with her attempts to flirt, and everything had come to a head all too quickly.

He'd caught her around the waist with a strength that frightened her and tossed her down on her back into a clean stack of hay. She'd lain there, her mind confused, while he stared down at her from his formidable height, his dark eyes glittering angrily. Her tank top had fallen off one smooth shoulder, and it was there that his attention wandered. He looked at her blatantly, letting his gaze go over her full breasts and down her flat stomach to the long, elegant length of her legs in their tight denim covering.

"You don't look half bad that way, Bess," he'd said

then, his voice taut and angry. He'd even smiled, but it hadn't been a pleasant smile. "If all you want is a little diversion with the hired hand, I can oblige you."

She'd gone scarlet, but that shock led quickly to another. He moved down beside her, his heavy hips suddenly square over her own while his arms caught his weight as his chest poised over hers. He laughed coldly at her sudden paleness.

"Disappointed?" he asked, holding her eyes. "As you can feel, little rich girl, you don't even arouse me. But once we get your clothes out of the way, maybe you can stir me up enough to give you what you want."

Bess closed her eyes even now at the shame his words had made her feel. She'd never felt a man's aroused body, but even in her innocence she knew that Cade was telling the truth. He'd felt nothing at all. She'd stiffened, her eyes tearing, her lower lip trembling, as the humiliation and embarrassment swamped her.

Cade had said something unpleasant under his breath and abruptly got to his feet. He was holding down a hand to help her up, but before she could refuse it or even speak, Gussie was suddenly in the barn with them, her dark eyes flashing as she took in the situation with a glance. She'd hustled a shaken Bess into the house, ignored Cade's glowering stare, and the next day the riding lessons became a memory.

Bess had often wondered why Cade had felt the need to be so cruel. It would have been enough to simply reject her, without crushing her budding femininity at the same time. If he'd hoped to discourage her, he'd succeeded. But her feelings hadn't vanished. They'd simply gone underground. There was a lingering nervousness of him in a physical way, but she knew in her heart that if he came close and took her in his arms, she'd cave in and give him anything he wanted, fear notwithstanding. He hadn't really touched her that day anyway. It had all been planned. But what hurt the most was that he hadn't wanted her and that he'd taunted her with it.

She rolled over with a long sigh. It was just her luck to be doomed to want the only man on earth she couldn't have. He'd thought she was teasing because he was poor and she was rich, but that wasn't the case at all. He couldn't see that his lack of material things had nothing to do with her emotional attraction to him.

He was a strong man, but that wasn't why she loved him. It was for so many other reasons. She loved him because he cared about people and animals and the environment. He was generous with his time and what little money he had. He'd take in a stray animal or a stray person at the drop of a hat. He never turned away a cowboy down on his luck, or a stranded traveler, even if it meant tightening the grocery budget a little more. He was hard and difficult, but there was a deep sensitivity in him. He saw beneath the masks people wore to the real person inside. Bess had seen his temper, and she knew that he could be too rigid and unreasonable when he wanted his own way. But he had saving graces. So many of them.

It was odd that he'd never married, because she knew of at least two women he'd been involved with over the years. The most recent, just before her twentieth birthday, had been a wealthy divorcée. That one had lasted the longest, and many local people thought that Cade was hooked for sure. But the divorcée had left Coleman Springs rather abruptly, and was never mentioned again by any of the Hollisters. Since then, if there were women in Cade's life, he'd carefully kept them away from his family, friends, and acquaintances. Cade was nothing if not discreet.

Bess herself had no real beaux these days, although she'd dated a few men for appearance' sake, to keep Gussie from knowing how crazy she was about Cade. No other man could really measure up to him, and it was cruel to lead a man on when she had nothing to offer him. She was as innocent as a child in so many ways, but Cade obviously thought she was as sophisticated as her outward image. That was a farce. If only he knew how long she'd gone hungry wanting him.

She closed her eyes and forced her taut muscles to relax. She had to stop worrying over the past and get some sleep. The funeral was tomorrow. They'd lay her poor father to rest, and then perhaps she and her mother could tie up all the loose ends and get on with the ordeal of moving and trying to live without the wealth they'd been accustomed to. That would be a challenge in itself. She wondered how she and Gussie would manage.

Chapter 4

As Bess expected, there was a crowd at the simple graveside service, but it wasn't made up just of friends and neighbors. It was a press holiday, with reporters and cameras from all over the state. On the fringe of the mob Bess caught a glimpse of Elise Hollister, stately and tall, standing with her three sons. She caught the older woman's eye, and Elise smiled at her gently. Then, involuntarily, Bess's eyes glanced at Cade. He looked very somber in a dark suit, towering over his mother and his brothers, Gary and Robert. Red-haired Rob was outgoing, nothing like Gary and Cade. Gary was bookish, and kept the accounts. He was a little shorter than Cade, and his coloring was lighter and he was less authoritative. Bess turned her attention back to what the minister was saying, aware of Gussie's subdued sobbing beside her.

The cemetery was on a small rise overlooking the distant river. It was a Presbyterian church graveyard with tombstones that dated back to the Civil War. All the Samsons were buried here. It was a quiet place, with live oaks and mesquite all around. A good place for a man's final resting place. Frank Samson would have approved.

"My poor Frank," Gussie whimpered into her handkerchief as they left the cemetery. "My poor, poor Frank. However will we manage without him?"

"Frugally," Bess said calmly. Her tears had all been shed the night before. She was looking ahead now, to the legal matters that would be pending. She'd never had to cope with business, but she certainly couldn't depend on Gussie.

She helped her mother into the limousine and sat back wearily on the seat as the driver climbed in and started the engine. Outside, cameras were pointed in their direction, but Bess ignored them. She looked very sophisticated in her black suit and severe bun atop a face without a trace of makeup. She'd decided early that morning that the cameras wouldn't find anything attractive in her face to draw them to it. They didn't either. She looked as plain as a pikestaff. Gussie, on the other hand, was in a lacy black dress with diamonds glittering from her ears and throat and wrists. Not diamonds, Bess reminded herself, because those had already been sold. They were paste, but the cameras wouldn't know. And Gussie had put on quite a show for them. She didn't look at her mother now. She was too disappointed in the spectacle she'd made of their grief. That, too, was like Gussie, to play every scene theatrically. She'd left the stage to marry Frank Samson, and that was apparent too.

"I don't want to sell the house," Gussie said firmly, glancing at her daughter. "There must be some other way."

"We could sell it with an option to rent," Bess said. "That way we could keep up appearances, if that's all that matters to you."

Gussie flushed. "Bess, what's gotten into you?"

"I'm tired, Mother," Bess replied shortly. "Tired, and worn out with grief and shame. I loved my father. I never dreamed he'd take his own life."

"Well, I'm sure I didn't either," Gussie wailed.

"Didn't you?" Bess turned in the seat to stare pointedly at the smaller woman. It was her first show of spirit in recent memory, and it almost shocked her that she felt so brave. Probably it was the ordeal of the funeral that had torn down her normal restraint, she thought. "Didn't you hound him to death for more jewels, more furs, more expensive vacations that he couldn't afford in any legal way?"

The older woman turned her flushed face to the window and dabbed at her eyes. "What a way to talk to your poor mother, and at a time like this."

"I'm sorry," Bess murmured, backing down. She always backed down. It just wasn't in her to fight with Gussie.

"Really, Bess, I don't know what's gotten into you lately," Gussie said haughtily.

"I'm worried about how we're going to pay those people back what they've lost," Bess said.

Gussie's eyebrows lifted. "Why should we have to

pay them back?" she exclaimed. "We didn't make them invest. It was all your father's fault, and he's dead."

"That won't make any difference, don't you see?" Bess said gently. "His estate will be liable for it."

"I don't believe that," her mother replied coolly. "But even if we are liable, your father had life insurance—"

"Life insurance doesn't cover suicide." Bess's voice broke on the word. It still hurt, remembering how it had happened, remembering with sickening clarity the bloodstained carpet under her father's head. She closed her eyes against the image. "No insurance does. We've forfeited that hope."

"Well, the lawyer will handle it," Gussie said. "That's what he gets paid for." She brushed lint off her jacket. "I really must have a new suit. I think I'll go shopping tomorrow."

Bess wished, for an instant, that she was a hundred miles away. The grief was hard enough to cope with, but she had Gussie as well. Her father had managed his flighty wife well enough, or at least it had seemed so to Bess. She had been protected and cosseted, just like Gussie. But she was growing up fast.

Since they had to talk to their attorney, Bess asked the driver to drop them by the lawyer's office on the way home. They could get a cab when they were through, she said, wondering even then how she'd pay for it. But the driver wouldn't hear of it. He promised to wait for them, an unexpected kindness that almost made Bess cry.

The limousine stopped at the office of their lawyer, Donald Hughes, a pleasant man with blue eyes and a kind heart, who was as much a friend as he was legal counsel. He sat down with Bess and Gussie and outlined what they'd have to do.

"As I've already told you, the house will have to go," he said, glancing from one woman to the other.

Bess nodded. "We've already faced that. Mother has a few jewels left—"

"I won't sell the rest of my jewels," Gussie broke in, leaning forward.

"But you'll have to," Bess began.

"I will not," Gussie said shortly. "And that's the end of it."

Bess sighed. "Well, I have a few pieces left. I can sell those. . . ."

"Not Great-aunt Dorie's pearls," Gussie burst out. "I absolutely forbid it!"

"They're probably fake anyway," Bess said, avoiding her mother's eyes. "You know Great-aunt Dorie loved costume jewelry, and they've never been appraised." In fact they had, just the other day. Bess had taken them to a jeweler and had been shocked at their value. But she wasn't telling their attorney that, or her mother. She had plans for those pearls.

"That's too bad. It would have helped swell the kitty," Donald said quietly. "Well, now, about the stocks, bonds, and securities . . ."

What it all boiled down to, Bess realized some minutes later, was that they were declaring bankruptcy. Creditors would have to settle for fifty cents on the dollar, but at least they would get some kind of restitution. But there would be nothing left for Bess and Gussie. It was a bleak picture he painted, of sacrifice and deprivation—at least it was to Gussie.

"I'll kill myself," she said theatrically.

Bess stared at her. "Wonderful," she said, her grief and misery making her lash out. "That's just what I need. Two suicides in my immediate family in less than a week."

Gussie had the grace to look ashamed. "I'm sorry," she mumbled.

"It won't be as bad as it sounds, Gussie," Donald told her kindly. "You'd be amazed how many people will sympathize with you. Why, I heard old Jaimie Griggs say yesterday how much he admired you for carrying on so valiantly."

"He did?" Gussie smiled. "How nice of him."

"And Bess's idea about the two of you renting the house is a sound one, provided you can find a buyer," Donald said. "Put it on the market and we'll see what develops. Meanwhile I'll need your signature on a few documents."

"All right," Gussie said, and she seemed to brighten at the thought that she might get to stay in her home.

"What about the Hollisters?" Bess said quietly. "You do know that Cade's going to need every penny back. We can't ask him to settle for fifty cents on the dollar, and he's the biggest investor."

"Yes." Donald sighed through his teeth. "Cade is going to have one big headache. He's careful with his money. He never puts up more than he can afford to lose, but he was generous with his investment in your father's venture. He'll have to cut back heavily to keep going if he doesn't recover that capital. They'll be in for some more lean times. A pity, when they'd just begun to see daylight financially."

"He did it of his own free will," Gussie said indignantly.

"Yes, so he did," Donald agreed. "But all the law will see is that he invested in a guaranteed market. Your father gave him that guarantee, in writing, and I'm sure he can produce it."

"Isn't that a bit unusual, in a risky venture like Dad's?" Bess asked, leaning forward.

"As a matter of fact, it is," Donald said. "But it's quite legal. Cade has the right to expect every penny of his investment back, under the terms of the contract."

"I can see myself now, eighty years old and still sending Cade a check for ten dollars every month." Bess began to laugh, and the laughter turned to tears. It seemed so hopeless. Her father was dead, the family was disgraced, and to top it all, she was going to be saddled with a debt that would last all her life, with no one to help. Gussie would be no more support than a broken stick. She'd be saddled with Gussie, too, wailing and demanding pretty things like a petulant child and giving Bess hell when she pointed out their circumstances. It was almost too much to bear.

"Oh, Bess, you mustn't," Gussie burst out, shocked by the tears. Bess never cried! "Darling, it will be all right."

"Of course it will," Bess said with a choke in her voice. She dabbed at her tears. "Sorry. I guess I'm just tired."

Donald nodded, but he knew very well what Bess was going to be up against with Gussie. She would have had a hard time without the older woman. With her the task would be well-nigh impossible.

Later that day, several neighbors came by the Samsons' bringing food, a custom in rural areas that Bess was grateful for. Elise Hollister had sent a fried chicken and some vegetables, but she hadn't come herself, and neither had Cade. Bess wondered why, but she accepted the food with good grace and thanks. Shortly after Maude had helped Bess set a table with the platters of food brought by their few friends, Gussie went up to bed with a headache. Bess got Great-aunt Dorie's pearls and drove to the Hollister home.

She rumbled quietly over several cattle grids, inside electrified wire fence stretched over rustic gray posts. The house wasn't palatial at all, but it looked comfortable. Her eyes roamed lovingly over the white clapboard, two stories tall, newly painted with gray rocking chairs and a swing on the porch. Around it were towering live oaks and pecan trees, and in the spring it was glorious with the flowers Elise painstakingly planted and nurtured. Now, in winter, it had a bleak, sad look about it.

Bess parked the car in the driveway and got out, grateful for the porch light. It was almost dark, and there was no moon.

She walked slowly up onto the porch. It had been a terrible day, and it showed no sign of getting better. She hadn't changed out of the black suit she'd worn to the funeral, nor had she added any makeup to her face or loosened her hair from the severe bun.

She knocked on the door, hearing a television set blaring in the background.

To her amazement Elise answered the door herself. She had Cade's dark eyes and silver hair that had been jet black in her younger days.

"Bess," she said gently. "What are you doing here?"

"I need to see Cade," Bess replied wearily. "Is he home?"

Elise was astute. She noticed the jewelry box clutched in Bess's slender hand. "Darling, we're not going to starve," the older woman told her. "Please, Bess, go home. You've had enough on you these past few days."

"Don't," Bess whispered, fighting tears. "I really can't bear sympathy, Elise, I'll just go to pieces, and I can't. Not yet."

The older woman nodded. "All right." She managed a quiet smile. "Cade's in his office. It's the second door on the right." She glanced toward the living room. "The boys are watching television, so you won't be disturbed."

"Thank you. For everything. The fried chicken was delicious, and mother said to thank you too."

Elise started to say something, but she stopped before the words got out. "It was the least I could do. I would have come, but the boys were busy with an emergency and there was nobody to drive me."

"You don't have to explain. We appreciate what you did," Bess said softly. "I wish I could cook."

"It's a shame Gussie wouldn't let Maude teach you," Elise said.

Bess sighed. "Maude leaves at the end of the week," she said. "We had to let her go, of course." She tried to smile. "I'll practice the trial-and-error cookery method. After I've burned up a few things, surely I'll get the hang of it."

Elise smiled. "Of course you will. If we can do anything . . ."

"Thank you." She touched the older woman's shoulder gently and turned down the long hall.

She knocked at the second door.

"Come in."

Cade sounded tired, too, and irritated. That wasn't encouraging. She opened the door and went in, leaning back against the cool wood for support. Her eyes cast briefly around the room. It was almost ramshackle compared with its counterpart at the Spanish House, with worn linoleum on the floor and equally worn throw rugs. The chairs were faded with age, and the paintings on the wall dated to the twenties. There was a small lamp on Cade's desk, along with stacks of ledgers and paperwork.

He sat at his desk, bent over one of the ledgers. He didn't look up for a minute, and Bess was shocked at the sheer fatigue she saw in his face. He had all the responsibility for the ranch these days and took care of all the other Hollisters. How he must hate the Samsons, she thought sadly, for what they were costing him now.

He glanced up and saw her, and the weariness was suddenly overlaid by bitterness.

"Hello, Bess," he said in a faintly surprised tone, leaning back. "Is this a social visit?"

"I expect you'd be delighted to throw me off the back steps if I dared, considering the mess we've landed you in," she said with what pride she had left. She moved forward and put the jewelry case down on the cluttered desk.

"What's this?" he asked.

She folded her hands in front of her. "Great-aunt Dorie's pearls," she said quietly.

His eyebrows shot up. He picked up the case and opened it, revealing the creamy-pink glow of those antique, priceless pearls. His expression gave nothing away, but she sensed that she'd shocked him.

"Does your attorney know about these?" he asked curtly.

She looked away from his piercing gaze. "I didn't think it was necessary," she said evasively. "Dad's enterprise cost you more than the other creditors. Those pearls will be almost enough to make up every penny."

"These are more than collateral," he said, closing the case and laying it on the desk. "They're a legacy. These should go to your oldest child."

Her eyes lingered on his chest. His blue work shirt was unbuttoned. "It's not likely I'll have children," she said. "The pearls don't matter."

"They will to your mother," he replied, standing. "And don't tell me she approved of your coming here. I doubt you even told her."

"She's not in much condition to notice what I do," she said uneasily.

He came around the desk slowly and perched on its edge to light a cigarette. In his half-leaning position, his jeans stretched sinuously across powerful leg muscles and narrow hips. He was devastating physically.

He leaned back and folded his arms across his chest. "How do you stand financially, after the other debts are paid?"

"We don't," she said simply. She had to fight the urge to move closer to him. He was so sensually appealing that her heart was nearly racing.

His chest rose and fell heavily. "Well, I won't pretend it's going to be easy, but I can make do with fifty cents on the dollar, and your attorney tells me you can manage that," he said, watching her face color. "Yes, I've spoken to him already."

"I should have guessed that you would."

"Why bring me the pearls, then?" he asked quietly. "Didn't you think I'd settle for what you had to give?"

She smiled. "I wasn't sure. You're first and foremost a businessman, and you stood to lose more than the other investors. I didn't want to see you lose Lariat."

"I'm not going to lose Lariat," he said curtly. "I'll hold on to it somehow."

She was staring at his dusty boots. He was a hard-working man. A hard man, period. Something in him appealed to her, despite the cold, sarcastic face he presented to the world. She sometimes thought that underneath there was a man who desperately needed to be loved. But Cade Hollister would never have admitted it. No one got close to him.

He was watching those expressions drift across her young face, and they weren't making it easy for him. Bess had worshipped him from afar for years, and knowing it had almost driven him crazy. There were so many reasons why he couldn't give in to the barely curbed hunger he felt for her. Her mother had a hold on her that Bess didn't seem able to break. Despite her lack of wealth now, she'd been born to it and he hadn't. There were all too many years between them. Besides those good reasons, he had Lariat and his family to think of. His first responsibility was to them, and they were in one hellacious financial pickle now, thanks to Bess's father.

He was surprised, too, at her continuing attraction

to him. He thought he'd convinced her that he didn't want her. But she still looked at him with those soft, sweet eyes that made him burn from head to toe. It had provoked him into near-violence once, and he'd humiliated her in a way that still haunted him. At the time it had seemed necessary to get her off the track, but now . . .

He stood up abruptly, irritated by her sudden, jerky backward movement. It angered him beyond all reason.

"For God's sake," he burst out, eyes blazing.

She bit her lower lip, her wide eyes searching his with faint apprehension.

He saw the fear and hated it. He had to control a wild urge to grab her, to bring her close and kiss the breath out of her and teach her not to be afraid of him. But he couldn't do that, and the knowledge made him wild. He crushed out the cigarette with muted violence.

"Don't flatter yourself, honey," he said bitingly. "You're hardly enough to make a man drunk with passion."

He'd made that clear long ago, so she didn't take offense. She looked down at her feet, her expression faintly defeated. "I know that already," she said. There was simply no fight in her, and that bothered him most of all. She was so damned vulnerable.

She looked up at him then with soft brown eyes that shot every scruple he had. The look burned between them like fire, ripping away his will, his restraint. All at once his hand shot out to catch her arm. He swung her around, right up against him, so that she could feel the warmth of his hard, fit body and see the faint beads of sweat clinging to the thick dark hair on his chest.

"Is that your best offer?" he asked deeply, and his eyes at close range were dynamite. He saw the puzzled look in her eyes and cursed himself for saying such a thing to her. She was so damned green, she didn't even know what he was talking about.

"You mean, the pearls?" she got out. "Well, everything else is gone already, except for some of Mama's jewelry. . . ."

He stared at her with unbridled contempt. "And of course, Mama won't give up her jewels, even to pay a debt, isn't that right?"

She felt herself going limp, feeling weary of defending her mother to him. "Cade, can't you find it in your heart to talk to me without making horribly sarcastic remarks about my mother?" Her big eyes pleaded with him.

He saw the tiredness then. Saw how the funeral had affected her. She was becoming far too pale, too thin, too worn for a woman her age. Like a leech, her mother had sapped her, robbed her of a normal girlhood. His dark eyes narrowed. He wondered if she'd ever realized that his sarcasm was more defensive than offensive.

His dark eyes moved over her like hands, exploring the roundness of her breasts and hips and her small waist. He knew what she felt. Even now she was almost trembling as he looked at her. She wanted him.

But wanting wouldn't be enough. There was still Gussie and Bess's lost life-style and her own inability to stand up to her own problems. In her present state he'd walk all over her, because she had hardly any spirit. That hurt him, to think that he could do even more damage to her spirit than Gussie had. He had a quick, hot temper that he wasn't shy about losing. Bess would knuckle under. The woman she could be would be submerged in his own strength.

There was a hunger in her soft brown eyes that he felt an urgent need to satisfy. He had to get her out of here, and quick.

But she smelled of gardenias and she looked as if he was every dream of perfection she'd ever had. Her eyes were making love to his, soft and hungry. Virgin eyes.

He touched a loose strand of Bess's soft hair and brushed it back from her long neck. Even the black suit she was wearing with that stark white blouse didn't detract from her appeal. If she'd worked at it, she could have been beautiful. But Mama wouldn't like the competition, so naturally Bess wasn't encouraged to dress up or fix her face and hair to her best advantage. He knew that, even if Bess didn't.

Her lips parted at the light touch on her hair. She stared up at him with eyes that were wide and excited.

"You want me like hell, don't you?" he asked quietly, his dark eyes holding hers.

She felt the ground moving under her feet. It was like having every dream of him she'd ever had come true. The look in his dark eyes, the feel of his hand in her hair, the way his gaze dropped suddenly to her soft mouth. She knew her legs were trembling. He already knew how affected she was, and she wondered if she could bear the humiliation.

"Cade . . . don't do this to me," she whispered

shakily as his fingers moved to her mouth and touched it, making it tremble.

"What am I doing to you, Bess?" he asked deeply, not quite in control anymore. The scent of her body was in his nostrils, drugging him, and he was more aware of her by the minute. He toyed with her collar, his knuckles brushing lazily against the soft skin of her throat, making her tremble with an avalanche of new sensations.

"I can't help what I feel," she whispered brokenly.

His eyes caressed the soft perfection of her mouth. Her lips were parted, a little swollen with passion. Her eyes were drowsy-looking despite their excitement. He saw her tongue brush her lips, and his breath caught.

He turned his hand so that his fingers could brush softly up and down the line of her throat. Her skin was like satin. It intoxicated him. He moved closer, towering over her, so close that the tips of her breasts touched him.

Bess looked up at him with all her untried dreams in her eyes. She was on fire for him. She wanted his hard mouth with a passion that was already white-hot, and he'd barely touched her. She was surprised and frightened by the intensity of emotion he aroused in her.

His dark head bent a little. "What would you give for my mouth right now, Bess?" he asked in a voice she didn't recognize, deep and slow and silky.

She felt his breath on her lips, and her restraint went flying. Damn her pride, she needed him . . . !

"Any . . . thing," she whispered shamelessly, her voice breaking on the word. "Don't you know already? Anything, Cade . . . !"

Her slender hands were on his arms, her nails digging into him, her body swaying against him. He couldn't help it. Years of suppressed hunger were overflowing inside him. His narrowed eyes fell to her mouth. He could bend his head a fraction of an inch and make all her dreams come true. He could take her mouth and taste its warm softness under the hard crush of his own. He could hold her and touch her, and for a space of seconds she could belong to him. He could feed on the soft, sweet desire that she'd saved up all these years for him. Only for him.

He was actually bending toward her, her breath mingling with his, her body begging to be held by him. And then he felt the weight of responsibility fall on him.

Bess was still a child emotionally, her mother's child.

That was what brought him to his senses. Bess wanted him, but that was all it was. The newness of desire and the illusion of hero worship were driving her. He could make her dreams come true, all right, but his would turn to nightmares because it was too soon. Perhaps years too soon.

He lifted his dark head and dropped his hand from her soft neck. "No," he said. He didn't say it in a rough way. It was only the one word, but firm enough to make her step away from him and blush.

She had to catch her breath audibly, because the feel of that powerful body so close to hers had made it almost impossible to breathe at all. Her soft brown eyes searched his dark ones as she pushed back an unruly strand of honey-brown hair. She looked and felt ashamed, especially when she remembered that she'd practically begged him to make love to her.

"You're too young and too green for me, Bess," he said coolly, forcing the words out. "Go home to Mama."

He reached behind him, picking up the jewelry case, and tossed it to her with as little care for what was inside as if he'd been throwing pebbles.

She caught it in her trembling hands. He didn't want her. Well, she knew that already, didn't she? He'd only been playing with her, taunting her. It was like what he'd done to her when she was twenty, rejecting her, throwing her away. Only this was more cruel, because he'd tempted her first, made her show him how badly she wanted him.

Her eyes closed on a wave of pain and shame. "If you won't take the pearls, you'll only get fifty cents on the dollar, like the other investors," she said in a ghost of her normal tone.

"I've already torn up that agreement your father signed with me," he said shortly, "You could have saved yourself the trip."

"That, and the humiliation," she said huskily.

"What humiliation?" he asked quietly. "I know that you want me. I've always known."

She turned away with tears streaming down her cheeks. "You'll get your money back, Cade. All of it, somehow," she said unsteadily.

She sounded a little wild, and the tears unsettled him. He wondered if she might take him seriously and go to some other man, and that whipped up a fury of sudden anger.

"You won't do anything stupid, will you?" he asked suddenly, moving forward.

"What do you mean?"

"Like letting Gussie offer you to some well-heeled, bald millionaire just to get enough money to pay me off?"

She took a deep, hurt breath as she felt behind her for the doorknob. "What do you care?" she cried, feeling reckless. "You don't even want me, you never did, so why play with me like a trout on a fishing line? You're cruel, and I think I hate you, Cade!"

He didn't flinch. Not outwardly, at least, except for the sudden angry glitter in his eyes. He cocked his head and gave her a cold smile. "Do you? Was that why you begged for my mouth? Because you hate me?"

Her face went from a blushing rose to a cold white in seconds. She gave in, as she always did, her eyes closing on a wave of shame.

"No. I don't. I only wish I could hate you," she whispered brokenly. "I've tried for years . . ." Tears choked her, and she blinked them away. "I came here because I was sorry for what you'd lost, because I wanted to help you. But you don't want help, least of all from me. I know you don't want me. I've always known that. I wish I was beautiful, Cade! I wish you wanted me so that I could push you away and watch you hurt as much as I do!"

She opened the door and ran through it, her heart broken. He was horrible. Cruel and cold and she didn't want him anymore, she hated him. . . .

She loved him! His mouth had been the end of the rainbow, the most exquisite promise of pleasure she'd ever known, and she'd wanted it with a pitifully evident desire. But he'd only been playing. And then he had to go and spoil everything with that cruel taunt . . . !

Cade meanwhile was glaring at the closed door with a jumble of emotions, foremost of which was anger at his own cruelty and Bess's helpless reaction to it. He'd never meant to humble her. He'd only wanted to protect her, even from himself. If he started kissing her, he wasn't sure he could stop. The last thing she needed now was the complication of a hopeless relationship. But he hadn't meant to hurt her.

He started after her, flaming with frustration and bad temper. "Damn circumstances," he muttered to himself. He hated making apologies. Not that he intended to make one now. But maybe he could rub a healing balm on the wound he'd inflicted.

But when he stepped out into the long hall, he found Bess halfway down it, sobbing into his mother's shoulder.

Elise looked at her tall, angry son with knowing, soulful eyes. That look was as condemning as Bess's had been. Worse. He glared at her, then at Bess's rigid back, and went into his office again. But he didn't slam the door. Oddly enough, he felt as if he'd just made the biggest mistake of his life.

"There, there," Elise murmured softly, smoothing Bess's soft hair as it fell out of the bun down her back. "It's all right, darling."

"I hate him," Bess whimpered. She clung, even though she'd sworn on her arrival that she didn't need sympathy. Yes, she did, desperately. Gussie had none for anyone except herself, and Bess had nobody else.

"Yes, I know you hate him." Elise hugged her close with a sigh. Poor little thing, with only Gussie for company at Spanish House. Elise and Gussie had been friends once, until Cade had made an accusation that had broken their friendship and made them enemies. Elise held no grudges even now, but Gussie hated Cade for the accusations he'd made and the way he'd embarrassed her in front of Elise. Bess didn't know about that scandal, and there was no reason to tell her. It was better left in the past, to her mind. It was only Cade and Gussie who kept it alive, and Elise had long since given up hope that the two of them would ever bury the hatchet.

All the same, she worried about Bess. At times like this she could have picked Gussie up and shaken her. Didn't she care enough about Bess to see that she was taking her father's death badly? The last thing she needed was to be here, letting Cade upset her. Elise, who'd wanted at least one daughter, had to content herself with the hope of daughters-in-law. Someday. Maybe.

Bess wept slowly, enjoying the luxury of tears. She was going to get over Cade Hollister if it killed her, now that she knew how he really felt about her. And she'd pay him back someday. It was going to be her goal in life. So it was a pity that no matter how hard she pictured her revenge, it always ended with his arms around her.

Chapter 5

Bess had herself under control by the time she went upstairs to say good night to Gussie. She'd wiped the tears away and even forced herself to smile as she carried her mother a cup of herbal tea and some cheese for a bedtime snack.

"Feeling better?" she asked Gussie.

The older woman stretched lazily. "A little, I suppose. It's very lonely without your father, Bess."

"Yes, I know," Bess said gently.

"I thought I heard the car leave while I was napping," Gussie said, eyeing her daughter. "Did you go out?"

"Just to the store for a minute, to get some more tea," she prevaricated.

"Oh. Well, you really should tell me when you're going out. I might have needed something."

Bess felt herself bristle. This was going to be unbearable. Now that her father was gone, she could already see Gussie's attention turning inward, to her own comfort. Bess was going to be trapped, just as Cade had said.

"Now, listen, Mother—" Bess began.

"I'm so tired and sleepy, darling. I simply must rest," Gussie said with a weary smile. "Sleep tight, baby."

Bess almost stood her ground, but that smile cut the ground out from under her. She stood up. "You, too, Mama."

"And don't forget to lock the doors."

"No, Mama."

"You're such a nice child, Bess." She lay back, sipping her tea.

Nice, Bess thought as she went to her own room. *Nice, but thick as a plank.* She was going to have to do something to shake Gussie out of her tearful, clinging mood. Perhaps that would work itself out in time. She had to hope it would.

Meanwhile she didn't dare tell her mother anything about going to see Cade with Great-aunt Dorie's pearls. It would be the final straw, to have to hear Gussie ranting about that.

That was unkind, Bess told herself as she put the pearls away in her drawer. Gussie did try, but she just didn't have many maternal instincts. Bess looked at the sheen of the pearls against their black velvet bed and touched them lightly. Save them for her eldest child, Cade had said. Her eyes softened as she thought about a child. Cade's child, dark-eyed and dark-haired, lying in her arms. It was the sweetest kind of daydream. Of course that's all it would ever be. Although his hunger for children was well known, and he made no secret of the fact that one day he wanted an heir very much, Cade seemed in no rush to involve himself with a woman. And now there would be no money and no time for romance. He was going to spend the next few months trying to save his inheritance, and Bess felt terrible that she'd had even a small part in seeing him brought to his knees. She only wished there was something she could do.

The things he'd said to her still hurt. Even though she could understand that he was frustrated about the financial loss, and her defense of her mother, his bitter anger had wounded her. Especially that crack about not wanting her. What made it so much worse was that it was true. He knew how she felt about him now, and maybe it was just as well that she and Gussie were leaving town. It would be hell to live near Cade and have him know how she felt.

He'd seemed for just a few seconds to want her as badly as she'd wanted him. But that was probably just her imagination. He'd been angry. Of course he'd started to come after her. She spent most of the night trying to decide why.

That night was the longest she'd ever spent. She couldn't sleep. Every time she closed her eyes, she saw her father's face. He'd been a wonderful father, a cheerful, smiling man who did anything Gussie wanted him to without protest. He had loved her mother so. But even that love hadn't been enough to make up for the disgrace of what he'd done. He'd betrayed his friends. He hadn't meant to. It had sounded like a perfectly respectable financial investment, but he'd been played for a fool, and that was what had driven him to suicide.

Bess cried for all of them. For the father she no longer had. For her mother, who was so weak and foolish and demanding. For Cade, who stood to lose everything on earth he loved. Even for herself, because Cade was forever beyond her reach.

She was up at the crack of dawn, worn and still half asleep. She dressed in an old pair of designer jeans and a long-sleeved pink shirt with her boots to go riding. It was cold, so she threw on a jacket as well. Gussie wouldn't awaken until at least eleven, so the morning was Bess's. She felt free suddenly, overwhelmed with relief because she could have a little time to herself after days of grief and mourning.

She went down to the stable for one last ride on her horse. Tina was a huge Belgian, a beautiful tan-and-white draft horse and dear to Bess's heart. She'd begged for the animal for her twentieth birthday, and her father had bought Tina for her. She remembered her father smiling as he commented that it would sure be hard to find a saddle that would go across the animal's broad back. But he'd produced one, and despite his faint apprehension about letting his only child have such an enormous horse, he'd learned, as Bess had, that Tina was a gentle giant. She was never mean or temperamental, and not once had she tried to throw Bess.

Giving her up would be almost as hard as giving up Spanish House. But there was no choice. There wouldn't be any place in San Antonio where she could afford to keep a horse. Tina had to go. There had already been two offers for her, but Bess had refused both. One was from a woman with a mean-looking husband, who'd said haughtily that he knew how to handle a horse, all it took was a good beating. The second offer had come from a teenage girl who wanted the horse desperately but wasn't sure she could come up with the money it would take to buy Tina and then to house and feed her. The girl's parents didn't even have a barn.

She sighed as she saddled Tina and rode her down to the creek. It was a beautiful day for winter, and even though her jacket felt good, it would probably be warm enough to go in her shirtsleeves later. Texas weather was unpredictable, she mused.

Lost in her thoughts, she didn't hear the other horse until it was almost upon her. She turned in the saddle to see Cade riding up beside her on his buckskin gelding.

Her heart ran away. Despite the way they'd parted company the night before, just the sight of him was heaven. But she kept her eyes averted so that he wouldn't see how hopeless she felt.

"I thought it was you," Cade said, leaning over the saddle horn to study her. "You sit that oversized cayuse pretty good."

"Thanks," she said quietly. Any praise from Cade was rare. She shifted restlessly in the saddle and didn't look at him. She was still smarting from his hurtful remarks of the night before, and she wondered why he'd approached her.

"But you still haven't got those stirrups right."

"No point now," she sighed. "She's going to be sold at auction. This is my last ride."

His dark eyes studied her in the silence of open country, flat land reaching to the horizon, vivid blue skies and not a sound except for an occasional barking dog. She was distant, and he had only himself to blame. He hadn't slept, remembering how he'd treated her the night before.

"If I could afford her, I'd buy her from you," he said gently. "But I can't manage it now."

She bit her lower lip. It was so kind. . . .

"Don't, for God's sake, start crying," he said. "I can't stand tears."

She forced herself not to break down. She shook her head to clear her eyes as she stared at the range and not at him. "What are you doing out here so early?"

"Looking for you," he said heavily. "I said some harsh things to you last night." He bent his head to light a cigarette, because he hated apologies. "I didn't mean half of them."

She turned in the saddle, liking the familiar creak of the leather, the way Tina's head came up and she tossed her mane. Familiar things, familiar sounds, that would soon be memories. "It's all right," she said. The almost-apology brought the light back into her life. She felt so vulnerable with him. "I guess you felt like saying worse, because of all the trouble we've caused you and your family."

"I told you before that it wasn't completely your father's fault."

"Yes, but—"

"What will you do?"

Her eyes glanced off his and back to the saddle horn.

"Go to San Antonio. Mama doesn't want to, but it's the only place I can find work."

"*You* can find work?" he exploded.

She cringed at the white heat in his deep, slow voice. "Now, Cade . . ."

"Don't you 'Now, Cade' me!" he said shortly. "There's nothing wrong with Gussie. Why can't she go to work and help out?"

"She's never had to work," she said, wondering why she should defend her mother when she agreed wholeheartedly with Cade.

"I've never had to wash dishes, but I could if it came to it," he returned. "People do what they have to do."

"My mother doesn't," she said simply. "Anyway," she added to divert him, "I can get a job as a copywriter. Advertising work pays well."

"I wouldn't know," he muttered. "I don't have much contact with cities or city professions. All I know is cattle."

"You know them pretty well," she said with a faint smile. "You were making money when all the other cattlemen were losing theirs."

"I'm a renegade," he said simply. "I use the same methods my great-grandfather did. They worked for him."

"They'll work for you, too, Cade," she said gently. "I know you can pull the ranch out of the fire."

He stared at her silently. She had such unshakable faith in what he could do. All that sweet hero worship was driving him to his knees, even though he knew it couldn't last. Once she got out from under Gussie's thumb and felt her wings, there'd be no stopping her. Then, maybe, when she could see him as a man and not a caricature of what he really was, there might be some hope for them. But that looked as if it was a long way off.

"Don't let your mother get her hands on those pearls," he said unexpectedly. "They'll go the way of anything else she can liquidate."

"Yes, I know," she said, agreeing with him for once. "I told her they were costume jewelry," she added with a faint smile.

"It won't work if she gets a close look at them," he murmured.

She knew that, too. "Why do you feel so strongly about them, Cade?" she asked.

"Because they're a legacy. Something that's been in your family a long time, a piece of history for the children you'll have one day."

She felt herself coloring. "I don't know that I'll ever have any."

"You will," he said. "So will I. I want half a dozen," he mused, letting his eyes run over the land, the horizon. "Ranches are tailor-made for big families. This one is big enough for my kids, and for Gary's and Robert's too. Gary's too city-minded to settle here, and I don't know about Robert. But it's in my blood. I'll never be able to leave it."

She'd known that already, but it was new to have him talk to her without the usual cold hostility in his voice. Perhaps it was because she was leaving. And maybe there was a little guilt for the things he'd said the night before.

"Anyway," he continued, "legacies shouldn't be used to get ready cash. Gussie isn't sentimental. You are."

She smiled shyly. "I guess I am, at that."

"Get down for a bit." He swung gracefully out of the saddle and helped her down, while she tried to control an irrational urge to throw her arms around him and hang on. Her heart was beating wildly when he put her down and moved quickly away to tie the horses separately to small trees.

He stood on the banks of the creek, leaning back against a big oak, smoking his cigarette while he studied the small flow of water over the rocks. He was wearing denims and a blue-checked shirt with his shepherd's coat and a battered old tan Stetson, and to Bess's eyes he looked the very picture of a working cowboy. His boots, like his hat, were worn with use, and he was wearing working spurs—bronc spurs, in fact, small rowels with pincer edges around them that looked fierce but only pulled the hair of the animal they were used on. A horse's hide was tough and not easily damaged if the right kind of spurs were worn, and Cade knew the right kind to wear.

"You've been breaking horses," she said, because she knew from experience that he only wore those particular spurs when he was riding new additions to the remuda.

"Helping Dally," he corrected. Dally was the ranch's wrangler, and a good one. "We compromised. He wanted to take three years and I had three weeks, so he turns his back while I help him break them to the saddle. Besides, it's good practice for the rodeo."

She knew that he competed at rodeos all around the Southwest and that he won a lot. He needed the money to help prop up Lariat.

"It's dangerous work." She remembered so well the

cowhand several years ago who'd had his back broken when a bronc slung him off against the barn wall. "You pulled that tendon. . . ."

"I barely limp at all now," he said. "And any ranch work is dangerous." He turned his head and looked at her, and she could see the light of challenge in his dark eyes. "That's why I enjoy it."

"Race-car drivers," she murmured. "Mountain climbers. Skydivers. Ranchers—"

"Not to mention little girls who buy oversized horses," he inserted, nodding toward Tina, who was towering over his own buckskin.

"She's terribly gentle."

"I guess so. Your father and I had words over her, but he finally convinced me that you'd be safe."

She went warm all over, to think that he'd been concerned about her. He'd never said anything to her, and neither had her father.

"But Gussie never cared, did she?" he asked pointedly, his cold eyes holding hers. "Not about seeing you trampled by an oversized horse or anything else. Unless it interfered with her comfort."

"Not again," she said, grimacing. "Cade . . ."

"She doesn't give a damn about you, can't you see that? My God, Bess, you've got enough problems without taking on Gussie for life."

"It won't be for life," she began.

"It will," he said solemnly. "She'll never let go. She's like a leech. She'll suck you dry and leave you the first time some rich man dangles a diamond over her head."

It was the truth. But she wasn't strong like Cade. She

never could say no to Gussie. How could she desert her own mother?

"You're thirty-four," she pointed out. "And you still live at home and take care of your own mother and both your brothers—"

"That's different," he returned curtly. "I'm strong enough to shoulder the responsibility."

"Oh, of course you are," she said softly, her eyes adoring him. "You've had to be. But the point I'm making is that you've got all that responsibility and you've never turned your back on your own people or refused to do for them. How can you expect me not to do for my mother?"

He stared at her quietly. "At home Gary keeps the books and Robert handles the sales. Gary's engaged and won't be around much longer, and Robert keeps talking about going to San Antonio to find work. I don't know how much longer they'll be here. But my mother takes care of a yardful of chickens and a gaggle of geese, which we use for pest control in the garden that she keeps every year. She sews and cleans and cooks. She cans and even helps out at roundup when she has to. I don't mind providing for a woman like that."

"I guess my mother would faint if she had to get near a horse," Bess mused. "But we lived in a different world from yours."

That was the wrong thing to say. It hurt him. No, he couldn't imagine Gussie around horses, or Bess cleaning and cooking and planting a garden. His face hardened. She was meant for some rich man's house, where everything would be done for her. A poor man was hardly her cup of tea.

"I've got to get back to work," he said curtly. He crushed out his cigarette under his boot. "When are you leaving for San Antonio?"

"Tomorrow," Bess said sadly. "We've left all the details to our attorney, and Tina goes to a stable this afternoon to be boarded until they sell her." She shrugged. "I don't have much luck with it, I'm too softhearted."

"Amen." He paused just in front of her, smelling of the whole outdoors and faint cologne and smoke, smells that were familiar and exciting because they always reminded her of him. "Don't kill yourself for Gussie."

She looked up, her eyes soft and misty with tears she didn't want to shed. "I'll . . . miss you," she said, and tried to smile.

"Do you think I won't miss you?" he asked, and it was the severest test of his control he'd ever had. The mask slipped, and some of the hunger he felt for her showed in his glittering dark eyes.

She almost gasped. It was such a shock, to know that he felt even a fraction of the longing she did.

"But you don't care about me," she whispered. "You don't even want me, you proved it—"

"I'm in an impossible situation here," he interrupted gruffly. "It isn't going to improve. You've got Gussie around your neck like an albatross and you have to get used to being an ordinary woman, not a debutante. Those are obstacles neither of us can get around."

Her lips parted. The hunger was so staggering that she felt her knees wobbling under her. "What if there . . . were no obstacles?" she asked breathlessly.

His jaw hardened and his eyes roved over her face. "My God, don't you know?" he asked roughly.

Her hand went out slowly toward his chest, but he caught her wrist and held it away from him. The contact was electric, his warmth penetrating her blood. "No," he said, letting go of her, watching her blush. "It's better not to start things when there's no hope of finishing them."

"I see." She did, but it hurt all the same. Her eyes searched his hungrily. "Good-bye, Cade."

The tears in her eyes made him feel homicidal. He could hardly bear them. "If things get too rough, let me know."

Tears overflowed down her cheeks, soundless, all the more poignant for the lack of sound.

"Stop that," he ground out and turned away, because he knew exactly what was going to happen if he didn't. He was already trembling with the need to grind her body into his and kiss the breath out of her. But kissing was intoxicating and addictive. If he started that with Bess, he might not be able to stop in time. Gentlemen didn't seduce virgins—he'd been raised to believe that, and his strict upbringing reared its head every time he looked at Bess with desire.

"I'm sorry I did that," Bess said after a minute, wiping her eyes. "You've been so much kinder about all this than I expected. That's all."

"I don't feel particularly kind," he said shortly. He turned back to her. "But if you need help, all you ever have to do is call. Watch yourself when Gussie has male friends in. Lock your bedroom door if they stay overnight."

"Mother wouldn't . . . !" she exclaimed.

"Like hell Mother wouldn't," he said. "You're so naive it's unreal. You can't see what she is."

"Neither can you," she stammered.

"You see what you want to," he said wearily. "And I'm tired of arguing with you about Gussie. It gets us nowhere. Be careful that she doesn't start shoving you at rich, eligible old men to help feather her nest." His eyes grew darker at the thought of it, and he felt a momentary twinge of fear.

"That's funny," she said with a faint smile, lowering her eyes. "You don't know how funny. Can you really see me as a femme fatale?"

"I can see you as a warm, loving woman," he said against his will, his voice deeper and softer than she'd ever heard it. "Once you come out of that shell, men are going to want you."

Her heart jumped. She lifted her eyes. "Even you?" she asked in a whisper, daring everything.

Careful, he told himself. *Careful.* He let his dark eyes wander over her face, but he didn't smile. "Maybe," he said noncommitally.

She laughed mirthlessly. "No, you wouldn't want someone like me," she said wistfully and averted her eyes from the probing look in his. "You'll want someone who's capable and strong, someone who can cope with ranch life and country living. I'm just a cream puff with an overbearing mother. . . ." Tears stung her eyes.

"Honest to God, Bess, if you don't stop that, I'm going to . . ." He bit down hard on his self-control. Keeping his hands off her was the hardest thing he'd ever done, and she didn't even realize the effect she was having on him.

"Sorry," she said. She laughed. "I'm always apologizing."

"You don't have much of a self-image," he said tightly. "Time will take care of that. Losing everything was tough on you, I know, but you may find that it was the best thing that ever happened to you. Hard times shape us. They'll shape you."

"Make a woman of me, you mean?" she asked shyly.

He drew in a short breath. "In a sense, yes. Go to San Antonio. Find your own place in life. That independence will be good for you. You'll marry one day, and it's important that a woman doesn't become only an extension of a man."

"That doesn't sound old-fashioned at all."

"In some ways I'm not," he murmured. His eyes narrowed thoughtfully on her face. "But Mother raised us in the church, even if she could never drag my father into one. The Bible looks upon some aspects of modern life as a sin."

She nodded. "Like sleeping around."

"Like sleeping around." He stared down at her quietly. "I'm not a fanatic about it, but I'd like to think the woman I marry had enough respect for herself to bring her chastity to the marriage bed. It seems to me," he mused deeply, "that this new morality is more for the man's sake than the woman's. The women are running all the risks, and the men are getting everything they want without the responsibilities of marriage."

She laughed gently. "Maybe so." She stared at the ground. "I never got to go to church, but I always thought it was so romantic to wait until I got married to be intimate with a man. Mama laughed at such an outdated notion, but my father never did. I think he approved."

"Your father was a good man," he replied. "I'll miss him too."

She looked up at him. "You can still have the pearls, Cade," she said softly.

He shook his head. "I'll get by." His eyes slid down to her mouth and stared at it until he thought his head was going to spin him to the ground. He wanted it so badly.

Bess saw that look and trembled with the need to go close to him, to offer her mouth, to experience even if only one time in her life the exquisite pleasure those hard, firm lips could give. She knew already that it would be everything she could want. Her lips parted as he looked at them, and the wave of hunger that swept over her almost brought her to her knees. *Just one kiss*, she pleaded silently. *One!*

He took one slow step toward her, his warmth enveloping her, the scent of him in her nostrils. She looked up, feeling his breath on her face, watching his eyes so intent on her mouth. She could see the very texture of his lips this close and she wanted them against her own.

"Please." She heard the soft plea and hardly realized that it had come from her own lips.

His jaw tautened. "I want it just that much," he said, biting off his words. His eyes caught hers. Tension strung between them like thunder building black on the horizon, the earth trembling as it waited for lightning to strike down against it. Bess searched Cade's dark eyes with that same anticipation, her heart slamming against her chest. It was going to happen . . . !

For one long, tense second it looked as if Cade wasn't going to be able to hold back. Then he forced himself to tear his eyes from hers, to take a step back and then another. His body protested, but for Bess's sake and his own, he didn't dare take the risk.

Watching him, Bess, felt her heart shaking her with its mad beat. The disappointment was almost physically painful. The way he'd been staring at her mouth had made her weak. But he'd had the strength to draw back before anything happened, because he didn't want complications. She wished that she could knock down all those obstacles he'd talked about. Life was so short. She'd go away, and he'd forget her. . . .

"You might write to us once in a while. Let us know how you're doing," he said unexpectedly.

"Would you write back?" she asked hesitantly.

He nodded. "Sure."

Her face lit up. It wasn't going to be the end of the world.

He slanted his hat over his brow and searched her face. "I've got something for you."

Her eyes sparkled. "For me?" she asked, surprised.

"It's not a diamond brooch, so don't get all excited," he muttered. He pulled a handkerchief out of his pocket and unfastened the knotted end. Inside was a small silver ring, inlaid with turquoise in the shape of a bird on its wide face.

"It's beautiful," she said softly.

"It has a history," he said. He took her right hand and slid the ring slowly onto her third finger, cradling her slender hand in his. "Someday I'll tell it to you. For now it's something to remind you that life goes on in spite of our problems."

"Are you sure you want me to have it?"

"I'm sure." His thumb rubbed over it while his fingers tightened slowly around hers. "It isn't worth much, but it's as much a legacy as your Great-aunt Dorie's pearls," he smiled faintly. "So take care of it."

"I'll never take it off," she promised. Her eyes went over it lovingly, and the expression on her face touched Cade. She was used to diamonds and pearls, but that little bit of silver seemed to touch her every bit as much as a mink coat would have touched her mother.

"You never were mercenary," he said quietly. "Or a snob. Once you've gotten over your father's death and learned how to manage your mother, you're going to be a heartbreaker."

She stared up at him quietly. "Be careful I don't break yours," she said with bravado.

Surprisingly he took her hand and put it over his heart. "I'm not sure I have one," he said simply. "It's been knocked around a good bit in recent years. But if you can find it, do your worst."

She reached up her free hand slowly and touched his hard mouth and then, when he stood very still and didn't protest, the rest of his lean, dark face.

"You won't forget me, will you?" she asked.

Her soft hands on his face had been heaven. He'd been busy imagining them on his bare chest, his shoulders, and his mind had to be dragged back from the exquisite images it had been contemplating. He caught her hand and pressed its soft palm to his mouth roughly. "No."

"I won't forget you either."

He sighed heavily, because this was harder than

he'd expected. "Come on. Time to get going. I've got two more horses to break. I only rode over to say good-bye."

She lingered at her horse, hoping that he might kiss her, but he didn't. He put her up into the saddle and rested one hand on her jean-clad thigh, his eyes dark and unsmiling as he looked up at her. When he didn't smile, that Comanche blood showed in his face, in the high cheekbones and stern expression.

"Remember what I told you about men," he said shortly. "You can't live like a hermit, but don't let Gussie railroad you into anything. Just be careful about the people you trust."

"You don't trust anybody, do you, Cade?" she asked gently.

"I trust my family and you. That's it." He turned to get back onto his own mount, looking as much a part of the buckskin as the saddle on its back. He was an excellent horseman. His mastery of horses and his skill with a rope had made him a natural in the rodeo arena, but Bess still worried about him.

She stared at him hungrily, hoping for a last-minute reprieve. That he'd propose marriage. That he'd ask her to wait for him. That he'd say, "Don't go."

He did none of those things. He stared at her for one long moment and then he turned his horse without a word, not even a good-bye, and went back the way he'd come. She watched him until he was a pinpoint in the distance, tears streaming down her cheeks. At least, she thought, she had one sweet memory to put under her pillow at night. She touched the silver ring on her finger and kissed it softly. She didn't really understand why Cade would give her a family heirloom when he hadn't said anything about a commitment, but it was the most wonderful present she'd ever received. She'd never part with it. It would remind her of Cade and help her cope with the hardships ahead.

And she knew Gussie was going to be the worst hardship of all.

Chapter 6

It took weeks for all the loose ends to be tied together, weeks during which Bess sometimes thought Gussie would drive her insane. She moped around the small apartment they'd taken in San Antonio, complaining about its size while she moaned about the loss of their fortune and grumbled about her late husband who was the cause of it all.

The sale of Spanish House was the final hurdle. A couple from Ohio bought it, and Bess breathed a sigh of relief when the papers were signed and the money advanced. Donald took over, paying out the last of the creditors. Gussie didn't know that Bess had given him Great-aunt Dorie's pearls, which were quietly sold to a jeweler for top dollar. She had to pay back Cade, so that he wouldn't lose Lariat. Despite what he'd said about the legacy and heritage of those pearls, she'd rather have lost them than let him lose his ranch.

The pearls were a small price to pay for the delight they were going to give Cade. But she made Donald promise not to tell him how she'd obtained the money. Let him think they realized a profit from the sale of the house and land, she told their attorney. She didn't want to tell Gussie, but inevitably she noticed that the pearls were missing.

"Where are Great-aunt Dorie's pearls?" she demanded petulantly. "They aren't in your jewelry box."

Bess was half angry that her mother should still be searching through her things after so many years. It was an old pattern that she'd always resented. "Why were you looking in my jewelry box?" Bess asked with faint indignation.

"Don't be absurd," Gussie said indifferently. "Where are they?"

Bess took a deep breath. No time like the present, she thought, to start as she meant to go on. "I sold them."

"You said they were costume jewelry!"

"I lied," Bess said with pretended calm. "We had debts to pay off. . . ."

"The debts were already paid off. That man," she began slowly, her temper rising. "You sold them to pay back Cade Hollister!"

Bess forced herself to breathe slowly. "I couldn't let his family lose Lariat because of us," she said.

"Damn his family and damn him!" Gussie burst out. "How dare you! How dare you sell an heirloom like those pearls!"

"It was a debt of honor," Bess began. "Dad would have—"

"Your father was a weak fool," Gussie said. "And so are you!"

Bess's lower lip trembled. Tears stung her eyes. She wouldn't cry, she wouldn't . . . but the tears spilled over.

Gussie wasn't moved. "I was going to buy a car with those pearls," she said angrily, "and you gave them away!"

That stopped the tears. Bess wiped them angrily from her cheeks and glared at her mother. Sell the pearls to buy a car, when they could barely meet their apartment rent and the money from the sale of the house was all but gone. She glared at Gussie.

"Yes, I sold them," she said, her voice shaking because it was the first time she'd ever spoken back. "And Cade will keep Lariat for his children. Children I'll never have, thanks to you. No man is ever going to want me because of you!"

Gussie turned her head warily, watching Bess as if she thought the younger woman had a fever. "That's enough, Bess."

"No, it isn't!" Bess's voice broke. "I can't take care of myself and you. Dad always looked after us, but I'm not Daddy. I'm not strong. I can't cope with a job and bills and you . . . !"

Gussie looked mortally wounded. "That my own child should speak to me like this," she said huskily. "After all I've done for you."

Bess's lips were trembling so hard that she could barely get words out. "You're making this so difficult," she whispered.

"I suppose I could always go on welfare," Gussie sniffed, reaching for a handkerchief. "And live in the streets, since my own child doesn't want me." She began to cry pitifully.

Bess knew it was an act. She knew that she should be strong, but she couldn't bear to hear Gussie cry. "Oh, Mama, don't," she moaned, going to Gussie, to hold her. "It's all right. We'll be fine, really we will."

"We could have had a nice car," Gussie sniffed.

"We couldn't have afforded gas and oil for it though," Bess murmured, trying to make a joke. "And somebody would have had to wash it."

Gussie actually laughed. "Well, it wouldn't have been me, you know; I can't wash a car." She hugged Bess back. "I know it's hard for you, but darling, imagine how it is for me. We were rich and now we have so little, and it's difficult."

"I know," Bess said gently. "But we'll get by."

"Will we?" Gussie sat up, rubbing her red eyes. "I do hope so." She sighed shakily. "Bess, you really will have to see about getting a job soon."

Bess started to argue, but Gussie was right. Her mother wasn't suited to any kind of work, and the most pressing problem was how they were going to live. After all the debts were paid, Bess and Gussie were left with little more than six hundred dollars and some of Gussie's jewelry.

"I'll start looking first thing in the morning," Bess said quietly.

"Good girl." Gussie got up. "Oh, damn the Hollisters," she muttered, glancing irritably at Bess. "I'll never forgive Cade for letting you pay off that debt in full. He could have refused the money, knowing how bad off we are."

Bess colored. "Mother, he's got debts of his own and Dad's investment scheme almost cost him Lariat. You know how he feels about heritage, about children."

"I don't want to talk about him. And don't you get any more ideas about that man. I won't let you get involved with him, Bess. He's the last man on earth for you. He'd break your spirit as easily as he breaks horses. I absolutely forbid you to see him, do you understand?"

"I'm twenty-three years old, Mother," Bess said uneasily. "I won't let you arrange my life."

"Don't be silly," Gussie laughed pleasantly. "You're a lovely girl and there are plenty of rich men around. In fact," she began thoughtfully, "I know of a family right here in San Antonio with two eligible sons. . . ."

Cade had been right. Bess stared at her mother in astonishment. "You aren't serious!" she burst out.

"It doesn't hurt to have contacts," Gussie was saying. "I'll phone them tonight and see if I can wrangle an invitation for us."

"I won't go," Bess said doggedly.

"Don't be silly. Of course you'll go. Thank God we still have some decent gowns left." Gussie waltzed out of the room, deep in thought and deaf to Bess's protests.

Bess didn't sleep. Gussie had upset her to the point of depression, and she was only beginning to realize what a difficult life it was going to be. Shackled with her flighty mother, there would never be any opportunity to see Cade again unless she fought tooth and nail. Not that Cade would try to see her. He was right in a way: there could never be a future for them with Gussie's interference. But it broke her heart.

At least Cade could keep Lariat now, she thought sadly. She'd done that for him, if nothing else.

The next morning she went out early to start looking for a job. She put her application in at two ad agencies and one magazine office, but her lack of experience was a strike against her and her typing skills were almost nonexistent. She and Gussie didn't have a typewriter for her to practice on and she couldn't afford to buy one. Perhaps she could rent one, she thought, and practice at night.

When she got back to the apartment at lunchtime, Gussie was in bright spirits. "We've got an invitation to dinner with the Rykers tonight," she said gaily. "They're sending a car for us at six. Do wear something sexy, darling. Jordan is going to be there. Daniel couldn't manage, he's in New York for a business meeting. Anna said she'd be delighted to see us both. You don't know her, of course, but she and I were at school together."

"Who is Jordan?" Bess asked warily.

"Jordan Ryker. Anna's eldest son. He's president of the Ryker Corporation. They make computers and that sort of thing. You'll like him, he's very handsome."

"I will not be railroaded into a blind date." Bess put her foot down.

"Don't start being difficult. We can't afford pride."

"I can," Bess said shortly. "I won't go."

"You most certainly will." Gussie turned and glared at her. "After what you did with our pearls, you owe me one little favor." She saw that belligerence wasn't going to work, so she changed tactics. "Now, darling, you'll enjoy yourself. I'm not trying to throw you at Jordan. It isn't even a date. We're just having dinner with old friends."

It couldn't be that simple, not with Gussie. Bess sighed wearily, knowing she was going to give in. She didn't have the heart to fight anymore. She'd lost Cade, and he was the only thing in life she might have cared enough to fight for.

"All right, Mama," she said. "I'll go."

"Lovely!" She held up a bracelet. "Isn't this adorable? I bought it today."

"What did you pay for that?" Bess asked, aghast at the gold bracelet.

"Just a few hundred—"

"Give it here." Before Gussie realized what was happening, Bess had taken the bracelet off. "It goes back. We can't afford things like this anymore."

"But it's all right," Gussie wailed. "I only charged it!"

"Charges have to be paid. Now where did you get it?"

Gussie told her, flushing when Bess started getting ready to take it back.

"I can't possibly live like this," Gussie wailed. "I must have a new winter coat, Bess, and my shoes are worn out. . . ."

"You have a new mink that Dad bought you last Christmas," Bess returned coolly, "and at least thirty pairs of shoes, all leather, none of which have been worn more than twice."

"They're out of style, and I won't be treated like this!"

"If you want to spend more money than we can afford, you could get a job," Bess offered.

Her mother looked horrified. "But what could I do?"

"Baby-sit little children. Be a receptionist. Wash dishes in a restaurant. Be a bartender."

Gussie's face paled. "You mean, work for the public? Oh, no, I couldn't do that," she gasped. "Suppose some of our friends saw me?"

"This is San Antonio," her daughter replied. "It won't shock anybody."

"I won't do it," Gussie said haughtily, and marched out of the room. "Besides, we still have our credit cards," she added, as if that magically alleviated all debt.

Bess couldn't help but laugh. Her mother was such a sweet, incorrigible idiot.

Bess felt old these days. She'd had her long hair trimmed, so it curved thick and shiny down her back, dropping in soft honey-colored waves over her shoulders. She looked sophisticated, more mature. She'd need to look older if she was going to get a job.

She'd cried about leaving the home where she'd grown up, the neighbors—Cade. Well, Cade was a part of the past already, she thought miserably. He hadn't called or written or been to see them since they'd moved to San Antonio, and the one letter she'd written to him had been returned to her unopened. It hadn't been a mistake either, because Cade's handwriting was bold and Bess had recognized it. She felt cold and miserable about that and finally decided that what he'd said to her that last day had been out of pity. He knew how she felt about him and he'd felt sorry for her. He'd been giving her a treat, a sweet send-off. That was the only explanation she could find for the ring he'd given her and the things he'd hinted at. Her heart felt like lead in her chest as the days went by. She'd gone almost out of her mind at first, but slowly she was getting used to the idea that he just didn't want her. Physically, perhaps, she thought, even though he'd never kissed her. But wanting wouldn't be enough eventually. Maybe it was just as well that he was keeping his distance. Someday she might be able to cope with losing him. For now she had other problems. She got up wearily and went to the store to return the bracelet.

Bess had put her long hair into a plaited bun and was just putting the final touches on her makeup when the doorbell rang. She listened, but at first she didn't hear the voices. Then as she put on her earrings, the ones that went with her sea-green strapless chiffon dress, the voices got louder and she suddenly recognized Cade's!

She ran out of her room, pausing just in time to hear her mother's triumphant voice telling him about their dinner invitation.

"She likes Jordan," Gussie was adding, "and the Rykers are a founding family of San Antonio. We're being well cared for—"

"Mother!" Bess gasped.

Gussie glared at her. "I was telling Cade about our invitation," she said innocently. "Don't talk long, darling. Jordan's chauffeur will be here to pick us up soon." She whirled out of the room, elegant in black silk, leaving Bess to face a coldly furious Cade. God only knew what Gussie had told him, because he looked murderous.

He was wearing a becoming dark charcoal-gray suit, that suited him. His equally dark eyes narrowed as he looked her over.

She took a slow breath, her heart going wild just at the sight of him. "Would you like to come in?" she asked hesitantly.

He lifted a careless eyebrow. "No. I don't think so. I came here to ask a question, but I don't think it's necessary anymore." His eyes went over her expensive dress and he smiled mockingly. "You don't seem much the worse for wear after paying me back, Bess, and you look all grown up."

"What did you want to ask me?" she murmured, letting her eyes wander slowly over his tanned face.

"I wanted to know where you got the money to give me."

"Oh." She breathed heavily. "I sent you a letter explaining it, but you sent it back unopened."

"I thought it might be a love letter," he said insolently.

She flushed. Her chin tilted. First Gussie, now Cade. It didn't seem possible that she could have so much antagonism in her life all at once. "Well, it wasn't. It was to explain what I sold to raise the money. I didn't want you to lose Lariat."

She meant the pearls, but he didn't know that. He was thinking about another rare commodity. His face hardened.

"You little fool!" he bit off. His hands caught her bare shoulders, gripping with such force that she was sure he'd bruised her as he pulled her out into the hall with him. The look in his eyes was frightening. Of all the things he'd expected, this was the last. The reason he'd come here today sat heavily on his chest. He was sick all over, thinking about Bess with some faceless man. Rage boiled up in him, choking him. He wanted to shake her senseless!

"Cade, what's the matter?" she gasped, shaken by the fury in his dark eyes as much as by the rage in his deep voice.

"What did you do for that money, Bess?" he demanded.

She jerked away from him, really frightened now. "What are you talking about!" she asked. "I just wanted you to have Lariat. . . ." she said, then broke off, astonished at his actions.

He couldn't even answer her. His tongue felt tied in knots. He just looked at her, hating her. After a minute he took a slow breath and let it out just as slowly.

"I came to ask how you were doing," he said finally. "But I can see that it was unnecessary. You've landed on your feet. Or, rather, on your back."

His tone was bristling with contempt. "On my back?" she echoed blankly, her eyes searching his for answers she couldn't find. He looked so strange. "Cade, are you all right?" she asked gently. "What's wrong?"

"She's already sold you to some damned rich man!" he accused.

Now she understood—not only what he was accusing her of but what he was so angry about. He was jealous! Her eyes widened as she gazed at his dark face and she had to force her feet not to dance a jig in the hall.

She understood all too well the anger he was feeling. His suit, while nice, was off a rack in some department store. His boots were expensive, but old and badly scuffed. Even his leather belt with its rodeo champion buckle was worn. He looked like a man at the bottom of the social ladder trying to make his way up, and Bess was wearing a designer gown that was only one season old and practically new. The differences between them were visible ones, and it struck her as odd that she'd never realized how proud Cade was, nor how reluctant he might be to make a pass at a rich woman. So many unanswered puzzle pieces fell into place when she understood all at once why he'd kept his distance for so long.

Her heart sang. She reached behind her and gently closed the apartment door. "Mama didn't sell me to anyone, Cade," she said quietly, her soft eyes smiling as they searched his furious ones.

"You're on your way to him now," he added, indicating her dress. His eyes lingered on her bare shoulders helplessly, with sudden hunger in his eyes.

"I'm on my way to dinner with some old friends of Mother's," she corrected. She touched his hand gently with hers, delighted at the way he tautened at the contact, at the unwilling curving of his hand into her touch. He looked down and saw the ring he'd given her, and all the hard lines went out of his face.

"You're still wearing it," he said quietly.

"Of course I am. You gave it to me. You're very possessive," she said, with gentle accusation, her heart racing as she felt the first stirrings of her femininity and realized its effect on him. He hadn't wanted her three years ago, but perhaps time had changed him, because he was looking at her now with open hunger.

"I suppose I am." He sighed heavily. "And blind as a damned bat. I don't know why I even assumed such a ridiculous thing. I know you're the last woman on earth who'd give herself to a total stranger for money."

The admission made her feel like flying. She smiled with all her heart. "I could have told you that, but I'm glad you decided it for yourself. What are you doing in San Antonio?"

"Selling off cattle mostly, but I had to find out how you got your hands on that money." He smiled ruefully. "You sold the pearls, didn't you?"

"Yes."

"I told you not to."

"Mama would have used them to buy a car. I decided that Lariat was a better investment," she added, and grinned. "Go ahead, throw them back in my face."

His eyebrows rose. "In a way I did. I gave Donald back everything except for the fifty cents on the dollar I asked for and told him to send it to you with my blessing."

She groaned. "Oh, no. Cade, you didn't!"

"I did it out of pride at the time," he admitted. "But the fact is, you need the money more than I do."

"Money is the last thing I need!" she cried. "Cade, if my mother gets her hands on anything, she'll spend it. I'm trying to make her see that we're going to have to work to support ourselves."

"Lots of luck," he said. "Gussie won't work. She'll get you a job instead."

She glared at him. "You might give me a chance."

He touched her cheek with a long, lean forefinger. "Yes. I might. You look lovely. Very expensive."

The feel of his finger made her knees weak. "You don't look bad yourself," she whispered huskily.

"Who is he, this man she's pushing you toward?" he persisted. His forefinger moved to her mouth and began to trace its exquisite bow shape very lightly.

"His name is Ryker," she said. "He owns a company of some sort. Cade, you're driving me crazy!" she protested, almost gasping at the sensations he was causing with his lazy touch against her mouth.

"What do you think it's doing to me?" he asked roughly. His eyes held hers until she felt the impact right to her toes. "The scent of you drowns me in gardenia blossoms, and that's what your mouth looks like to me right now, pink gardenia, petal soft. I want it, Bess," he breathed, letting his eyes fall to her mouth. "I want it so much I can hardly stand here and breathe without it."

She wanted it just as much. "I want it too, Cade," she whispered. She did. The thought of his kisses had kept her alive for years. Every day the longing grew worse. She moved a whisper closer to him, her face uplifted, her pulse throbbing at the flash of hunger in his dark eyes.

His lean hands slid to her shoulders and traced them, savoring the softness of her bare skin, the warmth under his hands. Her body would be like that, he thought in anguish. Her breasts would be even softer, and he could make their tips hard and flushed if he touched them. . . .

"My God, I'd give blood to touch you under that

dress," he whispered huskily. "I'd like to back you against the wall and crush you under me and kiss you until you moan out loud. But as sure as hell, Gussie's got radar and she'd come hotfoot to break it up."

Bess knew it was the truth, but she almost moaned out loud when he let go of her arms and moved away, leaving her trembling and weak.

"Besides all that, Bess," he added heavily, "kissing is addictive. That's why I didn't start anything before you left Coleman Springs."

He'd said something of the kind once before, but it was just as painful now as it had been then. She only knew that she'd die to kiss him, just once! "You might try it now, just to see," she whispered, her eyes on his hard mouth. "If it's addictive, I mean."

He smiled ruefully. "I might stick a handful of matches in my pockets and walk through a brushfire too. No way, honey. Go to your dinner party. I've got to get back to Lariat."

"I might decide to try kissing Mr. Ryker," she said threateningly, flirting with him for the first time in memory.

He read the mischief in her dancing eyes and actually smiled. "No, you won't."

"Why won't I?" she challenged.

He moved toward her, bending so that his warm breath touched her lips when he spoke. "Because you want me too much," he whispered. "You couldn't let another man touch you if you tried. I should have remembered that when I got hot under the collar about that money."

She stared into his dark eyes and couldn't deny it. She couldn't even breathe for the fever his nearness aroused in her. "Oh, Cade," she moaned under her breath. "I ache so . . . !"

"That works both ways," he said curtly. He moved away from her with a harsh laugh. "I've got to get out of here. I'll be in touch."

"But the money . . ."

"Damn the money," he said easily. His dark eyes searched over her face hungrily. "And to answer your earlier question, yes, I'm possessive—about the things and people I consider my own. Have a good time tonight, but don't let the proposed boyfriend touch you. I want to be the first." His eyes fell to her bodice, and she stopped breathing.

Her heart ran wild. But before she could get the words out, he'd turned and walked away without a backward glance, as if he'd forgotten that she existed. She stood watching him light a cigarette as he stepped into the elevator and it closed behind him.

Bess went back into the apartment in a daze. If she lived to be a hundred, she'd never understand Cade Hollister.

"Well, what did he want?" Gussie demanded as she came back into the living room.

"To tell me that he gave the money back to Donald."

Gussie brightened. "You mean we have money?"

"We did," Bess said, feeling suddenly capable of anything. "I'm going to tell Donald to buy back Great-aunt Dorie's pearls with what's left, and we'll put them away as a legacy."

"We can have a car . . . !" Gussie argued.

"No, we can't," Bess said firmly and waited for the explosion. Incredibly Gussie didn't say another word.

"We'll do very well without a lot of things we thought we needed, you'll see. Shouldn't you get your wrap? The chauffeur will be here any minute."

Gussie started to argue and then thought about Jordan Ryker and her plans to match him up with Bess. She couldn't really afford to antagonize Bess just yet, and obviously Cade Hollister hadn't made any headway, because Bess looked untouched and unruffled. She nodded and forced a smile.

"I'll do that," she told Bess.

Bess watched her go and then lifted her right hand to her lips and gently kissed the small silver ring Cade had given her. She could hardly believe what she'd heard him say, but now she had something to live for, something to fight for. Gussie wasn't going to find her quite as easy to manipulate from now on. Cade considered her his own. Perhaps her new state of poverty had made him decide that she was fair game now, or perhaps it was only that he wanted her after all. Either way she had a chance with him for the first time and she wasn't going to waste it.

She was going to be the independent, strong woman she knew she could be. She was already on the road to that independence, and she was awhirl with new feelings, new sensations. Cade was vulnerable, just a little, and that made her feel as if anything was possible. She could have danced on a cloud. Now all she had to do was escape the noose of her mother's suffocating attention and make Gussie understand that the past was dead. Then she could get a job, work hard, and prove to herself and Cade that she was capable of being the woman he needed. She could learn to cook and be independent. She might even learn to ride a horse as expertly as his mother, so that she could help out during roundup. She laughed at the thought, but it wasn't nearly as impossible now as it would have been when she was still Miss Samson of Spanish House. Oh, the wonder of being ordinary! If it hadn't been for her father's tragic death, she wouldn't have minded losing everything. For the first time she felt a sense of purpose, and a sense of self-worth. She could be a person instead of her mother's afterthought. That was a goal worth fighting for.

Chapter 7

Gussie came back with her coat over her arm, smiling at Bess. "You look delightful, dear. Jordan will be impressed."

"No matchmaking," Bess said firmly.

Gussie wavered. Bess was more assertive than she'd ever been, and Gussie didn't quite know how to take this new attitude. She proceeded cautiously. "I'm not trying to do that," she said. "It's just that I don't want you getting involved with Cade. It isn't only a question of different backgrounds, Bess. It goes much deeper than that. Haven't you noticed how hard he is, how domineering?" she asked with concern. "Darling, he'd break your spirit in no time. You'd end up just like poor Elise, and God knows, Coleman put her through one wringer after another their whole married life. I want more than that for you."

Bess was touched. Not that it affected her feelings for Cade, but it did at least make her mother's position a little clearer.

"I appreciate what you're saying, Mama," Bess said quietly. "And I understand it. But love doesn't just turn off."

"Love!" Gussie scoffed. "At your age it's just sexual attraction. Cade's no better—he wants you and that's all. A blind woman could see it."

Bess wanted to deny it, but she couldn't find the words. Yes, Cade did want her, she knew it now, even if she hadn't before. But Gussie was stepping cruelly on her dreams.

"I'm twenty-three," she told Gussie. "And I'm sorry that I'm not falling in line as usual, but from now on, I'm going to make my own decisions and live my own life." She was rigid as she said it, but she didn't let her mother see how unconfident she really was. She bluffed.

It worked, too. Gussie sighed. "You'll end up dominated and pregnant and poor. . . ."

"If I do, that will be my business," Bess said proudly. "It's time I made a few mistakes, I've never had the chance until now. And if you don't stop trying to live my life for me, I'll get out."

Gussie gaped. She simply didn't believe her ears. "You can't mean that! Why, you've always depended on me."

"That's true," Bess replied, amazed at the calm way she was able to stand up to Gussie, when she'd never managed it before. "But I'm not a child any longer.

You've got to stop treating me like one. I meant what I said, Mama," Bess added, standing her ground, even if she was secretly shaking in her high heels. It was hard saying no to Gussie. "I won't be used. Not by you nor by any of your 'rich young men.'"

"Well, darling, I didn't mean for you to prostitute yourself. . . ."

"I'll go to dinner tonight, because I promised. But there won't be any more arranged dates. I'm going to get a job, and so are you, Mother," she said, ignoring Gussie's flustered outburst. "If you live with me, you're going to have to pull your share of the load. I won't be your slave."

"I've just lost my husband, and now my only child is going to make a . . . a beast of burden of me!" she wailed, bursting into tears.

Bess was beginning to see through the tears. She smiled gently. "Mother, you'll look puffy at the Rykers' if you don't stop crying."

The tears dried up at once. Gussie fumbled for a handkerchief and wiped her eyes. "Yes, I suppose so," she sighed. "Well, we'll talk about it tomorrow." The doorbell rang in time to save her. "There's the chauffeur."

"We can talk, but it won't change anything," Bess said. She went to get her coat, a nice cashmere one that was two seasons old but still elegant. Its black wool highlighted her soft dark blond hair.

Gussie stared at her daughter without comprehending the change in her. It had to have something to do with Cade, she supposed, and her eyes glittered. Well, she'd keep that situation from developing. She wasn't about to have that man in her life or Bess's.

Unaware of her mother's thoughts, Bess was deep in her own and living in a fool's paradise. At least she knew Cade wanted her, she could build on that. But first she had to stop letting Gussie push her around like a pawn in a chess game. She had to start acting like an adult instead of Mama's little girl. She'd already made a start now, and it wasn't quite as hard as she'd imagined. She felt new already.

She went to the Rykers, and she found that she liked them. Anna Ryker was taller than Bess or Gussie and very dark, a charming woman with a noble Spanish heritage who was welcoming and outgoing. Her son Jordan was less enthusiastic. He was tall, like Cade, but husky, a big man with large dark eyes and a chiseled, wide mouth. He didn't smile when they were introduced, and he looked formidable. He had thick black hair, neatly combed, and thickly lashed black eyes. He was polite but very withdrawn and cool. He had to be in his late thirties, Bess thought, studying him. He didn't smile very much, and she had a feeling that business was very much the hallmark of his life. When he didn't ignore her, he made icy remarks about his lack of leisure and how difficult he could be at work.

After the meal Gussie subtly arranged to have Anna show her some paintings, deliberately leaving Bess alone with Jordan.

He leaned back in a dark red leather chair, smoking a thin cigar, his black eyes wary and faintly curious as he studied her.

"It's all right, you know," she sighed, sitting on the edge of her chair to study him with a weary smile. "I never attack men."

His dark eyebrows shot up, and something like a

twinkle danced in his black eyes. "Do I look nervous?" he asked dryly.

She laughed softly. "I wasn't sure." Her eyes lowered to the carpet. "I didn't want to come, but Mother insisted. Just lately I've realized that Lincoln abolished slavery, but I'm having to break it to her gently."

"You're something of a surprise," he said through a wisp of smoke. "I thought this evening was one of my mother's ongoing attempts to marry me off, so I haven't been on my best behavior." His lips twitched. "I had the idea that if I talked business and did my classic ax-murderer impression, you might turn tail and run."

"Oh, not at all," she said. "We homicidal maniacs really should stick together—it's safer that way."

He laughed, and she caught a flash of white teeth in his dark face. "Why does your mother want to throw you at eligible men?"

"She doesn't like the eligible man I want," she said simply. "He isn't a rich man, and he doesn't like her." Her eyes went to her hands in her lap. "He won't let me get close to him at the moment. But I'll never love anyone else."

"I'm sorry," he said, and sounded as if he meant it. "It seems we share similar problems. Except that the lady of my choice is engaged to another man." His broad shoulders rose and fell. "Not her fault exactly." He smiled bitterly. "I was never able to show my feelings. When I finally realized that she had no idea how I felt, it was too late." He took another draw from the cigar. "She never knew."

"If she isn't married, there's still time," she reminded him.

He shook his head. "I'm a bad marriage risk. I like my job too much, and I tend to spend too much time at it. I'd run a wife crazy in a month. If she loved me, it would be even worse." He leaned back. "No, I'm satisfied to die a bachelor. I have a horse I'm pretty fond of. . . ."

She laughed gently. "Mr. Ryker, you're being wasted on the horse."

"Thank you, Miss Samson, for your vote of confidence. If I ever need a character reference, you'll be the first on my list."

"Darling, do come and look at these paintings," Gussie called from the hall. "There's a van Gogh here!"

"Yes, Mother." She got up, glancing wryly at Jordan, who rose with her. "She loves art. We had quite a collection until we lost everything."

His eyes studied her quietly. "I'm sorry."

"Oh, I'm not," she said. "I think I had all my priorities mixed up. I rather like the idea of starting over and earning my own living." She smiled. "I think I may even like revolutions," she added with a pointed glance in her mother's direction.

"Allow me to support the cause." He rolled the cigar in his hand. "We own, among other concerns, an advertising agency, and I understand that you studied journalism in college."

She gasped. "Where did you find that out?"

"Oh, I had the usual incredibly fast background check done on your family early this morning," he said with a rakish smile. "By noon I knew that you were penniless, and I had a good idea why your mother was arranging to visit."

She went flaming red, but he took her hand and smiled.

"That was unforgivable," he said softly, "and I didn't mean it the way you're taking it. You remember very well how it is in our circles. I'm not a snob, but I'm no fool either. You said you want to earn your living, and I've got a job you can do. No strings. Try it for a month and if you don't like it, go with my blessing."

She was astonished at his speed. "But my typing is terrible, and I've never had a job—"

"You can start in the morning. You'll like the others. They're young and bright and energetic, and they won't think you're my mistress." He grinned. "In fact, I imagine most of them think I'm too somber to approach a woman."

She looked up at him warmly. "I think you're a very nice man," she said.

"Don't insult me." He propelled her into the hall. "Mother, I've just hired a new employee," he told Anna. "Meet our newest advertising whiz."

Gussie beamed, and seeing that smile, Bess could be forgiven for wondering if she'd gotten her mother's motives wrong. Had Gussie only wanted to help her find work? Or had there been a deeper, darker intent?

The next morning she reported to the Ryker Advertising Agency with her heart in her throat. She was wearing her best beige suit with a pink blouse, and her hair was pulled into a neat French plait at her nape. She hoped she looked businesslike but not too ritzy and standoffish. She was so nervous that she knew she was going to faint if anyone looked hard at her.

The receptionist was on the phone when she arrived. She had a card in her purse that Jordan had given her, with the name of a executive on it.

"Yes, may I help you?" the receptionist asked.

"I've come to see about a job," she began. "I was told to ask for Mrs. Terrell?"

"Certainly." The receptionist smiled and buzzed someone. Bess looked around the office, not wanting to eavesdrop. It was a beautiful place, full of huge potted plants with modern furniture and lots of light and sculpture. It had a welcoming personality.

"Miss Samson?"

She turned to find a tall, dark-haired woman smiling at her. The woman was wearing a vivid burgundy dress and she had a burgundy and black bow in her hair. "I'm Julie Terrell," she said, introducing herself, "and I guess you could call me the head honcho. Won't you come in?"

"It's very nice to meet you," Bess said uneasily as she followed Julie into a lavish office with a big drafting board and chair, computers, graphics charts, and a library that rivaled the one her family had prided itself on.

"Sit down." She indicated a comfortable uphol-stered chair for Bess as she seated herself behind the desk and leaned back, kicking her shoes off. "Wow, do my feet hurt! I've spent two days working up a presen-tation for a new client and I finished it at two this morning. I work on my feet," she added sheepishly. "They're the most abused part of my body. Now, let's hear about your qualifications."

"I don't have very many," Bess moaned. "I have a journalism degree, but I've never used it. . . ."

"Can you draw?"

"Why, yes," Bess said, surprised.

Julie handed her a sketch pad. "Draw something."

"What?"

"Anything you like."

Bess did a quick sketch of a rose and added a diamond ring around the stem just for fun and handed it to Julie.

"Very nice." She grinned. "Not just a rose, but a diamond as well. Yes, you've got a creative mind. Can you do layouts? Mechanicals?"

"Yes, I minored in art," she began, "but I thought writing—"

"Creating is what advertising is all about," Julie told her. "And your forte, very obviously, is art. Take your hair down, please."

Bess thought that this was surely the strangest interview she'd ever had in her life. "I beg your—"

"Take your hair down. We have an account coming up that's going to feature a harried secretary, and when we can save money by using staff instead of models, we use staff. Yes, your hair is perfect, just what I pictured, so we'll use you! There's a bonus for that," she added with a laugh. "Welcome to Ryker Advertising, and don't say a word if Nell accuses you of getting here through Jordan's bed. She's been crazy about the big boss for years, but it gets her nowhere. He doesn't look at women."

That was what Julie thought, but Bess didn't say a word. Apparently she didn't know that Jordan had recommended her for this job. "What's he like?" she asked.

Julie misunderstood and gave her a physical description. "Big," Julie said. "His mother is Spanish, but his father was Dutch. Interesting combination, and he's a complex man. I only know him from meetings. His mother sent you down, didn't she? She seems to be a lovely person. We all like her."

"Yes—" Bess began.

"Well, come on and I'll find you a spot." Julie, in bare stocking feet, wandered along the hall with Bess behind her.

There wasn't a large staff, and Bess had the impression that the agency was still in its early stages and was still a struggling concern. That made her like it even more, because it gave her the opportunity to grow with it. And since Julie was the boss, it meant that Jordan Ryker didn't have a chauvinistic bone in his body. He obviously hired by qualifications alone, because the office boasted three women and four men of whom one was black, one Mexican-American, and the other two white and middle-aged.

"All the men in the office are married, you notice," Julie said dryly when the introductions were over. "Mr. Ryker's idea apparently. I don't think he approves of office romances."

"I suppose it would cut down on productivity," Bess agreed, tongue-in-cheek. "I like it here already."

"You haven't met Nell yet," she said. "Well, brace yourself. Here goes."

Bess was nervous, expecting a Tartar. But Nell was delightful. She had dark hair and blue eyes and she bubbled. She was dressed in vivid colors, oranges and reds and browns, and she looked the way Bess imagined an autumn wind might dress if it wore clothing.

"A new victim!" Nell exclaimed. She pushed back her short pageboy and grinned. "Hi! I'm the office maniac. They usually hide me when company comes. Are you staying or just passing through? If you're staying, just remember that the big boss is mine. Private property. He doesn't know it yet, but I'm working on him real hard."

"Your secret is safe with me," Bess assured her. She smiled wistfully. "I've got a tall male problem of my own."

"Are you married?" Nell asked, peering at Bess's finger, on which the small turquoise-and-silver ring was worn. Bess had put it on her engagement finger last night and slept with her cheek on it. She'd resolved to wear it on her engagement finger from then on, and Cade could think what he liked.

"No, I'm not married," Bess said. "And not likely to be anytime in the near future unless I can tie up the man I want and marry him without his permission," she added dryly.

Nell grinned. "How old are you?"

"Twenty-three—almost twenty-four."

"A young person too," Nell declared. "I myself am twenty-eight, and Julie here is over-the-hill. She's thirty-three. Ancient."

"Speak for yourself, old relic," Julie returned. "Now, go away. I have to get Bess a desk and start her on the dog food account."

"Dog food." Nell put a hand to her head. "I see a dog wearing a crown, ordering his loyal subjects to eat nothing less royal than Goodbody's Prime Rib Treat."

"Nell does cost studies," Julie said. "She's also one of our best salespeople. She goes out and drags in new accounts." She glowered at the younger woman. "She doesn't do commercials or ads. No imagination," she added with a tsk-tsk. "Let's go, Bess, before she rubs off on you any more than she already has."

"Peasant," Nell scoffed, and went back to work.

"Fortunately you're meeting Nell on one of her more sedate days," Julie murmured dryly as they went back down the hall. "You should see her when she's being vivacious."

"No fish dinner for you today," Nell called after her. "You'll have to get a can of worms and catch your own."

"See what I mean?" Julie grinned.

Bess was given space in the office next to Julie's. Most of the so-called offices were only partitions in fact. Bess's place had a desk and a drafting table, along with a telephone, computer, printer, and modem.

"I hope I don't have to use that immediately," Bess said uneasily, nodding toward the computer.

"No problem. We give lessons," Julie said dryly. "Now sit down and I'll run you through this new account and you can work on some ideas for the presentation. But don't take too long. We only have this week to get it together."

After the first day Bess was sure that she wasn't intelligent enough to learn the operation of that computer. But the next day Nell removed Julie from the console, sat down, and proceeded to make English out of what had been Greek to Bess the day before. By the end of the second day Bess could pull up files, do graphics, and even print things out without help. She felt like a million dollars.

Gussie was watching Bess's progress with uneasiness. "I don't see why you won't just sell the pearls," she muttered later in the week while Bess was sprawled in the living room of the small apartment working on drawings for the ad campaign. "Having Donald buy them back with that money wasn't sensible."

"Yes, it was. They're a family legacy. And they're mine," she added, looking up. "Great-aunt Dorie gave them to me."

Gussie grimaced. "I'm sure she thought you'd use them to good advantage, not lock them up somewhere."

"If I took the money, it would be gone in a week, and you know it, Mother," she said. "This way we'll have them for an emergency. And have you thought any more about a job?"

"I most certainly have not." Gussie sat down irritably, crossing her legs. "I expected Anna to invite me to go with her and Jordan to Europe, but they left this morning. They won't be back for two months."

"Why should they have invited you?" Bess asked.

Gussie sniffed. "Well, they know I'm not suited to staying at home all the time. I thought they would, that's all."

"Did you ask them?" she exclaimed.

The older woman fidgited. "You never get anything unless you ask for it," she muttered. "I'm bored to death. And I don't want a job. I'm going shopping tomorrow," she added, daring her daughter to say anything.

Bess felt years older now that she had a job and a future. She sat up, her hair falling gracefully around her face, and glared at her mother. "If you go shopping, it had better be with your own jewelry and not with our joint charge cards, or I'll take back everything you buy. I swear I will. I refuse to spend my life in debt because you're trying to live in the past, Mama."

"You can't talk to me like that," Gussie snapped.

Bess glared back. "I just did."

Gussie got up, infuriated, and walked out of the room.

Bess put her work away, because the backlash from the argument continued for the rest of the night. It wasn't easy standing up to Gussie, and it upset her to have hard feelings with her mother. But she had to start somewhere. If she didn't, Gussie would walk all over her for the rest of her life.

She looked at the silver ring on her finger and touched it lovingly. At least Cade had cared a little, to give her such an heirloom. She kissed it softly, wondering where he was, what he was doing. Probably he wasn't even thinking about her, but she couldn't stop herself from dreaming about him.

The next day she finished the drawings she'd started for the dog food presentation and put them on Julie's desk before she went home. Julie was in a staff meeting and wouldn't be out until well after quitting time.

"I hope they'll do," Bess sighed.

Nell hugged her warmly. It was that kind of an office; everyone was open and friendly and affectionate. Bess, who'd never had real affection before, was overwhelmed and delighted by the feeling of belonging.

"They're terrific," Nell said. "Now, you go home and stop worrying."

"I'll try."

"It's Friday night. Poor Jordan, alone in Europe with his mother, when he could be here, taking me out on the town." Nell sighed. "I guess I'll read a romantic novel and throw myself off the roof."

"You nut."

Nell laughed gaily. "Not really. I love life too much. Have a nice weekend. Good night."

"Good night." Bess watched the older woman go and noticed that the minute Nell stepped outside the building, she changed. The bubbly personality seemed to go into eclipse, leaving a somber, quiet, very dignified woman. Bess's eyes narrowed thoughtfully. She wondered if Jordan Ryker had ever seen that side of Nell and figured that he probably hadn't. It might make all the difference, but then, his heart belonged to some other woman. Nell wouldn't be in the running anyway, she supposed. It was a pity, because a gay, happy person like Nell was just what a man like Jordan needed.

She took a cab home with her paycheck in hand. It was just for the week, but it looked like a small fortune to Bess, who'd become used to living without luxuries or pocket money.

The apartment was quiet when she entered it, beaming and feeling excited about her first check. But when she got into the living room and saw the boxes strewn across the sofa, her smile faded.

Gussie came out in a short fur jacket. Blue fox. She pushed back her hair. "Isn't it lovely?" she asked with faint hauteur. "It was on sale, so I bought it. And those things. And I'm not taking them back, and neither are you. I refuse to live like a pauper!"

Bess stared at the check in her hand. It wouldn't buy even one of the dresses on that sofa, much less several of them and a fox jacket. She turned and picked up the phone.

"What are you doing?" Gussie asked. "Bess!"

Bess dialed the number of the credit card company that she and her mother shared jointly, got an operator, and canceled the card. She also informed the operator that she was not responsible for her mother's purchases and that the company should know that her mother was without financial means.

"How could you! How dare you!" Gussie exploded. "You cannot do that. I forbid it!"

Bess turned, indignant and furious. She was working like a tiger and budgeting her own needs, only to have her mother out spending everything she could ever make. It was just too much to swallow.

"You listen to me," she said unsteadily. "I'm working for my living now, and it isn't going to be to support you in the style to which you've become accustomed. I am not buying fox jackets or designer dresses, and I'm not supporting you. When I told you that, I meant it. Either you take those things back or you get out and try to pay for them yourself."

"Take them back! Never!"

Gussie grabbed up two of the dresses and, staring contemptuously at Bess, she ripped them apart.

Bess felt her face go pale, but she didn't flinch. "If that's the way you want to wear them, suit yourself, but I'm not making any payments. If you won't move out, I will."

Gussie's face went red. "You won't. You can't make it without me."

"Hold your breath and see." Bess went into her bedroom, took out her suitcase, and began to pack. She hadn't expected Gussie to make it easy for her, but having to live like this was just impossible.

"You aren't going anywhere," Gussie said, but with less vigor.

Bess just kept packing. She was scared to death. She didn't know where she was going to go, or even if she could find an apartment, but she was certainly going to try. She at least had her paycheck. She could phone Donald tomorrow from the office and tell him what had happened.

Gussie began to cry. "What will I do without you?" she wailed. "I can't live by myself!"

Bess didn't answer her. She knew her face was almost white with fear and emotional strain, but she had to do this. It was now or never. If she didn't break free of Gussie this time, she never would.

"Where will you go?" Gussie moaned.

"I don't know," Bess said firmly. She picked up the suitcase. "But at least I won't have to worry about anyone's bills except my own."

The older woman sat down heavily on the couch, beside the ruins of the two dresses. She looked her age, for the first time in Bess's memory.

"You don't have to leave," she said dully. "I think I can find a place to go more easily than you can." She swallowed her tears and rubbed at her eyes with a pathetic kind of wounded pride. "You don't understand how hard it is for me. . . ."

"Yes, I do," Bess replied quietly. "But you don't understand the reverse. Daddy was always there to take care of our finances, to look after us. Neither of us ever had to lift a finger, and now we're paying for it." She sat down on a small chair, putting her suitcase down beside her. "But, Mama, I can't be Daddy. I can't take care of you. It's going to be all I can do to take care of myself, don't you see? I'm not strong."

Gussie lifted her head, and her eyes looked sad. "Neither am I," she replied. "I've never had to be. Bess, when I was a little girl, we were poor," she said, and it was the first her daughter had ever heard of her youth. "I had to go barefoot, and sometimes I was hungry because we were so poor. I had a brother, but he died when I was very young, and my parents never seemed to care as much for me as they had for him, so I never had a lot of love. When your father came along, I risked everything trying to get him to marry me." She grimaced. "He did, but only because I was carrying you." She averted her eyes from Bess's shocked face. "I suppose I was lucky in a way, because he grew to love me. But I never forgot my roots and I always felt that I wasn't good enough for him." She twisted the handkerchief in her hand. "Or for anybody else in his circle. I bought expensive clothes and tried to live up to the image he had of me, so I wouldn't embarrass him. Eventually I lost myself in the image. Now I'm not sure I know who I am anymore."

Bess had to work at comprehending it all. Gussie had never talked to her like this before, and she realized that it was the first time she'd seen her mother without the flighty-rich-woman mask she usually wore.

Gussie looked up, smiling faintly at her daughter's face. "Frank spoiled me rotten. I hate being poor again, and I've been fighting back. But it's not going to work, is it?" She leaned back wearily. "Bess, I can't get a job. I'd be hopeless at it, and I'd grow to hate my life.

I've been rich too long. I think you can adjust, but I never will."

"Then what will you do, Mama?" Bess asked solemnly. "The money's gone. We can't get it back. And really," she added with a tiny smile, "I can't see you as a matronly bank robber."

Gussie smiled. "Neither can I." She sighed. "I still have some friends who care about me. I'll travel, I think. I've got enough jewels left to manage to pay most of my expenses if I can impose on the hospitality of friends for some of the time, and I can. I've let enough of them impose on me when their luck was off, you know." She studied Bess quietly. "I hadn't realized what a pill I've been for you to swallow. But people tend to lean when you let them, darling, and you never said anything."

"I was a little intimidated," Bess murmured.

"Well, you've found your way now, haven't you? A job, and a good one, and new friends. You'll manage, even without Cade."

Bess's heart leaped. She didn't answer.

Gussie leaned forward. "You still don't understand, do you? Bess, Cade is a hard, strong man. He's not rich and he may never be. He needs a woman of his own kind, someone as strong as he is, someone who can stand up to him. . . ."

"What do you know about it?" Bess asked shortly.

"I knew his father," Gussie said simply. "And let me tell you, Coleman Hollister was one tough *hombre*. You were too young then to remember, but he used to break horses for your father from time to time when we had the riding stables just briefly. Elise worshiped the ground he walked on, and he walked all over her.

She was never able to stand up to him, and he hurt her a great deal. There was a major misunderstanding on Cade's part that ruined our friendship. I've never forgiven him for it." She lowered her eyes to the carpet. "He's just like his father." She looked up again. "And you're very much like Elise. He'd break your spirit in no time. You might not believe it, judging from the past few weeks, but I care for you. I don't want to see you hurt."

"I thought you didn't want me to get involved with Cade because you thought the Hollisters were beneath us socially," Bess murmured.

"That was a good enough excuse at the time. Cade, of course, saw right through it." She searched Bess's quiet eyes. "I know how you feel about him. But the past is going to get in the way forever, and Cade might not be above using you to get back at me. I can't be sure, so I've tried to keep you apart. It was for your own good, although I know you won't believe that."

"I love him," Bess said, her voice soft with pain. "I always have."

"I know. I'm sorry."

Bess looked at her suitcase. "So am I." She felt as if she'd been hit. Her mother's antagonism for Cade had puzzled her, but now she began to understand that there was more to it than she was being told. She was worried about what Gussie had said, about Cade using her to get even with her mother. Surely he wouldn't. But Gussie would make things difficult. "You must see that you and I are just not going to be able to stay together, the way things are."

"I can see that now." Gussie sat up straight. "I'll write to you, and you write back. Be careful who you go out with." She smiled. "Jordan Ryker isn't really a bad man, and you could do worse."

Bess wasn't going to get into another argument with her mother. "You take care of yourself," she said. "Even if you are a handful, I'm pretty fond of you."

Gussie actually laughed. "I'm fond of you too. And delighted to see that you do have a temper. I'd started to wonder." She dabbed at her eyes. "Well, I have to make one long-distance call." She gave Bess a rueful look. "I'll have to owe you for it too. I'm skint."

Bess laughed as well. "Okay."

She took her suitcase back to her room, amazed at the new things she'd learned about her own mother. It seemed that you never really knew people at all.

Now at least she understood some of Gussie's reasoning. But what had she meant about a misunderstanding? Had it had something to do with Cade's father? And what was it?

The questions nagged at her all night, but she didn't ask any more. Gussie managed to wrangle an invitation from some friends in Jamaica and she was going to be on a morning flight down there.

Bess was delighted at the change. She'd grown used to Gussie and she was going to miss her in a way. But in another way it was a taste of freedom that she'd never had. She could hardly wait to be truly on her own, for the first time in her life.

Chapter 8

Bess didn't go with Gussie to the airport. They said a quiet good-bye in the apartment, and Bess said it with mixed feelings. It was scary to be away from her mother for the first time, and at the same time it was like opening a new chapter in her life.

"Don't forget to write," Gussie said. "I'll send you the address. And I'm sorry to leave you with those things to return to the store," she added with a careless smile, "but I have to go."

"I'll take care of it," Bess said, thinking that it would probably be the last time and she shouldn't complain.

Gussie kissed her cheek. "Don't think too badly of me, Bess," she said seriously. "I do care about you."

"I care about you too," Bess replied. "Have a good time."

"With Carie Hamilton I'm bound to," she sighed. "She's a widow now, and we used to double-date years ago. She and her daughter are staying in one of the old plantation houses there, right on the beach. I imagine we'll have plenty of time to socialize."

"Send me a postcard," Bess said.

"Certainly." Her mother picked up her suitcase, grimacing. "I can't really remember the last time I had to carry my own things. But I suppose I'll get used to it, since I have to. Good-bye, darling. Good luck with the job."

"I'll be fine. So will you," Bess said.

Gussie paused, frowning worriedly. "Will you be all right on your own?" she asked, with maternal feelings she hadn't known she possessed. "It's a big city and you don't really know anyone here."

Bess had thought the same thing herself, but she couldn't backslide now. "I'll be fine," she repeated. She smiled, fighting back tears. "Don't worry about me. But do let me know that you arrived safely, will you?"

"Yes, I'll do that. Be careful." Gussie opened the door and the cab driver was standing there. She sighed and put down the case. "Oh, how lovely. Can you carry that for me, please? It's so nice to have a big, strong man to lug these heavy cases about. Good-bye, darling," she called to Bess, and followed the burly cab driver down the hall.

Bess watched her walk to the elevator, waved, and closed the door. She wiped away her tears and leaned back against the door. Well, she'd done it now. She was completely on her own. She had to make it now; she'd burned her bridges. And while it would be a little unnerving at first, Gussie was out of her life, temporarily at least, and she had a chance to be her own boss, to make her own decisions without having to argue for them or justify them.

The apartment was so small, hardly more than the size of a bedroom in the house she'd grown up in, and it was in a section of town that was far from the best San Antonio had to offer. The furniture was shabby and the curtains were dingy, but it was her home now, and she loved every crack and peeling bit of paint in it.

She made herself a cup of coffee and two pieces of cheese toast and sat down to eat before she went to work. She put on a creamy-beige knit suit, brushed out her hair so that it curled toward her face, dashed on some makeup, and started out the door. Then she remembered the fox jacket and the other things her mother had bought that had to be returned.

With a resigned sigh, she picked up the fox jacket and what was returnable of the things Gussie hadn't ripped, along with the sales ticket, and started out the door.

She carried them to work, because the department store wasn't open until ten. She could take them back on her lunch hour, she decided.

The presentation was being made that morning. She gave all her drawings to a nervous Julie, wished her luck, and settled down to work on the next ad campaign, this time for a new jeweler in town.

At lunch she went out alone to the department store, the fur jacket draped over one arm and the other things in their distinctive bag in her hand.

San Antonio was a big city. There were thousands and thousands of natives who lived here. But as fate would have it, there was a visitor in town that particular day, a familiar visitor who hailed from a ranch near Coleman Springs. And Bess turned a corner, with her mother's purchases in her hand, and almost collided with Cade Hollister.

He stopped dead. He was wearing a blue pin-striped suit with his best Stetson and boots, and he looked every inch an up-and-coming businessman.

His dark eyes gazed at what she was carrying. "What kind of job did you get?" he asked with a lifted eyebrow, and the old suspicion was in his eyes again. "Or did your new friend buy this for you?"

Bess sighed. Just like old times, she thought, he was ready to think the worst the minute he saw her.

"Well, actually—"

"Oh, there you are!" A tall, elegant brunette came around the corner before she could open her mouth and took Cade's arm with a familiarity that made Bess weak in the knees. No wonder he hadn't written. No wonder her last letter had gone unanswered. He'd already found another woman, and after the ring he'd given her and the things he'd said. . . . She knew her face was white.

The older woman was wearing a very expensive oyster wool suit with silk accessories, and she was a knockout.

"I'm sorry, I'd forgotten my purse, Cade," she said. Her eyes went to Bess and she smiled. "Hello. I'm Kitty."

"Hello," Bess replied numbly, because this was the last thing she'd expected, that Cade would have a woman with him.

Cade didn't have time to explain. After seeing the

hunted-doe look on Bess's face, he wanted to. Damn the luck, he thought angrily, she'd just have to think the worst. But as his eyes went again to that fox thing on her arm, he wondered why he should have to justify himself to her. It looked as if her mother had managed to find her a nice rich man, and here he was with bills piling up and having to sell off one of his best seed bulls to this brunette's husband just to stay alive.

Once more all the old, irritating differences between his life-style and Bess's came back to sit on his shoulder. He'd wondered ever since the last time he saw her how it was going to be when she got a taste of city life and her mother's close influence. Now he knew. Whatever hopes he'd been harboring were just so much smoke.

"We have to hurry. See you," Cade said curtly, as if he didn't mean it. His eyes cut at Bess's with icy contempt. He took the brunette's arm, smiling down at her in a way he'd never yet smiled at Bess, and led her down the street and through the door of a very expensive French restaurant.

Bess felt as if she'd been hit in the head, and she knew she was never going to get over it this time. Numbly she walked on toward the department store.

She barely realized what she was doing when she took the things back. She had to explain why she was returning them, but there was an understanding clerk who didn't ask any irrelevant questions and was very nice about it. Bess had the charges removed from her charge account and then wondered how she was going to manage the several hundred dollars the two damaged dresses had cost. Well, she thought, it was probably worth it to have Gussie temporarily out of her hair.

On the way back to work she had to pass the French restaurant again. She was torn between hunger for just one more glimpse of Cade and the realization that a quick, clean break was best. She forced herself not to look in the window as she passed it. Opening old wounds helped nobody. He thought she was getting expensive presents from other men. He didn't know that Gussie had left. He just assumed, as he always had. Well, she thought with a spark of temper, let him think it. If he couldn't trust her enough, even knowing how she felt about him, to stop from making unfounded assumptions about her character, she didn't need him. And he was one to look contemptuous, him with his elegant brunette! He was squiring other women around town, and he'd never even asked Bess out for a hamburger. But he seemed to expect her to wait forever just to have him turn up once in a blue moon to raise her hopes and then dash them with his usual arrogance. Well, not anymore! She'd had it with his moods. From now on he could go away and stay away.

Back at work she kept her mind on the job and appeared perfectly normal to her co-workers. But when she got to the apartment, she collapsed into tears, her momentary flare of spirit vanishing in the wake of cruel reality. He'd found another woman already. He was going out and having a good time, and Bess was just a bad memory to him. How quickly he'd erased her from his life, just as he'd said he would before she ever left Spanish House. He'd only come to see her that night to taunt her. Maybe there was even something in what Gussie had said, that he wouldn't be above taking out his revenge on Bess for whatever he held against Gussie. She brooded on that thought,

and it made her hurt. But she couldn't afford to let the
past affect her future. If she had to go on without
Cade, she'd just have to do it. The experience would
make her stronger at least.

But he wasn't all that easy to erase from her life. She
mourned him as surely as she'd mourned her father.
The days went by in a dull gray haze, and they seemed
to merge after a time. She felt as if she was just going
through the motions of living, without any real enthusiasm for it. When she'd lived at Spanish House, there
was always the possibility that any day might bring a
visit from Cade or a glimpse of him. But here in San
Antonio that wasn't likely. It was a trick of fate that
she'd run into him.

She wondered what he was doing here. He had business interests all over the place these days, but she
imagined he'd brought his lady love here for the cui-
sine. Odd that he'd be on a date in the middle of the
day, but then Cade didn't do anything by the book.
The woman had been really beautiful, and she seemed
friendly enough. But the thought of her in Cade's arms
broke Bess's heart. She'd lost so much in the past few
weeks, but it seemed unkind that she should keep
having Cade dangled over her head. Fate seemed determined to taunt her with him.

During the weeks that followed, Bess began to come
out of her shell. She put Cade in the back of her mind
and concentrated on learning how to live as an ordinary person. It wasn't really all that hard, adjusting to
being without a great deal of money. She found that
budgeting her salary was a delightful challenge. She
enjoyed mundane things such as going to the Laun-
dromat and the grocery store. She did her own hair

and nails instead of going to a beauty parlor, and she even learned to cook after a few near-fatal mistakes.

The apartment where she and Gussie had been staying didn't allow cooking, so Bess found a new one that did. It was just as small as the one she'd left, but it had charm. It was located in a group of older apartment buildings. It even reminded her of Spanish House, with its adobe facade and graceful arches, and most of the residents were elderly people who'd lived there for a long time. Bess made friends quickly, and some of the older ladies took an interest in her. She found herself on the receiving end of cuttings from flowers and small potted plants to set on her small balcony, because it was already early spring. They also gave her little things, such as homemade potholders and refrigerator magnets.

Work had become delightfully familiar. She was given bigger and better accounts as she went along. Her drawings improved, like her personality, and before long her status was elevated so that she wasn't only drawing mechanicals, she was writing copy as well. That brought her a small raise, and she began to feel her worth as a person. And to top it all, one of her ads was slated for a national television advertising campaign. She was so excited, to have accomplished so much so soon, and she wanted to share it with someone. But Gussie still hadn't sent her a telephone number where she could be reached, and nobody else would be interested. It took a little of the joy out of her achievement.

The thought of Gussie made her uncomfortable. In the back of her mind she worried that Gussie might run out of people to visit and come home. Then there was Cade, like a handsome ghost, haunting her dreams. She still wore the small silver ring on her hand, and it was something of a link to him. Even if he didn't want her, she wanted him. Love was hard to define, but it must have something to do with stubbornness, she told herself as night after lonely night passed. She couldn't give up, even knowing there was no hope.

Gussie sent a postcard saying that she was having fun and might come back in a few weeks to visit. But she didn't include a return address, and Bess wondered why. Gussie might not want her daughter to know where she was, she supposed, but it was an odd omission. So was the postmark, very dim, but it didn't look Jamaican.

But Bess was too busy to worry about it, with her greater responsibilities, because her job began to stretch into her leisure time. Not that she dated anyone, so the work was welcome. She purchased a small television so that she'd have something for company. But her biggest and best purchase was a small, older-model imported compact car. She had to learn how to use a stick shift, but she did well, and the sporty little red car became her pride and joy. It was a stretch to afford it, but it was getting hard to walk to work in the cold rain, and she wanted a way to get around because it was spring and the world was going green again.

The weather was getting warmer day by day. Green sprouts began to appear on lifeless-looking trees, and Bess felt as if she'd become reborn like those trees. She was a different woman from the shy, nervous, insecure one who'd left Coleman Springs back in January. Being around Nell and Julie had developed her personality and given her confidence. She'd found a thrift shop and managed to buy some nice clothes, and she was coping with housework and cooking very well indeed. Gussie was going to be surprised.

She wondered what Cade would think of the new Bess, but that didn't matter anymore. He had his gorgeous brunette, and she was sure that he wouldn't ever look her up again.

So it came as a shock when she answered a knock on her door late one spring night and found Cade himself standing on her doorstep.

She stared at him, stifling a crazy urge to rush into his arms and kiss him until she fainted.

"Yes?" she asked, trying to sound more poised than she felt.

His eyes went over her slowly. She was wearing a gold-and-cream caftan, and her honey-brown hair was loose and sexy around her shoulders, waving toward her soft eyes and her oval face, making her look soft and sweet and delectable. She seemed older than before, more confident.

"No warm welcome?" he taunted.

She only half-heard him. Her eyes were feeding on him. He was wearing the same blue pin-striped suit he'd been wearing when she'd seen him with his brunette lady friend, and he looked elegant, but she didn't give him the satisfaction of seeing her interest.

"Dream on," she said quietly. "You've already shown me what you think of me and how little I matter to you." Her brown eyes met his levelly. "I don't beat dead horses. Did you want something?"

His eyebrows shot up. That was new, that coolness. Was it real, or was she bluffing? "You've moved since I came to San Antonio last," he replied. He took out a cigarette and lit it, apparently content to stand in the hall all night as he propped his shoulder against the door facing to study her.

"I wanted an apartment with a kitchen," she said.

"You can cook?" he scoffed.

"As a matter of fact, yes, I can," she replied. "I can clean house and drive a stick-shift car, and all sorts of strange things. I can even hold down a job and make my own living." She forced a tiny smile. "If you're looking for helpless adulation, I'm afraid you just struck out, tall man. I'm all grown up now. I don't need a hero anymore."

One dark eye narrowed as he looked at her. She was different, all right. She was acting as if he was part of a past she'd outgrown. She was more poised and mature, and his eyes narrowed as he remembered the expensive wrap she'd been carrying that day he ran into her. This apartment was pretty ritzy too. Surely Bess didn't have a job that paid that kind of money. No, she was getting help. Gussie had railroaded her right into some rich man's hands, and he felt murderous. He wanted to throw things. Bess had been his. Damn his own stupidity for thinking that he had to protect her from him. He should have taken his chances before she got out of his reach. This wasn't the same woman he'd known in Coleman Springs.

"I didn't come here looking for a fan club," he replied with a mocking smile.

The way she looked in that caftan was making his blood sing, but she didn't seem to care if he looked at her anymore. That stung.

Even so, he couldn't help coming here any more

than he could make himself go away. The sight of her fed his heart. He'd been lonely, and he was only now realizing how lonely. "Can you make coffee?"

"Yes."

He tilted back the Stetson. "I've driven all the way from Coleman Springs. I could use something hot."

She felt her head spinning and she didn't want to be alone in her apartment with him, but her heart wouldn't let her send him away. Anyway, she told herself, she could keep a poker face and not let him see how he was affecting her.

"All right." She stood back to let him in.

He looked around him with narrow, hard eyes. It was a much better apartment than she and Gussie had been living in. There were good chairs and tables, and an expensive-looking sofa. His dark eyes flashed as he thought of the price of this apartment compared with the other one.

"Well, it's ritzy," he said, giving the room a cursory glance and sliding his eyes back to hers.

She could almost read his mind. As usual he was right back on the offensive.

"That's it, Cade, always expect the worst," she said. She put his coffee in front of him, without offering cream or sugar because she knew he didn't take it. But he looked at her hand with a stare that could have stopped a clock, and that was when she realized her mistake.

She was still wearing the ring he'd given her, and on her wedding finger. He couldn't seem to drag his eyes away from it.

"I liked it," she said defensively. "And it fits."

His dark eyes caught hers, asking questions that she

didn't want to answer. If she was that mixed up with another man, why wear his ring?

That stare disturbed her. She put her cup down. "Excuse me a minute."

She went into the bedroom, locked the door, and changed into a colorful sundress and sandals. She couldn't bear walking around half dressed with Cade in her apartment, especially at night. She was vulnerable with him, and it was going to be a strain to keep him from finding that out. She should have hidden the ring before he saw it, but it was so much a part of her hand now that it was difficult to think about putting it away.

Cade's dark eyes slid appreciatively over her slender body. "You've filled out," he murmured, wondering if her lover had brought about the new sensuality of her clothing and her graceful way of moving. "City living must agree with you."

"It isn't the city so much as the job," she said. "I'm doing very well, and I like the people I work with."

"Where does the rich man fit in?" he asked suddenly, his eyes pinning her. "Jordan Ryker, isn't it?"

She had to clamp down hard on her emotions. She smiled coolly. "Yes. Jordan Ryker. He's the big boss. A handsome, eligible bachelor with a very kind disposition."

"And rich, I suppose," he said cuttingly.

She nodded. "Filthy. Mother introduced us," she added, just to rile him. "He's really something."

He stared at her unsmiling. "So Gussie told me."

She stopped and stared at him. "Mother told you? When? That night you were here?"

He dropped his eyes to his coffee, glaring into it. "No."

It was getting more complicated by the second. She felt uneasy and didn't understand why. "Then, when?"

"Two days ago."

Her lips parted. She had a sinking feeling she knew why he was here. "You've seen her?" she asked.

"I can't move without tripping over her, in fact," he said through his teeth. He looked up. "My mother invited her to stay at Lariat. She's more than willing to forget the past and forgive. Gussie called her up with some sob story while I was out of town and wrangled an invitation. My mother feels sorry for her." His tone added, emphatically, that he didn't.

Bess knew she was going to faint if she didn't sit very, very still. "She's in Jamaica," she said.

"The hell she is," he replied with an insolent smile. "She talked Mother into an extended visit. Amazing, wouldn't you say, in view of the animosity she knows I have for her. I came up here to tell you that I want her out of my house." That wasn't why he'd come at all, but hearing her rave about Ryker had made him furious. She was missing the old life, and Ryker was one of her own kind. He'd been wrong right down the line, it seemed. Losing her wealth hadn't put her within his reach at all. She was still upper-class and he wasn't. He was going to lose her to a richer man in spite of all his hopes, and he had no one to blame but himself. She'd been vulnerable several weeks ago. He should have moved in while there was time, before he made the fatal mistake of not telling her why he was taking another woman to lunch. That had probably pushed her right into Ryker's arms.

He lashed out in pain, although she didn't know it. "She's your headache, not mine. I'm not going to support her."

"Who asked you to?" she returned. "You're the head of the household, aren't you? Tell her to go."

"I care too much about my mother's feelings to do that," he said quietly. "You'll have to send word that you need her here. God knows why you let her land on us in the first place."

"I didn't know where she was," she insisted, refusing to tell him that she'd thrown Gussie out in the first place. "She told me she was going to visit a friend in Jamaica."

"She didn't make it." he returned.

"So I gather." Bess groaned inwardly. She'd had a taste of freedom and now she was about to lose it again. Gussie was back and making trouble all over again. How could she have imposed herself on Elise and Cade? And why?

Bess leaned back in her chair. "I knew it was too easy," she murmured to herself.

"What was?" he asked.

"Nothing. It doesn't matter."

His dark eyes narrowed on her face. His lean hands wrapped around the coffee cup half-angrily. Gussie didn't concern him half as much as Bess's new love, but he wasn't going to admit that. He wanted to knock the stuffing out of Jordan Ryker. It was the tormenting thought of that man in Bess's life that had finally driven him to come here. The memory of her had haunted him day after day, and he couldn't bear to lose her. But it wasn't as easy as he'd thought it was going to be. Even though she wore his ring on her finger, Bess wasn't receptive at all, and she seemed actually to dislike having him here. Well, two could play at being antisocial.

"I want your mother out of my house by next weekend," he said curtly. "I don't give a damn how you do it. Just get her back here."

She'd been so happy, so carefree. Now she was going to have her flighty mother in her lap again, and the cycle would start all over. What had happened in Jamaica? Why had Gussie gone to Lariat? She frowned, feeling her security fall apart.

"I'll call her tonight," she said wearily. "I'll think of some reason to ask her to come back."

He felt guilty when he saw that hopeless look come back into her face. She'd seemed mature and poised until he mentioned Gussie, and then the facade had fallen away. She was almost shaking. He was letting his jealousy get the better of him, but he couldn't help it. He'd never really faced the possibility that he could lose Bess. Until now.

"You do that," he said, his voice reflecting his frustration.

She looked up at him. "Why do you hate her so, Cade?" she asked. "What has she ever done to you?"

Well, why not tell her, he thought irritably. He was tired of protecting her from the truth. His dark eyes flashed. "I'll tell you what she's done," he replied slowly. "She killed my father."

Bess felt as if her body had turned to stone. She stared at him with only faint comprehension. "What did you say?"

"She killed my father," he repeated coldly. "I stopped short of having her charged with it, but I know for a fact that she caused his death. I saw her hurrying out of a San Antonio hotel room just before I found him dying of a heart attack."

"She couldn't kill anyone!" Bess protested huskily, horrified at the revelation. "Mother is flighty and self-ish, but she's no murderess."

"She's capable of anything when she wants her own way. She was having an affair with my father," he added with a cold smile. "He had a heart attack in her arms, and she ran out of the room and left him there, dying, to save herself from the scandal!"

Bess got to her feet shakily, uncertain of her ground. He sounded convinced, and the hatred in his eyes was very real.

"She loved my father. . . ."

"She loved your father's money," he said harshly, rising from the chair with threatening ease. "But my father was good-looking, and women liked him, even your mother. She teased and tempted him until he betrayed my mother for her. She killed him, all right. My poor mother didn't even know, until I accused Gussie in front of her. She went white in the face, but she never denied it. Not once."

None of it made sense. Gussie wouldn't have done that to Frank Samson, not with his best friend. But Cade seemed so certain, and it explained his hatred for her mother. It even explained Gussie's hatred for him, because he'd revealed her part in Coleman Hollister's death.

"I can't believe it," she whispered brokenly. "Not my own mother! She isn't that kind of woman!"

But even as she said it, she saw the truth in Cade's eyes, and she knew he wasn't lying. But now that she knew why Gussie hated Cade, and why Cade hated Gussie, she knew that the past was going to be forever between them.

"Gussie said that you and Ryker are thick as thieves, and I guess it would take a rich man to buy you fox jackets and keep you in an apartment like this," he added, shocking her because she hadn't even seen Jordan Ryker lately. That was more of Gussie's attempt to keep her out of Cade's reach, she knew. But the fox jacket had been Gussie's. He'd never given her the chance to tell him she was returning it. She opened her mouth to tell him so.

But before she could speak, he caught her suddenly by the arms and jerked her against him. "All the years of waiting, hoping, holding back," he muttered under his breath, his eyes devouring her. "I've wanted you until you colored my life, but I wasn't good enough, was I, Bess? You were meant for better things than the life a poor cowboy could give you, Gussie said. Maybe she was right. But if Ryker's had you, there's no reason I can't, is there?" he bit off, jerking her against him. "No reason at all. . . ."

His mouth covered hers before she had time to consider what he was saying. His hand slid into the thick hair at her nape and held her head where he wanted it while he savored the first soft touch of her trembling lips under his mouth.

It was as if he'd never kissed a woman before. All of it was new and exciting. The way her breath caught, the taste of coffee on her mouth, the softness as his mouth stilled and hardened. His head was already spinning. The feel of her warm body in his arms aroused him as he'd never imagined any woman ever could, so quickly that he shuddered as he felt his own sudden, sharp arousal. Just being near her had always stirred him, but this was unexpected and staggering in its intensity.

He wanted her with an obsession that defied logic or reason. His hard arms swallowed her up while his mouth bit hungrily into hers, drowning her in the fierce sweetness of his ardor.

Bess had tautened with the first shock of his touch, but almost at once the intimacy overwhelmed her. Sensations piled on each other, the feel of his lips for the first time, the steely hardness of his chest and stomach and thighs against her, the rough demand of his mouth as it grew slower and rougher on the trembling of her soft lips. She felt his arms sliding even more closely around her yielding body, felt him groan softly as his lean hand slid down her back and pulled her close. And then she felt the full force of his sudden arousal, and her breath caught at the undisguised need. It was the first time in her life that she'd ever known such intimacy with a man, but it didn't frighten her. She gave in to him without the tiniest struggle, all her longing for him reflected in the clinging warmth of her arms around his hard waist, the response of her shy mouth.

She could hear his rough breathing mingling with the loudness of her own heartbeat as they kissed in the silence of the apartment. Whatever his reason, even anger, it was the sweetest pleasure in the world to feel his mouth moving on her lips, to have him holding her against his taut, muscular body. He might not have wanted her three years ago, but he wanted her now.

Heaven, she thought, after all the years of loneliness, of aching need. He was slow and very expert, and she loved the feel of his arms, the close contact with his hard, fit body. He smelled of spicy cologne and leather, and she thought that if she died now, she'd have had all life could offer. This was Cade, and she loved him more than the air she breathed. She relaxed into his taut body and let him kiss her, savoring every breathless second of the hard, smoky mouth slowly penetrating her own.

But even as she reveled in the crush of his mouth, she knew that she was going to have to stop him soon. He thought she was a tramp. He thought her mother was responsible for his father's death. There were too many reasons why she couldn't afford the luxury of letting him carry her to bed, even if her body was resisting reason.

"No," she whispered halfheartedly, pushing at his hard chest.

"Be still," he breathed into her mouth. "I won't hurt you," he whispered, and his mouth gentled. "Bess, I want you. Oh, God, I want you so much, honey . . . !"

He was losing control, second by second. His lean hands slid lower on her hips and pulled her up hard against the arch of his body, and his breath caught at the feel of all that sweet softness so close to him, even as her soft moan kindled fires in his blood.

For one long second she gave in to him, let him feel the hungry response of her lips, the sinuous warmth of her body. She was starving for the touch of him, for the hard warmth of his mouth on hers. Dreams came alive while he fed on her soft lips. She looked up and saw his dark brows knit, his eyes closed, thick black lashes on his cheeks as he pulled her even closer. He looked as desperate as she felt, and she closed her eyes and savored the fierce ardor that made her weak-kneed and breathless. She let him mold her to his hardness without fear. It was as natural as loving him to feel joy in his need of her, to glory in his response to her femininity.

But she had to stop him, because she could sense that he wasn't quite in control. He thought she'd already had a lover, for which she could thank her mother, and because of that suspicion, he wouldn't try to pull back. If she didn't get away, it would be too late to stop him in a very few minutes. She could feel a faint tremor in his arms already, and the arousal of his lean body was becoming more and more urgent.

"I can't, Cade," she whispered against his hard mouth, forcing herself to sound convincing this time.

"Why can't you?" he demanded, his breath quick and hard on her moistened lips. "Because I'm not rich enough?" he demanded, feeling a sense of anguish as he said it.

His mouth searched for hers again, but what he'd said had given her strength to get away. She ducked her head to avoid his lips, pulled out of his arms, and moved back. She was shaking from the double effect of his unexpected ardor and her own knowledge of her mother's betrayal of her father.

"Why?" he asked, his voice still a little shaken with the force of his ardor.

"Not like this," she whispered. "You're angry. . . ."

"Not angry enough to hurt you," he said gruffly.

"Not even if you were still the virgin you were three years ago."

"You laughed at me then," she said with a choke. "You showed me that you didn't want me . . . !"

His expression hardened. "I had to!" he said curtly. "It was even more impossible then than it is now. You were rich and I wasn't. I couldn't encourage you, but you almost made me lose my head. I had to make you stop flirting with me, and the only way to do it was to convince you that you left me cold. It took more self-control than I thought I had," he said, finishing wearily. "My God, I wanted you! I still do." He moved toward her. "And you want me. So no more games."

She knew he wouldn't stop this time. And once he touched her, she wouldn't want to stop him. She had to get away. Her hand reached behind her on the coffee table for her purse and she darted to the door, jerking it open.

"There's no need to run," he said, his eyes dark with desire and faint contempt. "You've wanted me for years, just as I've wanted you. We might as well satisfy each other. The only reason I held back this long was because you were a virgin."

She stared at him quietly. "Only . . . because of that?" she asked.

"Why else?" He moved closer, the faint scent of his cologne making her head spin as he stopped just in front of her, one lean hand touching her mouth, tracing it. "You and I were always worlds apart socially," he said bitterly. "I couldn't seduce a virgin, even to satisfy an obsessive hunger. But you don't have that restriction anymore, and I want you like hell. So come here, honey, and let's see how good we can be together."

"I don't want that," she stammered, backing through the open door.

"Why not?" he asked mockingly. "I can't marry someone like you—especially not with the past between us—but there's no reason we can't have each other. Not now that you're earning your money the hard way. And to think I believed you that first night you went out with Ryker," he added coldly. "I actually believed that you'd never let anyone touch you except me! Did you even love me, or was that just an act? Did you laugh behind your hand, thinking you could play me for a fool because you had money and I didn't?"

Tears stung her eyes. "How can you believe those things about me?" she whispered brokenly.

"How can I believe otherwise?" he shot back. "Your own mother said—"

"You're so quick to believe her, when you know she hates you, that she doesn't want me to even associate with you! You want to believe those things, don't you, Cade?" she cried. "You want to believe them because all you want from me is sex! Oh, what does it matter?" she moaned, hearing all her dreams torn to pieces. She'd loved him, and now he was confessing that all it had ever been with him was desire! "I can't take any more of you or my mother! I can't take any more!" She ran through the open doorway.

"Where do you think you're going at this hour of the night?" he called harshly, suddenly struck by the apparent hysteria on her face.

"As far away from you as I can get!" she burst out,

heading for the staircase that led down to the parking lot.

"Bess!" he burst out. He hadn't expected her to bolt and run. He went out the door after her, without considering how much his pursuit might affect her.

She panicked. She didn't know what he might do, and she couldn't let him overwhelm her with his ardor. He'd find out how innocent she was the hard way, but his conscience would force him to marry her. She didn't want him that way. Her mother had really fixed things this time, she thought miserably. She'd never forgive Gussie for this!

Gussie. As she ran, she saw the utter hopelessness of the future. She was going to be landed with her mother again. There would be no more peace, no more freedom. She was going to be hog-tied and owned, working herself to death to support Gussie's spending, and now that she understood Cade's reasons for hating her mother, she knew that it would have been impossible for him ever to have cared about her. She'd been living in a fool's paradise. It had just come abruptly to an end, thanks to Gussie and to Cade's own admission that it was only desire on his part, and she couldn't face it.

She ran for her small car and jumped in, locking the door. She drove out of the parking lot wildly because she could see Cade running toward her. She was too weak to last through another round of his ardent lovemaking, and she couldn't hide what she felt any longer. He was out for revenge and he'd only humiliate her again. It was only sex he wanted. He'd said so. He didn't love her, he never had, never would. He only wanted her. She couldn't bear it, she couldn't . . . !

She pulled out into traffic just as a speeding car rounded a corner and plowed right into the driver's side of her car. There was a sound of breaking glass and a hard thud, and a lightning bolt of pain. And then, nothing.

Cade reached the car seconds later. His face was white, his eyes so black that the driver of the car that had struck Bess's got out and ran for his life. But Cade didn't follow him. He fought to get the door open, but he couldn't. Bess was trapped in crushed metal. He couldn't get the other door open either. Somewhere voices rushed in on him, other hands helped, but they still couldn't free her. She was bleeding, and he knew with terrible certainty that she was badly hurt. Someone called an ambulance, and Cade began to pray.

Chapter 9

Cade didn't know how he stayed sane through the next few hours. Bess was cut out of the car by the local rescue unit and taken immediately to the nearest hospital emergency room. She was in a coma, with internal injuries and severe bleeding. The doctor was as kind as he could be, but the fact was she might die. Comas were unpredictable, and medical science was simply helpless. Either she'd come out of it or she wouldn't. It was in God's hands.

He sat in the intensive-care waiting room, smoking like a furnace, until his mother and Gussie got there.

"Has there been any change?" Gussie asked, looking pale and worried.

"None," Cade said curtly. He didn't look up.

"How did it happen?" Gussie asked without really

expecting an answer. "A car wreck, you said, but she's such a careful driver. I didn't even know she had a car." She buried her face in her hands and cried help-lessly. "My poor baby."

"It's all right, Gussie," Elise said gently, comforting her. "Cade, can they do anything?"

He shook his dark head. He didn't look at his mother, because she knew him too well. He didn't want her to see his anguish.

"I just don't understand why she was out driving in the middle of the night," Gussie said in a choked voice. "She never went out at night. She wouldn't even go out with men. . . ."

Cade's head jerked up and he stared at Gussie with barely concealed fury. "She wouldn't? That isn't what you said at Lariat!" he reminded her harshly, too cut up himself to worry about Gussie's feelings, if she had any. "You said she and Ryker were close."

She looked at him through red, puffy eyes, aware of Elise's pointed stare. "I hoped they would be," she faltered. "I haven't seen her for several weeks, you know. They might have been close." She ground her teeth together. "All right, I lied, hoping that you'd think she had someone so that you'd stay away from her. You're the last man on earth she needs. All of us know how Bess feels about you," she muttered defen-sively. "She worships the ground you walk on, but you'd walk all over her. She doesn't have the spirit to stand up to you."

"I'm not blind," Cade returned curtly. He glanced at Gussie and then away, but not before Gussie got a look at his eyes.

Gussie stopped sniffing and simply looked at him.

His face was as tormented as she imagined her own was. Why, he cared about Bess! She'd never stopped hating him long enough to consider his feelings, but they were written all over him now.

She almost reached out to him. Almost. But there had been too many bad feelings between them over the years. She wondered what he would say if he knew that her letting him think she'd been with his father that day had kept a devastating secret from him as well as from Elise—and that the truth would hurt him every bit as much as it would hurt his mother.

"I thought she was letting Ryker keep her," Cade said, grinding out his words. "The fancy apartment, that fox jacket. . . ."

Gussie took a deep breath. "She doesn't have a fox jacket," she said.

"She does. I saw her with it in town!"

She stared at him. "It was mine. At least I bought it." She lowered her eyes. "She took it back to the store. After she threw me out of the apartment," she added tightly, her face coloring. "That's why I went to Jamaica, because it was the only place I could go. She has a good job now, she could afford fox if she wanted it, but she said she wasn't supporting me. I went to Jamaica and then, when the welcome ran out, I had no place to go. If it hadn't been for Elise . . ." She looked past him at the other woman, and a long, quiet look passed between them. "I'll never forget what your mother did for me, Cade. Even though I know I don't deserve it."

Cade gaped at her. He knew his face had gone white. He'd accused Bess of something she hadn't done, he'd deliberately hurt her, and needlessly. He'd sent her into the path of that oncoming car. She might die, and it would be his fault. Out of jealousy and Gussie's interference, he'd attacked her. And all the while she'd been freeing herself of her mother's domination, working to earn what she had.

"You'd been to see her, hadn't you?" Gussie asked Cade suddenly.

"Thanks to you, yes," he returned, his heart ice-cold now from the terror of what he'd done. "You lied about Ryker."

Gussie's eyes filled with tears. "To protect Bess. Maybe to protect myself too," she said miserably. "Bess thought she loved you, and I knew I'd lose her forever if she was with you."

Cade stared down at his dusty boots. It wasn't the time for all that, for the past to start intruding again. Gussie was partly right too. The way he felt about Bess's mother, he would have kept them apart if he could. But now he didn't have a chance in hell with Bess. After what he'd said and done to her, he'd be lucky if she ever spoke to him again. He couldn't blame Gussie without blaming himself. Bess had accused him of always thinking the worst about her, of being willing to listen to any damaging gossip about her. His own jealousy had been his biggest enemy. He should have trusted her. He should have given her a chance to tell him about the fox jacket and about her mother. But he hadn't. Now she was lying in the hospital, maybe dying, and he had to live with the fact that he'd put her there. Gussie had dug the hole and he'd pushed Bess into it. He groaned and put his head in his hands.

"She'll be all right," Elise said gently, smoothing her

hand over Cade's shoulder. She looked across at Gussie, who was weeping. "We have to believe that she'll be all right."

"It's my fault," Gussie whimpered. "I pushed and pushed and demanded. I never realized how overbearing I was. I expected her to take Frank's place, and how could she?"

Cade didn't answer. He lifted his head and stared sightlessly ahead of him, memories flooding his mind, mental pictures of Bess laughing, running toward him, begging for his kisses. He had to believe she'd be all right, he thought, or he'd go mad.

In his mind he could hear the angry words he'd spoken, the accusations he'd made. He'd cut Bess to pieces with what he'd said to her, denying that he had any feelings for her aside from desire, demanding that she take Gussie back. He'd even acted as if he meant to attack her, so she had every reason in the world to run. And the irony of it was that she was the last human being on earth he'd hurt deliberately. He'd been angry, but only at first. Just before she'd pulled out of his arms, they'd been sharing the most exquisite tenderness with each other. Reality, after years of empty dreams, and if she'd only known it, she'd made a mockery of his claim not to care about her. A few more minutes of that tempestuous exchange and he'd have bared his soul to her. But she hadn't thought he was going to stop, and she'd run from him. He'd made it worse by chasing her, but he'd been so afraid that she was going to get hurt. And she had anyway.

Elise, seeing his tormented expression, took pity on him. "Isn't there a chapel?" Elise asked, rising. She took Gussie's arm. "Come on, dear, let's go find it. Cade?"

He shook his head. "I'll stay here, in case they need to tell us something." He didn't add that he'd already done, was still doing, his own share of praying. Life without Bess would lose its meaning completely. He wasn't sure if he could cope without her.

In some way that he didn't understand, Bess's adulation made him whole. It gave him strength. Now he was like a ship without a rudder, drifting without a direction. He'd worked for years to build Lariat into a successful ranch, mostly so that he'd have it to offer to Bess, if he could come to grips with the differences between them. There hadn't really been another woman in his heart, even if he'd known a few women over the years, including the divorcée whose attractions had momentarily dazzled him. And that physical attraction had only lasted as far as her bedroom. He'd seen the hardness under the beauty, and it had repelled him, along with her attitude toward sex. She liked three in a bed, but Cade only wanted two. It hadn't even bothered him when she left.

Cade glanced impatiently toward the nurses' station. He'd smoked a pack of cigarettes already, and he knew he was going to have to stop or he'd cough himself to death. But it was that or a quart of straight Kentucky bourbon, and he couldn't climb into a bottle, even if his heart was breaking in two.

He sighed wearily as he looked out the window. He hadn't told the others exactly how the accident happened because it hurt too much to admit it had been his fault. He didn't think he could live with himself if she was crippled. There had been some internal dam-

age, the doctor had said after a preliminary examination, and a good deal of bleeding, but she'd most likely
recover. Cade hadn't half-heard him; he was trying to
force an assurance from the doctor that she'd live.

"Excuse me . . ."

He turned to find a nurse watching him. She smiled
gently. "She's calling for someone named Cade. Would
that be you?"

His heart almost burst. She was calling for him! For
the first time since the accident he was able to hope.
"Yes." He quickly put the cigarette out in the ashtray
and followed the nurse into the intensive care unit,
and then to the small cubicle where Bess was hooked
up to all kinds of humming, buzzing, beeping machinery. There was an oxygen tube taped in her nose—to
replace the one he'd seen in her mouth earlier. She
was pale and there were bruises on her cheek, but her
eyes were open.

"Bess!" he whispered huskily. "How are you,
honey?"

I must be dead, she thought dizzily. Here was Cade
looking like his world had almost ended and calling
her honey.

"Cade?" she whispered.

"I'm here," he said, almost choking on the emotion
welling up in him.

"Two minutes," the nurse said gently. "We musn't
tire her."

He nodded and moved closer to Bess, touching her
bruised cheek with his hand. "I'm sorry," he whispered. "Oh, God, honey, I'm so sorry . . . !"

Definitely dead, she was telling herself, or dreaming. She managed to lift one hand and put it against his

lean, dark cheek. "I'm okay," she whispered. She could hardly see him, because she was full of drugs. "Cade, I'll be okay. I don't . . . blame you."

And that hurt most of all, that her first concern was for his feelings and not her own pain. He felt tears stinging his eyes and he hated his weakness almost as much as he blamed himself. He knew his face was giving him away, but he couldn't contain the guilt and fear that were raging in his mind. He brought her hand, palm up, to his mouth and kissed it.

She curled her fingers into his and gripped hard. "Am I dead?" she whispered, her eyelids drooping. "You're . . . my world, Cade. . . ."

She was asleep again. Her hand slid away from his face and he clasped it tight in both of his and bent to brush his mouth so carefully over her dry lips.

"You're my world, too, little one," he whispered brokenly. "For God's sake, don't die!"

But she didn't hear him. Not consciously. She drifted in and out for the rest of the day, aware of her mother's voice and Cade's between vivid, disturbing dreams.

Cade kept Gussie and his mother going, his own strength bolstering theirs. He still hadn't talked about how the accident had happened, and although Gussie and Elise knew that he'd somehow been involved, Gussie let it all slide after Bess was out of grave danger. But Elise was worried. Cade wasn't acting like himself, and she knew something was bothering him. He'd admitted that he'd gone to see Bess, but he was holding something back, something that was still tormenting him.

While Gussie was visiting Bess, Elise had Cade buy her a cup of coffee in the hospital coffee shop and found a corner table where they could sit and talk.

Outside in the hall, visitors and medical personnel walked past while the familiar intercom sounds and bells signaling the staff made a backdrop for the murmurings around the small white tables.

"What happened?" Elise asked gently, her dark eyes full of compassion. "I won't tell Gussie," she added. "But I think you need to tell someone."

He lit a cigarette, his dark eyes challenging a man nearby who was obviously a nonsmoker to say what he was thinking, before he turned his attention back to his mother. "I told her about Gussie and Dad. And I said some hard things to her, because of what Gussie had said about Bess and Jordan Ryker," he said quietly. "She ran out of the apartment to get away from me." He studied the cigarette with disgust. "I don't know why I smoke these damned things. Sometimes I think I do it just to make nonsmokers climb the walls." He put out the cigarette and leaned forward to slide his lean hands around his coffee cup. "I got to her before the ambulance did," he said. "She was trapped, and I couldn't get her out."

Elise wanted to put her arms around him as she had when he was a small boy and hold him until he stopped hurting. But he was a man now. Cade was curiously remote about affection. She knew that he cared for her, but his father had been standoffish and undemonstrative and he'd made Cade that way too.

"What did Gussie say to you about Bess?"

"That she was deeply involved with a rich business-man in San Antonio named Jordan Ryker." He smiled bitterly. "She's moved to a new, more expensive apartment and she wasn't exactly welcoming when I got there. To compound it all, I saw her with a fox jacket the day I was having a business lunch in San Antonio. I accused her of letting Ryker keep her."

Elise could almost feel his pain. "Do you really believe she would?"

"I did for a few fatal minutes," he said curtly. "She's changed since she's been in San Antonio. From what I hear about Ryker, he's attractive to women. Bess is human, and I haven't given her much encouragement," he added, his voice bitter. "In fact, she saw me with a business associate's wife in a perfectly innocent situation, but I let her believe I was dating the woman. I'd just seen her with that expensive jacket, and I couldn't bear the thought of her with another man. I cut her dead." His eyes fell to the coffee, oblivious of his mother's shocked delight. "After Gussie came to the ranch and fed me more of the same, I had to see Bess, to find out for myself."

"And got into an argument."

"Yes. She did argue back at least. She's not the same pliable little Bess she used to be, and she's got some spunk now. But I pushed her over the edge," he said bitterly. "I just want her to get well." His hands tightened around the hot cup. "You can't imagine what it did to me when I saw the other car fly around the corner and knew it was going to hit her." His eyes closed with a shudder as it all came flooding back. "Then I had to stand there and wait while the ambulance and rescue units got to her. My God, I almost went crazy. I couldn't get her out, and she was unconscious and badly hurt." He lifted the cup and took a small sip. "I thought I'd lost her."

"She's going to be all right." Elise smiled. "And you know she isn't blaming you, because she called for you after she came out of the coma."

"I can't be sure that it wasn't because of the drugs," he replied. "But even if she doesn't blame me, I blame myself, don't you see? Gussie's right. Bess is too gentle for a man like me. I can't help the way I am. It will take a strong woman to live with me."

"I loved your father, Cade," Elise replied, reading his thoughts. "He was a hard man, and he hurt me sometimes with his temper and his . . . one affair, just before he died," she said, with a haunted look in her eyes. "But I loved him, and in his way he loved me. It wasn't a modern relationship by any means, because Coleman never changed diapers or gave bottles or offered to help with the housework." She laughed softly. "I couldn't have imagined him doing those things. But he took care of me and you boys, he provided for us, and I wouldn't change one single thing about my life."

"What worked then won't work today," he said simply. "And I can't risk browbeating Bess that way."

"If she loves you, and you care about her, why don't you let those things work themselves out?"

"It isn't that easy." He drank the rest of his coffee. "She's a debutante. She's used to wealth and society and a different kind of life than I could give her. Ryker can give her everything she wants."

"Are you sure?" Elise asked seriously. "Because Bess doesn't seem mercenary to me."

"Her mother is," Cade returned. "And you, of all

people, know what Gussie is. She hasn't let go of Bess. She may never let go. Bess looked crushed when I told her to take Gussie back. I didn't know she'd thrown her out in the first place." He sighed at his mother's shocked expression. "You knew I didn't want Gussie on Lariat."

"Yes, I knew. But she hadn't anyplace to stay. She said she couldn't go back to Bess, although I didn't tell you that." Elise toyed with her napkin. "Gussie isn't a bad woman, Cade," she said, braving his temper. "She's what life has made her. I don't hold any grudges for what happened. It hurt very badly at the time, but Coleman is dead, and vendettas are a waste of emotional energy. Gussie and I were good friends before your father died. Besides that, Cade, we're churchgoing people. That means I have to believe in forgiveness. It's much more your war than mine now, dear."

He glared at her. "How can you stick up for her?"

She looked up. "I'm human enough to resent her part in Coleman's death," she replied. "But neither of us ever asked her side of it. We simply blamed her on circumstantial evidence."

"It was cut-and-dried . . . !"

"No." She put her hand over his. "We loved Coleman. We reacted to his death in a normal way. One day I want to hear Gussie's side of it. You can't live on hate, Cade."

"I'm not trying to live on it. I just don't want Gussie around."

"Well, there isn't much choice right now, is there? Bess can't stay in that apartment by herself, and Gussie will be less help than no one at all. She'll have a catering firm around to fix meals, and Bess will have a relapse when she sees the bills," she added with a twinkle in her dark eyes.

Cade laughed in spite of himself. "I guess so."You want to take them both back to Lariat, don't you?"

Elise smiled. "I like taking care of people. I wanted to be a nurse, but my father wouldn't hear of it. Back then ladies didn't work, you see," she whispered conspiratorially, "and certainly not in jobs that involved bathing men."

Cade's own eyes twinkled. "I can see my father letting you bathe him," he murmured, tongue-in-cheek.

Elise colored delicately, even at her age, and lowered her eyes. "You probably won't believe this, but I never once saw your father completely undressed. Our generation wasn't as laid-back—is that the word? —as yours."

"Laid-back is something city men are," he said dryly. "I'm bristling with old-fashioned ideas myself. But Robert and Gary are definitely laid-back. I suppose Gary told you that he wants to move in with Jennifer before they marry."

Elise grimaced. "I know. I don't approve."

"Neither do I, but short of locking him in the smokehouse, I don't see how we can stop him. He's twenty-five."

She nodded. "Well, they're engaged, and very much in love, and they're getting married." She shrugged. "The world has changed."

"Not in ways I like," he said. "But I guess it was inevitable. Back in the roaring twenties everybody thought the younger generation was going straight to hell, with booze and loose morals and women smoking and swearing, didn't they?" He chuckled. "Then came the thirties and forties, and it was back to early-Victorian attitudes."

"Indeed it was," his mother said, smiling reminiscently. "I remember trying on a pair of slacks just a few years before you were born, and Coleman had a fit! He made me take them back, because it wasn't decent for a woman to wear pants."

He glanced at her neat beige pantsuit. "He'd roll over in his grave now."

"Oh, I did finally wear him down," she asserted. "In his old age he was much more tolerant of new attitudes." Her eyes stared off into space. "I do miss him so terribly, Cade."

"Enough of that. You'll cry, and everyone will think it's my fault."

She pulled herself back and laughed. "As if you'd care."

"I care about you," he said gently, and smiled. "Even if you only hear that once or twice every ten years."

"Actions speak louder than words, don't they say?" She touched his hand gently. "You've taken great care of me, my darling. I hope you haven't decided to stay a bachelor, because you have the strength to be a very happy family man. You should marry and have children."

He stared at the graceful, wrinkled hand holding his and gave it a squeeze. "Maybe when I can get us a little further out of debt, I'll be able to think about it."

"Don't wait too long," Elise cautioned.

He nodded, but he was preoccupied and brooding. He only hoped that Bess hadn't been delirious when she'd said that he was her world. He didn't know if they could surmount the obstacles in their way, but more and more he wanted to try.

Bess drifted in and out of consciousness for the next two days. Cade had to leave long enough to put his brother Robert in charge of Lariat while he was away and delegate a meeting to Gary, but he came back prepared to stay the duration. Gussie, amazingly, had stayed, too, and so had Elise. Cade got two rooms at a nearby motel for himself and his mother, within walking distance of the hospital.

On the third day after the wreck Bess had been moved into a semiprivate room, where she lay propped up in bed worrying about her insurance while Cade sprawled lazily in a chair beside the bed and watched her.

"I've got coverage," she said, "but I think it only pays eighty percent. What will I do?"

"What the rest of us do," he mused. "Pay it off on the installment plan. You surely don't think that I pay cash for cattle when I buy them?"

"Well, yes, I did," she confessed. Her poor bruised face was still swollen, and she was having some pain in her side from the bruised ribs. The stitches in her abdomen bothered her, but she hadn't yet asked the reason for them. Apparently some internal damage had been done, but she hadn't been lucid enough to ask the doctor what was wrong.

Cade looked drawn and worn out. She found it surprising that he was still around, when she was obviously recovering all right. It was difficult to talk to him, because mostly he sat and scowled at the nurses and aides who came and went in the room and looked unapproachable. The argument they'd had before the accident was fresh in Bess's mind, and she imagined it was fresh in Cade's as well. He was a responsible man. Guilt would be eating him, because he'd think he had caused her to drive recklessly and get into the wreck.

"You and Gussie are coming back to Lariat with us," he said out of the blue. "Mother figured that Gussie would hire professional caterers to prepare meals for you and bankrupt you in a week."

Bess sighed wearily, and she didn't smile. "Most likely she would." Her drowsy eyes lifted to his. "But I don't want to impose on you," she added quietly. "You've got enough people to look after without being landed with us. And I know how you feel about Gussie." Her eyes lowered. "And about me."

He felt himself go stiff at the memory of the things he'd accused her of. "I suit myself as a rule, Bess," he replied easily. "If I didn't want you there, believe me, I could find reasons to leave you in San Antonio."

Bess grimaced. He felt sorry for her. Worse, he felt guilty. "It wasn't your fault," she murmured. "I didn't have to run like a shell-shocked thirteen-year-old and take my temper out on the car."

His dark eyes slid over her face. "I never meant to let it go that far. And despite the impression I might have given, I'd never have forced you," he said.

She felt her cheeks go hot at the memory.

Cade uncrossed his legs and got up, standing at the window with his hands in his gray slacks pockets. "Looking back isn't going to help the situation, Bess," he said. "I can't take back what happened." He turned toward her. "But I can give you a place to heal and take care of you and Gussie until you're back on your feet. I owe you that much."

She wanted to throw his offer back in his face, but she couldn't afford to. She sighed miserably and lowered her eyes to his boots. At least he didn't know how much she still cared for him. That was her ace in the hole. "I appreciate the gesture," she said. "And I won't embarrass you with any blatant displays of undying love."

His breath quickened. He wanted to tell her that he wouldn't mind blatant displays, that it would be heaven to have her run after him the way she used to. But he'd hurt her too badly this time, and the differences were still there. It was too soon.

"I ran into your doctor outside in the hall," he said to break the silence. "He said that if you keep improving, you can be discharged Friday. He'll take your stitches out before you leave, and I can run you back up here for your checkup in two weeks."

"When can I go back to work?"

"When he releases you."

He sounded irritable, and she imagined he felt it, too, being trapped by his own guilt into having two houseguests he hated added to his troubles.

"Maybe if I talk to Julie, she'll let me work on my assignment while I'm at your place," she said. "I've got everything I need at the apartment. I could pay you rent for Mother and me. . . ."

He said something harsh under his breath, then added more loudly, "Don't you ever offer me money again."

She felt the blood draining out of her face. "Why?"

she asked. "Because you think I'd get it from my rich lover?"

He stared at her without blinking. "Gussie admitted that she had exaggerated," he said. "And I over-reacted."

"How kind of you to admit it," she replied with more spirit than she knew she had. "But it's a day late and a dollar short. I don't owe you any explanations, so you just think what you like. And I won't go to Lariat with you. I'll stay in the apartment with Mother. That should please you," she added with a false smile, "since the entire purpose of your visit was to make sure she left Lariat."

He moved away from the bed, his hands in his slacks pockets, his dark hair catching the overhead light and gleaming like a raven's back. "That wasn't the entire purpose of it," he said quietly. "But this isn't the time or place to discuss what brought me there."

"What you said about my mother . . . and your fa-ther," she persisted, "was it true?"

"Ask your mother, Bess," he said shortly. "I can only give you one side of it. And as my mother is fond of saying, there are two sides to everything. I never both-ered to ask for Gussie's. I took what I saw at face value."

"It's hard to believe. She loved my father."

He stopped at the foot of the bed and stared at her intently for a long moment. "Are you experienced enough now to know that love and desire can exist separately?"

She glared at him. "You ought to know."

His eyebrow arched. "I know about desire," he mused. "Love is a different animal altogether."

Her fingers curled into the sheet, and she looked at it instead of him. "Trust you to compare it to something with four legs," she muttered.

"Where does Ryker fit into your life?" he asked, hoping to catch her off guard.

She lifted her eyes to his. "Jordan Ryker is none of your business. As you've gone to great pains to tell me, I'm out of your league. I'm decorative and useless and I may someday have to have my mother surgically removed from my back."

He laughed. He didn't mean to, because it wasn't funny, but the way she put it touched something inside him, and relief and delight mingled in the deep sound that escaped his throat.

"For two cents I'd tell Gussie what you just said."

"Be my guest," she replied. "I don't care anymore. My life is falling apart around my ears."

"None of that," he said firmly. "You can't give up and quit now that you're finally getting independent."

"What do you care?" she challenged, her brown eyes flashing at him. "You wouldn't want me if I came with french fries and tartar sauce!"

His dark eyes twinkled. "I've never seen you fight back before," he remarked. "I like you this way," he added, his voice deep and frankly sensual.

Her cheeks went hot, but she didn't drop her eyes. "Well, I don't like you any way at all. Why don't you go home and brand a calf or something?"

"I can't leave my mother alone with Gussie," he replied. "She'd have Mother signing notes for mink coats and luxury cars. Mother feels sorry for her."

"You sure don't," Bess guessed.

"You can tie a bow on that," he agreed.

"Has anyone called to ask about me?" she wanted to know.

His face closed up. "Ryker did, if that's what you want to find out," he said coldly, recalling that Gussie had spoken to him.

"How very nice of him," she said with a smile. "A man should care about his kept woman."

"Oh, hell, stop that," he muttered. Cade moved away from the bed. He looked as if he wanted to bite something. "Someone named Julie called too."

"She's my boss," she told him. "She's the office manager."

He glanced at her. "A woman?"

"Women can read and write and do math," she told him. "They can even manage offices if they're given a chance."

His eyebrows levered up. "Did I say they couldn't? My God, I know what women can do. My mother is one of the finest financial managers I've ever seen in action. She could run a damned corporation herself, except that she's softhearted enough to give it away to the first unfortunate who asked for it."

He sat back down in the chair beside the bed, his eyes going over her poor bruised face, her thin body in the cotton hospital gown. She looked much the worse for wear, but thank God she was alive.

"What do you do at that advertising agency?" he asked.

"I started out doing mechanicals." She smiled faintly at his curious stare. "That's the layout for printing ads and brochures and such. But now they're letting me come up with ideas of my own and do some copywriting as well. One of my ads is going to be used in a national campaign for a shampoo company."

"Good for you." He crossed one leg over the other. "Do you like the work?"

"Very much. And the people I work with are wonderful."

"Like Ryker?" he asked with a mocking smile.

"Mr. Ryker doesn't work in our office. He's downtown in a big building somewhere. He just owns the business. Julie runs it."

"But you do see him?" he persisted.

"Why does it matter?" she replied with equal stubbornness. "You went to great pains to warn me off, so why do you care what men I date?"

Cade got to his feet and paced some more. He felt restless and irritable and confined. "I guess I have been fighting it," he admitted, glancing out the window. "For a long time. Maybe for all the wrong reasons. But you were young and soft. Too soft," he said coldly. "You wouldn't have lasted a week on Lariat the way you were." He turned, his black eyes pinning her. "You're more mature, I'll hand you that, but you're still too full of illusions about me. I'm no storybook hero. I'm hard and disciplined and I've got a temper that could take a layer of skin off you. You're no match for me, cream puff. I need a tigress, not a sparrow."

"Was the brunette a tigress?" she said with soft malice. "Wasn't she a match for you?"

His head tilted toward her and his dark eyes kindled. That sounded very much like jealousy, so why not keep his secret and let her chew on the brunette for a while? "I don't talk about my women. Not even to my brothers, much less to you."

She averted her eyes, feeling embarrassment stick in her throat. "And I don't talk about my men, so you can stop asking me leading questions about Jordan Ryker."

He glared at her profile. "Done. Not that I give a damn about any of your men," he added with deliberate nonchalance. "All that concerns me is helping you get back on your feet."

"Thank you so much," she said. "I'll do my best to set new records for healing!"

He moved toward the door, trying not to smile. In the past her lack of spirit had annoyed him. Now she was developing it rapidly, and he liked the way she dueled with him. He liked the jealousy in her voice and the sparks of dark fire in her eyes. The old Bess would never have made it in his world, but this new one could. Although he did hope she wasn't going to take it to extremes, the verbal jousting aroused him.

"Leaving so soon?" she called gaily. "Do give my regards to your brothers," she added with a smile.

He turned at the door, his eyes narrow as a new complication presented itself. "Gary is engaged to Jennifer Barnes," he told her. "I'll appreciate it if you won't give him any encouragement."

That seemed to needle him. Good! "I wouldn't dream of trying to cut Jennifer out. On the other hand," she added, "Robert is still very much a single man. I trust you won't object if I speak to him?"

He didn't say another word. With anger smoldering in his eyes he opened the door and left the room. That was a curve he hadn't expected, and it haunted him for the rest of the day. Not only was Robert unattached, he was a born flirt, and he already liked Bess.

What a hell of a situation this could develop into, especially when Bess had every reason in the world for wanting to give him hell. What better way than to get involved with his brother?

He didn't come back for the rest of the day, leaving Gussie and Elise to talk to Bess and encourage her.

The doctor came to do his rounds after supper, and the two women left the room while he had a long, frank talk with Bess about her injuries. What he told her was so staggering that she didn't believe him at first. But when the knowledge began to penetrate, she burst into tears.

"I'm sorry," he said, patting her shoulder gently. "But the truth is always best. And it isn't impossible, you know. There are other ways. . . ."

"I knew I had stitches, but I never dreamed that much damage had been done," she said, weeping.

"I didn't want to tell you sooner, not until you were strong enough to face it," he replied. He was tall and elderly, and his voice was quiet with concern. "Believe me, we did our best. It just wasn't good enough." He paused. "I notice you've had a very persistent male visitor, and if he's involved with you, I thought you should be told, because he'll need to know."

Her eyes closed. "No, he won't," she whispered huskily. "Because there's no hope of any lasting relationship. He's a friend of the family, that's all. There's nothing between us."

"Miss Samson, don't let this prevent you from marrying," he pleaded softly. "It isn't the end of the world."

"Oh, yes it is," she whispered.

"Adoption is a very attractive alternative," he added. "You might consider it if you marry."

It might be attractive to some men, but it wouldn't be to Cade: she knew that already. He had such pride in his family's heritage. For years he'd talked about the heirs he was going to have someday, his sons who'd inherit Lariat after him. Now those children would be born to some other woman. As long as she'd been whole, she couldn't stop hoping. But now she felt that she was only half a woman. What good was hoping after what he'd said in her apartment anyway? He'd admitted that he'd never marry a woman like her, that all he could have offered her was a brief affair. So it was just as well that he didn't care, because this was one obstacle she couldn't overcome, even if she could have changed Cade's mind about her uselessness on a ranch and her inability to adjust to the hard life there. This was a stone wall, separating her from Cade forever.

Her eyes filled with tears as they searched the doctor's. "You're telling me that it's completely impossible, that there isn't a chance that I could ever have a child of my own?"

"Let me explain. You have one ovary left, but it was slightly damaged too. It is possible that you could conceive, it just isn't too likely. Not unless you married a man who was incredibly potent and all the factors were just exactly right. No, it isn't completely impossible, and I've seen too many miracles in my work to discount God's hand in things. But being realistic is best in the long run."

"I see." She had a little hope then, but not much. She managed a smile for him. "Thank you for being honest with me."

"It's the best thing, you know. I'll check on you again. Try to get some sleep."

"I'll do that." She watched him go. When she was alone, the room seemed to close in around her. She was scared to death, and there was no one she could tell. Least of all Cade.

Chapter 10

Gussie came in early the next morning to see her daughter, and this time she was alone. It was the first opportunity Bess had had to talk to her without anyone else present.

"You look a little brighter this morning," Gussie said, sitting down heavily in the chair beside the bed. "How do you feel, darling?"

"Worn," Bess said stiffly. Remembering what Cade had said about Gussie made her sick all over. It wasn't really all that hard to imagine Gussie chasing after a married man, despite the way she'd defended her to Cade. Gussie was a butterfly and she loved male adulation. And while Bess had always believed her mother loved her father, perhaps it was another part of her act. Gussie had been poor and she said herself that she'd tricked Frank Samson into marrying her by getting pregnant. Besides that, she'd ruined things between Bess and Cade and had indirectly caused the wreck. Bess was going to find it difficult to forgive her mother this time.

"You gave me quite a scare," Gussie said, a little hesitant because Bess didn't seem very glad to see her. In fact she seemed quite remote.

"I'll be all right," the younger woman said brusquely.

Gussie leaned back in her chair. "Why were you driving that late at night, and why in such a hurry? It was Cade, wasn't it?" she added coldly. "He came to see you, he said so. He caused you to have the wreck."

"We argued, but it wasn't anybody's fault," Bess said simply. "And don't start again about Cade," she added when her mother looked ready to argue. "He's been kind enough to let you stay at Lariat, and he's invited us both there while I recuperate. Isn't there some old saying about not biting the hand that feeds you?" she concluded with a flash of cold brown eyes.

Gussie's eyebrows went up. "Perhaps you're having a reaction to the medicine, Bess dear."

"Perhaps I'm having a reaction to you, Mother dear," came the terse reply. "Why did you impose on the Hollisters, of all people?"

Gussie grimaced. "Well, I couldn't find anywhere else to go," she muttered. "Jamaica went stale."

"They threw you out," Bess translated coolly.

Her mother ruffled. "They did not. I left of my own free will. Sort of." She shifted restlessly. "I told you, Bess, I can't make my own living. I don't know how to do anything."

"That's no excuse not to learn," she told her mother. "Living off other people is parasitic. There is no honor in it."

Gussie stared at Bess intently. "My darling, haven't you learned yet that money and honor don't mix? I won't be poor. I won't!"

"That's your affair," Bess told her. It was easier than she'd ever dreamed to stand up for herself. Now that she had the hang of it, she was almost enjoying it. "But I won't support you. And neither will Cade. You're the reason he came to see me, in fact," she said coolly. "He wanted me to get you away from Lariat, because his mother would be hurt if he ordered you off the place."

The older woman's face went curiously pale. "Yes, I suspected as much. He wasn't happy to have me around, and I'm ashamed to admit that I embroidered your relationship with Jordan Ryker. I only wanted to protect you. . . ."

"You don't have the right to interfere in my life, not even for noble motives," Bess said firmly. "And you know it."

Gussie lowered her eyes. "It's hard to let go," she said quietly. "Cade would never have let me see you again if you'd married him."

"Hasn't it dawned on you that Cade doesn't want to marry me?" she asked icily. "He never has. He's spent years chasing me away. Well, I finally got the message! You only brought the inevitable a little closer, so no harm done." Bess ignored her mother's stare and lifted herself back against the pillows, grimacing as the stitches caught.

Gussie wanted to tell her how Cade had looked outside in the waiting room while they lived through those first horrible few minutes. But Bess didn't even look receptive, and now she seemed resigned to giving up Cade forever. That should have made Gussie happy, but it didn't. She put herself in Bess's place and it hurt. Imagine loving a man beyond reason and having someone fight it tooth and nail, make the relationship impossible. It was the first time in years that she'd looked at anyone's viewpoint except her own. It made her feel a sense of shame. She'd grieved for the husband she loved, a husband she hadn't even known how much she loved until it was too late to tell him. She'd put herself first and Bess last, and now she didn't know how to get back on a motherly footing with her own daughter. Bess seemed to dislike her intensely, and how could she blame her? She'd been nothing but a burden to Bess.

"Cade isn't so bad," Gussie said slowly. "You could do worse."

"I could do better, too," Bess said, glaring at her mother. "Surely you'd rather I went after Mr. Ryker with no holds barred. After all, he's got money. He's rich."

Gussie felt sick at that mercenary statement. It reminded her of the way she'd sounded when she'd thrown Bess at him. But Jordan Ryker didn't strike her as a man who'd die for love of any woman. Oddly enough, she could picture Cade throwing himself under a bus to save someone he cared about, or even giving up a woman he loved to keep from hurting her. He'd done that for Bess, sacrificing his own need to protect her from being broken in spirit.

"There are things more important than money,"

Gussie said suddenly, because she'd only just realized it.

Bess lifted an eyebrow. "Really? You never used to think so."

The door opened abruptly, and Elise came in carrying two plastic cups of black coffee. "Here I am, I had to wait in line," she said, smiling at Bess. "Good morning. Are you feeling any better?" she asked, frowning as Bess confined her temper and Gussie took a calming breath. She handed a cup of coffee to Gussie, who looked pale and uneasy.

"Bess, what's wrong?" she asked, sitting down in the second chair.

"It's just reaction," Gussie said quietly. "That's all. She's had a hard few days."

"Yes. That's it," Bess agreed quietly. She drew in a breath and lay back on the pillows, exhausted and hurting. Gussie was singing a new song, but Bess didn't trust her. She'd been taken in once too often by her manipulative mother. And she wasn't about to be owned again, even if Gussie did sound as if she no longer minded about Cade. That was ironic, too, because Bess didn't dare let Cade near her again. She felt only half a woman now, and he needed a whole one to produce that family he wanted so badly.

"We've all been so concerned for you. Especially Cade," Elise said with a sigh. "He feels responsible."

"I was responsible," Bess corrected, and her eyes dared her mother to say a word.

"Anyway, we'll have you at Lariat by Friday afternoon, and I'm going to enjoy taking care of you. It's been ages since anyone's been confined to bed, and I have some marvelous recipes for trays," she added with a grin.

Bess had to smile at her enthusiasm. "It's very kind of Cade to let us come," she said. "I didn't want to put any more strain on him than he's already got."

"Cade doesn't mind responsibility," Elise said, smiling dreamily. "I was telling him just yesterday that he needs to marry and have a family of his own. He loves children, you know."

Bess did know, all too well. She said something polite and then quickly changed the subject. She couldn't bear to talk about children now. Especially Cade's children. Even if she could get close to him, he'd never want her the way she was now.

Friday morning Bess was up and dressed in a gray pantsuit Elise and Gussie had brought from her apartment. She was a little thinner than before, and she looked pale and drawn. She wasn't looking forward to the long drive to the ranch, but being in Cade's company, whatever the reason, was pure delight.

Cade came along to pick her up, and she didn't find out why until he'd signed her out and put her into his late-model Ford truck to drive her home.

"It's hard enough to squeeze three people into this cab," he murmured as he cranked the engine. "Four is pushing it. Mother and Gussie were able to get a ride with a friend of mine who had a business meeting up here." He glanced at her. "Put your seat belt on. I know it's going to be uncomfortable, but if I rolled this thing, you'd be in worse shape without it."

She hooked it slowly, still weak from days in bed.

"Are you planning to roll it?" she asked with graveyard humor.

"If I do, you'll be the first to know. Better crack a window. I'm having a nicotine fit."

He lit up and smoked while he drove. Out of the corner of her eye Bess watched him, adoring his strong profile and the way he sat, straight and tall. He had excellent posture, she mused, and the way his jeans and blue-checked Western shirt clung to those hard muscles made her head spin. It was such an unexpected treat to get to be alone with him. She had to bite her tongue to keep from telling him.

"You're pretty quiet. Feeling okay?" he asked a few miles down the long road toward Coleman Springs. The mesquite trees were green now, their feathery fronds swaying lazily in the soft spring breeze. There were wildflowers everywhere—Indian paintbrush, Mexican hat, Indian blanket, black-eyed Susan, and the state flower, the bluebonnet.

"On a day this beautiful, I'd have to feel okay," she murmured, her eyes following the land to the horizon.

"Your boss is a nice girl," he remarked. "She runs the office, you said?"

"Yes. And there's Nell. She's a live wire. We go out to lunch together sometimes." She moved and grimaced. "I'm glad they decided to let me go ahead with my latest project while I recuperate," she added. "I don't think I could stand being idle, now that I've found work I enjoy."

He glanced at her curiously. "That may not last when the newness wears off," he replied.

She smiled at him. "Well, it won't bother you one way or the other, I know."

"Do you, Bess?" he asked, and his eyes held hers so intently that she flushed before he looked back at the road.

That look disturbed her greatly. Knowing what she did about her barrenness, she didn't dare let him get close. It would be easier to keep him at a distance than to have to tell him the truth. She was going to have to walk a fine line while she was at Lariat. She only hoped she could.

He seemed to sense that uneasiness in her. A few miles from Lariat he pulled the truck onto a dirt road and parked it under a mesquite tree.

"What are we doing here?" she asked.

"I want to talk to you," he said simply. "There hasn't really been an opportunity since you've been in the hospital. At least here we won't be disturbed by nurses or relatives."

"What is there to talk about?" she parried, averting her eyes to the window. "I told you, I don't blame you for what happened."

He crushed out his cigarette in the ashtray with a heavy sigh. "It's eating me alive, Bess," he said finally. "I've got to know the truth about you and Ryker. I can't let it rest."

Her heartbeat quickened. He sounded odd. Not at all like Cade. She turned in the seat, her eyes wary.

"Mr. Ryker gave me a job," she said, so sick of the whole subject that she was driven to tell him the truth.

"And?"

She lowered her eyes to his booted feet. "And nothing."

"You haven't been out with him?" he persisted, although his expression was already lightening.

"If you can call one long dinner chaperoned by both our mothers going out with someone, I guess I did. Listen, Mr. Ryker isn't the kind of man who keeps a mistress. He's very much like you, in fact. He isn't interested in me. And nobody is keeping me. I make a good salary. That's why I can afford the new apartment. I told you, one of my ads is being used in a national campaign. I got a bonus. And the fox jacket was one Mama had bought that I was taking back. I threw her out of the apartment because she insisted on spending money I didn't have."

"Yes, I know. Gussie told me." He smiled slowly. "Glory be!" he murmured. "How you've changed, Miss Samson."

"You don't have to laugh at me," she said, glaring at him.

He couldn't help it. It was such a relief to know that all his inner torment had been for naught. He felt reborn.

"Imagine you throwing Gussie out," he mused. "What did she say?"

"Not a lot. And I guess she got back at me while she was with you and Elise and the boys, because she sure fed you a line of bull."

"And I fell for it," he agreed, the smile leaving his dark face. "My mother didn't. I suppose she knows you better than I do."

"It's just as well," Bess said, averting her eyes. "I appreciate your letting me stay at Lariat while I get better, but you don't need to worry that I might get ideas about why you're doing it. I'm not going to start chasing you again . . . Cade!"

His lean hand was against her cheek and he was

suddenly so close that she could feel the warmth of his body, smell the cologne he wore, the lingering traces of smoke on his breath as he stared into her eyes from point-blank range. She pushed at his chest nervously.

"What are you afraid of?" he asked huskily, his lips almost touching hers as he spoke.

"You," she whispered, her eyes filled with hopeless longing as she looked into his dark ones.

"I won't let you run this time," he whispered against her mouth. His eyes closed. His hands held her face steady while his mouth slowly parted her lips, smoky-tasting, gently expert, lifting her up into the sky.

She moaned. The impact of his kiss was shattering. This was nothing like the last time, when he'd been angry. This was a kind of tenderness she'd never associated with Cade, although she'd suspected sometimes that he was capable of it. She had no defense at all. She wanted him so, and the feel of his mouth and his hands was just heaven.

Her arms started to lift around him, but he caught them, holding them gently at her side while he pulled his lips from hers and stared down into her face. "No," he whispered. "We can't make love. You're still much too fragile."

Her face colored, and he bent and kissed it with exquisite tenderness, his lips lingering on her closed eyelids, her cheeks, her forehead.

"Cade, you . . . mustn't," she whispered brokenly.

"You can't fight me," he said quietly. "You'll give in every time, because you want it as much as I do. You want me."

Tears of helpless humiliation stained her cheeks. "Of course I want you," she admitted miserably. "I'll die wanting you. But it isn't enough, Cade. There's no future in it, you said yourself that it was only sex you wanted, that you could only offer me a brief affair . . . !"

"You talk too much," he murmured, and his mouth found hers again, savoring its soft, silky warmth, its faint trembling as he took it.

She kissed him back, her heart breaking inside her because it was only her body he wanted, not her heart. She couldn't give him a child, and when he knew, he probably wouldn't even want her body anymore.

One hand threaded itself through her long, soft hair and eased her head onto his shoulder, while his free hand moved to the buttons of her blouse.

"No!" she gasped, catching his fingers. Her face flamed.

He smiled slowly. "No?"

She didn't understand the smile. "You . . . you can't touch me like that," she whispered. "It isn't right."

"You little fraud," he murmured. His eyes had a devilish twinkle in them. "I actually thought Ryker was keeping you, when you've never even let a man touch your breasts."

Her blush deepened. "Cade!"

He smiled gently, and his hand caressed her slowly at her nape while he searched her misty eyes. "Are you sure you don't want me to touch you like that?" he asked in a slow, sensuous drawl. "You might like it."

"You're the one who said we mustn't start things we can't finish," she reminded him nervously.

"Oh, I said a lot of things," he agreed. His mouth brushed the tip of her nose. "I'll probably keep saying them, too, but once in a while I get hungry for a soft mouth under mine and the warmth of a woman's body."

The way he put it made it sound cheap. She froze, her body arching slightly away from him.

He let her go with obvious reluctance. "I see," he murmured, watching her retreat. "I put that badly, didn't I?"

"It doesn't matter," she said, averting her face. "Please stop playing games with me. I'm so green it's pitiful, and I don't know enough to laugh it off."

He watched her silently. "You're dead wrong about the game part," he said. "I don't play that kind of game with virgins. And I'm not laughing."

"You might as well be." She clenched her hands in her lap. "I'm a society girl, remember, decorative but totally useless. And you hate my mother, even if you do believe every lie she utters, as long as it's something bad about me."

It was going to be like that, was it? Cade thought, studying her set features. Well, he had plenty of time and she wasn't going anywhere. He could wear her down.

"Okay, honey," he said softly. "Just keep putting bricks in that wall you're building. When I get ready, I'll knock it down."

"I won't be one of your Saturday-night conquests!" she shouted.

His eyebrows arched as he turned the key in the truck's ignition. "I don't seduce women on Saturday night," he pointed out. He smiled slowly. "I like it best in the afternoon, so I don't have to find an excuse to leave the lights on."

She wanted to sink through the floorboard. He had the most awful way of making her feel naive. She quickly turned her attention to the landscape, bristling at the low laughter coming from behind the steering wheel.

Gussie and Elise were already at Lariat when Bess and Cade arrived, and Gary and Robert came out to meet them.

"Hi, Bess!" Robert said with enthusiasm. His red hair was almost standing on end as he opened the door and lifted her out before Cade could say a word. "You look great for an accident victim," he chuckled, turning with her in his arms. He was almost as tall as Cade and wiry. He had the same brown eyes, but he was freckled as well.

"Show-off," Gary scoffed, smiling at them. He was the middle son, dark-eyed like the other boys, but his hair was a light brown, and he was shorter than his brothers. He was the serious one. Cade had moods, but he could occasionally be as devilish as any cowboy. Gary never played. He was the bookkeeper and had the intelligent look of his profession.

"She doesn't weigh as much as a feather," Robert said with a chuckle.

Cade came around the truck with her suitcase. "Drop her and I'll beat the hell out of you," he told his brother, and he didn't smile when he said it.

Robert sobered up at once. "I won't drop her," he said defensively. He turned, grinning at Bess. "How long do we get to keep you? I'm learning chess and I need a new victim."

"I don't like chess," Bess confessed. "It's too logical."

"That's the best excuse I've ever heard for not playing it," Robert agreed.

"There's nothing wrong with logic," Gary protested as they went inside.

"Did Jennifer tell you that?" Robert asked, tongue-in-cheek.

Gary gave him a hard look. "We're glad to have you with us, Bess," he told her, and smiled. "If Robert gets to be too much of a pest, you just tell me and I'll find a client in Borneo for him to go and see about our cattle sales."

"You're a prince, Gary," Bess said.

"He's a—" Robert began.

"Robert!" Cade snapped.

"No need to start taking bites out of me when you're just home again," Robert teased. His eyes twinkled as he glanced over Bess's head at his older brother. "Save your energy for the rodeo Saturday."

Bess felt her heart stop beating. She stared at Cade, but he wouldn't look at her. "You're still on the rodeo circuit?" she asked hesitantly.

"Take her to her room, Robert. You can come back for the luggage," Cade said. He put the suitcase down in the sprawling living room with its huge rock fireplace and comfortable furniture. It had Elise's touch, because there were white Priscilla curtains at the windows and ruffled cushions on the chairs and flower arrangements on the end tables. But it was a functional room, too, with chairs big enough for men to sit comfortably in, and there was a huge oak desk in one corner.

"You're not going to bring the suitcase?" Robert

asked, but he was talking to thin air. Cade was out of the room, out of the house, seconds later.

"I shouldn't have mentioned the rodeo," Robert winced. He carried her along the hall and into the guest bedroom. It was white clapboard, like the rest of the house, with a handmade quilt at the foot of the bed and a white coverlet between the four towering bedposts. The room was done in dark antique furniture, with familiar white Priscilla curtains at these windows too. Bess loved it on sight.

"I thought he was through until fall," Bess said as Robert put her down gently on the bed, noticing that she winced when she moved.

"He was," he replied. "We got that additional financing we needed, but Cade doesn't want to grow old paying off the interest. He was always a damned good bronc rider, and he's great with a rope. We figure he'll do well."

"But it's so dangerous," Bess protested.

Robert pursed his lips. "Worried about him?"

"It's our fault that your family is in this trouble," she hedged. "I don't want any of you hurt because of us."

"Cade's practically indestructible," he reminded her, and smiled. "But if you promise to look that worried, I'll sign on for the calf wrestling myself. You can come and watch."

She shook her head. "I won't go to a rodeo. Besides," she added, trying to lighten the atmosphere, "I'm still a working girl. I've got an ad presentation to deliver."

"You can't possibly work all the time," Robert said.

"No, and I won't. But I'm not quite up to social events," she added meaningfully.

He smiled. "Okay. I'll leave you to get some rest.

Mom and Gussie were upstairs talking when you came. I'll see if they're through."

"Thanks."

He winked at her and went out. She didn't know Robert or Gary well, and it looked as if Robert might present a problem. He'd already set Cade off with his friendliness. Of course that might be a benefit in the long run. She had to keep Cade at bay, and being friendly to Robert might accomplish that.

Gussie came in minutes later, hesitant and a little unsure of herself. "Hello, darling. Did you make the trip all right?"

"Yes, thank you," Bess replied.

Her mother sat down in a chair beside the bed. "Don't you want to lie down?"

Bess was propped up against the pillows, her shoes off, still fully dressed. "I'm all right," she said.

"Can I do anything for you?" Gussie persisted.

"No, thank you."

The older woman sighed. She stared at her clasped hands. "You won't believe it, I know, but I'm sorry for what I tried to do. Cade does care for you in his way."

"I don't care for him anymore, in any way," Bess lied coldly. "So you don't need to worry."

Gussie frowned. "What do you mean?"

"I mean I like living alone," Bess said. "I'm perfectly happy with my life the way it is, and I don't need anyone to take care of me. If you'll make an effort to look after yourself, I won't have any problems."

Surprisingly her mother nodded. "I've been thinking about what you said. When you're better, and we can go back to San Antonio, I think I might have an idea about some kind of work I can do that I'd like."

Bess was shocked. That didn't sound like her mother. "You do?" she asked faintly.

"We can talk about it later," Gussie said. She got up, looking much younger than usual, with her hair in a ponytail and wearing jeans and a white blouse. "I know you don't think I'm much of a mother," she added. "But maybe I can change if I try." She patted Bess's hand. "I'm going to give Elise a hand with dinner. She thinks she can teach me to cook," she said, laughing. "I'll come back and see you later."

"Yes." Bess watched her leave and sat staring at the doorway after she'd gone. That didn't sound like Gussie at all. But perhaps her accident had had a sobering effect on her mother.

She wanted to ask Gussie about Cade's accusations. She wanted to hear her mother's side of it. But that might be disastrous at the moment. She was helpless and couldn't work, and she didn't feel right about starting more trouble for Cade.

Cade. Her eyes closed on a silent groan. She hadn't dreamed that he might go back to the rodeo circuit to make the money he needed to help bail Lariat out. He had his loan, but apparently that wasn't good enough for him. He wanted to pay it off, and he thought competition was the best way.

He was good, she couldn't deny that. She'd seen him ride broncs before. But anyone could have an accident. Even Cade.

She ran her fingers through her long honey-brown hair. He was in peak condition, and he didn't take unnecessary risks, but she had visions of him breaking his back or his neck in the arena. She couldn't bear to see him hurt.

Her eyes closed wearily. Life had been so simple a few months ago, and now everything had shifted and it was a new world that she had to cope with. She wondered if her life was ever going to straighten out and get on an even keel.

Chapter 11

Cade was quiet at supper, the only solemn note in a pleasant meal that left everyone else relaxed and contented. He didn't seem to notice. He brooded, hardly eating anything, and excused himself to go into his office with one long, silent glance at Bess. She colored, and he frowned slightly at the reaction. That was the one faint glimmer of hope, that she still reacted to him physically. It was enough to build on at least. In time she might forget his cruelty and learn to care for him all over again. She was a totally different proposition now, no longer the frightened child she'd been when she left for San Antonio. A woman with spirit and the need to stand on her own two feet could take anything he, or Lariat, threw at her. She'd grown into a woman he could marry. He only hoped he hadn't figured that out too late. He didn't like the way Robert was flirting with her, or her shy response to it. Robert was nearer her age than he was, and not as hard a man. He'd worried all through the meal, but that faint color in her cheeks dispelled some of it. He went off to his study to work with a lighter heart.

Bess averted her eyes from his intense scrutiny. He had to know that she was still vulnerable. She'd lost her head in the truck and let him kiss her, she'd kissed him back, and now he probably thought she was dying for love of him. That could be why he was keeping his distance, although he'd given the impression in the truck that he intended pursuing her in earnest.

Maybe it was better that he backed off, though, she told herself. After all, she didn't dare let him close now. Not only was she barren but he was knee-deep in guilt. Her life was becoming more tangled by the day.

Meanwhile Elise was passing around a plate of homemade pound cake. Gary and Robert had their heads together discussing sales, but they paused long enough to have dessert.

"Cade didn't wait for his," Elise said with a sigh.

Gussie got up, looking uncertain but determined all at once. "I'll take it to him," she said, and several pairs of shocked eyes watched her carry it on a saucer, with a fork, to his office.

She opened the door and went in without knocking. Cade looked up from his desk, where he was sitting, brooding over columns of figures that wouldn't balance no matter how hard he budgeted. He glared at Gussie.

"I didn't poison it," she said with forced humor as

she put the saucer and fork within his reach and sat down on the edge of the worn leather chair.

"You might as well have," he said coldly. "You've poisoned everything else."

Gussie stared down at her folded hands. Only Cade and his late father had ever made her feel so helpless and inadequate. "There's a reason for what you think you saw . . . the day your father died," she said quietly.

"Yes, and we both know damned well what it is, don't we?" he retorted.

Her head jerked up, and there was hurt and a certain amount of pride in her eyes. "Think what you want to about me," she said. "It's better than telling your mother the truth."

She started to get up, but he slammed his hand down on the desk, startling her.

"What truth?" he demanded, his voice flat and measured with cold rage. "That you were having an affair with him? We know that already."

"That's a lie," she said, meeting his glare levelly. "That's a bald-faced lie."

"You never denied it before."

"My daughter never hated me before! Some of that is your fault too," she said. "It was because of your ceaseless animosity that I stretched the truth about Bess. All right, I thought I was helping her, but it didn't bother me one bit to hurt you." She sighed. "Until I realized that I was only hurting Bess more in the process." Her shoulders slumped wearily. "You put me in an impossible position by accusing me in front of your mother. I couldn't tell the truth about what happened, so I had to take the blame and ruin a years-old friendship."

"Some friendship. Mother was your seamstress—"

"And my friend," she said quietly. Her eyes met his. "She loved your father."

"So did you, I gather," he returned harshly.

"I hated him!" she said with sudden venom. Cade stared at her expressionlessly and she laughed softly. "Are you that shocked? Did you really think he was so lovable? He was hard and selfish to a fault! He thought nothing of having affairs, and it didn't really bother him very much that Elise might one day find out about them!"

Cade rose slowly from his chair, his eyes blazing. "That's not true," he said. "My father was always faithful to my mother, except at the last, with you."

"Sit down, young man," Gussie said commandingly. "You're going to get the truth, for Bess's sake, and I hope you choke on it. Because you won't be able to tell Elise any more than I could."

"Are you capable of telling the truth?" Cade asked, but he backed down a little. She didn't look as if she were lying.

"Do you remember the Brindle girl?"

Cade frowned. He had known her over ten years ago, when Bess was barely a teenager, long before he saw her as a woman and began to burn for her. Daisy Brindle had been a special girl to him at the time, and her sudden departure from Coleman Springs had hurt and puzzled him. Now he realized that he hadn't thought about the girl in years. "Of course I remember her," he replied slowly. "I was dating her. After Dad died, she left town. . . ."

"Oh, she left town, all right," Gussie said quietly.

Cade felt the smoking cigarette burning in his fingers. He put it out with deliberation, because a nasty suspicion was beating at the back of his mind. Daisy . . . and his father? Bits and pieces of memory came back, of Daisy's sudden uneasiness when he brought her to the house, the tension when his father came around her.

"You're beginning to get the picture now, aren't you?" Gussie nodded. "Care to make a wild guess, Cade?"

"It couldn't be," he said slowly, but his eyes were admitting the possibility already.

"Well, it was," she said, pushing back her blond hair angrily. "Your father just couldn't resist the chance to cut you out with your pretty young brunette. He wasn't a rich man, but he had a way with women. It was about the time you bested him riding that Arabian crossbreed you bought, and he lost face with his men. He got even, in the most elementary way. It was your little Daisy Brindle he was with in that hotel room. He phoned you, didn't he, to ask you to bring some papers over to the Barnett Hotel. He phoned you from the desk, and I just happened to be coming out of the restaurant and overheard him give you the room number. When I looked outside and saw Daisy waiting for him, I understood the look on his face. He was going to let you find them together."

Cade felt sick all over. "For God's sake, why?"

"He thought it would pay you back for showing him up in front of his men, of course. He had a sadistic streak, as you, of all people, should know. He used it on Elise enough."

He put his head in his hands. He didn't even argue with her. It was all too obviously the truth. "Why did you get involved?"

"For Elise's sake," she said. "I thought I could head him off. Can't you see what a scandal it would have been? Not only a younger woman but *your* younger woman. Inevitably you'd have lost your temper and it would have been all over town in no time. It would have killed Elise. She didn't know he was having affairs at all."

"Neither did I," he said angrily.

"Well, Daisy wasn't the first, I'm sorry to say. He knew that I knew about him; one of his lovers was one of my acquaintances, and she talked. I walked around brooding about it for a long time before I finally decided that I had to do something. Not for your sake but for your mother's—there would have been such a scandal. Anyway he wasn't prepared to find me knocking at the door of his hotel room. I threatened to go straight to Frank and tell him. Your father was breaking horses for us, and it was a very profitable sideline that he didn't want to lose. He backed down and let me get her out, but I'd interrupted them at a rather . . . emotionally stressful moment," she added uncomfortably. "I told her what your father was planning. She was trembling so hard that she barely made herself decent before I pushed her out the door. When I turned to tell your father what I thought of him, he started gasping for breath and clutching his chest."

"So you ran to get help," Cade said as he realized it.

"That's exactly what I did," Gussie replied calmly. "But you'd just arrived at the hotel and you saw me and made the obvious assumption. My good deed turned to tragedy and destroyed the one friendship I'd ever managed to keep. I hated you for that. Over the years, making you pay was my one reason for living. Now, of course, having watched my daughter face death because of that hatred, it all seems rather pointless. So does protecting you and Elise from the truth. Nobility can be expensive. I've paid too much for mine already."

She got up, feeling less burdened. "I'm sorry. But it was time."

"Past time." He searched her face quietly. "It took me years to get over Daisy. I can't imagine why, now. She was nothing but a tramp apparently."

"She was in love," Gussie corrected him. "Your father was her whole world. She didn't know that he was only using her, and she felt guilty about betraying you. When he died, she was desperate to get away so that she wouldn't involve her family in the scandal. I gave her some money and drove her to the airport."

Cade sat back against the chair, his hands absently smoothing the arms. "Mother loved him."

"Of course she did, Cade. You don't stop loving people when they hurt you, any more than you throw a child out the door because it's been bad. Love lasts. Frank never believed what you did about me, you see," she said gently. "He loved me. That brings a kind of trust you can't imagine unless you've experienced it. I'm selfish, too, and spoiled, and I can't quite cope with life right now. But I've never lied to Frank, and he knew it. It very nearly killed me when he died. I went a little wild, and Bess suffered for it." She smiled ruefully. "But I think I'm growing up, just as she is. And you needn't worry that we're going to leech on you. As soon as Bess is able, we're going back to San Antonio, and I'm going to start taking care of myself." She got up. "Don't tell Elise, will you?" she added, pausing at the door. "She's suffered enough just from thinking it was a woman her own age. It's hard for a woman to lose out to someone half her age and beautiful. Don't do that to her. She's learned to live with it now. Let it be."

Cade only half-heard her. He'd hated her so much, for so long, that it was hard to accept that she was innocent. He drew in a slow breath, wanting to say so many things that he couldn't manage just yet.

"Thanks. For the cake," he said stiffly.

"It's safe to eat," she murmured. "Elise hid the rat poison the minute I offered to bring it to you."

A corner of his mouth tugged up, but he didn't say anything else. Gussie left him sitting there, alone.

It was something of a shock for Cade, if he could believe Gussie's confession. It was hard to think of it as a lie, because she hated him too much to bother with fabrications. He lit another cigarette and lifted it to his mouth. It seemed that he hadn't known his father at all, not in any private ways. It didn't bother him half as much that Daisy had betrayed him as it bothered him that his father hadn't even considered Elise Hollister's feelings. Gussie was right. His mother would have been destroyed if she'd found out. Even now the knowledge would hurt her terribly.

Well, knowing it did put a new complexion on something, he mused. At least it removed one barrier between Bess and himself. Not that there weren't plenty left—her new attitude of coolness toward him in any way except physically, and her accident, which he'd helped bring about, were others. Then there were the old differences, of class and wealth. He sighed. Those were the hardest to overcome. His dark eyes went slowly around the room, critical of the used furniture and the flaking paint on the walls and the long, bare light bulb hanging from the high ceiling on its twisted cloth cord. Bess was used to crystal chandeliers. Hell, even the apartment she was living in now was ritzier than his whole house.

He got up from the desk, forgetting the bookwork, and went down the hall and outdoors. He had to clear his head and stop brooding about things. If Bess still cared for him, after all he'd done to her, it wouldn't matter that he didn't have a lot to give her, he told himself. He had to hope that it didn't, anyway.

He hadn't mentioned to Gussie that he'd told Bess about her affair with his father—now he'd have to set that record straight as well, and it was going to be uncomfortable. He'd made all too many mistakes recently. A world of them. He was cool with Bess because he didn't want to play his hand too soon. But it was wearing on him, having to hold back, when what he wanted most was to sweep her into his arms and make passionate love to her. She wasn't in any condition for that just yet, and she was pulling away instead of reaching toward him. He was living from day to day while she healed, trying to manage the confusion of his own new feeling for her. Robert's adulation of her was his next biggest problem. He didn't want to hurt his brother, but Bess was his. Somehow he had to nip that situation in the bud before it became troublesome. He couldn't bear the thought of Bess belonging to anyone except him.

Meanwhile Robert was having the time of his life at the supper table entertaining Bess. She seemed to enjoy his wild stories about the cowhands and ranch life, and he was much too busy staring into her soft brown eyes to notice his brother Greg's worried scowl or his mother's curious glances.

It wasn't until Gussie came back that Robert began to wind down. He had chores, he said, and reluctantly excused himself.

"If you feel up to it, I'll carry you down to the barn tomorrow," he told Bess, his blue eyes full of fun. "We've got a calf in there."

"Just what she needs to recuperate," Elise murmured dryly, "the scent of the barn."

"Not to mention the hay," Greg seconded.

Robert glared at him. "Why don't you go and call Jennifer?"

Greg lifted his eyebrows. "I'll do that. But you'd better remember a few things yourself, little brother," he added with a meaningful stare that was instantly lost on Robert.

"He's vague," Robert said, grinning down at Bess. "But we have to overlook his behavior, because he's in love." He clasped his chest and gave a fair imitation of a Cupid sigh.

"Your day's coming," Greg warned.

"In fact, it's closer than you might think," he replied, his gaze warm and gentle on Bess's face.

Bess frowned slightly. Surely that look didn't mean what she thought it did? No, she moaned inwardly, not another complication. She liked Robert very much, but Cade was her heart. He always had been. Didn't Robert know that?

Gussie walked with her to her room after she'd said good night to Elise.

"Robert's got a crush on you," Gussie sighed. "I hope he knows it's hopeless."

"Is it?" Bess asked with a pointed look in her mother's direction. "I like Robert. He's very nice. Of course, he's not rich," she added cuttingly.

"You won't forget soon, will you, darling?" Gussie mused. She smiled. "Well, I'll work on you. I've already got Cade thinking."

Bess frowned as she sat gingerly on the edge of her bed. "What do you mean?"

"Cade and I had a nice talk, that's all," she replied. "About old times and misunderstandings. If it means anything to you, I'm through playing matchmaker or devil's advocate," she added seriously. "If you want Cade so much, I won't stand in the way or try to complicate things for you again. I was trying to protect you, I suppose. He's a hard man in some ways. But he does have a sensitivity that his father lacked, so he might not make mincemeat out of you after all."

Great, Bess thought bitterly. Now that she knew she was going to be barren, now that Cade was forever out of her reach, her mother had suddenly become her ally. It was hilarious, except that she didn't have the heart to laugh.

"I don't want Cade." She forced the words out and avoided her mother's eyes. "I'm going to be a career woman."

"Bosh!" Gussie scoffed. "You're meant for diapers and playpens, darling. You'd never be happy buried in business."

Bess knew her face had paled, but she averted it. "I'm tired, Mama. I need to get some rest."

Gussie watched her daughter curiously. "All right. I know I'm in your bad books. I even understand why. I won't force my company on you. Maybe one day we can talk about some things that have made me so hard to live with. Until then we'll take it one day at a time, okay? See? No coercion," she added with a gentle smile at Bess's curious stare. "No pleading. No tears. Just woman to woman. And I've told Cade that we're not going to sponge on him longer than necessary, by the way," she said as she paused at the door. "I think I may start a business of my own when we go back to San Antonio. But regardless of what I do, I won't be sponging on you either," she told her daughter. "I'm through being everybody's cross. I'm going to become a powerful business magnate and conquer Texas. Good night, dear."

Bess felt her forehead, but she didn't have fever, so maybe it wasn't a hallucination. She could hardly believe what she'd heard. She wondered if Cade had any part in that transformation. What could he and Gussie have talked about?

She put on her gown and climbed under the covers, half-hoping that Cade might come to say good night. She knew he didn't like Robert's attitude, and she wanted him to understand that she wasn't encouraging it. God knew why she should care, she told herself, when Cade was acting so distant. He'd been quiet and withdrawn since they'd come from San Antonio, almost as if he regretted his decision to let her and Gussie come here. She felt like an unwelcome visitor.

He was still apparently in his office, because he

hadn't made another appearance. But he didn't come, and Bess finally fell asleep from sheer fatigue.

The next morning Robert was in her room before her eyes were fully open, with a tray of coffee and ham biscuits that his mother had baked.

"How are you today?" he asked with a bright smile as he helped her sit up and then placed the tray across her lap. "You look pretty first thing in the morning."

"Thank you," she said self-consciously. She smiled back at him, but with reservations. He was quite obviously flirting with her, and she wasn't sure how to handle it. She didn't want to cause any more trouble than she already had, and she knew instinctively that Cade didn't like Robert paying attention to her.

Her big problem was that she had to discourage Cade from getting too close. He was already jealous, even though it was probably just sexual jealousy. She didn't dare let herself give in to him. Would it be wise, though, to encourage Robert's feeling for her just to keep Cade at bay? She didn't want to hurt Robert.

"Why the big frown?" Robert kidded. "Don't you like ham biscuits?"

"I like them very much. Thank you," she said. Her dark eyes lifted to his. "Robert . . ."

He drew in a steadying breath. "It's no go, isn't it?" he asked, searching her face. "It's still Cade."

She sighed miserably and dropped her eyes to the tray. "It's always been Cade," she confessed. "I must be a glutton for punishment. I know there's no future in it. . . ."

"Isn't there?"

The deep, quiet voice at the doorway startled them

both. Cade was lounging against the door, apparently drinking in every word. He wasn't smiling, and the look he was giving Bess was as possessive as the bridled anger he directed at Robert. Bess felt her heart shaking and wished she could get under the bed. She hadn't dreamed that he was nearby when she'd made that impulsive confession to Robert.

"I brought her breakfast," Robert began.

"So I see. Thank you," Cade replied politely. He didn't say another word, but his face spoke volumes.

Robert sighed. "No harm in finding out how things stand. I'll just wander along and jump off the barn."

"Don't be an idiot," Cade murmured, slapping the younger man affectionately on the shoulder as he passed him. "Try hanging out in church instead of bars. There are plenty of nice girls around if you look for them."

"But not Bess," he mused with a smile in his brother's direction.

"Bess is mine," Cade said, his eyes steady and covetous on Bess's shocked face.

"Your gain, my loss. Well, anyway, Bess, I smoked him out for you," Robert said, and winked at her as he left them together.

Bess was red-faced and confused. She met Cade's eyes with determination. "It wasn't fair to tell him that," she said. "I'm not your personal property."

"You're going to be," he replied calmly. "I'm sick to the back teeth of having to watch him moon over you."

"But he doesn't," she protested weakly.

"Yes, he does," he said seriously. "He's sensitive and

he's already halfway in love with you. Is it worth hurting him to avoid me?"

She groaned. "Don't say that."

"It's true. Besides they all know how it is with you," he added, his eyes narrowing. "You've been my shadow for years. Even if you've convinced yourself that your feelings have changed, you won't convince them without some work. You won't convince me either," he added, his eyes full of dark fires as they held hers. "I'd have to be blind not to know that you want me, and how much."

Her face flamed. She couldn't even deny it. "You yourself told me that desire didn't have much to do with caring about people."

"Sure I did," he agreed. "And it's true. But I don't think what you feel is purely physical. I never have."

She buried her face in her hands. He was stripping her soul naked, and she didn't have a comeback. She had to be strong, she had to!

He watched her, frowning. "Is it so embarrassing to talk about it, for God's sake?" he demanded. His gaze slid over her possessively, and she felt like her heartbeat was visible against the demure rounded neckline of her blue Juliet gown. "There was a time when you'd have given blood for my mouth on yours, and it wasn't that long ago. Now you're sitting there trying to pretend you don't know what I'm talking about."

"You don't want any kind of a relationship with a woman like me, remember?" she asked in a ghostly whisper. "All you can offer me is an affair. You said so."

Chapter 12

Cade registered those painful words with a sense of bitterness. He felt bad about the things he'd said to her. He'd been striking out at her because of jealousy, and yes, he'd said he couldn't offer her marriage, for all kinds of noble reasons. But when he'd come so close to losing her, reality had settled on him like a vulture. And now he felt more than a need to protect her. He wanted Bess. He especially wanted children. He was getting to the age where settling down wasn't so frightening a thing. Money would be scarce, with the family to think of, but they could manage. Anyway Greg and Robert were pulling their weight, and the ranch was pulling into the black. He could afford to start thinking about marriage now."

"I thought you'd been sleeping with Ryker," he said

after a minute. "I was jealous as hell and hurting. I lashed out because of it." He saw her startled expression and he smiled faintly. "Shocked? I've always been jealous of you. Even now, having to watch Robert with you tears me apart."

Her breath caught. So close to heaven, she thought, and she didn't dare let herself be caught in that sweet web.

"Robert's just being kind," she said huskily.

"Hell. Robert's halfway in love with you," he said shortly. "Thank God Greg's engaged. At least I don't have to worry about him."

She searched his face and almost smiled at the irritation there. "I'm not going to have an affair with Robert," she promised.

"I'm glad, because an affair is out of the question," he said shortly. His eyes narrowed. "Even with me."

Her heart jumped. "You said in San Antonio that an affair was all you had to offer. That you wouldn't ever want to marry someone like me."

He sighed angrily. "Oh, I was eloquent, wasn't I?" he muttered. "And you'll never forget a word I said." His dark eyes swept over her body in the gown, settling on her full, soft breasts, their tips suddenly hard where he was staring. His body echoed that hardness, and he clenched his teeth at the unexpected shock of pleasure before he forced his eyes back up to hers. "Look, you're wearing that on your engagement finger already," he pointed out, indicating the silver ring he'd given her. He took a steadying breath. "So why don't you just consider yourself engaged for a bit, and let's see where we go from there?"

He said it a little clumsily, and she realized that he'd

probably never asked a woman to marry him before. Her heart was in her eyes as she looked at him and dared to dream for a few precious seconds. He was asking her to marry him! Her pulse raced wildly as she stared at him, wishing. Wishing!

But she knew she couldn't. Why he'd made the proposal puzzled her, unless it was out of guilt or to save Robert. Probably, she thought miserably, it was the latter. He wouldn't have wanted Robert marrying a woman he wanted. He did want her, she realized, even though he felt nothing else for her. Even in her innocence she knew that men were sexually jealous sometimes, and Cade considered her his private property. He'd even told Robert she was, and he'd been angry when he'd said it.

"You don't have to get engaged to me to save Robert," she said, and then watched the shock that momentarily rippled over his features. It made her wonder if she'd accidentally hit on the truth, but surely he wouldn't ask her to marry him just for that reason! Or would he? An engagement wasn't a marriage, after all. An engagement could be broken when she was back at work and out of Robert's orbit.

"Bess . . ." he began, uneasy at her question. He hadn't meant it that way at all.

She sighed. "Anyway I don't want to get married right now. I'm only twenty-three, and I've just had a taste of freedom. I don't want to settle down yet. Now that I've started, I want to prove that I can make my own way in the world."

He scowled and his eyes narrowed as he looked around the room. It was neat and clean, but nothing disguised the age of the furniture or the worn spots in the rug, or the faded colors of the curtains and the bedspread. This room, like the others, had a single light bulb suspended on a cord instead of light fixtures or chandeliers.

"Your barn back at Spanish House was more luxurious than this room," he said quietly. "It would be a long drop from Spanish House to Lariat, wouldn't it, honey?" he demanded, furious because he'd never proposed to anyone before and Bess was acting as if he'd offered her a cup of coffee or something. "You wouldn't have elegant dresses or go to dinner parties or entertain rich people here, and you couldn't afford diamonds."

It might be the easy way out, to take advantage of the differences between them and play Miss Ingenue to his Rugged Cowboy, she thought. But she was too softhearted to hurt him that much.

"I know that," she said softly, her eyes involuntarily caressing on his dark, hard face. "Cade . . ." she began.

But he wouldn't listen. "And I guess kids would be out of the question for a career woman, too, wouldn't they?" he demanded, his eyes blazing. "God forbid that you should have to come home to take care of them."

Her knuckles went white as she gripped the coverlet, hating her body for what it could no longer give him—the sons he wanted. "I don't know that I want children," she said quietly.

He couldn't believe what he was hearing. He'd let her go to San Antonio. He'd forced himself not to do anything to tempt her to stay here. Now she'd become the independent, strong woman he'd known she could be—except that this new Bess was totally independent. She didn't want, or need, him. She didn't want his children. And what he had to offer wasn't enough. He wasn't rich enough to suit her. His pride bristled.

He felt wild. He wanted to throw things. He wanted to pull the ceiling down around him. Maybe all she'd ever felt for him was infatuation. Because if she loved him, really loved him, she'd have said yes without hesitation. He felt a coldness inside that was like ice against his rib cage. He was too late.

His silence brought her eyes up. He didn't show emotion very often, and his face was unreadable just now. She'd hurt his pride and she felt guilty, but it was better this way.

"Thank you for asking me, Cade," she said quietly, hiding her threatening tears. "You'll never know how much it meant . . ." She broke off because her voice trembled.

Cade was too bitterly hurt to notice the betraying quiver. He turned away. "Can I get you anything on my way out?" he asked in a voice that could have started fires.

She shook her head. "No. Thank you."

He strode toward the door without looking at her. "I'll have Mother look in on you later."

He went out without a word, without looking at her, without even a cold glance. His straight, muscular back was eloquent, and she felt the tears raining down on her pale cheeks the second the door closed behind him. She'd deliberately let him think that she'd only felt an infatuation, that she was on the road to being a career woman. She lifted the hand with the silver ring to her lips and kissed it with aching hunger. One little word, and she could have been his wife, his lover. She could have shared his life and taken care of him and slept in his arms every night. But it was inevitable that he'd wonder why she didn't conceive. And when he found out the truth, that she'd deliberately concealed it, he'd never forgive her. It was better to let him hate her than to face that certainty.

Even if it was relatively easy to make that decision, it was hell carrying it out. She cried herself to sleep that night and every night afterward. It was like being given a taste of heaven and then having it snatched away. She loved him more than her own life. But denying him the children he wanted would be more cruel in the long run than refusing him now. She had to keep that in mind.

But she dreamed of him all night every night, of his hungry kisses at her apartment, at the tenderness he'd shown her on the way back to Lariat from the hospital. She was haunted by the images of him, by the lost hopes and dreams. Only the little silver ring on her finger was left of that time, and she hadn't been able to remove it. Cade noticed, but he didn't say anything. He withdrew into himself, and while he was polite, he never sought her out or tried to be alone with her again. Her refusal had hurt him as nothing else ever had. He'd been so certain of her acceptance that the rebuff had sent him reeling. He'd thought she loved him, but she hadn't.

Meanwhile Robert was taking advantage of Cade's aloofness to entertain Bess. She made it clear that she had nothing to give him emotionally, and he'd accepted it with outward ease. But the way he looked at her sometimes made her uncomfortably aware that he wasn't as lighthearted as he pretended. He was hoping, despite what Cade had said, that she'd change her mind. Everyone was aware of Cade's animosity toward Bess. He openly avoided her when he wasn't glaring at her, and it gave Robert renewed hope.

Bess enjoyed Robert's company, his stories about the ranch, and his knowledge of marketing. He was the only friend she had right now and a soothing balm for the breach between Cade and herself. She only hoped Robert wasn't going to get hurt. Ignoring him hadn't accomplished anything, and even her blatant statement that she liked him as a friend didn't deter him. Greg worried and Cade muttered and cursed, but the friendship went on.

Gussie watched the new development with worry too. But despite the fact that Gussie was learning to cook and even helping Elise around the house, Bess was still wary of her. She wanted to prove to Bess that she wasn't totally useless, but Bess simply ignored her.

Eventually Gussie became desperate for the key to unlock her daughter's dislike.

"I wish you'd tell me what I've done, besides the obvious," Gussie said, sighing one day when everyone else had gone to town. Gussie was dusting in the living room while Bess sat quietly in an armchair reading a new detective novel that Robert had loaned her.

Bess looked up from the book, searching her mother's worried face. Gussie was trying, she understood that. But knowing that her mother had been responsible for such a tragedy in the Hollisters' past made it difficult. She couldn't bear the thought of how much it hurt Cade to know that her mother had caused his father's death. Cade had worshiped his father.

"How can Elise bear to have you in her home?" Bess asked finally.

Gussie stopped in midstride, her face white. "What?"

"It's an open secret, isn't it?" Bess asked. "Cade told me, the night I wrecked the car. He said that you killed his father—that you were having an affair with him."

Gussie sat down heavily on the sofa. "He told you that night?" she asked. "He told you, and upset you with it, and that was what made you run from him!"

"That, and the argument we had," Bess replied. She frowned. "How could you do that to Daddy . . . ?"

"I didn't." Gussie groaned. She put her face in her hands. "My God, I didn't." She looked up. "Hasn't Cade said anything to you since I took him the cake in his study? Hasn't he told you what I said?"

Bess closed the book. "No," she said. Cade never spoke to her.

"Bess, I know I've got my faults, but I've never committed adultery with anyone, least of all with Coleman Hollister," she said, and the very quietness of her tone was convincing. "He was having an affair, yes. He had several. But never with me."

"Then who was he having it with?" Bess asked curiously.

"With Cade's girlfriend," she replied. "That's right, a woman half Elise's age, and beautiful." She laughed bitterly. "Cade had bested him on a bronc," she continued. "So Coleman was going to get even. He called Cade to bring him some papers, and he was going to let Cade find him in bed with the girl. She didn't know. She was in love with him. I was at the hotel having lunch and I guessed what he was up to. I headed him off."

"And then Coleman had a heart attack while you were still there," Bess said, shocked that she'd believed her mother capable of such a thing in the first place.

"I was going for help when Cade got there," Gussie said simply. "He made the obvious assumption, and I couldn't contradict him without bringing the girl into it. It was Elise I was thinking of, but the girl was also the daughter of some friends of the family. It would have been a horrible scandal, and I thought it was kinder to let Elise think it was me than to hurt her like that. She'd have hurt twice as much because Cade was indirectly involved, don't you see?"

Bess did. Her eyes became cloudy, and she looked down at her feet. "I've always accused Cade of looking for the worst. I guess I've been doing the same thing, haven't I? I'm sorry I believed him." She looked up. "He doesn't know, does he?"

"Yes, he does," the older woman replied. "I got tired of the pretense. He won't tell Elise the truth any more than I will, but he had a right to know. Elise has forgiven me despite what she thinks I did. No friendship could ask more. Now I'm trying very hard to earn her respect and trust again."

"But it wasn't your fault," Bess argued.

"I stuck my nose in," Gussie said, smiling wistfully. "When you take on other people's trouble, you have to expect a few blows. I love Elise like a sister. I've never forgiven Cade for blurting it out in front of her. He forced me to keep quiet when he accused me. The only way I could have defended myself would have been to hurt Elise more."

"No wonder you've hated him so much."

"Not anymore," Gussie said. "Hatred is a waste of energy. I've decided to do something with all mine. I'm buying into a business, Bess," she added, leaning forward earnestly. "I can sell what's left of my jewelry to raise the capital I need."

"What kind of business do you have in mind?" Bess asked warily.

Gussie grinned. "A talent agency," she said.

Bess laughed softly. Her mother actually meant it. "But what do you know about job placement?"

"Lots," Gussie replied. "One of Frank's best friends is in the business. I phoned him several days ago and he's going to let me buy into his agency. He's promised to teach me the ropes when we get back to San Antonio. To start out, I'm going to work with him. Later on I may open a new branch and operate it myself."

"Mama!"

"Don't faint," Gussie laughed. "It's really me. I just figured it was time I stopped being a liability and became an asset. When I get my first paycheck, I'll treat you to dinner."

"Steak, of course," Bess murmured.

Gussie glared at her. "A burrito at Del Taco," she corrected. "I can't throw away money, I'm on a budget."

"Oh, I love you," Bess said with warmth.

Gussie could have cried when she saw the softness in her daughter's eyes, the love and respect. It would be worth anything not to have Bess mad at her anymore. She bent down to hug the younger woman.

"I love you, too, baby, even if I haven't said it very often or shown it very much." She stood up, brushing away tears. "I'll get my own apartment as soon as we get back," she added, "providing you're well enough to be left by yourself."

"You can stay with me. . . ." Bess offered hesitantly.

Gussie shook her head, smiling. "No. Now that we're both trying to be independent, it's best if we stick to our guns. We can visit without infringing on each other's freedom. Okay?"

Bess smiled. "Okay."

"Now, I'd better get back to work before the others come home." Gussie sighed. "Acres of dust around here, what with three grown men tracking dirt in and out. Honestly, you should see what Elise has to wash out of their jeans!"

Bess sat and listened to her, totally enchanted with this new person. At least this was one positive note in her life. It didn't make up for Cade, but it was nice all the same.

Robert was still her shadow. It was pleasant to have him to talk to, but she had a terrible feeling that it was more than friendship on his part. Even though she'd told him she had nothing to give, it made her feel guilty. And when Cade was home, it seemed to make him even colder when he saw his youngest brother in Bess's company. He didn't say anything or make sarcastic remarks. He simply withdrew into himself and became unapproachable. Somehow that was worse than shouting, because Bess sensed that she'd hurt him deeply.

It had been almost a month now since the accident, and Bess was up and around and feeling much better.

She'd been working on her presentation for the new ad campaign in her room at night and on the front porch during daylight, and it was almost done. Soon she'd be able to go back to work. She'd phoned the office every week to report her progress, and Jordan Ryker had called once or twice himself. He'd talked to Bess, but Cade had answered the phone. His dislike of Ryker and his fury at having him call Lariat were all too evident. Bess expected him to say something, but he never did. He simply ignored her afterward.

Bess was glad that she was making such progress, but Cade's coldness was beginning to affect her work and her sleep. She couldn't understand why he was so angry that she'd refused his proposal. He didn't love her. Was it pride or guilt that drove him? He asked Gussie or Elise about her progress, never her. She could have told him that she was feeling much better physically. Her abdomen was healing nicely, except for occasional twinges of discomfort. Looking at it, the scars weren't all that disfiguring. They were much less painful than the emotional ones of knowing that she could never bear a child.

Cade, meanwhile, was getting some scars of his own, and they were visible ones. He'd taken a bad toss in the bronc riding in New Mexico, and when he came home, he was limping again. The injury had aggravated the other tendon injury that had never had the chance to heal. Cade, being Cade, pushed himself until he dropped. But this time he'd added a few cuts and bruises to his face and arms as well.

Cade had signed up for two rodeos while Bess and Gussie had been staying at Lariat. There was another one in San Antonio a few weeks down the road. He'd won good money so far on the circuit, but Bess was holding her breath now. She'd told Cade that she didn't care for him, but it was hard to watch him without letting her dark, soft eyes show what she was feeling. Since he'd been back from New Mexico, his attitude had grown even more distant than before. He wouldn't even look at her, especially if Robert was in the same room with them. He skipped meals, presumably to avoid her, and he looked gaunt and driven. Bess couldn't help worrying about him, or letting it show that she did. But Cade didn't notice her sad scrutiny.

The Friday before Bess was scheduled to go back to San Antonio to work, Elise took Gussie with her to a garden club meeting. With Robert in Kansas City for the day, Greg in town working with the bookkeeper on taxes, and Cade out on the ranch, Bess was left alone in the house.

She was sitting on the porch swing, staring at her ad drawings without any particular interest, when she heard a horse riding up in the yard.

It was unusual for Cade to come home before dark. He looked perfectly at home in the saddle, his lean, elegant body in denim and chambray lazily echoing the motion of the bay under him, his Stetson at an arrogant slant across his dark, quiet face as he leaned over the pommel and stared at her.

She was wearing a colorful button-up tent sundress that didn't put too much pressure on her rapidly healing abdomen and was barefoot. He found her scribbling new ideas on the big sketch pad beside her, her honey-brown hair loose around her shoulders, just washed and fragrant as it waved gently in the breeze.

Her heart raced as it always did when he was anywhere in sight. All her dreams were centered on him. Her soft, dark eyes roamed over him lovingly, caressing his face, his broad shoulders tapering to narrow hips and long, powerful legs in worn black boots.

"For a woman who doesn't want me, you have covetous eyes," he remarked as he swung down out of the saddle and dropped the reins, leaving the horse to nibble at his mother's prize lilacs while he mounted the steps.

She colored, her perfect complexion exquisite with the faint blush in her cheeks. "Your horse is eating Elise's flowers," she said softly, watching the horse devour a particularly pretty blue columbine.

He lifted an eyebrow. "They'll grow back," he mused.

He picked up her sketch pad, sparing a glance at the neat artwork before he laid it on the glider and sat down beside her. He took off his hat and tossed it onto the sketch pad. His lean hand ran through his dark hair, pulling it back from his forehead. The breeze was pleasant, and patches of sunlight drifted onto the porch. Cade rocked the swing back into motion, one lean arm thrown carelessly behind Bess's shoulders.

"You're home early," she remarked quietly.

"I got through early." He turned, his dark eyes sliding over her face, down to the soft rise of her breasts under the thin fabric of her dress. "Where are Gussie and my mother?"

"Gone to a garden club meeting," she said. "Greg's still in town with the tax man, I guess."

"Estimated taxes are due," Cade mused. "Just when

I think we're ahead, we fall back a few thousand." He looked down at her. "Has Robert called?"

"No. Isn't he coming back tonight?" she said falteringly.

His dark eyes narrowed. "Why? Can't you stand it without him even for a day?"

She took a deep breath and lowered her eyes to the wild pastel colors of her dress. "Don't, Cade," she pleaded.

"Robert's in love," he said. "If you can't see it, you're either blind or too stubborn to admit it. I tried to warn you."

Her heart jumped. She knew it, but she didn't want to face it. "I'll be going back to San Antonio Monday," she said.

"He'll follow you there, with flowers and music and probably a ring. He wants you!"

Her eyes closed. "Why do you care?" she cried, lifting her wounded eyes to his. "You don't want me anymore . . . oh!"

He reached for her, and his hard mouth covered hers without warning. All the rage that had built up in him for weeks overflowed. He was beyond sanity now, giving in to the hunger that had haunted him night and day. All he knew, wanted, needed, and loved was in his arms.

"I go to bed aching at night and get up aching every morning," he said, groaning against her mouth, "and you don't think I want you? My God . . . Bess!"

He turned her, pressed her up against his wildly beating heart, against the smoky warmth of his mouth and the leather scent of his shirt. His tongue probed inside her mouth while his hand caught her nape and held it steady. He was trembling with the violence of his need, his mouth ravenous as it pressed deeper into hers, as his tongue penetrated rhythmically into the sweet darkness of her mouth.

She moaned and so did he as the fever caught them both, burning hot and wild. It had been so long since he'd touched her, so long since he'd kissed her. She shivered with the need to be even closer to him. She loved him so, would have died for him. Tears welled up behind her closed eyelids with the sheer joy of being close to him. His cold avoidance had hurt her so much. She'd thought he was through with her altogether, but as she felt the tremor in his hard arms, she relaxed into his body. He might not love her, but at least he still wanted her. If only she could have accepted his proposal. Oh, if only!

Her arms reached around his neck, her mouth yielded to the passionate fury of his. She didn't even protest when she felt his hand under her breast and his thumb probing the hard nipple.

The wind blew around them, the swing creaked as it moved. Cade lifted his head, his breath ragged, his lips faintly swollen and sensuous, poised above hers. His hand moved, and he watched her face as he caressed her, his thumb and forefinger gently kneading the hardness, and she gasped.

"A nipple this hard could make a man conceited," he breathed roughly, his dark eyes holding her embarrassed ones. "And eyes like yours could make him drunk. Open your mouth. I want all of it."

He bent over her hungrily, his parted lips biting at hers, teasing and tormenting her. Her teeth closed helplessly on his lower lip, trying to make him kiss her.

Eventually he did, and she clung to him, not protesting the way he touched her, lost in the scent and feel of him, the warm strength of him against her. At her hip she could feel the sudden hardness of his body as it reacted to their feverish lovemaking, and she wasn't afraid of it. She loved him so much that the reactions and responses of his body were as natural and acceptable to her as her own.

His mouth slid down her chin to the soft pulse in her throat and farther, to the warmth of her breast. His mouth opened and pressed down hotly over the nipple. She'd never felt anything remotely like the pleasure that shot, white-hot, through her loins. She cried out and arched under him, her fingers trembling as they ran through his cool, dark hair, holding him against her while the pleasure went on and on and on. . . .

He bit her and she jerked away, shocked. He lifted his head to look at her. His eyes were wild, and there was a reckless look in them that made her a little afraid.

"Do you like it?" he whispered roughly. "Or are you afraid of my teeth? I won't hurt your nipple."

She'd never dreamed that men said such things to women. She knew her face was scarlet, but the words were oddly arousing. Her nails dug into his shoulder as he rubbed his lips sensually across hers in a travesty of a kiss.

His fingers worked at the buttons on the front of the dress, and she was in such a sensual haze that it was more relief than fear when he opened them and unfastened the clasp of her front-closing bra.

He pulled the lacy fabric away and looked down at

the soft pink skin and hard mauve tips with pure masculine delight. His fingers brushed over their hardness very gently and then stroked their fullness while his eyes sought hers. "It's all very new to you, isn't it?" he asked, his expression stern and quiet and very adult. "I won't hurt you any more than I have to. Unbutton my shirt."

She was in a fog, or she might have realized what he meant and what he was planning. But she was dazed with pleasure and drowning in need. She tore the buttons away with trembling hands and then caught her breath at the pure sensual feast of his chest, with its bronzed muscles and the black hair that curled over them.

Her fingers roved through the thick coolness of hair and caressed him hungrily. She felt her body tighten as he suddenly stood up with her in his arms, so that her breasts pressed against his bare skin.

She shuddered and clenched her teeth at the screaming pleasure it gave her, her nails digging into his shoulders as she buried her face against his throat. "Cade," she moaned.

"Bite me," he said hoarsely, and when he felt her teeth, he shivered. She was everything he'd ever dreamed she could be. It wasn't the ideal solution to the problem, but it was the only one his tortured heart could find. If he made her pregnant, she'd marry him even if it was only for the child's sake. And he'd make her love him. She had once. If he was careful and gentle with her, he could draw that emotion out of her again. And she'd love their child, even if she didn't love *him* just yet.

Cradling her against his lean body, shivering with

the sweet thought of possessing her, he turned and carried her into the house. Behind them the horse lazily devoured every one of Elise's pink peonies, unnoticed by the human beings so entranced by each other.

Chapter 13

Bess couldn't fight her way out of the sensual web Cade had woven around her. She knew almost certainly that he wasn't going to stop, but she loved him too much to protest. She wanted him as badly as he wanted her. Monday she was leaving Lariat forever. This would be all she had of him for the rest of her life.

His mouth enslaved hers, drugging her senseless. He carried her into his bedroom, his body so feverish with desire that he could hardly walk. It was wrong. But even while his mind registered that, his body was throbbing with need, his arms faintly tremulous as they held and cherished Bess.

He loved her. It would only be this one time, he told himself, just this once to hold on to. He didn't dare admit what he was gambling to keep her. The faint hope that he might make her pregnant was pushed to the back of his mind while he fought all his repressions and principles. But it had been so long, and he loved her more than his own life. Losing her to Robert would kill him.

Bess felt him putting her down on the coverlet, and just for an instant she tried to protest. "Cade, don't," she whispered in a voice that was totally unconvincing. His strong hands pulled the dress away from her body.

"I can't stop, Bess," he whispered tenderly, his hands unsteady as they eased the fabric away from her soft pink skin. "I've got to have you. Sweetheart, I've got to," he whispered, his mouth suddenly on her bare belly as his hands swept her briefs away along with the dress. He felt the scars under his lips, but they didn't bother him. Bess was soft and sweet, and the scent of gardenias clung to her, making him drunk.

She moaned, and he pulled her hands to his hard, hair-covered chest and moved her fingers over the taut muscles. His mouth covered hers tenderly as his fingers worked at his belt and the zipper below it. He put her hands on him and groaned as he felt her touch him as she'd never dreamed of doing. It was intoxicating. Her hands moved experimentally, lightly touching, tracing, learning the hard lines of him. His nipples hardened when her fingers moved across them, and his flat belly rippled when her hands moved shyly back down again.

He was all muscle. Hard and warm and definitely male. He held her hands against him as he lifted his head and sought out her eyes.

His mouth was just above hers, his lips parted, his

eyes sensuous. "I dream of having you touch me like this," he said roughly. "I dream of taking you under me and feeling all that silky softness enveloping me. You are every dream I ever dreamed."

Her heart was turning cartwheels in her chest. He arched her back, and her soft breasts were under his mouth. He tasted her, the soft, moist suction making her whimper as he poised over her, his lean, fit body faintly trembling with hunger.

"I can't stop you," she said, moaning with her last breath of self-control, which dissolved with the sudden intimate touch of his hand as it moved down her flat belly. She cried out as the pleasure swept through her, sobbing while he found the right pressure, the right touch, to give her a taste of what was to come.

"We've gone too far to stop," he said softly. "We'll live with the consequences," he added, his eyes holding her wild ones for just an instant. "I'm going to cherish you. All our lives we'll have the memory of today," he whispered as he bent toward her.

She closed her eyes. He felt the same way she did, she thought headily. He wanted this one memory too. Perhaps that meant that he did care for her in some way.

He fit his lips against the soft contours of hers. His tongue probed inside and she gave in completely, on fire with the hunger to give in to him. All her noble principles flew through her mind, but her body was too hopelessly abandoned to care.

"Come to me," he murmured against her mouth.

She felt her body obeying him, coloring as her breasts pushed heavily against his hard chest and her bare belly felt the impact of stark male arousal.

"That's good," he breathed. His arms helped her, and his legs shifted slowly between hers, so that she was suddenly fitted into the shocking contours of his powerful body. "No, don't be afraid of it," he whispered when she stiffened at the stark intimacy. "I'm aroused, but I won't lose control. This is as natural as breathing for a man. You'll get used to it," he promised huskily as his mouth covered hers again, his weight pressing her gently into the mattress, the warmth and hardness of it making her tremble with new knowledge, new sensation. The feel of his hair-roughened chest over her bare breasts was as starkly pleasurable as the feel of his hips moving with exquisite tenderness over her own.

He tasted of smoke and mint, and what he was doing to her lips was fiercely arousing. He bit and teased them, tempted them until they opened. And then he moved down against them with a pressure that became swiftly invasive. His tongue pushed into her mouth with a slow, steady rhythm.

"Cade . . . oh, Cade, love me," she moaned, her voice breaking on the words.

He heard her, and his mind, like his body, blazed. She was soft and warm and he wanted her beyond bearing. His lean hands slid from her hips up her waist, to the outside of her breasts. He let them rest there, while his thumbs slowly, expertly, teased the soft curves, ever closer to the suddenly taut peaks. He heard Bess gasp, felt her fingers clutch him as she tried to fight. But he kept on, his mouth insistent, his hands more so, because he knew she wouldn't fight long.

And she didn't. The narcotic effect of desire washed over her with every sweep of his fingers. She began to tremble as he brushed his thumbs around the hard nipples, leaving her taut with feverish anticipation.

Her eyes opened as she gave in to the feeling he was arousing, and she looked into his dark eyes as she let him see how fiercely she wanted his hands.

"Is it good?" he whispered tenderly, and he didn't smile.

"Yes . . . !" she whispered back as his thumbs made one more foray almost, almost, almost to the place she wanted them. Her back arched and she trembled violently, her eyes holding his. "Touch . . . them," she pleaded brokenly.

"Soon, little one," he whispered. His dark eyes cherished her face as gently as his hands cherished her body. "Yes, it's a fever, isn't it? It burns. You want me to put my hands on you," he whispered sensuously. "You want my mouth on your breasts again."

She moaned at the images he was arousing. Her gasp was audible, and her need was visible. Her face was flushed, her eyes hauntingly beautiful as she moved toward him.

"Bess," he breathed, and this time his hand didn't stop. It swept across the hard tip and his fingers contracted suddenly, rhythmically on the soft, bare skin.

She cried out. It was like a consummation. Her wild eyes closed as her body clenched, and she arched her back, shuddering.

Cade could feel himself losing control at the sight of her like that. He'd always imagined that it would be slow and tender with Bess if he ever made love to her like this, that her responses would be shy and a little reticent. He'd never imagined her so passionate and responsive.

With a rough groan he bent and put his mouth over her breast, the heat and moisture of it penetrating as he cherished it.

She caught his head in her hands and pulled it closer, feeling the hot suction with a sense of inevitability. It had been this all along, this avalanche of feverish need. She'd sensed that, once out of control, it would sweep them both away. But there was no running from it now. She was as involved as he was, her body on fire for him, her mind washed away in her first experience of oblivious pleasure. Cade's mouth found bare, soft, warm skin, and he moaned against her body as he searched over it with his hands. It was the closest to paradise he could ever remember being. She smelled of gardenias and she tasted of rose petals, a softness that made ashes of his most erotic dreams. She was exquisite.

He kept her at fever pitch with hot, hungry kisses as he managed to get out of his clothes. She lay there, her eyes like saucers, her body trembling with hunger until he stood over her, his muscular body bare and fiercely masculine. He held her rapt gaze for a long moment, giving her time to understand the finality of what was going to happen. She stared at him with mingled fascination and fear, but she didn't turn away. His body clenched and he felt himself shudder when her eyes fell down the length of him and her lips parted.

He barely had the presence of mind to pull her dress under them before he fell down beside her. All that sweet curve of body, his to touch, to savor, to possess.

She felt his hands touching her and trembled with desire. She loved him. This would be the first time, and the only time, but she had to have it. She loved him too much to deny him, or herself, this one exquisite memory.

Her mouth met his halfway, and then she felt the unbearably sweet pleasure of his skin against her own, the clasp of his arms, the hardness of his muscular legs as they entwined with her soft ones.

His hands moved on her with slow expertise, gentling her for what was to come, tenderly arousing her all over again to the same fever pitch that had led to that first intimate touch. Only now he was touching her where she was most a woman, and she gasped and her body flinched involuntarily.

His head lifted and his dark eyes held hers while he probed gently. "I'm going to have to hurt you, sweetheart," he whispered. "But I'll be careful, and very, very slow."

Her voice broke as she saw him move above her, and there was one second of frightened regret.

"No," he whispered, his hands nudging her legs apart. "It's all right, Bess." His mouth brushed her eyes, closing them. "Close your eyes and listen. Listen, sweetheart." His hands slid under her hips and he whispered to her, starkly intimate things. He told her exactly what they were going to do, how he was going to do it. He teased her lips with his own while his body probed tenderly. The feel of him was beyond her wildest imaginings of intimacy. And still his voice went on and on, the words arousing, forming mental pictures, as he whispered about the pleasure that would follow the pain.

His lips brushed slowly over hers and his tongue teased them. He smiled softly and then he moved down again. His tongue slowly went into her mouth, easily penetrating, gently. She gasped at the first tiny stab of pain. He hesitated, whispering to her, his hands smoothing her hair, tracing her breasts gently. His mouth moved again, his tongue easing inside to touch hers, a little deeper this time. The pain was worse now.

"Don't try to pull away, *amada*," he whispered, the Spanish love word sounded exquisite in the stillness, which was broken only by her rapid breathing and his heartbeat. His hand clasped her hip, holding her. "Only a little longer now. Bear the pain for me. Think past it."

"It . . . hurts," she protested, her eyes wide and hurting.

He held her gaze, his lean fingers gently tracing her mouth. "Only a little longer," he whispered, carefully pushing against her. He saw the pain begin to go away, felt her gasp. "I'm . . . having you," he said, hoarsely as the pleasure began to uncoil in him. His breath sounded suddenly deeper, rougher. He bit at her mouth, the action slow and fierce and oddly arousing, like the changing rhythm of his damp, muscular body above her. "I'm having you, Bess," he whispered softly. The breathing grew ragged, and he pushed down, watching her pupils dilate, feeling her body suddenly accept him totally as she cried out softly. "There." He groaned, his jaw tightened, and he shivered with the incredible pleasure of possession. "My God . . . !"

"Cade!" she moaned.

"You're part of me," he whispered, awed by the enormity of what they were doing, by the almost awesome oneness. His eyes caressed her, adored her.

"Now we join," he said huskily. He caught her hands and curled them into his, pressing them down above her head. "Now. Yes, now . . . now, sweetheart. Now!" His hips lifted slowly and then pushed down, lifted again, pushed, and he shuddered with each deliberate movement, his face revealing the strain of his control. "Oh, God . . . it's so good . . . so good!"

Her body trembled. The stinging sensation was being consumed by a different sensation. Hot. Burning. But not pain. Her lips parted on a soft gasp as he shifted and she felt the sharp pleasure tear through her stomach.

"I'll make you cry out," he whispered, watching her face as he moved again. He saw the contortions begin and knew why. He felt a harsh pleasure, a masculine kind of pride in his own capability as he felt her shiver and knew that it was pleasure this time. "You're going to see rainbows." He breathed roughly as his mouth moved down toward hers. "I'm going to make you see rainbows, however long it takes!"

She moaned into his open mouth. Her fingers curled under his and she began to move with him as she felt the rhythm grow deeper and slower and more terrible. The pleasure was a living thing. Cade was part of her and she was part of him. They were one person, one creature. Her hips lifted to his, her legs tangled with his. Her breasts rose, only to be crushed softly by the descent of his hair-roughened muscles, and he looked down to watch. Her eyes followed his, drawn to the mystery that was a mystery no more. She swallowed and flushed. Her gaze lifted back to his, to find the same wonder and pleasure building in his black eyes.

"Pieces of a puzzle," he whispered huskily as he began to change the rhythm. "We fit together . . . like a puzzle. Male and female. Dark and light." His jaw clenched and he shivered as he began to feel the pleasure. "Oh, God, Bess!" he groaned. His eyes closed and he felt his body tightening. "I want you . . . !"

She echoed his words, her body gloriously surrendering to the strength and power of his, savoring his endurance when her own had given out. She let him take her then, and the ripple of pleasure caught her unaware as she heard his ragged, tortured breathing and felt the shudder of his body as he drove for fulfillment.

Somewhere in the fever of it she found a heady taste of the ultimate pleasure. But her joy was in his, because she felt and heard and saw the culmination of his pleasure. He didn't try to hide his face. He sensed her gaze and let her watch him. It increased the pleasure to such a degree that he heard his own voice cry out, unbearably strained in the quiet room.

A long time later she smoothed his black hair gently and kissed his closed eyes, his damp face, his hot throat as he lay over her, his weight formidable and beloved all at once.

"I love you," she murmured. She moved against him, sighing as she pulled him even closer. There should be guilt, she thought, but there was none. She'd loved no man except this one. She never would. To love him completely was as natural as breathing and this memory would last a lifetime.

He heard the words and wished he could be sure that she wasn't just saying them because he was her first man. He wanted her to mean them, but it was too soon yet.

He rolled onto his back and stretched his cramped muscles, aware of her rapt, curious gaze on the powerful, hair-roughened length of him. He was uncomfortable like this with women, as a rule, and he couldn't remember a time when he'd made love in the light, despite what he'd once said to Bess. But it was different with Bess. Everything was. Loving her had given him pleasure that made him burn even in the sated aftermath.

Bess moved, disturbed by his silence, and pulled the sheet up over her. She glanced at her dress, which had been under them, and at the faint red traces on it. She flushed, sitting up.

Cade's eyes found hers in the stillness of the room. She looked embarrassed and almost fragile like that.

"I'm sorry," he said quietly. "I never meant for that to happen." It wasn't quite the truth, but there was no need to upset her any more right now. His eyes ran down to the dress and he looked up, concerned. "Was it very bad?"

She shook her head. Her gaze fell to his body and she flushed, turning away.

He threw his legs off the bed half-angrily and got back into his clothes. The door was standing wide open, and he thanked God that the house had been empty. He hadn't even had the presence of mind to close and lock it, so lost had he been in Bess and his need to have her that nothing had registered except the desire he felt.

Her fingers clenched on the sheet as he stood up again, his shirt hanging open over the hard muscles and thick hair her hands had found such delight in. Now, sane again, she felt ashamed of what she'd let him do. He hadn't even said that he loved her, and now he looked as if he despised her. She felt tears moistening her eyes. All the reasons that had seemed so right in the heat of passion seemed irrational now, with the fever gone and cold reality staring them in the face. He couldn't ever respect her again because of what she'd let him do. Her tender memory had turned into a shaming nightmare.

Cade was feeling something similar. He'd wanted the hope of a child to tie Bess to him, and the fever that had burned in his blood had blinded him to the unfairness of what had seemed reasonable at the time. Now he felt a little ashamed. Bess had been a virgin and he'd seduced her. He'd given her one more reason to hate him, when she had enough as it was. He'd wanted her with him, but it wasn't fair to force her, to take her choices away.

He was vaguely aware of Bess's quiet gaze on him. He turned toward her with his shirt still unbuttoned, revealing damp, hair-matted chest, and his dark eyes searched her wan face as she sat there clutching the sheet over her breasts. His face hardened as he saw the telltale marks of his mouth on her soft skin, the faint redness created by its soft suction.

He reached for the cigarettes and lighter he kept in the drawer of his bedside table and lit one, blowing out a thick cloud of smoke as he went to the window and stared out.

Bess wanted to ask what he was feeling. She wanted him to explain why he hadn't even tried to stop. But she was too shy and too embarrassed and too ashamed.

She pulled the stained sundress over her head and buttoned it, aware of his quiet scrutiny. It would get her back to her own room at least. Then she could throw it away. She knew she'd never wear it again.

She stood up, and her eyes went to the door, which was standing wide open. She blushed, wondering how she could have lived with herself if anyone had come home and seen them.

"The house is empty," he remarked, his voice deep, subdued. "No one will be back for an hour or two."

She folded the material over the stain absently, her eyes downcast, her hair in a glorious tangle around her shoulders.

"Don't look like that," he said. "I feel bad enough as it is."

She turned toward him, her eyes searching his, but there was nothing showing in that poker face. "You didn't force me," she faltered, averting her eyes. "I'm as much to blame as you are."

He drew in a heavy breath. "Three years is a long time," he said absently. "I thought I could handle it, but you went right to my head."

She didn't understand. "Three years?" she echoed.

He lifted the cigarette to his mouth, drew, and blew out a cloud of smoke. "That's how long it had been for me," he replied. "I've been completely celibate since that last day I gave you riding lessons."

She didn't move. Her breath seemed suspended, deep in her chest. "But . . . surely, there were women who wanted you?" she began.

He smiled ruefully. "There are women who'd want any man if he was winning in rodeo competition. Rodeo fans." The smile faded. "A man has to want a woman back before he's capable with her." His eyes darkened, glittered. "I want you. Nobody else."

She sighed slowly. "You've been avoiding me since that last time we talked," she said. "I thought you'd given me up to Robert."

"Damn Robert," he said shortly. "He's my brother, and I love him, but I could have beaten the hell out of him with pleasure for the past couple of weeks. You're mine. I said it and I meant it. I'm not sharing you, least of all with my own brother."

"Cade . . ."

"Go ahead," he said challenging her with a mocking smile. "Tell me you could do that," he said, gesturing with his head toward the rumpled bed, "with Robert or any other man but me."

She couldn't. She shifted, wrapping her arms over her breasts. They were still a little sensitive from the touch of his hands and mouth. Just remembering made her color.

"I . . . I've never wanted anyone but you," she confessed, lowering her eyes to the bare floor. "I don't suppose I ever will."

"Then I think you'd better marry me."

There it was again, that question that made her feel so wonderful and so sorrowful all at once. She wasn't sure she had the strength to turn him down a second time, even if it was ultimately for his own good. She looked up, and everything she felt was in her eyes.

"Which is it?" she asked miserably. "Pity or shame or guilt?"

He put out the cigarette in a dish on the bedside table and moved toward her. His lean fingers touched her face, tilting her head back so that their eyes met. "Tell me you love me," he said.

He was hopeless. Impossible. Arrogant. She reached up and touched her mouth softly to him. "I love you," she whispered. "But I won't marry you."

"Why not?"

She pressed both trembling hands against his chest and stared at the hard muscle and damp, thick hair. "I've already told you why," she said. "I want to try my wings. I want my freedom for a little longer."

"And you think you can walk away from what we've just done together?" he asked gently.

She colored. "It's the wrong time of the month for me to get pregnant," she said, lying through her teeth, because any time of the month was the wrong time now.

"That wasn't what I meant." He sighed, pulling her forehead against his chest. "You don't understand how it is. Making love is addictive. You're going to want it again with me, just as I'm going to want it again with you. But my conscience won't let me play around with you, Bess. If you won't marry me, this isn't going to happen again."

She swallowed. "You mean, you'd find someone else."

"How?" he asked, looking into her eyes. "I wasn't kidding. I can't make love with other women. I haven't wanted anyone except you for three years."

"But—"

He put his forefinger over her lips. "If you're bound and determined to stay in San Antonio, then go ahead. I won't try to persuade you, and I won't compromise you any more than I already have. But if I've made you pregnant, I have a right to know."

"Yes." She stared up at him with her heart in her eyes, loving him so much that the thought of a child was tormented heaven. She'd have given anything to give him a son. But that was no longer possible and she just had to face it. At least she knew what it was to love him. Her fingers touched his broad chest, and she knew that she'd live on today all her life. Tears stung her eyes as she faced the idea of those long years without him.

"I shouldn't have let it go this far," he murmured when he saw the brightness of her eyes. "The first time should be a husband's right."

Her gaze met his and locked with it. "Then it would have been yours anyway," she whispered. "Because there won't ever be anybody else." The tears escaped her eyes and streamed down her cheeks. "Oh, Cade, you can't possibly imagine how much I love you . . . !"

He wrapped her up against him hungrily, his head bending over hers where it rested on his bare skin. He rocked her, his voice in her ear, murmuring endearments, his hands soothing her.

"Stay," he said huskily. "Take a chance on it."

"I can't." Her voice broke on the words. "I can't."

He wished he could understand what she was so afraid of. But maybe if he let her go, despite the agony it was going to mean, she might discover that she couldn't live without him. It was a gamble, like the one he'd just taken. But he'd been wrong to try to force her to stay by making her pregnant. He didn't have that right. He had to let her make the decision on her own. She loved him at least. That was in his favor.

She savored his warm strength, the feel and smell and hardness of him in her arms. He had to care about her, or why would he have gone to such lengths to keep her here? Cade wasn't the kind of man who seduced virgins. He had too much conscience, and too much respect for her. It was going to be hard for him, as old-fashioned as he was.

It was going to be hard for her, too, she admitted ruefully. Despite the modern attitudes of others, hers were cemented in the past, like Cade's. She'd lived too sheltered a life to accept life in the fast lane.

She pulled away from him at last, wiping her eyes.

He lifted her left hand and stared at the ring before his eyes met hers. His thumb rubbed over it gently. "You might consider yourself engaged now," he murmured. "That would ease my conscience a little." He smiled. "It might ease yours too. I think we're going to have hell living with what we've done otherwise."

It was only a little concession, she told herself. And did it really matter, because he didn't want anyone else, and neither did she. It was no less a bond than the feeling that kept them bound together already. But she had to remember that she couldn't give in to the need for his name. His child-hunger was the one impenetrable barrier between them, and not even love would make up for that.

"It will have to be a long engagement," she said after a minute.

Sheer joy danced in his eyes, but he wouldn't let her see. "Okay," he said carelessly. "That means you don't date, by the way," he added. "Unless you enjoy having your dates beaten bloody, that is."

She smiled softly. "Would you?"

"Now, I would," he agreed. The smile faded, and his eyes darkened as he looked down at her. "I'm your lover," he said. "Remember?"

She hid her eyes from him. "My first lover," she whispered.

He framed her face in his hands and lifted it. "I hope you dream about it every night of your life," he whispered against her mouth. "I hope the memory of it gives you hell."

"Thank you very much . . ." His mouth covered hers hungrily. He fitted her into the contours of his body, amazed to find that he was instantly aroused.

She felt it and tried to move back, but he caught her hips roughly and pushed them against his. Then he lifted his head and stared at her with mocking amusement.

"That used to happen every time I heard your voice," he said. "Now I can just look at you and it happens."

She colored at the way he said it, at the emotion in his voice, at the feel of his hard-muscled body so intimately close."

"How in hell can you still blush?" he asked, smiling.

"It's new," she said falteringly.

He bent and brushed his mouth softly over hers. "You might not believe it, honey, but it's new to me too." He lifted her by the waist until she was on a level with his dark eyes, close against him. "I don't guess I could change your mind about leaving on Monday?"

Her heart skipped. "No." She leaned forward helplessly and brushed her mouth softly over his. "I love you," she whispered. Her brows knitted. "I love you . . . !"

There was anguish in her voice. That disturbed him, but her mouth came back to his, and he gave in to the need to kiss her. His lips pushed hers gently apart and his tongue penetrated into the warmth of her mouth. He heard her moan and felt her tremble. He could almost have given her back those frantic words, but he didn't want her to feel trapped. She was softhearted, and if she knew how he really felt, she might sacrifice herself for his sake. He couldn't let her do that, he cared too much.

He lifted his head, drowning in the softness of her, the light in the soft brown eyes adoring him so openly. He shuddered with need and emotion. "I'll come to see you," he whispered.

She smiled. "Will you, really?"

"And keep your hands off your big, dark, sexy boss."

She grinned, leaning closer to bite his full lower lip gently. "I'll buy Nell a sexy nightdress and send her to see him," she whispered.

"And tonight," he added, "you'll tell Robert you're leaving and make it plain to him that you're off-limits."

The icy anger in his eyes made her weak in the knees. "Cade, I really wasn't leading him on," she said softly.

"I know that now," he replied. "But make it plain, just the same, or I will. And I think you have a pretty good idea of how I'd do it," he added.

She did. He'd set Robert up and let him find them kissing, or something equally traumatic for the younger man. She laid her cheek against his. "I'll tell him," she promised. She sighed, sliding her arms around his neck. "I'll miss you."

"You're holding back something," he said, startling her. "I'll find out what it is someday."

That's what she was afraid of. But she didn't say another word. She savored the nearness of him until the sound of an approaching car forced them apart. She felt cold and empty long before she went out the door ahead of him and down the hall to her own room to change clothes before their mothers came home.

Robert came back just in time for supper. But he noticed what the others had—a new kind of look that Cade and Bess were exchanging. It wasn't blatant, but it was a far cry from the hostility they'd been projecting. Bess's gaze was purely adoring. Robert sighed as he picked up his fork. He knew without being told that he'd lost her.

Chapter 14

Bess felt as if every eye in the room was on her, as if everyone could look at her and tell that she'd slept with Cade. It was her own conscience making her feel conspicuous, she knew, but it didn't make her any more comfortable. It didn't help that every time she looked at Cade, she colored and flicked her eyes back to her plate. It seemed devastating now, to remember how intimate they'd been, how beautiful it had been between them. Cade had been her life for years. The joy of what they'd shared was still brimming over inside her, despite the sting of guilt that accompanied what she'd let him do. They were engaged. She stared at the little silver ring and wished with all her heart that it could be a real engagement, followed by a real marriage.

Elise saw her touching the ring and smiled, because she knew the history of the ring as well as Cade did. "Is there something we should know about what's going on with you two?" Elise asked at last, eaten up with curiosity.

Bess went red, but Cade only laughed softly.

"I suppose this is as good a time as any," he replied. He took Bess's left hand in his and clasped it warmly. "Bess and I are engaged."

There were uproarious congratulations from everyone including Robert, who winked at Bess and shrugged, taking it in his stride. He'd always known how she felt about Cade, even though he'd hoped for a while that he might win her. But he gave in with grace, and his congratulations were sincere.

Cade let go of Bess's hand long enough to finish his meal and pushed the plate back, his dark eyes holding Bess's for a long moment while he lit a cigarette and leaned back in his chair.

"How was the sales trip?" he asked Robert.

The younger man was a good loser. He smiled at his older brother. "It went great," Robert replied with a grin. "We've got a potential buyer coming down next Tuesday to look over our operation. Big Jim's Texburgers."

Cade cocked an eyebrow. "That new fast-food chain?"

"Yes, and Big Jim himself is going to look us over." Robert blew on his nails and polished them on his shirt. "That could mean enough new revenue to get you out of the rodeo arena, big brother."

"Indeed it could," said Cade nodding. "Good job."

"No need to thank me. A new Jaguar would suit me very well."

"Dream on," Cade said chuckling.

"Bess, are you still leaving on Monday?" Elise asked gently.

"Yes," Bess said quietly. She avoided Elise's shocked look. Her soft eyes searched Cade's, and there was a deep sadness in them that he still couldn't quite understand. "I have to get back to my job, for now," she said falteringly.

"Don't worry, I'm not going to let her get away," Cade told his mother, and there was real intent in his eyes.

Gussie noticed the long look that passed between her daughter and Cade and felt the tension. She sat up straighter. "I'm going too," she announced. "I've got to get up Tuesday morning and go to work."

Cade dropped his lighter with a hard thud on the table. "What?" he asked.

Gussie gave him a haughty look. "Well, I'm not over the hill yet," she muttered. "I've got a good business head, Frank always said so. I'm going to use it." She turned to Bess. "You'll have to help me find an apartment Monday too." She smiled wickedly. "So that you don't get stuck with me."

Bess burst out laughing while the others stared at the two of them with faint surprise.

"What are you going to do?" Cade asked Gussie.

"I'm going to help run a talent agency," Gussie said, and without the old hostility. "I'm buying into a friend's business."

"And you'll do marvelously well," Elise said. She

touched her friend's hand gently. "I'm very proud of you."

Gussie smiled back at her. Cade sighed as he saw the friendship between the two women, feeling a little guilty because his mother still thought of Gussie as a home breaker. It was unfair that Gussie should suffer for trying to protect Elise. Someday, he promised himself, he was going to tell his mother the truth. Even if it was a little painful at first, in the long run it would be kinder. His father was dead. The truth couldn't hurt him now.

Greg came in just as the others were leaving the table. "I'm beat," he mumbled with a dry glance at Cade. "But it was worth it. Our accountant shaved a few thousand off our tax bill with the information I took him."

"It's been that kind of day." Robert grinned. "I got us a new customer, I think. We'll know next week. And Cade and Bess just got engaged."

Greg grinned. "Well, congratulations!" he said, laughing and shaking Cade's hand and hugging Bess gently. "And good for you, Robert. I see what you mean about it being that kind of day." He glanced at Cade. "Do you want to sit down with me and go over these figures?"

"Eat your supper first," Cade told him. "Then we'll talk." He looked at Bess and held out his hand. "Let's walk around for a bit," he said gently.

She put her cool hand into his big, warm one, tingling at the contact. She was all too aware of the indulgent smiles they were getting from the rest of the clan.

He had his cigarette in one hand as he linked the fingers of his free one with hers.

He glanced at her. She'd changed the stained sundress for jeans and a nice knit top with a demure rounded neckline and puffy sleeves. With her hair loose, she looked more deliciously feminine than ever. But she looked sad and preoccupied. His fingers closed around hers. "What's wrong?"

"I feel guilty," she confessed with a wan smile.

"Considering the way it happened, so do I," he replied. "I should have remembered from your apartment how easily you arouse me. I was in over my head before I had time to consider the consequences."

He stopped on the edge of the yard where it met the long dirt road that wound down to the highway. There was a crescent moon, and a patch of light that filtered down from the house, bright yellow in the darkness.

His dark eyes searched hers briefly before he turned his attention to the horizon, lifting the cigarette to his chiseled lips to take a long draw.

He exhaled a cloud of smoke and his hand curled closer around hers. "You're not ready for marriage. I should have taken that into consideration. You've been sheltered and protected all your life. You've been dominated by Gussie. Now you've got a chance to get out from under her thumb, and mine, and you want it. That's natural. I didn't have the right to try to force you into a decision just because I wanted it."

"I didn't resist all that hard," she murmured.

"Yes, but honey, you were a virgin," he replied, feeling that almost imperceptible jerk of her hand in his. "I made it impossible for you to resist. The kind of self-control you'd have needed takes years of practice."

"And I was a pushover," she said miserably.

His hand caught her chin and pulled it up, his dark

eyes searching hers. "No. You love me. That makes what we did an entirely different proposition. You gave me your body, but only after you'd given me your heart. How do you think I feel, knowing I took advantage of something you couldn't help?"

Her lips parted on a sigh. "You didn't take advantage," she said softly. "I wanted you to . . . to do what you did."

He drew her forehead to his chest, and his lean hand smoothed over her long hair with breathless tenderness. "I'm sorry I had to hurt you so badly." His lips touched her hair gently. "God, Bess, if you knew how much a man I felt with you when we came together . . . ! Knowing it was the first time, that you'd never let any other man touch you or look at you or hold you so intimately. It blew my mind." His hand actually trembled where it touched her hair. "I couldn't bear the thought that you might someday give that privilege to another man. I . . . needed so desperately to be the first." His chest rose and fell roughly. "Bess . . . I don't know how I'd manage if you stopped loving me."

That was an admission that curled her toes in her shoes and made her weak-kneed. She slipped her arms around his hard waist and pressed close, aware of his quick arousal and totally unembarrassed by it now. She laid her cheek against his chest and moved her hips even closer, aware of the sudden rough pressure of his hands against her lower spine as he held her there.

"I won't stop loving you," she whispered. "Not ever." That was true enough. She couldn't marry him, but she'd never be able to stop the way she felt.

"Feel how hard you turn me on, baby," he said, breathing his words into her ear, moving her gently against him, shuddering at the white-hot wave of pleasure that shot through him at the soft contact.

Her nails bit into his chest and her teeth clenched. She was on fire from the waist down. "Oh, Cade . . . we can't," she moaned.

"I know. Indulge me," he said, laughing with cold humor. "I can dream."

Her lips touched his hot throat and she felt his powerful body tense at even the light touch. "So can I. You're my whole world."

"If you get pregnant, Miss Samson, you're damned well marrying me whether you want to or not," he said shortly. He lifted his head and looked into her wide, dark eyes. "And if I hadn't had to hurt you so badly this afternoon, I'd back you into the barn wall and take you standing up right now, just to increase the odds in my favor!"

She shivered at the husky note of passion in his deep voice. The mental images he'd conjured made her blood run hot in her veins. She closed her eyes and let him press her hips even closer to his.

"Yes, you'd let me do that, wouldn't you?" he whispered. His hands had moved up under her knit top and over the thin, silky fabric covering her breasts to feel the hard tips. "You'd let me have you any way I wanted you, anytime. You're my woman. You always have been and you always will be."

She couldn't deny it. She sighed gently. "But you won't make me do it if I don't want to," she murmured.

His chest lifted and fell softly. "No. I won't make

you." He rubbed his cheek over her hair. "You'll marry me if there's a baby?"

"Yes," she agreed, because of course that was impossible.

His fingers tightened. "Only one time," he whispered absently. "I don't guess it's very likely."

He sounded disappointed. Dejected. Bess lifted her head, and her eyes searched his face. "Why do you want children so badly?" she asked.

He touched her soft mouth and smiled. "Lariat was more farm than ranch when my great-great-grandfather settled here in southern Texas. He invested in longhorns, and that tradition carried on until my grandfather started crossbreeding longhorns with Santa Gertrudis and Aberdeen Angus. Those crossbreeds have been money in the bank, and we're getting stronger every year. I expect to make Lariat pay, to fulfill the dreams of generations of Hollisters. To build a small empire here." His eyes glittered. "I want a son to come after me, to carry on the tradition. Several sons and daughters would be even better. Hollisters, to hold Lariat and look after it when I'm gone."

She shivered. "And . . . if you don't have children?"

"Oh, I'll have children," he said without a flicker of doubt. He smiled at her. He bent to her mouth. "You'll give them to me, when you've had your taste of freedom and you're ready to settle down. We'll make them in my bed, the way we started out this afternoon, with your body joining itself to mine in the heat of lovemaking. You and I are going to make a lot of babies . . . !" His mouth bit hungrily into hers. He put out the cigarette, and both arms went around her, lifting her against him while his hard mouth burned into hers until she moaned.

He felt her mouth open for him. His tongue went inside, gently probing and then rhythmically thrusting until she shuddered.

Then he lifted his head and held her away from him, his gaze possessive, arrogant. "If you want it again, you're going to have to marry me for it," he said huskily. "Think about that when you're back in your own bed in San Antonio. Now let's take that walk."

He lit a cigarette coolly before he caught her fingers in his and led her along to the corrals, his deep voice intoxicating as he explained his new breeding program to her and what it would mean financially.

Beside him, Bess felt her knees wobbling. This wasn't fair. He was using her own hunger against her to trap her into marriage. It would have been the most wonderful thing in the world, because she loved him so desperately and he did care about her somehow. But for his sake, she had to resist. Her job would keep her busy in the daytime. But how was she going to survive the nights, now that she knew how sweet Cade's hands and mouth could be?

All too soon she and Gussie said their good-byes and left Lariat. Bess threw herself back into her job. The ad presentation she'd been working on was finalized, with a few minor alterations, and shown to the client. He wanted one other minor change, and Bess was finally through.

"You did a great job," Julie Terrell said with a hug when she, Nell, and Bess were back in Julie's office after the client had left. "Imagine getting all that done while you were recuperating from an accident."

"And they say there are no heroes left." Nell grinned wickedly. "The *Times* must hear of this. I'll phone them collect."

"You do and I'll give their gossip columnist the juiciest kind of tidbit about you and an unnamed but extremely sexy older man you've got your eye on," Julie threatened the brunette.

Nell cleared her throat. "On second thought I do believe I have some new figures to work up. Good job, Bess. See you." She backed herself out of the office.

"We really should doll her up for the employees' barbecue in June and fling her at Mr. Ryker's feet," Bess mused.

"An excellent idea, Miss Samson," Julie returned. "This unrequited affair can't be allowed to go on. We have to save Nell from certain spinsterhood."

"I'll do my part." Bess stretched, her muscles sore from all the sitting. "It's so nice to be back to work. The flowers you all sent were lovely."

"So you've said, several dozen times." Julie chuckled. "They were our pleasure. We wanted to come and see you, but your Mr. Hollister wouldn't let anybody in. From what we hear, even Mr. Ryker was denied admittance." She grinned at Bess's wild color. "Didn't you know? I thought the aforesaid Mr. Hollister didn't have any designs on you . . . ?"

"Actually we got engaged while I was at Lariat," Bess said, finally giving up her most precious secret.

"Congratulations! We'll have to have a party."

"Not yet," Bess pleaded. "It's still hard for me to get used to the idea, and Cade hasn't given up trying to bulldoze me to the altar. I just want a little time." She lowered her eyes. "There's something he doesn't know."

"Care to tell a new friend who's first cousin to several clams?" Julie asked. "I know something's been on your mind since you've been back. But you're like me —a very private person. I hesitated to ask if you wanted to talk."

"I need to talk to somebody." Bess sighed. "I can't tell my mother. Even though we're better friends now than we were, she tells everything she knows. And there isn't anybody else." She sat down heavily. "I'm barren," she blurted it out. "The accident did some internal damage, and now I can't have a child."

"Oh, Bess." Julie sat down in the chair next to her, holding her hand tightly. "I'm so sorry. But if your Mr. Hollister still wants to marry you . . ."

"He doesn't know." She lifted tormented eyes. "I'm afraid to tell him. I don't know how to tell him. He's one of those old-line dynasty founders. He wants to leave Lariat to his sons to build on. How can I tell him that there won't ever be sons, or daughters for that matter?"

"Does he love you?" the older woman asked.

Bess shrugged. "He wants me," she said. "And in his way he cares about me. I'm not sure he knows what love is. If he loves me, he's never told me." Not even, she thought, at that moment of supreme intimacy. She colored, remembering.

"Some men have a hard time saying the words," Julie said. "That doesn't mean he doesn't feel them. You might give him the chance to decide for himself."

"If I do that, I've lost him forever." Her eyes closed.

"I'm trying to work up the courage, but every time I think I've got it, I draw back. He's going to hate me."

"Worrying about it is going to make it worse," she pointed out. "He might surprise you and not react at all."

"That would be a surprise, all right. You don't know Cade. I do." She stared down at her lap. "I'm such a coward."

"I wouldn't say that," Julie replied. "Is there any way I can help?"

Bess shook her head. "But thank you for listening. It helped just to get it out in the open. I'd better get back to work."

Julie walked with her to the door. "I'm always here if you need someone to listen," she said, smiling. "But whatever you decide to do, don't wait too long."

"No. I won't. If I . . . marry Cade, can I go on working here?" she asked.

"You idiot." Julie's mouth pulled down at one corner. "Do I look like the kind of boss who discriminates? I mean, look around, I've actually hired *men* to work here!"

Bess burst out laughing and walked off down the hall, shaking her head.

Three weeks had gone by, and there hadn't been a word from Cade. Gussie heard from Elise, who said that the boys were busy with moving the cattle to summer pasture and finishing the roundup, but there wasn't much news otherwise. Nothing specific about Cade, except that he was going to be competing in the San Antonio rodeo. Bess was sure that he'd come to see her while he was in town. It was still a couple of weeks away. She started planning what she was going to wear, and every night she dreamed about how it would be to see him again, to hear his voice, to touch him.

Only the ring on her finger was left to remind her of what had happened between them. She kissed it hungrily, drowning in her love for him. At least she had that one, sweet memory of him. Now, if she just had the courage not to give in to the aching desire to marry him. If she could just convince him that she didn't want to give up her job. She sighed. If only she could fly.

The long nights at her apartment were full of erotic dreams of Cade and nightmares about losing him forever. She didn't sleep well at all. Her most vivid memory was of Cade's careless kiss and confident, mocking smile just before she and Gussie had driven back to San Antonio from Lariat. Cade seemed to be sure that she wouldn't be able to stand it for long without him. He was right. By the end of the fourth week she was in agony with frustration and loneliness.

Gussie had been at work too. She stopped by the apartment to see Bess, aglow with her success and enthusiastic about her widowed business partner.

"It's very exciting, working for a living," Gussie said enthusiastically as they sat in the small kitchen in Bess's apartment and drank coffee.

Her mother even looked different, she thought, from the smart tailored suits to the very elegant short hairdo. Her mother had become a real dish. No more flamboyant clothes, no more ultra-young hair styles. Gussie was acting her age, and doing it with chic sophistication. She seemed to have grown up, like her daughter.

"I meant to call you last week, but they've given me a new assignment and I'm going crazy," Bess confessed. "What can you say about ballpoint pens that hasn't been said twenty thousand times?"

"You'll think of something," Gussie said confidently. "If I could find a job for an ex-marine gunnery officer with a yen to be a singer, believe me, you can advertise something to write with."

Bess's eyebrows lifted. "What did you find him a job doing?"

Gussie grinned. "Working for one of those singing telegram companies."

Bess threw up her hands. "Well, if I ever need a job, you're going to be the first person I go to see," she returned. She sipped her coffee, eyeing her mother. "Isn't it wild?" she asked softly. "Here we are, rich women with cultured life-styles, out on our own for the first time. And we're making it, by the sweat of our own brow."

"Thanks to you," Gussie acknowledged. "If you hadn't made me open my eyes, I'd still be out there sponging on my old friends." She hid her face in her beautifully manicured hands. "My gosh, I can't believe I imposed like that on them. I never thought I was such a selfish woman until Frank died and I saw myself the way others were seeing me."

"You were just lonely and afraid," Bess said, touching the older woman's arm gently. "So was I. We had to find our feet, but we did."

"Indeed we did." Gussie's eyes warmly approved her daughter's neat pantsuit and elegant coiffure. "If Cade could see you like this," she mused.

Bess flushed and lowered her eyes. "I'm trying not to think about Cade."

"Why? Darling, he cares about you so much. If you could have seen him when you were in the hospital," she added urgently, "you'd know how much he cares. It was what really changed my mind about him. I knew then that he'd never use you to try and get back at me, or for any other reason. I felt as sorry for him as I did for myself."

"He felt responsible," Bess replied. "Maybe he still does. He isn't a loving man. He's self-sufficient and very independent. He wants me, Mama, but that isn't love."

"For men it sometimes suffices," Gussie said gently. "Anyway, it will work out all by itself eventually. Meanwhile you just have a good time being your own boss for a while. Without any well-meaning help from me and Cade," she said, grinning.

Bess got up and hugged her warmly. "I love you, warts and all," she said, kissing the blond hair. "Now let's go and watch that new entertainment program and you can tell me about your partner."

The new partner was Jess Davis, and to hear Gussie talk, he was Superman on the side. It was pleasant to know that the older woman had found someone she could enjoy spending time with, enjoy working with. So far it was only a business relationship—Gussie made that very clear. But Bess had her suspicions, even though she was pretty sure that Gussie would take her time before she made any commitments. She'd loved Frank Samson, despite her faults. She still hadn't quite gotten over his death, at least not enough to be considering marriage so soon afterward.

Bess had hoped that Gussie knew something about Cade and how he was doing, but she didn't. It bothered Bess that Cade hadn't called or written. She'd expected that he would. Perhaps he'd expected her to make the first move. But it seemed as if she always made the first move these days, and now her hands were tied. It would be better for both of them if he let the engagement slide and didn't try to step it up. But it hurt Bess that he'd seemed not to care anymore. Unless it had been guilt on his part all along, and now that Bess was back at work and out of sight, perhaps he didn't feel guilty anymore.

She was sitting in her office late on a Friday afternoon, over six weeks since she'd left Lariat, when the door opened and she looked up from a mechanical she was finalizing, straight into Cade Hollister's dark eyes.

Chapter 15

It was like holding a bare electric wire, Bess thought, meeting that level stare. Like being caught in an electrical field. Jolts ran through her body, stiffened her, pushed her pulse rate up, quickened her breathing. Her body reacted to him immediately, her lips parting, her breasts swelling, her stomach tightening at just the sight of him. He was wearing gray slacks with a muted gray-and-beige plaid jacket, matching gray boots and Stetson, and he looked like an ad for a Western cologne. Her heart fed on him, dark-faced, somber, his powerful body unconsciously sensuous as he moved toward her, closing the door quietly behind him.

"It's been six weeks," he said without giving her a chance to say anything. His eyes ran over her gray pantsuit with the tiny white camisole top under it, the upswept elegance of her honey-brown hair in its coiffure, the white flower tucked in over her ear. She looked lovely. Radiant. "Are you pregnant?" he asked bluntly.

Her breath was stuck in her throat, along with any words she might have found to answer him. She was sure that she wasn't pregnant, although she was later than usual in her monthly rhythm. But the long weeks without Cade had melted her resolve, left her weak and wanting. She tingled all over with the need to run into his arms, to kiss him until they were both breathless, to rip open his shirt and run her hands through the thick hair on his chest. Her own hunger shocked her.

"I don't know," she blurted out, and flushed.

He took off his Stetson and dropped it into a chair, apparently unruffled by her reply. "Good. We'll get married and find out later," he said, half under his breath. His eyes glittered as he stared down at her from a scant few feet. "My God, come here!" he said, holding out his arms.

She got up from her chair even as he reached for her. He pressed her hungrily against him, and his hard mouth bit into hers with exquisite ferocity. She melted into him, no protest left, praying that her deception wouldn't be found out until he was as hopelessly in love as she was. Her mouth opened eagerly under his, bringing again the agonizing pleasure she remembered so well as his tongue thrust deep inside her mouth and her body clenched at the motion.

She moaned, and one lean hand slid down her body to arch her hips into the fierce arousal of his. She clung to him, giving him back the kiss as ardently as he offered it, drowning in him.

Neither of them heard the door open. But the soft, amused sound penetrated the fog of desire. Cade lifted his head, but he didn't let go of Bess or relinquish his tight hold on her.

Nell stood there, grinning wickedly as she glanced from Bess to Cade. "Well, when you two say 'Thank God, it's Friday,' you mean it, don't you?" She cleared her throat. "Just thought I'd mention the company picnic Sunday afternoon, if you can manage."

"I'll do my best," Bess said huskily, still trying to catch her breath. "Did Julie give you what we bought for you?"

"The dress, you mean?" Nell shifted restlessly. "Well, it won't work. I mean, Mr. Ryker could have anybody he wanted, and I'm just small fry. . . ."

"You're a dish," Bess returned. "And he's human. You just wear that dress, smile at him, and let nature take care of itself. By the way," she added, "he doesn't think women are attracted to him."

"That's helpful." Nell glanced up at Cade. "Uh, I'd better get going. Have a nice weekend." She stifled a giggle. "See you Monday if I don't see you Sunday."

"Yes." Bess felt Cade's breath on her mouth as the door closed and she looked up to surprise a devastating look in his dark eyes. "She's sweet on Mr. Ryker," she said falteringly.

"I'm sweet on you," he murmured. His teeth nipped lovingly at her lower lip, tugging it gently. "God, six weeks is too long, Bess."

"I know." She stretched up against him, pulling his

head down. "Kiss me," she whispered into his mouth. "I want to suffocate under your mouth . . . oh!"

The words had kindled his own hunger into a wild flame. He brought her even closer, his mind wavering while he tried to decide how much trouble they could get in if he pushed her back onto the desk and let nature take its course.

"We've got to stop or lock the door, honey," he said unsteadily, lifting his dark head with obvious reluctance. "There is such a thing as the point of no return, and we're standing on it."

Her hands slid down his hard arms with pure possession. "How soon are you going to marry me?" she asked, pushing the reasons against it to the back of her mind in the delicious joy of belonging to him and knowing he belonged to her.

"My God, how soon can I?" he asked. "Before they changed the damned law, we could have done it in one day. Now it will take three, I guess." He pressed his forehead against hers. "Monday we'll start the ball rolling. We'll get married on Thursday. You do get a lunch hour?" he asked huskily.

"Of course."

"It will have to be a small wedding. No fanfare. No bridesmaids," he warned.

"I don't care," she said, and meant it. "I love you. We can get married in a bus, for all it matters to me."

He smiled unsteadily. "Okay. A bus it is. How about on the Paseo del Rio?" he asked. "In a boat, with mariachis playing and flowers everywhere?"

She gasped. "Could we?"

He shrugged. "Why not?"

"Oh, Cade, that would be wonderful!"

"I'll make the arrangements." He framed her face in his hands and kissed her softly. "Let's go. I'll take you out to dinner and then we'll go to your apartment, where I'll say good night like a gentleman and swim back up to my hotel."

"Swim?"

"By then I'll need either a swim or a cold shower." He groaned, kissing her again. "Thursday can't come quickly enough to suit me."

She smiled under his mouth, because he sounded desperate. Where there was smoke, there was fire, didn't they say? Well, if he wanted her that badly and missed her so much, he had to care. She'd be the best wife in the whole world, and maybe then he wouldn't hate her when she finally told him the truth. . . .

It was a magical night. They ate on the Paseo del Rio, the River Walk that bordered the San Antonio River as it wound its way through the tree-lined city. They sat watching the river while they dined on steak and potatoes, with a mile-high strawberry pie and whipped cream dessert afterward. Cade looked at her with soft dark eyes that fed on her face, and her hands shook so badly from the scrutiny that she turned over her water glass and dropped her fork twice. It made her feel better that Cade's hands trembled when he tried to light his cigarette. If she was affected, so was he.

"Did you come just to see me?" she asked.

"In a way. I'm here for the rodeo. I have to go back when we finish and check my equipment. I'm staying over tonight so that I can get an early start in the morning. I've only signed up for two events, so I'll be through by tomorrow night. We can go to that picnic if you want to," he said with a smile.

"I'd like that," she said. "I can show you off to everybody."

He smiled as he linked her fingers with his. "You can show off your ring to Ryker," he said, lifting the hand that wore it. "Yes, I know, Nell's sweet on him. I just want him to know who you belong to. In case he had any ideas."

She smiled at his show of jealousy. She liked that possessive streak in him very much. "I don't know that I can bear to watch, but can I go with you to the rodeo tomorrow?"

"Sure. You can save me from the bronc if I fall under his hooves." He laughed at her expression. "I was kidding. Listen, honey, I've been doing this for a lot of years. It's dangerous, yes, but you can cut the risk if you're responsible and don't play around with your equipment or tempt fate. I'll be fine. There's a big purse. I can't afford to miss out."

"I'd give you back the pearls," she offered.

He shook his head. "You can keep those for our kids," he said and his eyes darkened and softened with the hunger for them.

Bess dropped her gaze to the table. *Tell him,* she thought. *Tell him now, before it goes farther. Be sure.* But she looked back up, and the expression on his face stopped her dead. She couldn't lose him now. She couldn't!

"Are you going back to Lariat Sunday?" she asked.

He shook his head. "Greg and Robert are looking out for things while I'm gone. These few days are ours. Yours and mine. I want to spend as much time as possible with you. I planned to be away a few days because I thought I might have to convince you to marry me," he added with a slow smile. "I had a long night in mind if you said no."

"Cade!"

"A man has to use whatever weapons he has." He sighed. "I couldn't have stood it much longer." His dark eyes blazed as he looked at her. "Amazing how vivid memories get as you move away from them," he said. "I can't sleep at night for remembering how it was."

She lowered her embarrassed eyes because she remembered too. "I don't sleep very well either," she confessed. Her fingers tightened in his grasp. "I thought I'd go crazy . . . !"

"That makes two of us." His jaw tightened as he searched her face. "Let's get out of here," he said huskily.

She lifted her face. She wanted to protest, to tell him that she couldn't do that with him again. But the look on his face made it impossible to say no. She got up from the table and followed him to the checkout counter. They walked to the car, hand in hand, without a word as the tension built to flashpoint between them. By the time they got back to Bess's apartment, she was trembling with it.

He closed the door behind them and leaned back against it, studying her with a gaze that made her knees tremble.

"While I can still think straight," he managed, "we'd better set some limits. Do you want to wait until we're married?"

He didn't have to put it into words. She knew what

he was asking. She put her purse down and leaned against the back of the sofa, looking at him. "Yes," she said quietly.

"So do I," he said, surprising her. "We jumped the gun, and I've regretted that a lot. The only good thing about it is that we've got the worst part out of the way. I'll never have to hurt you a second time. Our wedding night will be new for you because of that. I'm sorry I cheated you out of all of it."

She smiled softly. "I couldn't have stopped either," she confessed. "And like you said, Cade, we weren't playing games or making some casual entertainment out of it. We were committed, even then."

"And still are." He shouldered away from the door and moved toward her. "More than ever."

She stiffened a little as his lean hands slid past her hips to rest on the high back of the sofa. His body moved closer, so that she could feel the warmth and strength of his muscles, smell the cologne he wore, feel his coffee-scented breath on her lips as he searched her eyes.

"You said you'd tell me the story of this ring you gave me," she managed huskily.

He smiled. "I'll tell you on our wedding night," he replied. "It's a pretty special tale."

"Do . . . you want some more coffee?" she whispered, because his mouth was coming closer, and despite his assurances she wasn't sure that she could trust either one of them.

"Not really," he murmured just above her lips. "I want to lay you down on the sofa and ease my body on top of you." She blushed, and he chuckled softly. "Yes, you want it too. But we won't. However," he murmured, one hand going to the buttons of her jacket, "don't expect to get away from me as neat as you are right now." He pulled the jacket sensuously off her arms and studied the delicate, white lace-edged satin of her camisole with its pretty appliqués. Under it she was bare, and he could see that her nipples were rigid with desire.

His hand turned, so that just the backs of his fingers ran lightly over the fabric, deliciously abrasive against that tautness. She gasped, and he did it again, loving the way she clutched at his hard arms.

"On the sofa or on the bed, Bess?" he said breathily. "Because I've got to have more than this."

"The sofa . . . then." She gulped as he lifted her easily in his hard arms and moved away from the sofa. "It's . . . safer."

"Do you think so, little one?" His mouth settled softly on hers, teasing it, as he sat down on the cushions with Bess across his lap. "I'll bet you money that it's every bit as dangerous as the bed once we start touching."

She couldn't manage an answer. His hands were under the camisole, without much room to maneuver, but they were expert and sensuous all the same, rising up and down the soft slopes of her bare breasts without even coming close to the hard arousal of them.

"Oh, yes, that aches, doesn't it?" he asked with faint malice, his eyes dancing with pride as he watched her headlong reaction to him.

"I wish I could make you . . . ache as badly," she choked, arching as her body betrayed her will and she tried to force his hands the rest of the way.

"You'll learn," he murmured. "In the meantime I

like you just the way you are. It's exciting to teach you how to do this."

She gathered that from the wildness she saw glittering in his dark eyes. It was just as exciting to be taught, but she couldn't get the words out. He paused long enough to strip off his jacket and tie and unbutton his shirt. He drew her fingers inside, against damp hair and hard muscle, easing them along his chest. Her fingers moved involuntarily and suddenly discovered that a man's body was equally vulnerable to the same torment a woman's was.

It gave her a slight edge. She sighed and laid her cheek against his bare skin, liking the faint abrasion of all that hair covering him, smelling the soap and pure man scent of his powerful body as she returned his caresses.

She arched back, wanting the barriers out of the way, wanting his eyes on her. He seemed to sense it. His hands slowly eased the hem up, giving her plenty of time to refuse if she wanted to. But she was drowning in the same fire he was. She moved, but only to help him.

He stripped off the camisole and stared down at her with eyes blazing with desire. "It's been a long time since I've looked at you like this," he said quietly. His fingers trailed over the pale pink of her skin, up to the dark mauve aureoles with their hard tips. "You're firm. You don't even need to wear a bra, do you?"

She moved under his hand. "No. But it feels . . . uncomfortable without one. Men . . . men stare at me, so I wear jackets . . . Cade!"

His head had bent and his mouth was taking her inside, into the warm, moist suction of his lips while one hand supported her back and the other cupped the breast he was savoring.

Her hands clenched his thick, black hair. "Oh, don't stop," she wailed. "It feels . . . so good, Cade!"

She tasted of petals, cool and firm and sweet in his mouth. He lifted her so that her other breast was lying cool and soft against his bare chest, and he groaned at the intimate contact. His body was hardening already, coming alive with need for her.

She let him lay her down, her eyes open, dark and soft, looking up into his as he poised over her. She was trembling slightly, her trusting eyes telling him that he could do anything he wanted to her and she'd welcome him.

It gave him a sense of power, complicated by a sense of terrible responsibility. She'd already said that she didn't want to sleep with him until they were married.

His hands slid to her hips, cradling them, his eyes fell on her trembling legs as he caressed her slowly.

She could see his need. It was blatantly visible. "If you need to," she whispered, "I won't stop you."

He drew in a harsh breath. "You said you didn't want it tonight," he reminded them both.

"You're hurting," she whispered brokenly.

He groaned at the look in her eyes, the knowing compassion. He dragged her hand up his body and pressed it against him, shuddering with pleasure. "Yes, I'm hurting," he whispered. His fingers pressed harder over hers, and he saw her fascination even while he gloried in her shy acknowledgment of his capability. "But that's the best reason in the world to stop while I can. This kind of desire is violent, not like that long, slow session we had together in bed. I want you enough to throw you against the pillows and ravish you. That isn't what you need."

Her eyes widened. "Ravish . . . me?" she whispered.

He laughed helplessly at the look on her face when she said it. The laughter helped him defuse what they were feeling. He fell beside her, rolling over onto his back to hold her gently at his side while he fumbled above his head for a cigarette and lighter and ashtray on the coffee table.

"You're really going to stop?" she asked.

"If you could have seen your eyes," he said chuckling as he lit the cigarette and placed the ashtray on his chest. "My God."

"Well, nobody ever threatened to ravish me before, not even you," she pointed out. She sat up, all too aware of her bare breasts and his warm, appreciative eyes on them. She liked that, so she didn't try to cover herself. "What is it like to be ravished?"

"When you're a little more used to me, I'll show you," he murmured. "My God, they're beautiful," he whispered, involuntarily pressing his lips reverently to the soft swell of her breast, delighting in her gasp and the way she leaned closer. "All of you is beautiful."

"So are you," she replied, love dancing in her eyes.

"All of me?" he murmured dryly, his gaze falling to the place he'd made her touch.

She hid her face in his hairy chest with a laugh. "Stop that. It's too new to joke about. I've never touched anyone . . . !"

"Yes, I know. When we're married, I'll teach you how to do it properly, and without two layers of fabric in the way."

She knew her face was scarlet. It felt blazing hot as well. "And . . . and you'll touch me like that?" she whispered.

His arm contracted. "And in other ways," he replied quietly. "We've barely scratched the surface."

"I can't imagine anything more perfect than it was that day, Cade," she said softly. "Even if it did hurt at first."

"You were very much a virgin," he murmured. "And I had to push harder than I wanted to."

She gasped and clutched at him, remembering, shivering.

He lifted his head and looked down into her eyes. "I watched your face. I saw you become a woman."

She opened her mouth to the hard exploration of his. As the fevers began to burn again, she sighed, not protesting when he moved, so that his hips were square over hers, his arousal hard against her belly, his long legs entwined with hers, his bare chest faintly abrasive on her breasts. She moaned at the depth and ferocity of the kiss.

For one long, sweet minute she gave in completely. And then his mouth lifted and he moved back beside her, shuddering a little as he fought for control. He raised his cigarette to his mouth and took a long draw, reached for the ashtray, and tapped the cigarette against the clear glass edge.

"Are you all right?" she asked softly.

"Yes." He pulled her cheek to his chest, gently holding her there. His heartbeat all but shook him. "We're so good together, honey," he said huskily.

She brushed her lips over his shirt, one soft hand teasing him around the opening of it where thick hair curled out. But his fingers caught hers and stilled them.

"Don't," he said softly. "I'm too aroused already."

"Sorry." She flushed and then smiled at her own lack of knowledge. "I'm still learning."

"So am I," he murmured. He sighed heavily. "Bess, I've got to get out of here before something happens. I want you like hell." He got up with obvious reluctance and pulled her up with him. His dark eyes slid over her face possessively. "I'll pick you up at six if you want to come to the rodeo with me. We'll get breakfast on the way."

Her heartbeat shook her. It was new and fascinating to have Cade offering to take her anywhere, wanting to be with her. Such a change from the old days that she could hardly believe it was happening.

"Do you really want to marry me before we find out about . . ." she began.

"Yes." He bent and kissed her softly. "I've missed you so," he whispered huskily. "And judging by your reactions, you haven't been celebrating since we've been apart. We'll let the future take care of itself. Anyway, honey, if you aren't pregnant now, you will be before many more weeks," he added with a gentle laugh, and then kissed her, not seeing the pain in her eyes.

She let him out, watching him go with anguish. She didn't know how she was going to go through with it and live with her conscience. She owed him the truth. But she couldn't tell him. She didn't know how.

He picked her up just after daylight the next morning and had the misfortune to be seen by Señora Lopez next door, who was opening her living room curtains. She immediately closed them back, her expression eloquent.

"I'll have to tell her that we didn't spend the night together," Bess murmured, disturbed to have her favorite neighbor think ill of her. "I know it's the 1990s, but the *señora* is a devout Catholic and she doesn't move with the times." She sighed. "Until just now she didn't think I did either."

He chuckled, wrapping his long arm around her. "She can be forgiven for thinking the worst, it's early." He looked down at her with a rueful smile. "And it's true enough. You and I have slept together."

She colored prettily, pressing close to his side as they walked. "Oh, yes, we have," she whispered huskily.

His hand tightened roughly on her shoulder. "The sweetest memory of my life, Bess, right or wrong," he replied and brushed his lips against her forehead. "The next time I'll make it all come right for you."

She knew what he meant and her heart went wild. "You did that already," she whispered.

"Not the way I'm going to." He drew her along to the pickup truck and put her into the cab. "We'd better talk about something else." He chuckled, watching his hands shake as he lit a cigarette. His dancing eyes met hers. "You affect me pretty strongly these days. A man on a starvation diet gets nerves."

She laughed delightedly. It was incredible to see Cade admitting to nerves. And nice. She gave him an adoring look and fastened her seat belt. For once her conscience let her alone.

Chapter 16

Cade took Bess to the rodeo, and she sat in the stands and watched him bronc riding and calf roping with her heart in her throat. He looked so at home on a horse, so lean and powerful, that she could see other women eyeing him covetously. She smiled, because he was hers. He'd given nothing to any other woman for three years. That proved he was capable of fidelity. Even if he didn't love her, he wanted her enough to remain true to her. That spoke volumes about his character.

The bronc riding was the event she feared most. He'd come through the calf roping with ease and grace, but bronc riding was tricky. If he drew a really bad horse, or if something diverted his attention, he could be thrown and trampled. One competitor early on had suffered that indignity and had to be half-dragged, half-carried out of the arena with his hand clutching his ribs. Bess sat on the edge of her seat, praying every inch of the way.

Cade came out of the chute with his hand high, his spurred boots raking neatly from neck to flank on the opening jump and keeping the rhythm clean and neat as the seconds ticked away. The commentator was saying something about the skill it took to drag those spurs that distance while staying in the saddle and commending the way Cade was getting the last ounce of bucking out of that bronc. Before his voice died away, the buzzer sounded and Cade was looking for a way off the furious horse. He threw one leg over and jumped, landing with precision on both boots, but the bronc wheeled and snorted, bucking right toward him. Cade timed it perfectly while Bess sat shivering with fear. He waited until the horse was almost on him, then he dashed past it and leaped onto the corral, quickly easing over the fence and out of harm's way. There was a lot of laughter from the other competitors, and he was patted on the back while everyone waited for his time. They called it out, and the crowd went wild. He had the best score of the day. There were only two other competitors after him, both of whom were thrown before the first two seconds of their rides. Cade took top money and got a second place in calf roping. Bess sat in the stands beaming with pride, and when the awards were given out, she stood in the shelter of Cade's arm with her whole heart in her face as she looked up at him.

That night she lay in his arms on the sofa, curling close, and listened to him talk about the competition.

He was still winding down from the physical exertion of it, even though he'd borrowed her bathroom to have a long, hot shower. He was stiff and sore, and Bess had rubbed his broad shoulders and back with alcohol, trying to ignore his sensual innuendos when her hands stopped at the waistband of his jeans.

"We'll live at Lariat," he said, looking down at her quietly.

"Yes, I know."

"I guess it will take a lot of adjusting for you," he said, leaning back to smoke his cigarette. "There aren't many frivolities, and the plumbing leaves a lot to be desired."

She felt chills down her spine. She didn't know what else to say to convince him that his lack of wealth didn't matter to her. It never had. She loved him. "Cade, I'll be happy at Lariat," she said. "I hope I can make you happy too."

He sighed and bent to kiss her gently. "Well, we'll see how it works out," he said noncommitally. He glanced at his watch. "I've got to get back to the hotel. I'll be over early if you'll fix breakfast."

She got up, hesitating. "You . . . you don't want to stay?" she asked, looking so shyly curious that he smiled involuntarily.

He pulled her hands to his broad, bare chest, smoothing them over the thick hair on it. "Yes, I want to stay, sore muscles and all," he replied. "But I'm not going to. We're going to do it by the book. One lapse was enough, and I don't want people looking at you the way your next-door neighbor did this morning because of me." That had disturbed him, more than he wanted to admit. He didn't want people thinking Bess was easy.

"You mean Señora Lopez?" She smiled gently. "She's a very nice, very religious lady who doesn't approve of the modern world."

"Neither do I," he replied. He touched her mouth. "I feel bad about the way things have gone with you and me, Bess," he said worriedly. "I hate having so little control that I can't wait until our wedding night. I can't undo what happened, but I can prevent it from happening again until we're married."

She linked her arms around his neck with a tiny sigh. "I feel the same way, really. But I . . ." She lowered her face. "I'm a little afraid. Getting married is a big step." She looked up quickly. "I want to marry you very much. I just hope I can be what you want me to be." As she finished, she saw the lines of stress vanish from his face.

"You will be." He bent and kissed her warmly. "See you at breakfast."

"Okay. Good night." She let him out and watched him go with sad eyes. Thursday, she thought dreamily, she'd never have to watch him leave again.

He was at the apartment early the next morning, just as she'd dressed and was starting breakfast. It was as if they'd never been apart, she thought, watching him finish the last of his bacon. But there was an exquisite newness about their relationship that made her glow. Just to look at him fed her heart. What they were sharing now was precious. Being together was the end of the rainbow. Holding hands, looking at each other openly, caring. She felt as if she'd found the end of the rainbow, and it was Cade. All the long, lonely years were gone and forgotten as if they'd never been. She hated sleeping because it took her away from Cade. He was her whole life so suddenly, and apparently was enjoying it as much as she was. That was what was so beautiful, so incredible, that he expressed his feelings every time he looked at her or kissed her. If it was only desire, it was a tender kind of desire that put her first. She wondered if Cade realized how possessive he'd become.

He glanced up and saw that thoughtful stare. "What are you thinking?" he asked with a smile.

It was amazing how comfortable she was with him now, she mused, remembering a time when she was strung up and shivering every time he came near. Now he was like a part of her. "I was thinking how sweet it is to have breakfast with you," she confessed.

"I was thinking the same thing." He searched her eyes. "I feel married to you. I have for a long time. The wedding ring, the ceremony, they're necessary and I want them. But for three years there's been no time when I wanted anyone else."

She smiled. "I'm glad, because I felt the same way." She touched the back of his hand lightly. "Are you better today?"

"Still stiff," he murmured ruefully, "but with plenty to show for it, thank God."

"I wish you'd give it up," she said.

"I will, when the time comes. Don't nag."

She glowered at him. "I love you."

He grinned. "Yes, I know that. But I'm not going to throw myself under a horse's hooves to let you prove it. How about that company picnic? Still want to go?"

"Yes. I've got to fix some potato salad and ham. I'll

get started. Do you want to get the Sunday paper? It'll be just outside the door."

He got up with a sigh. "I guess your reputation's ruined by now," he said quietly. "I should have realized what your neighbors would think when they saw us coming out of your apartment together at daylight."

His concern for her reputation touched her. That was like him, that old-world courtesy and concern about honor. She turned, her eyes brimming with love. "I'll put a note on the door and invite the whole floor to the wedding," she said. "It's all right. Maybe Señora Lopez is still asleep," she added hopefully, knowing all the while that the *señora*, who had become a good friend, got up early every Sunday morning and went to Mass.

Cade hesitated at her expression. "Are you sure you want to risk having her see me again at this hour of the morning?" he asked quietly.

She smiled. "Yes, I'm sure."

He paused, then he nodded and went outside to get the paper, where he ran headlong into the small Mexican-American woman, Señora Lopez, who lived next door. He grinned at her hugely.

"Good morning. *Buenas días,*" he tried again.

She glowered at him, looking indignant.

"I only just got here," he persisted. "I came for breakfast yesterday and again this morning." He glowered. "Nothing's going on."

The elderly lady stared without saying a word.

Cade felt needles sticking in him at that wordless disapproval. "Oh, God," he groaned. "Bess! Help!" he called.

The Latin lady looked perplexed when she saw his expression and heard Bess's helpless laughter. Bess came running. "What's wrong?" she asked. "Oh, good morning, *señora,*" she flustered, turning scarlet.

"So much for your blasé attitude." Cade told Bess with a curt nod. "Serves you right. Come here." He pulled her close and held up her left hand to show it to the *señora.* "We're engaged. I don't have a loose moral attitude, no matter how it may look. Bess isn't a modern woman any more than I'm a modern man. I even go to church most Sundays."

"Ah." Señora Lopez relaxed, glad to have her dark suspicions disproved. "You are to be married, *sí?*"

"*Sí,*" Cade returned with a smile. "This Thursday. On the Paseo del Rio. You're invited. And nothing's going on," he repeated firmly.

The *señora* beamed. She hadn't really thought her sweet young neighbor was modern enough to have men staying with her in any casual way. And the *señor,* very proper and dignified when he defended Bess's reputation. She liked him. With the wedding so soon, it was understandable that the young couple would have much to discuss and would want to be together as early and as late as possible. Yes, there was love in Bess's eyes. And something dark and soft in the *señor's.* She nodded. "*¡Ay de mí,* it will be a privilege to attend such a wedding!" She clasped her hands. "*Señorita,* you have a wedding dress?"

Bess caught her breath. "No! I'll have to buy one."

"You will not! I have just the thing. Come."

The *señora* led them into her apartment. She gestured for them to wait while she went into her bedroom and came back after a minute with the most exquisite lace-trimmed white dress Bess had ever seen in her life, complete with glorious trailing mantilla.

"It was to have been my daughter's wedding gown. You remember, *señorita*, I told you about her," she prompted Bess, who remembered the poor tormented woman crying over her daughter's death. Bess and the long-widowed *señora* would sit outside in the evenings and had come to be friends. They talked, and Señora Lopez seemed to find Bess's company comforting. Although she never imposed, she was always bringing Bess cuttings of her profuse stock of flowers or cooking sweets for her to "fatten her up."

"But, I can't . . . !" Bess protested, even as her hands trailed lovingly over the gown that was obviously just her size.

"It will honor me if you will take it," Señora Lopez said gently. "Estrella would have liked you. I am sure that she would not mind that I give it to you. It should be worn, Bessita," she said, using the fond nickname she called Bess. "Please? *¿Por favor?*"

"All right. And thank you," Bess said fervently. "But only if you come to the wedding."

"Of course I will come. I must make sure that your oh-so-handsome *caballero* does not desert you at the altar," she said with a smile in Cade's direction.

"It would take an army to keep me away from the altar." Cade grinned, his eyes falling gently to meet Bess's.

Señora Lopez assessed their exchanged look and smiled, nodding to herself. Yes, this was going to be a good match. *Bonita.*

Bess carefully put the dress away, loving the way

Cade had looked at her when she held it up for Señora Lopez to see.

She packed up the potato salad and ham she was going to take to the company picnic, and she and Cade set off in jeans and matching chambray shirts with red bandannas at their necks, a perfect match except that Cade was wearing a Stetson and she wasn't.

The first sight they got was of the nervous Nell, sitting on a rock by herself while people all around her were talking and having a good time. Bess put her dishes on the table and uncovered them, settling back against Cade as Jordan Ryker stood up at the head of the table and called for silence.

Cade watched him, narrow-eyed, as the older man welcomed the employees, welcomed Bess back after her accident, and invited the company workers to dig in and have a good time.

Afterward he came up to Bess and grinned as he shook her hand. "You look refreshed and very pretty." He glanced at Cade and chuckled. "I hear I'm *persona non grata* in your book, Hollister," he added bluntly. "Let me assure you that the only designs I have on Bess are work-related. She's been a welcome addition to our ad agency staff. Julie thinks she's tops."

"So do I," Cade said quietly, pulling her close to his side. "The wedding's Thursday," he added.

"Congratulations!" Ryker shook Cade's hand and then Bess's. "Nice to see that someone got lucky." He sighed, trying to understand Cade's dark stare.

"Speaking of someone," Bess said. "If you won't think I'm meddling, there's a very nice girl here who worships the ground you walk on. If she wasn't too shy

to drop a handkerchief at your feet, you might find
that she isn't what she appears at all."

He frowned, and his dark eyes scanned the gathering. "Not Julie, surely?" His eyebrows arched and he
smiled amusedly.

"Julie is happily married," she pointed out.

"Yes. Just as her friend Nell was supposed to be," he
murmured. His eyes suddenly found Nell alone on her
rock, and his face hardened. "Amazing that she didn't
bring her fiancé along."

Bess all but gasped out loud. Surely it wasn't Nell
that he'd been pining over! But Nell wasn't engaged!

"Nell isn't engaged," she blurted out. "She's never
been engaged, as far as I know."

Ryker's scowl grew worse. "One of her former co-
workers told me. He showed me the ring he was giving her."

The light broke. Julie had told her about Nell's unfortunate run-in with a former employee. "A young
man named Barry Dennis?"

"Yes . . ."

"Nell pushed him down a manhole," she said.

His wide mouth parted on a breath. "What?"

"She pushed him down a manhole. He had designs
on her, in the worst way, and she couldn't stand him.
Julie said she tried everything to discourage him, because he always seemed to be hanging around her
every time you came near the office. So one day he
made a grab for her beside an open manhole and she
pushed him into it." She chuckled. "It was a sewer
they were working on. He climbed out cursing, but
Julie said it did the trick. He quit just after that and
went to work for your competition. For which Julie

says you should thank your lucky stars, because he cost you two accounts while he was trying to charm Nell."

Ryker stuck his hands deep inside his pockets, his dark eyes settled firmly on Nell. "Well, I'll be damned," he said absently. "And I thought . . . all this time."

"She has a picture of you in her desk," Bess said, shocking him into staring at her. "And the first thing she did when I walked into the office was tell me you were definitely off-limits, because someday she was going to get you if it killed her."

He smiled. He chuckled. He burst out laughing. "God, men are blind," he said under his breath. "Bess, you can have anything you want short of the agency for a wedding present. Now if you'll excuse me, I think I hear my name being cursed silently."

He strode off toward Nell, while Bess clung to Cade's hand and grinned with pure delight.

Nell looked up, and even at the distance Bess could see her face coloring. Ryker sat down slowly beside her, obviously having a hard time trying to make conversation. Nell looked equally flustered. But somehow Bess knew that that was going to work out.

"Cupid Samson," Cade whispered in her ear. "Nice going."

"I had no idea he was dying for the love of Nell," she whispered back. "Isn't it romantic?!"

He pulled her close and searched her eyes. "I know something more romantic. Being married to you on Thursday."

She sighed and nuzzled against him. He bent his head over hers and sighed. How amazing, she thought. For years he'd pushed her away at every opportunity, and now he couldn't seem to stay close enough. He was always holding her hand or keeping his arm around her, holding her as if he couldn't bear to lose contact. She felt that way, too, but it was new to find Cade staring at her with his desire plain in his eyes. He'd given her the impression that he hadn't liked her for years. But it was understandable, since she understood now how desperately he had wanted her. That pretended dislike had been his only defense. But he didn't need it anymore, and the sudden transition from enemy to lover sometimes made Bess's mind whirl. The closeness they were sharing was like nothing she'd dreamed of. Being away from Cade even overnight was excruciating now. She was counting the hours until they could be together all the time.

If only it would last, she thought as they moved to the long banquet table to fill their plates. It had to last!

Cade was hoping the same thing. At least now maybe he could stop worrying about Ryker. Nice to know that the other man was carrying a torch for someone besides Bess. He'd worried, because Ryker was successful and rich, and Gussie had built the man into a real threat. Sometimes he still felt keenly the differences between his way of life and Bess's, and in the back of his mind it bothered him that he might not be able to give her everything she wanted.

A tug on his jeans drew his attention looking down, he came eye to eye with a small, dark, laughing boy holding out a cookie.

"For me?" Cade asked, smiling. He knelt by the child, his eyes warm and soft. He was always that way with children, Bess recalled, watching him with a kind of pain that ate at her. He had an instant rapport with the child, who put its arms around his neck and allowed himself to be carried back to his searching parents without a hint of reluctance. Children gravitated toward Cade wherever he went. It used to fascinate Bess that even when he was his taciturn self, the children of his ranch workers hung around near him. They seemed to know that underneath that facade was a sensitive, loving man. Bess was only now finding out what kind of warmth his mask hid. But it hurt her terribly to see how much he loved children. She turned away and went back to the table to get some more food, which she didn't even taste, just to put the situation to the back of her mind.

She didn't see Nell and Mr. Ryker when she and Cade left to go back to the apartment. She hoped things would go as well for them as they had for Cade and herself.

"Tomorrow morning we get the ball rolling," he mused as they were watching television after supper. "Three more days, and you're mine forever."

"I'm yours forever right now, Mr. Hollister," she said, lifting her soft lips to his.

"Come here." He pulled her across his lap and held her, kissing her lightly from time to time, but nothing more intimate.

"He was cute, wasn't he? That little boy," he sighed. His fingers touched her breasts lightly over the fabric, and his eyes narrowed. "Are you going to nurse our children?" he asked suddenly.

She felt sick. "If we have children," she agreed.

He frowned. "I thought you weren't sure, about being pregnant."

She swallowed and prayed silently for forgiveness.

"I'm not," she said, burying her face in his warm throat. "Not sure, I mean."

"Well, there's plenty of time," he murmured. But he didn't mean it. He wanted a child with Bess. Now was the time, while they were both young enough to cope. Too, a child would cement their relationship, a child born of her love for him and his deep, hungry affection for her. It might make all the difference. His arm contracted. "Plenty of time," he repeated.

But was there? Bess wondered miserably. She felt his lips on her forehead, but he didn't try to kiss her deeply again. He left early that night to go back to his hotel room, and he seemed preoccupied. Bess hoped that he hadn't intuitively picked up anything from her. She knew she'd frozen when he mentioned the little boy, and he seemed vaguely disturbed by her attitude. She did want children so badly, but how could she tell him the truth without losing him? It was selfish, she told herself, horribly selfish to put her happiness before his. But she was so much in love that she couldn't force herself to say a word.

Love had a lot to answer for in her life, she thought miserably. She'd given in to Cade once before they were married, something she'd sworn to herself that she could never do. She hadn't counted on how heady it was to indulge in all those fantasies she'd had about him. She hadn't been able to draw back any more than he had. Well, at least he hadn't been stringing her along just to get her into bed, she thought ruefully. He was an honorable man, and she knew instinctively that he'd never have let it go so far if he hadn't meant to marry her. She frowned, wondering at his continued persistence about children. Had he seduced her with the idea of getting her pregnant, to coax her into marriage? Or was it just his usual child-hunger that he felt safe to indulge now? She remembered the way he'd been with that little boy and she felt uneasy. She was going to be cheating him when they married.

She only prayed that her love for him would be enough to make their marriage work.

They hadn't called Lariat to tell Elise and the boys about their wedding plans, and Bess hadn't called Gussie. They were going to wait until they got the license and phone everyone Tuesday night.

Bess did have regrets about not having a conventional wedding night, but Cade had suffered three years of abstinence and she couldn't blame him for wanting to go ahead and get married now. She felt the same way herself. The excitement kept her going as she tried to imagine what it was going to be like as Cade's wife.

Monday morning Nell was quiet and introspective, hardly communicative. Julie and Bess couldn't worm a word out of her about what had happened at the company picnic. She flushed and found excuses to go to other parts of the building every time it was mentioned.

Bess finally hemmed her up just before lunch, locking the door to her own office and staring the older woman down.

"I can't stand it anymore. I have got to know what happened!" Bess exclaimed.

Nell blushed to the roots of her hair. "Nothing," she muttered, her lower lip trembling and tears in her huge blue eyes. "He asked me how I was, then he mentioned that the weather sure looked fine. He looked at a bird, he lit a cigar and put it out, and then he invited me to go for a walk with him."

Bess was all eyes. "And . . . ?"

Nell rested her chin in her hands on the desk, looking bewildered and unsettled. "He . . . sort of kissed me."

"Sort of?"

Nell lifted her head. "Well, it was hard to tell," she muttered. "He aimed and missed and then I tripped over his feet and . . ." She covered her face with her hands.

"And . . . ?"

"Knocked him into the river," she groaned. "I was too ashamed to stay and face the music. He climbed out all dripping, and I just panicked and ran. I know he'll never speak to me again. I was so embarrassed! All those years of hoping he'd say something to me, and he finally does and I try to drown him!"

Bess got up and hugged her. "Hasn't it occurred to you that he doesn't know much about women?" she asked gently. "That he's awkward and maybe a little ungraceful because he's feeling this way? He told me that night Mother and I had dinner with the Rykers that he's not much of a ladies' man." She hesitated. "And that he was crazy about a woman who was engaged to someone else, who'd never noticed him."

Nell turned toward her. "Yes. That was the blonde he was carting around. . . ."

"It was you."

Nell's eyes widened. "I'm not engaged," she choked out.

"That Dennis man told Mr. Ryker you were engaged to him," Bess said, breaking it gently. Even so, Nell went white. "I'm sorry, but it's better if you know. He had the boss convinced. I told him at the picnic that you knocked Mr. Dennis down a manhole and that you weren't engaged, and that's when he made a beeline for you."

"And I knocked *him* into the river!" Nell was shaking. "Oh, what will I do? It was me . . . !" She sat down heavily, her face in her hands. "I never dreamed . . . !"

"So I see. May I make a suggestion? Stop worrying and let things take care of themselves. Believe me"— she grinned—"if Mr. Ryker feels the way you do, a little thing like near-drowning isn't even going to slow him down. Just take into consideration that he's as backward as you are with the opposite sex, and don't expect a playboy."

"What a morning," Nell whispered huskily. "I hope I last through the afternoon."

"Me too. Cade is out getting a marriage license." She grinned. "I can hardly wait until Thursday. You and Julie have to come." She pursed her lips. "And Mr. Ryker. I can't not invite him."

Nell colored prettily. "That would be . . . nice."

"Just what I thought. Please, for heaven's sake, don't get him between you and the water this time," she pleaded.

Nell's face burned bright, but she laughed. "If I get another chance, you'd better believe I won't mess it up. He liked me." She went out, shaking her head. "He really liked me. He thought I was engag . . . ooof!"

She walked right into Cade, who caught her before she fell.

"Thank God there aren't any bodies of water in here," she said absently, giving him a pleasantly blank look as she went out.

Cade opened his mouth to question Bess, but she just shook her head. "Never mind," she told him. "It's better not to ask. Did you apply for the license?"

"I did," he murmured smugly. "Now we get blood tests. I've found a place that can do them in twenty-four hours. Let's go."

"All right!" She grabbed her purse and his hand and followed him out. Everything, she thought, was falling into place gloriously!

It fell into place so well, in fact, that they were married Wednesday afternoon on the Paseo del Rio, on a boat, with a minister officiating and all the members of their respective families and friends gathered on the riverbank, along with some photographers and local reporters from the print and broadcast media. It was something of an event even for festive San Antonio, and Cade's recent wins at the rodeo made him more newsworthy than ever.

Bess hadn't considered that anyone might connect her with her father. But just as the ceremony began, one of thee reporters barged through the crowd and asked her how it felt to be marrying the man her father had almost ruined financially with that crooked investment scheme.

Bess never got a chance to answer. While she stood there trembling in Señora Lopez's beautiful white wedding gown, Cade's big fist shot out, and the reporter went into the river.

Jordan Ryker caught Nell's little hand in his and pulled her back protectively, smiling down at her. "At least it wasn't me this time," he murmured wryly, and looked delighted when she flushed and turned her face against his jacket.

"You snake in the grass." Gussie came out of the crowd like a gray-suited avenging angel. The reporter tried to climb back out of the river, and she helped him right back in, to the amusement of the crowd. "This is a wedding, not a news event. You stay there until it's over!"

The other reporters only grinned as the minister performed the ceremony. Cade slid the small white-gold band onto Bess's third finger, next to the small silver engagement ring. His dark eyes met hers as the minister had them recite the rest of the wedding service, and then he bent to lift her mantilla and kiss her for the first time as her husband.

Tears rolled down Bess's flushed cheeks. She looked up at him with her whole heart in her face.

"I love you," she whispered so that only he could hear.

He didn't return the words, but his eyes were very soft. He smiled at her, but before he could speak, even if he'd meant to, they were suddenly surrounded by well-wishers.

Bess had hoped that he might give the words back, if only for the sake of her pride. She didn't know how Cade really felt about her. She knew that he wanted her and that he liked her. He'd said often enough in the past that *love* wasn't a word he knew. But Bess was going to teach it to him, somehow.

Cade's looked down at her with a new kind of possessiveness. His wife, he thought proudly. She looked happy, but the reporter had managed to put a blight on the ceremony. He wished he'd hit the man harder. It only emphasized the life she'd led before, and what she was going to have to endure as his wife. He hoped that she could cope with the lack of luxuries at Lariat and get used to having his family around all the time. Now that they'd made it all legal, there were a lot of problems cropping up that he hadn't foreseen. Now that he had her, he was wondering if her love was going to be strong enough to endure the hardships of his life-style. She couldn't know that it had been a terrible strain on Lariat's budget to have even this small wedding. The minister, the mariachis, and the owner of the boat had to be paid. There had been the ring and the license—things she would have taken for granted. But Cade had lost plenty of money through that investment disaster. The rodeo money he'd won was a help, but it didn't get them far out of debt. He sighed. Bess could never be told just how badly off they were. She'd offer those damned pearls again, and he couldn't take them from her. He'd told her they should go to their children, and he meant it. He'd support her properly, somehow.

He remembered her voice at the end of the ceremony, whispering that she loved him. His chest swelled. Her love was part of his strength in some odd way. And he cared about her too. She was pretty and smart and accomplished, and she had the breeding he lacked.

He knew it was going to take time to adjust to being married, for her as well as for him, but they'd make it. He sighed and drew her close while they endured the congratulations and the press of reporters. He'd keep her happy somehow, he thought doggedly. And when the children came along, he'd be more than content. A child would make up for everything. She might even now be carrying their son. A faint smile touched his hard mouth as he looked down at her. Yes. A son. His chest swelled. And he'd be twice the father his own had been. He'd give his child love and attention, and he'd never turn his back on him. His arm tightened around Bess. Bess would be a good mother, too, once she had this independent streak of hers cured by some warm loving. She was class all the way, a real lady. Her family lineage would give his children a social acceptibility that he'd never had. It would open doors for them and give them pride in their heritage. She'd teach them the beautiful manners that she had, and the shame of poverty he'd always felt so keenly wouldn't exist for them. They'd never have to apologize for being low-class and rough, he thought bitterly. Even if they didn't have great wealth, they'd have respectability.

He looked down at her, smiling at his new wife. Miss Samson of Spanish House, he thought absently, and of all the men in Texas she could have had, she'd wanted him. That made him proud.

He lifted his chin. It would be a good marriage. He'd make her happy and she'd give him children. She'd help bring a new, better generation to Lariat, a more cultured and educated class of heirs. She'd come home and have babies and they'd live happily ever after. That settled, he reached out and hugged Robert and Gary and his mother. As an afterthought he even hugged Gussie. Life was looking up.

Chapter 17

They spent their wedding night at Bess's apartment. Cade had wanted their married life to begin at Lariat, but he was mindful of Bess's feelings. It would have been embarrassing for her, with his brothers and his mother in residence, and everyone giving them knowing looks. He could hardly ask the family to leave the house to give them privacy. Besides, he told himself, he and Bess had the rest of their lives.

He took her out to supper at the most expensive restaurant in town, mindful of his rented dinner jacket and her terribly expensive dress. It seemed more than anything to point up the vast differences between them and put a damper on his mood.

Bess touched the crepe de chine fabric of her cocktail dress when she saw his eyes on it, and instinctively she knew that he was thinking back. He didn't even own a dinner jacket and had had to rent one. Besides that, she thought guiltily, this meal was costing him an arm and a leg. If only she'd used her mind and protested, but even now it was difficult to get used to not going to the most expensive restaurants, the most expensive shops. Her whole life had been spent with wealth. Now she was still learning how to do without it, even though she loved Cade enough to live in a cave with him.

She touched his hand gently where it rested beside his water glass and smiled at him. "Can we afford this ritzy place?" she mused, with a twinkle in her eyes, "or should I order a salad and make us a nice chicken casserole back at the apartment?"

Her matter-of-fact remark took the lines out of his face. His hand curled around hers and he smiled. "Is that how I looked? I'm only planning to get married once in my life, Mrs. Hollister. I think we're entitled to a fancy meal."

She sighed. "It was a beautiful wedding," she said. "And thank you especially for removing the one blight from the landscape. I hope he catches cold," she said, remembering the pushy reporter.

He chuckled. "The river's not that warm even in summer," he agreed. "I'm sorry he did that. Nothing should have spoiled today for you."

"It isn't spoiled. I'm going to love you until I die, Cade Hollister," she said huskily, her smile fading as all the long years caught up with her and her eyes misted. "I never dreamed I'd be married to you, that I could live with you and . . ." She wiped away the tears, aware of his concerned gaze. "Sorry. All my dreams came true today, and I'm shaky."

His fingers linked with hers. "I'll take care of you," he said quietly. "We'll have a good life together." He rubbed his fingers against hers. "At least our kids won't have the childhood I did," he remarked with faint bitterness. "They won't be looked down on and made to feel worthless because they don't have breeding." His dark eyes met hers. "You'll teach them manners. They'll have all the advantages that my brothers and I didn't."

She stared at him for a long moment, a little unnerved by what he was saying. "Is that important?" she asked, feeling her way.

"Breeding? Of course it is." He let go of her hand and picked up his water glass, taking a sip. "I know I'm rough around the edges. I've got the biggest part of Lariat, but I'm still not much more than a glorified cowboy. But you're class, Mrs. Hollister," he said, eyeing her with pride of possession. "You're upper-crust all the way, a debutante with a rich background and excellent manners."

She'd always known that it was as much the illusion of what she was that Cade saw, even through the desire he felt for her. But it was rather shocking to have him put it into words and in such a way. Was that why he'd married her? To give him respectability? To improve the family bloodlines? She felt a twinge of fear.

"I'm just a woman," she said unsteadily. "Like other women. And I'm not a rich debutante anymore."

He scowled. Her tone disturbed him. "I know that."

She looked down at the table and slowly pulled her hand from under his. "I hope you didn't marry me for a status symbol," she said, laughing nervously. "Because I don't have much mileage in that respect. Whatever I was, now I'm just a copywriter for an ad agency."

He'd put it badly. He caught her hand back and held it. "Listen. I married you because I can't seem to get through the day without you anymore," he said, forcing the words out. "I want you. I want to have children with you. I'm not into status symbols, even if I made it sound that way. I'm proud of what you are. I'm proud that of all the men you could have had you wanted me."

She colored. It wasn't the speech she wanted, but it would do. She'd known that he didn't love her the way she loved him. Perhaps someday he would.

"I've never wanted anyone else," she said quietly. A long, tense silence fell between them, and it didn't ease even when the waiter brought their order. They ate in silence and left the restaurant in silence. Bess felt like crying.

Cade sensed the sadness he'd caused and could have crushed his impulsive tongue. He shouldn't have been thinking out loud. A woman wouldn't want to hear on her wedding day that her husband married her because she was well-bred. He hadn't meant it like that, but he had a hard time expressing emotion in words. He looked down at her, and his body began to burn. Well, he thought, there were other ways to let her know how he felt. Better ones.

But once they were back in her apartment, she shied away from him nervously, and his temper got away from him.

"Is that how it's going to be from now on?" he asked

icily. "Now that the ring's on your finger, you're going to have nerves and headaches?"

"Don't," she groaned. Her wide, hurt eyes held his. "I'm nervous. It's been a long few weeks, and then all the excitement of this week . . . I've been living on my nerves. And then tonight, you don't say that you love me or that you want to cherish me—you tell me that I'm a nice asset to the breeding program at Lariat. You made it sound as if you only wanted me because I had superior bloodlines and a classy background—just the way you'd buy a purebred heifer to breed to your best bull!"

His face paled. He couldn't have made it sound that way, could he? He started to speak, but she was in tears. She ran into the bedroom and threw herself across the bed, crumpling her black dress as she cried into the white coverlet.

He'd been clumsy. He muttered as he sat down beside her, his hand smoothing her long, disheveled hair. His eyes ran over the soft curves of her body, down to the elegant long legs in black hose that were so nicely revealed where the dress was pulled up. She was the prettiest woman he'd ever seen, and her body made him go taut with sudden need.

"Maybe we're both done in with nerves," he murmured. He pulled her up and turned her so that she was lying across his knees. His dark eyes met her tearful ones, and he brushed at the tears with an impatient hand. "But I've got the best cure in the world. And it won't be like breeding cattle," he said curtly, as his head bent to hers. He bit at her soft lips, enjoying her sudden lapse of breath, the kindling softness in her eyes. "I'm going to strip you down to your silky skin and enjoy you until dawn," he said sensuously, letting his hand slide down over her breasts, to her tiny waist and flat stomach and on to her silk-clad legs. "And you're going to enjoy me this time. I'm damned well going to ensure it. Come here."

His hand held her at her nape, bringing her mouth to his. His eyes closed, his brows knitting with pleasure, and he turned her into his arms.

She followed where he led. This time was nothing like the last, except for his exquisite tenderness. It was dark, but he left the lights on, encouraging her to look at him, to learn his body as he'd already learned hers, guiding her hands, smiling at her shy attempts to do what he wanted her to do.

Her body pressed warmly against the length of his, without a scrap of fabric between them, and she trembled with the pure joy of being so close to him, feeling his big, warm hands sliding lazily down her spine, rubbing her breasts against his hair-roughened chest, her hips against his.

His mouth slid onto hers as his hand moved down her body and made sure that she was ready for him. She shuddered at the intimate touch.

He lifted his swollen mouth from hers, and his dark eyes smiled tenderly into hers. "Does it still shock you to be touched this way?" he whispered and did it again. "This is how a man knows if his woman is ready for him, Bess. It's your body's own special way of making sure that I won't hurt you when we join."

She colored, but he made it sound so natural that she relaxed and didn't protest. Her eyes searched his when he slid a long, powerful leg across hers and levered himself above her.

"There's no rush," he whispered. "We've got all night, and I'm not going to pull away until you're completely satisfied this time."

"But, I was . . ." she protested huskily as he eased down over her. She gasped as she felt him intimately and gasped again when he pushed.

"It's all right," he said soothingly as the soft, slow joining began. It was still a little uncomfortable at first, but the tenderness of his hands and his mouth made her relax, so that her body made him welcome seconds later.

"It's a miracle, isn't it?" he whispered, shivering a little as he lifted his head to look into her eyes. "The way we fit together so perfectly when we love." His hands shaped her face, and he brushed his mouth with delicate mastery over hers, teasing it until her lips followed it and began to respond. Her hands were on his shoulders, resting shyly, but as the kiss and the overwhelming intimacy of their position began to work on her, her hands pulled at him and finally slid down to his hips, lightly touching but still hesitant.

"Cade . . . ?" Her voice broke as his hips lifted and then fell, a stab of remembered pleasure shaking her.

"Yes?" he whispered. His mouth settled softly on hers. "Don't be afraid. Feel the rhythm. Move with me. Slowly, honey, very, very slowly," he breathed into her mouth. "You're my wife. I'm going to take you as sweetly and as tenderly as I know how. I'm going to make love to you. . . ."

It felt like love. She began to whimper as his movements grew slower and deeper, as his lips burned down on her breasts and made her ache with the sensations that rippled through her taut body. She felt his hands on her skin, sliding over her, their deft exploration making her blaze. She tried not to think of how many women there must have been to make him so expert. He was hers now, she thought. Her own. Her husband. . . .

Her short nails dug into his lean flanks, and she felt him shudder and suddenly increase his movements, building the rhythm. His harsh breath in her ear became mingled with the softest kind of Spanish love words as his hands slid beneath her hips and his head lifted to watch.

Her eyes were drawn by his face as he looked down the length of their bodies. She flushed wildly. He caught the awed fascination in her eyes as his hands linked with hers above her head and the rhythm grew suddenly urgent and quick and fierce.

She gasped. His jaw clenched and his eyes blazed, his brows knit and his face strained as he arched his body against hers in a harsh drive for completion.

"Feel it. . . ." He groaned and still his eyes held her shocked ones as she began to shudder and weep under him. "Oh, God, feel it . . . ! Feel it, Bess, feel . . . it!"

She never knew when the shudders became convulsive, the pleasure so hot and sweeping that she cried out in a voice she knew she'd never used in her life. His face above her was a contorted blur, and when the spasms first hit her, she was afraid. His lean hands controlled the whip of her body, forcing her to completion in a frenzy that brought her into breathless, thoughtless oblivion. She cried out endlessly, vaguely aware of his own shuddering groan in the heated stillness around them.

His shivering body was damp in her arms. She

opened her eyes and looked to the ceiling. There was a dull, deep throb in her body and lingering heat. Her hands moved experimentally on Cade's broad back, moving over it with exquisite tenderness.

After a long, unsteady sigh he lifted himself off and rolled over onto his back beside her, stretching with a lazy, unconscious grace and apparently no inhibitions at all.

Bess stared at him, her eyes tracing the hair-roughened strength of his body from head to toe and back again. His eyes were open, quiet, soft, watching her while she watched him.

"Hello," she said, her voice soft with love.

"Hello." He slid his hand under her nape and brought her against him, wrapping her in one arm while he reached and fumbled for cigarettes, lighter, and ashtray with the other. He dragged a pillow behind him and eased himself into a sitting position, with Bess still cradled against his damp body.

The intimacy was as new as their marriage. Before, she'd been too self-conscious and guilty to enjoy what they'd done. But he was her husband now, and the lack of inhibition she felt with him was delicious. Her hand smoothed possessively over his chest and down to his flat stomach.

"Not yet," he murmured dryly, catching her fingers and dragging them to his mouth. He kissed them before he laid them on his chest, his cigarette still smoking in his hand. He put it to his mouth with a heavy sigh. "Men can't do that twice in a row without a little rest," he murmured, enjoying her blush. "While women, I believe, are capable of multiple—"

"Cade!"

He chuckled with pure delight at her expression. "So much for wifely sophistication. Come here and kiss me."

She lifted her lips to his, enjoying the feeling of possession and sharing. "Your mouth tastes of smoke," she whispered.

"Yours tastes of smoke, too, now," he whispered back. His eyes smiled into hers. "God, it was good this time," he said huskily. "Like being dropped off a balcony. I've never had it like that in my life, not even that first time we were together."

She hid her face in his throat. "I thought men always enjoyed it with women."

"In different degrees," he said quietly. He smoothed her hair. "You give me something I've never had before." His chest rose and fell heavily. "You give me peace, Bess."

What an odd way to put it, she thought, frowning. She stared across his broad, hairy chest. "I don't understand."

"Don't you?" He took another draw from the cigarette and shifted so that he could see her face on his bare shoulder. "You fulfill me completely," he said. "Until now that's never happened. It takes trust to feel that kind of satisfaction with another person. You have to give up control, to let go of all your inhibitions, your fears of letting your feelings show. At no other time is a man quite as vulnerable as in the throes of passion." He brushed his mouth over her temple. "Until tonight I've never relinquished control completely. I gave myself to you as surely as you gave your body to me."

She closed her eyes and smiled. "Oh." Her lips pressed soft, lazy kisses against his bare chest, and she felt the flat nipple suddenly go hard under her mouth. Frowning curiously, she lifted her head and looked at it.

"Yours do that when I kiss them," he pointed out.

She felt her cheeks go hot. "Yes, but I didn't know that yours would."

His eyes twinkled. "Surprise, surprise. And it's not the only thing that stands—"

She hit him. "You wicked man! Everything I've heard about you men is true, that you love to shock women, that you just lie awake thinking up embarrassing things to say . . . !"

"It's delicious," he said huskily. He put out the cigarette and threw her down on the bed with tender ferocity, looming over her with eyes that blazed with emotion. "Delicious, watching you blush, seeing you color. Most women these days are so damned blasé about sex, they make it as exciting as a drink of water. You get embarrassed when I talk to you like that, you blush when I look at you, and you go up in flames every time I touch you. My God, I've never felt more like a man in my life than I do with you! Experience be damned, I'm so proud I could strut." He bent and put his mouth hungrily on hers. "Even if it is a double standard," he murmured huskily, "it's sweet hell to put my hands on you and know that no other man ever has. If that sounds chauvinistic, I don't care."

She lifted her arms around him and held on. "There was never anyone I wanted but you," she whispered. "There never could be. It would be sacrilege to even let another man kiss me after you . . . !"

The emotion in her voice sent his heart spinning. He kissed her with aching hunger and eased down onto her, shivering with kindling need. "Is it too soon?" he whispered roughly. "I don't want to hurt you."

"You won't hurt me," she whispered back. "Oh, come here." She groaned, holding him. "I want you so!"

He cradled her under him and bent to her soft mouth. He wanted to love her so tenderly that she'd never get over the memory of it. Slowly, gently, he brought her body up to his, joined with it, curled his legs around her drawn-up knees so that they were in a position he'd never shared with a woman, curled together like shells. And that way he loved her, cherished her body with his in such a slow, tender lovemaking that she wept helplessly all through it, blinded by soft kisses and tender Spanish words in her ear and hands that were slow and sure. There was nothing fierce about it, nothing urgent until the final few seconds, when the feeling spiraled up into the night and broke past her lips in a sound that was more shattering moan than cry.

She shivered and felt him shiver as the exquisite pleasure rippled along their tightly joined bodies, silver-bright, petal-soft, in gentle explosions that went on and on and on.

He whispered her name in the midst of his satisfaction, his voice shaking like his powerful body. But there had been no violent urgency, nothing except the tenderness of two souls entwining.

"That . . . was loving," he whispered, his voice as shaken as his body. "My . . . God! My God!"

She heard reverence in his faint exclamations and repeated them in her mind. There couldn't have been that kind of pleasure without an intensity of feeling on both sides. It was then that she knew he was in love with her. It wasn't desire alone, as she thought it had been the first time. Then, he'd wanted her and lost control. But just now, that wasn't desire alone. She'd never imagined Cade giving that kind of tenderness to her, and she wept for the beauty and joy of being his wife.

"Don't cry," he whispered, kissing the tears away. "Don't. It was so beautiful."

"Yes. That's why," she whispered. Her eyes looked into his, seeing him only as a faint blur. "I love you so much . . . !" Her voice broke and her trembling arms encircled his neck as she hid her face against his damp throat. "I want to give you a child more than anything in the world." She did, but saying it aloud only tormented her and she cried more.

He didn't understand her emotional state, unless his lovemaking had shattered her. Probably it had, because it had certainly shattered him. He'd given and received more than ever before in his life. His hands soothed her, cradled her. He couldn't seem to make his body leave hers, though, and they were still in the same position they'd shared during that exquisite loving.

"We're still part of each other," he whispered. His eyes closed as he held her. "I can't . . . quite get enough of this closeness. Do you want me to move?"

"No," she said. "Oh, no, not ever."

"Do you feel it too?" he asked, lifting his head, searching her soft eyes. "The . . . oneness."

"Yes." She touched his face with trembling fingers, adoring it, worshiping its hard lines and stark strength. "Kiss me."

He bent and put his mouth on hers. Incredibly his body hardened. He gasped, and her eyes opened. She lifted her arms, offering herself.

"You won't hurt me," she promised when he hesitated. She closed her eyes and stretched up toward him with the first stirrings of her own femininity. "Cade, put your mouth on me . . . !" she pleaded, offering her breasts.

Chapter 18

Since Bess had been given the rest of the week off for a brief honeymoon, Cade put her in the truck and carried her, bag and baggage, to Lariat the next morning. The quicker she got used to living there the better, he told her.

She was nervous about the move. She hated her own anxieties. She liked his mother and brothers and she'd enjoyed her stay at the ranch when she'd come out of the hospital. But that had been different. She'd been an invalid, and Cade had been distant. Now they were close and it would show, and she didn't know if she could stand much teasing from Robert and Gary. Everything would be different. And at night she was going to be inhibited, because Cade's bedroom was right across the hall from Robert's.

He glanced at her disturbed expression. "What's wrong, honey?" he asked gently.

She turned toward him. "Just nervous, I guess," she said softly. Her loving eyes paused on his hard face. He looked more relaxed than she'd seen him in years, and the memory of the night before was there in his dark eyes as they briefly met hers.

He reached out a hand and caught hers, holding it in a strong clasp as he drove down the long highway out of San Antonio. It was a beautiful summer day, hot and airy. Everything was green and lazy out the windows of the old pickup truck.

"There's nothing to worry about," he assured her. "You're family now."

"Yes, but . . ." She gnawed her lower lip and frowned.

"But, what?"

She sighed. "Robert's room is just across the hall from yours. . . ."

"Oh. Yes, I see. And Gary's is next door. And you and I are noisy when we make love, aren't we?" he added with a slow, knowing look.

She lowered her eyes while her heart cut cartwheels in her chest. "Yes," she whispered, smiling shyly.

"Then let me surprise you, Mrs. Hollister, by telling you that we are now located downstairs in the old master bedroom, away from everyone." He grinned, glancing at her relieved face. "Not that it's going to matter tonight," he murmured dryly. "After what we did last night, I doubt if either of us is in any condition for protracted lovemaking."

That was true, she thought. It had been morning

before they finally slept, and she was a little uncomfortable even now.

"You're very thoughtful," she said.

"I care about you, cupcake," he returned easily. His fingers curled closer into hers as they rode down the long, sparsely settled road, seeing hardly any cars on the way. "Are you happy?"

"Happier than I ever dreamed of being," she said honestly. She ran her fingers over his long ones, enjoying their strength. Just to be allowed to touch him was a thrill. "Your hands are very dark," she remarked.

"Comanche blood," he reminded her, smiling. "Our kids will have some Indian from my side of the family and a lot of good Scotch-Irish from yours."

She stared at his hand, forcing her face not to give anything away. "Yes." She looked to the windshield. "You're sure you want me to give up the apartment?" she asked.

"Why not? There isn't much point in keeping it when we'll be living at Lariat and you'll be commuting. I don't want you away from me at night, Bess," he added firmly. "I'll want you to sleep in my arms even if we don't have each other every night."

She felt her body melting at the thought. Last night she'd curled up against him and slept as she'd never slept in her life, close and warm in his arms, against his bare flesh. It was an experience she couldn't wait to repeat.

"Yes, I want that, too," she said softly.

His fingers tightened quickly around hers before he let go of them to light a cigarette. "I'll have to teach you the cattle business, society girl," he teased in a deep and sensual voice. "You've got a lot to learn about ranches."

"And about you," she added. "I used to be so afraid of you," she recalled. "Nervous and shy and shaky with longing, all at once. I love looking at you, Cade. Do you mind?"

He glanced at her again, his eyes running down the green linen dress that clung so attractively to her figure. "No," he said. "I like looking at you too."

She leaned back against the seat with a long sigh. "Everything is new," she murmured. "Beautiful and bright. I've been so alone all my life, until now."

He felt that way too. As if his past was one long emptiness because Bess hadn't been part of him. She was now, and the longing for her grew with each passing day. Instead of satisfying his hunger, being with her increased it. He was bound to her in ways he'd never thought a woman could tie him. Bonded. He sighed, worrying about his independence. Marriage had been a big step for him, but he'd been afraid of losing Bess. And after that afternoon in his bed he hadn't been able to think of anything except how exquisite she looked without her clothes on. Maybe those weren't the best reasons for marriage, and he couldn't deny that her society background had influenced him somewhat in the decision. But she was getting to him, really getting to him. She was under his skin, in his bloodstream, in his mind. He felt as if he was losing control. She loved him, but if she ever had a mind to hurt him and his feelings for her went as deep as he was beginning to suspect they went, things could get complicated. For the first time he felt a faint apprehension. As long as only his body had been involved, it hadn't bothered him. Now his heart was gathering her in, and that did.

She saw his sudden frown and wondered about it. Probably he was wondering as she was about the family's reaction to their arrival, she told herself. Surely that was all.

"I still have my furniture and things to get out of the apartment," she pointed out.

"I'll send some of the boys up tomorrow to take care of it," he said easily. "And we'll send Señora Lopez some of the wedding cake Mama was baking for you when I called this morning."

"Oh, how sweet of her!" she burst out.

"She thinks you're pretty sweet, too, honey." He lifted his cigarette to his lips. "I've been pretty busy lately, but I'll make time to take you around and show you how things work on Lariat." He looked at her possessively. "We'll have a good life together."

"We still haven't talked about my salary going into the family budget."

"We will. That and the other finances. Things are going to be tight, but we'll make it."

She could believe that. Cade was a magician with money. It would work out, she told herself.

Elise was waiting at the door. She hugged Bess and stood aside so that Gussie could come forward to do the same.

"I hope you don't mind." Gussie grinned. "Elise and I thought a little celebration was in order."

"No, we don't mind," Cade returned, pulling Bess closer as Robert and Gary and Gary's fiancée, Jennifer, came into the room. They all hugged her, too, and finally they settled down to cake and coffee while Gussie took pictures of the couple for the family album.

It seemed like a happy gathering. But Bess couldn't help noticing how withdrawn Cade became as the afternoon wore on. He listened instead of talked, and when one of the men came to ask him something about ranch business, he got up and left the room, looking as if he was grateful for the excuse.

Bess started worrying then. As the rest of the week went by, she worried more. Because she was too uncomfortable to make love with Cade, the distance grew. He slept with her at night, but with his back to her, and they spent their time talking. He explained the cattle business to her, but she'd rather have heard sweet nothings and endearments. He acted as if her presence was trying, and she couldn't help thinking that he felt that way. Perhaps he'd had a different idea about marriage, and the reality was distasteful to him. Whatever the reason, Bess felt him slipping away from her.

Saturday night the boys had dates, and Elise went to a party for one of the women at her church. Bess and Cade were alone, but he was locked in his study with the books and she was watching television. This was ridiculous, she told herself. They were acting as if they'd already been married for years, yet they were on their honeymoon.

With an angry sigh, she got up and padded into the study on bare feet to see what he was doing. Her hair was loose, her yellow blouse highlighting her honey-brown hair as it waved toward her flushed face. Her jeans were tight, and Cade's eyes followed her long legs.

He felt irritated that she'd come looking for him, when he was doing his best to put some distance between them. He was finding marriage more disturbing than he'd expected, and his loss of freedom had begun to wear on him. Bess was lovely, and he wanted her for plenty of reasons. But he needed a little time to adjust to their new relationship, and she seemed determined to crowd him. He'd hoped that she'd get the idea when he pulled back, but she hadn't. He didn't want to come out and tell her to back off, but his temper was kindled by her persistence.

"I'm working on the books," he said. "When I finish, I'll come out, and we'll talk."

She stared at him quietly. "What's wrong?" she asked gently. "It's being married, isn't it?" she added insightfully and watched it register in his dark eyes before he could hide it. "Yes, I thought it might be. It's hard to be tied down when you never have been before, and harder to adjust to than you expected."

He sighed and put down the pencil he was holding. "I'll get used to it," he replied with a faint smile. "But things have changed pretty quickly. I've been alone for a long time."

"So have I." Her eyes ran hungrily over his dark face, down to his half-open blue-checked shirt, where bronzed muscles lay bare under thick, curling hair. "My gosh, I love to look at you," she breathed. "I don't think I've ever seen a man who looked sexier with his shirt open than you do."

His heart began to beat like a bass drum. He felt his body react suddenly, urgently, to her eyes and her husky voice. She was doing it to him again, seducing him with those soft, bedroom eyes.

"Isn't there anything on television you want to watch?" he asked curtly.

She moved closer to him, her eyes holding his, her blood burning. "Not really." She felt reckless. He was her husband and she wanted him. For the first time she felt free to express it, to show him how badly she wanted him.

Her hands went to the buttons of her shirt and she slowly undid them, her heart keeping time with her breathing. She hadn't worn a bra underneath because of the heat. She pulled the edges apart in front of Cade's steady, astonished gaze.

His jaw tightened as he saw the arousal of her pretty breasts, and his body reacted predictably. "Damn you, that's not fair," he said harshly.

She had to hold back a smile. His eyes were hungry, and she could see his arousal when he stood up. He wasn't indifferent. Not at all.

She walked around the desk and gently pushed him back down into his chair, sliding onto his lap facing him, overwhelmed with a sense of delicious freedom. Her fingers pulled his shirt aside and she leaned forward to rest her breasts on his hair-roughened chest, sighing as she nestled her face into his throat.

His big hands were already on her hips, pulling her closer. His heart was shaking him already, and when he bent and put his mouth on hers, it went crazy.

"This is insane." He groaned, his hands suddenly shaking as he reached for the zipper of her jeans. "For God's sake, stand up . . . !"

He jerked her jeans off while she fumbled with the fastenings on his. Then he dragged her back onto his lap and positioned her, looking up into her rapt, excited face as he lowered her gently, bringing them together in one long, sweet motion. He shivered as she enveloped him, but his eyes didn't leave hers, first above, then level with his, then below them.

"Hold on," he whispered. His mouth burrowed softly into hers and his hands tightened on her hips, showing her the motion, helping her body adjust itself to his as he built the rhythm gently.

She moaned sharply against his mouth when the pleasure began to sing through her. He felt her shudder and smiled harshly against her mouth. He laughed with feverish abandon, kissing her roughly while his hands pulled and lifted and the sounds they made together grew louder and more urgent.

When the pleasure burst through, she arched backward, her hair trailing to his thighs as she wept and shivered with the anguish of completion, her drawn face and body so beautiful that he deliberately delayed his own satisfaction just to watch hers.

And then it all went down in flames, his body convulsing under the softness of hers, while somewhere a clock struck the hour and he heard his own voice shouting her name.

He held her to him, trying to breathe while his body trembled helplessly in the aftermath. His hands gently stroked her damp back, soothing her. She was crying, huge tears rolling from her eyes onto his bare chest.

"I ought to throw you out on the porch and chase you to town with the truck," he breathed heavily. "Damn it, Bess . . . !" He burst out laughing. "My shy, innocent little wife, stripping for me in the office with the damned door standing wide open!"

"Yes. Just like last time, except that it's not wide

open," she pointed out. She clung closer. "Take me to bed, Cade," she whispered softly. "Love me some more."

He groaned. "Honey, I've got to do the books," he said.

But she moved sensually on him, and he shivered violently.

"You were saying?" she whispered unsteadily.

"I was saying to hell with the books," he muttered, standing up with her in his arms, his powerful body trembling from the feverish desire she'd kindled in him.

He turned, ignoring her clothes on the floor, and carried her down the hall and into the bedroom they shared, slamming the door and locking it behind them. Before he could put her down on the bed, she'd twisted up to take possession of his mouth again, glorying in her sense of control, in the wonder that she could undermine all his defenses and make him want her in such an uncontrollable way.

But she knew the next day that she'd made a mistake. By knocking him off balance, she'd put even more distance between them. He wanted her, and it made him helpless. She hadn't realized how that would hurt his pride until it was too late. He perceived her as trying to take control, and he was fighting it. Amazing, she thought, that she could do that to such a self-possessed, confident man. Amazing that she could make him want her badly enough to forget everything but the need to have her.

His dark eyes had glanced at her accusingly the

night before, when he'd finally laid her down on the bed and stood over her, as if he were deliberating his next move.

But it hadn't lasted long. He'd looked down at her with pure pleasure in his face and his hands had gone slowly to his jeans, to finish removing them, letting her watch as he stripped for her.

His body was powerful, muscular and hair-roughened all over his rippling chest and flat stomach and strong thighs. He was blatantly male, and her eyes worshiped every line of him, glorying in the sheer impact of him.

"You're beautiful," she whispered to him, aware of his dark eyes going over every inch of her, lingering on her firm breasts with their hard tips.

"Not as beautiful as you are, Mrs. Hollister." He'd moved to the bed, his dark eyes roving over her with blazing need. "I want a child," he said quietly. "I'm not going to do anything to prevent one, unless you insist."

She'd trembled a little. If only it could have been that simple. "I've never used anything," she whispered. "I don't want to either." She wanted to give him that child, but her body would never be able to, and she couldn't tell him so. She'd opened her arms to him then, hoping to make him so warm and welcome that he'd forget children in the pure delight of sharing her body. She had to keep him happy in bed, she told herself. He was a lusty, sensual man despite his cold, arrogant look, and if she could satisfy him, perhaps he wouldn't mind so much that she was barren. They could always adopt. . . .

* * *

But afterward, after she'd done everything she could think of to arouse and satisfy him, he'd withdrawn from her even more. Her very aggressiveness seemed to turn him off as surely as if she'd turned to ice in the night. From that time on he didn't touch her again. She went back to work the Monday after the wedding, and he seemed more relieved than disturbed by her absence during the day. Bess didn't know what to do. She knew instinctively that he didn't love her. He wanted her. But now she had to face the fact that desire might not be enough for him, and already he was losing interest in that side of their life together.

Not for the first time she wished that she and Gussie were close enough that she could really talk to her mother about such a problem. But they weren't. Gussie was kinder now than ever before, and friendly enough. But she didn't have the deep kind of emotional makeup that Bess did. Elise did. But how could Bess talk to her about what was going on with Cade without embarrassing them both? Her troubles seemed even larger because there was nobody she could share them with.

So she settled her mind on work to keep from going crazy. She loved her job and the people she worked with. It was inspiring and very challenging to come up with ideas that pleased management as well as the clients and herself. She learned that it was largely a team effort, because a lot of compromise came between her original idea and the finished advertisement.

Nell had gone on vacation for two weeks just after

Bess's honeymoon. She came back looking more tired than ever, her face giving nothing away.

"You look as bad as I feel," Bess said one morning after another long night in the big bed that Cade only shared after she'd gone to sleep. "You're miserable, aren't you?" she asked bluntly. "Can I help?"

Nell shrugged, looking tearful. "I thought he might call me," she said. "We held hands at the picnic, and he took me home. He even kissed me," she said, flushing at the memory. "Very nicely too. But I haven't seen or heard from him since."

"You've been on vacation," Bess pointed out. "And he's in California working on a hostile takeover bid."

"He's not in town?"

"He hasn't been since you left," Bess told her. "Feel better?"

Nell sighed. "Well, a little." She sat down, pushing her short dark hair away from her forehead. "How's married life?" she asked, forcing a smile.

"I don't know yet." Bess fingered her pencil. "He resents me. We haven't quite got our act together yet."

"He didn't seem resentful that first day he came here." Nell chuckled. "Talk about a hungry man . . . !"

Bess flushed. "Well, yes. But he doesn't like it when I make the first move."

"You know, there was an article about that in one of the women's magazines," Nell said seriously. "Something about aggressive women undermining a man's confidence and making him impotent. Isn't that absurd?" She frowned. "Although, you know, it's not really so farfetched. Men are naturally aggressive, and to have a woman put them on the defensive by being overbearing and demanding . . . I know one man who won't even date women anymore. He says he's afraid of being raped!"

Bess laughed helplessly. "You're a gold mine of information."

"I have to keep up with what's going on in the world. Someday I may need to know stuff like that." She crossed her long legs. "Why don't you put on a frilly dress and flirt with your handsome husband?"

"I don't want to be slapped down again," Bess told her.

"You never know how men will react until you try," Nell replied. "As for myself, I suddenly feel full of confidence. I think I'll phone Mr. Ryker's office and ask if he likes spaghetti. That's the only thing I can cook."

"That's the spirit!" Bess said.

Nell got up and then She sat down again. "Actually," she said, leaning forward, "it's frozen spaghetti in those little packets. He wouldn't like it. And I'm late on this presentation."

Bess watched with quiet concern as Nell turned back to her desk. She hid a lot of her feelings. She wasn't the outgoing, effervescent woman she projected. That was an image. A mask. Under it, Nell was insecure and shy and a little afraid of risking her heart. Bess thought sometimes that Cade was much that way himself. He didn't mind physical risks, but emotional ones . . . that was different. He didn't chance his heart, not even with his new wife. This was most of their problem, she decided with a weary sigh. Nell's idea about vamping him was nice, but vamping him had gotten her into enough trouble already. No, it was better to leave well enough alone and let him adjust at his own pace. Then maybe they could grow closer again.

But as the days turned to weeks and summer began to slip away, Bess saw her marriage go from bad to worse. Cade's anger turned to indifference before her eyes. He no longer tried to make love to her, or seemed to care what she did. They met at mealtimes and in the evening, but Bess spent most of her time at Lariat with Elise. Robert had a girlfriend now, and he and Gary were out a lot at night, so mostly it was just the two women.

"I shouldn't say anything," Elise said cautiously one night while Cade and the men had gone out to repair a broken fence. "But you and Cade seem so distant these days, Bess."

"Yes, I know." Bess lowered her eyes to the floor. "I think he's sorry he married me."

"Surely not," Elise said, smiling. "I can remember Cade staring up toward Spanish House when he was little more than a teenager, talking about marrying someone like the elegant Miss Samson when he grew up." She smiled at Bess's startled face. "Didn't you know? He adored you when he was a young man—not that he doesn't still. He was always going on about the cars and house and parties at Spanish House. Cade had ambition from the time he was a boy. He resented his father's roughness and the way we lived," she added quietly. "He wanted something more for Lariat. He got that from his grandfather," she added with a weary sigh. "Ben Hollister filled Cade's head full of dreams. He was always telling him stories about Lariat in the early days, about the parties and elegance and the famous people who used to come here when Desiree Hollister was alive. You might not believe it, but in its day Lariat was something of a showplace. This house was built when the old one burned down. The old one was like an antebellum mansion, and there was money here. Then Desiree died and old Ben just let it go out of grief." She put down the embroidery to sip coffee. "The house burned down and he built this one. Coleman was his only child, you know, and he let him run wild. He never tried to do for him what Desiree would have. As a result Coleman grew up rough and without some of the more desirable character traits. He brought Cade up the same way, and I was too afraid of him to say anything," she confessed quietly.

"He was intimidating," Bess recalled.

"That he was. I cared about him, in my way," she added. "But I never had many illusions about him, and I've never told any of the boys how I really felt. Coleman had one affair after another. There was even some talk about one of Cade's girlfriends. I've never said this to anyone else, but I was almost glad he had other women. I hated him that way most of all, because he never cared for my pleasure." She shivered a little. "So you can see why it was easy for me to forgive Gussie," she added with a sideways glance. "You can't be jealous of a man who hurts you."

Bess had to bite her tongue not to confess what Gussie had told her about that "affair." She didn't have the right to say anything, but she wanted to.

"Cade wants children right away," Bess blurted out.

"Yes, I know." Elise smiled at her. "Bess, a child

would be the best thing that could happen for both of you. Cade's reached the age where he feels his own mortality. He wants the security of children. He wants a family of his own to provide for, to work for."

"I do too," she replied, lowering her eyes. "He hasn't said anything, but I don't think he's happy that I haven't gotten pregnant yet." She didn't add that it would be impossible, or that even if she hadn't been barren, she would have needed a little cooperation from her husband.

"He's impatient," Elise said. "He's getting older and he's waited a long time for you. He does care for you very much."

"I only wish he loved me," Bess said softly. "Because I love him more than my own life."

"I know. I've always known." She patted Bess's hand. "Give it time. Everything will be all right."

But would it? That night when Cade came in, Bess was still awake, sitting up in bed in her pretty cotton pajamas with her hair around her shoulders, reading.

He stopped in the doorway and looked at her with cool, searching eyes. "Not sleepy? I hope you aren't in the mood for sex, because I can't oblige. I'm tired."

She blushed angrily as he closed the door and proceeded to the adjoining bathroom for a shower without bothering to look at her again.

By the time he came out again, in nothing but blue-striped pajama bottoms, his magnificent body bare from the waist up and his hair damp, she was fuming.

"You needn't worry about my base desires," she told him icily. "I can live without sex just fine, thanks."

He looked down at her with cool, indifferent eyes. "That wasn't the case when we first came back here, was it, Mrs. Hollister?" he asked with a mocking smile. "In fact you couldn't get enough of it."

She averted her eyes to the bedcover. Yes, he was still mad about her blatant seduction. Probably that had been eating him all this time and he'd just kept it bottled up. She tugged at the sheet. "I'm sorry about that," she stammered. "I thought that it might make up for . . . for the babies."

He stood very still. "You thought what?"

Her eyes closed. She had to tell him. They couldn't go on like this. The deceit was making her miserable, and so was her conscience. What Elise had said tonight about his child-hunger and the reasons for it had hurt.

"Cade, I can't give you a child," she said through stiff lips.

Chapter 19

Cade stared at her without speaking for one long, endless minute. He couldn't believe that he was hearing her properly.

"You mean you don't want my children, is that it?" he asked icily.

She felt tears in her eyes, and her vision blurred. "I mean," she said huskily, "that I can't bear a child. Ever. I'm . . . barren."

His chest rose and fell heavily. His jaw went hard, like his eyes. Barren. "How long have you known?" he asked in a deadly quiet tone. "Did you know when you married me?"

This was going to be the most damning part of her confession, and he was taking it every bit as hard as she'd expected him to. She couldn't blame him. She was shattering his dreams.

"Yes," she said, shouldering the responsibility.

His breathing was suddenly audible. "Didn't it occur to you that I had the right to know?"

She cringed inside at the accusation. "Of course you did," she said heavily. "But I knew you wouldn't want me if you knew the truth." Her eyes closed, missing the expression that crossed his face. "I loved you so much. I thought, God forgive me, that I'd steal a little happiness." She managed a smile as she lifted her misty eyes to his cold ones. "But it all went wrong even before you knew, didn't it? I loved you, but you only wanted me. And after that night, when I was aggressive, you never wanted me again." She shifted nervously on the bed. "You've been looking for an excuse to send me away, but you couldn't find one. Now you have it. You want children and I can't give them to you." She lowered defeated eyes to the bare wood floor. "I'm sorry."

He ground his teeth together. He couldn't get past the fact that Bess was barren. All these long years he'd wanted no one else. He'd married her and she'd sworn undying love. But she could lie to him that easily, she could deceive him. He'd been so besotted with her that he hadn't questioned her about why she hadn't become pregnant. He should have realized that something was wrong. God knew, she'd always turned aside his remarks about children, and she'd seemed depressed whenever she saw him with children.

"You knew how badly I wanted kids," he said with barely controlled fury. "You owed me the choice."

"I know that." She wiped away the tears with a

shaking hand. "I just don't quite fit in here, do I?" she asked with a tremulous smile. "I've tried. But you only want Lariat and those heirs you talked about to carry it on. I understand, really I do. I had dreams too. . . ." Her voice trailed away and the tears came back. Her eyes closed. "I know you won't want me here anymore. I can . . . I can leave tomorrow if you like." Even as she said it, she was hoping against hope that he'd ask her to stay.

"That might be the best thing for both of us," he said coldly. "You can get your apartment back, or one like it. We'll work out the details later."

"You mean, about a divorce," she said with forced calmness and nodded, missing the shocked look on his face. "Yes, I think that would be best too. I'll . . . I'll call Donald when I'm settled and he can get things started." She swallowed tears. "You don't have to worry about alimony. There isn't such a thing in Texas."

"Why didn't you tell me, damn it!" he demanded, anguish breaking through the calm.

"I thought you might care enough about me not to mind," she said, refusing to look at him. "I thought I could be good enough in bed to make you . . . to make up for what I couldn't give you. But that backfired, too, because you don't even want me anymore." Her voice broke and she bit her lower lip to stop from crying aloud.

Cade's face contorted. He stared at her, conflicting emotions tearing him apart. He had to have time. He had to deal with it. He couldn't do it now, it was too fresh a wound. She'd lied to him, she'd married him under false pretenses. She said she loved him, but she hadn't trusted him with the truth.

"No, I don't want you anymore," he replied tersely, striking back out of wounded pride and pain. "The woman I wanted doesn't exist anymore. She was sweet and kind and loving, not an aggressive little liar."

The words hit her like body blows, but she sat there calmly staring at him until she could speak again. "Is that what you thought of me?" she asked, laughing painfully. "I thought . . . men liked that sort of thing." She took a shaky breath. "Well, I'll know better next time, won't I? If there is a next time." Her world was collapsing, but she couldn't, didn't dare, break down. She felt sick from her head to her heels, and weak as water.

"Lots of luck. Maybe Ryker is still free," he said. His face contorted for an instant as he looked at her. "He might be just your style, society girl, and he probably wouldn't mind not having kids."

Her eyes closed and tears slipped from them. "I'm sorry," she whispered brokenly. "I love you so much, Cade. You can't know how badly I wanted a child with you!"

He couldn't find any words to say. He was hurting so badly himself that he couldn't see the pain he was causing her. All his dreams had died. He'd never have sons with Bess. There wouldn't be any children. Why hadn't she told him?

"I'll leave in the morning," she managed.

"Yes." He turned toward the door, walking numbly away from her. "I'll sleep in the guest room."

"Cade, please don't hate me!" she cried.

His back stiffened, but he didn't turn. "Good-bye,

Bess," he said gruffly, and forced himself not to look back.

The curt words hung in the room after he shut the door behind him. Bess collapsed in tears. Well, it was out in the open now, and he hated her. He'd thrown her out. He didn't want her anymore, because she wasn't a whole woman.

She couldn't even muster up enough hatred to pull her shattered emotions back together. It wasn't as if it was all her fault. He hadn't helped by attacking her in her apartment and frightening her into running away from him. That was why she was barren, after all. He hadn't even asked the reason and she hadn't volunteered it. But then, what difference would it have made? He might have felt guilty enough to let her stay, but guilt was a poor substitute for the love he couldn't give her. If he'd loved her, it wouldn't have mattered to him that she was barren, she was sure of it. Now she knew what he really felt for her. He thought she'd acted like a tramp when she'd seduced him, and it had made him not want her anymore. He thought she was cheap, and she felt it.

She wiped her eyes, trying not to think about tomorrow. Their marriage had been deteriorating anyway, but she loved Cade. She'd wanted nothing more than to live with him, but it had all gone wrong from the very beginning. Perhaps if she'd been honest with him at first, they wouldn't have come to this impasse. It all came down to trust, she thought. She hadn't trusted him, so she'd lost him. Her hopes for the future were as barren as her body now.

She got up before daylight, since she couldn't sleep anyway, and packed her things.

She was dressed for travel in a gray linen suit when she came downstairs with her suitcase and purse. She hadn't expected Cade to be up, even though he was an early riser, because it wasn't quite daylight. But he was, dressed in jeans and boots and a chambray shirt, prowling the hall with a cup of black coffee. He looked up when she came down the staircase, his dark eyes giving nothing away except the fact that he hadn't slept. She imagined she had equally dark circles under her own eyes.

"Good morning," she said politely, glad that her anguish didn't show, that her voice didn't tremble.

"You don't need to tell Donald any of the details when you talk to him," he said curtly. "Charge me with mental cruelty if you like," he added with a cold, mocking smile.

He had no idea how true a charge it would be, she thought. She felt queasy and hoped that she was going to be able to get out the door without fainting. All the pressure was really working on her system; she felt fragile.

"You're sure . . . ?" she asked, shelving her pride for an instant out of one last, lingering hope for a reprieve.

He ignored her soft plea. "I'm sure," he replied. "We were mismatched from the beginning. It's a long way from a mansion to a line cabin. I built a dream on an illusion. But the illusion won't keep me warm in the winter, or give me the sons I want for Lariat," he said with quiet meaning. "You'll find someone else. So will I."

She took slow breaths to keep from falling at his feet.

She knew her face must be white. He was killing her. Killing her . . .

"Then, good-bye, Cade," she said gently. "I've left a note for your mother, thanking her for everything. You can tell her what you like. Please say good-bye to your brothers for me."

He nodded irritably. "You'd better get started."

"Can't wait to get rid of me, can you?" she asked with graveyard humor. She bent and picked up her suitcase and started toward the door.

"Have you got enough money?" he asked, hating himself for even asking because it sounded as if he cared.

She glanced at him over her shoulder. "I don't want anything else from you, Cade, thank you. I've taken enough, in one way or another." Her eyes adored him, just for a few precious seconds. "Oh, be happy, my dear," she said on a broken sob.

He drew in a furious breath. "Get out!"

She shivered at his tone and swallowed down the tears. "I'll love you all my life," she whispered. She managed a wobbly smile. "Do you . . . do you want this back?" she asked, pausing to lift her left hand.

The little silver ring sparkled in the light, and he couldn't bear the sight of it. He'd never told her its story. Maybe it would have helped her to understand if he had. "No," he said.

"Someday you'll marry again, and you'll . . . you'll have those kids you want so much." She forced the words out. "I'll save the ring for them. Good-bye, Cade."

He didn't look at her again. He knew if he did, he'd go down on his knees and beg her to come back, and he didn't dare. This was the best thing he could do for both of them. He couldn't live without children and she couldn't give him any; it was just that simple and tragic. So he let her go. Long after he heard the car drive away, he remembered another time she'd left him, another time when she'd gone away in a car.

His blood ran cold. The accident. She'd wrecked the car because he'd upset her. He drew in a rough breath. What if she did it again?

He phoned down to the bunkhouse and woke one of his men and sent him to follow Bess back to San Antonio, just to make sure. He stared at the receiver when he'd hung it up. Why couldn't he stop caring, he wondered bitterly. She'd hurt him and cheated him, and he still cared about her. With a muffled curse he pulled his hat off the hat rack and stormed out the door to work.

Bess got to San Antonio in record time because the streets weren't crowded at that hour of the morning. Her first stop was the apartment house where she'd lived, and she was in luck because her old apartment hadn't been rented out yet. There had been a tenant who'd wanted it, but he'd canceled at the last minute. Bess took the key and went down the long walkway wearily. Thank God the apartment was furnished. Her few bits and pieces of furnishings from Spanish House were at Lariat. She hadn't thought to ask Cade to bring them up, but he was so coolly efficient that she knew he would. She hadn't expected him to let her stay, although she'd hoped that he might relent before she drove away. Then she'd hoped that he might come after her. But his mind seemed to be made up, and somehow she was going to have to learn to live without him.

Señora Lopez greeted her a little curiously. Bess made up some quick story about needing to stay in town on business, and that seemed to satisfy the little old lady.

Bess washed her face and unpacked before she left for work. She could always get some groceries when she came home, not that she had much appetite. At least the tears had slowed down. She felt numb and sick as she went back to her car and drove to work. Thank God she had her job. She'd never needed it so badly before.

No one questioned her sudden move back to San Antonio or the fact that she wasn't wearing her wedding band anymore. She didn't have the silver ring on either. She'd put it away in her jewelry chest so that she didn't have to look at it. But Nell was giving her long, sympathetic looks, so she had to have some idea of what was going on. One thing that Bess loved about her office was that no one invaded her privacy. They were supportive if she needed them, Julie and Nell most of all, but no one ever pried.

She called Donald in tears at the end of the first week, and told him that she and Cade were divorcing and asked him to handle the case. He'd come to San Antonio to talk her out of it, but she wouldn't be swayed. Donald didn't realize the whole truth of the matter, and she couldn't muster enough nerve to tell him the real reason Cade didn't want her anymore. It hurt too badly. She finally convinced him, paid him a retainer, and sent him off to get things started. There was no sense in postponing the inevitable, and Cade wouldn't want to continue to be tied to her. He wanted children. Since he no longer wanted Bess, she was certain that he could find another woman he desired enough to have children by.

Gussie came over the first week she was back at work, worried and obviously curious.

"Elise says that you've left Lariat, but she won't tell me anything," Gussie said quietly. "Darling, you've loved Cade for years. What's wrong? Can I help?"

The unexpected sympathy sent Bess running into the arms that had comforted her as a child, and she cried until her throat hurt from the tears. She felt terrible, as if she were dying of weakness and nausea, and the loss of Cade was responsible. She had to drag herself up out of bed every morning, and even that was a struggle. She felt as if all her strength was gone.

Gussie rocked her gently, smiling because for the first time in months her daughter actually seemed to need her. She sighed against the disheveled honey-brown hair. "It's all right, darling," she said. "Can't you talk to me about it?"

"He doesn't . . . doesn't *want* me anymore," she said, sobbing. Her body shook with misery. "He never loved me, but now he doesn't even want me, and I can't have babies, Mama." Tears rolled down her cheeks. "They say I'll never have babies because of the wreck . . . !"

"Oh, Bess." Gussie wrapped her up tight and cried with her. She didn't have to be told about Cade's child-hunger, or what it would mean to him to have to live with a woman who could never satisfy it. She understood everything now. She smoothed Bess's hair gently. "Just cry until it stops hurting, sweet. Mama's here. Mama's right here."

Afterward Bess made coffee and she and Gussie talked as they never had before, about the past and about the present. It made things so much easier to get it all off her chest. The hurting didn't stop, but it helped to talk about it.

"Give Cade time," Gussie said. "He may still come around. He's lived alone for a long time, and frankly, Bess, I think it was a mistake for him to move you into Lariat when you were just married. Elise thinks so, too. The two of you had no privacy at all. That's no way to begin a marriage."

"Cade wouldn't stay away from Lariat," she said. "He gave me no choice. But there's no hope of a reconciliation. You know that. He said so. Donald is proceeding with the divorce." She sipped black coffee. "It's what we both want. Cade will be free to find . . . someone else."

"I hope he chokes on whomever he finds," Gussie said with venom. "Love isn't conditional. If you love someone, you love them regardless of their inadequacies, and he did help you to have that wreck in the first place. He isn't blameless."

"He's never loved me, though," Bess said, ignoring her mother's vehement dialogue. "He wanted me, that was all it ever was. He wanted a society woman, a decoration for Lariat. He never even knew the real me. All he saw was the illusion." She put down the coffee cup. "Well, I'll get by. There must be men in the world who don't want children. . . ." Her voice broke and she began to cry again. "But I do! I wanted Cade's . . . !"

Gussie patted her shoulder gently, alarmed at the extent of Bess's emotional outburst. It wasn't like her to give way to tears, and she looked bad. "Darling, I think you should see a doctor," she said. "There's something in your complexion that I don't like, and you do seem terribly stressed. Will you do that, just for me?"

Bess wiped at her tears angrily. "Nell said that this morning. I'm just overwrought, though. And maybe it's that virus that's going around, the one that makes you nauseous. But I'll go. I'm tired all the time too. Maybe he can give me something to pep me up. I've got to fly to Missouri next week to do an ad presentation for a client, so I really have got to get better."

"I'll go with you if you like," Gussie volunteered.

Bess smiled at her. "Thanks. But I can manage. I'll call you when I find out what's wrong."

"Good girl. How about some more coffee?"

Bess got an appointment and went on her lunch hour the next day. The nausea was worse all the time. That was Cade's fault, she thought bitterly. He'd upset her so much that her whole system was falling apart.

She told the doctor as much, but he only smiled and began asking the obvious questions, especially about her period. She told him when the last one had been, frowning when she realized how long it had been. She'd had so much emotional stress, and she knew that that could affect her monthly routine, so she hadn't worried. But the doctor had her strip and did a pelvic examination and had samples taken for the lab.

"But I can't be pregnant," she said when he told her what he thought her problem was. Her eyes widened. "They told me I couldn't get pregnant."

"Yes, I know, I read the report. They didn't say you couldn't get pregnant," he told her. "They said it was unlikely, unless your husband was extremely potent and the timing was perfect. That ovary you have left is quite functional, if erratic. Yes, you can be pregnant. The tests will only confirm my diagnosis, Mrs. Hollister. You're about three months into pregnancy. At this stage there's not much guesswork."

She stared at him with blank eyes. She'd told Cade she couldn't have a child and he'd thrown her out. Now they were divorcing, all the doors were closing behind her, and she was pregnant. It was ironic. It was hilarious.

She began laughing and almost couldn't stop. Then she buried her face in her hands and started crying.

"It's all perfectly natural," the doctor told her with a gentle smile. He patted her shoulder. "I'll send you right over to Dr. Marlowe. He's an obstetrician and he loves pregnant women. He'll take excellent care of you. You need to be on prenatal vitamins and have regular checkups, especially during these first months. Come on, now."

He led her out to the nurse, who made the appointment for her and took the check from her trembling hands.

The doctor had said he'd call her to verify the diagnosis, but she knew he was right. There wasn't much doubt.

She went back to the office, wide-eyed and full of conflicting ideas about what she was going to do. She walked into Nell and excused herself and walked right past her into the office without another word.

"What's happened?" Nell asked, following her inside.

"Nothing. I don't know. I need to call Cade. Is it all right, do you think?" she asked.

"Of course it's all right. My gosh, I was wondering if you were ever going to do something."

Bess stared at her. "How about you, doing something?"

Nell flushed. "I can't invite the man who owns the company to supper," she said stiffly. "He'll think I'm after his money. And if he was interested, he'd have called me. Never mind my problems. Call your husband!"

Bess smiled at her. "Okay." She lifted the receiver as Nell went out and dialed Lariat's number with shaking fingers. Everything was going to be all right. She'd tell Cade and they'd laugh at the irony of it, and he'd tell her to come home. It would be all right.

"Hello?"

It was Cade. She hadn't really expected him to answer the phone himself, so she hesitated until he repeated the greeting more impatiently.

"Hello," she stammered. "It's me."

There was a stiff pause. "I got the divorce papers," he said with ice in his voice. "Donald had the sheriff serve them this morning. You didn't waste any time, did you, honey?"

She took a steadying breath. "It was your idea. . . ."

"What difference does it make now? I'm having the rest of your things sent up," he said coolly. "If I forgot anything, you can call Mother and have her get it to you. I'll be away for a few weeks. One of my business contacts has a resort in California, and a daughter who's marriage-minded. We might make a merger of it, so I don't want to waste any more time."

She felt the breath go out of her. "And you said I couldn't wait?" she whispered huskily.

"She's a redhead," he continued, driving the point home. "A real dish. So don't think I'm sitting down here in Coleman Springs eating my heart out for you, honey."

She closed her eyes. "I never thought that," she said. She touched her stomach, and tears welled up behind her eyelids. "I hope you'll find what you want."

"I already have." He forced the words out, hating them even as he said them. He missed her like hell and he knew he'd made a terrible mistake, but his pride wouldn't let him beg her to come back. She'd gone ahead with the divorce so quickly that his ego was badly bruised. If she was that anxious to be rid of him, he'd make sure she didn't think he was mourning her.

"Well . . . good-bye," she said.

"Why did you call?" he asked unexpectedly.

She thought of why she'd called, so excited, to tell him he was going to be a father, that she was carrying that impossible child she never thought she could give him. But what use was it now, when he'd already found someone else?

"Just to see how you were," she hedged. "I'm glad things are working out for you. Good-bye, Cade." She put the receiver down and leaned back in her chair. Well, that was that, she thought with a long, tired sigh. She was really on her own now, and how was she going to manage keeping it from her mother and Gussie until Cade was remarried and out of danger of mar-

rying her just for the child's sake? Maybe if she wore
big dresses and said she was getting fat. . . .

"That new client is here," Nell whispered around
the door, her face flushed, "and Mr. Ryker is with him!
Have you got a minute to talk to him about that airline
ad you're working up for the Texas commuter service?"

"You bet!" Bess said, forcing brightness into her
voice. "Bring him right in."

The client was a middle-aged man with no hair and
a nice smile. Mr. Ryker, big and dark and elegant,
deposited him with Bess to talk about ideas for the
advertising campaign. Mr. Ryker himself turned and
stared down at Nell quietly for a long moment before
he suddenly took her by the arm and half-dragged her
down the hall.

It looked promising, Bess thought, but she had far
too much on her tormented mind right now to pursue
the idea. She turned her mind back to the task of filling
seats on Mr. Hunter's Texas Air Taxi service.

Quitting time didn't come a minute too soon for
Bess. She waylaid Nell before the older woman could
get out the door, noticing with delight that Nell's lipstick was smeared and her eyes were unusually bright.

"So that was why he was dragging you down the
hall." Bess grinned, her own problems diminished by
the delight in Nell's face.

Nell flushed. "It was an interesting few minutes,"
she murmured, sighing. "He's taking me dancing tonight." She put her face in her hands. "He thought he
was too old for me, and I thought he was too rich to
care about someone like me. I guess we both had fixed
ideas about each other."

"I guess you did." Bess hugged her. "I'm so happy for you. At least your life is going on a happy medium."

"Yes, and yours isn't, is it?" Nell asked, searching Bess's sad eyes. "Can I do anything to help?"

"Not really, but thanks." She picked up her purse. "I guess I'll fix myself a steak and watch some television."

"Why not invite your husband up to share it with you?"

Bess's face closed up. "Because he won't be my husband in a few weeks, and right now he's on his way to spend some time with a redhead in California who wants to marry him."

"What?!"

"Oh, it gets better," Bess assured her with kindling anger. "He wants children, and we didn't think I could have any. So he's going to divorce me and marry this redhead so that he can have an heir. But I'm pregnant, and he won't let me tell him."

"Bess!" Nell leaned back against the door and caught her breath. "For God's sake, get down there and make him listen!"

"So he'll stay married to me out of guilt, or for the baby?" Bess asked with a sad smile. "We married for the wrong reasons in the first place."

"Well, don't bother telling me you've stopped loving him, because I won't believe it."

"I'll always love him," Bess said quietly. "And I'll have the baby." She smiled, touching her stomach. "Isn't it incredible?" she breathed, caught up in the beauty of her pregnancy already. "A little human being. They say they're perfectly formed at two months, you know, like miniature people." Her eyes grew dreamy. "And he's three months along. They'll do an ultrasound and I can see him." She laughed through tears. "I'm so happy I can't stand it."

"I hope the redhead puts your husband in a meat grinder and cooks him with eggs," Nell said shortly.

"And poison herself?" Bess said indignantly. "God forbid."

"You really aren't going to tell him?"

"He'll find out for himself one day." She went toward the door. "I'm going to tell Julie, but this has to be top secret for the time being, okay?"

"Okay."

"Meanwhile, good luck on your date." Bess grinned at her.

"I've got all my fingers crossed. If you need me, call, okay?" she added.

"Okay." She smiled at Nell with genuine warmth. "Thanks."

Julie took the news with the same incredulity that Nell had, and asked all the same questions.

"You won't fire me, will you?" Bess asked, only half-jokingly. "I know I've been a strain on the company insurance, but I've got two mouths to feed now."

"No problem there," Julie assured her. "You're one of the best ad people we've ever had. Even Mr. Ryker said so this afternoon. In fact"—she grinned—"he authorized a raise for you. I was on my way to tell you when you dropped by."

"Oh, how very nice of him!" she said enthusiastically.

"He's a nice man. Nell certainly thinks so, smeared lipstick and all," she added with a gleeful grin. "They're going to be one hot item around here, and I couldn't be happier for Nell. She's mooned over him for years. It's nice to see people finally get the happiness they deserve."

"Yes, it is," Bess agreed quietly, wishing hers had lasted.

"One more thing," Julie said, frowning as she got up. "Normally I wouldn't have mentioned this to you, because I had no idea you were pregnant. But we're going to have a fashion agency working with us on a presentation month after next, and it's going to involve modeling some maternity clothes at a charity benefit at the Paseo del Rio. Would you consider being a model? There's a bonus for it, and you do look radiant, even under the circumstances."

Bess smiled. "I'd enjoy it," she said. "If I get a discount on some of the clothes," she added.

Julie laughed. "Do it and I'll give them to you as part of the perks, okay?"

"Okay!"

"Now go home and rest and eat, or whatever pregnant people are supposed to do. I'm sorry about the mess you're in, but you have friends here, and we'll look out for you," she said firmly. "Not to mention that if you need a baby-sitter . . ."

"This is one baby who's hardly ever going to need one, because I don't think I'll be able to let him or her out of my sight at first," Bess said softly. "But I'll keep you in mind, and I appreciate the offer."

"Take care of yourself."

Bess nodded. She went home and put her feet up, dreaming about the future, trying not to think about Cade off at a resort with that redhead. It made her furious that he could slough her off so easily, and without so much as an apology. Let him have his stupid redhead. She could get along without Cade Hollister. After all, she'd had to get along without him for most of their married life.

It was so sad, remembering the way they'd begun, the sweetness of loving him, the warmth of his kisses, the anguished pleasure he'd taught her in the privacy of their bedroom. But that hadn't been enough for him. He'd thrown her away like an old shoe when he'd found out that she was barren. Now here she was pregnant. It was almost comical.

She wanted to call Elise and tell her, or tell Gussie. But something held her back. It was her secret. She wanted to keep it to herself just a little while longer, before it got out and everyone at Lariat knew.

She flew to Saint Louis for her presentation and came home with a big computer-corporation account for the company. Her clothes began to accentuate her image as a successful career woman—tailored suits and sedate accessories. She had her hair styled and wore it in a loose chignon which complimented her radiant face. Pregnancy gave her added color and vitality, rounded her body, and made her look more beautiful than she'd ever been. She even felt great, thanks to the prenatal vitamins Dr. Marlowe had prescribed. If it hadn't been for the loneliness and the anguish of losing Cade, her pregnancy would have been the high point of her life.

Even so, at night, she sat and read books on infants and how to take care of them and sorted through books of names, trying to decide what to name him or her. She had the ultrasound but not the amniocentesis, which could predict sex. She didn't really want to know if the baby was a boy or a girl. Not just yet. It was like waiting for a Christmas surprise package, and the uncertainty made it all the sweeter.

She was shopping on her lunch hour a few weeks after she'd left Lariat, when she ran into Robert Hollister.

He stared at her blankly for a long moment, trying to reconcile the woman who'd married his brother with this elegant, lovely creature staring up at him with such soft, startled eyes.

"Bess?" he asked, as if he wasn't quite sure she was.

Chapter 20

Bess was grateful that she was wearing a floppy, fashionable big top, because her condition was visible now at almost five months, and she didn't want Robert telling Cade.

"Well, hello, Robert," she said easily. "How are you?"

"Fine, thanks. How about you?" he asked.

She shrugged. "Couldn't be better." She smiled. "How are things at Lariat?"

His expression wavered. "Okay, I guess. Gary and Jennifer are getting married at the end of the month, and I'm about to pop the question to Audrey. Gary's leaving the ranch to go to work for an accounting firm in Houston." He grinned. "I'm going to Los Angeles with a marketing firm. Mama is opening a dress shop in Coleman Springs and plans to live above it with a widow who's a friend of hers. Cade's going to have Lariat all to himself," he added with a certain coldness in his voice. "He'll finally have exactly what he always wanted, full control. I hope it makes him happy. Lariat's the only thing he's ever really loved."

Bess knew that, but it hurt to hear it out loud. "He's . . . all right, then?" she asked, hating herself for voicing that tiny concern.

"No, of course he's not all right," he said heavily. He sighed. "My God, Bess, he's been hell to live with. Why do you think we're all heading for the windows and doors? He gets up raising hell in the morning and comes home raising hell at night. When he isn't doing that, he's working himself and the men to death or sitting in his study with a whiskey bottle."

"Cade doesn't drink," she pointed out huskily.

"Cade didn't used to drink," he replied. "He also didn't used to go around with dizzy redheads and wreck bars, but he's done a fair amount of that since you left," he added with a calculating look.

Her face closed up. "The dizzy redhead is going to be the new matriarch of Lariat. He told me so. He's going to make a merger with her daddy, and she's part of it."

"So that's what he's up to," he mused, smothering a grin. His eyes began to twinkle as if he had some private joke in his mind. He wiped the smile away. "Well, just between you and me, I don't think Cade is really that serious. Even though she's done everything but walk around naked in front of him. She's after him for sure." He studied her face. "Bess, what went wrong?" he asked. "There's never been anybody but you for

Cade, but he let you go and he won't even have your name mentioned. Why?"

She smoothed her hand over her purse. "We thought I couldn't have children," she said finally, letting the secret out. "The doctors said I wouldn't be able to, because of the wreck."

"My God." He touched her arm gently. "I'm so sorry. I know how he feels about kids. I guess he just couldn't take it. There wasn't any chance, then, was there?"

She shook her head. "He wanted children more than he wanted me. Don't worry about him, Robert. He'll enjoy his redhead. She can give him children," she said bitterly.

"That's not likely," Robert returned, hesitating. "Uh, I heard her telling Mama that she wasn't going to ruin her figure at twenty-five to produce any squalling brats."

"What did Cade say?" she asked.

"He didn't hear her. Gretchen and her daddy have been staying at Lariat for a few days, but they left this morning."

"How's your mother?" she asked. "And Gary?"

"Mama is sick about your divorce. So is Gary. Are you really going to let this divorce go through?" he asked quietly. "Because I think you might as well put a bullet in Cade if you do."

"Cade doesn't want me," she said stubbornly. "He said so."

"Well, he's a fool," Robert said with considerable venom. "I'm sorry he doesn't realize it." He studied her with piercing eyes, his red hair almost standing on end. "You look so different. Soft and pretty and radiant, in spite of everything. Gussie told Mama you'd been sick. I guess you're better now."

"Much better," she replied, moving suddenly when she felt the baby. It had been the most ecstatic discovery of her life when the first flutters began. They were like butterfly movements inside her stomach, and the first time she'd felt them, she cried. The baby was alive and happy and healthy, and her face began to glow with a creamy light as she smiled.

"Something wrong?" Robert asked, puzzled by that very visible radiance.

She held her breath. She almost told him. But she didn't dare. "No. Nothing at all."

"How's the job going?"

"Just great. I'm doing some modeling on the side." It was safe to tell him that. He wasn't the type to go to fashion shows. "At Henri's, the French restaurant. They're having a fashion show there tonight, and I get a bonus for helping out. It's for charity, so it should be great fun. I'm a little nervous, so I thought I'd buy some new makeup to cheer me up."

"I wouldn't have said you needed makeup," he murmured with a smile. "You look lovely."

"Thank you, Robert." She looked at her watch. "I've got to run. I'll be late for work. It was good to see you. Robert . . . don't tell Cade you saw me, okay?" she added gently. "He's got a new life, new priorities. Don't let the past interfere with his happiness."

Robert's face hardened. "Damn him for what he's done to you, Bess," he said coolly. "I hope he chokes on his pride. See you."

It took Bess the rest of the day to put Robert's disturbing remarks out of her mind. She wished she hadn't run into him, she didn't want to hear about Cade's redhead or his anger. That was part of the past. Not for the world was she going to admit how lonely she was or how hopelessly alone she felt.

She got dressed at the apartment in one of the ensembles she was to model at the benefit. It was a two-piece gold-and-cream evening dress, and it made her glow even more. She left her hair long and wavy around her bare shoulders and put on enough makeup for the cameras, along with a perfume she hadn't used in years. She looked presentable, she decided, and she was grateful that Gussie didn't know about the fashion show. She'd managed to fool her mother about her condition so far by wearing baggy, unconstructed clothes. But she was beginning to show, and very soon her pregnancy was going to be so far advanced that nobody would be fooled.

There was a huge crowd at Henri's for the fashion show. Bess went in through the employees' entrance along with Julie and the other models and hurriedly lined up the ensembles she'd be wearing with the shoes and other accessories for quick changes between presentations. She ran a brush through her hair and got in line, exchanging a nervous wink with Julie as the music started and she heard the announcer's soft voice.

Her cue came and she walked out onto the restaurant's carpeted floor with wobbly knees, but with a forced smile that made her look more relaxed than she was. She walked past the crowded tables as the announcer described her pregnancy outfit, pausing to explain prices to the patrons who asked.

She should have known Robert would say something to Cade. But somehow she hadn't expected it. When she moved around a hidden table in the corner of the room and came face-to-face with Cade and his redhead, she almost tripped and fell.

She recovered quickly, keeping the smile pinned to her face, but her eyes cursed Cade with every breath in her body.

He stared back at her with equal darkness, shadowed by pain and something deeper. He was wearing a dinner jacket and a pleated white shirt with his black tie, looking elegant and frightening. Beside him the redhead's hair was fashionably disheveled around a pale, freckled face with cold blue eyes. The woman was wearing a green dress that washed out her complexion, but it looked like pure silk and probably was. So his new woman was rich. That boded well for Lariat. She could help him build his empire.

Cade stood up slowly, towering over her. "What are you doing here," he asked coldly, "modeling that kind of outfit? Is it some kind of self-torment for you, or just a way to get back at me for the things I said to you?"

She didn't understand what he was saying. She tried to move around him. "I'm doing a job," she said. "And nothing I do is any concern of yours anymore," she added icily, glaring up at him. "Why did you come here? Did Robert tell you where I'd be?"

"Yes . . ." he began.

"You're Gretchen, aren't you?" Bess asked the redhead, forcing a bright smile for her. "Well, congratulations, I hear you're being groomed to replace me at Lariat. You're obviously rich and fertile, and that will suit Cade admirably."

Gretchen's eyes popped. She stared at Bess blankly. "I beg your pardon?"

"Haven't you told her that you're in the market for a brood mare?" she asked Cade. "Or are you keeping it a secret?"

"Look, it isn't that at all," Cade said quietly. He looked around, scowling at the attention they were drawing. "I've got to talk to you."

"We talked at Lariat, remember?" she asked him. Her eyes darkened. "You threw me out because you found out I was barren."

He actually winced. "I didn't know it was because of the wreck," he said, grinding out his words. "You told me nothing!"

She drew in a slow breath. "So that's why you came. Robert told you. I don't need your pity, as it happens, and I don't care about your conscience. I'm not part of your life anymore."

He reached out toward her, and she jerked back. "Don't you want to know the real irony, Cade?" she asked in a voice that was half whisper. She smiled shakily, furious that he should bring her successor here and flaunt her. She was hurt and hitting back, just as hard as she could.

"What irony?" he asked, fighting for time.

She reached down and pulled the gown tight across her swollen belly. She didn't say a word.

He scowled. "So, they put a pillow in to make you look—"

She moved closer, grabbing his hand, and suddenly put it flat right over their child. The expression on his dark face was worth every tear, every sleepless night, every anguished word, every miserable day since he'd asked her to leave.

"Oh, my God," he whispered, and his voice faltered. The lean fingers on her belly shook, pressing down, feeling, caressing. "Bess, my God . . . !"

She moved away from him in one swift step, her eyes hating him. "Take that back to Lariat with you and see how well you sleep now. You should have waited a few more weeks. Miracles still happen, you know. Then you'd have had the child you wanted, even if you didn't want his mother!"

He couldn't move. He felt the blood drain out of his face, and in slow motion he watched her give him one last icy smile before she turned with regal pride and went back the way she'd come, oblivious of the curious stares and soft whispers around her.

"Cade, what *is* she talking about?" Gretchen asked when he sat down. "Where did she get the idea that I was trying to take her place at Lariat?"

"From me, and from Robert, I'm afraid," he said heavily. "I'm sorry to put you in such a position. I was hoping against hope that she might be jealous and come home and give me hell about you. But she didn't care enough. Now I know why. She's carrying my child. I let her go, I made her go, and the reason for her possible barrenness was a car accident I caused. My God, I could shoot myself!"

"So I'm the scarlet woman." She grinned. "Robert should have asked me before he volunteered me for this mission, but since it's in such a good cause, and you are my future brother-in-law, I guess I can bear the shame. You really ought to go talk to Bess, though."

"You heard her. She doesn't want to talk to me. She hates me."

"You can't hate people you don't love," Gretchen said. "That sounds corny, but it's true. You aren't going to get anywhere until you take the first step."

"Maybe not. At this point I'm not sure a step will help." He got up wearily. "I'll be back."

He walked toward the place where the models vanished after each showing, his tall, elegant body drawing appreciative female eyes. He didn't even notice—his mind was on Bess, and the terrible way he'd treated her.

He found her putting on another maternity outfit. She glared at him.

"You can't come back here," she said. "It's the women's rest room, and I'm between turns."

"I'm here and I'm staying," he said curtly. "You can't drop a bombshell like that on me and expect me to sit down and watch you strut around a fancy restaurant."

"I don't strut—you do." She brushed her hair, the temper coloring her cheeks, darkening her eyes, so that he couldn't look away from her. "Your redhead will miss you," she said venomously.

"Jealous?" he taunted. "I didn't think you cared if I had other women. You wouldn't even come down to Lariat to check it out."

"I didn't care," she said shortly. "You threw me out."

He turned away, his hands deep in his pockets. He leaned against the wall with a weary sigh. "Yes, I did. God knows why."

"Simple. I couldn't give you a child, or so we thought." She lifted her chin pugnaciously. "I guess I got this one from a toilet seat," she added fiercely. "Or maybe I had a wild passionate affair with one of the men in the office. Maybe it's Mr. Ryker's!"

"It's mine," he said. "I know damned good and well you didn't go from me to another man."

"At least you've revised your former opinion of my morals," she snapped back. He looked blank. "Forgotten already? The night in your study when I flung myself at you . . . ?"

He actually flushed and averted his eyes. "We have to think about the baby."

"It's mine," she told him. "I'll have it and raise it. You can go back to Lariat and father a family of redheads!"

"God almighty, I'm not going to marry her!" he exploded. "I'm married to you . . . !"

"Sure. That's why you're out dating other people," she said. "And for your information, you're not going to be married to me much longer. The divorce will be final soon."

"Bess, you're my wife!" he said.

She smiled at him sweetly. "Not for much longer. Do go back to your date, Cade, before she thinks you don't love her anymore."

"I don't love her," he began.

"Well, you sure don't love me," she replied, and for an instant the hurt showed through. "Or want me. I guess you want the baby, but I won't stay married just to placate your conscience. You can have visitation rights, but I won't come back to Lariat. Now, do you mind? I'm trying to model clothes."

He took a slow breath, his eyes going over her softly,

warmly. "You're so beautiful like that," he said absently. "I've missed you almost beyond bearing."

She could have echoed that sentiment, but she wasn't going to give him the satisfaction. She straightened the skirt of her next ensemble, a black-and-white concoction. "I hope you and Gretchen will be very happy together. I don't imagine she'll ever try to rape you. . . ."

He caught her upper arms and pulled her against him with rough tenderness. "I loved what you did to me that night," he whispered curtly, lowering his voice so that only she could hear. "I didn't mean the things I said later. You had a hold on me that I couldn't break and you threw me off balance so bad that I felt like less than a man. I've been fighting it all this time, but you haunt me. I don't want to go back to Lariat alone."

Her legs were wobbly, but he wasn't going to know. She glared at him. "You won't be going home alone, Cade dear," she said. "Gretchen will be going with you." She brought her foot down hard on his instep, and when he groaned and stepped back, she brushed past him out into the restaurant just in time for her name to be called in the promenade.

After the show was over, Bess ducked out the back with a helplessly giggling Julie, who'd seen the whole thing.

"Poor man," she told Bess. "How could you!"

"Didn't you see why?" Bess asked, aghast. "She was hanging on his every word, damn her. Damn him too!"

"He'll limp for a week."

That reminded her of another time he'd limped, such a long time ago when he'd been hurt in the rodeo. Other unwanted memories came back of the times they'd been together, the long path they'd traveled to marriage and the tragic end of the relationship. He had Gretchen. Why was he here, upsetting her? His face as it had been when he discovered her condition flashed across her line of vision. Awe, delight, wonder, fierce possession—all those things had been in his dark eyes, along with a depth of feeling that shook her even in memory. She was carrying the child he wanted, and she knew he wasn't going to give it up easily. She was in for the fight of her life, but it was one she had to win. She couldn't live in the shadows of love. She couldn't live with Cade just to satisfy his guilt at his treatment of her or his hunger for the child they'd made.

She went back to her apartment in a miserable haze of emotional limbo, feeling as if she'd been beaten. Why hadn't Cade stayed away? Why had he come running to San Antonio with his kept woman the minute Robert had told him where Bess was going to be? It wasn't fair that he should haunt her.

She laid down and closed her eyes. Her hand found the mound of her belly and touched it, and she smiled at the sudden, fierce pressure of a tiny foot or hand hitting out so hard that she gasped and then teared up with delight.

"Well, hello, little one," she whispered, smiling as she left her hand there. "How are you tonight?"

It was a form of silent communication that was the most precious thing she'd ever experienced. She closed her eyes and lay back, everything else forgotten for the moment in the magic and mystery of creation.

*   *   *

The next day she started to work and walked into
Cade in the parking lot behind the office. Her eyes
opened wide, as if she didn't believe he was really
there.

He was wearing a tan suit and matching boots and
Stetson. He looked very good, and she had to tear her
eyes away from him.

"What do you want?" she asked icily.

"You of course," he replied. He stuck his hands in his
pockets. "But I can see that it's going to be a long,
uphill battle."

She almost smiled at the resignation in his voice.
"Look, why don't you just go and play with your red-
headed toy and leave me alone? I like my job, I'm
happy living alone, and the past is best left in the
past."

"You aren't happy," he said. "You're as dead without
me as I am without you."

"I don't have a redhead," she said sweetly. "But
don't worry, I'm working on it. A man in my office is
just about to become available, and I think he likes
kids . . . Cade!"

He'd lifted her in his hard arms, his face cold and
hard and furious as he turned and carried her back
toward his pickup truck. "I'll be damned if you're going to be available to any other man," he said curtly.

"If you can do it, so can I!" she cried, pushing angrily
at his chest. "You put me down! I hate you!"

"Yes, I know. You've got more reason to hate me
than anyone else alive, but that isn't going to slow me
down, Bess." He paused to open the cab of the truck,

balancing her carefully on one knee. "I'm taking you back to Lariat."

"In a pig's eye," she promised. "Officer!" she called, raising her hand to one of the security guards who patrolled the offices where she worked. "Could you come here, please?"

"Oh, my God, you wouldn't." Cade growled at her. "You wouldn't!"

"Like sweet hell I wouldn't," she whispered back, with ice dripping from her tones. "Officer, this gentleman is trying to abduct me," she informed the security guard. "Could you get him to put me down, do you think?"

"She's my wife," Cade told the man, his cold dark eyes making emphatic threats.

"A likely story," Bess said. "Am I wearing a wedding ring?"

She lifted her left hand, showing him how bare it was of rings. "You see," she said smugly, ignoring the flash of pain in Cade's eyes. "He and I are divorced, almost. He has a redheaded mistress," she added. "Of course, we're all good friends, and she knows that I'm having her lover's baby!"

"Oh, my God," Cade groaned. "Bess!"

"You louse," the security man told Cade. "Put that lady down or I'll make a citizen's arrest. You poor kid," he told Bess, slipping a protective arm around her as he glared at Cade's flash of fury. "Come on, I'll get you safely inside. You ought to be ashamed of yourself, you pervert!" he added over his shoulder.

Cade watched them go, torn between ripping the guard's head off and trying to plan his next move logically. He'd done nothing but make mistakes ever since he'd married Bess. He finally knew what was wrong with him and what to do about it, but convincing Bess was the problem. She might never let him get close to her again, and that was incredibly painful. He'd driven her away for fear of being vulnerable, but he was already vulnerable. He always had been. He just hadn't realized it.

He lit a cigarette and let out a cloud of smoke and a sigh. She looked pretty when she got mad at him, he thought with pursed lips and twinkling eyes. And pregnancy suited her. Robert had told him why she thought she was barren, which was what had catapulted him to San Antonio with Gretchen, Robert's fiancée, last night. Gretchen had been camouflage, to keep Bess from watching him go to pieces. Knowing that he'd caused her to be barren had put another complexion on things. He'd already decided that he'd rather have Bess than children, if it came down to it, and that there was nothing demeaning about loving her or occasionally letting her make the first move. He had his head on straight for the first time. Now if he could just get Bess to listen to him without trying to have him arrested. He shrugged his powerful shoulders and got back into the truck. Well, he could always try again later, he told himself.

Chapter 21

For the next few days Bess didn't see anything of Cade. She knew he hadn't given up, but it was like sitting on a time bomb, waiting for his next move. She felt a little guilty about the baby, knowing how badly he wanted it, but putting herself back into his hands again seemed foolhardy until she knew where she stood. The redhead was giving her fits, even in memory.

Gussie had heard about the confrontation in the restaurant, probably from Elise. She phoned and asked some probing questions, ending with the one she'd obviously wanted to ask first.

"Darling, are you pregnant?" she ventured finally.

"Yes," Bess confirmed it. She hesitated. "Didn't you

know?" she added when there was no surprise on Gussie's part.

"Well, yes, I did," her mother sighed. "Elise phoned me. Cade's told everybody. Elise said he's walked around in a daze ever since he came home from San Antonio, mumbling about buying baby beds and toys. Apparently he's getting a lot of odd looks from the men, because he sits and daydreams while they work. Strange, isn't it?" Gussie asked. "I mean, Cade isn't the daydreaming sort."

Bess knew that. It touched her that Cade was so engrossed in the baby. Then it irritated her that he should care when he had his redhead. He hadn't even made another attempt to patch things up with Bess.

"I have to go," Bess said irritably. "I'm working late for a few nights. One of our clients couldn't make up his mind on the ad he wanted until we were past the deadline for broadcast media." She sighed. "I'm putting in some hard time on the account, but the bonus will be nice. I can afford some nice things for the baby."

"Maybe we could go shopping," Gussie suggested. "At a reasonably priced store," she added on a soft, self-mocking laugh. "I'm going to be a doting grandmother, in case you wondered. I'm really looking forward to it. Some of my happiest times were spent just before and after you came along. Babies are so sweet."

"I can hardly wait," Bess admitted with a smile. "I'd better get back to work. Come and see me."

"Very soon," Gussie promised and rang off, leaving Bess wondering at Cade's attitude.

That night when she got off from work, very late,

after the office was empty, she set off across the dark parking lot with her heart in her throat.

This particular part of San Antonio wasn't the best place to be after dark. She wished she'd asked someone to stay with her, or that she'd had the foresight to move her car to the front of the office. Here she was, pregnant and alone, and what was she going to do if some mugger decided that she was fair game?

She looked around nervously as she heard voices, and all her nightmares seemed to converge as three teenagers in worn denims and old jackets, who were talking loudly as they came down the sidewalk.

Bess hoped that she could avoid trouble. She moved off the sidewalk and into the parking lot, her heart hammering under her beige linen dress. Surely they wouldn't bother her.

A wolf whistle came piercingly from behind her, followed by laughter and some remarks that made her face color. She quickened her pace, but behind her she heard footfalls and menacing whispers. *Oh, God, no,* she pleaded silently. Her car was still half the length of the parking lot away, and she was wearing high heels that were much too high for running.

"Don't run away," one of the boys drawled. He sounded drunk, which he probably was. "We won't hurt you, sweet thing."

"That's right, we just want to talk," a second boy agreed.

Bess turned, her purse tight under her arm, and stared at them with cold hauteur. "Leave me alone," she said quietly. "I don't want any trouble."

"Oh, neither do we," the taller of the three said,

laughing. He moved toward her, laughing even harder when she started to back away.

Bess was gathering her courage, her throat dry, when other footsteps came from behind her, quick, angry ones.

The boys apparently weren't too drunk to realize their sudden danger, because they scattered and ran for their lives. When Bess turned and saw Cade coming toward her, she couldn't blame them. Under the streetlights he was the picture of an old-time Texas cowboy, right down to the menacing pistol in one lean hand.

"Cade!" she burst out. She ran to him, all her pride and prejudice momentarily forgotten as she pressed hungrily into his arms and stood shaking against him.

"It's all right," he said huskily. He stuck the pistol back in his belt and held her. "You're safe, honey. Everything's all right now. They didn't hurt you, did they?"

"No, thanks to you," she said. She shivered, even though it was summertime and hot. Cade smelled of leather and dust and cattle, but the feel of him was sweet heaven. "I was stupid. I should have asked someone to stay over with me. I will next time."

"Let's get you home. I don't imagine your admirers will be back anytime soon," he mused, remembering with cold pleasure the fear he'd engendered. "Damned drunk kids."

"I don't guess they'd really have hurt me," she said, "but there were three of them and only one of me."

"Come on." He turned her and led her back toward where he'd left the pickup truck. His batwing chaps made leathery sounds as they walked, and she realized that he was in his working clothes.

"What are you doing here?" she asked.

"Watching you," he said. He glanced down at her. "I've been out here every night since you've had to stay over, just in case."

She could have cried at the protectiveness in his deep, slow voice. "That was kind of you," she said.

"I thought it was about time I tried being kind to you, Bess," he replied slowly. "I seem to have spent years cutting you to pieces." He opened the cab of the pickup and put her gently inside. "Mind the door," he said as he closed it.

He fastened her seat belt and then his before he cranked the truck and drove her back to her apartment house. "I'll drive you to work in the morning," he said. "Your car will be safe for tonight."

"Of course."

He got her inside and made a pot of coffee, then frowned as he poured it in the small kitchen. She changed into her gold-and-white caftan and sat down across the table from him.

"Should you have coffee?" he asked carefully, his dark eyes steady and quiet on her face.

"It's decaffeinated," she told him. "I don't drink a lot of it." She shifted, uneasy with him. "Thank you for what you did tonight."

"You're my responsibility," he said quietly. He looked into his coffee cup. "You're carrying my child."

She felt the pride and passion in the words and had to bite her tongue not to scream her anguish at him. Why didn't he go home to his redhead?

"How are things at Lariat?" she asked stiffly.

"Lonely." He smiled faintly, his eyes kindling as they slid over her flushed face and down to her mouth. "I don't guess you believe that, after the things I've said and done, but it's true. I don't sleep much these days."

She sipped her coffee, refusing to make any admissions. "I suppose your redhead sees to that," she replied with soft venom.

He searched her eyes quietly. "Stop and think for a minute," he said. "Despite what I said, and what you think, is it in my character?"

She blinked. "Is what in your character?"

"For me to go to some other woman while my child is growing in your body. For me to turn my back on you and sleep with someone else."

The thought hadn't really impinged on her consciousness before. Now she had to face it. She studied him for a long moment and knew that it wasn't in his character. Cade had integrity and he had honor.

"No," she said. "Even if you hated me, you'd have the divorce papers in hand before you'd start anything with another woman."

He smiled gently. "Good girl. Finish your coffee. You need some sleep."

She didn't understand him. Her lips touched the dark liquid briefly before she put the cup down. "Are you . . . are you going back to Lariat?" she asked.

He shook his head. He'd dropped the Stetson on the table, where it was still lying, dark and worn. "I'll sleep on the sofa. I can't leave you alone tonight, not after what happened. I'll be here if you get frightened in the night."

She bit her lower lip. He did care for her, in his way.

Perhaps if they hadn't had the past between them, their marriage might have worked. But he'd never felt that he was good enough for her, and she'd never felt that he wanted her, only an illusion of what she was.

"Thank you," she said simply as she got slowly to her feet. "I am . . . a little shaky."

"Can you dig me out a sheet?" he asked. "And a towel," he added with a rueful smile as he glanced down at himself. "I came straight from the holding pens. I could use a shower."

"Of course."

Why she should blush after weeks of marriage she didn't know. But thinking about Cade's lean, fit body without clothes made her tingle all over. She got him a towel and told him she'd thrown his clothes in the washer.

By the time he was through, wrapped up in her blue bath towel with his hair still damp, she had his clothes in the dryer.

He watched her spread the sheet over her sofa and put a pillow on the arm for him, her movements a little tremulous.

"Sorry," he murmured when she glanced at him shyly, "but unless you run to size thirty-two pajamas, I'm going to have to sleep raw."

She went red. "Oh."

His eyebrows arched and he chuckled with soft pleasure at the color in her cheeks. "Married and pregnant, and you can still look at me like that."

"I haven't ever felt that married," she hedged, averting her eyes. "So it's just as well you didn't contest the divorce."

"Oh, but I did," he replied lazily. "I had Donald stop it two weeks ago."

She knew she was gaping. Her eyes kindled with anger. "Well, he can just start it up again, Cade," she said shortly. "I've had it up to here with your stop-and-go attitude toward me and marriage, with your red-headed diversion, your bad temper, your condescending outlook, and . . . what are you doing?" She gasped.

He'd dropped the towel. His lips were pursed, his hands on his hips as he surveyed her embarrassment. "Just getting ready for bed, honey," he said pleasantly. "Go ahead. You were saying . . . ?"

"I can't talk to you like that!"

"Why not?" he asked.

She bit her lower lip and forced her eyes up to his amused dark face. She swallowed. "You threw me out because you thought I couldn't get pregnant . . . !" she accused miserably.

"And then I came up here and sat in restaurants and waited on street corners just for a glimpse of you," he mused gently. "I sat in your parking lot and watched you go to lunch with Nell. I sat in the parking lot where you live and watched you leave in the mornings for work and come home at night. My pride kept me from admitting what a fool I'd been, Bess, but it wasn't the baby that brought me back. It was the loneliness. I'd have told you that night at the restaurant that, if it came right down to it, I'd rather have you and me together for the rest of our lives than me and some other woman and a houseful of those kids I thought I couldn't live without." He shook his head. "Nobody else. Never. Only you, in my mind, in my heart. In my bed," he finished quietly.

She nibbled her lower lip, watching him. "And the redhead?"

He smiled lazily. "A dish, isn't she?" he murmured.

"Who is the redhead?" she asked, when something in his tone got through to her.

"Gretchen. She's Robert's fiancée, didn't I tell you . . . oof!"

She glared at him, watching with pure delight the shock in his eyes when her fist had connected with his diaphragm. "No, you didn't tell me, you conceited, overbearing, unfeeling—"

He stopped the tirade with his mouth, smiling against her soft, parted lips. He didn't touch her in any other way. He didn't have to. She hung there, her face lifted like a flower to the sun, her eyes squinting as they looked into his, her breath whispering in excited little flickers against his mouth.

"I love you," he whispered with aching softness. His teeth tugged gently at her lower lip and parted it as he bent again. "I wouldn't have minded if there could never have been a child. I don't want to live without you."

He said it with a stark simplicity that brought tears to her eyes. With a muffled sob she reached up to him and felt his arms gently enfold her. Her eyes closed as his mouth moved warmer, harder, against hers. Against her body she felt that sudden terrible need of his, felt him shiver with it.

She drew back a breath, searching his dark, quiet eyes. "I don't want to live without you either, Cade," she breathed.

His hands went to the buttons on either shoulder that held the caftan in place. "Let me love you," he whispered.

"Yes."

He eased the fabric away, his eyes slow and possessive on her swollen body, his hands tender as they traced every soft line of it.

"I want to know what the changes mean," he whispered huskily. "I want to know about this darkness"—his fingers touched her dusky nipples—"the swelling, the way it feels to have my baby inside you. . . . I want to know everything."

Her hands slid over his powerful thighs and up, watching him shudder without trying to hide the effect it had on him. "I want to know everything about you," she whispered. "I want to touch you."

He took her hands and guided them against his body, holding her gaze. "I could never do this before," he said quietly. "It was a hurdle I had to get over, letting you make the first move without feeling lessened as a man. I'm sorry I hurt your feelings about that night in my study. I wanted what you did to me, but it wounded my pride to admit it. I don't mind now." He bent and put his mouth gently on hers. "You can have me any way you want me, sweetheart," he whispered. "This is what married love should be. We'll learn it together."

She reached up to him, the last barriers down, the last inhibitions shattering as she realized just how far he was willing to go to make their marriage work. She smiled under his mouth and then she laughed, clinging to him as he lifted her and put her gently down the sofa.

"Here?" she whispered as he came down beside her, his hair-roughened muscles deliciously abrasive against her soft bareness.

"Why not?" he murmured dryly. "It's going to be a little crowded, but we'll manage . . . oh, yes," he whispered as he eased down over her, sparing her some of his weight as he shifted and moved into a sudden, stark intimacy with her willing body. His breath drew in sharply as he met her eyes, feeling her accept him easily, completely, in one long, slow movement that startled them both.

Her nails gripped him and he began to curve his body around hers in the old, familiar way, tenderly, his eyes steady and questioning.

"I don't want to hurt you," he whispered. His hips moved with sensual slowness. "Is this gentle enough, *amada*?"

Her body relaxed, cradling him, welcoming him. She touched his mouth with hers. "Yes. Oh, yes." Her arms slid around his broad shoulders and she felt the warm crush of him around her, over her, in a tender loving that she'd shared with him before.

Every motion was slow, exquisitely tender, every kiss softer than the one before. It was a kind of loving that brought every emotion, every nerve, every sense into play. She wept all through it, because the tenderness they gave each other was so beautiful. She watched him, adoring him while he whispered to her, soft words that increased the sweet tension spiraling upward. His hands trembled at the last, as he brought her hips up to his in one long, final shudder of feeling that burst from him in an anguished groan. She clung, her own body rippling with the same feverish completion, an agony of tenderness lifting them beyond anything she'd known with him before.

Her tears wet his cheek as it lay against hers, as his arms cradled her in the trembling aftermath.

"I don't know what we do together when we make love," he whispered wearily at her ear. "But whatever it is, it makes sex look like a pagan sacrifice by comparison. I can't believe the way I feel when it's over. As if I've touched you in ways that have nothing to do with the body at all."

"I know." She smoothed his damp hair and kissed his closed eyelids. "And as close as we are, it still isn't quite close enough," she whispered, smiling. "Oh, I do love you so, Cade."

"I love you just as much." His mouth brushed hers and he sighed gently, adoring her with his possessive gaze. "Well, so much for restraint," he mused, looking down their locked bodies. "I had planned to start courting you again. Flowers, fancy dinners, phone calls at two in the morning . . . all those romantic evenings. And here you fling yourself at me the first night and drag me into bed with you."

She lifted her eyebrows. "It is not a bed. It's a sofa."

"I want to live with you," he said, the quick humor fading away. "I want to take care of you and our child."

"Then I'll come home," she said simply. "Because I want to take care of you, too." She brushed her mouth softly against his nose. "I've never felt so alone."

"Neither have I." He sighed against her mouth. "Next time you decide to seduce me in the office," he whispered, "why don't you try bending me back over the desk."

She laughed under his hard mouth until the warm hunger kindled in her blood again. She moved, and he moved, and the laughter melted into something slower and sweeter altogether.

"Cade," she asked a long time later when they were curled up in bed together, "you never told me about my ring."

"Didn't I?" He was smoking a cigarette in the warm darkness. "Well, it belonged to my grandfather. It was given to him by his father, who married a Spanish grandee's daughter and lived very happily on the Spanish land grant that became Lariat. My grandfather gave it to his wife, Desiree, who was French. He used to show it to me when I was a boy and talk about the old days, when his wife was still alive. About the money and the cattle and the politics. He fed me dreams, and I had so little else that I ate them up. Those were raw, bad years when I was a kid. By the time Gary and Robert came along, things were a little better. But I got so damned tired of dressing in rags and being laughed at because my dad couldn't open his mouth without being profane or obscene and because he was forever getting into fights with people and landing in jail." He sighed heavily. "Bess, I wanted respectability. At first I convinced myself that that was why I wanted you."

"Yes," she said, "I had that figured out by myself. You wanted a rich debutante. I knew that it was the illusion you saw sometimes, not me."

"That might have been true at first." He drew her closer. "But after we got to know each other, especially after the day you let me make love to you completely, I forgot every motive I'd had. You loved me.

That became my strength. Lariat became less important to me, and you became more important. But I didn't realize what marriage was going to mean, that it was a two-way street. I took you down to Lariat, where we had no privacy, tossed you headfirst into my world, and left you to make adjustments. I couldn't cope with the togetherness because it meant sharing my deepest feelings."

"It was hard for me too."

"Not as hard as it was for me," he mused. "I never had shared them before, with anyone. And then you came into my study one night and made me notice you. My God," he breathed, "I never dreamed it could be like that between us! I get aroused every time I think about it. But I lost control and it shook me up, really shook me up. I was trying to cope with hurt pride, and then you told me you were barren. God forgive me, I went to pieces inside at the thought that there wouldn't be any children."

"I should have told you in the beginning," she said. "I didn't have the right to keep it from you."

"No, you should have told me that it was the accident that caused it," he said quietly. "I'd never have said a word, not if I'd had to bite my tongue off. You let me think that it had been a long-standing condition, and it was the thought of being lied to that hurt." He pressed his lips down gently on her forehead. "The day I let you go, I knew I'd made the biggest mistake of my life. But there was the matter of bending my pride enough to get you back, and before I could do it, the blessed sheriff was serving me with divorce papers."

"I was trying to be noble," she pointed out, "letting

you go so that you could find a nubile redhead to give you—"

His mouth cut her off, moving subtly on her soft lips. "Shut up," he whispered.

"Yes, Cade."

"I don't want a nubile redhead, or any other color head except yours," he said. "I love you. We'd have adopted children if that was the only way. And if this child is all we ever have, that's fine with me. I want you. With or without kids, with or without Lariat, with or without anything else. Bess, you're my heart," he whispered huskily. "You're my whole heart, honey."

She turned and pressed hard against him, tears stinging her eyes. "You're my world, Cade."

He kissed the tears away. "I'm sorry I gave you such a hard time. I'll make it up to you, somehow, some way. If it helps, I was just as miserable as you were."

She smiled. "Yes, we . . . oh!"

"What is it?" He put out the cigarette and turned on the bedside light, his face a study in quick concern. "Are you all right? I didn't hurt you when we made love . . . ?"

She was breathless with delight. She pulled aside the caftan to put his hand on her stomach. She pressed it down at one side and held it there, and then he felt it. The hard, quick flutter against his hand.

The look on his face was almost comical. It went from shock to awed delight, to wonder, and then to pure arrogance.

"He's strong," he whispered huskily. "I didn't know they moved this soon."

"Oh, yes," she laughed. "I've felt it for over a week now. Cade, isn't it a miracle?"

His hand smoothed over the soft mound. "It's a miracle all right. You never did explain it to me."

She did, mentioning what the doctor had said about the necessary combination for conception.

"They told you that your husband would have to be very potent for you to conceive?" he murmured with pride.

She colored. "Indeed they did, and you must be," she whispered. She pressed his fingers hard against their child. "Cade, we made a baby," she breathed, the wonder of it in her tone.

His eyes darkened. He bent and put his mouth softly over hers. "I feel just as awed as you do by it," he whispered. "Men don't think about babies when they're having sex. Not usually. But I thought about it every time with you. We give each other so much when we love. The baby is the proof of it, of what we feel for each other."

"That he is. I think he's going to be a boy," she said drowsily. She snuggled close with a long sigh as he reached for the light and turned it out. "Have you thought about names?" she murmured.

"Plenty of time for that, Mrs. Hollister," he murmured, smiling against her forehead as he pulled her closer. "Go to sleep."

"I like Quinn . . ."

"Quinn Alexander," he murmured.

She smiled. Trust Cade to give an imposing name like that to a little baby, she thought, and closed her eyes on the thought that it was just the right name for the heir of Lariat.

Chapter 22

Bess walked down the long airport concourse feeling as if she was walking on air. It had been a long two days, and she was tired, even if she did have a sense of accomplishment from her trip. She'd sold the account, and it would mean a big bonus. She knew just who she was going to spend it on too.

She smoothed her neat beige suit and adjusted the matching scarf, sure that she looked younger than her thirty years made her feel. Her bright dark eyes and lush, waving honey-brown hair and radiant smile caught the eye of a man on the aisle, who leaned back against one of the pillars and stared at her with open delight.

Her dark eyes spared him a glance. He was a dish. Tall, powerfully muscled, dressed in a very becoming

Western-cut suit in a light tan, with matching boots and a Stetson cocked over one eye. He made her knees wobble with that slow, sensual stare.

"Hello, pretty thing," he murmured in a deep Texas drawl. "Looking for trouble?"

She darted a mischievous eye at him. "And if I am?"

"Well, here it comes."

And he stood aside to let a small, dark-haired version of himself fling his small body at her, shouting, "Mommy, what did you bring me?" at the top of his six-year-old lungs.

"Quinn!" She laughed and dropped to her knees to meet the onrush, barely retaining her balance as she was overwhelmed by her son. Quinn Alexander had been something of a present, born on her twenty-fourth birthday. He still was a small surprise package.

"Careful, tiger," Cade chuckled. "Don't knock Mommy down."

"Mommy's very strong, thank you." She grinned up at him. She stood up with Quinn in her arms, ignoring his questions long enough to kiss his father with two days' loneliness in her warm mouth. "I missed you," she whispered huskily.

He kissed her hungrily, oblivious of curious stares from passersby, his mouth smiling warmly against hers. "Two nights is too long," he whispered. "Next time Quinn and I are going along." He lifted their son out of her arms. "We'd better get sweetheart here home. He's already turned two vendors gray-haired."

"My daddy's big as a bear," Quinn told his mother seriously as he held her hand and Cade's on the way out of the airport. "Jenny says there's a bear in her backyard, and it ate her dog."

"Her dog ran away to keep from having bows tied on his tail," Cade whispered over Quinn's head, and Bess laughed.

"What did you bring me, Mommy?" Quinn moaned. "I've been ever so good, haven't I, Dad?"

"That he has," his father had to admit, his dark eyes beaming down on their son. "He helped me pay bills this morning."

"I can imagine how. Have you heard from Mama?"

"She and your new stepfather are still on their honeymoon in Nassau. My mother wants us to come down to her house for lunch tomorrow."

"How about Gary and Robert?"

"They're sailing in the Gulf, as usual, with their wives." Cade sighed. "My God, I'm the only working man left in the family."

"They signed over their interest in Lariat when you bought them out year before last, darling," Bess reminded him. "They're making enough at their respective jobs to enjoy an occasional vacation."

"I guess so. How was the presentation?" he asked with a smile.

His pride in her work never ceased to amaze her. She'd always thought him a particularly chauvinistic kind of man before they married, but he'd been supportive and had encouraged her at her job. She was already in the job Julie had once occupied. Julie herself was an executive vice president. Nell was married —to Mr. Ryker, for five years now, and they had two children.

"The presentation was a great success. But it's going to be my last one for a while," she said, smiling up at him while they tried to keep their son from taking their hands in opposite directions on the way to the car. "I want to take it easy for a few months."

"Okay. If you want a vacation, we could—"

She glanced up at him dryly. "Cade, it isn't exactly going to be a vacation," she began. "Didn't you say six years ago that you'd manage with just one heir?"

He stopped, staring at her over their son's head. "Bess, you know what the doctors said. Once was a miracle . . ."

"So what is twice?" she asked, and tears of unbounded joy touched her eyelashes. "I fainted at the presentation," she whispered. "They got a doctor for me." She laughed through watery sniffles. "I'm pregnant!"

"God." He drew her close, wrapping her up against him, his free arm around his son, who was looking up curiously at them. "God, what a homecoming present," he whispered with the breath knocked out of him as he stared down at her with aching tenderness and love.

"I want a girl this time," she said laughing. She smiled down at young Quinn and touched his face gently. "We're going to have a new baby, young man," she told him. "And you and Daddy and I will take very good care of her."

"Him," Quinn said. "I want a baby brother."

"I'll settle for whatever I get, and so will you," Cade told him with a chuckle. He ruffled the hair that was already as dark as his own. "Although you were and are the light of my life, young man."

"I'm not a light," Quinn muttered grumpily.

Bess bent to kiss him. She looked up at Cade with a radiance in her eyes that almost blinded him.

"Six wonderful years," she whispered. "And now this. It's scary, so much happiness."

"Scary," he agreed. He sighed heavily. "I never dreamed we'd have two of them. A matched set. Our mothers will be ecstatic."

"Yes. They're better friends than ever these days."

"Because Gussie told mother the truth finally," he added. "I had to browbeat her into it, but I told her that secrets were much more damaging than the truth was. So she gave in, years too late. Mother already knew that Dad was a philanderer."

Bess's lips parted. She remembered what Elise had told her, but she hadn't let Cade know. She had to pretend surprise. "She knew about your father's affairs?"

"That's right. Someone had told her long ago. She pretended that she didn't know in order to protect Gary and Robert and me." He looked down at Quinn contemplatively. "I guess we'll be doing similar things for him, when he's older. And for this other one," he said softly, touching her belly.

"What other one?" Quinn frowned.

"The one who's going to look like you," his mother told him. She brushed back his unruly hair. "Your brother or sister."

"Where is she?" Quinn asked, looking around.

"Well?" Bess asked, lifting her eyebrows at Cade.

He cleared his throat and looked uncomfortable. "We'll talk about it at home, son," he said, glancing around them at the crowd of people. "Where we left that chocolate ice cream we had—"

"—for breakfast." Quinn nodded. "It was good, wasn't it, Daddy? And the cake—"

"Cake!" Bess exclaimed, wide-eyed. "You fed our child cake for breakfast?!"

"Well, ice cream too." He shrugged. "Honest to God, honey, you know I can't cook!"

"Cake and ice cream!"

"Chocolate." Quinn grinned. He pulled at her hand. "Let's go home, Mommy, and you can have some too."

"Not for lunch." Cade shuddered. "We'll eat the rest of the cookies instead," he added with a grin at Bess.

"I can see that I didn't come back a minute too soon," she said. "We'll stop by the store on the way home and get some ham and some salad fixings. . . ."

"Yuch!" Quinn said. "Me and Daddy don't want that awful stuff."

Cade looked at Bess and smiled slowly. "Yes, we do," he said. He pulled Bess close against his side. "As long as Mommy's here to fix it for us. Right?"

"Right." Quinn sighed. He winked up at his mother. She tightened her hold on his small hand as Cade guided them out of the terminal into the bright summer day. As Bess lifted her soft, dark eyes to her husband's, the radiance in her face made him catch his breath.

"Is something wrong?" she asked softly.

He laughed at his own reaction to her. He was denim to her lace, he thought, studying her. But in all the important ways, all the good ways, they were as alike as two people could get.

"No," he said, smiling slowly. "Nothing's wrong. Nothing at all." He linked his fingers into hers and lifted Quinn Alexander Hollister in his arms to carry him across the street. And his thoughts were warm and satisfying.

Praise for Harry Turtledove's
WORLDWAR:
IN THE BALANCE

"Readers will have a perfectly delightful time . . . Turtledove's storytelling and historiography now march in perfect step. World War II buffs will have a particular romp . . . But the readership will be much wider than this, and all will be glad that Turtledove plans three more volumes in *Worldwar*."
—*Chicago Sun-Times*

"Totally fascinating . . . With this engrossing volume, Turtledove launches a four-book alternate-history saga, possibly the most ambitious in the subgenre's history and definitely the work of one of alternate history's authentic modern masters."
—*Booklist*

"I literally could not put *Worldwar: In the Balance* down. I carried it with me to the doctor's office and to a dinner date the day it arrived! The novel is a tour de force in three acts."
—S. M. STIRLING

"A fast-paced, suspenseful work."
—*Chicago Tribune*

By Harry Turtledove
Published by Ballantine Books:

The Videssos Cycle:
   THE MISPLACED LEGION
   AN EMPEROR FOR THE LEGION
   THE LEGION OF VIDESSOS
   SWORDS OF THE LEGION

The Tale of Krispos:
   KRISPOS RISING
   KRISPOS OF VIDESSOS
   KRISPOS THE EMPEROR

The Time of Troubles:
   THE STOLEN THRONE
   HAMMER AND ANVIL *(forthcoming)*

NONINTERFERENCE
A WORLD OF DIFFERENCE
KALEIDOSCOPE
EARTHGRIP
DEPARTURES

THE GUNS OF THE SOUTH

WORLDWAR: IN THE BALANCE
WORLDWAR: TILTING THE BALANCE
WORLDWAR: UPSETTING THE BALANCE
WORLDWAR: FINDING THE BALANCE *(forthcoming)*

WORLDWAR: TILTING THE BALANCE

Harry Turtledove

A Del Rey® Book
BALLANTINE BOOKS • NEW YORK

A Del Rey® Book
Published by Ballantine Books

Copyright © 1995 by Harry Turtledove

All rights reserved under International and Pan-American Copyright Conventions. Published in the United States by Ballantine Books, a division of Random House, Inc., New York, and simultaneously in Canada by Random House of Canada Limited, Toronto.

Library of Congress Catalog Card Number: 95-92523

ISBN 0-345-38998-0

Manufactured in the United States of America

First Hardcover Edition: March 1995
First Mass Market Edition: February 1996

10 9 8 7 6 5 4 3 2 1

DRAMATIS PERSONAE

(Characters with names in CAPS are historical, others fictional)

HUMANS

ANIELEWICZ, MORDECHAI — *Leader of Jewish fighters in Poland*

Auerbach, Rance — *Captain, U.S. Army Cavalry*

Bagnall, George — *Flight engineer, RAF*

Barisha — *Tavern keeper in Split, Independent State of Croatia*

Berkowicz, Stefan — *Landlord in Lodz*

BLAIR, ERIC — *BBC talks producer, Indian Section, London*

Borcke, Martin — *Wehrmacht captain and interpreter in Pskov*

CHILL, KURT — *Wehrmacht lieutenant general, 122nd Infantry, in Pskov*

CHURCHILL, WINSTON — *Prime Minister, Great Britain*

COMPTON, ARTHUR — *Nuclear physicist with the Metallurgical Laboratory*

Cooley, Mary — *Waitress in Idaho Springs, Colorado*

Daniels, Pete ("Mutt") — *Sergeant, U.S. Army, in Illinois; former minor-league manager*

DIEBNER, KURT — *Nuclear physicist, Hechingen, Germany*

Donlan, Kevin — *U.S. Army private in Illinois*

Embry, Ken — *Pilot, RAF*

FERMI, ENRICO — *Nuclear physicist with the Metallurgical Laboratory*

FERMI, LAURA — *Enrico Fermi's wife*

Fiore, Bobby — *Lizard experimental subject; former baseball player*

1

FLEROV, GEORGI   *Soviet nuclear physicist*
Fritzie   *Cowboy in Chugwater,*
                        Wyoming
Fukuoka, Yoshi   *Japanese soldier in China*
GERMAN, ALEKSANDR   *Commander of Second*
                        Partisan Brigade in
                        Pskov
Goldfarb, David   *Radarman, RAF*
Gorbunova, Ludmila   *Pilot, Red Air Force*
GROVES, LESLIE   *Engineer; U.S. Army*
                        colonel
Harvey   *Civilian guard in Idaho*
                        Springs, Colorado
HEISENBERG, WERNER   *Nuclear physicist in*
                        Hechingen, Germany
Henry   *Wounded U.S. soldier in*
                        Chicago
Hexham   *U.S. Army colonel in*
                        Denver
Hicks, Chester   *U.S. Army lieutenant in*
                        Chicago
Higuchi   *Japanese scientist*
Hipple, Fred   *RAF group captain in*
                        Bruntingthorpe
HO-T'ING, NIEH   *Chinese Communist*
                        guerrilla officer
Horton, Leo   *RAF radarman in*
                        Bruntingthorpe
HULL, CORDELL   *U.S. Secretary of State*
Isaac   *Jew in Leczna, Poland*
Jacobi, Nathan   *BBC broadcaster in London*
Jäger, Heinrich   *Wehrmacht panzer colonel*
Jones, Jerome   *RAF radarman*
Karpov, Feofan   *Red Air Force colonel*
Kennan, Maurice   *RAF flight lieutenant in*
                        Bruntingthorpe
Klein, Sid   *U.S. Army captain in*
                        Chicago
Klopotowski, Roman   *Townsman in Leczna,*
                        Poland
Klopotowski, Zofia   *Daughter of Roman*
                        Klopotowski

KONIEV, IVAN	Red Army general
KURCHATOV, IGOR	Soviet nuclear physicist
Laplace, Freddie	U.S. Army private in Illinois
Larssen, Barbara	see Yeager, Barbara
Larssen, Jens	Nuclear physicist with the Metallurgical Laboratory
Leon	Jewish fighter in Lodz
Lidov, Boris	NKVD lieutenant-colonel in Moscow
Liu Han	Chinese peasant woman; Lizard experimental subject
Lo	Communist Chinese partisan
Maczek	U.S. Army captain in Illinois
Meinecke, Klaus	Sergeant; gunner on Heinrich Jäger's panzer
MOLOTOV, VYACHESLAV	Foreign Commissar, USSR
Morozkin, Sergei	Red Army interpreter in Pskov
MURROW, EDWARD R.	Radio news broadcaster
Nakayama	Japanese scientist
NISHINA, YOSHIO	Japanese nuclear physicist
Okamoto	Japanese Army major; interpreter and translator
Olson, Louise	Inhabitant of New Salem, North Dakota
Olson, Thorkil	Inhabitant of New Salem, North Dakota
Oscar	U.S. Army bodyguard in Denver
Peary, Julian	RAF wing commander in Bruntingthorpe
Petrovic, Marko	Captain, Independent State of Croatia
Potter, Lucille	Nurse in Illinois
RIBBENTROP, JOACHIM VON	German foreign minister
ROOSEVELT, FRANKLIN D.	President of the United States

Roundbush, Basil — *RAF flight officer in Bruntingthorpe*

RUMKOWSKI, MORDECHAI CHAIM — *Eldest of the Jews in the Lodz ghetto*

Russie, Moishe — *Former medical student; leader among Polish Jews; fugitive*

Russie, Reuven — *Son of Moishe and Rivka Russie*

Russie, Rivka — *Moishe Russie's wife*

Sawatski, Emilia — *Wife of Wladyslaw Sawatski*

Sawatski, Ewa — *Daughter of Wladyslaw and Emilia Sawatski*

Sawatski, Jozef — *Son of Wladyslaw and Emilia Sawatski*

Sawatski, Maria — *Daughter of Wladyslaw and Emilia Sawatski*

Sawatski, Wladyslaw — *Polish farmer*

Schultz, Georg — *Former Wehrmacht panzer gunner; Red Air Force mechanic*

Sharp, Hiram — *Physician in Ogden, Utah*

Shmuel — *Jewish fighter in Lodz*

Sholudenko, Nikifor — *NKVD man in the Ukraine*

Shura — *Whore in Shanghai*

SKORZENY, OTTO — *SS colonel*

Sobieski, Tadeusz — *Grocer in Leczna, Poland*

STALIN, IOSEF — *General Secretary of the Communist Party of the Soviet Union*

Sumner, Joshua ("Hoot") — *Justice of the peace in Chugwater, Wyoming*

Szabo, Bela ("Dracula") — *U.S. Army private in Illinois*

SZILARD, LEO — *Nuclear physicist with the Metallurgical Laboratory*

Tatiana — *Sniper and companion of Jerome Jones in Pskov*

TOGO, SHIGENORI — *Japanese foreign minister*

Tolya — *Groundcrew man, Red Air Force*

Tsuye — *Japanese scientist*

Ussishkin, Judah	*Doctor in Leczna, Poland*
Ussishkin, Sarah	*Wife of Judah Ussishkin; midwife in Leczna, Poland*
van Alen, Jacob	*U.S. Coast Guard lieutenant in Oswego, New York*
VASILIEV, NIKOLAI	*Commander, First Partisan Brigade in Pskov*
Vernon, Hank	*Ship's engineer in the Duluth Queen*
Victor	*Wounded U.S. soldier in Chicago*
Whyte, Alf	*RAF navigator*
Wittman, Rolf	*Driver in Heinrich Jäger's panzer*
Yeager, Barbara	*Former graduate student in medieval literature; Sam Yeager's wife*
Yeager, Sam	*U.S. Army corporal; liaison with Lizard POWs; former baseball player*
ZHUKOV, GEORGI	*Marshal of the Soviet Union*

THE RACE

Atvar	*Fleetlord, conquest fleet of the Race*
Bunim	*Official in Lodz*
Drefsab	*Intelligence agent and ginger addict*
Forssis	*Landcruiser gunner in Besançon, France*
Hessef	*Landcruiser driver in Besançon, France*
Ianxx	*Officer in Shanghai*
Kassnass	*Landcruiser unit commander in Besançon, France*
Kirel	*Shiplord of the 127th Emperor Hetto*

Nejas	*Landcruiser commander in Besançon, France*
Nossat	*Psychologist*
Ristin	*Lizard POW with the Metallurgical Laboratory*
Sherran	*The first male to circumnavigate Home*
Skoob	*Landcruiser gunner in Besançon, France*
Ssamraff	*Investigator in China*
Starraf	*Researcher in China*
Straha	*Shiplord of the 206th Emperor Yower*
Teerts	*POW in Japan*
Tessrek	*Psychologist*
Ttomalss	*Researcher in China*
Tvenkel	*Landcruiser gunner in Besançon, France*
Ullhass	*Lizard POW with the Metallurgical Laboratory*
Ussmak	*Landcruiser driver in Besançon, France*

For nostalgia's sake, Fleetlord Atvar called up the hologram of the Tosevite warrior he had often studied before the invasion fleet actually reached the world of Tosev 3. Nostalgia was an emotion that came easily to the Race: with a unified history of a hundred thousand years, with an empire that stretched over three solar systems and now reached out to a fourth, the past seemed a safe, comfortable place, not least because it was so much like the present.

The hologram sprang into being before the fleetlord: a stalwart savage, his pinkish face sprouting yellowish hairs, clad in soft iron mail and woven animal and plant fibers, armed with spear and rust-flecked sword, and mounted on a Tosevite quadruped that looked distinctly too scrawny for the job of carrying him.

Sighing, Atvar turned to the shiplord Kirel, who commanded the *127th Emperor Hetto*, bannership of the invasion fleet. He stabbed a fingerclaw at the image. "If only it had been so easy," he said with a sigh.

"Yes, Exalted Fleetlord." Kirel sighed, too. He turned both eye turrets toward the hologram. "It *was* what the probe led us to expect."

"Yes," Atvar said sourly. Preparing in its methodical way for another conquest, the Race had sent a probe across the interstellar void sixteen hundred years before (years of the Race, of course; Tosev 3 orbited its primary only about half as fast). The probe dutifully sampled the planet, sent its images and data back Home. The Race prepared the invasion fleet and sent it out, certain of easy victory: how much could a world change in a mere sixteen hundred years?

7

Atvar touched a control in the base of the holographic projector. The Tosevite warrior disappeared. New images took the Big Ugly's place: a Russki landcruiser, red star painted on its turret, lightly armed and protected by the Race's standards but well-designed, with sloped armor and wide treads for getting over the worst ground; an American heavy machine gun, with a belt full of big slugs that tore through body armor as if it were fiberboard; a Deutsch killercraft, turbojets slung under swept wings, nose bristling with cannon.

Kirel pointed toward the killercraft. "That one concerns me more than either of the others, Exalted Fleetlord. By the Emperor"—both he and Atvar briefly cast down their eyes at the mention of the sovereign—"the Deutsche did not have that aircraft less than two years ago, when our campaign began."

"I know," Atvar said. "All their aircraft—all Tosevite aircraft then—were those slow, awkward things propelled by rapidly rotating airfoils. But now the British are flying jets, too."

He summoned an image of the new British killercraft. It didn't look as menacing as the machine the Deutsche made: its wings lacked sweep and its lines were more graceful, less predatory. From the reports Atvar had read, it didn't perform quite as well as the Deutsch killercraft, either. But it was a quantum leap better than anything the British had put into the air before.

Fleetlord and shiplord stared glumly at the hologram. The trouble with the natives of Tosev 3 was that they were, by the Race's standards, insanely inventive. The social scientists attached to the fleet were still trying to figure out how the Big Uglies had gone from barbarism to a full-grown industrial civilization in the blink of an historical eye. Their solutions—or rather, conjectures—had yet to satisfy Atvar.

Part of the answer, he suspected, lay in the squabbling multiplicity of empires that divided up Tosev 3's meager land surface. Some of them weren't even empires in the strict sense of the word; the regime of the SSSR, for instance, openly boasted of liquidating its former ruling dynasty. The idea of impericide was enough to make Atvar queasy.

Empires and not-empires had competed fiercely among themselves. They'd been fighting a planetwide war when the Race arrived. Doctrine from earlier conquests said the Race ought to have been able to take advantage of their factionalism, play off one side against another. The tactic had worked

now and again, but not as well and not as often as doctrine suggested it would.

Atvar sighed and told Kirel, "Before I came to Tosev 3, I was like any sensible male: I was sure doctrine held all the answers. Follow it and you'd obtain the results it predicted. The males who designed our doctrines should have seen this world first; it would have broadened their horizons."

"This is truth, Exalted Fleetlord," the shiplord said. "One thing Tosev 3 has taught us is the difference between precept and experience."

"Yes. Well put," Atvar said. The last world conquest the Race had undertaken lay thousands of years in the past. The fleetlord had pored over the manuals of what had worked then, and in the Race's previous victory, even more thousands of years before that. But no one living had any practice using what was in the manuals.

The Tosevites, by contrast, conquered one another and dickered with one another all the time. They made deception and deceit into an art, and were perfectly willing to educate the Race as to their use. Atvar had learned the hard way how much—or rather, how little—Big Ugly promises were worth.

"The other trouble is, they make war the same way they conduct the rest of their dealings with us: they cheat," Atvar grumbled.

"Truth again, Exalted Fleetlord," Kirel said.

The fleetlord knew it was truth. Machine against machine, the Big Uglies could not match the Race: one landcruiser Atvar commanded, for instance, was worth anywhere between ten and thirty of its Tosevite opponents. The Big Uglies fought back with everything from mine-carrying animals trained to run under landcruiser tracks to set off their explosives to attacks that concentrated so many of their inferior weapons against the Race's thin-stretched resources that they achieved breakthrough in spite of lower technology.

Kirel might have plucked that thought from Atvar's head. "Will we resume our assault on the city by the lake in the northern section of the smaller continental mass? Chicago, the local name is."

"Not immediately," Atvar answered, trying to keep from his voice all the frustration he felt at the failure. Taking advantage of Tosev 3's truly abominable winter weather, the Americans had broken through the flanks of the assault force, cut off the

lead element, and wrecked most of it. It was the worst—and most expensive—embarrassment the Race had suffered on Tosev 3.

"We do not enjoy as many resources as we would like," Kirel observed.

Now Atvar had to say, "Truth." The Race was careful and thorough: the weapons they'd brought from Home would have conquered a hundred times over the Tosev 3 they thought they would find, very possibly without losing a male. But on the industrialized planet they discovered, they'd taken major losses. They'd inflicted far worse, but the Big Uglies' factories kept turning out weapons.

"We need to keep working to co-opt as much of their industrial capacity as we can," Kirel said, "and to wreck that part which persists in producing arms used against us."

"Unfortunately, the two goals often contradict each other," Atvar said. "Nor is our progress in destroying their fuel sources as great as they would wish us to believe, though we persist in those efforts."

The three males who had bombed the refineries at Ploesti, which supplied the Deutsche with much of their fuel, were convinced they'd wrecked the place. Since then, a pall of smoke had continuously lain over it, making reconnaissance difficult.

For as long as he could—for longer than he should have—Atvar believed with his pilots that that smoke meant the Deutsche could not control the refinery fires. But it wasn't so; he couldn't make himself think it was any more. The Big Uglies were shipping refined petroleum out of Ploesti every way they knew how: by water, by their battered rail network, by motorized conveyance, even by animal-drawn wagon.

The story wasn't much different at the other refinery complexes scattered across Tosev 3. They were easy to damage, hard to eliminate; since they were huge fire hazards just by existing, the Big Uglies had built them to minimize danger from explosions. They ferociously defended them and repaired bomb damage faster than the Race's alleged experts had thought possible.

Atvar's phone squawked at him. He welcomed the distraction from his own gloomy thoughts. "Yes?" he said into the speaker.

"Exalted Fleetlord, the male Drefsab awaits your pleasure in the antechamber," an aide reported.

"I am still conferring with the shiplord Kirel," Atvar said. "Tell Drefsab I shall see him directly when I'm finished."

"It shall be done, Exalted Fleetlord." The aide switched off.

Being reminded of Drefsab did nothing to improve Atvar's mood. "There's something else that hasn't worked as well as I'd hoped," he complained.

"What's that, Exalted Fleetlord?" Kirel asked.

"The whole problem with that vile Tosevite herb, ginger," Atvar said. "Drefsab recently tracked down and eliminated the Big Ugly who was a major supplier of the horrid drug, and I had hoped that would help us control our addicted males' demand for it. Unfortunately, a thicket of smaller dealers has sprung up to take the exterminated major supplier's place."

"Frustrating," Kirel observed, "to say nothing of dangerous to our cause."

Atvar swung one eye turret toward Kirel in a sidelong glance of suspicion. The commander of the bannership was the second highest ranking male in the fleet, his body paint less elaborate only than Atvar's own. If Atvar's policies led to disaster, he was the next logical choice as fleetlord. He was stable and conservative and had always acted loyal, but who could say when the fangs of ambition would begin to gnaw? Any remark that sounded like criticism made Atvar wary.

Not that ginger wasn't a problem. *One more thing we didn't learn from the probe,* Atvar thought. The cursed herb made males feel they were brighter and stronger than they really were; it also made them want to recapture that feeling as often as they could. They'd do almost anything to get ginger, even trade weapons and information to the Big Uglies.

"With the problem ginger poses to our security, it occurs to me that we may have been lucky the Big Uglies succeeded in blowing up the ship which carried the bulk of our nuclear weapons," the fleetlord said. "Otherwise, some male seeking pleasure for his tongue might have sought to convey one to the Tosevites in exchange for his precious herb."

"There's a pleasant thought!" Kirel exclaimed. "The Tosevites are barbarians without care for tomorrow—they would not hesitate to ruin their own planet if it meant defeating us."

"Truth," Atvar said glumly. After initial in-atmosphere bursts to wreck Tosevite communications with electromagnetic

pulse (unsuccessfully, because the Big Uglies' electronic devices were too primitive to use solid-state components), the Race had expended only two nuclear devices: against Berlin and Washington, centers of local resistance. But resistance had continued anyhow.

"Ironic that we have a greater obligation to maintain this world as nearly intact as possible than does the species that evolved on it," Kirel said. "Of course, the Tosevites are not aware our colonization fleet is on the way behind us."

"Indeed," Atvar said. "If it arrives and finds Tosev 3 uninhabitable, we will have failed here, no matter what else we accomplish."

"We also have to bear in mind that the Big Uglies are engaging in nuclear weapons research of their own, certainly with the material their guerrillas captured from us in the SSSR and, the evidence would suggest, with projects altogether their own as well," Kirel said. "Should one of those projects succeed, our problems here will become measurably more difficult."

"Immeasurably, you mean," Atvar said. The Big Uglies would not worry about what they did to Tosev 3, as long as that meant getting rid of the Race. "Deutschland, the SSSR, the United States, maybe those little island empires, too—Nippon and Britain—we have to keep both eye turrets on every one of them. The trouble is, a planet is a very large place. Their projects will not be easy to track down. But it must be done." He spoke as much to remind himself as to tell Kirel.

"It shall be done," the shiplord echoed loyally.

It had better be done, they thought together.

The horse-drawn wagon pulled to a stop in New Salem, North Dakota. Sam Yeager looked around. As a seventeen-year veteran of bush-league baseball and its endless travel, he was a connoisseur of small towns. New Salem might have had a thousand people in it; then again, it might not.

He scrambled out of the wagon. Barbara Larssen handed him his Springfield. He took the rifle, slung it over his shoulder, then held out a hand to help Barbara down. They clung to each other for a moment. He kissed the top of her head. The ends of her dark blond hair still showed traces of permanent wave. Most of it was straight, though; a long time had gone by since she'd got a permanent.

He didn't want to let her go, but he had to. He grabbed the rifle again, pointed it at the wagon. *Military routine,* he thought, and then, *military fiddlesticks.* But since he wore a corporal's stripes these days, he played the game by the rules. "Come on out, boys," he called.

Ristin and Ullhass, the two Lizard POWs who accompanied the Metallurgical Laboratory's wagon train on the way from Chicago to the Lab's planned new home in Denver, poked their heads up over the side of the wagon. "It shall be done, superior sir," they chorused in hissing English. They dropped down in front of Yeager and Barbara.

"Hard to think—things—so small could be so dangerous," Barbara murmured. Neither of the Lizards came up even to her shoulder.

"They aren't small with guns in their hands, or inside tanks, or inside planes, or inside their spaceships," Yeager answered. "I fought against them, remember, before my unit captured these boys."

"We thought you kill us," Ullhass said.

"We thought you kill us, then eat us," Ristin agreed.

Yeager laughed. "You'd been reading too much science fiction, both of you." He laughed again, more reflectively. If he hadn't been in the habit of reading science fiction himself to pass the time on trains and buses, he never would have volunteered—or been accepted—as the Lizards' principal guard, translator, and explainer of matters Earthly.

He'd been with them continuously for better than six months now, long enough to come to see them as individuals rather than mere creatures. They never had been much like the bug-eyed monsters he used to read about. They were short and skinny and, even dressed in multiple layers of warm clothes that hung on them like sacks, complained all the time about how cold it was (it wasn't just midwinter on the northern Great Plains, either; they'd complained about all but the hottest days back in Chicago, too).

By now, Yeager took for granted their turreted eyes that, chameleonlike, moved independently of each other, the green-brown scales they used for skin, their clawed hands and feet, their wide mouths full of little pointed teeth. Even the bifurcated tongues they sometimes used to lick their hard, immobile lips were just part of them, although he'd needed quite a while to get used to those.

"We will be warm tonight?" Ristin asked. Though he spoke English, at the end of the sentence he tacked on the little cough the Lizards used: sort of an audible question mark.

"We will be warm tonight," Sam answered in the Lizards' language, punctuating his sentence with a different cough, the one that put emphasis on his words.

He had reason for his confidence. The Lizards' bombers hadn't hit North Dakota badly: not much up here needed hitting, Yeager thought. The flat farming country reminded him of the flat farming country in eastern Nebraska where he'd grown up. New Salem could easily have been one of the little towns between Lincoln and Omaha.

The wagon had stopped not far from a snow-covered boulder with an unnaturally flat top. Barbara brushed off the snow with her sleeve. "Oh, it has a plaque on it," she said, and brushed away more snow so she could read the words on the bronze. She started to laugh.

"What's so funny?" Yeager asked. He absentmindedly tacked the interrogative cough onto that question, too.

"This is the Wrong Side Up Monument," she answered. "That's what the plaque says, anyhow. Seems one of the early farmers had just started breaking the ground so he could plant for the first time when an Indian came along, looked at a chunk of sod, set it back the right way, and said, 'Wrong side up.' The farmer thought about it, decided he was right, and went into dairying instead. This is part of a big dairy area now."

"We should eat well tonight, then." Yeager's mouth watered at the thought of milk, cheese, probably big steaks, too—the folk around here might well be inclined to do some slaughtering for their guests, because they wouldn't be able to keep feeding all their livestock now that the Lizards had made moving grain and hay on a large scale impossible.

More wagons from the convoy came into town, some carrying people but more loaded down with the equipment that had filled much of Eckhart Hall back at the University of Chicago. Not all the wagons would stop here tonight; they were spread out for miles along the highway and back roads that ran parallel to it, both to avoid looking interesting to the Lizards and to keep from taking too much destruction from an air attack if they did.

Enrico Fermi helped his wife Laura down from their wagon,

then waved to Yeager. He waved back. He still felt a rush of pride at hanging around with scientists and even helping them when they had questions for the Lizard prisoners. Till a few months ago, his closest brush with scientists had been with the near-supermen who populated the pages of *Astounding*.

The real ones, while bright enough, weren't a lot like their fictional counterparts. For one thing, a lot of the best ones—Fermi, Leo Szilard, Edward Teller, Eugene Wigner—were dumpy foreigners with funny accents. Fermi talked like Bobby Fiore's father (he wondered what had happened to his old roommate, the second baseman on the Decatur Commodores). For another, just about all of them, foreign and American, were much more *human* than their fictional analogs: they'd have a drink (or more than one), they'd tell stories, and they'd argue with their wives. Yeager liked them more for it, not less.

Steaks there proved to be, cooked over open flames and eaten by the fireside—no gas and no electricity in New Salem. Yeager cut his into very small pieces as he ate it: though he wouldn't be thirty-six for another couple of months, he had full upper and lower plates. He'd almost died in the influenza epidemic of 1918, and his teeth had rotted in his head. The only teeth of his own he had were the ones that gave everybody else trouble: seven or eight years after the epidemic, his wisdom teeth had come in fine.

Ullhass and Ristin, by contrast, held big chunks of meat up to their mouths and worried bites off them. The Lizards didn't chew much; they'd get a gobbet in and then gulp it down. The locals watched with undisguised curiosity—these were the first Lizards they'd ever seen. Yeager had watched that at every stop all the way across Minnesota and North Dakota.

"Where you going to put those critters tonight?" a man asked him. "We sure as hell don't want them getting loose."

"They're not critters. They're people—funny kind of people, but people," Yeager said. With small-town politeness, the man didn't argue, but obviously didn't believe him, either. Yeager shrugged; he'd seen that happen before, too. He asked, "Do you have a jail here?"

The local hooked a thumb into the strap of his denim overalls. "Yah, we do," he said. Yeager hid a smile—he'd heard "yah" for "yes" at every stop in North Dakota. Grinning, the local went on, "We'll put a drunk Indian in there every now

and again—or sometimes a drunk squarehead, too. Hell, I'm an eighth Sioux myself, even if my name is Thorkil Olson."

"That'd be perfect," Yeager said, "especially if you can put a board or a blanket or something over the window, if there is one. Lizards can't take as much cold as people can. Can you take us there, let me look it over?"

With Ristin and Ullhass safely behind bars, Yeager figured he had the night off. A lot of times, he'd had to stay alert because they were in the next room of a private house. He didn't think they'd try to escape; they risked both freezing and getting shot on a world not their own. You couldn't afford to take chances, though.

He and Barbara went home with Olson and his wife Louise, a pleasant, red-cheeked woman in her late forties. "Take the spare bedroom for the night, and welcome," Louise said. "We've rattled around the house since our boy George and his wife headed down to Kansas City so he could work in a defense plant." Her face clouded. "The Lizards are in Kansas City. I pray he's all right."

"So do I, ma'am," Yeager said. Barbara's hand tightened on his; her husband Jens, a Met Lab physicist, had never come back from a cross-country trip that had skirted Lizard-held territory.

"Plenty of blankets on the bed, folks, and Grandma's old thundermug under it," Thorkil Olson boomed as he showed them the spare room. "We'll feed you breakfast when you get up in the morning. Sleep tight, now."

There were plenty of blankets, heavy wool ones from Sears, with a goose-down comforter on top. "We can even get undressed," Yeager said happily. "I'm sick of sleeping in three, four layers of clothes."

Barbara looked at him sidelong. "Stay undressed, you mean," she said, and blew out the candle Olson had set on the nightstand. The room plunged into darkness.

Afterwards, Sam peeled off his rubber, then groped around under the bed till he found the chamber pot. "Something for them to cluck over after we leave," he said. He dove back under the covers as fast as he could; without them, the bedroom was a chilly place.

Barbara clung to him, for warmth, but for reassurance, too. He ran a hand down the velvety skin of her back. "I love you," he said softly.

"I love you, too." Her voice caught; she shoved herself against him. "I don't know what I would have done without you. I'd have been so lost. I—" Her face was buried in the hollow of his shoulder. A hot tear splashed down on him. After a few seconds, she raised her head. "I miss him so much sometimes. I can't help it."

"I know. You wouldn't be who you are if you didn't." Yeager spoke with the philosophy of a man who had spent his entire adult life playing bush-league ball and never come close to the majors: "You do the best you can with the cards you get dealt, even if some of them are pretty rotten. Me, I never got an ace before." Now he squeezed her.

She shook her head; her hair brushed softly across his chest. "But it's not fair to you, Sam. Jens is dead; he has to be dead. If I'm going to go on—if we're going to go on, I have to look ahead, not backwards. As you said, I'll do the best I can."

"Can't ask for more than that," Yeager agreed. Slowly, he went on, "Seems to me, honey, that if you hadn't loved your Jens a lot, and if he hadn't loved you, too, you wouldn't have been anybody I'd've wanted to fall in love with. And even if I had, just on account of you're such a fine-looking woman"—he poked her in the ribs, because he knew she'd squeak—"you wouldn't have loved me back. You wouldn't have known how to."

"You're sweet. You make good sense, too. You seem to have a way of doing that." Instead of clutching, now Barbara snuggled against him; he felt her body relax. The tip of her nipple brushed his arm, just above the elbow. He wondered if she felt like making love again. But before he could try to find out, she yawned enormously. Voice still blurry, she said, "If I don't get some sleep, God only knows what kind of wreck I'll be tomorrow." In the darkness, her lips found his, but only for a moment. "Good night, Sam. I love you." She rolled over onto her side of the bed.

"I love you, too. Good night." Sam found himself yawning, too. Even if she had been interested, he wasn't sure he could have managed two rounds so close together. He wasn't a kid any more.

He rolled over onto his left side. His behind brushed against Barbara's. They chuckled and moved a little farther apart. He popped out his dentures, set them on the nightstand. Inside a minute and a half, he was snoring.

* * *

Jens Larssen most cordially cursed the United States Army, first in English and then in the fragmentary Norwegian he'd picked up from his grandfather. Even as the oaths fell from his lips, he knew he was being unfair: if the Army hadn't scooped him up as he was making his way across Indiana, he might well have got himself killed trying to sneak into Chicago as the Lizard attacks on the city rose to a climax.

And even now, after General Patton and General Bradley had pinched off the neck of that attack, nobody would let him fly out to join the rest of the Met Lab team in Denver. Again, the brass had their reasons—save for combat missions, aviation had almost disappeared in the United States. Human aviation had almost disappeared, anyhow. The Lizards dominated the skies.

"Hellfire," he muttered, clinging to the rail of the steamer *Duluth Queen*, "the damn Army wouldn't even tell me where they'd gone. I had to go into Chicago and find out for myself."

That rankled; it struck him as security gone mad. So did everyone's refusal to let him send on any word to the Met Lab crew. He couldn't even let his wife know he was alive. Once more, though, the mucky-mucks had a point he couldn't honestly deny: the Met Lab was America's only hope of producing an atomic bomb like the ones the Lizards had used on Berlin and Washington, D.C. Without that bomb, the war against the aliens would probably fail. Nobody, then, could afford to draw any sort of attention toward the Metallurgical Laboratory or communicate with it in any way, for fear the Lizards would intercept a message and draw the wrong—or rather, the right—conclusions from it.

The orders he'd been given made just enough sense for him not to try disobeying. But oh, how he hated them!

"And now I can't even get into Duluth," he grumbled.

He could see the town, which lay by the edge of Lake Superior where it narrowed to its westernmost point. He could see the gray granite bluffs that dwarfed man's houses and buildings, and felt he could almost reach out and touch some of the homes atop these bluffs, the taller business buildings that climbed the steep streets toward them. But the feeling was an illusion; a sheet of blue-gray ice held the *Duluth Queen* away from the Minnesota town that had given it its name.

Jens turned to a passing sailor. "How far out on the lake are we?"

The man paused to think. His breath came out thick as smoke as he answered, "Can't be more than four, five miles. Up to less than a month ago, it was open water all the way in." He chuckled at Larssen's groan. "Some years the port stays open all winter long. More often, though, it'll freeze for twenty miles out, so this ain't so bad." He went on his way, whistling a cheery tune.

He'd misunderstood why Jens groaned. It wasn't at the cold weather; Jens had grown up in Minnesota, and spent enough time skating on frozen lakes to take for granted that water— even as massive a body of water as Lake Superior—turned to ice when winter came. But a month before, he could have gone straight into town. That ate at him. Probably the same blizzard that let Patton launch his attack against the Lizards had also finally frozen the lake.

In any other year, the *Duluth Queen* would have stopped sailing for the winter. The Lizards, though, had paid much more attention to knocking out road and rail traffic than to knocking out ships. Jens wondered what that meant about their home planet—maybe it didn't have enough water for them to take shipping seriously as a way of getting things from one place to another.

If that was so, the aliens were missing a trick. The *Duluth Queen* carried ball bearings, ammunition, gasoline, and motor oil to keep resistance to the Lizards strong in Minnesota; it would take back steel from Duluth and milled grain from Minneapolis to forge into new weapons and feed the people who fought and built.

Lots of little boats—boats small enough to haul across the ice, some of them even rowboats—clustered around the steamship. Deck cranes lowered crates to them and picked up others, with a lot of shouted warnings going back and forth with the goods. A quasi-harbor had sprung into being at the edge of the ice: crates from the *Duluth Queen* went back and forth toward town on man-hauled sledges, while others, outbound, were muscled onto the boats for transport out to the *Queen.*

Jens doubted the system was even a tenth as efficient as a proper harbor. But the proper harbor was icebound, and what the locals had worked out was a lot better than nothing. From his point of view, the only real trouble was that cargo was so

much more important than passengers that he couldn't get off the steamship.

The sailor came back down the deck, still whistling. Larssen felt like throttling him. "How much longer before you'll be able to start moving actual real live people off?" he asked.

"Shouldn't be more than another day or two, sir," the fellow answered.

"A day or two!" Jens exploded. He wanted to dive into Lake Superior and swim the mile or so over to the edge of the ice. He knew perfectly well, though, that he'd freeze to death if he tried it.

"We're doing the best we can," the sailor said. "Everything's screwed up since the Lizards came, that's all. Wherever you need to get to, people will understand that you've been held up."

That this was true made it no easier to bear. Unconsciously, Larssen had assumed that because the Lizards had been beaten back from Chicago and he was free to travel again without the Army trying to tie him down, the world would automatically unfold at his feet. But the world was not in the habit of working that way.

The sailor went on, "Long as you're stuck on board, sir, you might as well enjoy yourself. The grub's good here, and there aren't many places ashore where you'll find steam heat, running water, and electric lights."

"Isn't that the sad and sorry truth?" Jens said. The Lizards' invasion had badly disrupted the complex web the United States had become, and pointed out the hard way how much every part of the country depended on every other—and how ill-equipped most parts were to go it alone. Burning wood to keep warm and depending on muscles—animal or human—to move things about made America feel as if it had slipped back a century from 1943.

And yet, if Jens ever made it to Denver, he'd get back to work on a project that seemed to belong at least a hundred years in the future. The world to come would spring into being amidst the obtrusive reemergence of the past. And where was the present? *The present,* thought Jens, who had a weakness for puns, *is absent.*

He went below, to get out of the cold and to remind himself the present still existed. The *Duluth Queen*'s galley boasted not only electric lights but a big pot of hot coffee (a luxury that

grew rarer as stocks dwindled) and a radio. Jens remembered
his parents saving up to buy their first set in the late twenties.
It had felt like inviting the world into their parlor. Now, most
places, you couldn't invite the world in even if you wanted to.

But the *Duluth Queen* didn't depend on distant power
plants, now likely to be either wrecked or out of fuel, for electricity. It made its own. And so, static squawked and muttered
as Hank Vernon spun the tuning knob and the red pointer slid
across the dial. Music suddenly came out. The ship's engineer
turned to Larssen, who was getting a mug of coffee. "The An-
drews Sisters suit you?"

"They're okay, but if you can find some news, that would
be even better." Jens poured in cream. The *Duluth Queen* had
plenty of that, but no sugar.

"Let's see what I can do. I wish this was a shortwave set."
Vernon worked the knob again, more slowly now, pausing to
listen to every faint station he brought in. After three or four
tries, he grunted in satisfaction. "Here you go." He turned up
the volume.

Larssen bent his head toward the radio. Even through the
waterfall of static, he recognized the newscaster's deep, slow
voice: "—three days of rioting reported from Italy, where people went into the streets to protest the government's cooperation with the Lizards. Pope Pius XII's radio appeal for calm,
monitored in London, seems to have had little effect. Rioters
are calling for the return of Benito Mussolini, who was spirited
to Germany after being placed under arrest by the Lizards—"

Hank Vernon shook his head in bemusement. "Isn't it a hell
of a thing? A year ago, Mussolini was the enemy with a capital E because he was buddies with Hitler. Now he's a hero because the krauts got him away from the Lizards. And Hitler's
not such a bad guy any more, since the Germans are still fighting hard. Just because you're fighting the Lizards doesn't make
you a good guy in my book. Was Joe Stalin a good guy just
on account of he was fighting the Nazis? People say so, yeah,
but they can't make me believe it. What do *you* think?"

"You're probably right," Larssen answered. He agreed with
most of what the engineer had said, but wished Vernon hadn't
chosen just then to say it—his loud, nasal tones drowned out
Edward R. Murrow, to whom Jens was trying to listen.

Vernon, however, kept right on talking, so Jens got the news
in disconnected snatches: ration cuts in England, fighting be-

tween Smolensk and Moscow, more fighting in Siberia, a Lizard push toward Vladivostok, a passive resistance campaign in India.

"Is that against the English or the Lizards?" he asked.

"If it's all the way over in India, what the devil difference does it make?" the engineer said. On a cosmic scale, Larssen supposed he had a point, but for someone who was trying to catch up with what was going on in the world, losing any facts felt frustrating.

From the radio, Murrow said, "And for those who think the Lizard devoid of humor, consider this: outside of Los Angeles, the Army Air Force recently had occasion to build a dummy airport, complete with dummy planes. Two Lizard aircraft are said to have attacked it—with dummy bombs. This is Edward R. Murrow, somewhere in the United States."

"Nobody on the radio admits where they are any more, you notice that?" Vernon said. "From FDR on down, it's 'somewhere in the United States.' It's like if anybody knows where you are, you can't be a bigshot, 'cause if you were a bigshot and the Lizards knew where you are, they'd go after you. Am I right or am I right?"

"You're probably right," Jens said again. "You don't happen to have a cigarette, do you?" Now that he didn't get the chance to drink coffee often, one cup kicked the way three or four had in the good old days. The same was even more true of tobacco.

"Wish to hell I did," Vernon answered. "I smoked cigars myself, but I wouldn't turn down anything these days. I used to work on the rivers in Virginia, North Carolina, and we'd go right past the tobacco farms, never even think a thing about 'em. But when it can't get from where they grow it to where you want to smoke it—"

"Yeah," Larssen said. It was true of more than tobacco. That was why the Lizards didn't have to conquer the whole country to make the United States stop working. It was why the *Duluth Queen* sat off the ice and unloaded: anything to keep the wheels turning.

He stayed stuck for the next three days, biding his time and biting his nails. When he finally did get to descend into one of the small boats that was unloading the *Duluth Queen*, he almost wished he'd stayed stuck longer. Clambering down a

cargo net with a knapsack and a rifle slung over his shoulder was not his notion of fun.

One of the sailors lowered his Schwinn on a line. It banged against the side of the steamship a couple of times on the way down. Jens grabbed it and undid the knot. The line snaked back up to the *Duluth Queen*.

The small boat had a crew of four. They all looked at the bicycle. "You're not going anywhere far by yourself on that, are you, mister?" one of them said at last.

"What if I am?" Larssen had ridden a bicycle across most of Ohio and Indiana. He was in the best shape of his life. He'd always look skinny, but he was stronger than most people with bulging biceps.

"Oh, I won't say you couldn't do it—don't get me wrong," the crewman said. "It's just that—this is Minnesota, after all." He patted himself. He was wearing boots with fur tops, an overcoat over a jacket over a sweater, and earmuffs on top of a knitted wool cap. "You don't want to get stuck in a snow-storm, is what I mean. You do and you won't even start to stink till spring—and spring comes late around Duluth."

"I know what Minnesota's like. I was raised here," Jens said.

"Then you ought to have better sense," the sailor told him.

He started to come back with a hot reply, but it didn't get past his lips. He remembered all the winter days he'd had to stay home from school when snow made the going impossible. And his grammar school had been only a couple of miles from the farm where he'd grown up, the high school less than five. If a bad storm hit while he was in the middle of nowhere, he'd be in trouble and no doubt about it.

He said, "Things must move, or else you guys wouldn't be out here working in the middle of winter. How do you do it?"

"We convoy," the sailor answered seriously. "You wait until there's a bunch of people going the same way you are, and then you go along with 'em. Where you headin' for, mister?"

"Denver, eventually," Jens said. "Any place west of Duluth now, I guess." In a pocket of his overcoat he had a letter from General Patton that essentially ordered the entire civilized world to drop whatever it was doing and give him a hand. It had got him his cabin on the *Duluth Queen* . . . but the *Duluth Queen* was going from Chicago to Duluth anyhow. Even a sizzling letter from Patton probably couldn't call a land convoy

into being at the drop of a hat. But that sparked a thought. "Any trains still running?"

"Yeah, we try to keep 'em going, best we can, anyhow. I tell you, though, it's like playing Russian roulette. Maybe you'll get through, maybe you'll get your ass bombed off. If it was me, I wouldn't ride one, not now. The Lizards go after 'em on purpose, not for the hell of it like they do ships."

"I may take my chances," Larssen said. If the trains were running right, he could be in Denver in a couple of days, not a couple of weeks or a couple of months. If they weren't— He tried not to worry about that.

The boat drifted to a stop at the edge of the ice. Gunnysacks made the treacherous surface easier to walk on. The crew handed Larssen his gear, wished him good luck, and headed back to the *Duluth Queen*.

He headed over toward a dog-drawn sledge that didn't have too many crates in it. "Can I get a ride?" he called, and the driver nodded. He felt like a character out of Jack London as he got in behind the man.

The trip across the ice gave him more time to think. It also convinced him that if he was going to live in the twentieth century, he'd use its tools where he could. He'd do better even if the Lizards did bomb him while he was just partway to Denver. When at last he got into Duluth, he went looking for the train station.

The hauler aircraft rolled to a stop. Ussmak stared out the window at the Tosevite landscape. It was different from the flat plains of the SSSR where the landcruiser driver had served before, but that didn't make it any better, not as far as he was concerned. The plants were a dark, wet-looking green under sunlight that seemed too white, too harsh.

Not that the star Tosev adequately heated its third world. Ussmak felt the chill as soon as he descended from the hauler onto the concrete of the runway. Here, though, at least water wasn't falling frozen from the sky. That was something.

"Landcruiser crew replacements!" a male bawled. Ussmak and three or four others who had just deplaned tramped over to him. The male took their names and identity numbers, then waved them into the back of an armored transporter.

"Where are we?" Ussmak asked as the machine jounced into life. "Whom are we fighting?" That was a better question;

the names the Big Uglies gave to pieces of Tosev 3 meant little to him.

"This place is called France," a gunner named Forssis answered. "I served here for a while shortly after we landed, before the commander decided it was largely pacified and transferred my unit to the SSSR."

All the males let their mouths fall open in derisive laughter at that. Everything had seemed so easy in the days right after the landing. Ussmak remembered being part of a drive that had smashed Soviet landcruisers as if they were made of cardboard.

Even then, though, he should have had a clue. A sniper had picked off his commander when Votal, like any good landcruiser leader, stuck his head out the cupola to get a decent view of what was going on. And Krentel, the commander who replaced him, did not deserve the body paint that proclaimed his rank.

Well, Krentel was dead, too, and Telerep the gunner with him. A guerrilla—Ussmak did not know whether he was Russki or Deutsch—had blown the turret right off the landcruiser while they were trying to protect the crews cleaning up nuclear material scattered when the Big Uglies had managed to wreck the starship that carried the bulk of the Race's atomic weapons.

From his driver's position, Ussmak had bailed out of the landcruiser when it was stricken—out of the landcruiser and into radioactive mud. He'd been in a hospital ship ever since . . . till now.

"So whom are we fighting?" he repeated. "The Français?"

"No, the Deutsche, mostly," Forssis answered. "They were ruling here when we arrived. I hear the weapons we'll be facing are better than the ones they threw at us the last time I was here."

Silence settled over the transporter's passenger compartment. Fighting the Big Uglies, Ussmak thought, was like poisoning pests: the survivors kept getting more resistant to what you were trying to do to them. And, like any other pests, the Big Uglies changed faster than you could alter your methods of coping with them.

The heated compartment, the smooth ride over a paved highway, and the soft purr of the hydrogen-burning engine helped most of the males doze off before long: veterans, they

knew the value of snatching sleep while they had the chance. Ussmak tried to rest, too, but couldn't. The longing for ginger gnawed at him and would not let go.

An orderly had sold him some of the precious herb in the hospital ship. He'd started tasting as much out of boredom as for any other reason. When he was full of ginger, he felt wise and brave and invulnerable. When he wasn't—that was when he discovered the trap into which he'd fallen. Without ginger, he seemed stupid and fearful and soft-skinned as a Big Ugly, a contrast just made worse because he so vividly remembered how wonderful he knew himself to be when he tasted the powdered herb.

He didn't care how much he gave the orderly for his ginger: he had pay saved up and nothing he'd rather spend it on. The orderly had an ingenious arrangement whereby he got Ussmak's funds even though they didn't go directly into his computer account.

In the end, it hadn't saved him. One day, a new orderly came in to police up Ussmak's chamber. Discreet questioning (Ussmak could afford to be discreet then, with several tastes hidden away) showed that the only thing he knew about ginger was the fleetlord's general order prohibiting its use. Ussmak had stretched out the intervals between tastes as long as he could. But finally the last one was gone. He'd been gingerless—and melancholy—ever since.

The road climbed up through rugged mountains. Ussmak got only glimpses out the transporter's firing ports. After the monotonous flatlands of the SSSR and the even more boring sameness of the hospital ship cubicle, a jagged horizon was welcome, but it didn't much remind Ussmak of the mountains of Home.

For one thing, these mountains were covered with frozen water of one sort or another, a measure of how miserably cold Tosev 3 was. For another, the dark conical trees that peeked out through the mantling of white were even more alien to his eye than the Big Uglies.

Those trees also concealed Tosevites, as Ussmak discovered a short while later. Somewhere up there in the woods, a machine gun began to chatter. Bullets spanged off the transporter's armor. Its own light cannon returned fire, filling the passenger compartment with thunder.

The males who had been dozing were jerked rudely back to

awareness. They tumbled for the firing ports to see what was happening, Ussmak among them. He couldn't see anything, not even muzzle flashes.

"Scary," Forssis observed. "I'm used to sitting inside a landcruiser where the armor shields you from anything. I can't help thinking that if the Tosevites had a real gun up there, we'd be cooked."

Ussmak knew only too well that not even landcruiser armor guaranteed protection against the Big Uglies. But before he could say as much, the transporter driver came on the intercom: "Sorry about the racket, my males, but we haven't rooted out all the guerrillas yet. They're just a nuisance as long as we don't run over any mines."

The driver sounded downright cheery; Ussmak wondered if he was tasting ginger. "I wonder how often they do run over mines," Forssis said darkly.

"*This* male hasn't, or he wouldn't still be driving us," Ussmak said. A couple of the other landcruiser crewmales opened their mouths at him.

After a while, the mountains gave way to wide, gently rolling valleys. Forssis pointed to neat rows of gnarled plants that clung to stakes on south-facing slopes. He said, "I saw those when I was in this France place before. The Tosevites ferment alcoholic brews from them." He ran his tongue over his lips. "Some have a very interesting flavor."

The passenger compartment had no view straight forward. The driver had to make an announcement for the males he was hauling: "We are coming into the Big Ugly town of Besançon, our forward base for combat against the Deutsche. You will be assigned to crews here."

All Ussmak had seen of Tosevite architecture was the wooden farming villages of the SSSR. Besançon was certainly different from those. He didn't quite know what to make of it. Compared to the tall, blocklike structures of steel and glass that formed the cities of Home, its buildings seemed toys. Yet they were very ornate toys, with columns and elaborate stone- and brickwork and steep roofs so the frozen water that fell from the sky hereabouts would slide off.

The Race's headquarters in Besançon was on a bluff in the southeastern part of the town. Not only was the place on high ground, Ussmak discovered on alighting from the transporter

that a river flowed around two sides of it. "Well sited for defense," he remarked.

"Interesting you should say that," the driver answered. "This used to be a Big Ugly fortress." He pointed to a long, low, gloomy-looking building. "Go in there. They'll process you and assign you to a crew."

"It shall be done." Ussmak hurried toward the doorway; the cold was nipping at his fingers and eye turrets.

Inside, the building was heated to the point of comfort for civilized beings—Ussmak hissed gratefully. Otherwise, though, the local males were mostly using the furnishings they'd found. A planet was a big place, and the Race hadn't brought enough of everything to supply all its garrisons. And so a personnel officer seemed half swallowed by the fancy red velvet chair in which he sat, a chair designed to fit a Big Ugly. The male had to stretch to reach the computer on the heavy, dark wood table in front of him; the table was higher off the ground than any the Race would have built.

The personnel officer turned one eye toward Ussmak. "Name, specialization, and number," he said in a bored voice.

"Superior sir, I am Ussmak, landcruiser driver," Ussmak answered, and gave the number by which he was recorded, paid, and would be interred if he got unlucky.

The personnel officer entered the information, used his free eye to read Ussmak's data as they came up. "You were serving in the SSSR against the Soviets, is that correct, until your landcruiser was destroyed and you were exposed to excess radiation?"

"Yes, superior sir, that is correct."

"Then you've not had combat experience against the Deutsche?"

"Superior sir, I am told the guerrilla team that wrecked my vehicle was part Deutsch, part Soviet. If you are asking whether I've faced their landcruisers, the answer is no."

"That is what I meant," the personnel officer said. "You will need to maintain a higher level of alertness hereabouts than was your habit in the SSSR, landcruiser driver. Tactically, the Deutsche are more often clever than perhaps any other Tosevite group. Their newest landcruisers have heavier guns than you will have seen, too. Combine these factors with their superior knowledge of the local terrain and they become opponents not to be despised."

"I understand, superior sir," Ussmak said. "Will my land-cruiser commander be experienced?" *I hope.*

The personnel officer punched at the computer again, waited for a response to appear on the screen. "You're going to be assigned to Landcruiser Commander Hessef's machine; his driver was wounded in a bandit attack here in Besançon a few days ago. Hessef compiled an excellent record in España, south and west of here, as we expanded out of our landing zone. He's relatively new to the northern sector."

Ussmak hadn't known España from France until the moment the personnel officer named them. And no matter what that officer said about the superior skills of the Deutsche, to Ussmak one band of Big Uglies seemed pretty much like another. "I'm glad to hear that he has fought, superior sir. Where do I report to him?"

"The hall we are using as a barracks is out the door through which you entered and to your left. If you do not find Hessef and your gunner—whose name is Tvenkel—there, try the vehicle park down past the antiaircraft missile launcher."

Ussmak tried the vehicle park first, on the theory that any commander worth his body paint took better care of his landcruiser than he did of himself. Seeing the big machines lined up in their sandbagged revetments made him eager to get back to the work for which he'd been trained, and also eager for the tight-knit fellowship that flowered among the males of a good landcruiser crew.

Crewmales working on their landcruisers directed him to the one Hessef commanded. But when he walked into its stall, he found it buttoned up tight. That presumably meant Hessef and Tvenkel *were* back at the barracks. *Not a good sign,* Ussmak thought as he began to retrace his steps.

He longed to feel a part of something larger than himself. That was what the Race was all about: obedience from below, obligation from above, all working together for the common good. He'd known that feeling with Votal, his first commander, but after Votal died, Krentel proved such an incompetent that Ussmak could not bond to him as subordinate was supposed to bond to superior.

Then Krentel had got himself killed, too, and Ussmak's original gunner with him. That worsened the driver's feeling of separation, almost of exclusion, from the rest of the Race. The long stay in the hospital ship and his discovery of ginger had

pushed him even further out of the niche he'd been intended to fit. If he couldn't have ginger any more, crew solidarity would have been a good second best. But how could he really feel part of a crew that didn't have the simple sense to treat their landcruiser as if their lives depended on it?

As he walked back past the missile launcher, bells began to ring down in the town of Besançon. He turned to one of the males. "I'm new here. Are those alarms? Where should I go? What should I do?"

"Nothing—take no notice of them," the fellow answered. "The Big Uglies just have a lot of mechanical clocks that chime to divide up the day and night. They startled me at first, too. After a while here, you won't even notice them. One is spectacular for something without electronics. It must have seventy dials, and these figures all worked by gears and pulleys come out and prance around and then disappear back into the machine. When you get some slack time, you ought to go see it: it's worth turning both eye turrets that way."

"Thanks. Maybe I will." Relieved, Ussmak kept on toward the barracks building. Just as he pushed the door open, the sweet metallic clangor ceased.

Even the cots the males were using had formerly belonged to the Big Uglies. The thin mattresses looked lumpy, the blankets scratchy. They were undoubtedly woven from the hair of some native beast or other, an idea that made Ussmak itch all by itself. A few males lounged around doing nothing in particular.

"I seek the landcruiser commander Hessef," Ussmak said as some of those males turned an eye or two toward him.

"I am Hessef," one of them said, coming forward. "By your paint, you must be my new driver."

"Yes, superior sir." Ussmak put more respect into his voice than he truly felt. Hessef was a jittery-looking male, his body paint sloppily applied. Ussmak's own paint was none too neat, but he thought commanders should adhere to a higher standard.

Another male came up to stand beside Hessef. "Ussmak, I introduce you to Tvenkel, our gunner," the landcruiser commander said.

"Be good to have a whole crew again, go out and fight," Tvenkel said. Like Hessef, he couldn't quite hold still. His body paint was, if possible, in even worse shape than the

landcruiser commander's—smeared, blotched, daubed on in a hurry. Ussmak wondered what he'd done to deserve becoming part of this substandard crew.

Hessef said, "Sitting around the barracks all day with nothing to do is as boring as staying awake while you go into cold sleep."

Then why aren't you out tending to your landcruiser? Ussmak thought. But that wasn't something he could say, not to his new commander. Instead, he answered, "Boredom I know all about, superior sir. I just spent a good long while in a hospital ship, recovering from radiation sickness. There were times when I thought I'd been in that cubicle forever."

"Yes, that could be bad, just staring at the metal walls," Hessef agreed. "Still, though, I think I'd sooner stay in a hospital ship than in this ugly brick shed that was never made for our kind." He waved to show what he meant. Ussmak had to agree: the barracks was indeed a dismal place. He suspected even Big Uglies would have found themselves bored here.

"How did you get through the days?" Tvenkel asked. "Recovering from sickness makes time pass twice as slowly."

"For one thing, I have every video from the hospital ship's library memorized," Ussmak said, which drew a laugh from his new crewmates. "For another—" He stopped short. Ginger was against regulations. He didn't want to make the commander and gunner aware of his habit.

"Here, drop your gear on this bed by ours," Hessef said. "We've been saving it against the day when we'd be whole again."

Ussmak did as he was asked. The other two males crowded close around him, as if to create the unity that held a good landcruiser crew together. The rest of the males in the barracks looked on from a distance, politely allowing Ussmak to bond with his new comrades before they came forward to introduce themselves.

Quietly, Tvenkel said, "You may not know it, driver, but the Big Uglies have an herb that makes life a lot less boring. Would you care to try a taste, see what I mean?"

Ussmak's eyes both swung abruptly, bored into the gunner. He lowered his voice, too. "You have—ginger?" He hesitated before he named the precious powder.

Now Tvenkel and Hessef stared at him. "You know about

ginger?" the landcruiser commander whispered. His mouth fell open in an enormous grin.

"Yes, I know about ginger. I'd love a taste, thanks." Ussmak wanted to caper like a hatchling. Instead, the three males looked at each other for a long time, none of them saying anything. Ussmak broke the silence: "Superior sirs, I think we're going to be an *outstanding* crew."

Neither commander nor gunner argued with him.

The big Maybach engine coughed, sputtered, died. Colonel Heinrich Jäger swore and flipped up the Panther D's cupola. "More than twice the horsepower of my old Panzer III," he grumbled, "and it runs less than half as often." He pulled himself out, dropped down to the ground.

The rest of the crew scrambled out, too. The driver, a big sandy-haired youngster named Rolf Wittman, grinned impudently. "Could be worse, sir," he said. "At least it hasn't caught fire the way a lot of them do."

"Oh, for the blithe spirit of the young," Jäger said, acid in his voice. He wasn't young himself. He'd fought in the trenches in the First World War, stayed in the Weimar Republic's *Reichswehr* after it was over. He'd switched over to panzers as soon as he could after Hitler began rearming Germany, and was commanding a company of Panzer IIIs in the Sixteenth Panzer Division south of Kharkov when the Lizards came.

Now, at last, the *Reich* had made a machine that might make the Lizards sit up and take notice when they met it. Jäger had killed a Lizard tank with his Panzer III, but he was the first to admit he'd been lucky. Anybody who came out alive, let alone victorious, after a run-in with Lizard armor was lucky.

The Panther he now stood beside seemed decades ahead of his old machine. It incorporated all the best features of the Soviet T-34—thick sloped armor, wide tracks, a powerful 75mm gun—into a German design with a smooth suspension, an excellent transmission, and better sights and gun control than Jäger had ever imagined before.

The only trouble was, it was a brand-new German design. Bumping up against the T-34 and the even heavier KV-1 in 1941 had been a nasty surprise for the *Wehrmacht*. The panzer divisions had held their own through superior tactics and started upgunning their Panzer IIIs and IVs, but getting better

tanks became urgent. When the Lizards arrived, *urgent* turned mandatory.

And so development had been rushed, and the Panther, powerful machine that it was, conspicuously lacked the mechanical reliability that characterized older German models. Jäger kicked at the overlapping road wheels that carried the tracks. "This panzer might as well have been built by an Englishman," he growled. He knew no stronger way to condemn an armored fighting vehicle.

The rest of the crew leaped to their panzer's defense. "It's not as bad as that, sir," Wittman said.

"It has a real gun in it, by Jesus," added Sergeant Klaus Meinecke, "not one of the peashooters the English use." The gun was his responsibility; he sat to Jäger's right in the turret, on a chair that looked like a black-leather-covered hockey puck with a two-slat back.

"Having a real gun doesn't matter if we can't get to where we're supposed to use it," Jäger retorted. "Let's fix this beast, shall we, before the Lizards fly by and strafe us."

That got the men moving in a hurry. Attack from the air had been frightening enough when it was a *Shturmovik* with red stars painted on wings and fuselage. It was infinitely worse now; the rockets the Lizards fired hardly ever missed.

"Probably the fuel lines again," Wittman said, "or maybe the fuel pump." He rummaged in one of the outside stowage bins for a wrench, attacked the bolts that held the engine louvers onto the Panther's rear deck.

The crew was a good one, Jäger thought. Only veterans, and select veterans at that, got to handle Panthers: no point in frittering away the important new weapon by giving it to men who couldn't get the most out of it.

Klaus Meinecke grunted in triumph. "Here we go. This gasket in the pump is *kaput*. Do we have a spare?" More rummaging in the bins produced one. The gunner replaced the damaged part, screwed the top back onto the fuel pump case, and said, "All right, let's start it up again."

The crew had to take off the jack to get at the starter dog clutch. "That's poor design," Jäger said, and pulled a piece of paper and pencil out of a pocket of his black panzer crewman's tunic. *Why not stow jack vertically between exhausts, not horizontally below them?* he scribbled.

Cranking up the Panther was a two-man job. Wittman and

Meinecke did the honors. The engine belched, farted, and came back to life. After handshakes all around, the crew climbed back into the machine and rolled on down the road.

"We'll want to look for a good patch of woods where we can take cover for the night," Jäger said. Such a patch might be hard to find. He checked his map. They were somewhere between Thann and Belfort, heading down to try to hold the Lizards away from the latter strategic town.

Jäger stuck his head out of the drum-shaped cupola. If he was where he thought he was— He nodded, pleased with his navigation. There ahead stood Rougement-le-Château, a Romanesque priory now in picturesque ruin. Navigating through the rugged terrain of Alsace and the Franche-Comté was a very different business from getting around on the Ukrainian steppe, where, as on the sea, you picked a compass heading and followed it. If you got lost here, heading across country wasn't so easy. More often than not, you had to back up and retrace your path by road, which cost precious time.

The woods were still leafless, but Jäger found a spot where bare branches interlaced thickly overhead. Behind scattered clouds, the pale winter sun was low in the west. "Good enough," he said, and ordered Wittman to pull off the road and conceal the Panther from prying eyes in the sky.

Within the next half hour, four more tanks—another Panther, two of the new Panzer IVs with relatively light protection but a long 75mm gun almost as good as the Panther's, and a huge Tiger that mounted an 88 and armor poorly sloped but so thick and heavy that it made the panzer slower than it should have been—joined him there. The crews swapped rations, spare parts, and lies. Somebody had a deck of cards. They played skat and poker till it got too dark to see.

Jäger thought back to the splendid organization of Sixteenth Panzer when the division plunged into the Soviet Union. Back then, the thought of getting tanks into action by these dribs and drabs would have caused apoplexy in the High Command. That was before the Lizards had started plastering the German rail and road networks. Now any movement toward the front was counted a success.

He squeezed butter and meat paste from their tubes onto a chunk of black bread. As he chewed, he reflected that a lot of things had happened to him that he never would have expected before the Lizards came. He'd fought against the alien invaders

side by side with a band of Russian partisans, most of them Jews.

He hadn't had much use for Jews before then. He still didn't have a whole lot of use for them, but now he understood why the Jews of Warsaw had risen against the town's German occupiers to help the Lizards take it. Nothing the aliens did to them could come close to what they'd suffered at the hands of the *Reich.*

And yet those same Polish Jews had let him cross their territory, and hadn't even confiscated from him all the explosive metal that had been his booty from the joint German-Soviet raid on the Lizards. True, they'd taken half to send it to the United States, but they'd let him deliver the rest to his own superiors. Even now, German scientists were working to avenge Berlin.

He took another bite. Even that wasn't the strangest. Had anyone told him on June 22, 1941, that he would—have an affair with? fall in love with? (he still wasn't sure about that himself)—a Soviet pilot, his most likely reaction would have been to punch the teller in the eye for calling him a fairy. On the day the war with the Soviet Union started, no one in Germany knew the Russians would use female fliers in combat.

He hoped Ludmila was all right. They'd first met in the Ukraine, where she'd plucked him and his gunner (he hoped Georg Schultz was all right, too) off a collective farm and taken them to Moscow so they could explain to the Red Army brass how they'd managed to kill a Lizard panzer. He'd written to her after that—she had some German, he a little Russian—but got no answer.

Then they'd come together at Berchtesgaden, where Hitler had pinned on him the German Cross in gold (a medal so ugly he wore only the ribbon these days) and she'd flown in Molotov for consultation with the *Führer.* He smiled slowly. That had been as magical a week as he'd ever known.

But what now? he wondered. Ludmila had flown back to the Soviet Union, where the NKVD would not look kindly upon her for sleeping with a Nazi . . . any more than the *Gestapo* was pleased with him for sleeping with a Red. "Screw 'em all," he muttered, which drew a quizzical glance from Rolf Wittman. Jäger did not explain.

A motorcycle came put-putting slowly down the road, its headlight dimmed almost to extinction by a blackout slit cap.

With the Lizards' detectors, even that could be dangerous, but not so dangerous as driving a winding French road in pitch darkness.

The motorcycle driver spotted the panzers off under the trees. He stopped, throttled down, and called, "Anyone know where I can find Colonel Heinrich Jäger?"

"Here I am," Jäger said, standing up. *"Was ist los?"*

"I have here orders for you, Colonel." The driver pulled them out of his tunic pocket.

Jäger unfolded the paper, stooped down and held it in front of the motorcycle headlamp so he could read it. *"Scheisse,"* he exclaimed. "I've been recalled. They just put me back in front-line service, and now I've been recalled."

"Yes, sir," the driver agreed. "I am ordered to take you back with me."

"But why?" Jäger said. "It makes no sense. Here I am an experienced fighter for *Führer* and *Vaterland* against the Lizards. But what good will I do in this Hechingen place? I've scarcely even heard of it."

But he had heard of it, and fairly recently, too. Where? When? He stiffened as memory came. Hechingen was where Hitler had said he was sending the explosive metal. Without another word, Jäger walked over to his Panther, got on the radio, and turned command over to the regimental lieutenant-colonel. Then he slung his pack onto his shoulders, went back to the motorcycle, climbed on behind the driver, and headed back toward Germany.

☆ **II** ☆

Ludmila Gorbunova did not care for Moscow. She was from Kiev, and thought the Soviet capital drab and dull. Her impression of it was not improved by the endless grilling she'd had from the NKVD. She'd never imagined the mere sight of green collar tabs could reduce her to fearful incoherence, but it did.

And, she knew, things could have been worse. The *chekists* were treating her with kid gloves because she'd flown Comrade Molotov, second in the Soviet Union only to the Great Stalin, and a man who loathed flying, to Germany and brought him home in one piece. Besides, the *rodina*—the motherland— needed combat pilots. She'd stayed alive through most of a year against the Nazis and several months against the Lizards. That should have given her value above and beyond what she got for ferrying Molotov around.

Whether it did, however, remained to be seen. A lot of very able, seemingly very valuable people had disappeared over the past few years, denounced as wreckers or traitors to the Soviet Union or sometimes just vanished with no explanation at all, as if they had suddenly ceased to exist . . .

The door to the cramped little room (cramped, yes, but infinitely preferable to a cell in the Lefortovo prison) in which she sat came open. The NKVD man who came in wore three crimson oblongs on his collar tabs. Ludmila bounced to her feet. "Comrade Lieutenant-Colonel!" she said, saluting.

He returned the salute, the first time that had happened since the NKVD started in on her. "Comrade Senior Lieutenant," he acknowledged. "I am Boris Lidov." She blinked in surprise; none of her questioners had bothered giving his name till now, either. Lidov looked more like a schoolmaster than an NKVD

man, not that that meant anything. But he surprised her again, saying, "Would you like some tea?"

"Yes, thank you very much, Comrade Lieutenant-Colonel," she answered—quickly, before he changed his mind. The German attack had deranged the Soviet distribution system, that of the Lizards all but destroyed it. These days, tea was rare and precious.

Well, she thought, *the NKVD will have it if anyone does.* And sure enough, Lidov stuck his head out the door and bawled a request. Within moments, someone fetched him a tray with two gently steaming glasses. He took it, set it on the table in front of Ludmila. "Help yourself," he said. "Choose whichever you wish; neither one is drugged, I assure you."

He didn't need to assure her; that he did so made her suspicious again. But she took a glass and drank. Her tongue found nothing in it but tea and sugar. She sipped again, savoring the taste and the warmth. "Thank you, Comrade Lieutenant-Colonel. It's very good," she said.

Lidov made an indolent gesture, as if to say she didn't need to thank him for anything so small. Then he said idly, as if making casual conversation, "You know, I met your Major Jäger—no, you've said he's Colonel Jäger now, correct?—your Colonel Jäger, I should say, after you brought him here to Moscow last summer."

"Ah," Ludmila said, that being the most noncommittal noise she could come up with. She decided it was not enough. "Comrade Lieutenant-Colonel, as I have said before, he is not *my* colonel by any means."

"I do not necessarily condemn," Lidov said, steepling his fingers. "The ideology of the fascist state is corrupt, not the German people. And"—he coughed dryly—"the coming of the Lizards has shown that progressive economic systems, capitalist and socialist alike, must band together lest we all fall under the oppression of the ancient system wherein the relationship is slave to master, not worker to boss."

"Yes," Ludmila said eagerly. The last thing she wanted to do was argue about the dialectic of history with an NKVD man, especially when his interpretation seemed to her advantage.

Lidov went on, "Further, your Colonel Jäger helped perform a service for the people of the Soviet Union, as he may have mentioned to you."

"No, I'm afraid he didn't. I'm sorry, Comrade Lieutenant-

Colonel, but we talked very little about the war when we saw each other in Germany. We—" Ludmila felt her face heat. She knew what Lidov had to be thinking. Unfortunately—from her point of view—he was right.

He looked down his long, straight nose at her. "You like Germans well, don't you?" he said sniffily. "This Jäger in Berchtesgaden, and you attached his gunner"—he pulled out a scrap of paper, checked a name on it—"Georg Schultz, *da*, to the ground crew at your airstrip."

"He is a better mechanic than anyone else at the airstrip. Germans understand machinery better than we do, I think. But as far as I am concerned, he is only a mechanic," Ludmila insisted.

"He is a German. They are both Germans." So much for Lidov's words about the solidarity of peoples with progressive economic systems. His flat, hard tone made Ludmila think of a trip to Siberia on an unheated cattle car, or of a bullet in the back of the neck. The NKVD man went on, "It is likely that Comrade Molotov will dispense with the services of a pilot who forms such un-Soviet attachments."

"I am sorry to hear that, Comrade Lieutenant-Colonel," Ludmila said, though she knew Molotov would have been glad to dispense with the services of any pilot, given his attitude about flying. But she insisted, "I have no attachments to Georg Schultz save those of the struggle against the Lizards."

"And to Colonel Jäger?" Lidov said with the air of a man calling checkmate. Ludmila did not answer; she knew she was checkmated. The lieutenant-colonel spoke as if pronouncing sentence: "Because of this conduct of yours, you are to be returned to your former duties without promotion. Dismissed, Comrade Senior Lieutenant."

Ludmila had been braced for ten years in the *gulag* and another five of internal exile. She needed a moment to take in what she'd just heard. She jumped to her feet. "I serve the Soviet state, Comrade Lieutenant-Colonel!" *Whether you believe me or not,* she added to herself.

"Prepare yourself for immediate departure for the airport," Lidov said, as if her mere presence polluted Moscow. An NKVD flunky must have been listening outside the door or to a concealed microphone, for in under half a minute a fellow in green collar tabs brought in a canvas bag full of her worldly goods.

Before long, a *troika* was taking her from the Kremlin to the airport on the edge of Moscow. The sleigh's runners and the hooves of the three horses that drew it kicked up snow gone from white to gray thanks to city soot. Only when her beloved little U-2 biplane came into view on the runway did she realize she'd been returned to this duty, which she wanted more than any other, as if it were a punishment. She chewed on that a long time, even after she was in the air.

"I'm bloody lost," David Goldfarb said as he pedaled his RAF bicycle through the countryside south of Leicester. The radarman came to an intersection. He looked for signs to tell him where he was—and looked in vain, because the signs taken down in 1940 to hinder a feared German invasion had never gone back up.

He was trying to get to the Research and Development Test Flying Aerodrome at Bruntingthorpe, to which he'd been ordered to report. *South from the village of Peatling Magna,* his directions read. The only trouble was, nobody had bothered to tell him (for all he knew, nobody was aware) *two* roads ran south from Peatling Magna. He'd taken the right-hand track, and was beginning to regret it.

Peatling Magna hadn't looked *magna* enough to boast two roads when he rolled through it; he wondered if there could possibly be a Peatling Minima, and, if so, whether it was visible to the naked eye.

Ten minutes of steady pedaling brought him into another village. He looked around hopefully for anything resembling an aerodrome, but nothing he saw matched that description. A matronly woman in a scarf and a heavy wool coat was trudging down the street. "Begging your pardon, madam," he called to her, "but is this Bruntingthorpe?"

The woman's head whipped around—his London accent automatically made him out to be a stranger. She relaxed, a little, when she saw he was in RAF dark blue and thus had an excuse for poking his good-sized nose into a place where he didn't belong. But even though she used the broader vowels of the East Midlands, her voice was sharp as she answered, "Bruntingthorpe? I should say *not*, young man. *This* is Peatling Parva. Bruntingthorpe lies down that road." She pointed east.

"Thank you, madam," Goldfarb said gravely. He bent low over his bicycle, rode away fast so she wouldn't hear him start

to snicker. Not Peatling Minima—Peatling Parva. The name fit; it had looked a pretty *parva* excuse for a village. Now, though, he was on the right track and—he looked at his watch—near enough on time that he could blame his tardiness on the train's getting into Leicester late, which it had.

He hadn't gone far toward Bruntingthorpe when he heard a screaming roar, saw an airplane streak across the sky at what seemed an impossible speed. Alarm and fury coursed through him—had he come here just in time to see the Lizards bomb and wreck the aerodrome?

Then he played in his mind the film of the aircraft he'd just seen. After the Lizards destroyed the radar station at Dover, he'd been an aircraft spotter the old-fashioned way, with binoculars and field telephone, for a while. He recognized the Lizards' fighters and fighter-bombers. This aircraft, even if it flew on jets, didn't match any of them. Either they'd come up with something new or the plane was English.

Hope replaced anger. Where was he more likely to find English jet aircraft than at a research and development aerodrome? He wondered why the powers that be wanted him there. He'd find out soon.

The village of Bruntingthorpe was no more prepossessing than either of the Peatlings. Not far away, though, a collection of tents, corrugated-iron Nissen huts, and macadamized runways marred the gently rolling fields that surrounded the hamlets. A soldier with a tin hat and a Sten gun demanded to see Goldfarb's papers when he pedaled up to the barbed-wire fence and gate around the RAF facility.

He surrendered them, but could not help remarking, "Seems a fairish waste of time, if anyone wants to know. Not bloody likely I'm a Lizard in disguise, is it?"

"Never can tell, chum," the soldier answered. "Besides, you might be a Jerry in disguise, and we're not dead keen on that even if the match there won't be played to a finish."

"Can't say I blame you." Goldfarb's parents had got out of Russian-ruled Poland to escape pogroms against the Jews. By all accounts, the Nazis' pogroms after they conquered Poland had been a hundred times worse, bad enough for the Jews there to make common cause with the Lizards against the Germans. Now, from the reports that leaked out, the Lizards were beginning to make things tough on the Jews. Goldfarb sighed. Being a Jew wasn't easy anywhere.

The sentry opened the gate, waved him through. He rode over to the nearest Nissen hut, got off his bicycle, pushed down the kickstand, and went into the hut. Several RAF men were gathered round a large table there, studying some drawings by the light of a paraffin lamp hung overhead. "Yes?" one of them said.

Goldfarb stiffened to attention: the casual questioner, though just a couple of inches over five feet tall, wore the four narrow stripes of a group captain. Saluting, Goldfarb gave his name, specialization, and service number, then added, "Reporting as ordered sir!"

The officer returned the salute. "Good to have you with us, Goldfarb. We've had excellent reports of you, and we're confident you'll make a valuable member of the team. I am Group Captain Fred Hipple; I shall be your commanding officer. My speciality is jet propulsion. Here we have Wing Commander Peary, Flight Lieutenant Kennan, and Flight Officer Roundbush."

The junior officers all towered over Hipple, but he dominated nonetheless. He was a dapper little fellow who held himself very erect; he had slicked-down wavy hair, a closely trimmed mustache, and heavy eyebrows. He spoke with almost professional precision: "I am told that you have been flying patrols aboard a radar-equipped Lancaster bomber in an effort to detect Lizard aircraft prior to their reaching our shores."

"Yes, sir, that's correct," Goldfarb said.

"Capital. We shall make great use of your experience, I assure you. What we are engaged in here, Radarman, is developing a jet-propelled fighter aeroplane to be similarly equipped with radar, thus facilitating the acquisition and tracking of targets and, it is to be hoped, their destruction."

"That's—splendid, sir." Goldfarb had always thought of radar as a defensive weapon, one to use to detect the enemy and send properly armed planes after him. But to mount it on a fighter already formidably armed in its own right ... He smiled. This was a project in which he would gladly take part.

Flight Officer Roundbush shook his head. He was as big and blond and blocky as Hipple was spare and dark. He said, "It'd be a lot more splendid if we could make the bloody thing fit in the space we have for it."

"Which is, at the moment, essentially nil," Hipple said with a rueful nod. "The jet fighter you may have seen taking off a

few moments ago, that little Gloster Pioneer, is not what one would call lavishly equipped with room. It was, in fact, in the air more than a year before the Lizards came." Bitterness creased his face. "As I had produced a working jet engine as far back as 1937, I find the delay unfortunate, but no help for it now. When the Lizards descended, the Pioneer, though intended only as an experimental aircraft, was rushed into production to give us as much of an equalizer as was possible."

"Might as well be tanks," Roundbush murmured. Both the German invasion of France and the fighting in the North African desert had shown severe deficiencies in British armor, but the same old obsolescent models kept getting made because they did work, after a fashion, and England had no time to tool up to build anything better.

Group Captain Hipple shook his head. "It's not as bad as that, Basil. We have managed to get the Meteor off the ground, after all." He turned back to Goldfarb. "The Meteor is more a proper fighter than the Pioneer. The latter carries a single jet engine placed in back of the cockpit, whereas the former has two, of an improved design, mounted on the wings. The improvement in performance is considerable."

"We also have a considerable production program laid on for the Meteor," Flight Lieutenant Kennan said. "With luck, we should be able to put large numbers of jet fighters into the air by this time next year."

"Yes, that's so, Maurice," Hipple agreed. "Of all the great powers, we and the Japanese have proved most fortunate, in that the Lizards did not invade either island nation. From the depths of space, I suppose we seemed too small to be worth troubling over. We've endured a worse blitz than the Jerries gave us, but life does go on despite a blitz. You should know that, eh, Goldfarb?"

"Yes, sir," Goldfarb said. "It got a bit lively at Dover now and again, but we came through." Though only a first-generation Englishman, he had a knack for understatement.

"Exactly." Hipple's nod was vehement, as if Goldfarb had said something important. The group captain went on, "As Flight Lieutenant Kennan and I have noted, our industrial capacity is still respectable, and we shall be able to get considerable numbers of Meteors airborne within a relatively short period. What point to it, however, if, once airborne, they are shot down again in short order?"

"Which is where you come in, Goldfarb," Wing Commander Peary said. He was a slim fellow of medium height with sandy hair starting to go gray; his startling bass voice seemed better suited to a man of twice his bulk.

"Exactly," Hipple said again. "Julian—the wing commander—means we need a chap with practical experience in airborne radar to help us plan its installation in Meteors as quickly as possible. Our pilots must be able to detect the enemy's presence at a distance comparable to that at which he can 'see' us. D'you follow?"

"I believe so, sir," Goldfarb said. "From what you say, I gather you intend the Meteor to have a two-man cockpit, pilot and radar observer. With the sets we have, sir, a pilot would be hard-pressed to tend to them and fly the aircraft at the same time."

The four RAF officers exchanged glances. Goldfarb wondered if he'd just stuck his foot in it. That would be lovely, a lowly radarman affronting all his superiors within five minutes of arriving at a new posting.

Then Julian Peary rumbled, "This is a point which was much debated during the design of the aircraft. You may be interested to know that the view you just expressed is the one which prevailed."

"I'm—pleased to hear that, sir," Goldfarb said, with such transparent relief that Basil Roundbush, who seemed not overburdened with military formality, broke into a large, toothy grin.

Group Captain Hipple said, "Having established your level of expertise with such dispatch, Radarman, you give me hope you will also be able to assist us in reducing the size of the radar set to be carried. The fuselage of the Meteor is rather less spacious than the bomb bay of the Lancaster where you were previously ensconced. Perhaps you'll have a look at these drawings with us so you can get a notion of the volume involved—"

Goldfarb stepped up to the table. With no more fanfare than that, he found himself a part of the team. He said, "I don't know the solution to one problem we faced in the Lanc."

"Which is?" Hipple asked.

"Of course, the Lizards' guided rockets can knock down a plane at longer range than any guns that we have can hit back. One of those rockets definitely seems to home in on our radar

transmissions—probably the same sort the Lizards used to knock out our ground stations. Turning off the set made that particular rocket go wild, but it also left us blind—something I shouldn't fancy if I were in the midst of a dogfight."

"Indeed not." Hipple nodded vigorously. "Even under ideal circumstances, the Meteor does not pull us level with the Lizards; it merely reduces our disadvantage. We remain deficient in speed and, as you say, in armament as well. To have to engage enemy aircraft without being able to detect them past the range of the pilot's eye would be a dreadful handicap. I do not pretend to be an expert in radar; as I said, engines are my speciality." He turned to the other officers. "Suggestions, gentlemen?"

Basil Roundbush said, "Can your airborne radar set emit more than one frequency, Goldfarb? If so, perhaps switching between one and the next might, ah, confuse the rocket and cause it to miss without losing radar capacity."

"That might work, sir; I honestly don't know," Goldfarb said. "We weren't any too keen on experimenting, not up above Angels Twenty, if you know what I mean."

"No quarrel there," Roundbush assured him. "We'd have to try it on the ground first: if a transmitter there survived by shifting frequencies, the result might be worth testing in aircraft as well."

He paused to scribble some notes. Goldfarb was delighted research and development had not stopped because of wartime emergencies, and even more delighted to be a part of the effort at Bruntingthorpe. But he'd already promised himself that, when the radar-equipped Meteors flew, he'd be in the rear seat of one of them. Having become part of an aircrew, he knew he'd never again be content to stay on the ground.

Moishe Russie was tired of staying underground. The irony of his position hit him in the teeth like a rifle butt in the hands of an SS man. When the Lizards came to Earth, he'd thought they were the literal answer to his prayers; absent their arrival, the Nazis would have massacred the Jews in the Warsaw ghetto, and in the others they'd set up throughout Poland.

The Jews had been looking for a miracle then. When Moishe declared that he'd had one, he gained enormous prestige in the ghetto; before, he'd been just another medical student slowly starving to death along with everyone else. He'd

urged the Jews to rise, to help throw the Germans out and let the Lizards in.

And so he'd become one of the Lizards' favorite humans. He'd broadcast propaganda for them, telling—truthfully—of the horrors and atrocities the Nazis had committed in Poland. The Lizards came to think he would say anything for them. They'd wanted him to praise their destruction of Washington, D.C., and say it was as just as the devastation that had fallen on Berlin.

He'd refused . . . and so he found himself here, hiding in a ghetto bunker that had been built with the Nazis, not the Lizards, in mind.

His wife Rivka picked that moment to ask, "How long have we been down here?"

"Too long," their son Reuven chimed in.

He was right; Moishe knew he was right. Reuven and Rivka had been cooped up in the bunker longer than he had; they'd gone into hiding so the Lizards couldn't use threats against them to bend him to their will. After that, the Lizards put a gun to his head to make him say what they wanted. He did not think of himself as a brave man, but he'd defied them even so. They hadn't killed him. In a way, what they did was worse— they killed his words, broadcasting a twisted recording that made him seem to say what they wanted even when he hadn't.

Russie had had his revenge; he'd made a recording in a tiny studio in the ghetto that detailed what the Lizards had done to him, and the Jewish fighters had managed to smuggle it out of Poland to embarrass the aliens. After that, he'd had to disappear himself.

Rivka said, "Do you even know, Moishe, whether it's day or night up there?"

"No more than you do," he admitted. The bunker had a clock; both he and Rivka had been faithful about keeping it wound. But the clock had only a twelve-hour dial, and after a while they'd lost track of which twelve hours they were in. Even by candlelight, he could see the dial from where he stood: it was a quarter past three. But did that mean bustling afternoon or dead of night? He had no idea. All he knew was that, at the moment, everyone here was awake.

"I don't know how much longer we can stand this," Rivka said. "It's no fit life for a human being, hiding down here in the darkness like a rat in its hole."

"But if it's the only way we can go on, then go on we will," Moishe answered sharply. "Life in wartime is never easy—do you think you're in America? Even if we are underground, we're better off now than when the Nazis ruled the ghetto."

"Are we?"

"I think so. We have plenty of food—" Their other child, a daughter, had died during the Nazi occupation, of dysentery aggravated by starvation. Moishe had known what he needed to do to save her, but without food and medicine he'd been helpless.

But now Rivka said, "So what? We could see our friends before, share our troubles. If the Germans beat us on the streets, it was just because we happened to be there. If the Lizards spy us, they'll shoot us on sight."

Since that was manifestly true, Moishe chose the only ploy left to him: he changed the subject. "Even now, our people are better off under the Lizards than they were under the Germans."

"Yes, and that's thanks in large part to you," Rivka retorted. "And what have you got for it? Your whole family, buried alive!" So much anger and bitterness clogged her voice that Reuven started to cry. Even as he comforted his son, Moishe blessed the little boy for short-circuiting the argument.

After he and Rivka got Reuven calmed down again, Moishe said carefully, "If you feel you must, I suppose you and Reuven can go back above ground. Not that many people knew you by sight; with God's help, you might go a long time before you were betrayed. Anyone who wanted to curry favor with the Lizards could gain it by turning me in. Or a Pole might do it for no better reason than that he hates Jews."

Rivka sighed. "You know we won't do that. We won't leave you, and you're right, you can't come up. But if you think we're well off here, you're *meshuggeh.*"

"I never said we were well off," Russie answered after a brief pause to search his memory and make sure he really hadn't said anything so foolish. "I only said things could be worse, and they could." The Nazis could have shipped the whole Warsaw ghetto to Treblinka or that other extermination camp they were just finishing when the Lizards came, the one they called Auschwitz. He didn't mention that to his wife. Some things, even if true, were too horrific to use as fuel in a quarrel.

The argument petered out. Reuven got sleepy, so they put him to bed. That meant they needed to go to bed themselves not much later; they couldn't get much sleep when the boy was awake and bouncing off the walls of the cramped bunker.

Noises woke Rivka first, then Moishe. Reuven snored on, even when his parents sat up. Noises in the cellar of the block of flats that concealed the bunker were always frightening. At times, Jewish fighters whom Mordechai Anielewicz led came down with fresh supplies for the Russies, but Moishe always wondered if the next appearance would be the one that brought the knock on the plasterboard panel hiding the doorway.

Rap, rap, rap! The sharp sound echoed through the bunker. Russie started violently. Beside him, Rivka's lips pulled back from her teeth, her eyes widened, and the skin all over her face tightened down onto the bones in a mask of fear. *Rap, rap, rap!*

Russie had vowed he wouldn't go easily. Moving as quiet as he could, he slid out of bed, grabbed a long kitchen knife, and blew out the last lamp, plunging the bunker into darkness blacker than any above-ground midnight.

Rap, rap, rap! Shoving and scraping noises as the plasterboard panel was dislodged and pushed aside. The bunker door itself was barred from the inside. Moishe knew it wouldn't hold against anyone determined to break it down. He raised the knife high. The first one who came through—Jewish traitor or Lizard—would take as much steel as he could give. That much he promised himself.

But instead of booted feet pounding on the door or a battering ram crashing against it, an urgent Yiddish voice called, "We know you're in there, *Reb* Moishe. Open this *verkakte* door, will you? We have to get you away before the Lizards come."

A trick? A trap? Automatically, Moishe looked toward Rivka. The darkness he'd made himself stymied him. "What to do?" he called softly.

"Open the door," she answered.

"But—"

"Open the door," Rivka repeated. "Nobody in the company of the Lizards would have sworn at it that way."

It seemed a slim reed to snatch. If it broke, it would pierce more than his hand. But how could he hold the invaders at bay? All at once, he realized they didn't have to come in after

him. Suppose they just stood back and sprayed the bunker with machine-gun bullets ... or started a fire and let him and his wife and child roast? He let the kitchen knife clatter to the floor, fumbled blindly for the bar, lifted it out of its rest, and pushed the door open.

One of the two Jews in the cellar carried an oil-burning lantern and a pistol. The lantern wasn't very bright, but dazzled Moishe anyhow. The fighter said, "Took you long enough. Come on. You have to hurry. Some *mamzer* talked where he shouldn't, and the Lizards'll be here soon."

Belief took root in Russie. "Get Reuven," he called to his wife.

"I have him," she answered. "He's not quite awake, but he'll come—won't you, dear?"

"Come where?" Reuven asked blurrily.

"Out of the bunker," Rivka said, that being all she knew. It was plenty to galvanize the boy. He let out a wild whoop and bounded out of bed. "Wait!" Rivka exclaimed. "You need your shoes. In fact, we all need our shoes. We were asleep."

"At half past eight in the morning?" the Jew with the lantern said. "I wish I was." After a moment, though, he added, "Not down here, though, I have to admit."

Moishe had forgotten he wore only socks. As he pulled on shoes and tied the laces, he asked, "Do we have time to take anything with us?" The books on a high shelf had become more like siblings than friends.

But the other Jew impatiently waiting outside, the one with a German Mauser slung on his back, shook his head and answered, "*Reb* Moishe, if you don't get moving, you won't have time to take yourself."

Even the low-ceilinged cellar seemed spacious to Moishe. He started to pant on his way up the stairs; he'd had no exercise at all in the bunker. The gray, leaden light at the top of the stairwell made him blink and set his eyes to watering. After so long with candles and oil lamps, even a distant hint of daylight was overwhelming.

Then he walked out onto the street. Thick clouds hid the sun. Dirty, slushy snow lay in the gutters. The air was hardly less thick and smoky than it had been in his underground hideaway. All the same, he wanted to throw his arms wide and dance like a Chasid to let loose his delight. Reuven *did* caper, coltlike; with a child's compressed grasp of time, he must have

felt he'd been entombed forever. Rivka walked steadily beside him, but her pale face was alight with joy and wonder, too.

Pale— Moishe looked down at his own hands. Beneath dirt, they were white and transparent as skimmed milk. His wife and son were just as pale. Everyone grew pallid through a Polish winter; but if he and his family lost any more color, they'd disappear.

"What's the date?" he asked, wondering how long he'd been cooped up in the bunker.

"Twenty-second of February," the Jew with the lantern answered. "A month till spring." He snorted. Spring seemed more likely a year away than mere weeks.

The first Lizard Moishe saw on the street made him want to run back to the bunker. The alien, though, paid him no special attention. Lizards had as much trouble telling humans apart as people did with Lizards. Moishe glanced over to Reuven and Rivka. The aliens' difficulties in that regard had helped the Jews spirit the two of them away from right under their snouts.

"In here," the fighter with the pistol said. The Russies obediently went up a stairway and into another block of flats. The halls smelled of cabbage and unwashed bodies and urine. In an apartment at the back of the third floor, more of Anielewicz's warriors waited. They whisked Moishe and his family inside.

One of them grabbed Moishe by the arm and hustled him over to a table set out with a bar of yellow-tan soap, an enameled basin, a pair of shears, and a straight razor. "The beard, *Reb* Moishe, has to come off," he said without preamble.

Moishe drew back in dismay. A protective hand rose to cover his chin. The SS had cut off the beards—and sometimes the ears and noses—of Jews in the ghetto for sport.

"I'm sorry," the fellow—bearded himself—said. "We're going to move you, we're going to hide you. Look at yourself now." He picked up a fragment of what might once have been a full-length mirror, thrust it in Moishe's face.

Moishe perforce looked. He saw—himself, paler than usual, his beard longer and fuzzier than usual because he hadn't bothered trimming it while in the bunker, but otherwise the same rather horse-faced, studious-looking Jew he'd always been.

The fighter said, "Now imagine yourself clean-shaven. Imagine a Lizard with a photograph of you as you are now looking at you—and walking on to look at someone else."

The closest Moishe could come to seeing himself beardless

was remembering what he'd looked like before his whiskers sprouted. He had trouble bringing the youth across the years and putting that face on the man he'd become.

Then Rivka said, "They're right, Moishe. It will make you different, and we need that. Please, go ahead and shave."

He sighed deeply, a token of surrender. Then he took the mirror from the fighter and leaned it on a shelf so he could see what he was doing. He picked up the shears and rapidly clipped as short as he could the beard he'd worn his whole adult life. What he knew about shaving was all theoretical. He splashed his face with water, then lathered the strong-smelling soap and spread it over cheeks and chin and neck.

Reuven snickered. "You look funny, Father!"

"I feel funny." He picked up the razor. The bone grip molded itself to his hand, like the handle of a scalpel. The comparison seemed even more apt a few minutes later. He thought he'd seen less blood flow at an appendectomy. He nicked his ear, the hollow under his cheekbone, his chin, his larynx, and he made a good game try at slicing off his upper lip. When he rinsed himself, the water in the basin turned pink.

"You look funny, Father," Reuven said again.

Moishe peered into the scrap of mirror. A stranger stared back at him. He looked younger than he had with the beard, but not really like his earlier self. His features were sharper-edged, bonier, more defined. He looked *tougher* than he'd expected. The dried blood here and there on his face might have had something to do with that; it gave him the air of a boxer who'd just lost a tough match.

The fellow who'd handed him the mirror patted him on the back and said, "Don't worry, *Reb* Moishe. They say it gets easier with practice." He wasn't speaking from experience; his own gray-brown beard reached halfway down his shirtfront.

Russie started to nod, then stopped and stared. It hadn't occurred to him that he'd have to do this more than once. But of course the fighter was right—if he wanted to keep up his disguise, he'd have to go on shaving. It struck him as a great waste of time. Even so, after he rinsed and dried the razor, he stuck it into a pocket of his long, dark coat.

The man with the pistol who'd plucked him from the bunker said, "All right, I think we can get you out of here now without too many people recognizing you."

His own mother wouldn't have recognized him . . . but she

was dead, like his daughter, of intestinal disease aggravated by
starvation. He said, "If I stay in Warsaw, sooner or later I'll be
spotted."

"Of course," the fighter said. "So you won't stay in Warsaw."

It made sense. It was like a kick in the belly just the same.
He'd spent his whole life here. Till the Lizards came, he'd
been sure he would die here, too. "Where will I—where will
we—go?" he asked quietly.

"Lodz," the fellow answered.

The word tolled through the room like the deep chime of a
funeral bell at a Catholic church. The Germans had done their
worst to the Lodz ghetto, second largest in Poland after Warsaw's, just before the Lizards came. Many of the quarter-
million Jews who had lived there were shipped to Chelmno
and Treblinka, never to come out again.

Russie's newly bared face must have shown his thoughts all
too clearly. The Jewish fighter said, "I understand how you
feel, *Reb* Moishe, but it's the best place. No one, not even,
God willing, a Lizard, would think to look for you there, and
if you're needed, we can bring you back in a hurry."

He could not fault the logic, but when he looked at Rivka,
he saw the same sick dread in her eyes that he felt himself. The Jews of Lodz had passed into the valley of the shadow of death. Going to live in a town where that shadow had
fallen . . .

"Some of us still survive in Lodz," the fighter said. "We'd
not send you there otherwise, you may be sure of that."

"Let it be so, then," Russie said with a sigh.

The fighter with the pistol drove the horse-drawn wagon out
of Warsaw. Russie sat beside him, feeling horribly visible and
vulnerable. Rivka and Reuven huddled in back along with several other women and children amid scraps and rags and odd-
shaped pieces of sheet metal: the stock of a junkman's trade.

The Lizards had a checkpoint on the highway just outside of
town. One of the males there carried a photograph of Russie
with his beard. His heart thuttered in alarm. But after a cursory
glance, the Lizard turned to his comrade and said in his own
language, "Just another boring bunch of Big Uglies." The
comrade waved the wagon ahead.

After a couple of kilometers, the fighter pulled over to the
side of the road. The women and children who had served to

camouflage Reuven and Rivka got down and started walking back to Warsaw. The fighter flicked the reins, clucked to the horse. The wagon rattled down the road toward Lodz.

Liu Han looked mistrustfully at the latest assortment of canned goods the little scaly devils had brought into her cell. She wondered what was most likely to stay down this time. The salty soup with noodles and bits of chicken, perhaps, and the canned fruit in syrup. She knew she wouldn't touch the stew with the thick gravy; she'd already given that back twice.

She sighed. Being pregnant was hard enough anywhere. It was even worse imprisoned here in this airplane that never came down. Not only was she alone in the little metal room except when the scaly devils brought Bobby Fiore to her, but almost all her food was put up by foreign devils like him and not to her taste.

She ate what she could, wishing she were back in her Chinese village or even in the prison camp from which the little scaly devils had plucked her. In either place, she would have been among her own kind, not caged all alone like a songbird for the amusement of her captors. If she ever got out of here, she vowed she would free every bird she could.

Not that getting out seemed likely. She shook her head—no indeed. Her straight black hair tumbled over her face, over her bare shoulders—the scaly devils, who wore no clothes themselves, allowed their human prisoners none and kept the cell too warm to make them comfortable anyhow—and across her newly tender breasts. Her hair hadn't been long enough to do that when the little devils brought her up here. It was now, and growing toward her waist.

She belched uncomfortably and got ready to dash for the plumbing hole. But what she'd eaten decided to stay where it belonged. She wasn't sure exactly how far gone she was, not in here where the little scaly devils never turned off the light to let her reckon the passage of days. But she wasn't throwing up as much as she had at first. Her belly hadn't started to swell, though. Getting close to four months was the best guess she could make.

Part of the floor, instead of being metal like the rest, was a raised mat covered with slick gray stuff that looked more like leather than anything else but didn't smell like it. Her body, sweaty in the heat, stuck to the mat when she lay down on

it, but it was still better for resting than anywhere else in the cell. She closed her eyes, tried to sleep. She'd been sleeping a lot lately, partly because she was pregnant and partly because she had nothing better to do.

She was just dozing off when the door to her cell hissed open again. She opened one eye, sure it would be the little devil who came in to take away the cans after every meal. Sure enough, in he skittered, but several others came with him. A couple of them had body paint more ornate than she was used to seeing.

One, to her surprise, spoke Chinese after a fashion. Pointing to her, he said, "You come with us."

She quickly got to her feet. "It shall be done, superior sir," she said, using one of the phrases she'd learned of the little devils' language.

The devils fell in around her at more than arm's length. She was on the small side, an inch or so above five feet, but she towered over the scaly devils, enough so to make them nervous around her. She joined them eagerly enough; any trip out of her cell was unusual enough to count as a treat. And maybe, better still, they would take her to Bobby Fiore.

They didn't; they led her in the opposite direction from his cell. She wondered what they wanted with her. Wondering made her hopeful and anxious by turns. They might do anything at all to her, from setting her free to taking her away from Bobby Fiore and giving her to some new man who would rape and beat her. She had no say. She was just a prisoner.

What they did reached neither extreme. They took her down an oddly curved stairway to another deck. She felt lighter there than she should have; her stomach didn't like it. But much of her fear went away. She knew they'd brought Bobby Fiore here, and nothing too bad had happened to him.

The scaly devils escorted her into a chamber full of their incomprehensible gadgetry. The devil sitting behind the desk surprised her by speaking fair Chinese: "You are the female human Liu Han?"

"Yes," she answered. "Who are you, please?" Her own language tasted sweet in her mouth. Even with Bobby Fiore, she spoke a curious mixture of Chinese, English, and the little devils' tongue, eked out with much gesture and dumb show.

"I am called Nossat," the scaly devil answered. "I am a—I

do not know it, your language has an exact word for it—I am a male who studies how you humans think. I am colleague to Tessrek, who spoke with your mate Bobby Fiore."

"Yes, I understand," Liu Han said. That was the little scaly devil with whom Bobby Fiore had spoken down here. What had he called the devil Tessrek? English had a name for what that devil did—*psychologist*, that was it. Liu Han relaxed. Talking could not be dangerous.

Nossat said, "You are going to lay an egg in the time to come? No, your kind does not lay eggs. You are going to give birth? Is that what you say, 'give birth'? You will have a child?"

"I am going to have a child, yes," Liu Han agreed. Of themselves, the fingers of her right hand spread fanlike over her belly. She had long since resigned herself to being naked in front of the scaly devils, but she remained automatically protective of the baby growing inside her.

"The child is from matings between Bobby Fiore and you?" Nossat said. Without waiting for her to reply, he stuck one of his thin, clawed fingers into a recess on the desk. A screen, as if for motion pictures, lit up behind him. The picture that moved upon it was of Bobby Fiore thrusting atop Liu Han.

She sighed. She knew the little scaly devils took pictures of her while she made love, as well as any other time they chose. They had mating seasons like farm animals, and were utterly uninterested in matters of the flesh at any other time. The way people mated the whole year round seemed to fascinate and appall them.

"Yes," she answered as the picture played on, "Bobby Fiore and I made love to start this baby." Before long, it would begin to kick inside her, hard enough to feel. She remembered what a marvel that was from the boy she'd borne her husband before the Japanese killed him and the child.

Nossat stuck his finger into a different recess. Liu Han was not sorry to see the picture of her joined gasping to Bobby Fiore fade. A different moving picture took its place, this one of an immensely pregnant black woman giving birth to her baby. Liu Han watched the woman with more interest than the birth process: she knew about that, but she'd never before seen a black, man or woman. She hadn't known the palms of their hands and soles of their feet were so pale.

"This is how your young are born?" Nossat said as the baby's head and then shoulders emerged from between the straining woman's legs.

"What else could it possibly be?" To Liu Han, the little scaly devils were an incomprehensible blend of immense and terrifying powers on the one hand and childishly abysmal ignorance on the other.

"This is—dreadful," Nossat said. The motion picture kept running. The woman delivered the afterbirth. It should have been over then. But she kept on bleeding. The blood was hard to see against her dark skin, but it spread over and soaked into the ground where she lay. The little scaly devil went on, "This female died after the young Tosevite came out of her body. Many females in the land we hold have died bearing their young."

"That does happen, yes," Liu Han said quietly. It was not something she cared to think about. Not just bleeding, but a baby trying to come out while in the wrong position, or fever afterwards . . . so many things could go wrong. And so many babies never lived to see their second birthday, their first outside their mother.

"But it's not right," Nossat exclaimed, as if he held her personally responsible for the way people had their babies. "No other kind of intelligent creature we know puts its mothers in such danger just to carry on life."

Liu Han had never imagined any kind of intelligent creatures but human beings until the little scaly devils came. Even after she knew of the devils, she hadn't thought there could be still more varieties of such creatures. Irritation in her voice, she snapped, "Well, how do you have your babies, then?" For all she knew, the little devils might have been assembled in factories rather than born.

"Our females lay eggs, of course," Nossat said. "So do those of the Rabotevs and Hallessi, over whom we rule. Only you Tosevites are different." His weird eyes swiveled so that one watched the screen behind him while the other stayed accusingly on Liu Han.

She fought to keep from laughing, fought and lost. The idea of making a nest—out of straw, maybe, like a chicken's—and then sitting on it till the brood hatched was absurd enough to tickle her fancy. Hens certainly didn't seem to have trouble

laying eggs, either. It might be an easier way to do the job. But it wasn't the way people did it.

Nossat said, "Your time to have the young come out of your body is now about a year away?"

"A year?" Liu Han stared at him. Didn't the little scaly devils know *anything*?

But the devil said, "No—this is my mistake, for two years of the Race, more or less, make one of yours. I should say—should have said—you are half a year from your time?"

"Half a year, yes," Liu Han said. "Maybe not quite so long."

"We have to decide what to do with you," Nossat told her. "We have no knowledge of how to help you when the young is born. You are only a barbarous Tosevite, but we do not want you to die because we are ignorant. You are our subject, not our enemy."

Fear blew through Liu Han, a cold wind. Give birth here, in this place of metal, with only scaly devils beside her, without a midwife to help her through her pangs? If the least little thing went wrong, she *would* die, and the baby, too. "I will need help," she said, as plaintively as she could. "Please get some for me."

"We are still planning," Nossat said, which was neither yes nor no. "We will know what we do before your time comes."

"What if the baby is early?" Liu Han said.

The little devil's eyes both swung toward her. "This can happen?"

"Of course it can," Liu Han said. But nothing was *of course* for the little scaly devils, not when they knew so little about how mankind—and, evidently, womankind—functioned. Then, suddenly, Liu Han had an idea that felt so brilliant, she hugged herself in delight. "Superior sir, would you let me go back down to my own people so a midwife could help me deliver the baby?"

"This had not been thought of." Nossat made a distressed hissing noise. "I see, though, from where you stand, it may have merit. You are not the only female specimen on this ship who will have young born. We will—how do you say?— consider. Yes. We will consider."

"Thank you very much, superior sir." Liu Han looked down at the floor, as she had seen the scaly devils do when they

meant to show respect. Hope sprang up in her like rice plants in spring.

"Or maybe," Nossat said, "maybe we bring up a—what word did you use?—a midwife, yes, maybe we bring up a midwife to this ship to help you here. We will consider that, too. You go now."

The guards took Liu Han out of the psychologist's office, led her back to her cell. She felt heavier with each step up the curiously curving stairway that returned her to her deck—and also because the hope which had sprouted now began to wilt.

But it didn't quite die. The little scaly devils hadn't said no.

A blank-faced Nipponese guard shoved a bowl of rice between the bars of Teerts' cell. Teerts bowed to show he was grateful. Feeding prisoners at all was, in Nipponese eyes, a mercy: a proper warrior would die fighting rather than let himself be captured. The Nipponese were in any case sticklers for their own forms of courtesy. Anyone who flouted them was apt to be beaten—or worse.

Since the Nipponese shot down his killercraft, Teerts had had enough beatings—and worse—that he never wanted another (which didn't mean he wouldn't get one). But he hated rice. Not only was it the food of his captivity, it wasn't something any male of the Race would eat by choice. He wanted meat, and could not remember the last time he'd tasted it. This bland, glutinous vegetable matter kept him alive, although he often wished it wouldn't.

No, that was a falsehood. If he'd wanted to die, he had only to starve himself to death. He did not think the Nipponese would force him to eat; if anything, he might gain their respect by perishing this way. That he cared whether these barbarous Big Uglies respected him showed how low he had sunk.

He lacked the nerve to put an end to himself, though; the Race did not commonly use suicide as a way out of trouble. And so, miserably, he ate, half wishing he never saw another grain of rice, half wishing his bowl held more.

He finished just before the guard came back and took away the bowl. He bowed again in gratitude for that service, though the guard would also have taken it even if he hadn't finished.

After the guard left, Teerts resigned himself to another in-definitely long stretch of tedium. So far as he knew, he was the

only prisoner of the Race the Nipponese held here at Nagasaki. No cells within speaking distance of him held even Big Ugly prisoners, lest he somehow form a conspiracy with them and escape. He let his mouth fall open in bitter laughter at the likelihood of that.

Six-legged Tosevite pests scuttled across the concrete floor. Teerts let his eye turrets follow the creatures. He had nothing in particular against them. The real pests on Tosev 3 were the ones who walked upright.

He drifted away into a fantasy where his killercraft's turbofans hadn't tried to breathe bullets instead of air. He could have been back at a comfortably heated barracks talking with his comrades or watching the screen or piping music through a button taped to a hearing diaphragm. He could have been snapping bites off a chunk of dripping meat. He could have been in his killercraft again, helping to bring the pestilential Big Uglies under the Race's control.

Though he heard footsteps coming down the corridor toward him, he did not swing his eyes to see who was approaching. That would have returned him to grim reality too abruptly to bear.

But then the maker of those footsteps stopped outside his cell. Teerts quickly put fantasy aside, like a male saving a computer document so he can attend to something more urgent. His bow was deeper than the one he'd given the guard who fed him. "*Konichiwa,* Major Okamoto," he said in the Nipponese he was slowly acquiring.

"Good day to you as well," Okamoto answered in the language of the Race. He was more fluent in it than Teerts was in Nipponese. Learning a new tongue did not come naturally to males of the Race; the Empire had had but one for untold thousands of years. But Tosev 3 was a mosaic of dozens, maybe hundreds, of languages. Picking up one more was nothing out of the ordinary for a Big Ugly. Okamoto had been Teerts' interpreter and interrogator ever since he was captured.

The Tosevite glanced down the hall. Teerts heard jingling keys as a warder drew near. Another round of questions, then, the pilot thought. He bowed to the warder to show he was grateful for the boon of leaving the cell. Actually he wasn't; as long as he stayed in here, no one hurt him. But the forms had to be observed.

A soldier with a rifle tramped right behind the warder. He covered Teerts as the other male used the key. Okamoto also drew his pistol and held it on Teerts. The pilot would have laughed, except it wasn't really funny. He only wished he were as dangerous as the Big Uglies thought he was.

The interrogation room was on an upper floor of the prison. Teerts had seen next to nothing of Nagasaki. He knew it lay by the sea; he'd come here by ship after being evacuated from the mainland when Harbin fell to the Race. He didn't miss seeing the sea. After that nightmare voyage of storms and sickness, he hoped he'd never see—much less ride upon—another overgrown Tosevite ocean again.

The guard opened the door. Teerts walked in, bowed to the Big Uglies inside. They wore white coats rather than uniforms like Okamoto's. *Scientists, not soldiers,* Teerts thought. He'd come to realize the Tosevites used clothing to indicate job and status as the Race used body paint. The Big Uglies, however, were much less systematic and consistent about it—*typical of them,* he thought.

Nonetheless, he was glad not to face another panel of officers. The military males had been much quicker than scientists to resort to the instruments of painful persuasion in the interrogation room.

One of the men in white addressed Teerts in barking Nipponese, much too fast for him to follow. He turned both eye turrets toward Major Okamoto, who translated: "Dr. Nakayama asks whether, as has been reported, all members of the Race who have come to Tosev 3 are male."

"Hai," Teerts answered. *"Honto."* Yes, that was the truth.

Nakayama, a slim male on the small side for a Tosevite, asked another long question in his own tongue. Okamoto translated again: "He asks how you can hope to keep Tosev 3 with males alone."

"We don't, of course," Teerts answered. "We who are here make up the conquest fleet. Our task is to subjugate this world, not to colonize it. The colonization fleet will come. It was being organized even as we set out, and will arrive in this solar system about forty years from now."

So long a gap should have given the males of the conquest fleet plenty of time to get Tosev 3 into good running order for the colonists. It would have done just that, had the Big Uglies been the pre-industrial savages the Race thought they were.

Teerts still thought they were savages, but, worse luck, they were anything but pre-industrial.

All three Nipponese in white started talking volubly at one another. Finally one of them put a question to Teerts. "Dr. Higuchi wants to know whether you mean your years or ours."

"Ours," Teerts said; would he waste his time learning Tosevite measurements? "Yours is longer—I don't remember how much."

"So, then, this colonization fleet, as you call it, will arrive on our planet in fewer than forty years' time as we reckon it?" Higuchi said.

"Yes, superior sir." Teerts suppressed a sigh. It should have been so easy: smash the Big Uglies, prepare the planet for full exploitation, then settle down and wait till the colonists arrived and were thawed out. When at last he smelled mating pheromones again, Teerts might even have sired a couple of clutches of eggs himself. Raising hatchlings, of course, was females' work, but he liked thinking of passing on his genes so he could contribute to the future of the Race.

The way things looked now, this world might still be troublesome when the colonization fleet got here. And even if it wasn't, his own chance of being around to join the colony's gene pool wasn't big enough to be visible to the naked eye—he couldn't see it, at any rate.

He had a while to think of such things, because the Nipponese were chattering furiously among themselves again. Finally the male who hadn't addressed him before spoke through Major Okamoto: "Dr. Tsuye wishes to know the size of the colonization fleet as opposed to that of the conquest fleet."

"The colonization fleet is not opposed to the conquest fleet," Teerts said. Clearing up the idiom took a couple of minutes. Then he said, "The colonization fleet is larger, superior sir. It has to be: it carries many more males and females as well as what they will need to establish themselves here on Tosev 3."

His answer produced more sharp colloquy among the Nipponese. Then the one named Tsuye said, "This colonization fleet—is it, ah, as heavily armed as your invasion fleet?"

"No, of course not. There would be no need—" Teerts corrected himself. "There was thought to be no need for including many weapons with the colonization fleet. It was assumed that you Tosevites would already be thoroughly subdued by the time the colonists arrived here. We hadn't counted on your re-

sisting so ferociously." *I hadn't counted on being shot down,* the pilot added to himself.

His words seemed to please the Nipponese. They bared their flat, square teeth in the facial gesture they used to show they were happy. Major Okamoto said, "All Tosevites are brave, and we Nipponese the bravest of the brave."

"Hai," Teerts said. *"Honto."* The interrogation broke up not long after that. Okamoto and the guard, who had waited outside, escorted Teerts back to his cell. That evening, he found small chunks of meat mixed in with his rice. That had only happened a couple of times before. Flattery, he thought as he gratefully swallowed them down, had got him something.

Mutt Daniels looked at his hand: four clubs and the queen of hearts. He discarded the queen. "Gimme one," he said.

"One," Kevin Donlan agreed. "Here you go, Sarge." The new card was a diamond. None of the other soldiers in the game would have known it from Mutt's face. He'd played countless hours of poker on trains and bus rides as a minor-league (and, briefly, major-league) catcher and as a longtime minor-league manager. He'd played in the trenches in France, too, in the last war. He didn't care to risk a big roll of money when he gambled, but he won more often than he lost. Every so often he'd stolen a pot on a busted flush, too.

Not tonight, though. One of the privates in his squad, a big hunkie named Bela Szabo who was universally called Dracula, had drawn three cards and raised big when it was his turn to bet. Mutt pegged him for at least three of a kind, maybe better. When the action came round to him, he tossed in his cards. "Can't win 'em all," he said philosophically.

Kevin Donlan, who couldn't possibly have been as young as he looked, hadn't learned that yet. Calling Szabo was okay if you had two little pair, but raising back struck Mutt as foolhardy. Sure as hell, Dracula was holding three kings. He scooped up the folding money.

"Son, you gotta watch what the other guy's doin' better'n that," Daniels said. "Like I told you, you ain't gonna win 'em all." If nothing else, years of managing in the minors had pounded that home as a law of nature. Mutt chuckled. The life he'd lived beat the hell out of the one he'd have had if he hadn't played ball. Likely he'd still be watching a mule's hind end on the Mississippi farm where he'd been born and raised.

Like trains in the distance, shells rumbled by overhead. Everybody looked up, though the roof of the barn where they sheltered held the sky at bay. Szabo cocked his head, gauging the sound. "Southbound," he said. "Those are ours."

"Probably landing on the Lizards in Decatur right now," Kevin Donlan agreed. A moment later, he added, "What's funny, Sarge?"

"I reckon I've said I was managing the Decatur team in the Three-I League when the Lizards came," Mutt answered. "Matter of fact, I was on the train from Madison to Decatur when we got strafed right outside o' Dixon, upstate. This here's the closest I've come to makin' it to where I was goin' since, and most of a year's gone by now."

"This here"—the barn—was on a farm just south of Clinton, Illinois, about halfway between Bloomington and Decatur. The Americans had taken Bloomington in an armored blitz. Now it was slow, tough work again, trying to push the Lizards farther back from Chicago.

More shells hissed through the sky, these from the south. "Goddamn, the Lizards are quick with counterbattery fire," Donlan said.

"They're dead on, too," Mutt said. "I hope our boys moved their guns before those little presents came down on 'em."

The poker game went on by lantern light, shelling or no shelling. Mutt won a hand with two pair, lost expensively to a straight when he was holding three nines, didn't waste money betting on a couple of others. Another American battery opened up, this one a lot closer. The thunder of the big guns reminded Mutt of bad weather back home.

"Hope they blow all the Lizards in Decatur straight to hell," Szabo said.

"Hope one of 'em lands on second base at Fan's Field and blows the center-field fence out to where it belongs," Daniels muttered. It was 340 down each foul line at the Decatur ballpark, a reasonable poke, but dead center was only 370, a pain in the ERA to every Commodore pitcher who took the mound.

Small-arms fire rattled only a few hundred yards away, some M-1s and Springfields, some from the automatic rifles the Lizards carried. Before Mutt could say a word, everybody in the latest hand grabbed his money from the pot, stuffed it into a pocket, and reached for his weapon. Someone blew out

the lantern. Someone else pushed the barn door open. One by one, the men emerged.

"You want to be careful," Mutt said quietly. "The Lizards have those damn night sights, let 'em see like cats in the dark."

Dracula Szabo laughed, also softly. "That's why I got me this here Browning Automatic Rifle, Sarge. Put out enough lead and some of it'll hit somebody." He wasn't much older than Donlan, young enough to be gut-sure no bullet could possibly find him. Mutt knew better. France had convinced him he wasn't immortal, and several months fighting the Lizards drove the lesson home again.

"Spread out, spread out," Daniels called in an urgent whisper. To his ear, the men sounded like a herd of drunken rhinos. Several were new recruits; by virtue of having lived through several encounters with the Lizards, Mutt was reckoned suitable for showing others how to do likewise.

"How many Lizards you think there are, Sarge?" Kevin Donlan asked. Donlan wasn't eager any more; he'd been through enough of the tough defensive fighting outside Chicago to be sure his number could come up. The question came in a tone of intelligent professional concern.

Daniels cocked his head, listened to the firing. "Damfino," he said at last. "Not a whole bunch, but I wouldn't peg it tighter'n that. Those rifles o' theirs shoot so fast, just a couple can sound like a platoon."

Off to one side lay the concrete ribbon of US 51. A couple of soldiers charged straight down it. Daniels yelled at them, but they kept going. He wondered why they didn't paint big red-and-white bull's-eyes on their chests, too. He dodged from bush to upended tractor to hedgerow, making himself as tough a target as he could.

That wasn't the only reason he fell behind most of the squad. He had fifty-odd years and a pot belly under his belt, though he was in better shape now than he had been before the Lizards came. Even in his long-gone playing days, he'd been a catcher, so he'd never moved what anybody would call fast.

He was panting and his heart thudded in his chest by the time he half jumped, half fell into a shell hole at the edge of the American firing line. Somebody not far away was screaming for a medic and for his mother; his voice was ebbing fast.

Cautiously, Mutt raised his head and peered into the night to

see if he could pick up muzzle flashes from the Lizards' rifles. Over there, a yellow-white flicker . . . He raised his Springfield to his shoulder, squeezed off a round, worked the bolt, fired again. Then he threw himself flat again.

Sure enough, bullets cracked by, just above the hole where he hid. If he could pick up the Lizards' muzzle flashes, they could find his as well. And if he fired again from here, he was willing to bet some turret-eyed little scaly sharpshooter would punch his ticket for him. The Lizards weren't human, but they were pretty fair soldiers.

He scrambled out of the hole and crawled across cold ground over to something made of bricks—a well, he realized when he got behind it. Szabo was making a hell of a racket with that BAR; if he wasn't hitting the Lizards, he was sure making them keep their heads down. Even more warily than before, Daniels looked south again.

He saw a flash, fired at it. In the night, it was the next closest thing to shooting blind. No more flickers of light came from that spot, but he never found out whether it was because he'd scored a hit or the Lizard moved to a new firing spot, as he'd done himself.

After fifteen or twenty minutes, the firing faded. The Americans slowly moved forward to discover the Lizards had pulled out. "Just a recon patrol," said another sergeant who, like Mutt, was trying to round up his squad and not having much luck.

"Don't rightly recall the Lizards doin' a whole lot o' that, not at night and not on foot," Daniels said with a thoughtful frown. "Ain't been their style."

"Maybe they're learning," the other noncom answered. "You don't really know what the other fellow's doing till you sneak around and see it with your own eyes."

"Yeah, sure, but the Lizards, they mostly fight one way," Mutt said. "Don't know as how I like 'em learnin' how to do their job better. That'll mean they got more chance of shootin' my personal, private ass off."

The other sergeant laughed. "Somethin' to that, pal. I don't know what we can do about it, though, short of giving their patrols enough lumps to make 'em try something else instead."

"Yeah," Mutt said again. He blew air out through his lips to make a whuffling noise. This hadn't been too bad—just a little

skirmish. As far as he could tell, he didn't have anybody dead or even hurt. But if the Lizards were skirmishing outside of Clinton, it was liable to be a good long while yet before he saw Decatur.

☆ **III** ☆

Clip-clop, clip-clop. Colonel Leslie Groves hated slowness, hated delay, with the restless passion of an engineer who'd spent a busy lifetime fighting inefficiency wherever it reared its head. And here he was, coming into Oswego, New York, in a horse-drawn wagon because the cargo he had in his charge was too important to risk putting it on an airplane and having the Lizards shoot it down. *Clip-clop, clip-clop.*

Rationally, he knew this slow, safe trip didn't stall anything. The Met Lab team, traveling by the same archaic means he was using himself, wasn't close to Denver yet and couldn't work with the uranium or whatever it was that the British had fetched over to the United States from eastern Europe.

Clip-clop, clip-clop. Riding alongside the wagon was a squadron of horse cavalry, an antique arm Groves had long wished would vanish from the Army forever. The horsemen were useless against the Lizards, as they had been for years against any Earthly mechanized force. But they did a first-class job of overawing the brigands, bandits, and robbers who infested the roads in these chaotic times.

"Captain, will we reach the Coast Guard station by sunset?" Groves called to the commander of the cavalry unit.

Captain Rance Auerbach glanced westward, gauged the sun through curdled clouds. "Yes, sir, I believe so. Only a couple more miles to the lake shore." His Texas drawl drew looks here in upstate New York. Groves thought he should be wearing Confederate gray and maybe a plume in his hat, too; he was too flamboyant for olive drab. That he called his horse Jeb Stuart did nothing to weaken that freewheeling image.

The wagon rolled past a wooden ballpark with a sign that

67

read, OTIS FIELD, HOME OF THE OSWEGO NETHERLANDS, CANADIAN-AMERICAN LEAGUE. "Netherlands," Groves said with a snort. "Hell of a name for a baseball team."

Captain Auerbach pointed to a billboard across the street. In faded, tattered letters it proclaimed the virtues of the Netherland Ice Cream and Milk Company. "Bet you anything you care to stake they ran the team, sir," he said.

"No thank you, Captain," Groves said. "I won't touch that one."

Otis Field didn't look as if it had seen much use lately. Planks were missing from the outer fence; they'd no doubt helped Oswegians stay warm during the long, miserable winter. The gaps showed the rickety grandstand and the dugouts where in happier—and warmer—times the opposing teams had sheltered. Stands and dugout roofs also had the missing-tooth effect from vanished lumber. If the Netherlands ever returned to life, they'd need somewhere new to play.

From long experience, Groves reckoned Oswego a town of twenty or twenty-five thousand. The few people out on the streets looked poor and cold and hungry. Most people looked that way these days. The town didn't seem to have suffered directly in the war, though the Lizards were in Buffalo and on the outskirts of Rochester. Groves guessed Oswego wasn't big enough for them to have bothered pulverizing it. He hoped they'd pay for the omission.

On the east side of the Oswego River stood the U.S. Military Reservation, with the earthworks of Fort Ontario. The fort dated back even further than the French and Indian War. Holding enemies at bay now, unfortunately, wasn't as simple as it had been a couple of centuries before.

The Coast Guard station was a two-story white frame building at the foot of East Second Street, down by the cold, choppy gray waters of Lake Ontario. The cutter *Forward* was tied up at a pier out in the lake. A seaman policing up outside the station spied the wagon and its escort approaching. He ducked into the building, calling loudly, "The U.S. Cavalry just rode into town, sir!"

Groves smiled at that, in amusement and relief. An officer came out of the station. He wore a U.S. Navy uniform; in time of war, the Coast Guard was subsumed into the Navy. Saluting, he said, "Colonel Groves?"

"Right here." Groves ponderously descended from the wagon. Even with wartime privation, he carried well over two hundred pounds. He returned the salute and said, "I'm afraid I wasn't given your name"—the Coast Guardsman had two broad stripes on his cuffs and shoulder blades—"Lieutenant, ah . . . ?"

"I'm Jacob van Alen, sir," the Coast Guardsman said.

"Well, Lieutenant van Alen, I gather the messenger got here ahead of us."

"From what Smitty yelled, you mean? Yes, sir, he did." Van Alen had an engaging grin. He was a tall, skinny fellow somewhere close to thirty, very blond, with an almost invisible little mustache. He went on, "Our orders are to give you whatever you want, not to ask a whole lot of questions, and never, ever put your name on the radio. I'm paraphrasing, but that's what they boil down to."

"It sounds right," Groves agreed. "You'd be better off forgetting we even exist once we're gone. Impress that on your sailors, too; if they start blabbing and any word of us gets out, they'll be arrested and tried as traitors to the United States. That comes straight from President Roosevelt, not from me. Make sure your people understand it."

"Yes, sir." Van Alen's eyes sparkled. "If they hadn't told me to keep my big mouth shut, I'd have at least a million questions for you; you'd best believe that."

"Lieutenant, believe me—you don't want to know." Groves had seen the slagged ruin a single Lizard bomb had made of Washington, D.C. If the Lizards had that power, the United States had to have it, too, to survive. But the idea of a uranium bomb chilled him. Start throwing those things around and you were liable to end up with an abattoir instead of a world.

"What you say has already been made very clear to me, Colonel," van Alen said. "Suppose you tell me what it is you want me to do for you."

"If the Lizards weren't in Buffalo, I'd have you sail me all the way to Duluth," Groves answered. "As it is, you're going to take me across to the Canadian side so I can continue on the overland route."

"To wherever you're going." Van Alen raised a hand. "I'm not asking, I'm just talking. One thing I do need to know, though: whereabouts on the Canadian side am I taking you? It's a biggish country, you know."

"I have heard rumors to that effect, yes," Groves said dryly. "Sail us across to Oshawa. They should be expecting me there; if a messenger got through to you, no reason to think one didn't make it to them."

"You're right about that. The Lizards haven't hit Canada as hard as they've hit us."

"By all I've heard, they don't care for cold weather." Now Groves held up a broad-palmed hand. "I know, I know—if they don't care for cold weather, what are they doing in Buffalo?"

"You beat me to it," the Coast Guardsman said. "Of course, they did get there in summertime. I hope they had themselves a hell of a surprise along around November."

"I expect they did," Groves said. "Now then, Lieutenant, much as I'd like to stand around shooting the breeze"—something he loathed—"I have a package to deliver. Shall we get moving?"

"Yes, sir," van Alen answered. He glanced toward the wagon from which Groves had got down. "You won't be bringing that aboard the *Forward*, will you? Or the horses?"

"What are we supposed to do for mounts without 'em?" Captain Auerbach demanded indignantly.

"Captain, I want you to take a good look at that cutter," Jacob van Alen said. "It carries me and a crew of sixteen. Now there's what, maybe thirty of you folks? Okay, we can squeeze you onto the *Forward*, especially just for one fast run across the lake, but where the hell would we stow those animals even if we could get 'em on board?"

Groves looked from the *Forward* to the cavalry detachment and back again. As an engineer, he was trained in using space efficiently. He turned to Auerbach. "Rance, I'm sorry, but I think Lieutenant van Alen knows what he's talking about. What is that, Lieutenant, about an eighty-foot boat?"

"You have a good eye, Colonel. She's a seventy-eight-footer, forty-three tons displacement."

Groves grunted. Thirty-odd horses weighed maybe twenty tons all by themselves. They'd have to stay behind, no doubt about it. He watched Captain Auerbach unhappily making the same calculation and coming up with the same result. "Cheer up, Captain," he said. "I'm sure the Canadians will furnish us with new mounts. They don't know what we're carrying, but they know how important it is."

Auerbach reached out to stroke his mount's velvety muzzle. He answered with a cavalryman's *cri de coeur*: "Colonel, if they took your wife away and issued you a replacement, would you be satisfied with the exchange?"

"I might, if they issued me Rita Hayworth." Groves let both hands rest on his protuberant belly. "Trouble is, she probably wouldn't be satisfied with me." Auerbach stared at him, let out an amazingly horsey snort, and spread his palms in surrender.

Lieutenant van Alen said, "Okay, no horses. What about the wagon?"

"We don't need that either, Lieutenant." Groves walked over, reached in, and pulled out a saddlebag that had been fixed with straps so he could carry it on his back. It was heavier than it looked, both from the uranium or whatever it was the Germans had stolen from the Lizards and from the lead shielding that—Groves hoped—kept the metal's ionizing radiation from ionizing him. "I have everything required right here."

"Whatever you say, sir." What van Alen's eyes said was that the pack didn't look important enough to cause such a fuss. Groves stared stonily back at the Coast Guardsman. Here, as often, looks were deceiving.

Regardless of what van Alen might have thought, he and his crew efficiently did what was required of them. Inside half an hour the *Forward*'s twin gasoline engines were thundering as the cutter pulled away from the dock and headed for the Canadian shore.

As Oswego receded, Groves strode up and down the *Forward*, curious as usual. The first thing he noticed was the sound of his shoes on the deck. He paused in surprise and rapped his knuckles against the cutter's superstructure. That confirmed his first impression. "It's made out of wood!" he exclaimed, as if inviting someone to contradict him.

But a passing crewman nodded. "That's us, Colonel— wooden ships and iron men, just like the old saying." He grinned impudently. "Hell, leave me out in the rain and I rust."

"Get out of here," Groves said. But when he thought about it, it made sense. A Coast Guard cutter wasn't built to fight other ships; it didn't need an armored hull. And wood was strong stuff. Apart from its use in shipbuilding, the Russians and England both still used it to build highly effective aircraft

(or so the Mosquito and LaGG were reckoned before the Lizards came). Even so, it had taken him aback here.

Lake Ontario had a light chop. Even Groves, hardly smooth on his feet, effortlessly adjusted to it. One of his cavalrymen, though, bent himself double over the port rail puking his guts out. Groves suspected the sailors' ribbing would have been a lot more ribald had the luckless fellow's friends not outnumbered them two to one and been more heavily armed to boot.

The *Forward* boasted a one-pounder mounted in front of the superstructure. "Will that thing do any good if the Lizards decide to strafe us?" Groves asked the Coast Guardsman in charge of the weapon.

"About as much as a mouse giving a hawk the finger when the hawk swoops down on it," the sailor answered. "Might make the mouse feel better, for a second or two, anyhow, but the hawk's not what you'd call worried." In spite of that cold-blooded assessment, the man stayed at his post.

The way the Coast Guardsmen handled their jobs impressed Groves. They knew what they needed to do and they did it, without fuss, without spit and polish, but also without wasted motion. Lieutenant van Alen hardly needed to give orders.

The trip across the lake was long and boring. Van Alen invited Groves to take off his pack and stow it in the cabin. "Thank you, Lieutenant, but no," Groves said. "My orders are not to let it out of my sight at any time, and I intend to take them literally."

"However you like, sir," the Coast Guardsman said. He eyed Groves speculatively. "That must be one mighty important cargo."

"It is." Groves let it go at that. He wished the heavy pack were invisible and weightless. That might keep people from jumping to such accurate conclusions. The more people wondered about what he was carrying, the likelier word was to get to the Lizards.

As if the thought of the aliens were enough to conjure them out of thin air, he heard the distant scream of one of their jet planes. His head spun this way and that, trying to spot the aircraft through scattered clouds. He saw the contrail, thin as a thread, off to the west.

"Out of Rochester, or maybe Buffalo," van Alen said with admirable sangfroid.

"Do you think he saw us?" Groves demanded.

"Likely he did," the Coast Guardsman said. "We've been buzzed a couple times, but never shot at. Just to stay on the safe side, we'll crowd your men down below, where they won't show, and look as ordinary as we can for a while. And if you won't leave that pack in the cabin, maybe you'll step in yourself for a bit."

It was as politely phrased an order as Groves had ever heard. He out-ranked van Alen, but the Coast Guardsman commanded the *Forward*, which meant authority rested with him. Groves went inside, jammed his face against a porthole. With luck, he told himself, the Lizard pilot would go on about his business, whatever that was. Without luck . . .

The throb of the engines was louder inside, so Groves needed longer to hear the shriek the Lizard plane made. That shriek grew hideously fast. He waited for the one-pounder on the foredeck to start banging away in a last futile gesture of defiance, but it stayed silent. The Lizard plane screamed low overhead. Through the porthole, Groves saw van Alen looking up and waving. He wondered if the Coast Guard lieutenant had gone out of his mind.

But the jet roared away, the scream of its engine fading and dopplering down into a deep-throated wail. Groves hadn't known he was holding his breath until he let it out in one long sigh. When he couldn't hear the Lizard plane any more, he went out on deck again. "I thought we were in big trouble there," he told van Alen.

"Naah." The Coast Guardsman shook his head. "I figured we were all right as long as they didn't notice all your men on deck. They've seen the *Forward* out on the lake a good many times, and we've never done anything that looks aggressive. I hoped they'd just assume we were out on another cruise, and I guess they did."

"I admire your coolness, Lieutenant, and I'm glad you didn't have to show coolness under fire," Groves said.

"You can't possibly be half as glad as I am, sir," van Alen answered. The Coast Guard cutter sailed on toward the Canadian shore.

In the midst of the trees—some bare-branched birches, more dark pine and fir—the ice-covered lake appeared as suddenly

as a rabbit out of a magician's hat. "By Jove," George Bagnall exclaimed as the Lancaster bomber ducked down below tree-top height to make it harder for Lizard radar to pick them up. "That's a nice bit of navigating, Alf."

"All compliments gratefully accepted," Alf Whyte replied. "Assuming that's actually Lake Peipus, we can follow it straight down to Pskov."

From the pilot's seat next to Bagnall, Ken Embry said, "And if it's not, we don't know where the bloody hell we are, and we'll all be good and Pskoved."

Groans filled the earphones on Bagnall's head. The flight engineer studied the thicket of gauges in front of him. "It had better be Pskov," he told Embry, "for we haven't the petrol to go much farther."

"Oh, petrol," the pilot said airily. "We've done enough bizarre turns in this war that flying without petrol wouldn't be that extraordinary."

"Let me check my parachute first, if you don't mind," Bagnall answered.

In fact, though, Embry had a point. The aircrew had been over Cologne on the thousand-bomber raid when Lizard fighters started hacking British planes out of the sky by the score. They'd made it back to England and gone on to bomb Lizard positions in the south of France—where they were hit. Embry had set the crippled bomber down on a deserted stretch of highway by night without smashing or flipping it. If he could do that, maybe he *could* fly without petrol.

After getting to Paris and being repatriated with German help (that still grated on Bagnall), they'd been assigned to a new Lanc, this one a testbed for airborne radar. Now, the concept being deemed proved, they were flying a set to Russia so the Reds would have a better chance of seeing the Lizards coming.

Ice, ice, close to a hundred miles of blue-white ice, with white snow drifted atop it. From the bomb bay, Jerome Jones, the radarman, said, "I looked up Pskov before we took off. The climate here is supposed to be mild; the proof adduced is that the snow melts by the end of March and the ice on the lakes and rivers in April."

More groans from the aircrew. Bagnall exclaimed, "If that's what the Bolshies make out to be a mild climate, what must they reckon harsh?"

"I'm given to understand Siberia has two seasons," Embry said: "Third August and winter."

"Good job we have our flight suits on," Alf Whyte said. "I don't think there's another item in the British inventory that would do in this weather." Below the Lanc, Lake Peipus narrowed to a neck of water, then widened out again. The navigator went on, "This southern bit is called Lake Pskov. We're getting close."

"If it's all one lake, why has it got two names?" Bagnall asked.

"Supply the answer and win the tin of chopped ham, retail value ten shillings," Embry chanted, like an announcer over the wireless. "Send your postal card to the Soviet Embassy, London. Winners—if there are any, which strikes me as unlikely—will be selected in a drawing at random."

After another ten or fifteen minutes, the lake abruptly ended. A city full of towers appeared ahead. Some had the onion domes Bagnall associated with Russian architecture, while others looked as if they were wearing witches' hats. The more modern buildings in town were scarcely worth noticing among such exotics.

"Right—here's Pskov," Embry said. "Where's the bloody airfield?"

Down in the snow-filled streets, people scattered like ants when the Lancaster flew by. Through the bomber's Perspex windscreen, Bagnall spied little flashes of light. "They're shooting at us!" he yelled.

"Stupid sods," Embry snarled. "Don't they know we're friendly? Now *where's* that bleeding airfield?"

Away to the east, a red flare rose into the sky. The pilot swung the big, heavy aircraft in that direction. Sure enough, a landing strip appeared ahead, hacked out of the surrounding forest. "It's none too long," Bagnall observed.

"It's what we've got." Embry pushed forward on the stick. The Lancaster descended. The pilot was one of the best. He set the bomber down at the back edge of the landing strip and used up every inch braking to a stop. The tree trunks ahead were looking very thick and very hard when the Lancaster finally quit moving. Embry looked as if he needed to will himself to let go of the stick, but his voice was relaxed as he said, "Welcome to beautiful, balmy Pskov. You have to be balmy to want to come here."

No sooner had the Lancaster's three-bladed props spun to a stop than men in greatcoats and thick padded jackets dashed out of the trees to start draping it with camouflage netting. Groundcrews had done that back in England, but never with such élan. The outside world disappeared in a hurry; Bagnall could only hope the bomber disappeared from outside view as quickly.

"Did you see?" Embry asked quietly as he disconnected his safety belt.

"See what?" Bagnall asked, also freeing himself.

"Those weren't all Russians out there covering us up. Some of them were Germans."

"Bloody hell," Bagnall muttered. "Are we supposed to give them the airborne radar, too? That wasn't in our orders."

Alf Whyte stuck his head out from the little black-curtained cubicle where he labored with map and ruler and compasses and protractor. "Before the Lizards came, Pskov was headquarters for Army Group North. The Lizards ran Jerry out, but then they left themselves when winter started. It's Russian enough now for us to land here, obviously, but I expect there will be some leftover Nazis as well."

"Isn't that wonderful?" By Embry's tone, it was anything but.

The cold hit like a blow in the face when the aircrew left the Lanc. They were an abbreviated lot, pilot, flight engineer (Bagnall doubled as radioman), navigator, and radarman. No bomb-aimer on this run, no bombardiers, and no gunners in the turrets. If a Lizard jet attacked, machine guns weren't going to be able to reply to its cannon and rockets.

"Zdrast'ye," Ken Embry said, thereby exhausting his Russian. "Does anyone here speak English?"

"I do," two men said, one with a Russian accent, the other in Germanic tones. They looked suspiciously at each other. Some months of joint battle against a common foe had not eased the memory of what they'd been doing to each other before the Lizards came.

Bagnall had done some German before he left college to join the RAF. That was only three years ago, but already most of it had vanished from his brain. Like most undergraduates taking German, he'd come upon Mark Twain's "The Awful German Language." *That* he remembered, especially the bit

about sooner declining two beers than one German adjective.
And Russian was worse—even the alphabet looked funny.

To Bagnall's surprise, Jerome Jones started speaking
Russian—halting Russian, but evidently good enough to be understood. After a brief exchange, he turned back to the air
crew and said, "He—Sergei Leonidovich Morozkin there, the
chap who knows a bit of English—says we're to accompany
him to the *Krom*, the local strongpoint, I gather."

"By all means let us accompany him, then," Embry said. "I
didn't know you had any Russian, Jones. The chaps who put
this mission together had a better notion of what they were
about than I credited them for."

"I doubt that, sir," Jones said, unwilling to give RAF higher-
ups any credit for sense. But he had reason on his side: "When
I was at Cambridge, I was interested for a while in Byzantine
history and art, and that led me to the Russians. I hadn't the
time to do them properly, but I did teach myself a bit of the
language. That wouldn't be in any of my papers, though, so no
one would have known of it."

"Good thing it's so, all the same," Bagnall said, wondering
if Jones was a Bolshevik himself. Even if he was, it didn't
matter now. "My German is villainous, but I was about to trot
it out when you spoke up. I wasn't what you'd call keen on
trying to speak with our Soviet friends and allies in the language of a mutual foe."

The German who spoke English said, "Against the
Eidechsen—I am sorry, I do not know your word; the Russians
call them *Yashcheritsi*—against the invaders from the sky, no
men are foes to one another."

"Against the Lizards, you mean," Bagnall and Embry said
together.

"Lizards." Both the German and Morozkin, the anglophone
Russian, echoed the word to fix it in their minds; it was one
that would be used a good deal in days to come. The German
went on, "I am *Hauptmann*—Captain *auf Englisch, ja?*—
Martin Borcke."

As soon as the men of the aircrew had introduced themselves in turn, Morozkin said, "Come to *Krom* now. Get away
from airplane."

"But the radar—" Jones said plaintively.

"We do. Is in box, *da?*"

"Well, yes, but—"

"Come," Morozkin said again. At the far end of the air-strip—a long, hard slog through cold and snow—three-horse sleighs waited to take the Englishmen into Pskov. Their bells jangled merrily as they set off, as if in a happy winter song. Bagnall would have found the journey more enjoyable had his Russian driver not had a rifle slung across his back and half a dozen German potato-masher grenades stuffed into his belt.

Pskov had been built in rings where two rivers came together. The sleigh slid past churches and fine houses in the center of town, many bearing the scars of fighting when the Germans had taken it from the Soviets and when the Lizards struck north.

Closer to the joining of the two streams were a marketplace and another church. In the market, old women with scarves around their heads sold beets, turnips, cabbages. Steam rose from kettles of borscht. People queued up to get what they needed, not with the good spirits Englishmen displayed on similar occasions but glumly, resignedly, as if they could expect nothing better from fate.

Guards prowled the marketplace to make sure no one even thought of turning disorderly. Some were Germans with rifles and coal-scuttle helmets, many still wearing field-gray great-coats. Others were Russians, carrying everything from shotguns to military rifles to submachine guns, and dressed in a motley mixture of civilian clothes and khaki Soviet uniform. Everyone, though—Germans, Russians, even the old women behind their baskets of vegetables—wore the same kind of thick felt boot.

The sleigh driver had on a pair, too. Bagnall tapped the fellow on the shoulder, pointed at the footgear. "What do you call those?" He got back only a smile and a shrug, and regretfully tried German: *"Was sind sie?"*

Comprehension lit the driver's face. *"Valenki."* He rattled off a couple of sentences in Russian before he figured out Bagnall couldn't follow. His German was even slower and more halting than the flight engineer's, which gave Bagnall a chance to understand it: *"Gut—gegen—Kalt."*

"Good against cold. Thanks. Uh, *danke. Ich verstehe.*" They nodded to each other, pleased at the rudimentary communication. The *valenki* looked as if they'd be good against cold; they were thick and supple, like a blanket for the feet.

The sleigh went past a square with a monument to Lenin and then, diagonally across from it, another onion-domed church. Bagnall wondered if the driver was conscious of the ironic juxtaposition. If he was, he didn't let on. Letting on that you noticed irony probably wasn't any safer in the Soviet Union than in Hitler's Germany.

Bagnall shook his head. The Russians had become allies because they were Hitler's enemies. Now the Russians and Germans were both allies because they'd stayed in the ring against the Lizards. They still weren't comfortable company to keep.

The horses began to strain as they went uphill toward the towers that marked old Pskov. As the beasts labored and the sleigh slowed, Bagnall grasped why the fortress that was the town's beginning had been placed as it was: the fortress ahead, which he presumed to be the *Krom*, stood on a bluff protected by the rivers. The driver took him past the tumble-down stone wall that warded the landward side of the fortress. Some of the tumbling down looked recent; Bagnall wondered whether Germans or Lizards were to blame.

The sleigh stopped. Bagnall climbed out. The driver pointed him toward one of the towers; its witches'-hat roof had had a bite taken out of it. A German sentry stood to one side of the doorway, a Russian to the other. They threw the doors wide for Bagnall.

As soon as he stepped over the threshold, he felt as if he'd been taken back through time. Guttering torches cast weird, flickering shadows on the irregular stonework of the wall. Up above, everything was lost in gloom. In the torchlight, the three fur-clad men who sat at a table waiting for him, weapons in front of them, seemed more like barbarian chieftains than twentieth-century soldiers.

Over the next couple of minutes, the other Englishmen came in. By the way they peered all around, they had the same feeling of dislocation as Bagnall. Martin Borcke pointed to one of the men at the table and said, "Here is *Generalleutnant* Kurt Chill, commander of the 122nd Infantry Division and now head of the forces of the *Reich* in and around Pskov." He named the RAF men for his commander.

Chill didn't look like Bagnall's idea of a Nazi lieutenant general: no monocle, no high-peaked cap, no skinny, hawk-nosed Prussian face. He was on the roundish side and badly

needed a shave. His eyes were brown, not chilly gray. They had an ironic glint in them as he said in fair English, "Welcome to the blooming gardens of Pskov, gentlemen."

Sergei Morozkin nodded to the pair who sat to Chill's left. "Are leaders of First and Second Partisan Brigades, Nikolai Ivanovich Vasiliev and Aleksandr Maksimovich German."

Ken Embry whispered to Bagnall, "There's a name I'd not fancy having in Soviet Russia these days."

"Lord, no." Bagnall looked at German. Maybe it was the steel-rimmed spectacles he wore, but he had a schoolmasterly expression only partly counteracted by the fierce red mustache that sprouted above his upper lip.

Vasiliev, by contrast, made the flight engineer think of a bearded boulder: he was short and squat and looked immensely strong. A pink scar—maybe a crease from a rifle bullet—furrowed one cheek and cut a track through the thick, almost seallike pelt that grew there. A couple of inches over and the partisan leader would not have been sitting in his chair.

He rumbled something in Russian. Morozkin translated: "He bid you welcome to forest republic. This we call land around Pskov while Germans rule city. Now with Lizards"—Morozkin pronounced the word with exaggerated care—"here, we make German-Soviet council—German-Soviet *soviet, da?*" Bagnall thought the play on words came from the interpreter; Vasiliev, even sans scar, would not have seemed a man much given to mirth.

"Pleased to meet you all, I'm sure," Ken Embry said. Before Morozkin could translate, Jerome Jones turned his words into Russian. The partisan leaders beamed, pleased at least one of the RAF men could speak directly to them.

"What is this thing you have brought for the Soviet Union from the people and workers of England?" German asked. He leaned forward to wait for the answer, not even noticing the ideological preconceptions with which he'd freighted his question.

"An airborne radar, to help aircraft detect Lizard planes at long range," Jones said. Both Morozkin and Borcke had trouble turning the critical word into their native languages. Jones explained what a radar set was and how it did what it did. Vasiliev simply listened. German nodded several times, as if what the radarman said made sense to him.

And Kurt Chill purred, "You have, *aber natürlich*, also brought one of these radar sets for the *Reich*?"

"No, sir," Embry said. Bagnall started to sweat, though the room in this drafty old medieval tower was anything but warm. The pilot went on, "Our orders are to deliver this set and the manuals accompanying it to the Soviet authorities at Pskov. That is what we intend to do."

General Chill shook his head. Bagnall sweated harder. No one had bothered to tell the RAF crew that Pskov wasn't entirely in Soviet hands. Evidently, the Russians who'd told the English where to fly the set hadn't thought there would be a problem. But a problem there was.

"If there is only one, it shall go to the *Reich*," Chill said.

As soon as Sergei Morozkin translated the German's English into Russian, Vasiliev snatched up the submachine gun from the table in front of him and pointed it at Chill's chest. *"Nyet,"* he said flatly. Bagnall needed no Russian to follow that.

Chill answered in German, which Vasiliev evidently understood. It also let Bagnall understand some of what was going on. The Nazi had courage, or at least bravado. He said, "If you shoot me, Nikolai Ivanovich, Colonel Schindler takes command—and we are still stronger around Pskov than you."

Aleksandr German did not bother gesticulating with the pistol on the table. He simply spoke in a dry, rather pedantic voice that went well with his eyeglasses. His words sounded like German, but Bagnall had even more trouble with them than he had in following Kurt Chill. He guessed the partisan was actually speaking Yiddish. To stay up with that, they should have kept David Goldfarb as crew radarman.

Captain Borcke made sense of it. He translated: "German says the *Wehrmacht* is stronger around Pskov than Soviet forces, yes. He asks if it is also stronger than Soviet and Lizard forces combined."

Chill spoke a single word: "Bluff."

"Nyet," Vasiliev said again. He put down his weapon and beamed at the other partisan leader. He'd found a threat the Germans could not afford to ignore.

Bagnall did not think it was a bluff, either. Germany had not endeared itself to the people of any of the eastern lands it occupied before the Lizards came. The Jews of Poland—led by, among others, a cousin of Goldfarb's—had risen against the

Nazis and for the Lizards. The Russians might do the same if this Chill pushed them hard enough.

He might, too. Scowling at the two partisan brigadiers, he said, "You may do this. The Lizards may win a victory through it. But this I vow: neither of you will live long enough to collaborate with them. We will have that radar."

"Nyet." This time Aleksandr German said it. He switched back to Yiddish, too fast and harsh for Bagnall to follow. Captain Borcke again did the honors: "He says this set was sent to the workers and people of the Soviet Union to aid them in their struggle against imperialist aggression, and that surrendering it would be treason to the Soviet state."

Communist rhetoric aside, Bagnall thought the partisan was dead right. But if Lieutenant General Chill didn't, the flight engineer's opinion counted for little.

And Chill was going to be hard-nosed about it. Bagnall could see that. So could everyone else in the tower chamber. Captain Borcke edged away from the RAF air crew to one side, Sergei Morozkin to the other. Both men slid a hand under their coats, presumably to grab for pistols. Bagnall got ready to throw himself flat.

Then, instead, he hissed at Jerome Jones: "You have the manuals and such for the radar, am I right?"

"Of course," Jones whispered back. "Couldn't very well come without them, not when the Russians are going to start making them for themselves. Or they will if anyone comes out of this room alive."

"Which doesn't look like the best wager in the world. How many sets have you got?"

"Of the manuals and drawings, you mean? Just the one," Jones said.

"Bugger." That put a crimp in Bagnall's scheme, but only for a moment. He spoke up in a loud voice: "Gentlemen, please!" If nothing else, he succeeded in distracting the Germans and partisans from the bead they were drawing on each other. Everyone stared at him instead. He said, "I think I can find a way out of this dispute."

Grim faces defied him to do it. Trouble was, he realized suddenly, the Germans and Russians really wanted to have a go at each other. In English, Kurt Chill said, "Enlighten us, then."

"I'll do my best," Bagnall answered. "There's only the one radar, and no help for that. If you hijack it, word will get back to Moscow—and to London. Cooperation between Germany and her former foes will be hampered, and the Lizards will likely gain more from that than the *Luftwaffe* could from the radar. Is this so, or not?"

"It may be," Chill said. "I do not think, though, there is much cooperation now, when you give the Russians and not us this set." Captain Borcke nodded emphatically at that.

There was much truth in what the German general said. Bagnall was anything but happy about sharing secrets with the Nazis, and his attitude reflected that of British leaders from Churchill on down. But setting the *Wehrmacht* and the Red Army back at each other's throats wasn't what anyone had had in mind, either.

The flight engineer said, "How is this, then? The radar itself and the manuals go on toward Moscow as planned. But before they do"—he sighed—"you make copies of the manuals and send them to Berlin."

"Copies?" Chill said. "By photograph?"

"If you have that kind of equipment here, yes." Bagnall had been thinking of doing the job by hand; Pskov struck him as a burnt-out backwater town. But who could say what sort of gear the division intelligence unit of the 122nd Infantry—or whatever other units were in the area—had available?

"I'm not sure the higher-ups back home would approve, but they didn't anticipate this situation," Ken Embry murmured. "As for me, I'd say you've managed to saw the baby in half. King Solomon would be proud."

"I hope so," Bagnall said.

Sergei Morozkin was still translating his suggestion for the partisan leaders. When he finished, Vasiliev turned to Aleksandr German and said with heavy humor, "*Nu,* Sasha?" It had to be more Yiddish—Bagnall had heard that word from David Goldfarb.

Aleksandr German peered through his spectacles at Chill the German. Having Goldfarb in the aircrew for a while had made Bagnall more aware of what the Nazis had done to Eastern European Jews than he otherwise would have been. He wondered what went on behind German's poker face, how much hatred seethed there. The partisan did not let on. After a while, he sighed and spoke one word: "*Da.*"

"We shall do this, then." If Chill was enthusiastic about Bagnall's plan, he hid it very well. But it gave him most of what he wanted, and kept alive the fragile truce around Pskov.

As if to underline how important that was, Lizard jets streaked overhead. When bombs began to fall, Bagnall felt something near panic: a hit anywhere close by would bring all the stones of the *Krom* down on his head.

Through the fading wail of the Lizards' engines and the ground-shaking crash of the bombs came the rattle of what sounded like every rifle and submachine gun in the world going off at once. Pskov's defenders, Nazis and Communists alike, did their best to knock down the Lizards' planes.

As usual, their best was not good enough. Bagnall listened hopefully for the rending crash that would have meant a fighter-bomber destroyed, but it never came. He also listened for the roar that would warn of a second wave of attackers. That didn't come, either.

"Anyone would think that flying more than a thousand miles would take us out of the bloody blitz," Alf Whyte complained.

"They called it a world war even before the Lizards came," Embry said.

Nikolai Vasiliev shouted something at Morozkin. Instead of translating it, he hurried away to return a few minutes later with a tray full of bottles and glasses. "We drink to this—how you say?—agreement," he said.

He was pouring man-sized slugs of vodka for everyone when a partisan burst in, shouting in Russian. "Uh-oh," Jerome Jones said. "I didn't catch all of that, but I didn't care for what I understood."

Morozkin turned to the RAF air crew. "I have—bad news. Those—how you say?—Lizards, they bomb your plane. Is wreck and ruin—is that what you say?"

"That's what we say," Embry answered dully.

"Nichevo, tovarishchi," Morozkin said.

He didn't translate that, maybe because it was so completely Russian that doing so never occurred to him. "What did he say?" Bagnall demanded of Jerome Jones.

" 'It can't be helped, comrades'—something like that," the radarman answered. " 'There's nothing to be done about it,' might be a better rendering."

Bagnall didn't care a pin for fine points of translation. "We're stuck here in bloody Pskov and there's bloody nothing to be done about it?" he burst out, his voice rising to a shout.

"Nichevo," Jones said.

Science Hall was a splendid structure, a three-story red brick building on the northwest corner of the University of Denver campus. It housed the university's chemistry and physics departments, and would have made a fine home for the transplanted Metallurgical Laboratory from the University of Chicago. Jens Larssen admired the facility intensely.

There was only one problem: he had no idea when the rest of the Met Lab team would show up.

"All dressed up with no place to go," he muttered to himself as he stalked down a third-floor corridor. From the north-facing window at the end of that corridor, he could see the Platte River snaking its way south and east through town, and beyond it the state capitol and other tall buildings of the civic center. Denver was a pretty place, snow still on the ground here and there, the air almost achingly clear. Jens delighted in it not at all.

Everything had gone so perfectly. He might as well have been riding the train in those dear, vanished pre-Lizard days. He wasn't bombed, he wasn't strafed, he had a lower Pullman berth more comfortable than any bed he'd slept in for months. He had heat on the train, and electricity; the only hint there was a war on was the blackout curtain on the window and a sign taped alongside it: USE IT. IT'S YOUR NECK.

An Army major had met him when the train pulled into Union Station, had taken him out to Lowry Field east of town, had arranged a room for him at the Bachelor Officers' Quarters. He'd almost balked at that—he was no bachelor. But Barbara wasn't with him, so he'd gone along.

"Stupid," he said aloud. Going along even once had got him tangled up again in the spiderweb of military routine. He'd had a taste of that in Indiana under George Patton. The local commanders were less flamboyant than Patton, but no less inflexible.

"I'm sorry, Dr. Larssen, but that will not be permitted," a bird colonel named Hexham had said. The colonel hadn't sounded sorry, not one bit. By *that* he meant Larssen's going

out of town to find out where the rest of the Met Lab team was.

"But why?" Jens had howled, pacing the colonel's office like a newly caged wolf. "Without the other people, without the equipment they have with them, I'm not much good to you by myself."

"Dr. Larssen, you are a nuclear physicist working on a highly classified project," Colonel Hexham had answered. He'd kept his voice low, reasonable; Jens supposed he'd got on the fellow's nerves as well as the other way round. "We cannot let you go gallivanting off just as you please. And if disaster befalls your colleagues, who better than you to reconstruct the project?"

Larssen hadn't laughed in his face, but he'd come close. Reconstruct the work of several Nobel laureates—by himself? He'd have to be Superman, able to leap tall buildings at a single bound. But there was just enough truth in it—he'd been part of the project, after all—to keep him from taking off on his own.

"Everything is fine," Hexham had told him. "They're heading this way; we know that much. We're delighted you're here ahead of them. That means you can help get things organized so they'll be able to hit the ground running when they arrive."

He'd been a scientist at the Met Lab, not an administrator. Administration had been a headache for other people. Now it was his. He went back to his office, wrote letters, filled out forms, tried the phone three or four times, and actually got through once. The Lizards hadn't hit Denver anywhere near the way they'd plastered Chicago; to a large degree, it still functioned as a modern city. When Jens turned the switch on the gooseneck lamp on his desk, the bulb lit up.

He worked a little longer, then said the hell with it and went downstairs. His bicycle waited there. So did a glum, unsmiling man in khaki with a rifle on his back. He had a bike, too. "Evening, Oscar," Jens said.

"Dr. Larssen." The bodyguard nodded politely. Oscar wasn't his real name, but he answered to it. Jens thought it amused him, but his face didn't show much. Oscar had been detailed to keep him safe in Denver—and to keep him from leaving town. He was depressingly good at his job.

Larssen rode north up University, turned right toward Lowry

Field. Oscar stuck to the physicist like a burr. Jens was in good shape. His bodyguard, he was convinced, could have made the Olympic team. All the way back to BOQ, he sang, "I'm Only a Bird in a Gilded Cage." Oscar joined in the choruses.

But in the next morning, instead of biking back to the University of Denver, Larssen (Oscar in his wake) reported to Colonel Hexham's office. The colonel looked anything but delighted to see him. "Why aren't you at work, Dr. Larssen?" he said in a tone that probably turned captains to Jell-O.

Jens, however, was a civilian, and a fed-up civilian at that. "Sir, the more I think about my working conditions here, the more intolerable they look to me," he said. "I'm on strike."

"You're what?" Hexham chewed toothpicks, maybe in lieu of scarce cigarettes. The one he had in his mouth jumped. "You can't do that!"

"Oh yes I can, and I'm going to stay on strike until you let me get in touch with my wife."

"Security—" Hexham began. Up and down, up and down went the toothpick.

"Stuff security!" Jens had wanted to say that—he'd wanted to scream it—for months. "You won't let me go after the Met Lab. Okay, I guess I can see that, even if I think you're pushing it too far. But you as much as told me the other day you know where the Met Lab wagon train is, right?"

"What if I do?" the colonel rumbled. He was still trying to intimidate Larssen, but Larssen refused to be intimidated any more.

"This if you do: unless you let me send a letter—just an ordinary, handwritten letter—to Barbara, you get no more work out of me, and that's that."

"Too risky," Hexham said. "Suppose our courier is captured—"

"Suppose he is?" Jens retorted. "I'm not going to write about uranium, for God's sake. I'm going to let her know I'm alive and in one piece and that I love her and I miss her. That's all. I won't even sign my last name."

"No," said Hexham.

"No," said Larssen. They glared at each other. The toothpick twitched.

Oscar escorted Larssen back to BOQ. He lay down on his cot. He was ready to wait as long as it took.

* * *

The fat man in the black Stetson paused in the ceremony first to spit a brown stream into the polished brass spittoon near his feet (not a drop clung to his handlebar mustache) and then to sneak another glance at the Lizards who stood in one corner of his crowded office. He half shrugged and resumed: "By the authority vested in me as justice of the peace of Chugwater, Wyoming, I now pronounce you man and wife. Kiss her, boy."

Sam Yeager tilted Barbara Larssen's—Barbara *Yeager*'s— face up to his. The kiss was not the decorous one first post-wedding kisses are supposed to be. She molded herself against him. He squeezed her tight.

Everybody cheered. Enrico Fermi, who was serving as best man, slapped Yeager on the back. His wife Laura stood on tip-toe to kiss Sam's cheek. Seeing that, the physicist made a Latin production out of kissing Barbara on the cheek. Everybody cheered again, louder than ever.

Just for a second, Yeager's eyes went to Ullhass and Ristin. He wondered what they made of the ceremony. From what they said, they didn't mate permanently—and to them, human beings were barbarous aliens.

Well, to hell with what they think of human beings, he thought. As far as he was concerned, having Fermi as his best man was almost—not quite—as exciting as getting married to Barbara. He'd been married once before, unsuccessfully, and he'd sometimes thought about marrying again. But never in all the hours he'd spent reading science fiction on trains and buses between one minor-league game and the next had he thought he'd really get to hobnob with scientists. And having a Nobel Prize winner as your best man was about as hob a nob as you could find.

The justice of the peace—the sign on his door said he was Joshua Sumner, but he seemed to go by Hoot—reached into a drawer of the fancy old rolltop desk that adorned his office. What he pulled out was most unjudicial: a couple of shot glasses and a bottle about half full of dark amber fluid.

"Don't have as much here as we used to. Don't have as much here as we'd like," he said as he poured each glass full. "But we've still got enough for the groom to make a toast and the bride to drink it."

Barbara eyed the full shot dubiously. "If I drink all that, I'll just go to sleep."

"I doubt it," the justice of the peace said, which raised more whoops from the predominantly male crowd in his office. Barbara turned pink and shook her head in embarrassment but took the glass.

Yeager took his, too, careful not to spill a drop. He knew what he was going to say. Even though he hadn't expected to have to propose a toast, one leaped into his mind the moment Sumner said he'd need it. That didn't usually happen with him; more often than not, he'd come up with snappy comebacks a week too late to use them.

Not this time, though. He raised the shot glass, waited for quiet. When he got it, he said, "Life goes on," and knocked back the shot. The whiskey burned its way down his throat, filled his middle with warmth.

"Oh, that's good, Sam," Barbara said softly. "That's just right." She lifted the shot glass to her lips. She started to sip, but at the last moment drank it all down at once as Sam had. Her eyes opened very wide and started to water. She turned much redder than she had when the justice of the peace flustered her. What should have been her next breath became a sharp cough instead. People laughed and clapped anyhow.

Joshua Sumner said, "Don't do that every day, you tell me?" He had the deadpan drollness that goes with many large men who are sparing of speech.

As the wedding party filed out of the justice of the peace's office, Ristin said, "What you do here, Sam, you and Barbara? You make"—he spoke a couple of hissing words in his own language—"to mate all the time?"

"An agreement, that would be in English," Yeager said. He squeezed Barbara's hand. "That's just what we did, even if I am too old to mate 'all the time.' "

"Don't confuse him," Barbara said with a cluck in her voice.

They went outside. Chugwater was about fifty miles north of Cheyenne. Off against the western horizon, snow-cloaked mountains loomed. The town itself was a few houses, a general store, and the post office that also housed the sheriff's office and that of the justice of the peace. Hoot Sumner was also postmaster and sheriff, and probably none too busy even if he did wear three hats.

The sheriff's office (fortunately, from Yeager's point of

view) boasted a single jail cell big enough to hold the two Lizard POWs. That meant he and Barbara got to spend their wedding night without Ristin and Ullhass in the next room. Not that the Lizards were likely to pick that particular night to try to run away, nor, being what they were, that they would make anything of the noises coming from the bridal bed. Nevertheless . . .

"It's the principle of the thing," Sam explained as he and the new Mrs. Yeager, accompanied by cheering well-wishers from the Met Lab and from Chugwater, made their way to the house where they'd spend their first night as man and wife. He spoke a little louder, a little more earnestly, than he might have earlier in the day: when they found they were going to host a wedding, the townsfolk had pulled out a good many bottles of dark amber and other fluids.

"You're right," Barbara said, also emphatically. Her cheeks glowed brighter than could be accounted for by the chilly breeze alone.

She let out a squeak when Sam picked her up and carried her over the threshold of the bedroom they'd use, and then another one when she saw the bottle sticking out of a bucket on a stool by the bed. The bucket was ordinary galvanized iron, straight out of a hardware store, but inside, nestled in snow— "Champagne!" she exclaimed.

Two wineglasses—not champagne flutes, but close enough— rested alongside the bucket. "That's very nice," Yeager said. He gently lifted the bottle out of the snow, undid the foil wrap and the little wire cage, worked the cork a little—and then let it fly out with a report like a rifle shot and ricochet off the ceiling. He had a glass ready to catch the champagne that bubbled out, then finished filling it the more conventional way.

With a flourish, he handed the glass to Barbara, poured one for himself. She stared down into hers. "I don't know if I ought to drink this," she said. "If I have a whole lot more, I *will* fall asleep on you. That wouldn't be right. Wedding nights are supposed to be special."

"Any night with you is special," he said, which made her smile. But then he went on more seriously, "We ought to drink it, especially now that we've opened it. Nobody has enough of anything any more to let it go to waste."

"You're right," she said, and sipped. An eyebrow rose.

"That's pretty good champagne. I wonder how it got to the great metropolis of Chugwater, by God, Wyoming."

"Beats me." Yeager drank, too. He didn't know much about champagne; he drank beer by choice and whiskey every so often. But it did taste good. The bubbles tickled the inside of his mouth. He sat down on the bed, not far from the stool with the bucket.

Barbara sat down beside him. Her glass was already almost empty. She ran a hand along his arm, let it rest on his corporal's chevrons. "You were in uniform, so you looked fine for the wedding." She made a face. "Getting married in a gingham blouse and a pair of dungarees isn't what I had in mind."

He slid an arm around her waist, then drained his glass of champagne and pulled the bottle from its bed of snow. It held just enough to fill them both up again. "Don't worry about it. There's only one proper uniform for a bride on her wedding night." He reached behind her, undid the top button of her blouse.

"That's the proper uniform for bride and groom both," she said. Her fingers fumbled as she worked at one of his buttons. She laughed. "See—I told you I shouldn't have had that champagne. Now I'm having trouble getting you out of soldier's uniform and into bridegroom's."

"No hurry, not tonight," he said. "One way or another, we'll manage." He drank some more, then looked at the glass with respect. "That takes me to a happier place than I usually go when I've had a few. Or maybe it's the company."

"I *like* you, Sam!" Barbara exclaimed. For some reason— maybe it was the champagne—that made him feel better than if she'd said *I love you.*

Presently, he asked, "Do you want me to blow out the candles?"

Her eyebrows came together in thought for a moment. Then she said, "No, let them burn, unless you really want it to be dark tonight."

He shook his head. "I like to look at you, honey." She wasn't a Hollywood movie star or a Vargas girl: a little too thin, a little too angular, and, if you looked at things objectively, not pretty enough. Sam didn't give two whoops in hell about looking at things objectively. She looked damn good to him.

He ran his hands over her breasts, let one of them stray

down her belly toward where her legs joined. She stretched luxuriously and made a noise like a purring cat, down deep in her throat. His tongue teased a nipple. She grabbed the back of his head, pulled him against her.

After his mouth had followed his hand downward, she rubbed at the soft flesh of her inner thighs. "I wish there were more razor blades around," she said in mock complaint. "Your face chafes me when you do that."

He touched her, gently. Her breath sighed out. She was wet. "I thought you liked it while it was going on," he said, grinning. "Shall I get that rubber now?"

"Wait." She sat up, bent over him, and lowered her head. It was the first time she'd ever done that without being asked. Her hair spilled down and tickled his hipbones.

"Easy, there," he gasped a minute later. "You do much more and I won't need to bother with a rubber."

"Would you like that?" she asked, looking up at him from under her bangs. She still held him. He could feel the warm little puffs of breath as she spoke.

He was tempted, but shook his head. "Not on our wedding night. Like you said, it ought to be perfect. And it's for something else."

"All right, let's do something else," she said agreeably, and lay back on the bed. He leaned over the side and pulled a rubber out of the back pocket of his chinos. But before he could peel it open, she grabbed his wrist and repeated, "Wait." He gave her a quizzical look. She went on, "I know you don't like those all that much. Don't bother tonight—if we're going to make it perfect, that will help. It should be okay."

He tossed the rubber onto the floor. He wasn't fond of them. He wore them because she wanted him to, and because he could see why she didn't want to get pregnant. But if she felt like taking a chance, he was eager to oblige.

"It does feel better without overshoes," he said. He guided himself into her. "Oh, God, does it!" Their mouths met, clung. Neither of them said anything then, not with words.

"I always said you were a gentleman, Sam," Barbara told him as he rolled off her: "You keep your weight on your elbows." He snorted. She said, "Don't go away now."

"I wasn't going anywhere, not without you." He put an arm around her, drew her close. She snuggled against him. He liked that. In some ways, it seemed more intimate than making love.

You could make love with a stranger; he'd done it in a fair
number of minor-league whorehouses in minor-league towns.
But to snuggle with somebody, it had to be somebody who really mattered to you.

As if she'd picked the thought out of his head, Barbara said,
"I love you."

"I love you, too, hon." His arms tightened around her. "I'm
glad we're married." That seemed just the right thing to say on
a wedding night.

"So am I." Barbara ran the palm of her hand along his
cheek. "Even if you are scratchy," she added. He tensed, ready
to grab her; sometimes when she made jokes in bed, she'd
poke him in the ribs. Not tonight—she turned serious instead.
"You made exactly the right toast this afternoon. 'Life goes
on' . . . It has to, doesn't it?"

"That's what I think, anyhow." Yeager wasn't sure whether
she was asking him or trying to convince herself. She still
couldn't be easy in her mind about her first husband. He had
to be dead, but still . . .

"You have the right way of looking at things," Barbara said,
serious still. "Life isn't always neat; it's not orderly; you can't
always plan it and make it come out the way you think it's
supposed to. Things happen that nobody would expect—"

"Well, sure," Yeager said. "The war made the whole world
crazy, and then the Lizards on top of that—"

"Those are the big things," she broke in. "As you say, they
change the whole world. But little things can turn your life in
new directions, too. Everybody reads Chaucer in high-school
English, but when I did, he just seemed the most fascinating
writer I'd ever come across. I started trying to learn more
about his time, and about other people who were writing then
. . . and so I ended up in graduate school at Berkeley in medieval literature. If I hadn't been there, I never would have met
Jens, I never would have come to Chicago—" She leaned up
and kissed him. "I never would have met you."

"Little things," Sam repeated. "Ten, eleven years ago, I was
playing for Birmingham down in the Southern Association.
That's Class A-1 ball, the second highest class in the minor
leagues. I was playing pretty well, I wasn't that old—if things
had broken right, I might have made the big leagues. Things
broke, all right. About halfway through the season, I broke my
ankle. It cost me the rest of the year, and I wasn't the same

ballplayer afterwards. I kept at it—never found anything I'd rather do—but I knew I wasn't going anywhere any more. Just one of those things."

"That's just it." She nodded against his chest. "Little things, things you'd never expect to matter, can turn up in the most surprising ways."

"I'll say." Yeager nodded, too. "If I hadn't read science fiction, I wouldn't have gotten chosen to take our Lizard POWs back to Chicago or turned into their liaison man—and I wouldn't have met you."

To his relief, she didn't make any cracks about his choice of reading; someone who dove into Chaucer for fun was liable to think of it as the literary equivalent of picking your nose at the dinner table. Instead, she said, "Jens always had trouble seeing that the little things could make—not a big difference, but a *surprising* difference. Do you see what I'm saying?"

"Mm-hmm." Yeager kept his answer to a grunt. He didn't have anything against Jens Larssen, but he didn't want his ghost coming between them on their wedding night, either.

Barbara went on, "Jens wanted things just so, and thought they always had to be that way. Maybe it was because his work was so mathematically precise—I don't know—but he thought the world operated that way, too. That sort of need for exactitude could be hard to live with sometimes."

"Mm-hmm." Sam grunted again, but something loosened in his chest even so. He never remembered her criticizing Jens before.

No sooner had that thought crossed his mind than she said, "I guess what I'm trying to tell you, Sam, is that I'm glad I'm with you. Taking things as they come is easier than trying to fit everything that happens into some pattern you've worked out."

"That calls for a kiss," he said, and bent his head down to hers. She responded eagerly. He felt himself stirring, and knew a certain amount of pride: if you couldn't wear yourself out on your wedding night, when were you supposed to?

Barbara felt him stirring, too. "What have we here?" she said when the kiss finally broke. She reached between them to find out. Yeager's lips trailed down her neck toward her breasts again. Her hand tightened on him. His found the dampness between her legs.

After a while, he rolled onto his back: easier to stay hard for

a second round that way, especially if you weren't in your twenties any more. He'd learned Barbara didn't mind getting on top every so often.

"Oh, yes," he said softly as she straddled him. He was glad she hadn't made him put on a rubber tonight; you could feel so much more without one. He ran his fingers lightly down the smooth curve of her back. She shivered a little.

Afterwards, she didn't pull away, but sprawled down on top of him. He kissed her cheek and the very corner of her mouth. "Nice," she said, her voice sleepy. "I just want to stay right here forever."

He put his arms around her. "That's what I want, too, hon."

Oscar appeared in the doorway of Jens Larssen's BOQ room. "Colonel Hexham wants to see you, sir. Right away."

"Does he?" Larssen had been sprawled out on the cot, reading the newest issue of *Time*—now getting on toward a year old—he could find. He got up in a hurry. "I'll come." He hadn't been "sir" to Oscar since he'd gone on strike, not till now. Maybe that was a good sign.

He didn't think so when the guard escorted him back into the colonel's office. Hexham's toothpick was going back and forth like a metronome, his bulldog face pinched and sour. "So you won't do any work unless you write your miserable letter, eh?" he ground out, never opening his mouth wide enough for the toothpick to fall out.

"That's right," Jens said—not defiantly, but more as if stating a law of nature.

"Then write it." Hexham looked more unhappy than ever. He shoved a sheet of paper and a pencil across the desk at Jens.

"Thank you, sir," Larssen exclaimed, taking them gladly. As he started to write, he asked, "What made you change your mind?"

"Orders." Hexham bit the word off. *So you've been overruled, have you?* Jens thought as he let the pencil race joyously across the paper. Trying to get a little of his own back, the colonel went on, "I will read that letter when you're done with it. No last names, no other breaches of security will be permitted."

"That's fine, sir. I'll go back to Science Hall the minute I'm done here." Larssen scrawled *Love, Jens* and handed the paper

back to Colonel Hexham. He didn't bother waiting for
Hexham to read it, but started out to keep his end of the bargain. If you worked at it, he thought, you could make things
go the way they were supposed to.

☆ **IV** ☆

Bobby Fiore almost wished he was still on the Lizards' space-ship. For one thing, as far as he was concerned, the food had been better up there. For another, all the human beings on the spaceship had been aliens, guinea pigs. Plopped down in the middle of God only knew how many Chinamen, he was the alien in this refugee camp.

His lips quirked wryly. "I'm the only guinea here, too," he said out loud.

Speaking English, even to himself, felt good. He didn't get much chance to do it these days, even less than he'd had when he was up in space. Some of the Lizards there had understood him. Here nobody did; if the Lizard camp guards spoke any human language—not all of them did—it was Chinese. Only Liu Han knew any English at all.

His face set in a frown. He hated depending on a woman; it made him feel as if he were eight years old again, and back in Pittsburgh with his mama. He couldn't help it, though. Except for Liu Han, nobody for miles around could speak with him.

He rubbed his chin. He needed a shave. The first thing he'd done when the Lizards dumped him here was get a razor and get rid of his beard. Not only did shaving make him stand out less from everybody else, a razor was a handy thing to have in a fight. He'd seen enough barroom brawls to know that; he'd been in a few, too.

The funny thing was how little notice he drew. He wore wide-legged pants and baggy shirts that reminded him of paja-mas, the same as the Chinese (even with them, he was cold a lot of the time—and he wasn't used to *that* after the spaceship,

97

either), which helped him fit in. A lot of the locals were too busy to pay him any mind, too; they made stuff for the Lizards out of straw and wicker and leather and scrap metal and God only knew what all else, and they worked hard.

But what really surprised him was that his looks weren't so far out of place. Sure, he still had his big Italian nose; his eyes were too round and his hair was wavy. But eyes and hair were dark; a blond like Sam Yeager would have stood out like a sore thumb. And his olive skin wasn't that different from the color of the people around him. As long as he stayed clean-shaven, he wasn't that remarkable.

"I'm even tall," he said, smiling again. Back in the States, five-eight was nothing. Even here he wasn't huge, but for a change he was bigger than average.

Sudden shouts not far away—even when he didn't speak the language, Fiore knew fury and outrage when he heard them. He turned toward the sudden racket. Being taller than most let him see over the crowd. A man was running his way with a hen under each arm. Behind him, screeching like a cat with its tail stuck in a door, dashed a skinny woman. The chicken thief gained ground with every stride.

Fiore looked down to the dirt of the street. A nice-sized rock lay there, just a couple of feet away. He snatched it up, took a couple of shuffling steps sideways to get a clear shot at the man, and let fly.

When he was playing second base for the Decatur Commodores, he'd had to get off accurate throws to first with a runner bearing down on him with spikes high. Here he didn't even need to pivot. He hadn't done any throwing since the Lizards took him up into space, but he'd played pro ball for a lot of years. The smooth motion was still there, automatic as breathing.

The rock caught the fellow with the chickens right in the pit of the stomach. Fiore grinned; he couldn't have placed it any better with a bull's-eye to aim at. The would-be thief dropped the chickens and folded up like an accordion. His face was comically amazed as he fell—he had no idea what had hit him.

The two chickens ran away, squawking. The screeching woman started kicking the fellow who'd swiped them. She might have been better advised to chase them, but she seemed to put revenge ahead of poultry. The chicken thief couldn't

even fight back. He'd had the wind knocked out of him, and had to lie there and take it.

One of the chickens darted past Fiore. It disappeared between two huts before he could decide to grab it for himself. "Damn," he said, kicking at the dirt. "I should've brought that home for Liu Han." Somebody else—almost certainly not its proper owner—would enjoy it now.

"Too bad," he muttered. He'd eaten some amazing things since the Lizards stuck him here. He'd thought he knew what Chinese food was all about. After all, he'd stopped at enough chop suey joints on the endless road trips that punctuated his life. You could fill yourself up for cheap, and it was usually pretty good.

The only familiar thing here was plain rice. No chop suey, no crunchy noodles, no little bowls of ketchup and spicy mustard. No fried shrimp, though that made sense, because he didn't think the camp was anywhere near the ocean. Not even fried rice, for God's sake. He wondered if the guys who ran the chop suey places were really Chinese at all.

The vegetables here looked strange and tasted stranger, and Liu Han insisted on serving them while they were still crunchy, which meant raw as far as he was concerned. He wanted a string bean—not that there *were* any string beans—to keep quiet between his teeth, not fight back. His mama had cooked vegetables till they were soft, which made it Gospel to him.

But Liu Han's mama had had different ideas. He wasn't about to cook for himself, so he ate what Liu Han gave him.

If the vegetables were bad, the meat was worse. Papa Fiore had known hard times in Italy; every once in a while, he'd slip and call a cat a roof rabbit. Roof rabbit seemed downright tempting compared to some of the things for sale in the camp marketplace: dog meat, skinned rats, elderly eggs. Bobby had quit asking about the bits and strips of flesh Liu Han served along with her half-raw vegetables: better not to know. That was one of the reasons he regretted not grabbing the chicken—for once, he would have been sure of what he was eating.

The woman quit kicking the chicken thief and started after the bird that hadn't come near Fiore. That hen had sensibly decided to go elsewhere. The woman stopped screeching and started wailing. What with all the racket she made, Fiore decided he was on the chicken's side. That wouldn't help the

bird; if it stayed anywhere in camp, it would end up in somebody's pot pretty damn quick.

Fiore picked his way through the crowded, narrow streets back toward his hut. He was glad he had a good sense of direction. Without it, he wouldn't have gone out past his own front door. Nobody here had ever heard of street signs, and even if signs hung on every corner, they wouldn't have been in a language he could read.

Liu Han was chattering away in Chinese with a couple of other women when he walked in. They turned and stared at him, half in curiosity, half in alarm. He bowed, which was good manners here. "Hello. Good day," he said in his halting Chinese.

The women giggled furiously, maybe at his accent, maybe just at his face: as far as they were concerned, anybody who wasn't Chinese might as well have been a nigger. They spoke rapidly to each other; he caught the phrase *foreign devil*, which they applied to those not of their kind. He wondered what they were saying about him.

They didn't stay long. After good-byes to Liu Han and bows to him—he had been polite, even if he was a foreign devil—they headed back to wherever they lived. He hugged Liu Han. You still couldn't tell she was pregnant when she wore clothes, but now he felt the beginning of a bulge to her belly when they embraced.

"You okay?" he asked in English, and added the Lizards' interrogative cough at the end.

"Okay," she said, and tacked on the emphatic cough. For a while, the Lizards' language had been the only one they had in common. Nobody but the two of them understood the mishmash they spoke these days. She pointed to the teapot, used the interrogative cough.

"*M'goi*—thanks," he said. The pot was cheap and old, the cups even cheaper, and one of them cracked. The Lizards had given them the hut and everything in it; Fiore tried not to think about what might have happened to whoever was living there before.

He sipped the tea. What he wouldn't have given for a big mug of coffee with sugar and lots of cream! Tea was okay once in a while, but all the time every day? Forget it. He started to laugh.

"Why funny?" Liu Han asked.

"Up there"—their shorthand for the spaceship—"you eat my kind food." Most of the canned goods the Lizards fed them with came from the States or from Europe. Fiore made a horrible face to remind her how well she'd liked them. "Now I eat your kind food." He made the face again, but this time he pointed to himself.

A mouse scuttled across the floor, huddled against the baked-clay hearth to get warm. Liu Han didn't carry on the way a lot of American women would have. She just pointed at it.

Fiore picked up a brass incense burner and flung it at the mouse. His aim was still good. He caught the rodent right in the ribs. It lay there twitching. Liu Han picked it up by the tail and threw it out. She said, "You"—she made a throwing gesture—"good."

"Yeah," he said. With their three languages and a lot of dumb show, he told her how he'd nailed the chicken thief. "The arm still works." He'd tried explaining about baseball. Liu Han didn't get it.

She made the throwing gesture. "Good," she repeated. He nodded; this wasn't the first mouse he'd nailed. The camp was full of vermin. It had been a jolt, especially after the metallic sterility of the spaceship. It was also another reason not to want to know too much about what he ate. He'd never worried about what health departments back in the U.S.A. did. But seeing what things were like without them gave him a new perspective.

"Should make money, arm so good," Liu Han said. "Not do like here."

"God knows that's so," Fiore answered, responding to the second part of what she'd said. Most Chinamen, he thought scornfully, threw like girls, shortarming it from the elbow. Next to them, he looked like Bob Feller. Then he noticed the key word from the first part. "Money?"

He didn't need much, not in camp. He and Liu Han were still the Lizards' guinea pigs, so they didn't pay rent for the hut and nobody dared haggle too hard in the marketplace. But more cash never hurt anybody. He'd made a little doing the hard physical work—hauling lumber and digging trenches—he'd started playing ball to avoid. And he won more than he lost when he gambled. Still . . .

Mountebanks did well here, among people starved for any other entertainment: jugglers, clowns, a fellow with a trained

monkey that seemed smarter than a lot of people Fiore knew. All the baseball skills he had—throwing, catching, hitting, even sliding—were ones the people here didn't use. He'd never thought about turning baseball into a vaudeville act, but you could do it.

He bent to kiss Liu Han. She liked that—not just that he did it, but that he made a production of it. She needed to know he kept caring for her. "Baby, you're brilliant," he said. Then he had to stop and explain what brilliant meant, but it was worth it.

Ussmak was unenthusiastic about leaving the nice warm barracks at Besançon. The cold outside made his muzzle tingle. He hurried toward his landcruiser, whose crew compartment had a heater.

"We'll kill all the stupid Deutsch Big Uglies as far as the eye can see, then come back here and relax some more. Shouldn't take long," Hessef said. The landcruiser commander let the lid to his cupola fall with a clang.

That's the ginger talking, Ussmak thought. Hessef and Tvenkel had both tasted just before they started this mission: ginger was cheap and easy to come by here in France. They'd both laughed at him for declining—he'd used even more than they had while sitting around waiting for something to happen.

But he still thought combat was different. The Big Uglies were barbarous, but he knew they could fight. He'd had landcruisers wrecked around him; he'd lost crewmales. And the Deutsche were supposed to be more dangerous than the Russki had been. That was plenty to make him want to go at them undrugged.

Tvenkel had sneered, "Don't worry about it. The landcruiser just about fights itself."

"Do what you want," Ussmak had answered. "I'll taste plenty when we get back, I promise you that." He missed the confidence and exuberance ginger gave him, but he didn't think he really was smarter when he tasted—he only felt that way. A lot of tasters failed to draw the distinction, but he thought it was there.

At Hessef's blithe order, he started the landcruiser's engine. Part of a long column, the big, heavy machine rumbled out of the fortress and through the narrow streets of Besançon. Big Uglies in their ridiculous clothes stared as it went past. Some

of the Big Uglies yelled things. Ussmak hadn't learned any Français, but the tone didn't sound friendly.

Males of the Race, aided here and there by Tosevites in low, flat-topped cylindrical hats, held back local traffic until the column passed by. Most of the traffic was Big Uglies on foot or on the two-wheeled contraptions that used their own body energy for propulsion. Others sat atop animal-drawn wagons that seemed to Ussmak something straight out of an archaeology video.

One of the animals let a pile of droppings fall to the street. None of the Big Uglies rushed to clean it up; none of them seemed to notice it was there. Hessef spoke to Ussmak from the landcruiser's intercom: "Filthy creatures, aren't they? They deserve to be conquered, and we're going to do it." An unnatural confidence filled his voice.

But for the landcruisers, only a couple of motorized vehicles moved in Besançon. Both of them had big metal cylinders rising from the rear like tumors. "What are those things?" Ussmak asked. "Their engines?"

"No," Tvenkel answered. The gunner went on, "They're built to burn petroleum by-products, like Tosevite landcruisers. But they can't get those by-products any more. The gadgets you see extract burnable gas from wood. They're ugly makeshifts like most of what the Big Uglies do, but they work after a fashion."

"Oh." Up in the fortress that overlooked Besançon, Ussmak had grown used to smells he'd never smelled before. Now that he saw what produced some of those smells, he wondered what they were doing to his lungs.

The operations order said the landcruisers were to proceed northeast from Besançon. Through the town, however, they rumbled northwest. Ussmak wondered if that was right, but didn't say anything about it. All he was doing was following the male in front of him. You couldn't possibly get in trouble if you did that.

The male in front of him—and all the males in the column, right up to the lead driver, who had to make his own decisions—proved to know what they were doing. They rattled across a bridge (to the relief of Ussmak, who wasn't sure it would take his landcruiser's weight), past the earthworks of yet another fort, and then out onto a road that led in the proper direction.

Ussmak undogged his entry hatch and stuck out his head. Driving unbuttoned gave him the best view, even if the breeze in his face was chilly. *Shouldn't be dangerous here,* he thought. Nothing even slightly out of the ordinary had happened since he came to Besançon. He'd become convinced the area was thoroughly pacified.

Up ahead, something went *whump.* Ussmak recognized that noise from the SSSR: somebody had driven over a land mine. Sure enough, landcruisers started going off the road on either side to get around a disabled vehicle. From the commander's cupola, Hessef said, "Ah, will you look at that? It's blown the track right off him."

The ground to either side of the paved road was soft and soggy: not surprising, Ussmak supposed, since the highway ran parallel to the river that flowed through Besançon. He didn't think anything of it until a landcruiser, and then another one, bogged down in the muck.

From the woods to the north of the road came another sound with which Ussmak had become intimately familiar in the SSSR: a sharp, fast, harsh *tac-tac-tac.* He slammed the hatch with a clang. "They're shooting at us!" he screamed. "That's an egg-addled machine gun, that's what that is!" Bullets ricocheting from the landcruiser's composite armor underscored his words.

In the turret, Hessef shouted in high excitement. "I see muzzle flashes, by the Emperor! There he is, Tvenkel, right over there! Bring the turret around—that's the way. Give him some with the machine gun, and then a round of high explosive. We'll teach the Big Uglies to fool with *us!*"

Ussmak let out a slow hiss of wonder. Hessef's sloppy commands weren't anything like the ones that had been drilled into the landcruiser crews in endless days of simulator training and exercises back on Home. Ussmak realized he was listening to the ginger talking again. An adjutant monitoring Hessef would have swelled up as if he had the gray staggers.

However unorthodox the orders, though, they accomplished their purpose. Hydraulics whirred as the turret smoothly traversed. The coaxial machine gun opened up. Heard from inside the landcruiser, it wasn't loud at all. "Fool with us, will they?" Tvenkel yelled. "I'll teach them this world belongs to the Race!" He fired a long, long burst. Not being turned toward the Big Uglies with the machine gun, Ussmak at first had trou-

ble judging how effective Tvenkel's shooting was. But then more bullets pattered off the landcruisers like pebbles thrown at a metal roof. They did no more damage than pebbles would have, but showed the Tosevite gunners were still in business.

"Give 'em the real thing," Hessef said. Again, thick armor muffled the cannon's roar, though the landcruiser rocked slightly on its treads as it took up the recoil.

"There, that's done it," Tvenkel said with satisfaction. "We put enough rounds on that machine gun so the Big Uglies running it won't bother their betters again." As if to underscore his words, bullets stopped hitting the landcruiser.

Ussmak peered through his forward vision slits. Some of the other vehicles in the column were already moving ahead. A moment later, Hessef said, "Forward."

"It shall be done, superior sir." Ussmak released the brake, put the landcruiser into low gear. It rumbled forward. He steered very close to the machine that had thrown a track, keeping one of his own on the paved road to make sure he didn't bog down. As soon as he was past the crippled landcruiser, he sped up to try to recapture some of the time everyone had lost shooting at the Big Uglies and their machine gun.

Hessef said, "Not bad at all. The column commander reports only two wounds, neither serious. And we obliterated those Tosevites."

The ginger was still talking through him, Ussmak thought. Landcruiser crews shouldn't have taken any casualties from a nuisance machine gun. Besides which, Hessef was ignoring the disabled fighting vehicle and the delay that sprang from the little firefight. If you'd tasted ginger a while before, such setbacks were too small to be worth noticing. Had Ussmak tasted along with the rest of the crew, he wouldn't have noticed them, either. Without a particle of the herb in him, though, they bulked large. He wondered just how clever he really was after a good taste.

From behind and to the left, bullets clattered off the landcruiser's rear deck and the back of the turret. The Big Uglies at their machine gun had lived through the firestorm around them after all.

"Halt!" Hessef screeched. Ussmak obediently hit the brake. "Five rounds high explosive this time," the commander or-

dered. "Do you hear me, Tvenkel? I want those maniacal males blown to bloody bits."

"So do I," the gunner said. He and his commander agreed perfectly, just as training said members of a landcruiser crew should. The only trouble was that the tactic on which they agreed struck Ussmak as insane.

The landcruiser's main armament boomed, again and again. And Hessef's was not the only crew that had halted. Through his vision slits, Ussmak watched several other landcruisers stop so they could pour fire down on the Tosevites who had had the temerity to annoy them. The driver wondered if their commanders were tasting, too.

When the barrage was done, Hessef said, "Forward," in tones of self-satisfaction. Ussmak obeyed again. Not much later, the landcruiser column came to an enormous hole blown in the highway. "The Big Uglies can't stop us with nonsense like that," Hessef declared. And sure enough, the armored fighting vehicles swung off the road one by one.

The machine just in front of Ussmak's rolled over a mine and lost a track. As soon as it slewed to a stop, a concealed Tosevite machine gun opened up. The landcruisers again returned fire with cannon and machine guns.

The column was very late reaching its assigned destination.

Heinrich Jäger paced through the cobblestoned streets of Hechingen. Up on a spur of the Schwäbische Alb stood Burg Hohenzollern. Its turrets, seen mistily through fog, made Jäger think of medieval epic, of maidens with long golden tresses and of the dragons that coveted them for their own dragonish reasons.

The trouble these days, however, was Lizards, not dragons. Jäger wished he were back at the front so he could do something useful about them. Instead, he was stuck here with the best scientific minds of the *Reich*.

He had nothing against them: on the contrary. They were far more likely to save Germany—to save mankind—than he was. But they thought they needed him to help them do it, and in that, as far as he could see, they were badly mistaken.

He'd watched soldiers make the same kind of mistake. If a detachment from the quartermaster's office brought a new model field telephone to the front-line soldiers, they were au-

tomatically seen as experts on the gadget, even if the only thing they knew about it was how to get it out of its crate.

So with him now. He'd helped steal the explosive metal from the Lizards, he'd hauled it across the Ukraine and Poland. Therefore, the presumption ran, he had to know all about it. Like a lot of presumptions, that one presumed too much.

Coming up the street toward him, munching on a chunk of black bread, was Werner Heisenberg. In spite of the bread, Heisenberg looked very much the academic: he was tall and serious-looking, with bushy hair combed straight back, fluffy eyebrows, and an expression mostly, as now, abstracted.

"*Herr Doktor Professor,*" Jäger said, touching the brim of his service cap. No matter how bored he was, he remained polite.

"Ah, Colonel Jäger, good day. I did not see you." Heisenberg chuckled uneasily. Being taken for the traditional absentminded professor had to embarrass him, not least because he really wasn't that way. Up till now, he'd always seemed plenty sharp—and not just brilliant, which went without saying—to Jäger. He went on, "I am glad to find you, though. I must thank you again for the material you have given us to work with."

"To serve the *Reich* is my pleasure and my duty," Jäger answered, politely still. If Heisenberg had ever seen combat, he didn't show it. He could thank Jäger for bringing the explosive metal, but he didn't really know what that meant, or how much blood had been spilled to get him his experimental material.

He proceeded to prove that, saying, "A pity you could not have fetched us a bit more. Theoretical calculations indicate the amount we have is marginal for the production of a uranium explosive. Another three or four kilos would have been most beneficial."

That did it. Jäger's boredom boiled away in fury. "Dr. Diebner had the courtesy to be grateful for what was provided rather than to complain about it. He also had the sense, sir"—Jäger loaded the title with scorn—"to remember how many lives were lost obtaining it."

He'd hoped to make Heisenberg ashamed. Instead, he flicked him on his vanity. "Diebner? Ha! He has not even his *Habilitation*. He is, if you ask me, more tinkerer than physicist."

"He knows what war entails, which is more than you seem

to. And, by all accounts, he and his group are further along than yours in setting up the apparatus to produce more of this explosive metal for ourselves after we expend what we procured from the Lizards."

"By no means is his work theoretically sound," Heisenberg said, as if he were accusing the other physicist of embezzlement.

"I don't care about theory. I care about results." Jäger automatically reacted like a soldier. "Without results, theory is irrelevant."

"Without theory, results are impossible," Heisenberg retorted. The two men glared at each other. Jäger wished he hadn't bothered to greet the physicist. By the expression on his face, Heisenberg wished the same thing.

Jäger shouted, "The metal is more real to you than the men who fell getting it." He wanted to clout Heisenberg down from his cloud, make him glimpse, however distantly, the world beyond equations. He also wanted to kick him in the teeth.

"I tried to express to you a civil good day, Colonel Jäger," Heisenberg said in tones of ice. "That you return it to me with such, such recriminations I can take only as the mark of an unbalanced mind. Believe me, Colonel, I shall trouble you no further." The physicist stalked off.

Still steaming, Jäger stalked, too, in the opposite direction. He jumped and almost grabbed for his sidearm when someone said, "Well, Colonel, what was that in aid of?"

"Dr. Diebner!" Jäger said. "You startled me." He took his hand away from the flap of his holster.

"I shall try not to do that again," Kurt Diebner said. "I can see it might not be healthy for me." Where Heisenberg looked like a professor, Diebner at first glance seemed more likely to be a farmer. He was in his thirties, with a broad, fleshy face and a receding hairline which he emphasized by slicking down his dark hair with grease and combing it straight back. He wore his baggy suit as if he'd been out walking the fields in it. Only the thick glasses that showed how nearsighted he was argued for a different interpretation of his character.

Jäger said, "I had a—disagreement with your colleague."

"I saw that, yes." Behind the glasses, amusement glinted in Diebner's eyes. "I don't believe I have ever seen Dr. Heisenberg so provoked; he normally cultivates an Olympian imperturbability. I came round the corner only for the tail end

of the—disagreement, you said?—and was wondering what touched it off."

The panzer colonel hesitated, since his compliments for Diebner had helped set Heisenberg off. At last he said, "I was concerned that Professor Heisenberg did not, ah, fully realize the difficulties in getting this metal to you nuclear physicists so you could exploit it."

"Ah." Diebner turned his head, peered this way and that; unlike Jäger and Heisenberg, he was careful about who heard him speak. His big thick spectacles and their dark rims gave him the air of a curious owl. "Sometimes, Colonel Jäger," he said when he was sure the coast was clear, "from the top of the ivory tower it is hard to see the men struggling down in the mud."

"This may be so." Jäger studied Diebner. "And yet—forgive me, *Herr Doktor Professor*—it seems to me, a colonel of panzers admittedly ignorant of all matter pertaining to nuclear physics, that you, too, dwell in this ivory tower."

"Oh, I do, without a doubt." Diebner laughed; his plump cheeks shook. "But I do not dwell on the topmost floor. Before the war, before uranium and its behavior became so important to us all, Professor Heisenberg concerned himself almost exclusively with the mathematical analysis of matter and its behavior. You have perhaps heard of the Uncertainty Principle which bears his name?"

"I'm sorry, but no," Jäger said.

"Ah, well." Diebner shrugged. "Put me in charge of a panzer and I would be quickly killed. We all have our areas of expertise. My gift is in physics, too, but in experimenting to see what the properties of matter actually are. Then the theoreticians, of whom Professor Heisenberg is among the best, use these data to develop their abstruse conclusions over what it all means."

"Thank you. You have clarified that for me." Jäger meant it—now he understood why Heisenberg had sneeringly called Diebner a tinkerer. The difference was something like the one between himself and a colonel of the General Staff. Jäger knew he didn't have the broad strategic vision he'd need to succeed as a man with the *Lampassen*—the broad red stripes that marked a General Staff officer—on his trousers. On the other hand, a General Staff officer wasn't likely to have acquired the

nuts-and-bolts knowledge (often in the literal sense of the words) to run a panzer regiment.

Diebner said, "Do try to bear with us, Colonel. The difficulties we face are formidable, not least because we are under such desperate pressure of time and strategy."

"I follow," Jäger said. "I wish I were back with my unit, so I could use what I have learned to help hold the Lizards out of the *Reich* and let you complete your work. I am badly out of place here."

"If you advance our building of the uranium bomb, you will have done more for the *Reich* than you could possibly accomplish in the field. Believe me when I say this." Now Diebner looked earnest, like a farmer solemnly explaining how excellent his beets were.

"If." Jäger remained unconvinced that he could do anything useful here at Hechingen: he was about as valuable as oars on a bicycle. He came up with a plan, though, one that made him smile. Diebner smiled back; he seemed a very decent fellow. Jäger felt a little guilty at going against him, but only a little.

When he got back to his quarters, he drafted a request to be returned to active duty. On the space in the form that asked his reason for seeking the transfer, he wrote, *I am of no use to the physicists here. If confirmation is required, please inquire of Professor Heisenberg.*

He sent the request off with a messenger and awaited results. They were not long in coming—the application got approved faster than he had thought possible. Diebner and a couple of the other physicists expressed regret that he was leaving. Professor Heisenberg said not a word. He'd no doubt had his say to the office who'd called or telegraphed about Jäger.

Maybe he thought he'd had his revenge. As far as Jäger was concerned, the distinguished professor had done him a favor.

Yea, though I walk through the valley of the shadow of death, I shall fear no evil, for Thou art with me. Lodz constantly put Moishe Russie in mind of the Twenty-third Psalm, and of that valley. Lodz, though, had only walked into the valley, not through it. The shadow of death still lay over the town.

In Warsaw, thousands in the ghetto had died of starvation and disease before the Lizards came. Starvation and disease had walked the streets of Lodz, too. But the Nazis hadn't let

them work alone here. They'd started shipping Jews off to
their murder factories. Maybe the memory of those death trans-
ports was what made Lodz still seem caught in the grip of a
nightmare.

Russie walked southeast down Zgierska Street toward the
Balut Market square to buy some potatoes for his family. Up
the street toward him came a Jewish policeman of the Order
Service. His red-and-white armband bore a six-pointed black
star with a white circle in the center, marking him as an underofficer. He had a truncheon on his belt and a rifle across his
back. He looked like a tough customer.

But when Russie tugged at the brim of his hat in salute, the
Order Service man returned the gesture and kept on walking.
Emboldened, Russie turned and called after him: "How are the
potatoes today?"

The policeman stopped. "They're not wonderful, but I've
seen worse," he answered. Pausing to spit in the gutter, he
added, "We all saw worse last year."

"Isn't that the sad and sorry truth?" Russie said. He headed
on down to the market while the Order Service man resumed
his beat.

More policemen roamed the Balut Market square, to keep
down thievery, maintain order—and cadge what they could.
Like the underofficer, they still wore the emblems of rank
they'd got from the Nazis.

That helped make Lodz feel haunted to Russie. In Warsaw
the *Judenrat*—the Jewish council that had administered the
ghetto under German authority—collapsed even before the Lizards drove out the Nazis. Its police force had fallen with it.
Jewish fighters, not the hated and discredited police, kept order
there now. The same held true in most Polish towns.

Not in Lodz. Here, the walls of the buildings that fronted
the market square were plastered with posters of balding,
white-haired Mordechai Chaim Rumkowski. Rumkowski had
been Eldest—puppet ruler—of Lodz's Jews under the Nazis.
Somehow, he was still Eldest of the Jews under the Lizards.

Russie wondered how he'd managed that. He must have
jumped from the departing train to the arriving one at just the
right instant. In Warsaw, there were stories that he'd collaborated with the Nazis. Russie had asked no questions of that sort
since he got into Lodz. He didn't want to draw Rumkowski's

attention toward him and his family. For all he knew, the Eldest would turn him over to Zolraag, the local Lizard governor.

He got into line for potatoes. The lines moved fast; the Order Service men saw to that. They were fierce and fussy at the same time, a manner they must have learned from the Germans. Some of them still wore German-style jackboots, too. As with the ghetto stars on their armbands, the boots raised Russie's hackles.

When he reached the front of the line, such worries fell away. Food was more important. He held out a burlap bag and said, "Ten kilos of potatoes, please."

The man behind the table took the bag, filled it from a bin, plopped it onto a scale. He'd had endless practice; it weighed ten kilos on the dot. He didn't hand it back to Russie. Instead, he asked, "How are you going to pay? Lizard coupons, marks, zlotys, Rumkies?"

"Rumkies." Russie pulled a wad of them out of his pocket. The fighter who'd driven him into Lodz had given him what seemed like enough to stuff a mattress. He'd imagined himself rich until he discovered that the Lodz ghetto currency was almost worthless.

The potato seller made a sour face. "If it's Rumkies, you owe me 450." The potatoes would have cost only a third as many Polish zlotys, the next weakest currency.

Russie started peeling off dark blue twenty-mark notes and blue-green tens, each printed with a Star of David in the upper left-hand corner and a cross-hatching of background lines that spiderwebbed the bills with more *Magen Davids*. Each note bore Rumkowski's signature, which gave the money its sardonic nickname.

The potato seller made his own count after Moishe gave him the bills. Even though it came out right, he still looked unhappy. "Next time you come, bring real money," he advised. "I don't think we're going to take Rumkies a whole lot longer."

"But—" Russie waved to the ubiquitous portraits of the Jewish Eldest.

"He can do what he wants in here," the potato seller said. "But he can't make anybody outside think Rumkies are good for anything but wiping your behind." The merchant's shrug was eloquent.

Russie started back to his flat with the potatoes. It was on the corner of Zgierska and Lekarska, just a couple of blocks

from the barbed wire that had sealed off the ghetto of Lodz—
Litzmannstadt, the Nazis had renamed it when they annexed
western Poland to the *Reich*—from the rest of the city.

Much of the barbed wire remained in place, though paths
had been cut through it here and there. In Warsaw, Lizard
bombs had knocked down the wall the Germans made. Of
course, that barrier had looked like a fortification and most of
this one didn't. But something else went on here, too. The potato seller had said that Rumkowski could do what he wanted
inside the ghetto. He'd meant it scornfully, but Moishe thought
his words held a truth he hadn't intended. He had the feeling
Rumkowski liked being a big fish, no matter how small his
pond was.

At least there were enough potatoes to go around these days.
The Lodz ghetto had been as hungry as Warsaw's, maybe hun-
grier. The Jews inside remained gaunt and ragged, especially
compared to the Poles and Germans who made up the rest of
the townsfolk. They weren't actively starving any more,
though. From where they'd been a year before, that wasn't just
progress. It felt like a miracle.

A horse-drawn wagon clattered up behind Russie. He
stepped aside to let it pass. It was piled high with curious-
looking objects woven out of straw. "What are those things,
anyway?" Russie called to the driver.

"You must be new in town." The fellow pulled back on the
reins, slowed his team to an amble so he could talk for a
while. "They're boots, so the Lizards won't freeze their little
chicken feet every time they go out in the snow."

"Chicken feet—I like that," Russie said.

The driver grinned. "Every time I see two or three Lizards
together, I think of the front window of a butcher's shop. I
want to go down the street yelling, 'Soup! Get your soup fixings here!' " He sobered. "We were making straw boots for the
Nazis before the Lizards came. All we had to do was make
'em smaller and change the shape."

"Wouldn't it be fine to make what we wanted just for ourselves, not for one set of masters or another?" Russie said
wistfully. His hands remembered the motions they'd made
sewing seams on field-gray trousers.

"Fine, yes. Should you hold your breath? No." The driver
coughed wetly. *Tuberculosis,* said the medical student Russie
had once been. The driver went on, "It'll probably happen

about the time the Messiah comes. These days, stranger, I'll take small things—my wife's not embroidering little eagles for *Luftwaffe* men, a *kholereye* on them, to wear on their shoulders. You ask me, *that's* fine."

"It is fine," Russie agreed. "But it shouldn't be enough."

"If God had asked me when He was making the world, I'm sure I could have done much better for His people. Unfortunately, He seems to have been otherwise engaged." Coughing again, the driver flicked the reins and sent the wagon rattling on down the street. Now at least he could go outside the ghetto.

More posters of Rumkowski were plastered on the front of Russie's block of flats. Under his lined face was one word—WORK—in Yiddish, Polish, and German. His hope had been to make the industrious Jews of Lodz so valuable to the Nazis that they would not want to ship them to extermination camps. It hadn't worked; the Germans were running trains to Chelmno and other camps until the day the Lizards drove them away. Russie wondered how much Rumkowski had known about that.

He also wondered why Rumkowski fawned so on the Lizards when only horror had come from his efforts at accommodating the Nazis. Maybe he didn't want to lose the shadowy power he enjoyed as Jewish Eldest. Or maybe he just didn't know any other way to deal with overlords so much mightier than he. For the Eldest's sake, Russie hoped the latter was true.

Shlepping the potatoes up three flights of stairs as he walked down the hallway to his flat, years of bad nutrition and weeks of being cooped up inside the cramped bunker had taken their toll on his wind and on his strength generally. He tried the door. It was locked. He rapped on it. Rivka let him in.

A small tornado in a cloth cap tackled him just above the knees. "Father, Father!" Reuven squealed. "You're back!" Ever since they'd come out of the bunker—where they'd been together every moment, awake and asleep—Reuven had been nervous about his going away for any reason. He was, however, starting to get over that, for he asked, "Did you bring me anything?"

"Sorry, son; not this time. I just went out for food," Moishe said. Reuven groaned in disappointment. His father pulled his cap down over his eyes. He thought that was funny enough to make up for the lack of trinkets.

People sold toys in the market square. How many of them, though, used to belong to children who'd died in the ghetto or been taken away to Chelmno or some other camp? When even something that should have been joyous, like buying a toy, saddened and frightened you because you wondered why it was for sale, you began to feel in your belly what the Nazis had done to the Jews of Poland.

Rivka took the sack of potatoes. "What did you have to pay?" she asked.

"Four hundred and fifty Rumkies," he answered.

She stopped in dismay. "This is only ten kilos, right? Last week ten kilos only cost me 320. Didn't you haggle?" When he shook his head, she rolled her eyes toward the heavens. "Men! See if I let you go shopping again."

"The Rumkie's worth less every day," he said defensively. "In fact, it's almost worthless, period."

As if she were explaining a lesson to Reuven, she said, "Last week, the potato seller's first price for me was 430 Rumkies. I just laughed at him. You should have done the same."

"I suppose so," he admitted. "It didn't seem to matter, not when we have so many Rumkies."

"They won't last forever," Rivka said sharply. "Do you want us to have to go to work in the Lizards' factories to make enough to keep from starving?"

"God forbid," he answered, remembering the wagon full of straw boots. Making things for the Germans had been bad enough; making boots and coats for the aliens who aimed to conquer all mankind had to be worse, although the wagon driver hadn't seemed to think so.

Rivka laughed at him. "It's all right. I got us some nice onions from Mrs. Jakubowicz downstairs for next to nothing. That should cancel out your foolishness."

"How does Mrs. Jakubowicz come by onions?"

"I didn't ask. One doesn't, these days, but she had enough of them that she didn't gouge me."

"Good. Do we have any of that cheese left?" Moishe asked.

"Yes—plenty for today, with some left over for tomorrow, too."

"That's very good," Moishe said. Food came first. The ghetto had taught him that. He sometimes thought that if he ever got rich (not likely) and if the war ever ended (which

seemed even less likely), he'd buy himself a huge house, live in half of it, and fill the other half with meat and butter (in separate rooms, of course) and pastries and all manner of wonderful things to eat. Maybe he'd open a delicatessen. Even in wartime, people who sold food didn't go as hungry as those who had to buy it.

The part of him that had studied human nutrition said cheese and potatoes and onions could keep body and soul together a long time. Protein, fat, vitamins (he wished for something green, but that would have been hard to come by in Poland in late winter even before the war), minerals. Unexciting food, yes, but food.

Rivka carried the sack of potatoes into the kitchen. Moishe trailed after her. The apartment was scantily furnished—just the leftovers of the people who had lived, and probably died, here before his family came. One thing it did boast, though, was a hot plate, and Lodz, unlike Warsaw even now, had reliable electricity.

Rivka peeled and chopped up a couple of onions. Moishe drew back a few paces. Even so, the onions were strong enough to make tears start in his eyes. The onions went into the stew pot. So did half a dozen potatoes. Rivka didn't peel them. She glanced over to her husband. "Nutrients," she said seriously.

"Nutrients," he agreed. Potatoes in their jackets had more than potatoes without. When potatoes were most of what you ate, you didn't want to waste anything.

"Supper in—a while," Rivka said. The hot plate was feeble. It would take a long time to boil water. Even after it did, the potatoes would take a while to cook. When your stomach was none too full, waiting came hard.

Without warning, a huge *bang!* rattled the windows. Reuven started crying. As Rivka rushed to comfort him, sirens began to wail.

Moishe followed his wife out to the front room. "It frightened me," Reuven said.

"It frightened me, too," his father answered. He'd tried to forget how terrifying an explosion out of the blue could be. Hearing just one took him back to the summer before, when the Lizards had forced the Germans out of Warsaw, and to 1939, when the Nazis had pounded a city that couldn't fight back.

"I didn't think the Germans could hurt us any more," Rivka said.

"I didn't, either. They must have gotten lucky." Moishe spoke as much to reassure himself as to hearten his wife. Believing they were safe from the Nazis was as vital to them as to every other Jew in Poland.

Bang! This one was louder and closer. The whole block of flats shook. Glass tinkled down on the floor as two windows blew in. Faint in the distance, Moishe heard screams. The rising bay of the sirens soon drowned them out.

"Lucky?" Rivka asked bitterly. Moishe shrugged with as much nonchalance as he could find. If it wasn't just luck—He didn't want to think about that.

"The Deutsche got lucky," Kirel said. "They launched their missiles when our antimissile system was down for periodic maintenance. The warheads did only relatively minor damage to our facilities."

Atvar glowered at the shiplord, though it was only natural that he try to put the best face on things. "Our facilities may not be badly damaged, but what of our prestige?" the fleetlord snapped. "Shall we give the Big Uglies the impression they can lob these things at us whenever it strikes their fancy?"

"Exalted Fleetlord, the situation is not so bad as that," Kirel said.

"No, eh?" Atvar was not ready to be appeased. "How not?"

"They fired three more at our installations the next days and we knocked all of those down," Kirel said.

"This is less wonderful than it might be," Atvar said. "I presume we expended three antimissile missiles in the process?"

"Four, actually," Kirel said. "One went wild and had to be destroyed in flight."

"Which leaves us how many such missiles in our inventory?"

"Exalted Fleetlord, I would have to run a computer check to give you the precise number," Kirel said.

Atvar had run that computer check. "The precise number, Shiplord, is 357. With them, we can reasonably expect to shoot down something over three hundred of the Big Uglies' missiles. After that, we become as vulnerable to them as they are to us."

"Not really," Kirel protested. "The guidance systems on

their missiles are laughable. They can strike militarily significant targets only by accident. The missiles themselves are—"

"Junk," Atvar finished for him. "I know this." He poked a claw into a computer control on his desk. The holographic image of a wrecked Tosevite missile sprang into being above the projector off to one side. "Junk," he repeated. "Sheet-metal body, glass-wool insulation, no electronics worthy of the name—"

"It scarcely makes a pretense of being accurate," Kirel said.

"I understand that," Atvar said. "And to knock it out of the sky, we have to use weapons full of sophisticated electronics we cannot hope to replace on this world. Even at one for one, the exchange is scarcely fair."

"We cannot show the Big Uglies how to manufacture integrated circuits," Kirel said. "Their technology is too primitive to let them produce such sophisticated components for us. And even if it weren't, I would hesitate to acquaint them with such an art, lest we find ourselves on the receiving end of it in a year's time."

"Always a question of considerable import on Tosev 3," Atvar said. "I thank the forethoughtful spirits of Emperors past"—he cast his eyes down to the floor, as did Kirel—"that we stocked any antimissiles at all. We did not expect to have to deal with technologically advanced opponents."

"The same applies to our ground armor and many other armaments," Kirel agreed. "Without them, our difficulties would be greater still."

"I understand this," Atvar said. "What galls me still more is that, despite our air of superiority, we have not been able to shut down the Big Uglies' industrial capacity. Their weapons are primitive, but continue to be produced."

He had once more the uneasy vision of a new Tosevite landcruiser rumbling around a pile of ruins just after the Race's last one had been lost in battle. Or maybe it would be a new missile flying off its launcher with a trail of fire, and no hope of knocking it down before it hit.

Kirel said, "Our strategy of targeting the Tosevites' petroleum facilities has not yet yielded the full range of desired results."

"I am painfully aware of this," Atvar replied. "The Big Uglies are better at effecting makeshift repairs than any rational being could have imagined. And while their vehicles and air-

craft are petroleum-fueled, the same is not true of a large proportion of their heavy manufacturing capacity. This also makes matters more difficult."

"We are beginning to get significant amounts of small-arms ammunition from Tosevite factories in the areas under our control," Kirel said, resolutely looking at the bright side of things. "The level of sabotage in production is acceptably low."

"That's something, anyhow. Up till now, these Tosevite facilities have produced nothing but frustration for us," Atvar said. "The munitions they turn out are good enough to damage us, but not of sufficient quality or precision to be useful to us in and of themselves. We cannot merely match them bullet for bullet or shell for shell, as they have more of each. Ours, then, must have the greater effect."

"Indeed so, Exalted Fleetlord," Kirel said. "To that end, we have recently converted a munitions factory we captured from the Français to producing artillery ammunition in our calibers. The Tosevites manufacture the casings and the explosive charges; our only contribution to the process is the electronics for terminal guidance."

"Something," Atvar said again. "But when our supply of seeker heads runs out—" In his mind, that ugly, smoke-belching landcruiser came out from behind the pile of ruins again.

"Such stocks are still fairly large," Kirel said. "Again, we now have factories in Italia, France, and captured areas of the U.S.A. and the SSSR beginning to turn out brakes and other mechanical parts for our vehicles."

"This is progress," Atvar admitted. "Whether it proves sufficient progress remains to be seen. The Big Uglies, unfortunately, also progress. Worse still, they progress qualitatively, where we are lucky to be able to hold our ground. I still worry about what the colonization fleet will find here when it arrives."

"Surely the conquest will be complete by then," Kirel exclaimed.

"Will it?" The more Atvar looked ahead, the less he liked what he saw. "Try as we will, Shiplord, I fear we shall not be able to prevent the Big Uglies from acquiring nuclear weapons. And if they do, I fear for Tosev 3."

Vyacheslav Molotov detested flying. That gave him a personal reason for hating the Lizards to go along with reasons of

patriotism and ideology. Ideology came first, of course. He hated the Lizards for their imperialism, for the efforts to cast all of mankind—and the Soviet Union in particular—back into the ancient economic system, with the aliens taking the role of masters and reducing mankind to slaves.

But beneath the imperatives of the Marxist-Leninist dialectic, Molotov also despised the Lizards for making him fly here to London. This trip wasn't as ghastly as his last one, when he had flown in the open cockpit of a biplane from just outside Moscow to Berchtesgaden to beard Hitler in his den. He'd been in a closed cabin all the way—but he'd been no less nervous.

True, the Pe-2 fighter-bomber that had brought him across the North Sea was more comfortable than the little U-2 he'd used before. But it was also more vulnerable. The U-2 seemed too small for the Lizards to notice. Not so the machine he'd flown in yesterday. If he'd gone down into the cold, choppy gray water below, he knew he wouldn't have lasted long.

But here he was, at the heart of the British Empire. For the five major powers still resisting the Lizards—the five major powers which, before the Lizards came, had been at war with one another—London remained the most accessible common ground. Large parts of the Soviet Union, the United States, and Germany and its European conquests lay under the aliens' thumb, while Japan, though like England free of invaders, was next to impossible for British, German, and Soviet representatives to reach.

Winston Churchill strode into the Foreign Office conference room. He nodded first to Cordell Hull, the American Secretary of State, then to Molotov, and then to Joachim von Ribbentrop and Shigenori Togo. As former enemies, they stood lower on his scale of approval than did the nations that had banded together against fascism.

But Churchill's greeting included all impartially: "I welcome you, gentlemen, in the cause of freedom and in the name of His Majesty the King."

Molotov's interpreter murmured the Russian translation for him. Big Five conferences got along on three languages: America and Britain shared English, while Ribbentrop, a former German ambassador to the Court of St. James's, was also fluent in that tongue. That left Molotov and Togo linguis-

tically isolated, but Molotov, at least, was used to isolation—serving as foreign commissar for the only Marxist-Leninist state in a capitalist world was good pariah training.

The envoys delivered their replies. When Molotov's turn came, he said, "The peasants and workers of the Soviet Union express through me their solidarity with the peasants and workers of worldwide humanity against our common foe."

Ribbentrop gave him a dirty look. Getting the Nazi's goat, though, was no great accomplishment; Molotov thought of him as nothing more than a champagne salesman jumped up beyond his position and his abilities. Churchill's round pink face, on the contrary, remained utterly imperturbable. For the British Prime Minister, Molotov had a grudging respect. No doubt he was a class enemy, but he was an able and resolute man. Without him, England might have yielded to the Nazis in 1940, and he had unhesitatingly gone to the support of the Soviet Union when the Germans invaded a year later. Had he thrown his weight behind Hitler then in the crusade against Bolshevism he'd once preached, the USSR might have fallen.

Cordell Hull said, "It's a good idea that we get together when we can so we can plan together the best way of ridding ourselves of the damned Lizards." As he had been at previous meetings, Molotov's interpreter was a little slower in translating for Hull than he had been for Churchill: the American's dialect differed from the British English he'd learned.

"Ridding ourselves of the Lizards now is not our only concern," Shigenori Togo said.

"What could possibly be of greater concern to us?" Ribbentrop demanded. He might have been a posturing, pop-eyed fool, but for once Molotov could not disagree with his question.

But Togo said, "We also have now a future concern. Surely you all hold captives from among the Lizards. Have you not observed they are all males?"

"Of what other gender could warriors properly be?" Churchill said.

Molotov lacked the Englishman's Victorian preconceptions on that score: female pilots and snipers had gone into battle—and done well—against both the Germans and the Lizards. But even Molotov reckoned that a tactic of desperation. "What are you implying?" he asked of the Japanese foreign minister.

"Under interrogation, a captive Lizard pilot has informed us

that this enormous invasion force is but the precursor to a still larger fleet now traveling toward our planet," Togo replied. "The second fleet is termed, if we understand correctly, the colonization fleet. The Lizards intend not merely conquest but also occupation."

He could have created no greater consternation if he'd thrown a live grenade onto the gleaming mahogany surface of the table in front of him. Ribbentrop shouted in German; Cordell Hull slammed the palm of his hand down onto the tabletop and shook his head so that the fringe of hair he combed over his bald crown flailed wildly; Churchill choked on his cigar and coughed harshly.

Only Molotov still sat unmoved and unmoving. He waited for the hubbub to die down around him, then said, "Why should we allow this to surprise us, comrades?" He used the last word deliberately, both to remind the other dignitaries that they were in the struggle together and to irk them on account of their capitalist ideology.

Speaking through an interpreter had its advantages. Among them was getting the chance to think while the interpreter performed his office. Ribbentrop started off in German again (a mark of indiscipline, to Molotov's mind), then switched to spluttering English: "But how are we to defeat these creatures if they throw at us endless waves of attack?"

"This is a question you Germans should have asked yourselves before you invaded the Soviet Union," Molotov said.

Hull raised a hand. "Enough of that," he said sharply. "Recriminations have no place at this table, else I would not be sitting here with Minister Togo."

Molotov dipped his head slightly, acknowledging the Secretary of State's point. He enjoyed twitting the Nazi, but enjoyment and diplomacy were two separate things.

"The depths of space between the stars are vaster than any man can comfortably imagine, and traveling them, even near the speed of light, takes time, or so the astronomers have led me to believe," Churchill said. He turned to Togo. "How long have we before the second wave falls on us?"

The Japanese foreign minister answered, "The prisoner states that this colonization fleet will reach Earth in something under forty of his kind's years. That is less than forty of our years, but by how much he does not know."

The interpreter leaned close to Molotov. "I am given to un-

derstand that two of the Lizards' years are more or less equal to one of ours," he murmured in Russian.

"Tell them," Molotov said after a moment's hesitation. Revealing information of any sort went against his grain, but joint planning required this.

When the interpreter finished speaking, Ribbentrop beamed. "So we have twenty years or so, then," he said. "This is not so bad."

Molotov was dismayed to see Hull nod at that. To them, he concluded, twenty years hence was so far distant that it might as well not exist. The Soviet Union's Five-Year Plans forced a concentration on the future, as did continued study of the ineluctable dynamics of the historical dialectic. As far as Molotov was concerned, a state that did not think about where it would be twenty years from now did not deserve to be anywhere.

He saw intense concentration on Churchill's face. The Englishman had no dialectic to guide him—how could he, when he represented a class destined for the ash-heap of history?—but was himself a student of history of the reactionary sort, and thus used to contemplating broad sweeps of time. He could look ahead twenty years without being dizzied at the distance.

"I shall tell you what this means, gentlemen," Churchill said: "It means that, even after we have defeated the Lizards even now encroaching on the green hills of Earth, we shall have to remain comrades in arms—even if not comrades in Commissar Molotov's sense—and ready ourselves and our world for another great battle."

"I agree," Molotov said. He was willing to let Churchill twit him without mercy if that advanced the coalition against the Lizards. Next to them, even a fossilized conservative like Churchill was reminted in shiny progressive metal.

Ribbentrop said, "I agree also. I must say, however, that certain countries now preaching the gospel of cooperation would do well to practice it. Germany has noted several instances of new developments transmitted to us incompletely or only with reluctance, while others at this table have shared more equally and openhandedly."

Churchill's bland face remained bland. Molotov did not change expression, either—but then he rarely did. He knew Ribbentrop was talking about the Soviet Union, but declined to feel the least bit guilty. He was still sorry that Germany had

succeeded in smuggling even half his share of explosive metal back to his homeland. That hadn't been part of the Soviet plan. And Churchill couldn't be enthusiastic about sharing British secrets with the power that had all but brought Britain to her knees.

"Minister Ribbentrop, I want to remind you that this notion of sending new ideas runs both ways," Cordell Hull said. "You haven't shared your fancy long-range rockets with the rest of us, I notice, nor the improved sights I hear tell about in your new tanks."

"I will investigate this," Ribbentrop said. "We shall not be less forthcoming than our neighbors."

"While you are investigating, you ought to look into the techniques involved in your Polish death camps," Molotov said. "Of course, the Lizards have publicized them so well that I doubt many secrets are left any more."

"The *Reich* denies these vicious fabrications advanced by aliens and Jews," Ribbentrop said, sending Molotov an angry glare that made him want to smile—he'd hurt the German foreign minister where it mattered. And Germany could deny all she pleased; no one believed her. Then Ribbentrop went on, "And in any case, *Herr* Molotov, I doubt whether Stalin needs any instruction in the art of murder."

Molotov bared his teeth; he hadn't expected the normally fatuous German to have such an effective comeback ready. Stalin, though, killed people because they opposed him or might be dangerous to him (the two categories, over the years, had grown closer together until they were nearly identical), not merely because of the group from which they sprang. The distinction, however, was too subtle for him to set it forth for the others around the mahogany table.

Shigenori Togo said, "We need to remember that, while we were enemies, we now find ourselves on the same side. Things which detract from this should be left by the wayside as inessential. Perhaps one day we shall find the time to pick them up once more and reexamine them, but that day is not yet."

The Japanese foreign minister was the appropriate man to speak to both Molotov and Ribbentrop, as his country had been allied with Germany and neutral to the Soviet Union before the Lizards came.

"A sensible suggestion," Hull said. His agreement with

Togo meant something, for the United States and Japan had the same reasons for hatred as Russians and Germans.

Molotov said, "As best we can, then, we shall maintain our progressive coalition and continue the struggle against the imperialist invaders, at the same time seeking ways to share the fruits of technical progress among ourselves?"

"As best we can, yes," Churchill said. Everyone else around the table nodded. Molotov knew the qualification would weaken their combined effort. But he also knew that, without it, the Big Five might have balked at sharing anything at all. An agreement with an acknowledged flaw was to his mind better than one that could blow up without warning.

They were keeping the fight alive. Past that, little mattered now.

☆ V ☆

The air–raid siren at Bruntingthorpe began to howl. David Goldfarb sprinted for the nearest slit trench. Above the siren came the roar of the Lizards' jets. It seemed to grow impossibly fast.

Bombs started falling about the time Goldfarb dove headlong into the trench. The ground shook as if it were writhing in pain. Antiaircraft guns hammered. The Lizard planes screamed past at just above treetop height. Their cannon were pounding, too. Through everything, the siren wailed on.

The jets streaked away. The AA around Bruntingthorpe sent a last few futile rounds after them. Shell fragments pattered down from the sky like jagged metal hail. Stunned, half deafened, filthy, his heart pounding madly, Goldfarb climbed to his feet.

He glanced down at his watch. "Bloody hell," he muttered, and then, because that didn't have enough kick, *"Gevalt."* Hardly more than a minute had gone by since the air raid warning began.

In that minute, Bruntingthorpe had been turned upside down. Craters pocked the runway. One of the bombs had struck an airplane in spite of the camouflaged revetment in which it huddled. A column of greasy black smoke rose into the cloudy sky.

Goldfarb looked around. "Oh, bloody *fucking* hell," he said. The Nissen hut where he'd been studying how to fit a radar into the Meteor jet fighter was just a piece of rubble. Part of the curved roof of corrugated galvanized iron had been blown fifty feet away.

The radarman scrambled out of the trench and dashed toward

the Nissen hut, which was beginning to burn. "Group Captain Hipple!" he shouted, and then called in turn the names of the other men with whom he'd been working. A dreadful fear that he would hear no reply rose in him.

Then, one by one, the heads of the RAF officers popped up out of the trench close by the hut. Only the top of Hipple's cap was visible; he really was very short. "That you, Goldfarb?" he called. "Are you all right?"

"Yes, sir," Goldfarb said. "Are you?"

"Quite, thanks," Hipple answered, scrambling out spryly. He looked around at the hut, shook his head. "There's a good deal of work up in smoke. I'm glad we salvaged what we did." As the other officers got out, he waved Goldfarb over to see what he meant.

The bottom of the slit trench was covered with manila folders and the papers that had spilled out of them. Goldfarb stared from them to Hipple and back again. "You—all of you— stopped to grab papers when the air raid alarm went off?"

"Well, the work upon which we are engaged here is of considerable importance, don't you think?" Hipple murmured, as if he hadn't imagined doing anything but what he'd done. He probably hadn't. Had Goldfarb been in the Nissen hut with the others, the only thing he would have thought about was getting to cover as fast as he could.

Groundcrew men had already emerged from their shelters. They swept and pushed chunks of tarmac off onto the winter-brown grass to either side of the newly hit runways, or else tossed them into the craters the bombs had made. Others started dragging up lengths of pierced-steel planking material to put over the holes until they could make more permanent repairs.

Flight Lieutenant Kennan pointed toward the burning aircraft. "I do hope that's not one of our Pioneers."

"Not in that revetment, sir." Flight Officer Roundbush shook his head. "It's only a Hurricane."

"*Only* a Hurricane?" Kennan looked scandalized; he'd flown one during the Battle of Britain. "Basil, if it weren't for Hurricanes, you'd have had to trim that mustache of yours down to a toothbrush and start learning German. The Spitfires grabbed the glory—they look like such thoroughbreds, after all—but Hurricanes did more of the work."

Roundbush's hand went protectively to the bushy blond

growth on his upper lip. "I beg your pardon, sir. Had I realized the Hurricane stood between my mustache and war's desolation, I should have spoken of it with more respect—even if it is as obsolete as a Sopwith Camel these days."

If possible, Kennan looked even more affronted, not least because Roundbush was in essence right. Indeed, against the Lizards a Sopwith Camel might have been of more use than a Hurricane, simply because it contained very little metal and so was hard for radar to pick up.

Before Kennan could return to the verbal charge, Group Captain Hipple said, "Maurice, Basil, that's quite enough." They shuffled their feet like a couple of abashed schoolboys.

Wing Commander Peary jumped back down into the trench, started rummaging through file folders. "Oh, capital," he said a minute later. "We didn't lose the drawings for the installation of the multifrequency radar in the Meteor fuselage."

At the same time as Goldfarb breathed a silent sigh of relief, Basil Roundbush said, "I had to save those. David would have smote me hip and thigh if I'd left them behind."

"Heh," Goldfarb said. He wondered if Roundbush was using that pseudo-Biblical language to mock his Jewishness. Probably not, he decided. Roundbush made fun of everything on general principles.

"Shall we gather up our goods and see who will give us a temporary home?" Hipple said. "We shan't have a hut of our own for a while now."

Planes were taking off and landing on the damaged runways by that afternoon. By then, Goldfarb and the RAF officers were back at work in a borrowed corner of the meteorological crew's Nissen hut. The inside of one of the temporary buildings was so much like that of another that for a few minutes at a time Goldfarb was able to forget he wasn't where he had been.

The telephone rang. One of the weathermen picked it up, then held it out to Hipple. "Call for you, Group Captain."

"Thank you." The jet engine specialist took the phone, said, "Hipple here." He listened for a couple of minutes, then said, "Oh, that's first-rate. Yes, we'll be looking forward to receiving it. Tomorrow morning some time, you say? Yes, that will do splendidly. Thanks so much for calling. Good-bye."

"What was that in aid of?" Wing Commander Peary asked.

"There may be some justice in the world after all, Julian," Hipple answered. "One of the Lizard jets which strafed this base was later brought down by antiaircraft fire north of Leicester. The aircraft did not burn upon impact, and damage was less extensive than in most other cases where we have been fortunate enough to strike a blow against the Lizards. An engine and the radar will be sent here for our examination."

"That's wonderful," Goldfarb exclaimed; his words were partly drowned by similar ones from the other members of his team and from the meteorologists as well.

"What happened to the pilot?" Basil Roundbush asked, adding, "Nothing good, I hope."

"I was told he used one of the Lizards' exploding seats to get free of the aircraft, but he has been captured by Home Guards," Hipple answered. "Perhaps it might be wise for me to seek to have him placed here so we can draw on his knowledge of the parts of his aircraft once he gains some command of English."

"I've heard the Lizards sing like birds once they get to the point where they can talk," Roundbush said. "They're supposed to be even worse than the Italians for that. It's odd, if you ask me."

Maurice Kennan walked into the trap: "Why's that?"

"Because they all come with stiff upper lips, of course." Roundbush grinned.

"You're one of the brightest Britain has to offer?" Kennan said, groaning. "God save us all."

Goldfarb groaned, too—Basil Roundbush would have been disappointed if he hadn't—but he was also smiling. He'd seen this kind of chaffing at the radar station in Dover at the height of the Battle of Britain, and then again with the Lancaster crew testing airborne radar. It made men work better together, lessened their friction against one another. Some, like Group Captain Hipple, didn't need such social lubrication, but most mere mortals did.

They labored on until well past eight, trying to make up for time lost to the Lizard raid. They didn't catch up; Goldfarb spent most of his time looking for the papers he needed, and didn't always find them. The other four men, being more concerned with engines than radar, had grabbed those file folders first and his as an afterthought.

When Fred Hipple yawned and stood up from his stool, that

was a signal for everyone else to knock off, too: if he'd had enough, they didn't need to be ashamed to show they were worn. Goldfarb felt it in the shoulders and in the small of the back.

Hipple, a man of uncommon rectitude, headed for the refectory and then, presumably, for his cot—such, at least, was his usual habit. Goldfarb, though, had had a bellyful—in both the literal and figurative senses of the word—of the food the RAF kitchens turned out. After a while, stewed meat (when there was meat), soya links, stewed potatoes and cabbage, dumplings the size, shape, and consistency of billiard balls, and stewed prunes got to be too much.

He climbed onto his bicycle and headed for nearby Bruntingthorpe. Nor was he surprised to hear the rattling squeak of another bicycle's imperfectly oiled chain right behind him. Looking back over his shoulder in the darkness would have been an invitation to go straight over the handlebars. Instead, he called, "A Friend In Need—"

Basil Roundbush's chuckle came ahead to him. The flight officer finished the catch phrase: "—is a friend indeed."

A few minutes later, they both pulled up in front of A Friend In Need, the only pub Bruntingthorpe boasted. Without the RAF aerodrome just outside the hamlet, the place would not have had enough customers to stay open. As things were, it flourished. So did the fish-and-chips shop next door, though Goldfarb fought shy of that one because of the big tins of lard that showed up in its refuse bins. He was not nearly so rigid in his Orthodox faith as his parents, but eating chips fried in pig's fat was more than he could stomach.

"Two pints of bitter," Roundbush called. The publican poured them from his pitcher, passed them across the bar in exchange for silver. Roundbush raised his pint pot in salute to Goldfarb. "Confusion to the Lizards!"

They both drained their pints. The beer was not what it had been before the war. After the first or second pint, though, you stopped noticing. Following immemorial custom, Goldfarb bought the second round. "No confusion to us tomorrow, when they fetch the damaged goods," he declared. He said no more, not off the base.

"I'll drink to that, by God!" Roundbush said, and proved it. "The more we can learn about how they do what they do, the better our chance of keeping them from doing it."

The innkeeper leaned across the waxed oak surface of the bar. "I've still got half a roasted capon in the back room, lads," he said in a confidential voice. "Four and six, if you're interested—"

The slap of coins on the bar gave his sentence its end punctuation. "Light meat or dark?" Goldfarb asked when the bird appeared: as an officer, Roundbush had the right to choose.

"I fancy breasts more than legs," Roundbush answered, and added, after the perfect tiny pause, "and I like light meat better, too."

So did Goldfarb, but he ate the dark without complaint; it was vastly better than anything they made back at the aerodrome. The two RAF men each bought another round. Then, regretfully, they rode back to the base. Keeping bicycles on a steady course seemed complicated after four pints of even bad bitter.

The headache Goldfarb had the next morning told him he probably shouldn't have drunk the last one. Basil Roundbush looked disgustingly fresh. Goldfarb did his best to keep Group Captain Hipple from noticing he was hung over. He thought he succeeded, and got help because no one was working at his best, not only because of yesterday's raid, but also because everyone was looking forward to examining the wreckage from the Lizard plane.

Said wreckage did not arrive until nearly eleven, which put everyone, even the patient, mild-mannered Hipple, on edge. When it finally happened, though, the arrival was a portent: the fragments came to Bruntingthorpe aboard a pair of 6×6 GMC trucks.

The big rumbling American machines seemed to Goldfarb almost as great a prodigy as the cargo they bore. Next to them, the British lorries he was used to were awkward makeshifts, timid and underpowered. If the Lizards hadn't come, thousands of these broad-shouldered bruisers would have been hauling men and equipment all around England. As it was, only the earliest handful of arrivals were working here. The Yanks had more urgent use for the rest on their own side of the Atlantic.

That a couple of the precious American lorries had been entrusted with their present cargo spoke volumes about how important the RAF reckoned it. The lorries also boasted winches, which helped get the pieces out of the cargo compartments: ra-

dar and engine, especially the latter, were too heavy for convenient manhandling.

"We have to get these under cover as quickly as we can," Hipple said. "We don't want Lizard reconnaissance aircraft noting that we're trying to learn their secrets."

Even as he spoke, men from the groundcrew were draping camouflage netting over the wreckage. Before long, it looked pretty much like meadow from above. Goldfarb said, "They'll expect us to rebuild the Nissen hut they wrecked yesterday. When we do, it might be worthwhile to move this gear into it. That way, the Lizards won't be able to tell we have it."

"Very good suggestion, David," Hipple said, beaming. "I expect we'll do that as soon as we have the opportunity. Yet no matter how quickly they can run up a Nissen hut, we shan't wait for them. I want to attack these beasts as rapidly as possible, as I'm certain you do also."

There Hipple was right. Even though it was gloomy under the netting, Goldfarb got to work right away. The Lizard plane must have come down on its belly rather than nose first, a happy accident that had indeed kept it from being too badly smashed up. Part of the streamlined nose assembly remained in place in front of the parabolic radar antenna.

The antenna itself had escaped crumpling. It was smaller than Goldfarb had expected; for that matter, the whole unit was smaller than he'd expected. The Lizards had mounted it in front of their pilot—that was obvious. It was good design; Goldfarb wished the set that would go into the Meteor was small enough to imitate it.

Some of the sheet metal around the radar had torn. Peering through a gap, Goldfarb saw bundles of wires with bright-colored insulation. *Coded somehow,* he thought, wishing he knew which color meant what.

Even wrecked, the finish of the Lizard aircraft was very fine. Welds were smooth and flat, rivets countersunk so their heads lay flush with the metal skin. Even tugging with pliers at a tear in the metal to widen it so he could reach inside felt like tampering to Goldfarb.

Behind the radar antenna lay the magnetron; he recognized the curved shape of its housing. It was the last piece of apparatus he did recognize. Things that looked like screws held it to the rest of the unit. They did not, however, have conventional heads. Instead of openings for a flat-blade or Phillips-

head screwdriver, they had square cavities sunk into the centers of the heads.

Goldfarb rummaged through the tools on his belt till he found a flat-blade screwdriver whose blade fit across the diagonal of one of the Lizard screws. He turned it. Nothing happened. He gave the screw a hard look that quickly turned speculative and tried to turn it the other way. It began to come out.

Bad language was coming from the RAF men working on the engine. Suspecting he knew why, Goldfarb called, "The screws are backwards to ours: anticlockwise tightens, clockwise loosens."

He heard a couple of seconds' silence, then a grunt of satisfaction. Fred Hipple said, "Thank you, David. Lord only knows how long that would have taken to occur to us. One can sometimes become too wedded to the obvious."

Goldfarb fairly burst with pride. This from the man who had designed and patented the jet engine almost ten years before the war began! *Praise indeed*, he thought.

The bad language from the engine crew faded away as the officers got the casing off and started looking at the guts. "They use fir-tree roots to secure the turbine blades, sir," Julian Peary said indignantly. "Pity you had so much trouble convincing the powers that be it was a good notion."

"The Lizards have had this technology in place rather longer than we have, Wing Commander," Hipple answered. Despite long thwarting by RAF indifference and even hostility, he showed no bitterness.

"And look," Basil Roundbush said. "The blades have a slight twist to them. How long ago did you suggest that, sir? Two years? Three?"

Whatever Hipple's answer was, Goldfarb didn't hear it. He'd loosened enough screws himself to get off a panel of the radar's case. He had a good notion of what he'd find inside: since physical laws had to be the same all through the universe, he figured the Lizard set would closely resemble the ones he was used to. Oh, it would be smaller and lighter and better engineered than RAF models, but still essentially similar. Valves, after all, remained valves—unless you went to the United States, where they turned into tubes.

But the second he got a good look at the radar, the flush of pride he'd felt a little while before evaporated. Hipple and his

team could make some sense of what they saw inside the jet engine. The parts of the radar set remained a complete mystery to Goldfarb. The only thing of which he could be certain was that it had no valves ... or even tubes.

What took their place was sheets of grayish-brown material with silvery lines etched onto them. Some had little lumpy things of various shapes and colors affixed. Form said nothing about function, at least not to Goldfarb.

Basil Roundbush chose that moment to inquire, "How goes it with you, David?"

"I'm afraid it doesn't go at all." Goldfarb knew he sounded like a bad translation from the French. He didn't care: he'd found the simplest way to tell the truth.

"Pity," Roundbush said. "Well, I don't suppose we need every single answer this morning. One or two of them may possibly wait until tonight."

Goldfarb's answering laugh had a distinctly hollow ring.

Mutt Daniels drew the cloth patch through the barrel of his tommy gun. "You got to keep your weapon clean," he told the men in his squad. Telling—even ordering—accomplished only so much. Leading by example worked better.

Kevin Donlan obediently started in on his rifle. He obeyed Daniels like a father (or maybe, Mutt thought uneasily, like a grandfather—he was old enough to be the kid's grandfather, if he and his hypothetical child had started early). Other than that, though, he had a soldier's ingrained suspicion of anyone of higher rank than his own—which in his case meant just about the whole Army. He asked, "Sarge, what are we doing in Mount Pulaski anyways?"

Daniels paused in his cleaning to consider that. He wished he had a chaw; working the wad of tobacco in his mouth always helped him think. He hadn't come across one in a long time, though. He said, "Near as I can see, somebody looked at a map, saw 'Mount,' and figured this here was high ground. Hell of a mountain, ain't it?"

The men laughed. Mount Pulaski was on higher ground than the surrounding hamlets—by twenty, thirty, sometimes even fifty or sixty feet. It hardly seemed worth having spent lives to take the place, even if it did also sit at the junction of State Roads 121 and 54.

Bela Szabo said, "They finally figured out we weren't about

to take Decatur, so they figured they'd move us someplace new and see how many casualties we can take here." Szabo wasn't much older than Kevin Donlan, but had a couple of extra lifetimes' worth of cynicism under his belt.

But Mutt shook his head. "Naah, that ain't it, Dracula. What they're really after is seein' how many fancy old-time buildings they can blow to hell. They're gettin' right good at it, too."

The Mount Pulaski Courthouse was his case in point here. Almost a hundred years old, it was a two-story Greek Revival building of red-brown brick with a plain classical pediment. Or rather, it had been: after a couple of artillery hits, more of it was rubble than building. But enough still stood to show it would have been worth saving.

"You boys hungry?" a woman called. "I've got some ducks and some fried trout here if you are." She held up a big wicker picnic basket.

"Yes, ma'am," Mutt said enthusiastically. "Beats the sh— pants off what the Army feeds us—when they feed us." Quartermaster arrangements had gone to hell, what with the Lizards hitting supply lines whenever they could. If it hadn't been for the kindness of locals, Daniels and his men would have gone hungry a lot more than they did.

The woman came up to the front porch of the wrecked house where the squad was sitting. None of the young soldiers paid her any particular mind—she was a year or two past forty, with a tired face and mouse-brown hair streaked with gray. Their attention was on the basket she carried.

Springfields and M-1s still came with bayonets, even if nobody was likely to use them in combat any more. They turned out to make first-rate duck carvers, though. The roast ducks were greasy and gamy. Mutt still ate duck in preference to trout; the only fish he cared for was catfish.

"Mighty fine, ma'am," Kevin Donlan said, licking his fingers. "Where'd you come by all this good stuff, anyhow?"

"Up in Lincoln Lakes, six, seven miles north of here," she answered. "They aren't real lakes, just gravel pits filled with water, but they're stocked with fish and I can use a shotgun."

"Found that out," Mutt said. His teeth had stumbled on birdshot a couple of times. You could break one that way if you weren't lucky. He tossed aside a leg bone gnawed bare, then went on, "Mighty kind of you to go to so much trouble

for us, uh"—his eyes flicked to her left hand to see if she wore a ring—"Miss . . ."

"I'm Lucille Potter," she answered. "What's your name?"

"Pleased to meet you, Miss Lucille," he said. "I'm M—uh, Pete Daniels." He thought of himself as Mutt these days; he had for years. But that didn't seem the right way to introduce yourself to a woman you'd just met. The kids might ignore her—they were younger than most of the players he'd managed—but she didn't look half bad to him.

Only trouble was, the kids wouldn't let him get away with being Pete. Some of them started rolling in the dirt; even Kevin Donlan snorted. Lucille looked from one of them to the next. "What's so funny?" she asked.

Resignedly, Daniels said, "My name's Pete, but they usually call me Mutt."

"Is that what you'd rather be called?" she asked. When he nodded, she went on, "Why didn't you say so, then? There's nothing wrong with that."

Her brisk tones made a couple of the soldiers look abashed, but more of them didn't care what she said, even if she had brought them food. The matter-of-fact common sense in her words made him eye her speculatively. "You a schoolteacher, ma'am?"

She smiled. That made some of her tiredness fall away and let him see what she'd looked like when she was twenty-five or so. No, she wasn't bad at all. She said, "Pretty good guess, but you didn't notice my shoes."

They were white—an awfully dirty white now—with thick, rubbery soles. "You're a nurse," Mutt said.

Lucille Potter nodded. "I sure am. I've been doing a doctor's work since the Lizards came, though. Mount Pulaski only had Doc Hanrahan, and somebody's bomb—God knows whose—landed in his front yard just when he was coming out the door. He never knew what hit him, anyhow."

"Lord, I wish we could take you with us, ma'am," Kevin Donlan said. "The medics we got, they ain't everything they oughta be. 'Course, what is these days?"

"That purely is a fact," Daniels agreed. The Army tried hard, the same as it did with supplies. As with supplies, war's disruption was too great to permit hurt men proper care. He suspected his grandfathers in the War Between the States hadn't risked much worse medical treatment. Doctors knew a

lot more nowadays, but so what? All the knowledge in the world didn't matter if you couldn't get your hands on the medicines and instruments you needed to use it.

Lucille Potter said, "Why the hell not?"

Mutt gaped at her, startled twice—first at the casual way she swore and then by how she fell in with Donlan's suggestion, which had been more wistful than serious. Mutt said, "But, ma'am, you're a woman." He thought that explained everything.

"So?" Lucille said—evidently she didn't. "Would you care if I was digging a bullet out of your leg? Or do you think your boys here are going to gang-rape me the second your back is turned?"

"But—But—" Mutt spluttered like a man who can't swim floundering out of a creek. He felt his face turn red. His men were staring at Lucille Potter with their mouths open. *Rape* wasn't a word you said around a woman, let alone a word you expected to hear from one.

She went on, "Maybe I should bring my shotgun along. You think that might make 'em behave?"

"Y'all mean it," he said, surprised again, this time into a Southernism he seldom used.

"Of course I mean it," she said. "Get to know me for a while and you'll find out I hardly ever say things I don't mean. People in town were stupid, too, till they started coming sick and breaking bones and having babies. Then they found out what I could do—because they had to. You can't afford to wait around like that, can you? If you give me five minutes, I'll go home and get my black bag. Or"—she shrugged—"you can do without."

Mutt thought hard. Whatever the trouble she brought with her, could it be worse than the hurts they'd take that would go bad without a doctor? He didn't think so. But he also wanted to find out why she was volunteering, so he asked, "How come you want to leave this town, if you're the only thing even halfway close to a doctor here?"

"When the Lizards held this part of the state, I had to stay here—I was the only one around who could do anything," Lucille answered. "But now that proper human beings are back in charge, it'll be easier to bring a real doctor around. And an awful lot of what I've been doing lately is patching up hurt

soldiers. I hate to put it so plain, Mutt, but I think you people are liable to need me worse than Mount Pulaski does."

"That makes sense," Mutt said. Glancing at Lucille Potter, he got the feeling she would make sense a lot of the time. He rubbed his chin. "Tell you what, Miss Lucille. Let's take you over to Captain Maczek, see what he thinks about the idea. If it's all right with him, I like it." He looked over to the men in his squad. They were all nodding. Mutt suddenly grinned. "Here—bring some of this duck along with you. That'll help put him in the right kind of mood."

Maczek was around the corner, eating with another squad from the company. He was maybe half Mutt's age, but not altogether lacking in sense. Mutt grinned again to see him digging a spoon in what looked like a can of baked beans. He held up the duck leg. "Got something better'n that for you, sir—an' here's the lady who shot the bird."

The captain stared in delight at the duck, then turned to Lucille. "Ma'am, my hat's off to you." He took himself literally, doffing his net-covered helmet. The sweaty blond hair underneath it stuck up in all directions.

"Pleased to meet you, Captain." Lucille Potter gave her name, shook Maczek's hand with a decisive pump. Then the captain took the drumstick and thigh from Daniels and bit into it. Grease ran down his chin. His expression turned ecstatic.

"You know what else, sir?" Mutt said. He told Maczek what else.

"Is that a fact?" Maczek said.

"Yes, sir, it is," Lucille said. "I'm not a proper doctor, and I don't claim to be one. But I've learned a hell of a lot these past few months, and I'm a lot better than nothing."

Maczek absently took another bite of duck. As Mutt had, he eyed the men around him. They'd all been listening with eager curiosity. You couldn't run an army by asking what everybody thought all the time, but you didn't ignore what people thought, either, not if you were smart. Maczek wasn't stupid, anyhow. He said, "I'll clear it with the colonel later, but I don't think he'll say no. It's irregular as all get out, but this whole stinking war is irregular."

"I'll go get my tools," Lucille said, and strode off to do just that.

Captain Maczek watched her no-nonsense walk for a few seconds before he turned back to Daniels. "You know, Ser-

geant, if you'd come along to me with some little chippy you'd found, I'd have been very angry at you. But this one—I think she may do. If I've ever seen a female who can take care of herself, she's it."

"Reckon you're right, sir." Mutt pointed to the bones Maczek was still holding. "And we already know she can handle a shotgun."

"That's true, by God." Maczek laughed. "Besides, she's old enough to be a mother for most of the men. You have anybody in your squad with an Oedipus complex, you think?"

"With a what, sir?" Mutt frowned—just because Maczek had been to college, he didn't need to show off. And besides— "She's not bad-lookin', I don't think."

Captain Maczek opened his mouth to say something. By the glint in his eye, it would have been lewd or rude or both. But he didn't say it—he was too smart an officer to make fun of his noncoms, especially in front of a bunch of listening soldiers. What he did finally say was, "However you like, Mutt. But remember, she's going to be medic for the whole company, maybe the battalion, not just your squad."

"Yeah, sure, Captain, I know that," Daniels said. To himself, he added, *I saw her first, though.*

The U-2 droned through the night just above the treetops. The cold slipstream buffeted Ludmila Gorbunova's face. It was not the only reason her teeth chattered. She was deep inside Lizard-held territory. If anything went wrong, she wouldn't make it back to her dirt airstrip and the cramped little space she shared with the other female pilots.

She forced such thoughts from her mind, concentrated on the mission at hand. That was the only way to get through them, she'd learned: keep your mind firmly fixed on what you had to do *now*, then what you had to do *next*, and so on. Look ahead or off to one side and you were in trouble. That had been true against the Nazis; it was doubly so against the Lizards.

"What I have to do *now*," she said aloud, letting the slipstream fling her words away behind her, "is find the partisan battalion."

Easier said than done, in what looked like endless stretches of forest and plain. She thought her navigation was good, but when you were flying by compass and wristwatch, little errors

always crept in. She thought about gaining altitude so she could see farther, but rejected the idea. It would also have made it easier for the Lizards to spot her.

She worked the pedals and the stick, swung the U-2 into a wide, slow spiral to search the terrain below. The little wood-and-fabric biplane responded beautifully to the controls, probably better than it had when it was new. Georg Schultz, her German mechanic, might be—was—a Nazi, but he was also a genius at keeping the aircraft not only flying but flying well in spite of an almost complete lack of spare parts.

There down below—was that a light? It was, and a moment later she spotted the other two with it. She'd been told to look for an equilateral triangle of lights. Here they were. She buzzed slowly overhead, hoping the partisans had all their instructions straight.

They did. As soon as they heard the sewing-machine whine of the U-2's little Shvetsov engine, they set out two more lights, little ones, that were supposed to mark out the beginning of a stretch of ground where she could land safely. Her mouth went dry, as it did every time she had to land at night on a strip or a field she'd never seen before. The *Kukuruznik* was a rugged machine, but a mistake could still kill her.

She lined up on the landing lights, lost altitude, killed her airspeed—not that the U-2 had much to lose. At the last moment, the lights disappeared: they must have had collars, to keep them from being seen at ground level. Losing them made her heart thump fearfully, but then she was down.

The biplane bounced along over the field. Ludmila hit the brakes hard; every meter she traveled was one more meter in which a wheel might go into a hole and flip the U-2 over. Fortunately, it did not need many meters in which to stop.

Men—dark shapes in darker night—came running up and got to the *Kukuruznik* while the prop was still spinning. "You have presents for us, Comrade?" one of them called.

"I have presents," Ludmila agreed. She heard the mutters when they heard her voice—variations on the theme of *a woman!* She was used to that; she'd been dealing with it ever since she joined the Red Air Force. But there were fewer such murmurs among the partisans than there had been at some air force bases to which she'd flown. A fair number of partisans were women, and most male partisans understood that women could fight.

She climbed down from the front cockpit, set a foot in the metal stirrup on the left side of the fuselage that gave access to the rear one. She didn't go up into it, but started handing out boxes. "Here we are, Comrades: presents," she said. "Rifles— with ammunition . . . submachine guns—with ammunition."

"The weapons are good, but we already have most of the weapons we need," a man said. "But next time you come, Comrade Pilot, bring us lots more bullets. It's the ammunition we're short of—we use a lot of it." Wolflike chuckles rose from the partisans' throats.

From back in the crowd of fighters, someone called, "Comrade, did you fetch us any 7.92mm ammunition? We have a lot of German rifles and machine guns we could use more if we had bullets for them."

Ludmila hauled out a canvas bag that clinked metallically. The partisans' murmurs turned appreciative; a couple of them clapped gloved hands together in delight. Ludmila said, "I am told to tell you: you cannot expect this bounty on every resupply run. We have to scavenge German cartridges—we don't manufacture them. The way things are, we have a hard enough time manufacturing our own calibers."

"Too bad," said the man who had asked about German ammunition. "The Mauser is not a great rifle—accurate, *da*, but a slow, clumsy bolt—but the Nazis make a very fine machine gun."

"Maybe we can work a trade," the fellow who'd first greeted Ludmila said. "There's a mostly German band of fighters back around Konotop, and they use our weapons just as we use theirs. They might swap some of their caliber for some of ours."

Those couple of sentences spoke volumes about the anguish of the Soviet Union. Konotop, a hundred fifty kilometers east of Ludmila's native Kiev, had been in German hands. Now it belonged to the Lizards. When would the Soviet workers and people be able to reclaim the *rodina*, the motherland?

Ludmila started handing out cardboard tubes and pots of paste. "Here you are, Comrades. Because wars are not won only by bullets, I bring also the latest posters by Efrimov and the Kukryniksi group."

That drew pleased exclamations from the partisans. Newspapers hereabouts had been forced to echo the Nazi line; now they slavishly reproduced Lizard propaganda. Radios, especial-

ly those able to pick up signals from land still under human control, were few and far between. Posters gave one way of striking back. They could go up on a wall in seconds and show hundreds the truth for days.

"What do the men of Kukryniksi do this time?" a woman asked.

"It's one of their better ones, I think," Ludmila said, which was no small praise, for the team of Kupryanov, Krylov, and Sokolov probably turned out the best Soviet poster art. She went on, "This one shows a Lizard in Pharaoh's headdress lashing Soviet peasants; the caption reads, 'A Return to Slavery.' "

"That is a good one," the partisan leader agreed. "It will make the people think, and make them less likely to collaborate with the Lizards. We will post it widely, in towns and villages and at collective farms."

"How much collaboration goes on with the Lizards?" Ludmila asked. "This is something of which our authorities need to be aware."

"It's not as bad as what went on with the Germans at first," the man answered. Ludmila nodded; little could be as bad as that. Large segments of the Soviet populace had welcomed the Nazis as liberators in the early days of their invasion. If they'd played on that instead of working to prove they could be even more savage and brutal than the NKVD, they might have toppled the Soviet regime. The partisan went on, "We do have collaboration, though. Many people passively accept whatever power they find above them, while others welcome the rather indifferent rule of the Lizards as superior to the hostility they had known before."

"Hostility from the fascists, you mean," Ludmila said.

"Of course, Comrade Pilot." The partisan leader's voice was innocence personified. No one could safely speak of hostility to the people from the Soviet government, though that shadow lay across the whole of the *rodina.*

"You called the Lizards' rule indifferent," Ludmila said. "Explain that more fully, please. Intelligence is worth more than many rifles."

"They take crops and livestock for themselves; in the towns, they try to set up manufacturers that might be useful to them: forges and chemical works and such. But they care nothing for what we do as people," the partisan said. "They do not forbid

worship, but they do not promote it, either. They do not even forbid the Party, which would be only elementary prudence on their part. It is as if we are beneath their notice unless we take up arms against them. Then they hit hard."

That much Ludmila already knew. The other perplexed her. By the sound of his voice, it perplexed the partisan, too. They were used to a regime that minutely regulated every aspect of its citizens' lives—and disposed of them without mercy when they didn't meet its expectations . . . or sometimes even if they did. Simple indifference seemed very alien by contrast. She hoped her superiors would have a better idea of what to make of it.

"Does anyone have letters for me?" she asked. "I'll be glad to take them along, though with the post as disrupted as it is, they may be months on the way."

The partisans queued up to hand her their notes to the outside world. None of them had envelopes; those had been in short supply before the Lizards came. The papers were folded into triangles to show they came from soldiers: the Soviet mail system carried such letters, albeit slowly, without a postage fee.

When she had the last letter, Ludmila climbed back into the front cockpit and said, "Would you please swing my aircraft around nose for tail? If I landed safely on this strip, I'd like to take off down the same ground."

The little U-2 was easy to haul around by hand; it weighed less than a thousand kilos. Ludmila had to explain to someone how to turn the prop. As always on these missions, she had an anxious moment wondering whether the engine would start—no mechanical starter here if it didn't. But it was still warm from the flight in, and kicked over almost at once.

She released the brake, pushed the stick forward. The *Kukuruznik* jounced over the rough field. A few partisans ran alongside, waving. They soon fell behind. The takeoff run was longer than the one she'd needed to land. That meant she was going over some new terrain (to say nothing of the holes she might have missed while she was landing). But after a last couple of jolts, the biplane made an ungainly leap into the air.

She swung the U-2 north and west, back toward the base from which she'd set out. Finding it again would take the same kind of search she'd needed to locate the partisans' makeshift airstrip. A base that advertised its presence soon drew the

attention of the Lizards. Once that happened, the base was unlikely to remain present for long.

Not that she had any guarantees of getting back safely, anyhow. U-2s were detected and destroyed less often than any
other Soviet aircraft; Ludmila's best guess was that they were
too small and light and flimsy to be noticed most of the time.
But *Kukuruzniks* did not always come home, either.

Off in the distance, she saw flashes, like heat lightning on a
summer evening: someone's artillery, probably the Lizards'.
She glanced at her watch and compass, made the best position
estimate she could. When she landed, she'd report it to Colonel
Karpov. Maybe one day before too long, the partisans would
fire a rack of *Katyusha* rockets that way.

Stars twinkled through gaps in the clouds. A couple of
times, she spotted brief twinkles of light on the ground, too:
muzzle flashes. They made the stars seem less safe and
friendly.

Watching the compass and her watch, she flew on toward
the base. When she thought she was overhead, she looked
down and saw—nothing. That failed to surprise her; finding it
on the first try by dead reckoning was no likelier than plunging
your hand into a haystack and bringing out a needle between
thumb and forefinger.

She began another search spiral. Now she watched her fuel
gauge, too. If she was lost and had to set down in a field, she
wanted to do it while she still had power, not dead stick.

Just when she was beginning to worry she might have to do
exactly that, she spied the lights she'd been looking for. She
gratefully made for them; knowing where you were made you
feel ever so much more in control of things.

The airstrip had supposedly been leveled. As a matter of
fact, it was no smoother than the one the partisans had marked
off for her. Ludmila's teeth clicked together at every jolt until
the U-2 stopped. She told herself the roughness made the runway harder to spot. Was that consolation enough for the
bruises she'd have wherever her safety harness touched her?
Maybe.

She unbuckled the harness, got out of the plane while the
prop was still spinning. The groundcrew ran up, hauled the
Kukuruznik away to its between-missions home in a camouflaged revetment. "Where's Colonel Karpov?" she asked.

"He went to bed an hour ago," somebody answered. "It is

close to three in the morning. You have anything so important it won't keep till dawn?"

"I suppose not," she said. The Lizard artillery wasn't something he had to know about right now. She followed the *Kukuruznik* toward its shelter.

Ludmila would have bet as much money as she had that she'd find Georg Schultz waiting at the revetment. Sure enough, there he was. *"Alles khorosho?"* he asked in his usual mixture of German and Russian.

"Gut, da," she answered, mixing the languages the same way.

He scrambled up into the cockpit. No lantern was lighted, not even beneath the camouflage netting; the Lizards had gadgets that could pick up the tiniest gleam. That didn't stop Schultz from starting to work on Ludmila's biplane. He tested the pedals and other controls, leaned out to say, "Left aileron cable not good—feels a little loose. Come light, I fix."

"Thank you, Georgi Mikhailovich," Ludmila answered. She hadn't noticed anything wrong with the cable, but if Schultz said it needed tightening, she was willing to believe him. His understanding for machinery was, to her way of thinking, all but uncanny. She flew the aircraft; Georg Schultz projected himself into it as if he were part plane himself.

"Nothing else bad," he said, "but here—you leave on floor." He handed her a folded triangle of paper.

"Thank you," she said again. "Our post is unreliable enough without me losing a letter before it ever gets into the mail." She wasn't sure how much of that he understood, but found herself yawning enormously. She was too tired to try to dredge up German to make things clear for him. If Colonel Karpov was asleep, she saw no reason she shouldn't grab a couple of hours for herself, too.

She shrugged out of her parachute harness—not that she'd have much chance to use a chute if she got hit while she was hedgehopping the way she usually did—and stowed it in the cockpit, then started out of the revetment toward her sleeping quarters. As she passed Georg Schultz, he patted her on the backside.

Ludmila took a skittering half step, half jump. She whirled around in fury. This wasn't the first time such things had happened to her since she'd joined the Red Air Force, but somehow she'd thought Schultz too *kulturny* to try them.

"Don't you ever do that again!" she blazed in Russian, then switched to German to drive it home: *"Nie wieder, verstehst du?"* It was the *du* of insult, not intimacy. She added, "What would your Colonel Jäger think if he found out what you just did?"

Schultz had been the gunner in the tank Jäger commanded; he thought highly of his former leader. Ludmila hoped reminding him of that would bring him to his senses. But he just laughed quietly and said, "He would think I wasn't doing anything he hadn't done himself."

A short, deadly silence followed. Ludmila broke it in tones of ice: "That is none of your business. If it will not make you keep your hands where they belong, maybe this will: remember, you are the only Nazi on a base full of Red Air Force men. They leave you alone because you work well. But they do not love you. *Verstehst du das?*"

He drew himself to stiff attention, did his best to click his heels in soft felt *valenki*, shot out his arm in a defiant Hitlerite salute. "I remember very well, and I do understand." He stomped away.

Ludmila wanted to kick him. Why couldn't he have just said he was sorry and gone on about his business instead of getting angry, as if she had somehow wronged him instead of the other way round? Now what was she supposed to do? If he was that angry with her, did she still want him working on her aircraft? But if he didn't, who would?

The answer to that formed in her mind with the question: some quarter-trained Russian peasant who hardly knew the difference between a screwdriver and a pair of pliers. She could do some work herself, but not all, and she knew she didn't have Schultz's artist's touch with an engine. Her show of temper was liable to end up getting her killed.

But what should she have done? Let him treat her like a whore? She shook her head violently. Maybe she should have responded with a joke instead of a blast, though.

Too late to worry about it now. Slowly, tiredly, she walked over to the building that sheltered the women pilots. It wasn't much of a shelter: the walls were dirt-filled sandbags and bales of hay like the revetments that protected the aircraft, the roof camouflage netting over straw over unchinked boards. It leaked and let in the cold. But no one here, Colonel Karpov included, had quarters any better.

The door to the improvised barracks had no hinges, and had to be pushed aside. Inside was a blackout curtain. Ludmila pulled the door closed before she went through the curtain. *Let no light leak out* was a rule she took as much for granted as *take off into the wind.*

The barracks held little light to leak, anyhow: a couple of candles and an oil lamp were enough to keep you from stumbling over blanket-wrapped women snoring on straw pallets, but that was about all. Yawning, Ludmila stumbled toward her own place.

A white rectangle lay on top of her folded blankets. It hadn't been there when she went out on her mission a few hours earlier. "A letter!" she said happily—and from a civilian, too, or it would have been folded differently. Hope flared in her, painfully intense: she hadn't heard from anyone in her family since the Lizards came. Maybe they were safe after all, when she'd almost given up on them.

In the dim light, she had to pick up the letter to realize it was in an envelope. She turned it over, bent her head close to it to look at the address. She needed a moment to notice part of it was written in the Roman alphabet, and the Cyrillic characters were printed with a slow precision that said the person who used them wasn't used to them.

Then her eyes fixed on the stamp. Had anyone told her a year before that she'd have been glad to see a picture of Adolf Hitler, she'd either have thought him mad or been mortally insulted—probably both. "Heinrich," she breathed, doing her best to pronounce the H at the beginning of the name, which was not a sound the Russian language had.

She tore the envelope open, eased out the letter. To her relief, she saw Jäger had considerately printed: she found German handwriting next to indecipherable. She read, *My dear Ludmila, I hope this finds you safe and well. In fact, I have to hope it finds you at all.*

In her mind's eye she could see one corner of his mouth quirking upwards as he set his small joke down on paper. The perfection and intensity of the image told her how much she missed him.

I was on duty in a town I cannot name lest the censor reach for his razor, he went on. *I will be leaving in the next day or two, though, and going back to a panzer outfit I also cannot name. I wish I were returning to you instead, or you to me. So*

much easier to travel long distance by plane than by horse or even by panzer.

She remembered some of his stories of crossing Lizard-occupied Poland on horseback. That made anything she'd done in her U-2 seem tame by comparison. In the letter, he went on, *I wish we could be together more. Even at best, we have so little time on this world, and with the war we do not have the best. Yet without it, we would not have met, you and I, so I suppose I cannot say it is altogether a bad thing.*

"No, it isn't," she whispered. Having an affair with an enemy might be stupid (a feeling Jäger no doubt shared with her), but she couldn't make herself believe it was a bad thing.

The letter continued, *I thank you for looking out for my comrade Georg Schultz; your country is so vast that only great luck could have brought him to your base, as you said when we were last together. Greet him for me; I hope he is well.*

Ludmila didn't know whether to laugh or cry when she read that. Schultz was well, all right, and she had looked out for him, and all he wanted was to get her pants down. She wondered whether he had enough sense of shame to be embarrassed if she showed him Jäger's letter.

She didn't have to decide now. She wanted to finish the letter and get a little sleep. Everything else could wait. She read, *If fate is kind, we will meet again soon in a world at peace. If it is less kind, we will meet again though the war goes on. It would have to be very cruel to keep us from meeting again at all. With love and the hope you stay safe—Heinrich.*

Ludmila folded the letter small and stuck it in a pocket of her flying suit. Then she took off her leather helmet and goggles, but none of the rest of the outfit, not even her *valenki.* The inside of the barracks was cold. She lay down on the straw, pulled the blanket up over her head, and fell asleep almost at once.

When she woke the next morning, she found one hand in the pocket where she'd put the letter. That made her smile, and resolved her to answer it right away. Then she had to figure out whether to show it to Schultz. She decided she would, but not this minute. Time enough when they were calmer, not actively angry at each other. Meanwhile, she still had to make her report to Colonel Karpov.

* * *

The Nipponese guard handed Teerts his bowl of food. He bowed polite thanks, turned one eye toward it to see what he'd got. He almost hissed with pleasure: along with the rice, the bowl was full of chunks of some kind of flesh. The Big Uglies had been feeding him better lately; by the time he finished the meal, he was almost content.

He wondered what they were up to. Captivity had taught him they were not in the habit of doing gratuitous favors for anybody. Up till now, captivity had taught him they weren't in the habit of doing any favors whatever. The change made him suspicious.

Sure enough, Major Okamoto and the usual stone-faced, rifle-toting guard marched up to the cell door not long after the bowl was taken away. As the door swung open, Okamoto spoke in the language of the Race: "You will come with me."

"It shall be done, superior sir," Teerts agreed. He left the cell with no small relief. His step seemed lighter than it had in a long time; going upstairs to the interrogation chamber of the Nagasaki prison felt like good exercise, not a wearing burden. *Amazing what something close to proper food can do,* he thought.

Again, the Nipponese inside the chamber wore the white robes of scientists. The Big Ugly in the center chair spoke. Major Okamoto translated: "Dr. Nishina wishes to discuss today the nature of the bombs with which the Race destroyed the cities of Berlin and Washington."

"Why not?" Teerts answered agreeably. "These bombs were made from uranium. In case you do not know what uranium is, it is the ninety-second element in the periodic table." He let his mouth fall slightly open in amusement. The Big Uglies were so barbarous, they would surely have not the slightest notion of what he was talking about.

After Okamoto relayed his answer to the Nipponese scientists, he and they talked back and forth for some time. Then he returned his attention to Teerts, saying, "I do not have the technical terms I need to ask these questions in proper detail. Give them to me as we speak, please, and do your best to understand even without them."

"It shall be done, superior sir," Teerts said, agreeable still.

"Good." Okamoto paused to think; his rubbery Big Ugly features made the process easy to watch. At length, he said, "Dr. Nishina wishes to know which process the Race uses to

separate the lighter, explosive kind of uranium from the more common heavy kind."

Teerts bit down on that as if it were an unsuspected bone in his meat. Not in his wildest nightmares—and he'd had some dreadful ones since his capture—had he imagined that the Big Uglies had the slightest clue about atomic energy, or even that they'd heard of uranium. If they did—He abruptly realized they might be dangerous to the Race, not just the horrid nuisances they'd already proved themselves.

To Major Okamoto, he said, "Tell the learned Dr. Nishina that I do not know which processes he means." He had to work not to turn an eye turret toward the instruments of torture in the interrogation chamber.

Okamoto fixed him with a stare he'd come to identify as hostile, but passed his words on to Nishina without comment. Nishina spoke volubly in reply, ticking off points on his fingers as if he were a male of the Race.

When he was through, Okamoto translated: "He says theory shows several ways which might accomplish this. Among them are successive barriers to a uranium-containing gas, heating the gas so that part of it which has the lighter kind of uranium rises more than the other, using a strong electromagnet"—a word that took a good deal of backing and filling to get across—"and using rapid spinning to concentrate the lighter kind of uranium. Which of these does the Race find most efficient?"

Teerts stared at him. He was even more appalled than he had been when his killercraft got shot down. That had affected only his own fate. Now he had to worry about whether the Race had any idea what the Tosevites were up to. They might be barbarians—by everything Teerts had seen, they *were* barbarians—but they were also alarmingly knowledgeable . . . which meant it behooved Teerts to be more than cautious in his answers. He'd have to do his best to avoid giving away any information at all.

He took so long figuring that out that Okamoto snapped, "Don't waste time dreaming up lies. Answer Dr. Nishina."

"I beg your pardon, superior sir," Teerts said, and added, "*Gomen nasai*—so sorry," from his limited stock of Nipponese. "Part of the problem is my not having enough words to give a proper answer, and another part is my own ignorance,

for which I again beg pardon. You must remember that I am—I was—a pilot. I had nothing at all to do with uranium."

"You certainly were glib enough talking about it a little while ago," Okamoto said. "You do not want to make me disbelieve you. Some of the tools back there are very sharp, others can be made hot, and still others can be hot and sharp at the same time. Do you want to learn which is which?"

"No, superior sir," Teerts gasped with utmost sincerity. "But I truly am ignorant of the knowledge you seek. I am only a pilot, not a nuclear physicist. What I know of flying, I have freely told you. I am not an expert in the matter of atomic weapons. What little I know of nuclear energy I learned in school as I was growing from hatchlinghood. It is no more and no less than any other ordinary male of the Race would know."

"This is difficult to believe," Okamoto said. "You spoke quite a lot about uranium just a little while ago."

That was before I realized how much you knew about it, Teerts thought. He wondered how he was going to escape with his integument intact. He knew he couldn't lie to the Nipponese; he didn't know how much they knew, and the only way to find out—getting caught—would involve the painful penetration of that integument.

He said, "I do know that atomic weapons do not necessarily use uranium alone. Some involve, I am not sure how, hydrogen as well—the very first element." *Let the Japanese chew on that paradox for a while,* he thought: how could a weapon involve the lightest and heaviest elements at the same time?

After Okamoto interpreted, the team of Big Ugly scientists chattered for a while among themselves. Then Nishina, who seemed to be their spokesman, put a question to Okamoto. The major translated for Teerts: "The uranium explosion, then, is hot enough to make hydrogen act as it does in the sun and convert large amounts of matter to energy?"

Horror filled Teerts. Every time he tried to escape from this hideous mess in which he found himself, he sank deeper instead. The Big Uglies knew about fusion. To Teerts, the product of a civilization that grew and changed at a glacial pace, knowing about something was essentially the same as being able to do it. And if the Tosevites could make fusion bombs . . .

Major Okamoto knocked him out of his appalled reverie by snapping, "Answer the learned Dr. Nishina!"

"I beg your pardon, superior sir," Teerts said. "Yes, everything the learned doctor says is true."

There. He'd done it. Any day now, he feared, the Nipponese would start using nuclear weapons against the Race on the mainland—which still struck Teerts as nothing more than a big island; he was used to water surrounded by land, not the other way around.

He heard Okamoto say *"Honto,"* confirming his answer to the Nipponese scientist's question. The cold of the interrogation room sank deeply into his spirit. The Nipponese hardly seemed to need him. By their questions, they had all the answers already, just waiting to be put into practice.

Then Nishina spoke again: "We return to the question of getting the lighter uranium, the kind which is explosive, out of the other, more common, type. This as yet we have not succeeded in doing; indeed, we have only just begun the attempt. That is why we will learn from you how the Race solves this problem."

Teerts needed a moment to understand that. The Race had been shocked when they reached Tosev 3 to discover how advanced the Big Uglies were. Before Teerts was captured, pilots had talked endlessly about that; they'd expected no opposition, and here the Tosevites were, shooting back—not very well, and from inadequate aircraft, but shooting back. How could they have learned to build combat aircraft in the eight hundred local years since the Race's probe examined them?

Now, for the first time, Teerts got a glimmering of the answer. The Race made change deliberately slow. When something new was discovered, extrapolationists performed elaborate calculations to learn in advance how it would affect a long-stable society, and how best to minimize those effects while gradually acquiring the benefits of the new device or principle.

With the Big Uglies, the tongue was on the other side of the mouth. When they found something new, they seized it with both hands and squeezed until they got all the juice out. They didn't care what the consequences five generations—or even five years—hence would be. They wanted advantages now, and worried about later trouble later, if at all.

Eventually, they'd probably end up destroying themselves with that attitude. At the moment, it made them far more deadly opponents than they would have been otherwise.

"Do not waste time thinking up lies. I warned you before," Major Okamoto said. "Tell Dr. Nishina the truth at once."

"By what I know, superior sir, the truth is that we do not use any of these methods," Teerts said. Okamoto drew back his hand for a slap. Afraid that would be the start of a torture session worse than any he'd yet known, Teerts went on rapidly, "Instead, we use the heavier form of uranium: isotope is the term we use."

"How do you do this?" Okamoto demanded after a brief colloquy with the Nipponese scientists. "Dr. Nishina says the heavier isotope cannot explode."

"There is another element, number ninety-four, which does not occur in nature but which we make from the heavier, nonexplosive—Dr. Nishina is right—isotope of uranium. This other element is explosive. We use it in our bombs."

"I think you are lying. You will pay the penalty for it, I promise you that," Okamoto said. Nevertheless, he translated Teerts' words for the Big Uglies in the white coats.

They started talking excitedly among themselves. Nishina, who looked to be the senior male, sorted things out and relayed an answer to Okamoto. He said to Teerts, "I may have been wrong. Dr. Nishina tells me the Americans have found this new element as well. They have given it the name plutonium. You will help us produce it."

"Past what I have already said, I know little," Teerts warned. Despair threatened to consume him. Every time he'd revealed something new to the Nipponese, it had been with the hope that the technical difficulties of the new revelation would force them off the road that led toward nuclear weapons. Instead, everything he told them seemed to push them further down that road.

He wished a plutonium bomb would fall on Nagasaki. But what were the odds of that?

☆ **VI** ☆

WELCOME TO CHUGWATER, POPULATION 286, the sign said. Colonel Leslie Groves shook his head as he read it. "Chugwater?" he echoed. "Wonder why they call it that."

Captain Rance Auerbach read the other half of the sign. " 'Population 286,' " he said. "Sounds like Jerkwater'd be a better name for it."

Groves looked ahead. The cavalry officer had a point. It didn't look like much of a town. But cattle roamed the fields around it. This late in winter, they were on the scrawny side, but they were still out there grazing. That meant Chugwater had enough to eat, anyhow.

People came out to look at the spectacle of a cavalry company going through town, but they didn't act as impressed as townsfolk had in Montana and farther north in Wyoming. One boy in ragged blue jeans said to a man in overalls who looked just like him, "I liked the parade a couple of weeks ago better, Dad."

"You had a parade through here a couple of weeks ago?" Groves called to a heavyset man whose black coat, white shirt, and string tie argued that he was a person of some local importance.

"Sure as hell did." The pear-shaped man spat a stream of tobacco juice into the street. Groves envied him for having tobacco in any form. He went on, "Only thing missing then was a brass band. Had us a whole slew o' wagons and soldiers and foreigners who talked funny and even a couple of Lizards—silly-lookin' little things to cause all the trouble they do, aren't they?"

"Yes, now that you mention it." Excitement coursed through

154

Groves. That sounded very much like the Met Lab crew. If he was only a couple of weeks behind them, they'd be into Colorado by now, not too far from Denver. He might even catch them before they got there. Whether he did or not, the lead-lined saddlebag in his wagon would push their work forward once they got themselves settled. Trying to make his hope a certainty, he asked, "Did they say what they were up to?"

The heavyset man shook his head. "Nope. They were right close-mouthed, as a matter of fact. Friendly enough people, though." His chest inflated, although not enough to stick out over his belly. "I married off a couple of 'em."

One of the other men on the sidewalk, a stringy, leathery fellow who looked like a real cowboy, not the Hollywood variety, said, "Yeah, go on, Hoot, tell him how you laid the bride, too."

"You go to hell, Fritzie," the pear-shaped man—Hoot—said. *A cowboy named Fritzie?* Groves thought. Before he had time to do more than marvel, Hoot turned back to him. "Not that I would've minded: pretty little thing, a widow I think she was. But I do believe the corporal she married would have kicked my ass around the block if I'd even looked at her sideways."

"You'd've deserved it, too," Fritzie said with a most uncowboylike giggle.

"Oh, shut up," Hoot told him. Again, he returned to Groves: "So I don't know what they were doing, Colonel, only that there were a lot of 'em, heading south. Toward Denver, I think, not Cheyenne, but don't make me swear to that."

"Thank you very much. That helps," Groves said. If they weren't talking about the crew from the University of Chicago, he'd eat his hat. He'd made better time coming across Canada and then down through Montana and Wyoming than they had traveling straight west across the Great Plains. Of course, his party had only the one wagon in it, and that lightly loaded, while theirs was limited to the speed of their slowest conveyance. And they'd have been doing a lot more scrounging for fodder than his tight band. If you couldn't think in terms of logistics, you didn't deserve to be an Army engineer.

"You folks going to put up here for the night?" Hoot asked. "We'll kill the fatted calf for you, like the Good Book says. 'Sides, there's nothin' between here and Cheyenne but miles and miles of miles and miles."

Groves looked at Auerbach. Auerbach looked back, as if to

say, *You're the boss.* Groves said, "I know things are tight, Mister, uh—"

"I'm Joshua Sumner, but you may as well call me Hoot; everybody else does. We got plenty, at least for now. Feed you a nice thick steak and feed you beets. By God, we'll feed you beets till your eyeballs turn purple—we had a bumper crop of 'em. Got a Ukrainian family up the road a couple miles, they showed us how to cook up what they call borscht—beets and sour cream and I don't know what all else. They taste a sight better that way than what we were doing with 'em before, I tell you for a fact."

Groves was unenthusiastic about beets, with or without sour cream. But he didn't think he'd get anything better farther south on US 87. "Thanks, uh, Hoot. We'll lay over, then, if it's all right with you people."

Nobody in earshot made any noises to say it wasn't. Captain Auerbach raised his hand. The cavalry company reined in. Groves reflected that a couple of the old-timers on the street had probably seen cavalry go through town before, back before the turn of the century. The idea left him unhappy; it was as if the Lizards were forcing the United States—and the world—away from the twentieth century.

Such worries receded after he got himself outside of a great slab of fat-rich steak cooked medium-rare over a wood fire. He ate a bowl of borscht, too, not least because the person who pressed it on him was a smiling blonde of about eighteen. It wasn't what he would have chosen for himself, but it wasn't as bad as he'd thought it would be, either. And somebody in Chugwater made homebrew beer better than just about anything that came out of a big Milwaukee brewery.

Hoot Sumner turned out to be sheriff, justice of the peace, and postmaster all rolled into one. He gravitated to Groves, maybe because they were the leaders of their respective camps, maybe just because they were about the same shape. "So what brings you through town?" he asked.

"I'm afraid I can't answer that," Groves said. "The less I say, the less chance the Lizards have of finding out."

"As if I'm gonna tell 'em," Sumner said indignantly.

"Mr. Sumner, I have no way of knowing whom you'd tell, or whom they'd tell, or whom *they'd* tell," Groves said. "What I do know is that I have orders directly from President Roosevelt that I tell no one. I intend to obey those orders."

Sumner's eyes got big. "Straight from the President, you say? Must be something important, then." He cocked his head, studied Groves from under the brim of his Stetson. Groves looked back at him, his face expressionless. After close to a minute of that tableau, Sumner scowled in frustration. "Goddamn, Colonel, I'm glad I don't play poker against you, or I'd be walking home in my long johns, I think."

"Hoot, if I can't tell you anything, that means I really can't tell you anything," Groves said.

"Thing is, though, a small town like this one here runs on gossip. If we can't get any, we'll just shrivel up and die," Sumner said. "The folks who came through a couple weeks ago were just as tight-lipped as you people are—they wouldn't't've said shit if they had a mouthful, if you know what I mean. All this stuff going through us, and we don't even get to find out what the hell it is?"

"Mr. Sumner, it's altogether possible that you and Chugwater don't want to know," Groves said. His face did twist then, in annoyance at himself. He shouldn't have said anything at all. How many mugs of that good home brew had he drunk?

He consoled himself with the thought that he'd learned something from Sumner. If the previous set of travelers had been as secretive as he was, the odds were even better than good that they came from the Metallurgical Laboratory.

The justice of the peace said, "Hellfire, man, those people even had an Eyetalian with 'em, and ain't Eyetalians supposed to be the talkingest people on the face of the earth? Brother, not this one! Nice enough feller, but he wouldn't give you the time of day. What kind of an Eyetalian is that?"

A smart one, Groves thought. It sounded like Enrico Fermi to him . . . which just about nailed things down.

"Only time he unbent *a*-tall," Sumner went on, "was when he did best man duty at the wedding I told you about—kissed the bride right pert, he did, even though his own wife—not a bad looker herself—was standing right there beside him. Now *that* sounds like an Eyetalian to me."

"Maybe so." Groves wondered where Sumner got his ideas about how Italians were supposed to act. Not in the great metropolis of Chugwater, Wyoming—or at least Groves hadn't seen any here. *Most likely from Chico Marx,* he thought.

Wherever he got those ideas, though, Sumner was no fool in matters directly under his own eye. Nodding to Groves, he

said, "Stands to reason your business, whatever it is—and I won't ask any more—is somehow connected with that other crowd. We hadn't seen hardly anybody from the outside world since things went to hell last year, and then two big bunches both goin' the same direction, almost one on top of the other. You gonna tell me it's a coincidence?"

"Mr. Sumner, I'm not saying yes and I'm not saying no. I am saying we'd all be better off—you and me and the country, too—if you didn't ask questions like that." Groves was a career Army man; to him, security was as natural as breathing. But civilians didn't, wouldn't, think that way. Sumner set a finger alongside his nose and winked, as if Groves had told him what he wanted to know.

Gloomily, Groves sipped more homemade beer. He was afraid he'd done just that.

"Ah, the vernal equinox," Ken Embry exclaimed. "Harbinger of mild weather, songbirds, flowers—"

"Oh, shut your bleeding gob," George Bagnall said, with heartfelt sincerity.

Breath came from both Englishmen in great icy clouds. Vernal equinox or not, winter still held Pskov in an iron grip. The oncoming dawn was just beginning to turn the eastern horizon gray above the black pine forests that seemed to stretch away forever. Venus blazed low in the east, with Saturn, far dimmer and yellower, not far above her. In the west, the full moon was descending toward the land. Looking that way, Bagnall was painfully reminded of the Britain he might never see again.

Embry sighed, which turned the air around him even foggier. He said, "I'm not what you'd call dead keen on being demoted to the infantry."

"Nor I," Bagnall agreed. "That's what we get for being supernumeraries. You don't see them handing Jones a rifle and having him give his all for king and country. He's useful here, so they have him teaching everything he can about his pet radar. But without the Lanc, we're just bodies."

"For commissar and country, please—remember where we are," Embry said. "Me, I'd sooner they tried training us up on Red Air Force planes. We are veteran aircrew, after all."

"I'd hoped for that myself," Bagnall said. "Only difficulty with the notion is that, as far as I can see, the Red Air Force, whatever may be left of it, hasn't got any planes within God

knows how far from Pskov. If there's damn all here, they can hardly train us up on it."

"Too true." Embry tugged at his *shlem*—sort of a balaclava that didn't cover his nose or mouth—so it did a better job of keeping his neck warm. "And I don't like the tin hat they've kitted me out with, either."

"Then don't wear it. I don't fancy mine, now that you mention it." Along with Mauser rifles, both Englishmen had received German helmets. Wearing that coal scuttle with its painted swastika set Bagnall's teeth on edge, to say nothing of worrying him lest he be mistaken for a Nazi by some Russian more eager for revenge against the Germans than to attack the Lizards.

"Don't like to leave it off, either," Embry said. "Puts me too much in mind of the last war, when they went for a year and a half with no tin hats at all."

"That is a poser," Bagnall admitted. Thinking about the infinite slaughter of World War I was bad enough anyhow. Thinking how bad it had been before helmets was enough to make your stomach turn over.

Alf Whyte came walking toward them. He had his helmet on, which made his silhouette unnervingly Germanic. He said, "You chaps ready to find out about the way our fathers fought?"

"Sod our fathers," Bagnall muttered. He stamped his feet up and down. Russian felt boots kept them warm; boots were the one part of his flying suit he'd willingly exchanged for their local equivalents.

Other small groups of men gathered in Pskov's market square, chatting softly among themselves in Russian or German. It was a more informal muster than any Bagnall had imagined; the occasional female voice among the deeper rumbles only made the scene seem stranger.

The women fighters were as heavily bundled against the cold as their male counterparts. Pointing to a couple of them, Embry said, "They don't precisely put one in mind of Jane, do they?"

"Ah, Jane," Bagnall said. He and Alf Whyte both sighed. *The Daily Mirror*'s marvelous comic-strip blonde dressed in one of two ways: very little and even less. Bagnall went on, "Even Jane would dress warmly here. And the Russians, even

dressed like Jane, wouldn't much stir me. The ones I've seen are most of them lady dockwallopers or lorry drivers."

"Too right," Whyte said. "This is a bloody place." All three Englishmen nodded glumly.

A couple of minutes later, officers—or at least leaders— moved the fighters out. Bagnall's rifle was heavy; it made him feel lopsided and banged his shoulder at every step he took. At first it drove him to distraction. Then it became only a minor nuisance. By the time he'd gone a mile or so, he stopped noticing it.

He did expect to see some difference in the way the Russians and Germans went off to war. German precision and efficiency were notorious, while the Red Army, although it had a reputation for great courage, was not long on spit and polish. He soon found what such clichés were worth. He couldn't even tell the two groups apart by their gear: many Russian partisans bore captured German equipment, while about an equal number of Hitler's finest eked out their own supplies with Soviet stocks.

They even marched the same way, in loose, widespread groups that got looser and more spread out as the sun rose. "We might do well to emulate them," Bagnall said. "They have more experience at this kind of thing than we do."

"I suppose it's to keep too many from going down at once if they're caught out in the open by aircraft," Ken Embry said.

"If we're caught out in the open, you mean," Alf Whyte corrected him. As if with one accord, the three RAF men spread out a little farther.

Before long, they entered the forest south of Pskov. To Bagnall, used to neat, well-trimmed English woods, it was like stepping into another world. These trees had never been harvested; he would have bet money that many of them had never been seen by mortal man till this moment. Pine and fir and spruce held invaders at bay with their dark-needled branches, as if the only thing they wanted in all the world was for the men to go away. The occasional pale gray birch trunks among them startled Bagnall each time he went past one; they reminded him of naked women (he thought again of Jane) scattered among matrons properly dressed for the cold.

Off in the distance, something howled. "A wolf!" Bagnall said, and grabbed for his rifle before he realized there was no immediate need. Wolves had been hunted out of England for

more than four hundred years, but he reacted to the sound by
instinct printed on his flesh by four hundred times four hundred generations.

"We're rather a long way from home, aren't we?" Whyte
said with a nervous chuckle; he'd started at the wolf call, too.

"Too bloody far," Bagnall said. Thinking about England
brought him only pain. He tried to do it as little as he could.
Even battered and hungry from war, it felt infinitely more welcoming than wrecked Pskov, tensely divided between Bolsheviks and Nazis, or than this forbidding primeval wood.

In amongst the trees, the almost eternal ravening wind was
gone. That let Bagnall grow as nearly warm as he'd been since
his Lancaster landed outside Pskov. And Jerome Jones had
said the city was known for its mild climate. Trudging through
snow as spring began gave the lie to that, at least if you were
a Londoner. Bagnall wondered if spring ever truly began here.

Alf Whyte said, "What precisely is our mission, anyhow?"

"I was talking with a Jerry last night." Bagnall paused, and
not just to take another breath. He had a little German and no
Russian, so he naturally found it easier to talk with the *Wehrmacht* men than with Pskov's rightful owners. That bothered
him. He was so used to thinking of the Germans as enemies
that dealing with them in any way felt treasonous, even if they
loved the Lizards no better than he.

"And what did the Jerry say, pray tell?" Whyte asked when
he didn't go on right away.

Thus prompted, Bagnall answered, "There's a Lizard ... I
don't know what exactly—forward observation post, little garrison, something—about twenty-five kilometers south of
Pskov. We're supposed to put paid to it."

"Twenty-five kilometers?" As a navigator, Whyte was used
to going back and forth between metric and imperial measures.
"We're to hike *fifteen miles* through the snow and then fight?
It'll be nightfall by the time we get there."

"I gather that's part of the plan," Bagnall said. Whyte's
scandalized tone showed what an easy time England had had
in the war. The Germans and, from what Bagnall could gather,
the Russians took the hike for granted: just one more thing
they had to do. They'd done worse marches to get at each
other the winter before.

He munched cold black bread as he shuffled along. While
he paused to spend a penny against the trunk of a birch tree,

a Lizard jet wailed by, far overhead. He froze, wondering if the enemy could have spotted the advancing human foes. The trees gave good cover, and most of the fighters wore white smocks over the rest of their clothes. Even his own helmet had white-wash splashed across it.

The leaders of the combat group (or so his German of the night before had called it) took no chances. They hurried the fighters along and urged them to scatter even more widely than before. Bagnall obeyed, but worried. He'd thought nothing could be worse than fighting in these grim woods. But suppose he got lost in them instead? The shiver that brought had noth-ing to do with cold.

On and on and on. He felt as if he'd marched a hundred miles already. How was he to fight after a slog like this? The Germans and Russians seemed to think nothing of it. A British Tommy might have felt the same, but the RAF let machines carry warriors to combat. In a Lanc, Bagnall could do things no infantry could match. Now, quite literally, he found the shoe on the other foot.

The sun swung through the sky. Shadows lengthened, deep-ened. Somehow, Bagnall kept up with everyone else. As shad-ows gave way to twilight, he saw the men ahead of him going down on their bellies, so he did, too. He slithered forward. Through breaks in the forest he saw a few houses—huts, real-ly—plopped down in the middle of a clearing. "That's it?" he whispered.

"How the devil should I know?" Ken Embry whispered back. "Somehow, though, I don't think we've been invited here for high tea."

Bagnall didn't think the village had ever heard of high tea. By its look, he wondered if it had heard of the passing of the tsars. The wooden buildings with carved walls and thatched roofs looked like something out of a novel by Tolstoy. The only hint of the twentieth century was razor wire strung around a couple of houses. No one, human or Lizard, was in sight.

"It can't be as easy as it looks," Bagnall said.

"I'd like it if it were," Embry answered. "And who says it can't? We—"

Off in the distance a small *pop!* interrupted him. Bag-nall had been involved in dropping countless tons of bombs and had been on the receiving end of more antiaircraft fire than he cared to think about, but this was the first time he'd done

his fighting on the ground. The mortar fired again and again, fast as its crew—Bagnall didn't know whether they were Russians or Germans—could serve it with bombs.

Snow and dirt fountained upward as the mortar rounds hit home. One of the wooden houses caught fire and began to burn merrily. Men in white burst from the trees and dashed across the clearing. Bagnall wondered if the village really was a Lizard outpost after all.

He fired the Mauser, worked the bolt, fired again. He'd trained on a Lee-Enfield, and vastly preferred it to the weapon he was holding. Instead of angling down to where it was easy to reach, the Mauser's bolt stuck straight out, which made quick firing difficult, and the German rifle's magazine held only five rounds, not ten.

Other rifles started hammering, and a couple of machine guns, too. Still no response came from the village. Bagnall began to feel almost sure they were attacking a place empty of the enemy. Relief and rage fought in him—relief that he wasn't in danger after all, rage that he'd made that long, miserable march in the snow.

Then one of the white-cloaked figures flew through the air, torn almost in two by the land mine he'd stepped on. And then muzzle flashes began winking from a couple of the village buildings as the Lizards returned fire. The charging, yelling humans began to go down as if scythed.

Bullets kicked up snow between Bagnall and Embry, whacked into the trees behind which they hid. Bagnall hugged the frozen earth like a lover. Shooting back was the last thing on his mind. This was, he decided in an instant, a much uglier business than war in the air. In the Lanc, you dropped your bombs on people thousands of feet below. They shot back, yes, but at your aircraft, not at your precious and irreplaceable self. Even fighter aircraft didn't go after you personally—their object was to wreck your plane, and your gunners were trying to do the same to them. And even if your aircraft got shot down, you might bail out and survive.

It wasn't machine against machine here. The Lizards were doing their best to blow large holes in his body so he'd scream and bleed and die. Their best seemed appallingly good, too. Every one of however many Lizards there were in the village had an automatic weapon that spat as much lead as one of the raiders' machine guns and many times as much as a bolt-action

rifle like his Mauser. He felt like Kipling's Fuzzy-Wuzzy charging a British square.

But you couldn't charge here, not if you felt like living. The Russians and Germans who'd tried it were most of them down, some chewed to bits by a hail of bullets, others shredded like the first luckless fellow by stepping on a mine. The few still on their feet could not go forward. They fled for the shelter of the woods.

Bagnall turned to Embry, shouted, "I think we just stuck our tools in the meat grinder."

"Whatever gave you that idea, dearie?" Even in the middle of battle, the pilot managed to come up with a high, shrill falsetto.

In the gathering gloom, one of the houses in the village began to move. At first Bagnall rubbed his eyes, wondering if they were playing tricks on him. Then, after Mussorgsky, he thought of the Baba Yaga, the witch's hut that ran on chicken's legs. But as the wooden walls fell away, he saw that this house moved on tracks. "Tank!" he screamed. "It's a bleeding tank!"

The Russians were yelling the same thing, save with a broad *a* rather than his sharp one. The Germans screamed *"Panzer!"* instead. Bagnall understood that, too. He also understood that a tank—no, two tanks now, he saw—meant big trouble.

Their turrets swiveled toward the heaviest firing. Machine guns opened up on them as they did so; streams of bullets struck sparks from their armor. But they'd been made to withstand heavier artillery than most merely Earthly tanks commanded—the machine guns might as well have been firing feathers.

Their own machine guns started shooting, muzzle flashes winking like fireflies. One of the raiders' machine guns—a new German one, with such a high cyclic rate that it sounded like a giant ripping an enormous canvas sail when it opened up—abruptly fell silent. It started up again a few seconds later. Bagnall admired the spirit of the men who had taken over for its surely fallen crew.

Then the main armament of one of the tanks spoke, or rather bellowed. From less than half a mile away, it sounded to Bagnall like the end of the world, while the tongue of flame it spat put him in mind of hellmouth opening. The machine gun stopped firing once more, and this time did not open up again.

The other tank's cannon fired, too, then slowed so it pointed

more nearly in Bagnall's direction. He scrambled deeper into the woods: anything to put more distance between himself and that hideous gun.

Ken Embry was right with him. "How the devil do you say, 'Run like bloody hell!' in Russian?" he asked.

"Not a phrase I've learned, I'm afraid, but I don't believe the partisans need our advice in that regard," Bagnall answered. Russians and Germans alike were in full retreat, the tanks hastening on their way—and hastening too many of them into the world to come—with more cannon rounds. Shell splinters and real splinters blown off trees hissed through the air with deadly effect.

"Someone's reconnaissance slipped up badly," Embry said. "This was supposed to be an infantry outpost. No one said a word about going up against armor."

Bagnall only grunted. What Embry had said was self-evidently true. Men were dying because of it. His main hope at present was not being one who did. Through the crash of the cannon, he heard another noise, one he didn't recognize: a quick, deep thutter that seemed to come out of the air.

"What's that?" he said. Beside him, Embry shrugged. The Russians were running faster than ever, crying *"Vertolyet!"* and *"Avtozhir!"* Neither word, unfortunately, meant anything to Bagnall.

Fire came out of the sky from just above treetop height: streaks of flame as if from a *Katyusha* launcher taken aloft and mounted on a flying machine instead of a truck. The woods exploded into flame as the rocket warheads detonated. Bagnall shrieked like a lost soul, but couldn't even hear himself.

Whatever had fired the rockets, it wasn't an ordinary airplane. It hung in the sky, hovering like a mosquito the size of a young whale, as it loosed another salvo of rockets on the humans who had presumed to attack a Lizard position. More deadly shrapnel flew. Buffeted, half stunned by the blast, Bagnall lay flat on the ground, as he might have during a great earthquake, and prayed the pounding would end.

But another helicopter came whickering up from the south and poured two more salvos of rockets into the raiders' ranks. Both machines hovered overhead and raked the forest with machine-gun fire. The tanks came crashing closer, too, smashing down everything that stood in their way but the bigger trees.

Somebody booted Bagnall in the backside, hard. "Get up and run, you bloody twit!" The words were in English. Bagnall turned his head. It was Ken Embry, his foot drawn back for another kick.

"I'm all right," Bagnall said, and proved it by getting up. As soon as he was on his pins again, adrenaline made him run like a deer. He fled north—or, at any rate, away from the tanks and the helicopters' killing ground. Embry matched him stride for desperate stride. Somewhere in their mad dash, Bagnall gasped out, "Where's Alf?"

"He bought his plot back there, I'm afraid," Embry answered.

That hit Bagnall like—like a machine-gun round from one of the deathships up there, he thought. Watching Russians and Germans he didn't know getting shot or blown to bits was one thing. Losing someone from his own crew was ten times worse—as if a flak burst had torn through the side of his Lancaster and slaughtered a bombardier. And since Whyte was—had been—one of the three other men in Pskov with whom he could speak freely, he felt the loss all the more.

Bullets still slashed the woods, most of them, though, behind the fleeing Englishmen now. The Lizards' tanks did not press the pursuit as aggressively as they might have. "Maybe they're afraid of taking a Molotov cocktail from someone up a tree whom they don't spy till too late," Embry suggested when Bagnall said that out loud.

"Maybe they are," the flight engineer said. "I'm damned sure I'm afraid of them."

The gunfire and rockets and cannon rounds had left his ears as dazed as any other part of him. Dimly, as if from far away, he heard screams of terror and the even more appalling shrieks of the wounded. One of the helicopters flew away, then, after a last hosing of the woods with bullets, the other one. Bagnall looked down at his wrist. The glowing hands of his watch said only twenty minutes had gone by since the first shots were fired. Those twenty minutes of hell had stretched for an eternity. Though not ordinarily a religious man, Bagnall wondered how long a real eternity of hell would seem to last.

Then his thoughts snapped back to the present, for he almost stumbled over a wounded Russian lying in a pool of blood that looked black against the snow at night. *"Bozhemoi,"* the Russian moaned. *"Bozhemoi."*

"My God," Bagnall gasped, unconsciously translating. "Ken, come over here and help me. It's a woman."

"I hear." The pilot and Bagnall stooped beside the wounded partisan. She pressed a hand against her side, trying to stanch the flow of blood.

As gently as he could, Bagnall undid her quilted coat and tunic so he could see the wound. He had to force her hand away before he could bandage it with gauze from his aid kit. She groaned and thrashed and weakly tried to fight him off. *"Nemtsi,"* she wailed.

"She thinks we're Jerries," Embry said. "Here, give her this, too." He pressed a morphia syrette into Bagnall's hand.

Even as he made the injection, Bagnall thought it a waste of precious drug: she wasn't going to live. Her blood had already soaked the bandage. Maybe a hospital could have saved her, but here in the middle of a frozen nowhere ... *"Artzt!"* he yelled in German. *"Gibt es Artzt hier?* Is there a doctor here?"

No one answered. He and Embry and the wounded woman might have been alone in the woods. She sighed as the morphia bit into her pain, took a couple of easy breaths, and died.

"She went out peacefully, anyhow," Embry said; Bagnall realized the pilot hadn't thought she'd make it, either. He'd done her the last favor he could by freeing her death from agony.

Bagnall said, "Now we have to think about staying alive ourselves." In the middle of the cold woods, after a crushing defeat that showed only too clearly how the Lizards had seized and held great stretches of territory from the mightiest military machines the world had known, that seemed to require considerable thought.

Liu Han called, "Come and see the foreign devil do amazing things with stick and ball and glove. Come and see! Come and see!"

Mountebanks of all sorts could be sure of an audience in the Chinese refugee camp. Behind her, Bobby Fiore tossed into the air the leather-covered ball he'd had made. Instead of catching it in his hands, he tapped it lightly with his special stick—a *bat*, he called it. The ball went a couple of feet into the air, came straight down. He tapped it up again and again and again. All the while, he whistled a merry tune.

"See!" Liu Han pointed to him. "The foreign devil juggles without using his hands!"

A spattering of applause came from the crowd. Three or four people tossed coins into the bowl that lay by Liu Han's feet. Some others set rice cakes and vegetables on the mat next to the bowl. Everyone understood that entertainers had to eat or they wouldn't be able to entertain.

When no donations came for a minute or so, Bobby Fiore tapped the ball up one last time, caught it in his free hand, and glanced toward Liu Han. She looked out into the crowd and said, "Who will play a game where, if he wins, the foreign devil will look ridiculous? Who will try this simple game?"

Several men shouted and stepped toward her. Nothing delighted Chinese more than making a European or American into an object of ridicule. Liu Han pointed toward the bowl and the mat: if they wanted to play, they had to pay. A couple of them made their offerings without a word, but one asked belligerently, "What is this game?"

Bobby Fiore handed her the ball. She held it up in one hand, bent to pick up a flat canvas bag stuffed with rags which she displayed in the other. Then she put the bag back on the ground, gave the ball to the belligerent man. "A simple game, an easy game," she said. "The foreign devil will stand well back and then run toward the bag. All you have to do is stand in front of it and touch him with the ball before he reaches it. Win and you get back your stake and twice as much besides."

"That *is* easy." The man with the ball puffed out his chest and tossed a silver trade dollar into the bowl. It rang sweetly. "I will put the ball on him, no matter what he does."

Liu Han turned to the crowd. "Clear a path, please. Clear a path so the foreign devil can run." Chattering among themselves, the people moved aside to form a narrow lane. Bobby Fiore walked down it. When he was almost a hundred feet from the man with the ball, he turned and bowed to him. The arrogant fellow did not return his courtesy. A couple of people clucked reproachfully at that, but most didn't think a foreign devil deserved much courtesy.

Bobby Fiore bowed again, then ran straight at the man with the ball. The Chinese man clutched it in both hands, as if it were a rock. He set himself for a collision as Fiore bore down on him.

But the collision never came. At the last instant, Fiore threw himself to the ground on his hip and thigh and hooked around the clumsy lunge the man made with the ball. His foot came

down on the stuffed bag. *"Safe!"* he yelled in his own language.

Liu Han didn't quite know what *safe* meant, but she knew it meant he'd won. "Who's next?" she called, taking the ball from the disgruntled Chinese man.

"Wait!" he said angrily, then turned and played to the crowd: "You all saw that! The foreign devil cheated me!"

Fear coursed through Liu Han. She called Bobby Fiore *yang kwei-tse*—foreign devil—herself, but only to identify him. In the angry man's mouth, it was a cry to turn an audience into a mob.

Before she could answer, Fiore spoke for himself in clumsy Chinese: "Not cheat. Not say let win. He quick, he win. He slooow." He stretched the last word out in a way no native Chinese would have used, but one insultingly effective.

"He's right, Wu—you missed him by a *li*," someone yelled from the crowd. The miss hadn't really been a third of a mile, but it hadn't been close, either.

"Here, give *me* the ball now," someone else said. "I'll put it on the foreign devil." He said *yang kwei-tse* the same way Liu Han did, to name Bobby Fiore, not to revile him.

Liu Han pointed to the bowl. As Wu stamped away, the next player tossed in some paper money from Manchukuo. It wasn't worth as much as silver, and Liu Han did not like it because of what Manchukuo's Japanese puppet masters had done to China—and to her own family, just before the Lizards came. But the Japanese were still fighting hard against the Lizards, which gave them prestige they hadn't had before. She let the bills lay, handed the man the ball.

Bobby Fiore brushed dirt off his pants, shooed the spectators back so he could take his running start. The Chinese man stood in front of the bag, holding the ball in his left hand and leaning left, as if to make sure Fiore wouldn't use on him the trick that had fooled the first player.

Bobby Fiore ran down the aisle of chattering Chinese, as before. When he got within a couple of strides of the waiting Chinese, he took a small step in the direction the fellow was leaning. "Ha!" the man cried in triumph, and brought the ball down.

But Bobby Fiore was not there to be tagged. After that small step made the man commit himself, Fiore took a long, hard stride on his other leg, changing directions as nimbly as any

acrobat Liu Han had ever seen. The man tagged to the left; Bobby Fiore slid to the right. *"Safe!"* he yelled again.

The man with the ball ruefully flipped it to Liu Han. His sheepish grin said he knew he'd been outsmarted. "Let's see if this fellow can put the ball on the foreign devil," he said, now using the label almost in admiration. "If I couldn't, I'll make a side bet he can't, either."

Another man set down a meaty slab of pork ribs to pay for the privilege of trying to tag Bobby Fiore. The fellow making side bets did a brisk business: now that Fiore had gone one way and then the other, what tricks could he have left?

He promptly demonstrated a new one. Instead of going right or left, he dove straight toward the bag on his belly, snaked a hand through his opponent's legs, and grabbed the bag before the ball touched his back. *"Safe!"* Now a couple of people in the crowd raised the victory cry with him.

He kept running and sliding as long as men were willing to pay to try to put the ball on him. Sometimes he'd hook one way, sometimes the other, and once in a while he'd dive straight in. A couple of people did manage to guess right and tag him, but Liu Han watched the bowl fill with money and the mat with food. They were doing well.

When the sport began to seem routine rather than novel, Liu Han called, "Who wants revenge?" She tossed the ball up and down in her hand. "You can throw at the foreign devil now. He will not dodge, but if you hit him anywhere but his two hands, you win three times what you wager. Who will try?"

While she warmed up the crowd, Bobby Fiore put on the padded leather glove he'd had made along with the ball. He stood in front of the wall of a shack, then made a fist with his other hand and pounded it into the glove, as if confident no one would be able to touch him.

"From how close do we get to throw?" asked the man who'd been making side bets.

Liu Han paced off about forty feet. Bobby Fiore grinned at her. "Do you want to try?" she asked the man.

"Yes, I'll fling at him," he answered, dropping more money into the bowl. "I'll put it right between his ugly round eyes, you see if I don't."

He tossed the ball into the air once or twice, as if to get the feel of it in his hand, and then, as he'd said, threw it right at

Bobby Fiore's head. *Whack!* The noise it made striking that peculiar leather glove was like a gunshot. It startled Liu Han, and startled the people in the crowd even more. A couple of them let out frightened squawks. Bobby Fiore rolled the ball back to Liu Han.

She stooped to pick it up. Before long, that wouldn't be easy, not with her belly growing. "Who's next?" she asked.

"Whoever it is, he can wager with me that he misses, too," said the fellow who liked to make side bets. "I'll pay five to one if he hits." If he couldn't beat Bobby Fiore, he was convinced nobody could.

The next gambler paid Liu Han and let fly. *Wham!* That wasn't ball hitting glove, that was ball banging against the side of the shack—the man had thrown too wildly for Bobby Fiore to catch his offering. Fiore picked up the ball and tossed it gently back to him. "You try again," he said; he'd practiced the phrase with Liu Han.

Before the fellow could take another throw at him, the old woman who lived in the shack came out and screamed at Liu Han: "What are you doing? Are you trying to frighten me out of my wits? Stop hitting my poor house with a club. I thought a bomb landed on it."

"No bomb, grandmother," Liu Han said politely. "We are only playing a gambling game." The old woman kept on screaming until Liu Han gave her three trade dollars. Then she disappeared back into her shack, obviously not caring what happened to it after that.

The fellow who hadn't thrown straight took another shot at Bobby Fiore. This time he was on target, but Fiore caught the ball. The man squalled curses like a scalded cat.

If the old woman had thought that first ball was like a bomb landing, she must have figured the Lizards had singled out her house for bombardment practice by the time the next hour had passed. One of the things Liu Han discovered about her countrymen during that time was that they didn't throw very well. A couple of them missed the shack altogether. That sent boys chasing wildly after the runaway ball, and meant Liu Han had to pay small bribes to get it back.

When no one else felt like trying to hit the quick-handed foreign devil, Liu Han said, "Who has a bottle or clay pot he doesn't mind losing?"

A tall man took a last swig from a bottle of plum brandy, then handed it to her. "Now I do," he said thickly, breathing plummy fumes into her face.

She gave the bottle to Bobby Fiore, who set it on an upside-down bucket in front of the wall. He walked back farther than the spot from which the Chinese had taken aim at him.

"The foreign devil will show you how to throw properly," Liu Han said. This last stunt made her nervous. The bottle looked very small. Bobby Fiore could easily miss, and if he did he'd lose face.

His features were set and tight—he knew he could miss, too. His arm went back, then snapped forward in a motion longer and smoother than the Chinese had used. The ball flew, almost invisibly fast. The bottle shattered. Green glass flew every which way. Chatter from the crowd rose to an impressed peak. Several people clapped their hands. Bobby Fiore bowed, as if he were Chinese himself.

"That's all for today," Liu Han said. "We will present our show again in a day or two. I hope you enjoyed it."

She picked up all the food the show had earned them. Bobby Fiore carried the money. He also hung onto ball and bat and glove. That made him different from all the Chinese men Liu Han had known: they would have added to her burden without a second thought. She'd already seen up in the plane that never came down that he had the strange ways ascribed to foreign devils. Some of them, such as his taste in food, annoyed her; this one she found endearing.

"Show good?" he asked, tacking on the Lizards' interrogative cough.

"The show was very good." Liu Han used the emphatic cough to underline that, adding, "You were very good too there, especially at the end—you took a chance with the bottle, but it worked, so all the better."

Of necessity, she spoke mostly in Chinese, which meant she had to repeat herself several times and go back to use simpler words. When Fiore understood, he grinned and slipped an arm around her thickening waist. She dropped an onion so she could break away to pick it up. Showing affection in public was one foreign devil way she wished he would forget in a hurry. It not only embarrassed her, but lowered her status in the eyes of everyone who saw her.

As they approached the hut they shared, she stopped fretting over such relatively trivial concerns. Several little scaly devils stood outside, two with fancy body paint and the rest with guns. Their unnerving turreted eyes swung toward Liu Han and Bobby Fiore.

One of the little devils with fancy paint spoke in hissing but decent Chinese: "You are the human beings who live in this house, the human beings brought down from the ship *29th Emperor Fessoj*?" The last three words were in his own language.

"Yes, superior sir," Liu Han said; by his perplexed look, Bobby Fiore hadn't understood the question. Even though the scaly devil used words that were individually intelligible, she had trouble following him, too. Imagine calling the airplane that never came down a ship!

"Which of you is carrying the growing thing that will become a human being in her belly?" the devil with the fancy paint asked.

"I am, superior sir." Not for the first time, Liu Han felt a flash of contempt for the little scaly devils. They not only couldn't tell people apart, they couldn't even tell the sexes apart. And Bobby Fiore, with his tall nose and round eyes, was unique in this camp, yet the little devils didn't recognize him as a foreign devil.

One of the gun-carrying little devils pointed at Liu Han and hissed something to a companion. The other devil's mouth fell open in a devilish laugh. They found people preposterous, too.

The little devil who spoke Chinese said, "Go in this little house, the two of you. We have things to say to you, things to ask of you."

Liu Han and Bobby Fiore went into the hut. So did the two little devils with elaborate paint on their scaly hides, and so did one of the more drably marked guards. The two higher-ranking little devils skittered past Liu Han so they could sit on the hearth that also supported the hut's bedding. They sank down on the warm clay with rapturous sighs—Liu Han had seen they didn't like cold weather. The guard, who liked it no better, had to stand where he could keep his eyes on the obviously vicious and dangerous humans.

"I am Ttomalss," the scaly devil who spoke Chinese said—a stutter at the front of his name and a hiss at the end. "First I ask you what you were doing with these strange things." He

turned his eye turrets toward the ball and bat and glove Bobby Fiore held, and pointed at them as well.

"Do you speak English?" Fiore asked in that language when Liu Han had put the question into their peculiar jargon. When neither little scaly devil answered, he muttered, "Shit," and turned back to her, saying, "You better answer. They won't follow me any more than I follow them."

"Superior sir," Liu Han began, bowing to Ttomalss as if he were her village headman back in the days (was it really less than a year before?) when she'd had a headman . . . or a village, "we use these things to put on a show to entertain people here in this camp and earn money and food for ourselves."

Ttomalss hissed to translate that to his companion, who might not have known any human language. The other scaly devil hissed back. Ttomalss turned his words into Chinese: "Why do you need these things? We give you this house, we give you enough to get food you need. Why do you want more? Do you not have enough?"

Liu Han thought about that. It was a question that went straight to the heart of the *Tao*, the way a person should live. Having too much—or caring in excess about having too much—was reckoned bad (though she'd noticed that few people who had a lot were inclined to give up any of it). Cautiously, she answered, "Superior sir, we seek to save what we can so we will not be at want if hunger comes to this camp. And we want money for the same reason, and to make our lives more comfortable. Can this be wrong?"

The scaly devil did not reply directly. Instead, he said, "What sort of show is this? It had better not be one that endangers the hatchling growing inside you."

"It does not, superior sir," she assured him. She would have been happier for his concern had it meant he cared for her and the baby as persons. She knew it didn't. The only value she, the baby, and Bobby Fiore had to the little devils was as parts of their experiment.

That worried her, too. What would they do when she'd had the child? Snatch it away from her as they'd snatched her away from her village? Force her to find out how fast she could get pregnant again? The unpleasant possibilities were countless.

"What do you do, then?" Ttomalss demanded suspiciously.

"Mostly I speak for Bobby Fiore, who does not speak Chinese well," she said. "I tell the audience how he will hit and catch and throw the ball. This is an art he brings with him from his own country, and not one with which we Chinese are familiar. Things that are new and strange entertain us, help us pass the time."

"This is foolishness," the little devil said. "The old, the familiar, should be what entertains. The new and strange—how could they be interesting? You will not be—what is the word?—familiar with them. Is this not frightening to you?"

He was even more conservative than a Chinese, Liu Han realized. That rocked her. The little scaly devils had torn up her life, to say nothing of turning China and the whole world on their ear. Moreover, the little devils had their vast array of astonishing machines, everything from the cameras that took pictures in three dimensions to the dragonfly planes that could hover in the sky. She'd thought of them as flighty gadgeteers, as if they were Americans or other foreign devils with scales and body paint.

But it wasn't so. Bobby Fiore had almost burst with excitement at the idea of bringing something new into the prison camp and making a profit from it. She'd liked the notion, too. To the scaly devil, it seemed as alien and menacing as the devil did to her.

Her wool-gathering irritated Ttomalss. "Answer me," he snapped.

"I'm sorry, superior sir," she said quickly. She didn't want to get the little devils annoyed at her. They might cast her and Bobby Fiore out of this home, they might take her back to the plane that never came down and turn her into a whore again, they might take her baby away as soon as it was born . . . or they might do any number of appalling things she couldn't imagine now. She went on, "I was just thinking that human beings like new things."

"I know that." Ttomalss did not approve of it; his blunt little stump of a tail switched back and forth, like an angry cat's. "It is the great curse of you Big Uglies." The last two words were in his own language. Liu Han had heard the little scaly devils use them often enough to know what they meant. Ttomalss resumed, "Were it not for the mad curiosity of your kind, the Race would have brought your world under our sway long ago."

"I am sorry, but I do not follow you, superior sir," Liu Han said. "What does this have to do with preferring new entertainments to old? When we see the same old thing over and over, we grow bored." How getting bored at old shows was tied to the devils' not conquering the world was beyond her.

"The Race also has this thing you call growing bored," Ttomalss admitted, "but with us it comes on more slowly, and over a long, long time. We are more content with what we already have than is true of your kind. So are the other two races we know. You Big Uglies break the pattern."

Liu Han did not worry about breaking patterns. She did wonder if she'd understood the scaly devil aright. Were there other kinds of weird creatures besides his own? She found it hard to believe, but she wouldn't have believed in the scaly devils a year earlier.

Ttomalss stepped forward, squeezed at her left breast with his clawed fingers. "Hey!" Bobby Fiore said, and started to get to his feet. The scaly devil with a gun turned it his way.

"It's all right," Liu Han said quickly. "He's not hurting me." That was true. His touch was gentle; although his claws penetrated her cotton tunic and pricked against her skin, they did not break it.

"You will give the hatchling liquid from your body out of these for it to eat?" Ttomalss asked, his Chinese becoming awkward as he spoke of matters and bodily functions unfamiliar to his kind.

"Milk, yes," Liu Han said, giving him the word he lacked.

"Milk." The scaly devil repeated the word to fix it in his memory, just as Liu Han did when she picked up something in English. Ttomalss continued, "When you mate, this male"—he pointed at Bobby Fiore—"chews there, too. Does he get milk as well?"

"No, no." Liu Han had all she could do not to laugh.

"Then why do this?" Ttomalss demanded. "What is its— function, is that the proper word?"

"That is the proper word, yes, superior sir." Liu Han sighed. The little devils talked so openly about mating that her own sense of shame and reticence had eroded. "But he does not draw milk from them. He does it to give me pleasure and to arouse himself."

Ttomalss gave a one-word verdict: "Disgusting." He spoke

in his own language to the other little devil with fancy paint. That one and the guard both swung their eyes from Liu Han to Bobby Fiore and back again.

"What's going on?" Fiore demanded. "Honey, they asking filthy questions again?" Though he liked publicly showing affection in a way in which no Chinese would have felt easy, he was and had stayed far more reticent than Liu Han in speaking of intimate matters.

"Yes," she answered resignedly.

The scaly devil with fancy paint who didn't speak Chinese sent several excited sentences at Ttomalss, who turned to Liu Han. "You use the *kee-kreek*? This is our speech, not yours."

"I am sorry, superior sir, but I do not know what the *kee-kreek* is," Liu Han said.

"The—" Ttomalss made the little devils' interrogative cough. "Do you understand now?"

"Yes, superior sir," Liu Han said. "Now I understand. Bobby Fiore is a foreign devil from a country far away. His words and my words are not the same. When we were up in the plane that never came down—"

"The what?" Ttomalss interrupted. When Liu Han explained, the little devil said, "Oh, you mean the ship."

Liu Han still wondered how it could be a ship if it never touched water, but the little devil seemed insistent about the point, so she said, "When we were up in the ship, then, superior sir, we had to learn each other's words. Since we both knew some of yours, we used those, too, and we still do."

Ttomalss translated for the other little scaly devil, who spoke volubly in reply. "Starraf"—Ttomalss finally named the other devil—"says you could do without all this moving back and forth between languages if you spoke only one, as we do. When your world is all ours, all you Big Uglies who survive will use our language, just as the Rabotevs and Halessi, the other races in the Empire, do now."

Liu Han could see that having everyone speak the same language would be simpler: even other dialects of Chinese were beyond her easy comprehension. But the unspoken assumptions in the scaly devil's words chilled her. Ttomalss seemed very sure his kind would conquer the world, and also that they would be able to do as they pleased with its people (or as many of them as were left when the conquest was complete).

Starraf spoke again, and Ttomalss translated: "You have shown, and we have seen at other places, that you Big Uglies are not too stupid to learn the tongue of the Race. Maybe we should begin to teach it in this camp and others, so that you can begin to be joined to the Empire."

"Now what?" Bobby Fiore asked.

"They want to teach everyone how to talk the way we do," Liu Han answered. She'd known the scaly devils were overwhelmingly powerful from the moment they first descended on her village. Somehow, though, she'd never thought much about what they were doing to the rest of the world. She was only a villager, after all, and didn't worry about the wider world unless some part of it impinged on her life. All at once, she realized the little devils didn't just want to conquer mankind; they aimed to make people as much like themselves as they could.

She hated that even more than she hated anything else about the little scaly devils, but she hadn't the slightest idea how to stop it.

Mordechai Anielewicz stood at attention in Zolraag's office as the Lizard governor of Poland chewed him out. "The situation in Warsaw grows more unsatisfactory with each passing day," Zolraag said in pretty good German. "The cooperation between you Jews and the Race which formerly existed seems to have disappeared."

Anielewicz scowled; after what the Nazis had done to the Warsaw ghetto, hearing the word "Jews" in German was plenty to set his teeth on edge all by itself. And Zolraag used it with arrogance of a sort not far removed from that of the Germans. The only difference Anielewicz could see was that the Lizards thought of all humans, not just Jews, as *Untermenschen*.

"Whose fault is that?" he demanded, not wanting Zolraag to know he was concerned. "We welcomed you as liberators; we shed our blood to help you take this city, if you remember, superior sir. And what thanks do we get? To be treated almost as badly under your thumb as we were under the Nazis."

"That is not true," Zolraag said. "We have given you enough guns to make your fighters the equal of the *Armija Krajowa*, the Polish Home Army. Where you were below them, we set you above. How do you say we treat you badly?"

"I say it because you care nothing for our freedom," the Jewish fighting leader answered. "You use us for your own purposes and to help make slaves of other people. We have been slaves ourselves. We didn't like it. We don't see any reason to think other people like it, either."

"The Race *will* rule this world and all its people," Zolraag said, as confidently as if he'd remarked, *The sun* will *come up tomorrow.* "Those who work with us will have higher place than those who do not."

Before the war, Anielewicz had been a largely secularized Jew. He'd gone to a Polish *Gymnasium* and university, and studied Latin. He knew what the Latin equivalent of *work together* was, too: collaborate. He also knew what he'd thought of the Estonian, Latvian, and Ukrainian jackals who helped the German wolves patrol the Warsaw ghetto—and what he'd thought of the Jewish police who betrayed their own people for a crust of bread.

"Superior sir," he said earnestly, "with the guns we have from you, we can protect ourselves from the Poles, and that is very good. But most of us would rather die than help you in the way you mean."

"This I have seen, and this I do not understand," Zolraag said. "Why would you forgo such advantage?"

"Because of what we would have to do to get it," Anielewicz answered. "Poor Moishe Russie wouldn't speak your lies, so you had to play tricks with his words to make them come out the way you wanted them. No wonder he disappeared after that, and no wonder he made you out to be liars the first chance he got."

Zolraag's eye turrets swung toward him. That slow, deliberate motion held as much menace as if they'd contained 38-centimeter battleship guns rather than organs of vision. "We are still seeking to learn more of these events ourselves," he said. "*Herr* Russie was an associate, even a friend, of yours. We wonder how and if you helped him."

"You questioned me under your truth drug," Anielewicz reminded him.

"We have not learned as much with it as we hoped from early tests," Zolraag said. "Some early experimental subjects may have deceived us as to their reactions. You Tosevites have a gift for being difficult in unusual ways."

"Thank you," Anielewicz said, grinning.

"I did not mean it as a compliment," Zolraag snapped.

Anielewicz knew that. Since he'd been up to his eyebrows in getting Russie away and in making the recording in which Russie blasted the Lizards, he was less than delighted to learn the Lizards had found their drug was worthless.

Zolraag resumed, "I did not summon you here, *Herr* Anielewicz, to listen to your Tosevite foolishness. I summoned you here to warn you that the uncooperative attitude of you Jews must stop. If it does not, we will disarm you and put you back in the place where you were when we came to Tosev 3."

Anielewicz gave the Lizard a long, slow, measuring stare. "It comes to that, does it?" he said at last.

"It does."

"You will not disarm us without a fight," Anielewicz said flatly.

"We beat the Germans. Do you think we cannot beat you?"

"I am sure you can," Anielewicz said. "Superior sir, we will fight anyhow. Now that we have guns, we will not give them up. You will beat us, but one way or another we will manage to hurt you. You will probably set off the Poles, too. If you take our guns away, they'll fear you'll take theirs, too."

Zolraag didn't answer right away. Anielewicz hoped he'd managed to distress the Lizard. The Race was good at war, or at least had machines of almost invincible power. When it came to diplomacy, though, they were as children; they had no feel for the likely effects of their actions.

The Lizard governor said, "You do not seem to understand, *Herr* Anielewicz. We can hold your people hostage to make sure you turn in your rifles and other weapons."

"Superior sir, you are the one who does not understand," Anielewicz answered. "Whatever you want to do to us, we went through worse before you came. We will fight to keep that from happening again. Will you start up Auschwitz and Treblinka and Chelmno and the rest again?"

"Do not make disgusting suggestions." The German death camps had revolted all the Lizards, Zolraag included. They'd gotten good propaganda mileage out of them. There, Russie and Anielewicz and other Jews had felt no compunctions about helping the Lizards tell the world the story.

"Well, then, in that case we have nothing to lose by fighting," Anielewicz said. "We were getting ready to fight the Nazis even though we had next to nothing. Now we have guns.

If you are going to treat us the way the Nazis did, do you think we'd not fight you? What would we have to lose?"

"Your lives," Zolraag said.

Anielewicz spat on the floor of the governor's office. He didn't know whether Zolraag knew how much scorn the gesture showed, but he hoped so. He said, "What good are our lives if you push us back into the ghetto and starve us once more? No one will do that to us again, superior sir, no one. Do what you like with me. The next Jew you pick as puppet leader will tell you the same—or his own people will deal with him."

"You are serious in this matter," Zolraag said in tones of wonder.

"Of course I am," Anielewicz answered. "Have you talked with General Bor-Komorowski about taking guns away from the Home Army?"

"He did not seem pleased with the idea, but he did not reject it in the way you have," Zolraag said.

"He's politer than I am," Anielewicz said, adding *the alter kacker* to himself. Aloud, he went on, "That doesn't mean you'll get any real cooperation from him."

"We get no real cooperation from any Tosevites," Zolraag said mournfully. "We thought you Jews were an exception, but I see it is not so."

"We owed you a lot for throwing out the Nazis and saving us from the death camps," Anielewicz said. "If you'd treated us as free people who deserved respect, we would have worked with you. But you just want to be another set of masters and treat everyone on Earth the way the Nazis treated us."

"We would not kill the way the Germans did," Zolraag protested.

"No, but you would enslave. When you were through, not a human being on this world would be free."

"I do not see that this matters," Zolraag said.

"I know you don't," Anielewicz said—sadly, for Zolraag was, given the limits of his position, a decent enough being. Some of the Germans had been that way, too; not all by any means enjoyed exterminating Jews for the sake of extermination. But enjoy it or not, they'd done it, as Zolraag resented freedom now.

That ate at Anielewicz's. Nineteen hundred years before,

Tacitus had remarked with pride that good men—the one in particular he had in mind was his father-in-law—could serve a bad Roman emperor. But when a bad ruler required good men to do monstrous things, how could they obey and remain good? He'd asked himself the question more times than he could count, but never yet found an answer.

Zolraag said, "You claim we cannot make you obey by force. I do not believe this, but you say it. Let us think ... does this language have a word for thinking of something so as to examine it?"

" 'Assume' is the word you want," Anielewicz said.

"Assume. Thank you. Let us assume, then, that what you say is true. How in this case are we to rule you Jews and have you obey our requirements?"

"I wish you would have asked that before events drove a wedge between you and us," Anielewicz answered. "The best way, I think, is not to force us to do anything that would damage the rest of mankind."

"Even the Germans?" Zolraag asked.

The Jewish fighting leader's lips curled in what was not a smile. Zolraag knew his business, sure enough. What the Nazis had done to the Jews in Poland—all over Europe—cried out for vengeance. But if the Jews collaborated with the Lizards against the Germans, how could they say no to collaborating with them against other peoples as well? That dilemma had sent Moishe Russie first into hiding and then into flight.

"Don't use us as your propaganda front." Anielewicz knew he wasn't answering directly, but he could not force himself to say yes or no. "Whether you win your war or lose it, you make the rest of the world hate us by doing that."

"Why should we care?" Zolraag asked.

The trouble was, he sounded curious, not vindictive. Sighing, Anielewicz replied, "Because that would give you your best chance of ruling here quietly. If you make other people hate us, you'll also make us hate you."

"We gave you privileges early on, because you did help us against the Germans," Zolraag said. "By our way of thinking, you abused them. Issuing threats will not make us want to give you more. You may go, *Herr* Anielewicz."

"As you say, superior sir," Anielewicz answered woodenly. *Trouble coming,* he thought as he left the Lizard governor's office. He'd managed to get Zolraag to hold off on trying to dis-

arm the Jews, or at least he thought he had, but that wasn't concession enough.

He sighed. He'd found a hiding place for Russie. Now he was liable to need one himself.

☆ **VII** ☆

"I wish we were in Denver," Barbara said.

"Well, so do I," Sam Yeager answered as he helped her out of the wagon. "The weather can't be helped, though." Late-season snowstorms had held them up as they made their way into Colorado. "Fort Collins is a pretty enough little place."

Lincoln Park, in which several Met Lab wagons were drawn up, was a study in contrasts. In the center of the square stood a log cabin, the first building that had gone up on the Poudre River. The big gray sandstone mass of the Carnegie Public Library showed how far the area had come in just over eighty years.

But Barbara said, "That's not what I mean." She took his arm and steered him away from the wagon. He looked back toward Ulhass and Ristin, decided the Lizard POWs weren't going anywhere, and let her guide him.

She led him over to a tree stump out of earshot of anybody else. "What's up?" he asked, checking the Lizards again. They hadn't poked their heads out of the wagon; they were staying down in the straw where it was warmer. He was as sure as sure could be that they wouldn't pick this moment to make a break, but ingrained duty made him keep an eye on them anyhow.

Then Barbara asked him something that sounded as if it came out of the blue: "Remember our wedding night?"

"Huh? I'm not likely to forget it." As Sam remembered, a broad smile spread over his face.

Barbara didn't smile back. "Remember what we didn't do on our wedding night?" she persisted.

"There wasn't a whole lot we didn't do on our wedding night. We—" Yeager stopped when he took a close look at

Barbara's half-worried, half-smiling expression. A light went on inside his head. Slowly, he said, "We didn't use a rubber."

"That's right," she said. "I thought it would be safe enough, and even if it wasn't—" Her smile grew broader, but still had a twist in it. "My time of the month should have started a week ago. It didn't, and I've always been very steady. So I think I'm expecting a baby, Sam."

Had it been a normal marriage in a normal time, he would have shouted, *That's wonderful!* The time was anything but normal, the marriage very new. Yeager knew Barbara hadn't wanted to get pregnant. He set down his rifle, took her in his arms. They clung to each other for a couple of minutes. "It'll work out," he said at last. "One way or another, we'll take care of it, and it'll be okay."

"I'm scared," she said. "Not many doctors, or equipment, and us in the middle of the war—"

"Denver's supposed to be better off than most places," he said. "It'll be all right, honey." *Please, God, make it all right,* he thought, something that would have been closer to a real prayer if God had given any signs lately of listening. After another few seconds, he went on, "I hope it's a girl."

"You do? Why?"

"Because she'd probably look just like you."

Her eyes widened. She stood up on tiptoe to give him a quick kiss. "You're sweet, Sam. It wasn't what I expected, but—" She kicked at the dirty snow and at the mud that showed through it. "What can you do?"

For a career minor leaguer, *What can you do?* was an article of faith that ranked right alongside the commandments Moses had brought down from the mountain. Actually, Yeager knew there was something you could do if you wanted to. But finding an abortionist wouldn't be easy, and the procedure was liable to be more dangerous than having the baby. If Barbara brought it up, he'd think about it then. Otherwise, he'd keep his mouth shut.

She said, "We'll just do the best we can, that's all. Right?"

"Sure, honey," Sam said. "Like I said, we'll manage. The idea kind of grows on me, you know what I mean?"

"Yes, I do." Barbara nodded. "I didn't want this to happen, but now that it has . . . I'm scared, as I said, but I'm excited, too. Something of ours, to go on after we're gone—that's something special, and something wonderful."

"Yeah." Yeager saw himself tying a little girl's shoes, or maybe playing catch with a boy and teaching him to hit well enough to get all the way to the top in pro ball. What the father might have done, the son *would*. He would, anyhow, if the Lizards were beaten and there ever was pro ball again. Sam should have been in spring training, getting ready for yet another season on the road, hoping to move up as better players got drafted, still with a ghostly chance at a big-league slot and glory. As it was . . .

Someone shouted, "Back to the wagons, everybody. They're going to billet us at the college on the south edge of town."

Yeager hadn't thought Fort Collins big enough to boast a college. "You never can tell," he muttered, which would have been a good handle for the whole past year. Hand in hand, he and Barbara walked back toward Ullhass and Ristin. "Careful getting up there," he warned as she scrambled in.

She made a face at him. "For God's sake, Sam, I'm not made out of cut glass. If you start treating me as if I were going to fall to pieces any minute now, we'll have trouble."

"Sorry," he said. "I've never had to worry about anybody expecting before."

The wagon driver's head whipped around. "You gonna have a baby? That's great. Congratulations!"

"Thanks," she said. As the wagon rattled forward, she shook her head wryly. Yeager knew she wasn't as delighted as she might have been. He wasn't, either. He couldn't imagine a worse time to try to raise a kid. But all they could do now was give it their best shot.

Sure enough, the Colorado State College of Agriculture and the Mechanic Arts sat on the southern border of Fort Collins. Its red and gray brick buildings clustered along an oval drive that ran through the heart of the campus. The cafeteria wasn't far from the south end of the drive. Women in surprisingly clean white dished out fried chicken and biscuits. That was good, but the burnt-grain brew they called coffee tried to bite off Yeager's tongue.

"Where do we sleep tonight?" he asked as he walked out of the cafeteria.

"Girls' dormitory," a soldier answered, pointing northward. Grinning, he went on, "Jeez, I dreamed for years of getting into one o' those, but it just ain't the same this way."

The only rooms in the dorm with doors that locked from the

outside were the rest rooms. Fortunately, it had three, so Sam didn't feel guilty about commandeering one for the Lizard prisoners to use during the night. He and Barbara had a two-coed room for themselves. Looking at the steel-framed cots, he said, "I think I'd sooner have been quartered with some nice, friendly people back in town."

"It'll be all right for one night," she said. "It's easier for them to keep track of us if we're together here instead of scattered around Fort Collins."

"I suppose so," he said, unenthusiastic still. But then, as he set his rifle down, he exclaimed, "I'm going to be a father! How about that?"

"How about that?" Barbara echoed.

Only one candle lit the room. Her face was hard to read. Electricity had taken the mystery out of night, turned it bright and certain as day. Now mystery was back, with a vengeance. Yeager studied the shifting shadows. "We'll do the best we can, that's all," he said, as he had when she first gave him the news.

"I know," she answered. "What else can we do? And," she added, "if anyone can take care of me and help me take care of a baby, I know it's you, Sam. I do love you. You know that."

"Yeah. I love you, too, hon."

She sat down on one of the cots, smiled over at him. "How shall we celebrate the news?"

"No booze around. No firecrackers . . . I guess we'll just have to make our own fireworks. How does that sound?"

"It sounds good to me." Barbara took off her shoes, then stood up for a moment so she could slide out of her slacks and panties. When she sat down again, she made a face and bounced back to her feet. "That wool blanket *scratches*. Wait a second; let me turn down the sheet."

Some happy time later, Sam asked, "Do you want me to put on a rubber, in case you're wrong?"

"Don't bother," she said. "I'm regular as clockwork; even getting sick doesn't throw me off. And I haven't been sick. The only thing that could make me this late is a bun in the oven. And since there's one in there, we don't need to worry about keeping the oven door closed."

"Okay." Sam poised himself over her. She tilted her hips up to ease his way, locked her legs and arms around him. After-

wards, he rubbed at his back; she'd clawed him pretty hard. "Maybe you should get knocked up more often," he said.

Barbara snorted and poked him in the ribs, which almost made him fall off the narrow cot. Then she leaned over and kissed him on the tip of his nose. "I love you. You're crazy."

"I'm happy, is what I am." He squeezed her against him, tight enough to make her squeak. She was all the woman he'd ever wanted and then some: pretty, bright, sensible, and, as he'd just delightedly found out again, a handful and a half in bed. And now she was going to have his baby. He stroked her hair. "I don't know how I could be any happier."

"That's a sweet thing to say. I'm happy with you, too." She took his hand, set it on her belly. "That's ours in there. I wasn't expecting it, I wasn't quite ready for it, but"—she shrugged—"it's here. I know you'll make a good father."

"A father. I don't feel like a father right now." He let his hand slide lower, through her little nest of hair to the softness it concealed. His fingertip traced small, slow circles.

"What *do* you feel like?" she whispered. The candle burned out about then. They didn't need it.

The next morning, Yeager woke still a little worn. *Feels like I played a doubleheader yesterday.* He grinned. *I did.*

The cot squeaked when he sat up. The noise woke Barbara. Her cot squeaked, too. He wondered how much racket they'd made the night before. At the time, he hadn't noticed.

Barbara rubbed her eyes, yawned, stretched, looked over at him and started to laugh. "What's so funny?" he asked. He didn't sound as grumpy as he would have a few months before; he'd finally got used—or resigned—to facing the day without coffee.

She said, "You have a large male leer pasted all over your face. That's what's funny."

"Oh." Now that he thought about it, that *was* funny. "Okay." He put his corporal's uniform back on. The last time it had been washed was in Cheyenne. He'd got used—or resigned—to dirty clothes, too. Just about everybody's clothes were dirty these days; it wasn't as if Corporal Sam Yeager stood out as a special slob. He slung his rifle over his shoulder and said, "I'm going downstairs to turn Ristin and Ullhass loose. They'll be glad to see the light of day, I expect."

"Probably. It seems mean to keep them locked up all night long." Barbara laughed again, this time at herself. "I've been

with them so long now that I think of them as people, not as Lizards."

"I know what you mean. I do the same thing myself." Yeager considered, then said, "Come on, you get dressed, too. Then we can go over to the cafeteria with them and we'll have breakfast."

Breakfast was bacon and eggs. The bacon came in great thick slices and was obviously home-cured; it took Yeager back to the smokehouse on the Nebraska farm where he'd grown up. The stuff that came in packages of cardboard and waxed paper just didn't have the same flavor.

The Lizard POWs wouldn't touch eggs, maybe because they were hatched themselves. But they loved bacon. Ristin ran his long, lizardy tongue around the edges of his mouth to get rid of grease. "That is so good," he said, adding the emphatic cough. "It reminds me of *aasson* back on Home."

"Not salty enough for *aasson*," Ullhass said. He reached for the salt shaker, poured some onto the bacon, took another bite. "Ah—better." Ristin held out his hand for the salt shaker. He, too, hissed with pleasure after he'd sprinkled the bacon.

Sam and Barbara exchanged glances: the bacon had salt enough for any human palate. In the manner of an *Astounding* reader, Yeager tried to figure out why the Lizards wanted it with even more. They'd said Home was hotter than Earth, and its seas smaller. Maybe that meant they were saltier, too, the way Salt Lake was. When he got to Denver, he'd have to ask somebody about that.

Back to the wagons. Ullhass and Ristin scrambled aboard theirs, then all but disappeared under the straw and blankets they used to fight the cold. Yeager was about to help Barbara up—no matter what she said, he wanted to make sure she took extra care of herself—when a fellow on horseback came trotting up the oval drive toward them. He was dressed in olive drab and wore a helmet instead of a cavalryman's hat, but he put Yeager in mind of the Old West just the same.

Most of the Met Lab wagons were untenanted. Some didn't even have their teams hitched to them yet: a lot of people were still eating breakfast. The rider reined in when he saw Yeager and Barbara. He called to her, "Ma'am, you wouldn't by any chance know where to find Barbara Larssen, would you?"

"I am—I was—I am Barbara Larssen," she said. "What do you want?"

"Right the first time," the cavalryman exclaimed happily. "Talk about your luck." He swung down from his horse, walked over to Barbara. *Maybe it's his boots that make him look that way,* Yeager thought. They were tall and black and shiny and looked as if they'd hurt like hell if he had to walk more than a few feet in them. He reached inside his coat, pulled out an envelope, handed it to Barbara and said, "This here is for you, ma'am." Then he stumped back to his horse, remounted, and rode off, trappings jingling, without a backward glance.

Yeager watched him go before he turned back to Barbara. "What do you suppose that's all about?" he said.

She didn't answer right away. She was staring down at the envelope. Sam took a look at it, too. It didn't have a stamp or a return address, just Barbara's name scrawled hastily across it. Her face was dead pale when she lifted it to him. "That's Jens' handwriting," she whispered.

For a couple of seconds, it didn't mean anything to Yeager. Then it did. "Oh, Jesus," he muttered. He felt as if a Lizard shell had just landed next to where he was standing. Through stunned numbness, he heard himself say, "You'd better open it."

Barbara nodded jerkily. She almost tore the letter along with the envelope. Her hands shook as she unfolded the sheet of paper. The note inside was in the same handwriting as her name had been. Yeager read over her shoulder:

Dear Barbara, I had to twist arms to get them to let me write this and send it to you, but I finally managed to do it. As you'll gather, I'm already in the town you're going toward. I had some interesting (!!) times getting back to the town from which we both left, but came through them all right. I hope you're OK, too. I'm so glad you'll be here soon—I miss you more than I can say. With all the love there is, Jens. There was a row of X's under the signature.

Barbara looked at the letter, then at Yeager, then at the letter again. She held it in her right hand. Her left hand, which didn't seem to know what her right was doing, pressed at her belly through the ratty wool sweater she was wearing.

"Oh my God," she said, maybe to herself, maybe to Yeager, and maybe to God, "what am I supposed to do now?"

"What are we supposed to do now?" Yeager echoed.

She stared at him, as if consciously reminded of his pres-

ence for the first time. Then she noticed her hand, fingers spread fan-fashion, stretched over her belly. She jerked it away.

He flinched as if she'd hit him. Her face twisted when she saw that. "Oh, Sam, I'm sorry," she exclaimed. "I didn't mean—" She started to cry. "I don't know what I meant. Everything's just turned upside down."

"Yeah," he said laconically. He startled himself by laughing.

Barbara glared through tears. "What could possibly be funny about this, this—" She gave up in the middle of the sentence. Yeager didn't blame her. No words were strong enough to fit the mess they'd just landed in.

He said, "Last night I found out I was going to be a father, and now I don't even know if I'm a husband any more. If that isn't funny, what is?"

He wondered if it would be too risqué for Hollywood to touch. Probably. Too bad. He could all but see Katharine Hepburn and Cary Grant and somebody else—Robert Young, maybe—to play the guy who didn't get her, all of them going through their antics bigger than life up on the screen. It would be a great way to kill a couple of hours, and you'd come out of the theater holding your sides.

But it wasn't the same when it really happened to you, not when you were wondering whether you had the Cary Grant part or the Robert Young one . . . and when you were afraid you knew the answer.

Barbara's small smile was the sun coming out from behind rain clouds. "That is funny. Like something out of a silly movie—"

"I just thought the very same thing," he said eagerly. Any sign that they were on the same wavelength felt doubly welcome.

The clouds covered the sun again. Barbara said, "Somebody's going to get hurt, Sam; I'm going to have to hurt somebody I love. That's the last thing in the world I want, but I don't see how I can help it."

"I don't, either," Yeager said. He did his best not to show his worry, his fear. It wouldn't help, any more than it would have at the tryout for his first pro team half a lifetime ago. Would he make it or wouldn't he?

Show them or not, the worry and fear were there. How could Barbara pick him? She'd been married to Jens for years and years, while she'd only known him a matter of months,

and they hadn't even been lovers for most of that time. And besides, with a choice between a nuclear physicist and a minor league outfielder with an ankle that told him when it was gonna rain, whom would she take?

But she was carrying his kid. That had to count for something. Didn't it? Lord, if this was any kind of normal time, lawyers would be coming out of the woodwork like cockroaches. Maybe cops, too. Bigamy, adultery . . . Maybe the chaos the Lizard invasion had brought wasn't such a bad thing after all.

He sucked in a deep breath. "Honey?"

"What is it?" Barbara asked warily. She'd been reading the letter again. He couldn't blame her for that, either, but just the same he wished she hadn't been.

He took her hands in his. She let him do it, but she didn't grab hold of him back the way she usually did. The edge of the sheet of paper scraped against the side of his palm. He made himself ignore it, concentrated on what he had to do as if he were trying to pick up the spin of a curveball right out of the pitcher's hand.

"Honey," he said again, and then paused to feel for the perfect words even though Barbara knew a thousand times more about words than he'd learn if he lived to be a hundred. He went on, one tough phrase at a time, "Honey, the most important thing in the whole world for me—is for you to be happy. So you—go ahead and do—whatever it is you've got to do—and that'll be all right with me. Because I love you and—like I said—I want you to be happy."

She started crying again, hard this time, and buried her head in the hollow of his shoulder. "What am I supposed to do, Sam?" she said between sobs, her voice so small and broken he could hardly understand her. "I love you, too, and Jens. And the baby—"

He kept his arms around her. He wasn't more than an inch from breaking down and blubbering himself, either. Enrico Fermi picked that precise moment to walk up, hand in hand with his wife Laura. "Is something wrong?" he asked, concern in his accented voice.

"You might say so, sir," Yeager answered. Then he remembered the physicist needed to know Jens Larssen was alive, too. He patted Barbara on the back and said, "Honey, you'd better show Dr. Fermi the letter."

She handed it to Fermi. The physicist put on reading glasses, peered owlishly through them at the sheet of paper. "But this is wonderful news!" he exclaimed, his face lighting up in a smile. He spoke rapidly in Italian to his wife. She answered more hesitantly. Fermi's smile went out. "Oh," he said. "It is, ah, complicated." He nodded to himself, pleased at finding the right word. "*Sì*, complicated."

"It sure is," Yeager said bleakly.

"It's more than just complicated," Barbara added. "I'm going to have a baby."

"Oh," Fermi said again, this time echoed by Laura. He tried again: "Oh, my." He was completely at home in abstruse realms of thought which Sam Yeager knew he could never enter. But when it came to merely human ways of messing up your life, the Nobel laureate was just as lost as anybody else. Somehow that heartened Sam.

"We like to say congratulations." Laura Fermi's accent was thicker than her husband's. She spread her hands helplessly. "But—"

"Yeah," Yeager said. "But—"

Fermi handed the letter back to Barbara. He said, "You are good people. One way or another, I am sure you will work this out in the fashion that is best for all of you." He touched a hand to the brim of his hat and walked on with his wife.

At first, Yeager was touched at the physicist's compliment. Then he realized Fermi had just said, *It's not my problem, Jack.* He started to get angry. But what was the point of that? The man was right. One way or another, he and Barbara and Jens would work it out.

The only trouble was, he had no idea what that way might be.

They made about thirteen miles that day, almost all of them in silence. Barbara seemed lost in her own thoughts, and Sam didn't want to break in. He had plenty on his mind, too; maybe she also avoided intruding on him. Ullhass and Ristin, oblivious to what was going on around them, chattered with each other, but whenever they ventured into English, the answers they got were so monosyllabic, they soon gave up.

The St. Louis Hotel on St. Louis Avenue in Loveland had seen better days. The food wasn't up to college cafeteria standards, and the room Sam and Barbara got wasn't much bigger than the one at the college dorm. It wasn't very clean, either.

It had a double bed. At first Sam was glad to see that; sleep-

ing with Barbara warm and soft beside him was one of the joys of his life. Doing other things on a roomy mattress was wonderful, too. Or it had been, anyhow.

Barbara looked at the bed, at him, back again. He could see the same set of thoughts going through her mind as were in his. He didn't say anything. It wasn't really up to him.

Barbara quickly scanned the rest of the room. Other than the bed, it held only a night table, a couple of rickety chairs, and a chamber pot—the plumbing didn't work, then. She shook her head. "I'm not going to put you on the floor, Sam," she said. "That wouldn't be right."

"Thank you, hon." He'd slept hard while he was out in the field against the Lizards. He knew he could do it . . . but doing it with his wife in the room would have been unbearably lonely.

"This is even more complicated than I thought it was going to be," Barbara said. She managed a shaky laugh. "They said it couldn't be done."

"Yeah—tell me about it." Sam sat down on one of the chairs, pulled off his shoes and let them fall to the threadbare carpet with two loud clunks.

Barbara peeled back the bedspread. The blankets underneath were the best thing about the room; there were lots of them and they were nice and thick. She clucked approvingly, opened her suitcase and took out a long cotton flannel nightgown. "We won't have to sleep in all our clothes tonight," she said. She reached up to her neck to pull off her sweater, then froze, her eyes on Sam.

"Do you want me to turn my back?" he asked, though every word hurt.

He watched her think about it. That hurt, too. But finally she shook her head. "No, never mind, don't be silly," she said. "I mean, we're married, after all—kind of married, anyway."

Kind of married, indeed, Yeager thought, and had another vision of swarming lawyers. He got out of his shirt and chinos while she was taking off the sweater and slacks. The flannel nightgown rustled as it slid down over her smooth skin. He liked to sleep with as few clothes as the weather would allow. Tonight, with all those heavy blankets, that meant socks and boxer shorts and undershirt. He dove under the covers in a hurry; the room itself was cold.

Barbara slipped in beside him. She blew out the candle on

the night table. Darkness enfolded them; with the blinds closed and the curtains drawn, it was almost absolute. "Good night, honey," he said, and without thinking, leaned over for a kiss. He got it, but her lips didn't welcome his the way they had before.

He got back to his own side of the bed in a hurry. They lay together on the same mattress, but a Maginot Line might have sprung up between them. He sighed and wondered if he'd ever go to sleep. He tossed and turned and turned and tossed and felt Barbara doing the same, but they were both careful not to bump into each other. After some time that seemed forever but probably was before midnight, he drifted off.

He woke in the wee small hours, needing to use the chamber pot. Regardless of how he and Barbara had kept apart from each other awake, they'd come together in sleep, maybe for warmth, maybe for no real reason at all. Her nightgown had ridden up a lot; her bare thigh sprawled across his legs.

He cherished the feeling, wondering if he'd ever know it again, wondering if he was just sticking pins in himself for staying with her now when he didn't think she'd end up picking him. But what the hell? He'd played umpteen seasons of ball, stubbornly hoping he'd catch a break. Why be different here?

And he did have to use the pot. He slid away as gently as he could, hoping not to wake her. But he did; the mattress shifted as her head came off the pillow. "Sorry, hon," he whispered. "I need to get up for a second."

"It's okay," she whispered back. "I have to do the same thing. Go ahead and go first." She rolled over to her own side, but not, this time, as if she thought she'd get leprosy from touching him. He groped around by the bed, found the chamber pot, did what he had to do, and handed the pot to her.

The flannel nightgown rustled again as she hiked it up. She used the pot, too, then slid it out of the way and got back into bed. Yeager did, too. "Good night again," he said.

"Good night, Sam." To his surprise and delight, Barbara slid across to his side of the bed and gave him a hug. His arms slid around her, squeezed her to him. She was good to hang on to in the middle of the night. Too soon, though, she slipped away, and he knew that if he tried to hold her there, he was liable to lose her forever.

He tossed and turned for another long while before he went

back to sleep. He wondered what that hug meant for his future, trying to read it the same way he'd tried to gauge managers' oracular pronouncements in years gone by to see whether he was liable to get promoted or shipped down.

As with a lot of those pronouncements, he couldn't figure out exactly what the hug foretold. He just knew he was gladder with it than he would have been without it. He also knew this mess wouldn't unravel quickly, no matter what. More than the other, that thought calmed him and helped him fall asleep at last.

Heinrich Jäger set a hand on the stowage compartment that rode atop the track assembly of his Panther. The steel was warm against his palm—spring came to France more quickly than to Germany, and far more quickly than to the Soviet Union, where he'd waited out last winter.

The panzer crews stood by their machines, waiting for him to speak. Sunlight dappled down through trees in new leaf. With their black coveralls, the tankers looked like splotches of shadow. Their panzers were painted in what the camouflage experts called ambush pattern—red-brown and green splotches over ocher, and then smaller ocher patches over the red-brown and green. It was the best scheme the *Wehrmacht* had come up with for making its vehicles invisible from the air. Whether it was good enough—they were about to find out.

"Fuel pump aside," Jäger said, giving his Panther an affectionate thwack, "this is the best human-made panzer in the world." The crewmen of the Tigers attached to his unit glared at him, as he'd known they would. They liked their massive beasts' 88mm gun better than the Panther's 75, even if the Panther was more maneuverable and had its armor properly sloped.

"But," Jäger went on, and let the word hang in the air, "if you try to fight the Lizards straight up with your machines, the only thing you'll do is get yourselves killed. The Fatherland can't afford that. Remember it. Think of yourselves as going up against T-34s in a Panzer II."

That got their attention in the way he wanted. Next to one of the tough Soviet machines, a Panzer II, with its 20mm cannon and cardboard-thin protection, was a crew's worth of "sad duty to inform you" letters waiting to happen. And yet, despite

Without much hope and without fear, they'd try to accomplish it.

Jäger climbed up onto the turret of his Panther, slid down inside through the open cupola. Beneath and behind him, the big Maybach engine thundered into life. He wished it were a diesel like the ones the Russians used; a petrol power plant didn't just burn when it got hit—it exploded.

"Down the road southwest," he told the driver over the intercom. "We're looking for good defensive positions, remember. We want to be in ambush before we run into the Lizards nosing north from Besançon."

As seemed their habit since the blitzkrieg that followed their arrival on Earth, the Lizards were moving on Belfort slowly and methodically—with luck, even more slowly than they'd planned, because they had a way of overreacting to harassment fire from German infantry and French guerrillas. With more luck, Jäger's panzer regiment—panzer combat group was a better name for it, given the mixed and mixed-up nature of his command—would slow them further. With a whole lot more luck, he might even stop them.

The Panther had a much smoother ride than the Panzer III in which he'd advanced into Russia. The interleaved road wheels had a lot to do with that. Not feeling as if his kidneys were shaking loose was a pleasant novelty. Now if the damned fuel pump wouldn't keep breaking down . . .

In spite of the engine's rumble and the rattle and squeak and grind of the treads, riding with his head and shoulders out of the cupola was pleasant on a bright spring day. New grass sprouted in meadows and in cracks in the macadam of the road. In a normal year, traffic would have smashed that latter hopeful growth flat, but the column of German panzers might have been the first motorized traffic the road had known in months. Here and there in the grass, wildflowers made bright splashes of red and yellow and blue. The air itself smelled green and growing.

To Jäger's right, Klaus Meinecke sneezed sharply, once, twice, three times. The gunner pulled a handkerchief from the breast pocket of his tunic, and let out a long, mournful honk. "I hate springtime," he mumbled. His eyes were puffy and tracked with red. "Miserable hay fever kills me every year."

Nothing makes everybody happy, Jäger thought. They ran through Montbéliard, where the big Peugeot works stood idle

for want of fuel and raw materials, then followed the road that paralleled the Doubs River southwest toward Besançon—and toward the Lizards surely on the way up toward Belfort.

Jäger's head swiveled up and down, back and forth, watching every moment for the airplane or helicopter that could turn his panzer into a funeral pyre. Meinecke chuckled. "You've got the *deutsche Blick* all right, Colonel," he said.

"The German glance?" Jäger echoed, puzzled. "What's that?"

"They recruited me for Panthers out of the Afrika Korps, not the Russian war," the gunner explained. "It was a joke we made there, a takeoff on the *deutsche Gruss*, the German salute. We were always on the lookout for aircraft, first British, then from the Lizards. Spot one and it was time to find a hole in the ground."

Before the Lizards came, Jäger had envied the tankers who fought in North Africa. The war against the British there was clean, gentlemanly—*war as it should be,* he thought. Both sides in Russia had fought as viciously as they could. Jäger thought of the massacres of Jews at Babi Yar and other places. A miracle the Polish Jews hadn't killed him on his way back to Germany.

He didn't care to brood on that too long; it made him wonder about what his country had been doing in the lands it had conquered. Instead he said, "So what was it like in the desert after the Lizards came?"

"Bad," Meinecke answered. "We'd been beating the British, they were brave, but their panzers didn't match up to ours, and their tactics were pretty bad. If we'd had proper supplies, we'd have mopped them up, but everything kept going to the Eastern Front."

"We never had enough, either," Jäger put in.

"Maybe not, Colonel, but a lot even of what was supposed to go to us ended up on the bottom of the Mediterranean. But you asked about the Lizards. They mopped up the Tommies and us both. They *liked* the desert, and we couldn't hide from their planes there. Talk about the *deutsche Blick—Gott in Himmel!* The Tommies had it, too."

"Misery loves company," Jäger said. Then, still looking around, he suddenly called "Halt!" to the Panther's driver.

The big battle tank slowed, stopped. Jäger stood tall in the cupola, waving the column to a halt behind him. He studied

the little ridge that rose off to one side of the road. It was covered with old brush and saplings, and its crest could have been more than four hundred meters from the roadway. He'd have to scout out what lay behind, check his line of retreat—the one thing you couldn't do was stand toe-to-toe with the Lizards, or before long you wouldn't have any toes left.

He ordered the Panther up the rise to the crest. The longer he looked at the setup, the better he liked it. He didn't think he'd come across a better defensive position, anyhow.

At his command, most of the German panzers deployed hull down on the reverse slope of the ridge line. He sent three or four Panzer IVs and a Tiger forward to meet the Lizards ahead of his main position and, with luck, bring them back all unsuspecting into the ambush he'd set up.

That left nothing to do but wait and stay alert. In back of the ridge lay a pond fed by a small stream. A fish leaped out of the water after a fly, fell back with a splash. Somewhere in his gear, Jäger had a couple of hooks and a length of light line. Pan-fried trout or pike sounded a lot better to him than the miserable rations he'd been eating.

A Frenchman in civilian clothes came out of the bushes on the far side of the pond. Jäger wasn't surprised to see he had a rifle on his back. He waved to the Frenchman, who returned the gesture before stepping back into the undergrowth. Before the Lizards came, the French underground had nipped at the Germans who occupied their country. Now they worked together against the new invaders: in French eyes, the Germans were the lesser of two evils.

That's something, anyhow, Jäger thought. In Poland, the Lizards had seemed the lesser of two evils to the Jews. From what he'd learned, he couldn't blame them for feeling that way.

A couple of times, he'd tried talking with officers he trusted about what Germany had done in the east. It hadn't worked: he'd been met by a refusal to listen that almost amounted to saying, *I don't want to know.* He hadn't brought up the subject now for some time.

Away in the distance, he heard the harsh, abrupt bark of a panzer cannon. At the same time, a shout sounded in his earphones: "Engaging lead element of enemy panzer column! Will attempt to carry out plan as outlined. Will—" The transmission cut off abruptly; Jäger feared he knew why.

More booms: from the Panzer IV's 75mm guns; heavier,

deeper ones from the Tiger's 88; and, sharp as thunderclaps, from the Lizards' cannon. Then another sort of roar, lower and more diffuse, with smaller blasts and cheery *pop-pop*s all mixed in with it. That was the sound of a panzer brewing up.

"Armor-piercing," Jäger said quietly. The loader slammed a black-nosed shell into the breech of the cannon. Out of sight down the road, another panzer exploded. Jäger bit his lip; those were men, comrades-in-arms, dying nastily. *And,* the officer part of him whispered, *if all my panzers get killed before any make it back here, what good is my ambush?* He was inured to sacrificing men; throwing them away was something else again.

He stood up in the cupola, made a hand sign: *be ready.* Panzer commanders passed it down the line. He didn't want to use radio, not now. The Lizards were too good at picking up their foes' signals. As if from very far away, he felt his heart thudding in his chest, his bowels loosening. That was what fear did to your body. It didn't have to rule you if you didn't let it.

Up the road, motor going flat out, men inside probably shaken to blood pudding, raced a Panzer IV. It sounded like an explosion in a smithy, roaring and clattering and clanking as if it were about to fall to pieces.

Behind it, almost silent by comparison, glided a Lizard panzer, then another and another and another. Jäger knew they were toying with the Panzer IV. They had a way of stabilizing their guns so they shot accurately even on the move, but they were enjoying the chase for a while before they ended it.

Let's see how they enjoy this, he thought, and yelled, "Fire!"

Because his head was outside the cupola, the bellow of the cannon half stunned him. Flame and smoke spurted from the gun's muzzle. "Hit!" he cried in delight. It was a solid hit, too, right at the join between the turret and body of the Lizard panzer. The turret tilted, almost torn out of its ring; Jäger wouldn't have wanted to be inside when that 6.8-kilo round came knocking.

But the Lizards made their panzers tough. That shell would have torn the turret right off a British tank or a Soviet T-34, and turned either of them into an inferno on the instant. Not only did this one not catch fire, its driver threw it into reverse and did his best to escape the trap in which he found himself. "Hit him again!" Jäger shouted. His gunner required no urging—the second shot punctuated Jäger's sentence.

All the rest of the hull-down German panzers along the ridge line opened up, too. The Lizards offered them a target tankers dream about: the less heavily armored flanks and engine compartments of their vehicles. One of those vehicles brewed up in a flash of orange and blue flame—somebody's round had penetrated to something vital. Jäger wondered if that had been a Panther's kill or a Tiger's: the heavier panzer's 88 fired a correspondingly more massive shell, but the Panther's gun had a higher muzzle velocity and would pierce just as much armor, maybe more.

The Lizards did not react well to being taken in flank. Jäger had counted on that: they were even more vulnerable to the unexpected than Soviet troops. For a crucial few seconds, they either tried to back out of trouble like the panzer Jäger had hit or traversed their turrets toward the concealed German armor without shifting the tanks themselves. That let the Germans keep pounding away at their more vulnerable sides and rears. Another Lizard panzer turned into a fireball, then another.

But the Lizards did not stay stupid forever. One by one, they turned toward the Germans' fire. No German panzer gun could beat their front glacis plates. Jäger's gunner tried. His shell buried itself almost to the drive bands, but did no damage anyone could find.

Then the aliens started shooting back. They had only small targets at which to aim, but they didn't need anything big: their fire-control arrangements were even better than the ones the new Panthers boasted. And while a Panther shell couldn't quite shift one of their turrets, the Lizards' projectiles smashed German panzer turrets as if they were anvils dropping on cockroaches.

Two tanks down from Jäger, a Panzer IV was abruptly beheaded. Shells cooking off inside, its turret smashed down the rear slope of the ridge and skidded into the pond. The hull exploded in flames, too, and started a fire in the brush.

Then a Tiger got hit. Its turret flew off, too, which rocked Jäger; he'd hoped the 100mm of armor there might be proof against anything the Lizards could throw at it. No such luck, though. Now he got on the radio. "Fall back!" he ordered. Keep things moving, keep them confused: that was how you got whatever chance you had against the Lizards. In a set-piece battle, you were dead.

As if he were back on the other side of the rise, Jäger saw

what the Lizard panzer commander would be thinking: if they came straight up the slope and charged after the retreating Germans, they'd keep presenting their invulnerable frontal armor to his comrades and him. Then they could destroy the panzer force at their convenience and press on up the road toward Belfort.

He got on the command frequency again: "Peel off to either side as you retreat. We'll want to get some decent shots at their flanks when they come after us."

His Panther backed through the little stream that fed the pond; water sprayed up on either side. Sure enough, just as he'd guessed, a couple of Lizard panzers breasted the rise and advanced on the Germans. They were too confident of their own invincibility; had he been an instructor on a training ground, he would have lowered their mark. The proper tactical solution was to stay hull down on the reverse slope and pound the Germans while exposing as little of themselves as possible.

He remembered his first big fight with the Lizard panzers, in the Ukraine. They'd made the same mistake then, and he'd killed one of their tanks with a Panzer III—he was one of a bare handful of German tankers who could say that.

This time, though, he didn't get a chance to put a shell into the enemy's belly, where his armor was thinnest. One of the Lizards fired. A Panzer IV went up in gouts of flame. But the Germans were hitting back, too, and their high-velocity armor-piercing shells could hurt the Lizards when they hit the right spot. One of the Lizard panzers slewed to a halt, road wheels wrecked by a shell. That made the machine only marginally less dangerous; its main armament still worked, and its turret swung toward a Panther. It took the German panzer out with one shell straight through the sloped front plate that was supposed to deflect enemy fire.

More rounds slammed into the disabled Lizard panzer. Hatches popped open in the turret and at the driver's position in the front of the hull. Lizards jumped out. Machine guns chattered. The Lizards went down. Jäger felt some sympathy for them—they'd fought bravely, if not with a lot of brains. That didn't keep him from yelling like a wild-west Indian when they fell.

A moment after the last Lizard bailed out and was shot down, the disabled panzer brewed up. A smoke ring, perfect as any an old man with a cigar in his mouth might make but

twenty times as big, blew out of the commander's open cupola. Then all the ammunition stowed in there must have cooked off at once, for the panzer went up in a fireball that sent blazing debris flying for a hundred meters.

A Lizard helicopter fluttered over the ridge just then, rockets stabbing out from it like knives of fire. Machine gunners opened up on it, but it was armed against their fire. But a Panzer IV, traversing its cannon toward the second Lizard tank, happened to line up on the flying machine. Jäger never knew whether the commander gave the order or the gunner acted on his own initiative. Either way, the 75mm shell tore through the helicopter's belly and swatted it out of the air in flames. Jäger screamed with delight.

The commander of the other Lizard panzer that had come over the ridge should have pulled back then. The panzer's turret swung back and forth, as if the Lizards inside couldn't make up their minds on a target. The Germans had no such hesitation—and Panthers and Tigers, though far from a match for the Lizard machine, could hurt it when they got a chance like this one. Even the new Panzer IVs, though hideously vulnerable to return fire, had in their long 75s main armament little inferior to what the Panthers carried.

When the Lizard did decide to go back, it was too late. Smoke and almost transparent blue flames boiled from the enemy panzer's engine compartment. That crew bailed out, too. Jäger didn't know if they all perished; the smoke was too thick for him to be sure. If they didn't, though, it wasn't for lack of effort.

"Forward the Panthers," he ordered. "Tigers and IVs lay back to support."

"How many Panthers are still running?" Klaus Meinecke asked. Jäger blinked; the gunner's question hadn't occurred to him, but it was a damn good one. It would be a hell of a thing to go swarming over the ridge to confront the Lizards ... alone. But no. At least two other machines rumbled past the flaming hulks of friends and foes to renew the fight against the Lizards on the Belfort road.

The smartest thing the Lizards could have done was to keep right on moving toward Belfort, make the Germans react to them. With their rotten fuel pumps, the Panthers would surely have broken down if pushed hard. And the Lizard panzers were faster than the ones Jäger commanded, anyhow. Guderian

and Manstein had invented the drill: first force your opening, then worry about what happens next.

But the Lizards in this column didn't have a Guderian leading them. Jäger stuck his head and torso out of the cupola to see what they were about. They still waited on the road, face-on toward the ridge line. "Halt hull down," he called to his comrades. He also ordered his own panzer to halt; no sense in exposing more of it to enemy fire than he had to.

For the moment, standoff. Jäger saw no point in firing from his present position. He'd just waste ammunition and announce to the Lizards where he was. About the only way he could hurt them from here would be to put one right down a cannon barrel. He laughed at that and muttered, "If I want a miracle, I'll ask for it in church."

The Lizards weren't eager to swarm up the ridge any more, though, not when the two that had tried it didn't come back. They weren't used to armor fights where their foes had a decent chance of doing them in. Jäger didn't think they were afraid; he'd stopped underestimating enemies after his first couple of weeks in Russia. He did think he'd made the Lizards thoughtful.

He was about to order his reserves to try a flanking maneuver using the ridge for cover when a shell slammed into the side of the northernmost Lizard panzer. Another followed a few seconds later and set the armored vehicle ablaze. Jäger was still trying to figure out who was doing the shooting when the Lizard crew bailed out of their panzer and ran for the brush. Machine-gun fire cut them down.

Jäger whooped. "It's that Panzer IV!" he yelled. "They should have chased it down and killed it, but they got busy with us and forgot all about it." He'd forgotten all about it, too, but he didn't have to admit that, even to himself.

The Lizards certainly had left it out of their plans. Its unexpected return to action did the same thing to them that the unexpected in combat often did to the Russians: it panicked them and sent them into a retreat they didn't have to make. Jäger fired a couple of rounds at them from the ridge line, just to remind them he was there, but didn't pursue—coming out into the open against them was asking to get shot up.

Klaus Meinecke looked up from his gunsight, a grin stretched wide across his face. "By God, Colonel, they're as

sensitive about their flanks as any virgin I ever tried to lay," he exclaimed.

"So they are." Jäger laughed, too, but under the coarse joke lay a grain of truth. He had seen the same thing fighting the Red Army. Come straight at them and they'd die in place by thousands sooner than yielding a meter of ground. Flank them out—or even threaten to flank them out—and they were liable to run like rabbits. Half to himself, he said, "They aren't quick to adapt, not even a little."

"No, sir," the gunner agreed. "And they've paid for being slow, that they have."

"You're right." Jäger sounded wondering, even to himself. His men had killed at least five Lizard panzers—to say nothing of a helicopter—in this fight. They'd lost more than that— Tigers, Panthers, Panzer IVs—but they'd done the enemy some real damage. He wondered how long it had taken the *Wehrmacht*'s armor to kill five Lizard panzers last year. Weeks probably, maybe months. Panzer IIs, Panzer IIIs, Czech machines impressed into action, Panzer IVs with the stubby 75mm guns for infantry support—they were all toys, set against the Lizards' tanks.

He must have said that aloud, for Meinecke answered, "That was last year. This is now. And who knows what they'll come up with next? Maybe a Tiger with sloped armor and a really long-barreled 88. That'd make the Lizards sit up and think."

It made Jäger sit up and think, too. He liked the idea. Then he looked around again. Now he didn't see smoke and flame and shattered flesh and metal. He saw that his comrades were still here and the Lizards had fled. "We held the position," he exclaimed.

"We did, by God!" The gunner sounded as surprised— almost dazed—as Jäger felt. "I'm not used to that."

"Nor I," Jäger said. "I've been part of a partisan raid that stung them, but every time I went up against them in regular combat, I always ended up retreating ... till now." He started thinking about what needed to happen next. "Now we can bring some infantry forward, send 'em down the road to screen for us."

"Infantry!" Meinecke spoke the word with a tanker's ingrained scorn. "What's infantry going to do against panzers?"

"Give us warning when they're on the move, if nothing else," Jäger answered. "Snipers may pick off a commander or

two; the Lizards come out of their cupolas when they think it's safe, same as we do. Maybe even an unbuttoned driver. And I hear they're going to get some sort of antipanzer rocket the Americans have passed on to us."

"That'd be something, if it works," the gunner said. "The Lizards have hurt us plenty with rockets."

"I know. They've hurt us with their panzers, too, a lot worse than they did today." Jäger scratched his head. His hair was matted with greasy sweat. "I haven't seen them foolish that way before—those couple that charged straight at us. They should have known better. I wonder why they didn't."

"Don't know that, sir," Meinecke said, "but I'm not going to complain about it. You?"

"No," Jäger said.

Ussmak desperately wanted a taste of ginger. He needed to feel strong and bright and in control of things, even if he knew he wasn't. Back in the turret of the landcruiser, Hessef and Tvenkel were undoubtedly dipping their tongues into the supply of the drug they'd brought along. Undoubtedly, too, it made them see the fight from which they'd just retreated as a small thing, hardly more than some cracked pavement on the path to the Race's inevitable victory.

Ussmak wished he could feel the same way. But no matter how much he craved ginger, he didn't trust it any more. Ginger could make you do stupid things, things stupid enough to get you killed. Two landcruisers had swarmed over that rise after the Deutsche. Neither one had come back.

Everything had seemed so easy when he started out on the plains of the SSSR: easier even than the training simulators, for those had assumed an opposition of a quality to match his own, and the Soviets' machines didn't come close, while their tactics weren't anything special, either.

When he'd got into Besançon, the males had warned him the Deutsche were better at armored warfare. Now he knew what they'd meant. Nobody'd paid any attention to that rise until the Deutsche started shooting from it. They'd lured the Race's landcruisers right into an ambush, he realized. They were just Big Uglies—they shouldn't have been able to trick males of the Race like that.

And their landcruisers weren't just inflammable targets any more. These were a lot bigger and heavier than the Soviet

tanks he'd faced in the SSSR, let alone the little Deutsch models. Their guns could hurt, too.

Hessef's voice came over the audio button taped to Ussmak's hearing diaphragm: "Come on back here. We've got enough herb to share with you, even if you didn't bring any of your own."

"I'll be there soon, superior sir," Ussmak answered. Just blind luck, he thought, that Hessef hadn't gone charging after the Big Uglies himself and gotten his landcruiser—and Ussmak with it—blown to bits.

He wanted to pop the hatch above his reclining seat and get a little fresh if chilly air, but he knew that wasn't a good idea. The side of the road closer to the river offered no cover for Big Uglies with guns, but any number of Tosevite raiders might be lurking in the woods that led up onto the mountain slopes to the west, just waiting for a male to show himself, even for a moment.

As with landcruisers, the Big Uglies' personal weapons were less effective than those of the Race: most of their individual firearms could shoot only one bullet at a time, while their machine guns were too heavy and clumsy to be easily portable. As with the landcruisers again, though, you didn't want to make a mistake or you'd find that one of those inferior weapons was plenty good enough to kill you.

Ussmak crawled back through the fighting compartment, then, and stuck his head up through the opening in the bottom of the turret. "Here you are, just another shell to be expended," Tvenkel exclaimed. "Well, as long as you are here, you might as well have a taste."

Before Ussmak could say no as he'd intended, his tongue shot out and licked the little mound of ginger from the palm of the gunner's hand. He opened and closed his jaws several times, gulped the powder down his throat.

"That's *good*," he exclaimed. With the herb buzzing through him, he felt like a brand-new male. All his worries, all his fears, ebbed away. "I wish we had the Big Uglies in our sights again." Part of him knew that was just the ginger talking, but none of him cared.

"So do I," Tvenkel said fiercely. "If they think I'd miss 'em again at that range, I tell you they're wrong."

So Tvenkel had missed when he should have hit, had he? Under the influence of the ginger, Ussmak felt almost as much

contempt for him as he did for the Big Uglies. *The bungling incompetent couldn't hit a city if he was in the middle of it,* he thought.

Hessef said, "We didn't do as well as we should have." His voice held melancholy uncertainty; the drug was wearing off, leaving crushing sadness and emptiness behind. He also sounded more thoughtful than usual as he continued, "Maybe Ussmak is right: maybe we should go into combat without tasting first."

"I think that would be a good idea, superior sir," Ussmak said. At the moment, he would have thought any ideas good that agreed with his own. He went on, "We may think we do well when we taste the herb, but in fact we don't." The contrast between belief and reality hit him with stunning force, almost as if his own words came not from his mouth but from one of the great departed Emperors of the past.

"It may be so," Hessef agreed mournfully. He was sliding down from his peak of omnipotent euphoria, sure enough.

"Nonsense, superior sir." Tvenkel must have had another taste just before he gave one to Ussmak, for he still sounded ginger-certain about things. "Just bad luck, that's all. Can't hit everything all the time—and these Big Uglies had the advantage of position on us."

"Yes, and how did they get it?" Ussmak answered his own question: "They got it because we rushed ahead without taking proper notice of our surroundings and we did that because too many of us were tasting." His mouth fell open. Here he was complaining about tasting while he had a head full of ginger. The irony struck him as deliciously funny.

"We should smash them anyhow," Tvenkel declared.

"When we first landed, we would have, I think," Hessef said. "Now we face tougher landcruisers . . . and ours remain the same."

"Still better by far than anything the Big Uglies have," Tvenkel said with an angry hiss; the herb was making him confident to the point of being combative. "Even these new machines are slow and weak next to ours."

"That's so," Hessef said, "but they're not as slow or as weak as the ones we met before. And who can say what the Tosevites will build next?" He shivered a little. Just as Tvenkel was arrogant under the influence of ginger and ignored real

problems, Hessef saw those problems magnified in the depression that came when the drug wore off.

"If we conquer them, they won't build anything next," Tvenkel said.

Ussmak liked that idea. Since he was riding his taste of ginger up to the heights, he felt as Tvenkel did: that the Race could accomplish whatever it desired, and that nothing would be allowed to stand in its way. But he had learned that what he felt when he tasted was not to be relied upon, which was something few other ginger tasters seemed to have realized. He tried to stand outside himself, to look at what the ginger did to him as if it were happening to someone else.

He said, "We had better conquer them soon, or they will build their new machines. And every one they do build makes them that much harder to overcome."

"Retreating from their landcruisers isn't going to make conquering them any easier," Hessef said, almost moaning. "But losing five machines in battle against them doesn't get the job done, either. The Emperor only knows what they're saying about that back in Besançon." He cast down his eyes at the mention of the Race's sovereign, and didn't raise them again right away. Sure enough, after-ginger depression held him in its claws.

"Superior sir, what you need is another taste," Tvenkel said. He took out a vial of ginger, poured some into his hand, offered it to Hessef. The landcruiser commander's tongue flicked out. The powdered drug disappeared.

"Ah, that's better," Hessef said as the ginger began to take hold of him once more.

"Why is it better?" Ussmak wondered aloud. "The world is still the same as it was before you tasted, so how have things really changed?"

"They've changed because now I have this lovely powder inside of me. No matter how ugly the Big Uglies outside the landcruiser are, I don't have to worry about it. All I have to do is sit here in my seat and not think about a thing."

And if some Tosevite chooses this moment to sneak up on us with a satchel charge, we're all liable to die because you're not thinking. Ussmak held that to himself. Despite all he'd been through, despite the herb coursing through him, the subordination drilled into him since his hatchling days remained strong.

In any case, he didn't think the Big Uglies had pursued the Race's retreating landcruisers. Why should they have? They'd kept the Race from pushing north, which was what they'd had in mind. They didn't have to conquer, they just had to resist. *For how long?* Ussmak wondered. The answer slammed into him like a cannon shell: *till we have no equipment left.*

Five landcruisers gone today in this engagement alone. Hessef was right: they would be gnashing their teeth in Besançon over that news. Ussmak wondered how many landcruisers the Race had left, all over Tosev 3. In the first heady days of the invasion, it hadn't seemed to matter. They advanced as they would, and swept all before them. They didn't sweep any more; they had to fight. And when they fought, they got hurt.

Oh, so did the Tosevites. Though his ginger euphoria was starting to ebb, Ussmak still acknowledged that. Even in the botched engagement from which the Race's landcruisers had just retreated, they'd killed many more enemy vehicles than they'd lost themselves. When transcribing his after-action report onto disk, the unit commander would probably be able to present the engagement as a victory.

But it wasn't a victory. The clarity of thought the drug brought to Ussmak let him see that only too well. The Big Uglies were losing landcruisers at a prodigal rate, yes, but they were still making them, too, and making them better than they had before. Ussmak wondered how many landcruisers remained aboard the freighters that had fetched them from Home. Even more than that, he wondered what the Race would do when no more landcruisers were left on those freighters.

When he said that aloud, Hessef answered, "That's why we'd better conquer quickly: if we don't, we'll have nothing left to do the job with." Even the landcruiser commander's new taste of ginger didn't keep him from seeing as much for himself.

"We'll beat them. It's our destiny—we are the Race," Tvenkel said. The herb left him confident still. He gave his gun's autoloader an affectionate slap.

Thus reminded of the device, Hessef said, "We ought to perform maintenance on that gadget. We expended a lot of rounds today. It goes out of adjustment easily, and then we're left with main armament that won't shoot."

"It'll be all right, superior sir," Tvenkel said. "If it hasn't gone wrong, odds are it won't."

Ussmak expected Hessef to come down angrily on the gunner for that: maintenance was as much a part of a landcruiser crew's routine as eating. But Hessef kept quiet—the ginger made him more confident than he should have been, too. Ussmak didn't like that. If the autoloader wouldn't feed shells into the cannon, what good was the landcruiser? Good for getting him killed, that was all.

Though the gunner outranked him, Ussmak said, "I think you ought to service the autoloader, too."

"It's working fine, I tell you," Tvenkel said angrily. "All we need is to top up on ammunition and we'll be ready to go out and fight some more."

As if on cue, a couple of ammunition carriers rolled up to the landcruisers. One was a purpose-built vehicle made by the Race, but the other sounded like a Tosevite rattletrap. Ussmak went back to the driver's position, undogged the hatch, and peered out. Sure enough, it was a petroleum-burning truck; its acrid exhaust made him cough. When the driver—a male of the Race—got out, Ussmak saw he had wooden blocks taped to the bottoms of his feet to let him reach the pedals from a seat designed for bigger beings.

Tvenkel climbed out through the turret, hurried over to the ammunition carriers. So did the gunners from the rest of the landcruisers in the unit. After a low-voiced comment from one of the resupply drivers, one of them shouted, "What do you mean, only twenty rounds per vehicle? That'll leave me less than half full!"

"And me!" Tvenkel said. The rest of the gunners echoed him, loudly and emphatically.

"Sorry, my friends, but it can't be helped," the male driving the Tosevite truck said. His foot blocks made him tower over the angry gunners but, instead of dominating them, he just became the chief target of their wrath. He went on, "We're a little short all over the planet right now. We'll share what we have evenly, and it'll come out well in the end."

"No, it won't," Tvenkel shouted. "We're facing real landcruisers here, don't you see that, with better guns and tougher armor than anybody else has to worry about. We need more ammunition to make sure we take them out."

"I can't give you what I don't have," the truck driver an-

swered. "Orders were to bring up twenty rounds per land-cruiser and that's what we brought, no more, no less."

The Race didn't need to run out of landcruisers to find itself in trouble against the Big Uglies, Ussmak realized. Running out of supplies for the landcruisers it had was less dramatic, but would do the job just fine.

ward. "Octant want to build up enough rounds for long-
range and that's what we bought, no more, no less."

The Race didn't need to run out of landcruisers to find itself
in trouble against the Big Uglies, Ussmak realized. Running
out of supplies for the landcruisers it had was just as dangerous would do the job just fine.

☆ **VIII** ☆

After darkness, light. After winter, spring. As Jens Larssen
peered north from the third floor of Science Hall, he thought
that light and spring had overtaken Denver all at once. A week
before, the ground had been white with snow. Now the sun
blazed down from a bright blue sky, men bustled across the
University of Denver campus in shirtsleeves and without hats,
and the first new leaves and grass were beginning to show
their bright green faces. Winter might come again, but no one
paid the possibility any mind—least of all Jens.

Spring sang in his heart, not because of the warm weather,
not for the new growth on lawns and trees, not even because
of early arriving birds warbling in those trees. What fired joy
in him was at first sight much more prosaic: a long stream of
horse-drawn wagons making their slow way down University
Boulevard toward the campus.

He could wait up here no longer. He dashed down the stairs,
his Army guard, Oscar, right behind him. When he got to the
bottom, his heart pounded in his chest and his breath came
short with exercise and anticipation.

Jens started over to his bicycle. Oscar said, "Why don't you
just wait for them to get here, sir?"

"Dammit, my wife is in one of those wagons, and I haven't
seen her since last summer," Jens said angrily. Maybe Oscar
didn't breathe hard even in bed.

"I understand that, sir," Oscar said patiently, "but you don't
know *which* one she's in. For that matter, you don't even know
if she's in any of the ones coming in today. Isn't the convoy
broken into several units to keep the Lizards from paying too
much attention to it?"

The right way, the wrong way, and the Army way, Jens thought. This once, the Army way seemed to have something going for it. "Okay," he said, stopping. "Maybe you're smarter than I am."

Oscar shook his head. "No, sir. But my wife isn't on one of those wagons, so I can still think straight."

"Hmm." Aware he'd lost the exchange, Larssen turned toward the wagons, the first of which had turned off University onto East Evans and was now approaching Science Hall. *I'll have the best excuse in the world for getting out of BOQ now,* he thought.

He didn't recognize the only man aboard the lead wagon: just a driver, wearing olive drab. Oscar *had* had a point, he reluctantly admitted to himself. A lot of these wagons would just be carrying equipment, and the only people aboard them would be soldiers. He'd have felt a proper fool if he'd pedaled up and down the whole length of the wagon train without setting eyes on Barbara.

Then he saw Leo Szilard sitting up alongside another driver. He waved like a man possessed. Szilard returned the gesture in a more restrained way: so restrained, in fact, that Jens wondered a little. The Hungarian physicist was usually as open and forthright a man as anyone ever born.

Larssen shrugged. If he was going to read that much into a wave, maybe he should have chosen psychiatry instead of physics.

A couple of more wagons pulled up in front of Science Hall before he saw more people he knew: Enrico and Laura Fermi, looking incongruous on a tarp-covered hay wagon. "Dr. Fermi!" he called. "Have you seen Barbara? Is she all right?"

Fermi and his wife exchanged glances. Finally he said, "She is not that far behind us. Soon you will see her for yourself."

Now what the devil was that supposed to mean? "Is she all right?" Larssen repeated. "Is she hurt? Is she sick?"

The Fermis looked at each other again. "She is neither injured nor ill," Enrico Fermi answered, and then shut up.

Jens scratched his head. Something was going on, but he didn't know what. Well, if Barbara was just a few wagons behind the Fermis, he'd find out pretty soon. He walked up the stream of incoming wagons, then stopped dead in his tracks. Ice ran up his spine—what were two Lizards doing here attached to the Met Lab crew?

He relaxed a bit when he saw the rifle-toting corporal in the wagon with the Lizards. Prisoners might be useful; the Lizards certainly knew how to get energy out of the atomic nucleus. Then all such merely practical thoughts blew out of his head. Sitting next to the corporal was—

"Barbara!" he yelled, and sprinted toward the wagon. Oscar the guard followed more sedately.

Barbara waved and smiled, but she didn't jump down and run to him. He noticed that, but didn't think much of it. Just seeing her again after so long made the fine spring day ten degrees warmer.

When he fell into step beside the wagon, she did get out. "Hi, babe, I love you," he said, and took her in his arms. Squeezing her, kissing her, made him forget about everything else.

"Jens, wait," she said when lack of oxygen forced him to take his mouth away from hers for a moment.

"The only thing I want to wait for is to get us alone," he said, and kissed her again.

She didn't respond quite the way she had the first time. That distracted him enough to let him notice the corporal saying, "Ullhass, Ristin, you two just go on along. I'll catch up with you later," and then getting down from the wagon himself. His Army boots clumped on the pavement as he walked back toward Jens and Barbara.

Jens broke off the second kiss in annoyance that headed rapidly toward anger. Oscar had enough sense to keep his distance and let a man properly greet his wife. Why couldn't this clodhopper do the same?

Barbara said, "Jens, this is someone you have to know. His name is Sam Yeager. Sam, this is Jens Larssen."

Not, my husband, Jens Larssen? Jens wondered, but, trapped in the rituals of politeness, he grudgingly stuck out a hand. "Pleased to meet you," Yeager said, though a dark blond eyebrow quirked up as he spoke. He was a handful of years older than Larssen, but considerably more weathered, as if he'd always spent a lot of time outdoors. *Gary Cooper type,* Jens thought, not that the corporal was anywhere near so good-looking.

"Pleased to meet you, too, pal," he said. "Now if you'll excuse us—" He started to steer Barbara away.

"Wait," she said again. He stared at her, startled. She was

looking down at the ground. When she raised her eyes, she looked not to him but to this Yeager character, which not only startled Jens but made him mad. The corporal nodded. Now Barbara turned toward Jens. In a low voice, she went on, "There's something you have to know. You and Sam have— something in common."

"Huh?" Jens gave Yeager another look. The soldier was human, male, white, and, by the way he talked, might well have sprung from the Midwest. Past that, Larssen couldn't see any resemblance between them. "What is it?" he asked Barbara.

"Me."

At first, he didn't understand. That lasted only a heartbeat, maybe two; the way she said it didn't leave much room to doubt what she meant. Numbness filled him, to be replaced in an instant by all-consuming rage.

He almost threw himself blindly at Sam Yeager. He'd always been a peaceable man, but he wasn't afraid of a fight. After attacking a Lizard tank when Patton's troops drove the aliens back from Chicago, the idea of taking on somebody carrying a rifle didn't faze him.

Then he took another look at Yeager's face. The corporal wasn't toting that rifle just for show. Somewhere or other, he'd done some work with it. The way his eyes narrowed as he watched Jens said that louder than words. Jens hesitated.

"It wasn't the way it sounds," Barbara said. "I thought you were dead; I was sure you had to be dead. If I hadn't been, I never would have—"

"Neither would I," Yeager put in. "There's names for people who do stuff like that. I don't like 'em."

"But you did," Jens said.

"We did it the right way, or the best way we knew how." Yeager's mouth twisted; those weren't the same, not here. He went on, "Up in Wyoming a little while back, we got married."

"Oh, Lord." Larssen's eyes went to Barbara, as if begging her to tell him it was all some dreadful joke. But she bit her lip and nodded. Something new washed over Jens then: fear. She wasn't just telling him she'd made a mistake with this miserable two-striper. She really had a thing for him.

"There's more," Yeager said grimly.

"How could there be more?" Jens demanded.

Barbara held up a hand. "Sam—" she began.

Yeager cut her off. "Hon, he's gotta know. The sooner all the cards are on the table, the sooner we can start figuring out what the hand looks like. Are you gonna tell him, or shall I?"

"I'll do it," Barbara said, which surprised Jens not at all: she'd always been one to take care of her own business. Still, she had to gather herself before she brought out a blurted whisper: "I'm going to have a baby, Jens."

He started to say, "Oh, Lord," again, but that wasn't strong enough. The only things that were, he didn't want to say in front of Barbara. He thought he'd been afraid before. Now— how could Barbara possibly want to come back to him if she was carrying this other guy's child? She was the best thing he'd ever known, most of the reason he'd kept going across Lizard-held Ohio and Indiana . . . and now this.

He wished they'd started their family before the Lizards came. They'd talked about it, but he kept reaching for the rubbers in the nightstand drawer—and times he hadn't (there were some), nothing happened. Maybe he was shooting blanks. Yeager sure as hell wasn't.

Jens also wished, suddenly, savagely, that he'd screwed the ears off the brassy blond waitress named Sal when the Lizards held them and a bunch of other people in that church in Fiat, Indiana. She'd done everything but send up a flare to let him know she was interested. He'd stayed aloof, figuring he'd be back with Barbara soon, but when he finally got back to Chicago, she was already gone, and now that he'd finally caught up with her—she was pregnant by somebody else. Wasn't that a kick in the nuts? It sure was. And he'd gone and wasted his chance.

"Jens—Professor Larssen, I guess I mean—what *are* we gonna do about this?" Sam Yeager asked.

He was being as decent as he could. Somehow, that made things worse, not better. Worse or better, though, he'd sure found the sixty-four-dollar question. "I don't know," Jens muttered with a helplessness he'd never felt while confronting the abstruse equations of quantum mechanics.

Barbara said, "Jens, I guess you've been here a while." She waited for him to nod before she went on, "Do you have some place where we could talk for a while, just the two of us?"

"Yeah." He pointed back toward Science Hall. "I've got an office on the third floor there."

"Okay, let's go." He wished she'd headed off with him with-

out a backwards glance, but she didn't. She turned back to
Sam Yeager and said, "I'll see you later."

Yeager looked as unhappy about her going with Jens as Jens
felt about her looking back at the corporal, which oddly made
him feel a little better. But Yeager shrugged—what else could
he do? "Okay, hon," he said. "You'll probably find me riding herd on the Lizards." He mooched after the wagon that had
held him and Barbara and the aliens.

"Come on," Jens said to Barbara. She fell into step beside
him, their strides matching as automatically as they always did.
Now, though, as he watched her legs move, all he could think
of was them locked around Sam Yeager's back. That scene
played over and over in his mind, in vivid Technicolor—and
brought pain just as vivid.

Neither of them said much as they walked back to Science
Hall, nor as they climbed the stairs. Jens sat down behind his
cluttered desk, waved Barbara to a chair. The minute he did
that, he knew it was a mistake: it felt more as if he was having
a conference with a colleague than talking with his wife. But
getting up and coming back around the desk would have made
him look foolish, so he stayed where he was.

"So how did this happen?" he asked.

Barbara looked at her hands. Her hair tumbled over her face
and down past her shoulders. He wasn't used to it so long and
straight; it made her look different. Well, a lot of things had
suddenly turned different.

"I thought you were dead," she said quietly. "You went off
across country, you never wrote, you never telegraphed, you
never called—not that the phones or anything else worked very
well. I tried and tried not to believe it, but in the end—what
was I supposed to think, Jens?"

"They wouldn't let me get hold of you." His voice shook
with fury ready to burst free, like a U-235 nucleus waiting for
a neutron. "First off, General Patton wouldn't let me send a
message into Chicago because he was afraid it would foul up
his attack on the Lizards. Then they wouldn't let me do anything to draw attention to the Met Lab. I went along. I thought
it made sense; if we don't make ourselves an atomic bomb, our
goose is probably cooked. But, Jesus—"

"I know," she said. She still would not look at him.

"What about Yeager?" he demanded.

More rage came out in his voice. Another mistake: now

Barbara did look up, angrily. If he attacked the bum, she was going to defend him. *Why shouldn't she?* Larssen asked himself bitterly. If she hadn't had a feel for him, she wouldn't have married him (God), wouldn't have let him get her pregnant (God oh God).

"After you—went away, I got a job typing for a psychology professor at the university," Barbara said. "He was studying Lizard prisoners, trying to figure out what makes them tick. Sam would bring them around—he helped capture them, and he's sort of their keeper, I guess you'd say. He's very good with them."

"So you got friendly," Jens said.

"So we got friendly," Barbara agreed.

"How did you get—more than friendly?" With an effort, Larssen kept his voice steady, neutral.

She looked down at her hands again. "A Lizard plane strafed the ship that was taking us out of Chicago." She gulped. "A sailor got killed— horribly killed—right in front of us. I guess we were both so glad just to be alive that—that— one thing led to another."

Jens nodded heavily. Things like that could happen. *Why do they have to happen to me, God?* he asked, and got no answer. As if twisting the knife in his own flesh, he asked, "And when did you get married to him?"

"Not even three weeks ago, up in Wyoming," Barbara answered. "I needed to be as sure as I could that that was something I really wanted to do. I figured out I was expecting the evening we got into Fort Collins." Her face twisted. "A soldier on horseback brought your letter the next morning."

"Oh, for Christ's sake," Jens groaned.

"What's the matter?" Barbara asked, worry in her voice.

"Nothing anybody can help now," he said, though he wanted to twist a knife, not in his own flesh, but in Colonel Hexham's. If the miserable blunder-brained, brass-bound, regulation- and security-crazy son of a bitch had let him write a letter when he first asked, most of this mess never would have happened.

Yeah, she and Yeager still would have had their fling, but he could deal with that—she'd thought he was dead, and so had Yeager. She wouldn't have married the guy, or got pregnant by him. Life would have been a hell of a lot simpler.

Jens asked himself a new and unsettling question: how

would things go between Barbara and him if she decided to give Yeager the brush and come back to him forever? How would he handle her giving birth to the other man's kid and then raising it? It wouldn't be easy; he could see that much.

He sighed. So did Barbara, at almost the same moment. She smiled. Jens stayed stony-faced. He asked, "Have the two of you been sleeping together since you found out?"

"In the same bed, you mean?" she said. "Of course we have. We traveled all the way across the Great Plains like that—and it still gets cold at night."

Though he habitually worked with abstractions, he wasn't deaf to what people said, and he sure as hell knew evasion when he heard it. "That's not what I meant," he told her.

"Do you really want to know?" Her chin went up defiantly. Pushing her made her angry, all right; he'd been afraid it would, and he was right. Before he could answer what might have been a rhetorical question, she went on, "As a matter of fact, we did, night before last. And so?"

Jens didn't know *and so*. Everything he'd looked forward to—everything except work, anyhow—had crumbled to pieces inside the last half hour. He didn't know whether he wanted to pick up those pieces and try to put them together again. But if he didn't, what did he have left? The answer to that was painfully obvious: nothing.

Barbara was still waiting for her answer. He said, "I wish to God it had been me instead."

"I know," she said, which was not the same as *I wish it had, too*. But something—maybe the naked longing in his voice—seemed to soften her. She continued, "It's not that I don't love you, Jens—don't ever think that. But when I thought you were . . . gone forever, I told myself life went on, and I had to go on with it. I can't turn off what I feel about Sam as if it were a light switch."

"Obviously," he said, which made her angry again. "I'm sorry," he added quickly, though he wasn't sure he meant it. "The whole thing is just fubar."

"Fubar? What's that?" Barbara's eyes lit up. She lived for words. When she found one she didn't know, she pounced.

"I picked it up from the Army guys I was with for a while," he answered. "It stands for 'fouled'—but that's not what they usually say—'up beyond all recognition.' "

"Oh, like snafu," she said, neatly cataloging it.

After that, silence stretched between them. Jens wanted to ask the one question he hadn't put to her—"Will you come back to me?"—but he didn't. Part of him was afraid she'd say no. A different part was just as much afraid she'd say yes.

When he didn't say anything, Barbara said: "What are we going to do?"

"I don't know," he answered, which was honest enough to make her nod soberly. He went on, "In the end, it's more or less up to you, isn't it?"

"Not altogether." Her left hand spread over her belly; he wondered if she knew it had moved. "For instance, do you want me back—under the circumstances?"

Since he'd been asking himself the same thing, he couldn't exclaim *Yes!* the way he probably should have. When a couple of seconds passed without his saying anything, Barbara looked away. That frightened him. He didn't want to throw her out, either. He said, "I'm sorry, dear. Too much landing on me all at once."

"Isn't that the sad and sorry truth?" She shook her head wearily, then got to her feet. "I'd better get downstairs and help with the work, Jens. I've sort of turned into assistant Lizard liaison person."

"Wait." He had work, too, a load that was going to quadruple now that the Met Lab was finally here. But that didn't have to start at this precise instant. He got up, too, hurried around the desk and took her in his arms. She held him tight; her body molded itself to his. It felt so familiar, so right. He wished he'd had the sense to lock his office door: he might have tried to drag her down to the floor then and there. It had been so long . . . He remembered the last time they'd made love on the floor, with Lizard bombs falling all over Chicago.

She tilted her face up, kissed him with more warmth than she'd shown down on East Evans. But before he could try dragging her down to the floor even with the door unlocked, she pulled away and said, "I really should go."

"Where will you stay tonight?" he asked. There. That brought it out in the open. If she said she'd stay with him, he didn't know what *he'd* do—not go back to the BOQ, that was for sure.

But she just shook her head and answered, "Don't ask me that yet, please. Right now I don't even know which end is up."

"All right," he said reluctantly; *he'd* been up when they held each other.

Barbara walked out of the office. He listened to her footsteps receding down the hallway and then in the stairwell. He went back to his desk, looked out the window behind it. There she came, out of Science Hall.

And there she went, over to Sam Yeager. No doubt who he was, even from three floors up: plenty of men in Army uniforms standing around, but only one of them stayed by the two Lizard prisoners. Jens felt like a Peeping Tom as he watched his wife hug and kiss the tall soldier, but he couldn't make himself tear his eyes away. When he compared the way she held Yeager to how she'd embraced him, a cold, inescapable conclusion formed in his mind: wherever she slept tonight, it wouldn't be with him.

At last Barbara broke free of the other man, but her hand lingered affectionately at his waist for an extra few seconds. Jens made himself turn away from the window and look at his desk. *No matter what happens to the rest of my life, there's still a war on and I have a ton of work to do,* he told himself.

He could make himself lean forward in the chair. He could make himself pull a report from the varnished pine IN basket and set it on the blotter in front of him. But, try as he would, he couldn't make the words mean anything. Misery and rage strangled his brains.

If that was bad, pedaling back to the BOQ with a silent Oscar right behind him felt ten times worse. "I won't take it," he whispered again and again, not wanting the guard to hear. "I won't."

Normal life. Moishe Russie had almost forgotten such a thing could exist. Certainly he'd known nothing of the sort for the past three and a half years, since the Stukas and broadwinged Heinkel 111s and other planes of the Nazi war machine began dropping death on Warsaw.

First the bombardment. Then the ghetto: insane crowding, disease, starvation, overwork—death for tens of thousands, served up a centimeter at a time. Then another spasm of war as the Lizards drove the Germans from Warsaw. And then that strange time as the Lizards' mouthpiece. He'd thought that was close to normal; at least he and his family had had food on the table.

But the Lizards were as eager to put shackles on his spirit as the Nazis had been to squeeze work out of his body and then let it die . . . or to ship him away and just kill him, regardless of how much work was left in him.

Then God only knew how long underground in a dark sardine tin, and then the flight to Lodz. None of that had been even remotely normal. But now here he was, with Rivka and Reuven, in a flat with water and electricity (most of the time, at least), and with no sign the Lizards knew where he'd gone.

It wasn't paradise—but what was? It was a chance to live like a human being instead of a starving draft horse or a hunted rabbit. *This, by now, is my definition of normal?* Russie asked himself as he strode down Zgierska Street to see what the market had to offer.

He shook his head. "Not normal," he insisted aloud, as if someone had disagreed with him. *Normal* would have meant going back to medical school, where the worst he would have had to endure was hostility from the Polish students. He itched to be able to start learning again, and to start practicing what he'd learned.

Instead, here he came, ambling along down a street in a town not his own, clean-shaven, doing his best to act like a man who'd never had a thought in his life. This was safer than the way he'd been living, but . . . normal? No.

As usual, the Balut Market square was packed. Some new posters had gone up on the dirty brick walls of the buildings surrounding the square. Bigger than life, Mordechai Chaim Rumkowski looked down on the ragged men and women gathered there, his arms and hands outstretched in exhortation. WORK MEANS FREEDOM! the poster cried in Yiddish, Polish, and German.

ARBEIT MACHT FREI. A shiver ran down Russie's back when he saw that in German. The Nazis had put the same legend above the gates of their extermination camp at Auschwitz. He wondered if Rumkowski knew.

He got in line to buy cabbage. More of Rumkowski's posters stood behind the peddler's cart. So did other, smaller ones with big red letters that announced WANTED FOR THE RAPE AND MURDER OF A LITTLE GIRL in the three most widely spoken languages of Lizard-held Poland.

Who could be such a monster? Russie thought. His eyes, drawn by those screaming red letters, looked to the picture on

the poster. It was one of the fancy photographs the Lizards took, in full color and giving the effect of three dimensions. Moishe noticed that before he realized with horror that he recognized the face on the poster. It was his own.

The poster didn't call him by his proper name—that would have given the game away. Instead, it styled him Israel Gottlieb. It said he'd committed his ghastly crimes in Warsaw and was being sought all over Poland, and it offered a large reward for his capture.

His head whipped wildly back and forth. Were people staring at him, at the poster, getting ready to shout at him or grab him and drag him to the cobblestones? He'd never imagined the Lizards would come up with such a devilish way of trying to bring him back into their hands. He felt as if they'd set the mark of Cain on his forehead.

But none of the men in hats or caps, none of the women in head scarves, acted as if the mark were visible. Few even glanced at the poster; of those who did, none looked from it to Russie.

His eyes went to it once more. On that second examination, he began to understand. The Lizards' photo showed him as he had been when he was speaking on the radio for Zolraag: in other words, bearded and in a dark homburg rather than clean-shaven and with a flat gray cloth cap of the sort he wore these days. To him, the difference seemed minuscule: it was, after all, his own face. But nobody else seemed to have the faintest suspicion he was the alleged monster whose visage would undoubtedly be used to frighten children.

Bristles rasped under his fingers as he rubbed his chin. He needed a shave. From here on out, he'd shave every day, no matter what: putting it off till tomorrow was liable to make him resemble himself too much.

He finally reached the head of the line, bought a couple of cabbages, and asked the price of some green onions the peddler had in a little wicker basket on his cart. When the fellow told him, he clapped a hand to his forehead and exclaimed, "*Ganef! You* should grow like an onion—with your head in the ground."

"An onion should grow from your *pippuk*," the vegetable seller retorted, answering one Yiddish execration with another. "Then it would be cheaper."

They haggled for a while, but Russie couldn't beat the man

down to a price that wouldn't leave Rivka furious at him, so he gave up and left, carrying his cabbages in a canvas bag. He thought about stopping to buy a cup of tea from a fellow with a battered tin samovar, but decided that would be tempting fate. The sooner he got out of the square, the fewer eyes would have a chance to light on him.

Going out, though, was swimming against the tide. The Balut Market square had filled even fuller when he stood in line. Then, abruptly, the swarm of people coming in slowed. Russie looked up just in time to keep from being run over by Chaim Rumkowski's coach.

The horse that drew the four-wheeled carriage snorted in annoyance as the driver, a hard-faced man in a gray greatcoat and quasimilitary cap, hauled back on the reins to stop it. The driver looked annoyed, too. Russie touched the brim of his own cap and mumbled, "Sorry, sir." He'd had plenty of practice fawning on the Germans, but doing it for one of his own people grated even harder on him.

Mollified, the driver dipped his head, but from behind him came the querulous voice of an elderly man:

"You up there—come here." Heart sinking, Russie obeyed. As he walked back toward Rumkowski, he saw that the driver's bench still sported a neat sign left over from the days of German domination: WAGEN DES AELTESTEN DER JUDEN (coach of the Eldest of the Jews), with the same in smaller letters in Yiddish below.

He wondered if the Eldest still wore a yellow Star of David on his right breast, as the Nazis had required the ghetto Jews to do. No, he found to his relief, although he could still see where the star had been sewn onto Rumkowski's herringbone tweed overcoat.

Then Moishe stopped worrying about small things, for sitting beside Rumkowski, almost hidden by his bulk, was a Lizard. Russie didn't think he had ever seen this particular alien, but he couldn't be sure. He felt as if all the posters with his picture on them were growing hands and pointing straight at him.

Rumkowski pointed straight at him, too, with a stubby forefinger. "You should be careful. You were almost badly hurt."

"Yes, Eldest. I'm sorry, Eldest." Russie looked down at the ground, both to show humility and to keep Rumkowski and the Lizard from getting a good look at him. The aliens had as

much trouble telling people apart as people did with their kind, but he did not want to find himself an exception to the rule.

The Lizard leaned forward to see him without being blocked by Rumkowski's body. Its eye turrets swiveled in a way Russie knew well. In fair German, it asked him, "What do you have in that bag?"

"Only a couple of cabbages." Russie had the presence of mind not to add *superior sir*, as he had learned to do back in Warsaw. That would just let the Lizard know he was familiar with the usages of its kind.

"How much did you pay for these cabbages?" Rumkowski asked.

"Ten zlotys, Eldest," Moishe said.

Rumkowski turned to the Lizard and said, "You see, Bunim, how we have flourished under your rule. A few months ago, these cabbages would have been many times as dear. We are always grateful for your aid, and will do whatever we can to continue deserving your favor."

"Yes, of course," Bunim said. Had he been a human, Russie would have thought his voice full of contempt: how could one not feel contemptuous of such an abject thing as Rumkowski had become? Yet the Lizards, even more than the Germans, assumed themselves to be the *Herrenvolk*, the master race. Perhaps Bunim accepted sycophancy from the Eldest simply as his due.

Rumkowski pointed to his own propaganda posters on the walls of the market square. "We know our debt, Bunim, and we work hard to repay it."

Bunim swung one eye toward the posters while keeping the other on Russie. Moishe made ready to fling the cabbages at his scaly face and flee. But the Lizard just said, "Continue on this course and all will be well."

"It shall be done, superior sir," Rumkowski said in the hissing language of the Race. Moishe had all he could do to keep his face blank and stupid; if he was just an ordinary *shlemiel* on the street, he had no business understanding the Lizards' speech. The Eldest seemed to remember he was there. "Take your food home to your family," he said, dropping back into Yiddish. "We may not be so hungry as we once were, but I know the memory lingers."

"You're right about that." Russie touched the brim of his cap. "Thank you, Eldest." He scuttled away from the carriage

as fast as he could without seeming to be running for his life. Acrid sweat dripped from his armpits and down his back.

Along with the fear came anger. Rumkowski had *chutzpah* and to spare, if he thought to impress anyone by talking about how hungry "we" had been. His fleshy frame didn't look to have missed many meals under German control of the ghetto, and he'd earned his food with the sweat and the blood of his fellow Jews.

But that, dreadful as it was, was also by the way. For now, the only thing that truly mattered to Russie was that he'd got away with the toughest test his flimsy disguise was ever likely to face. He wasn't surprised the Lizard had failed to recognize him; the Lizard might not have known who he was even if he'd still had his beard.

But Chaim Rumkowski . . . Rumkowski was a Lizard puppet as Moishe had been a puppet. It wouldn't have been too surprising if he'd seen Moishe's face in a Lizard photograph or in one of the propaganda films Zolraag and his minions had taken back when he and Russie got along. But if he had, he didn't associate it with a shabby Jew carrying cabbages home to his wife.

"And a good thing, too," Moishe said.

When he got back to his block of flats, he waved to Reuven, who was kicking a ball around with a couple of other boys and dodging in and out amongst passersby on the street. That game would have been impossibly dangerous before the war, when whizzing motorcars killed children every week.

These days, even the Eldest of the Lodz ghetto rode in a carriage like a nineteenth-century physician on his rounds; the only motor vehicle in the ghetto that Moishe knew about was the fire engine. People got about on bicycles or in carts hauled by their fellow men, or most often, afoot. And so sport got safer for little boys. *Even the worst wind blows in a little good with it,* Russie thought.

He carried the cabbages upstairs to his apartment. Rivka pounced on them. She did no more than raise an eyebrow when he told her how much he'd paid, from which he concluded he hadn't done too badly. "What else did they have down there?" she asked.

"*Tzibeles*—green onions—but I couldn't get a decent price for them, so I didn't buy any," he said. Rivka positively beamed; by her expression, she'd expected him to spend all

their money for one dried-up little onion. He went on, "That's not all," and told her about the posters.

"That's terrible," she said, before he even had a chance to let her know what they claimed he'd done. When he did, she clenched her fists and ground out, "It's worse than terrible—it's filthy."

"So it is," Moishe answered. "But the pictures show me the way I used to be, and I look different now. I proved it after I got these cabbages."

"Oh? How?"

"Because the Eldest of the Jews and the Lizard he had in the carriage with him both spoke to me, and neither one of them had the least idea who I was even though my picture was plastered all over the market square." Russie spoke as if he'd been through something that happened every day, hoping not to alarm Rivka. He alarmed himself instead; all the fright he'd felt came back in a rush.

And he frightened his wife. "That's it," she said in a voice that brooked no argument. "From now on, you don't go out of the flat unless it's a matter of life or death—any you do go out, it turns into a matter of life or death."

He could not disagree with that. He did say, "I had been thinking of going to the hospital and offering my services there. Lodz—and especially its Jews—still has far too much sickness and not enough people trained in medicine."

"If you were only putting your own neck in the noose, that would be one thing," Rivka said. "But if they catch you, Moishe, they catch Reuven and me, too. They won't be very happy with us, either; remember, we disappeared right under their snouts when we went into hiding."

"I know," he answered heavily. "But after being cooped up so long under Warsaw, the idea of having to stay here leaves me sick."

"Better you should be left sick than left dead," Rivka said, to which he had no good reply. She went on, "I'm a better shopper than you, anyhow, and you know it. We'll save money with you at home."

He knew that, too. Had he gone straight from the Warsaw bunker to close confinement in this flat, he could have borne it easily enough. But a taste of freedom left him hungry for more. It had been the same in Warsaw. If the Lizards had treated its Jews the same way the Germans had, people there

might well have accepted it, simply because it was what they'd grown used to. After a spell of mild rule, though, tough strictures would have been hard to reimpose. He'd certainly rebelled when the Lizards tried to make him into nothing but their mouthpiece.

Rivka inspected the cabbages, peeled off a couple of wilted outer leaves, and threw them away. That was a measure of how far they'd come. In the days when the Nazis ruled the ghetto, wilted cabbage leaves would have been something to fight over. Their being just garbage again showed that the family wasn't in the last stages of starving to death any more.

The rest of the cabbage, chopped, went into the soup pot with potatoes and a big white onion from a vegetable basket by the counter. Moishe wished for a roasted pullet or barley and beef soup with bones full of marrow. Cabbage and potatoes, though, you could live a long time on that, even without meat.

"It certainly seems like a long time, anyhow," he muttered.

"What's that?" Rivka asked.

"Nothing," he answered loyally, thinking of all the vitamins and other nutrients in potatoes and cabbages and onions. But man did not live by nutrients alone, and the soup, however nourishing the medical part of him knew it to be, remained uninspiring despite Rivka's best efforts.

She put a lid on the soup pot. The hot plate would eventually bring it to a boil. Moishe had given up on quickly cooked food—not that soup cooked quickly any which way. Rivka said, "I wonder how long Reuven will play outside."

"Hmm." Moishe sent her a speculative look. She smiled back. Just for a moment, the tip of her tongue appeared between her teeth. He did his best to sound severe: "I think you're just trying to butter me up." He listened to himself. Severe? He sounded eager as a bridegroom.

As a matter of fact, he *was* eager as a bridegroom. He took a couple of quick steps across the kitchen. Rivka's arms went around him at the same time his went around her. After a few seconds, she said, "For this, I may even like you better clean-shaven. Your mustaches used to tickle my nose when we kissed."

"If you like it so well—" he said, and resumed. His hand cupped her breast through the wool of her dress. She made a

small noise deep in her throat and pressed herself tighter against him.

The door opened.

Moishe and Rivka jumped away from each other as if they had springs in their shoes. From the doorway, Reuven called, "Is there anything to eat? I'm hungry."

"There's a heel of bread in here you can have, and I'm making soup," Rivka answered. "Your father brought home a couple of lovely cabbages." Her shrug to Moishe was full of humorous frustration.

He understood the feeling because he shared it. In the insanely overcrowded Warsaw ghetto, concerns about privacy had fallen to pieces, because so little was to be had. People did what they did, and the other people crammed into a flat with them, no matter how young, pretended not to notice. But decorum had returned to the family as soon as they were out of that desperate overcrowding.

Reuven wolfed down the bread his mother gave him, then sat on the kitchen floor to stare expectantly at the soup pot. Above him, Rivka said "Tonight" to Moishe.

He nodded. His son let out an indignant squawk: "The soup won't be ready till *tonight?*"

"No, I was talking about something else with your father," Rivka said.

Partway appeased, Reuven resumed his pot watching. The idea of privacy had come back after they were no longer stuffed into a flat like sardines. But food . . . they all still worried about food, even though they weren't starving any more. If they hadn't, Moishe wouldn't have noticed Rivka throwing out the wilted cabbage leaves, wouldn't have counted that as a sign of their relative affluence.

"Do you know," he said out of the blue, "I think I understand Rumkowski better."

"*Nu?*" Rivka said. "Tell me. How he could go on dealing with the Lizards, and with the Nazis before them—" She shivered.

Moishe explained his thoughts about the cabbage leaves, then went on, "I think Rumkowski's the same way, only about power, not food. However he thought of it when this was a Nazis ghetto, he can't change his mind now. He's—fixated, that's the word." It came out in German; Yiddish didn't have

a term for the precise psychological concept Moishe was trying to get across. Rivka nodded to show she followed.

Reuven said, "You threw out some cabbage leaves, Mama?" He got up and went over to the garbage can. "May I eat them?"

"No, just leave them there," Rivka said, and then again, louder, "Leave them there, I told you. You're not going to starve to death before the soup is done." She stopped with a bemused look on her face.

Progress, Moishe thought. He shook his head. To such had he been reduced that he measured progress by the existence of garbage.

Rasputitsa—the time of mud. Ludmila Gorbunova squelched across the airstrip, her boots making disgusting sucking and plopping noises at every step. Each time she lifted one, more mud clung to it, until she thought she was carrying half a *kolkhoz*'s worth on each foot.

The mud came to Russia and the Ukraine twice a year. In the fall, the rains brought it. The fall *rasputitsa* could be heavy or light, depending on how much rain fell for how long before it turned to snow and froze the ground.

The spring *rasputitsa* was different. When the spring sun melted the snow and ice that had accumulated since last fall, millions of square kilometers turned into a bog. That included roads, none of which was paved outside the big cities. For several weeks the only ways to get around were by *panje* wagons, which were almost boat-shaped and had wheels high enough to get down through the glop to solid ground, and by widetracked T-34 tanks.

That also meant most aviation came to a halt during the *rasputitsa.* The Red Air Force flew off dirt strips, and all the dirt was liquid for the time being. Taxiing for takeoffs and landings wasn't practical; just keeping aircraft from sinking into the swamp wasn't easy.

As usual, one model proved the exception: the U-2. With skis of the same sort the little biplane used to operate in heavy snow, it could skid along the surface of the mud until it gained enough speed to take off, and could also land in muck . . . provided the pilot set it down as gently as if eggs were under the skis. Otherwise it dug its nose into the ground and sometimes flipped, with unfortunate results for all concerned.

The mud in the revetment that housed Ludmila's U-2 was heavily strewn with straw, which meant she didn't even sink to her ankles, let alone to midcalf as she had outside. She didn't squelch as much, either.

Georg Schultz was adjusting one of the struts that joined the U-2's upper and lower wings when she came into the revetment. *"Guten Tag,"* he said cautiously.

"Good day," she returned, also in German, also cautiously. He hadn't made any unwelcome advances since she'd rounded on him for trying it, and he had kept on maintaining her *Kukuruznik* with his usual fanatic attention to detail. They still weren't easy around each other: she'd caught him watching her when he didn't think she'd notice, while he had to be nervous she'd speak to her fellow Russians about what he'd done. A thoroughgoing fascist, he was tolerated only for his mechanical skills. If the Russians found a reason not to tolerate him, he wouldn't last long.

He stuck a screwdriver into a pocket of his coveralls, came to attention so stiff it mocked the respect it was supposed to convey. "The aircraft is ready for flight, Comrade Pilot," he reported.

"Thank you," Ludmila answered. She did not call him "Comrade Mechanic" in return, not because it sounded unnatural to her in German, but because Schultz used for sarcasm what should have been a term of egalitarian respect. She wondered how he'd survived in Hitlerite Germany; in the Soviet Union that attitude would surely have seen him purged.

She checked the fuel level and the ammunition loads herself: no such thing as being too careful. When she was satisfied, she stepped out of the revetment and waved for groundcrew men. She, they, and Schultz manhandled the *Kukuruznik* out onto the runway. It stayed on top of the mud more easily than they did.

When Schultz yanked at the prop, the little Shvetsov five-cylinder radial began to buzz almost at once. The engine's exhaust fumes made Ludmila cough, but she nodded approvingly at its note. Nazi and lecher though he was, Georg Schultz knew his work.

Ludmila released the brake, applied the throttle. The U-2 slid down the airstrip, mud splattering in its wake. When she'd built up the speed she needed (not much), she eased back on the stick and the biplane abandoned the boggy earth for the freedom of the sky.

With the *rasputitsa* below her, Ludmila could savor the beginnings of spring. The slipstream that slid over the windscreen no longer turned her nose and cheeks to lumps of ice. The sun shone cheerily out of a blue sky with only a few plump white clouds, and would not disappear below the horizon when later afternoon came. The air smelled of growing things, not of the mud in which they grew.

She wished she could fly higher to see more. This was a day when flying was a joy, not a duty. But just when, for a moment, she was on the verge of forgetting why she flew, she skimmed low over the rusting hulks of two T-34s, one with its turret lying upside down fifteen meters away from the hull. She wondered whether the Germans or Lizards had killed the Soviet tanks.

Either way, the melancholy sight reminded her someone would kill her, too, if she failed to remember she was in the middle of a war. With every second, Lizard-held territory drew closer.

After so many missions, flying into country the alien imperialist invaders controlled had begun to approach the routine. She'd dropped small bombs on them and shot at them, smuggled in weapons and propaganda for the partisans. Today's mission was different.

"You are to pick up a man," Colonel Karpov had told her. "His name is Nikifor Sholudenko. He has information valuable to the Soviet Union. What this information is, I do not know, only its importance."

"I understand, Comrade Colonel," Ludmila had answered. The more one knew, the more one could be . . . encouraged to tell if captured.

An apple orchard halfway between Konotop and Romni. That's what he'd said, at any rate. It would have been easy if she'd been able to fly straight over Konotop on a course for Romni. Well, it would have been easier, anyhow. But the Lizards held Konotop in their little clawed hands. Flying over it would have resulted in the untimely demise she'd so far managed to forestall.

And so, as usual, she flew a track that reminded her of what she'd learned in biology of the twists of the intestines within the abdominal cavity, all performed less than fifty meters off the ground. If everything went perfectly, the last jink would

put her right at the orchard. If things went as they usually did—*well*, she told herself, *I'll manage somehow.*

Off to her left, she watched a Lizard tank struggling to pull three or four trucks from the morass into which they'd blundered. The tank wasn't having a much easier time moving than the trucks. Ludmila's lips skinned back from her teeth in a predator's grin. If she hadn't been under orders, she could have shot up the convoy. But deviating from the mission assigned would have caused her more grief than it was worth.

Another change of course and—if everything had gone right—the apple orchard should have been a couple of kilometers dead ahead. It wasn't, of course. She began a search spiral, not something she was happy to do in broad daylight: too much chance of flying past Lizards who weren't so preoccupied as that last bunch had been.

There! Bare-branched trees beginning to go green, with here and there the first white blossoms that before long would make the orchard look as if snow had fallen on it, though all the rest of the world was verdant with spring. A man waited in amongst the trees.

Ludmila looked around for the best place to land her plane. One stretch of boggy ground seemed no different from another. She'd hoped the partisans would have marked off a strip, but no such luck. After a moment, she realized no one had told her this Sholudenko was connected with the partisans. She'd assumed as much, but what were assumptions worth? Not a kopeck.

"As close to the orchard as I can," she said, making the decision aloud. She'd landed on airfields which were just that—fields—so often that she took one more such landing for granted. Down she came, killing her airspeed and peering ahead to make sure she wasn't about to go into a hole or anything of the sort.

She was down and sliding along before she saw the old gnarled roots sticking out of the ground. She realized then, too late, that the orchard had once been bigger than it was now. She couldn't wrench back on the stick and take off again; she wasn't going fast enough.

The *Kukuruznik* didn't need much room to land. God willing (a thought that welled up unbidden through her Marxist-Leninist education and training), everything would be all right.

She almost made it. But just when she started to believe she

would, the tip of her left ski caught under a root as thick as her arm. The U-2 tried to spin back around the way it had come. A wing dug into the ground; she heard a spar snap. The prop smacked the ground and snapped. One wooden blade whined past her head. Then the *Kukuruznik* flipped over onto its back, leaving Ludmila hanging upside down in the open pilot's cabin.

"*Bozhemoi*—my God," she said shakily. No, the dialectic somehow didn't spring to mind when she'd just done her best to kill herself.

Squelch, squelch, squelch. Someone, presumably the fellow who'd been standing in the apple orchard, was coming up to what had been her aircraft and was now just so much junk. In a dry voice, he said, "I've seen that done better."

"So have I," Ludmila admitted. ". . . Comrade Sholu-denko?"

"The same," he said. "They didn't tell me you would be a woman. Are you all right? Do you need help getting out?"

Ludmila took mental inventory. She'd bitten her lip, she'd be bruised, but she didn't think she'd broken anything but her aircraft and her pride. "I'm not hurt," she muttered. "As for the other—" She released the catches of her safety harness, came down to earth with a wet splat, and, filthy, crawled out from under the U-2. "Here I am."

"Here you are," he agreed. His Russian, like hers, had a Ukrainian accent. He looked like a Ukrainian peasant, with a wide, high-cheekboned face, blue eyes, and blond hair that looked as if it had been cut under a bowl. He didn't talk like a peasant, though: not only did he sound educated, he sounded cynical and worldly-wise. He went on, "How do you propose to take me where I must go? Will another aircraft come to pick up both of us?"

It was a good question, one for which Ludmila lacked a good answer. Slowly, she said, "If they do, it won't be soon. I'm not due back for some hours, and my aircraft has no ra-dio." No U-2 that she knew of had one; poor communications were the bane of all Soviet forces, ground and air alike.

"And when you do not land at your airstrip, they are more likely to think the Lizards shot you down than that you did it to yourself," Sholudenko said. "You must be a good pilot, or you would have been dead a long time ago."

"Till a few minutes ago, I thought so," Ludmila answered

ruefully. "But yes, you have a point. How important is this information of yours?"

"*I* think it has weight," Sholudenko said. "Someone in authority must have agreed with me, or they would not have sent you to do tumbling routines for my amusement. How large my news bulks in the world at large ... who can say?"

Ludmila slapped at the mud on her flying suit, which spread it around without getting much of it off. Tumbling routines ... she wanted to hit him for that. But he had influence, or he wouldn't have been able to get a plane sent after him. She contented herself with saying, "I don't think we should linger here. The Lizards are very good at spotting wreckage from the air and coming round to shoot it up."

"A distinct point," Sholudenko admitted. Without a backwards glance at the U-2, he started north across the fields.

Ludmila glumly tramped after him. She asked, "Do you have access to a radio yourself? Can you transmit the information that way?"

"Some, at need. Not all." He patted the pack on his back. "The rest is photographs." He paused, the first sign of uncertainty he'd shown. *Wondering whether to tell me anything,* Ludmila realized. At length he said, "Does the name Stepan Bandera mean anything to you?"

"The Ukrainian collaborator and nationalist? Yes, but nothing good." During the throes of the Soviet Revolution, the Ukraine had briefly been independent of Moscow and Leningrad. Bandera wanted to bring back those days. He was one of the Ukrainians who'd greeted the Nazis with open arms, only to have them throw him in jail a few months later. *No one loves a traitor,* Ludmila thought. *You may use him if that proves convenient, but no one loves him.*

"I know of nothing good to hear," Sholudenko said. "When the Lizards came, the Nazis set him free to promote solidarity between the workers and peasants of the occupied Ukraine and their German masters. He paid them back for their treatment of him, but not in a way to gladden our hearts."

Ludmila needed a few seconds to work through the implications of that. "He is collaborating with the Lizards?"

"He and most of the Banderists." Sholudenko spat on the ground to show what he thought of that. "They have a Committee of Ukrainian Liberation that has given our patriotic partisan bands a good deal of grief lately."

"What is the *rodina*, the motherland, coming to?" Ludmila said plaintively. "First we had to deal with those who would sooner have seen the Germans enslave our people than live under our Soviet government, and now the Banderists prefer the imperialist aliens to the Soviet Union and the Germans. Something must be dreadfully wrong, to make the people hate government so."

No sooner were the words out of her mouth than she wished she had them back again. She did not know this Nikifor Sholudenko from a hole in the ground. Yes, he dressed like a peasant, but for all she knew, he might be NKVD. In fact, he probably *was* NKVD, if he had pictures of Banderists in his knapsack. And she'd just criticized the Soviet government in front of him.

Had she been so foolish in 1937, she'd likely have disappeared off the face of the earth. Even in the best of times, she'd have worried about a show trial (or no trial) and a stretch of years in the *gulag*. She suspected the Soviet prison camp system still functioned at undiminished efficiency; most of it was in the far north, where Lizard control did not reach.

Sholudenko murmured, "You do like to live dangerously, don't you?"

With almost immeasurable relief, Ludmila realized the world wasn't going to fall in on her, at least not right away. "I guess I do," she mumbled, and resolved to watch her tongue more closely in the future.

"In the abstract, I could even agree with you," Sholudenko said. "As things are—" He spread his hands. That meant that, as far as he was concerned, this conversation was not taking place, and that he would deny anything she attributed to him if the matter came to the attention of an interrogator.

"May I speak—abstractly—too?" she asked.

"Of course," he said. "The constitution of 1936 guarantees free expression to all citizens of the Soviet Union, as any schoolgirl knows." He spoke without apparent irony, yet his hypothetical schoolgirl had to know also that anyone trying to exercise her free speech (or any of the other rights guaranteed—or entombed—in the constitution) would discover she'd picked a short trip into big trouble.

Somehow, though, she did not think Sholudenko, for all his cynicism, would betray her after giving her leave to speak.

Maybe that was naive on her part, but she'd already said enough to let him ruin her if that was what he had in mind, and so she said, "It's terrible that our own Soviet government has earned the hatred of so many of its people. Any ruling class will have those who work to betray it, but so many?"

"Terrible, yes," Sholudenko said. "Surprising, no." He ticked off points on his fingers like an academician or a political commissar. "Consider, Comrade Pilot: a hundred years ago, Russia was entirely mired in the feudal means of production. Even at the time of the October Revolution, capitalism was far less entrenched here than in Germany or England. Is this not so?"

"It is so," Ludmila said.

"Very well, then. Consider also the significance of that fact. Suddenly the revolution had occurred—in a world that hated it, a world that would crush it if it could. You are too young to remember the British, the Americans, the Japanese who invaded us, but you will have learned of them."

"Yes, but—"

Sholudenko held up a forefinger. "Let me finish, please. Comrade Stalin saw we would be destroyed if we could not match our enemies in the quantity of goods we turn out. Anything and anyone standing in the way of that had to go. Thus the pact with the Hitlerites: not only did it buy us almost two years' time, but also land from the Finns, on the Baltic, and from the Poles and Rumanians to serve as a shield when the fascist murderers did attack us."

All that shield had been lost within a few weeks of the Nazi invasion. Most of the people in the lands the Soviet Union had annexed joined the Hitlerites in casting out the Communist Party, which spoke volumes on how much they'd loved falling under Soviet control.

But did that matter? Sholudenko had a point. Without ruthless preparation, the revolution of the workers and peasants would surely have been crushed by reactionary forces, either during the civil war or at German hands.

"Unquestionably, the Soviet state has the right and duty to survive," Ludmila said. Sholudenko nodded approvingly. But the pilot went on, "But does the state have a right to survive in such a way as to make so many of its people prefer the vicious Germans to its own representatives?"

If she hadn't still been shaky from flipping her airplane, she wouldn't have said anything so foolish to a probable NKVD man, even "abstractly." She looked around the fields through which they were slogging. No one was in sight. If Sholudenko tried to place her under arrest ... well, she carried a 9mm Tokarev pistol in a holster on her belt. The comrade might have a tragic accident. If he did, she'd do her best to get his precious pictures back to the proper authorities.

If he contemplated arresting her, he gave no sign of it. Instead, he said, "You are to be congratulated, Comrade Pilot; this is a question most would not think to pose." It was a question most would not dare to pose, but that was another matter. Sholudenko went on, "The answer is yes. Surely you have been trained in the historical use of the dialectic?"

"Of course," Ludmila said indignantly. "Historical progress comes through the conflict of two opposing theses and their resulting synthesis, which eventually generates its own antithesis and causes the struggle to recur."

"Congratulations again—you are well instructed. We stand in the historical process at the step before true communism. Do you doubt that Marx's ideal will be fulfilled in our children's time, or our grandchildren's at the latest?"

"If we survive, I do not doubt it," Ludmila said.

"There is that," Sholudenko agreed, dry as usual. "I believe we should have beaten the Hitlerites in the end. The Lizards are another matter; Party dialecticians still labor to put them into proper perspective. Comrade Stalin has yet to speak definitively on the subject. But that is beside the point—you might have asked the same question had the Lizards never come, *da*?"

"Yes," Ludmila admitted, wishing she'd never asked the question at all.

Sholudenko said, "If we abandon the hope of our descendants' living under true communism, the historical synthesis will show that reactionary forces were stronger than those of progress and revolution. Whatever we do to prevent that is justified, no matter how hard it may be for some at present."

By everything she'd learned in school, his logic was airtight, however much it went against the grain. She knew she ought to shut up; he'd already shown more patience with her than she had any right to expect. But she said, "What if, in seeking

to move the balance our way, we are so harsh that we tilt it against us?"

"This, too, is a risk which must be considered," he said. "Are you a Party member, Comrade Pilot? You argue most astutely."

"No," Ludmila answered. Then, having come so far, she took one step further: "And you, Comrade—could you be from the People's Commissariat for the Interior?"

"Yes, I could be from the NKVD," Sholudenko answered evenly. "I could be any number of things, but that one will do." He studied her. "You needed courage, to ask such a question of me."

That last step had almost been one step too far, he meant. Picking her words with care, Ludmila said, "Everything that's happened over the past year and a half—it makes one think about true meanings."

"This I cannot deny," Sholudenko said. "But—to get back to matters more important than my individual case—the dialectic makes me believe our cause will triumph in the end, even against the Lizards."

Faith in the future had kept the Soviets fighting even when things looked blackest, when Moscow seemed about to fall late in 1941. But against the Lizards—"We need more than the dialectic," Ludmila said. "We need more guns and planes and tanks and rockets, and better ones, too."

"This is also true," Sholudenko said. "Yet we also need the people to work and struggle for the Soviet state, not on behalf of imperialist invaders, whether from Germany or the depths of space. The dialectic predicts that on the whole we shall have their support."

Instead of answering, Ludmila stooped by the edge of a little pond that lay alongside the field through which she and Sholudenko were walking. She cupped her hands, scooped up water, and scrubbed mud from her face. She pulled up dead grass and did her best to scrape her leather flying suit clean, too, but that was a bigger job. Eventually the mud there would dry and she could knock most of it off. Till then she'd just have to put up with it. Plenty of foot soldiers had gone through worse.

She straightened up, pointed to the pack on Nikifor Sholudenko's back. "And for those who choose to ignore the teaching of the dialectic—"

"*Da*, Comrade Pilot. For those folk, we have people like me." Sholudenko smiled broadly. His teeth were small and white and even. They reminded Ludmila of a wolf's fangs just the same.

Mutt Daniels crouched in a foxhole on the edge of Randolph, Illinois, hoping and praying the Lizard bombardment would ease up before it smeared him across the small-town landscape.

He felt naked with just a hole in the ground for cover. Back in France during the Great War, he'd been able to dive into a deep dugout when German shells came calling. If you were unlucky, of course, a shell would come right in after you, but most of the time a dugout was pretty safe.

No dugouts here. No proper trench lines, either, not really. This war, unlike the last one, moved too fast to let people build elaborate field fortifications.

"Plenty of foxholes, though," Matt muttered. The local landscape looked like pictures of craters on the moon. The Lizards had taken Randolph last summer in their drive on Chicago. Patton's men had taken it back in the pincers movement that brought them into Bloomington, six or eight miles north. Now the Lizards were moving again. If Randolph fell, they'd be well positioned to drive back into Bloomington.

Yet another shell crashed into the ground, close enough to lift Daniels into the air and fling him back to earth as if body-slammed by a wrestler. Dirt pattered down on him. His lungs ached from the blast when he drew in a shaky breath.

"Might as well be between Washington and Richmond, the way we're goin' back and forth here," Daniels said. Both his grandfathers had fought for the South in the War Between the States; as a small boy, he'd listened avidly to the tales they told, tales that grew taller with each passing year. No matter

how tall the tales got, though, France and now this convinced him his grandfathers hadn't had it as tough as they'd thought.

More shells whistled overhead, these southbound from Bloomington. Mutt hoped they were registered on the Lizard guns, but they probably weren't; the Lizards outranged American artillery. Giving Lizard infantry a taste of what he was going through wasn't the worst thing in the world, either. A flight of prop-driven fighters screamed by at treetop height. Mutt touched his helmet in salute to courage; pilots who flew against the Lizards didn't last long.

Once the planes zipped out of sight, he didn't spot them again. He hoped that meant they were returning to base by a different route instead of getting knocked down. "No way to find out for sure," he said.

He abruptly stopped being interested, too, because Lizard shelling picked up again. He embraced the ground like a lover, pressed his face against her cool, damp neck.

Some of the blasts that shook him where he lay were explosions of the same sort he'd known in France. Others had a sound he'd first met retreating toward Chicago: a smaller bang, followed by a pattering as of hail.

"Y'all want to look sharp," he called to the scattered members of his squad. "They're throwin' out them goddamn little mines again." He hated those little baseball-sized blue explosives. Once a regular shell went off, at least it was gone. But the Lizards' fancy ammo scattered potential mutilation over what seemed like half an acre and left it sitting there waiting to happen. "Instant goddamn mine field," Mutt said resentfully.

After a while, the barrage let up. Daniels grabbed his tommy gun and took a cautious peek out of the foxhole. If the *Boches* had been doing that shelling, they'd follow up with an infantry attack just as sure as you were supposed to hit the cutoff man. But the Lizards didn't always play by the book Mutt knew. Sometimes they fooled him on account of that. *More often,* he thought, *they hurt themselves.*

So here: if they wanted to drive the Americans out of Randolph, they'd never have a better chance than now, while the shelling had stunned and disorganized their human foes. But they stayed back in their own lines south of town. The only sign of action from them was a single plane high overhead, its path through the sky marked by a silvery streak of condensation.

Mutt gave the aircraft a one-finger salute. "Gonna see how bad you beat on us before you send in the ground-pounders, are you?" he growled. "Mis'able cheap bastards." What was infantry for, after all, if not to pay the butcher's bill?

His battered eardrums made the quiet that followed the barrage seem even more intense than it was. The short, sharp *bang!* that punctuated it wouldn't have seemed worth noticing, save for the shriek right after.

"Oh, shit," Mutt exclaimed. "Somebody went and did somethin' dumb. Goddamn it to hell, why don't nobody never listen to me?" He'd thought minor-league ballplayers were bad at paying attention to what a manager told them. Well, they were, but they looked like Einsteins when you set 'em next to a bunch of soldiers.

He scrambled out of the foxhole. His body was skinnier and sprier than it had been while he was wearing his Decatur Commodores uniform, but he'd have cheerfully gone back to fat and flab if anybody offered him the choice.

No one did, of course. He crawled over battered ground and through ruined buildings toward where that shriek had come from. Memory wasn't his only guide; a low moaning kept him on course.

Kevin Donlan lay just outside a shell hole, clutching his left ankle. Below it, everything was red ruin. Mutt's stomach did a slow lurch. "Jesus Christ, kid, what did you do?" he said, though the answer to that was all too obvious.

"Sarge?" Donlan's voice was light and clear, as if his body hadn't really told him yet how bad he was hurt. "Sarge, I just got out to take a leak. I didn't want to piss in my hole, you know, and—"

Next to what he had, swimming a river of piss was nothing. No point telling him that, though, not now. "Miss Lucille!" Mutt bawled. While he waited for her, he got a wound bandage and a packet of sulfa powder out of a pouch on Donlan's belt. He dusted the powder onto the wound. He wondered if he ought to get the remains of Donlan's shoe off his foot before he started bandaging it, but when he tried, the kid started screaming again, so he said the hell with it and wrapped the bandage over foot, shoe, and all.

Lucille Potter scrambled up a minute later, maybe less. In dirty fatigues and a helmet, she looked like a man except that

she didn't need a shave. The helmet bore a Red Cross on a white circle; the Lizards had learned what that mark meant, and weren't any worse than people about respecting it.

She looked at the way blood was soaking through the bandage, clicked her tongue between her teeth. "We've got to get a tourniquet on that wound, Sergeant."

Mutt looked down at Donlan. The kid's eyes had rolled up in his head. Mutt said, "You do that, Miss Lucille, he's gonna lose the foot."

"I know," she said. "But if we don't do it, he's going to bleed to death. And he'd lose the foot anyhow; no way to save it with a wound like that." Her sharp stare dared him to argue. He couldn't; he'd seen enough wounds in France and Illinois to know she was right.

She cut Donlan's torn trousers, took out a length of bandage and a stick, and set the tourniquet. "Hell of a thing," Daniels said, to himself and her both: another young soldier on crutches for the rest of his life.

"It's hard, I know," Lucille Potter answered. "But would you rather have him dead? Ten years from now, if this war ever ends, would he rather we'd let him die?"

"I reckon not," Daniels said. In his younger days in Mississippi, a lot of the older white men he'd known were shy an arm or a leg or a foot from the States War. They weren't glad of it, naturally, but they got on better than you'd expect. When you got right down to it, people were pretty tough critters.

He sent a runner over to Captain Maczek. Where the captain was, the company field telephone would be, too. After that, there was nothing to do but wait. Donlan seemed pretty shocky. When Mutt remarked on it, Lucille Potter said, "It's probably a blessing in disguise—he won't feel that foot as much."

The forward aid station wasn't much more than a quarter of a mile back of the line. A four-man litter team got to Donlan in less than fifteen minutes. The boss of the team, a corporal, looked at the youngster's ruined foot and shook his head. "Nothing much we'll be able to do about that," he said. "They'll have to take him back into Bloomington, and I expect they'll chop it off there."

"You're almost certainly right," Lucille said. All the litter bearers stared when she spoke. She stared right back, daring

them to make something out of it. None of them did. She went on, "The sooner he goes back, the sooner they can treat him."

The team got Donlan onto the stretcher and carried him away. "Too stinkin' bad," Mutt said. "He's a good kid. Ain't this war a—" He stopped, inhibited in his language by a woman's presence. After a sigh, he resumed, "Lord, I wish I had me a cigarette, or even a chaw."

"Filthy habits, both of them," Lucille Potter said, her voice so sharp he turned to give her an irritated look. Then, with a wry chuckle, she added, "I wish I had a smoke, too. I ran out of tobacco months ago, and I miss it like anything."

"Might be some back in Bloomington," Mutt said. "We ever get a real lull, could be I'd send Szabo back there to see how the foraging is. You want to liberate somethin' from where it rightly belongs, ol' Dracula's the man for the job."

"He's certainly good at coming up with home brew and moonshine," Lucille said, "but people make those around here. Illinois isn't tobacco country, so we can't get hold of bootleg cigars."

"Can't get hold of much of anything these days," Mutt said. "I'm skinnier'n I've been for close to thirty years."

"It's good for you," she answered, which made him give her another resentful glance. She was on the lean side, and looked to have always been that way: not an ounce of excess flesh anywhere. What did she know about what felt comfortable and what didn't?

He wasn't in a mood to argue, though, so he said, "I just hope Donlan's gonna make out okay. He's a good kid. Hell of a thing to be crippled so young."

"Better than dying. I thought we already settled that," Lucille Potter answered. "I'm just glad the field telephone was working and the litter crew was on the ball. If they hadn't gotten here inside of about another ten minutes, I was going to take his foot off myself." She tapped her little black bag. "I've got some ether in here. He wouldn't have felt anything."

"You know how?" Daniels asked. Battlefield wounds were one thing, but cutting into a man on purpose . . . He shook his head. He was sure he couldn't do it.

Lucille said, "I haven't had to do an amputation yet, but I've read up on the technique. I—"

"I know that," Mutt broke in. "Every time I see you, you got a doctor's book in your hand."

"I have to. Nurses don't operate, and I wasn't even a scrub nurse to watch doctors work. But a combat medic had better be able to do as much as she can, because we're not always going to have a lull like this one to get our casualties back to the aid station. Does that make sense to you?"

"Yeah," Daniels said. "You usually do—" Off to the left, small arms began to chatter on both sides of the line. Mutt interrupted himself to scramble into the shell hole from which unlucky Kevin Donlan had emerged to relieve himself. Lucille Potter jumped in beside him. Her only combat experience was what she'd had in the past few weeks, but *take cover* was a lesson you learned in a hurry, at least if you wanted to keep on living.

Then the artillery started up again, the Lizards firing steadily, the Americans in bursts of a few rounds here, a few rounds there, a few somewhere else. They'd learned the hard way that if their pieces stayed in one place for more than a short salvo, the Lizards would zero in on them and knock them out.

The ground began tossing like the stormy sea, though Mutt had never been in a natural storm that made such a god-awful racket. He pushed Lucille down flat on her belly, then lay on top of her to protect her from splinters as best he could. He didn't know whether he did it because she was a woman or because she was the medic. Either way, he figured, she needed to stay as safe as possible.

As suddenly as it had begun, the barrage stopped. Mutt stuck his head up right away. Sure as hell, Lizard ground troops were scurrying forward. He squeezed off a long burst with his tommy gun. The Lizards flattened out on the ground. He didn't know whether he'd hit any of them; the tommy gun wasn't accurate out past a couple of hundred yards.

He wished he had one of the automatic weapons the Lizards carried. Their effective range was something like double that of his submachine gun, and their cartridges packed a bigger kick, too. He'd heard of dogfaces who toted captured specimens, but keeping them in the right ammo was a bitch and a half. Most of the weapons the Lizards lost went straight back to the high-forehead boys in G-2. With luck, the Americans would get toys just as good one of these days.

That train of thought abruptly got derailed. He moaned, down deep in his throat. The Lizards had a tank with them.

Now he understood what the poor damned Germans had felt like in France in 1918 when those monsters came clanking their way and they couldn't stop them or even do much to slow them down.

The tank and the Lizard infantry screening it slowly advanced together. The aliens had learned something since the winter before; they'd lost a lot of tanks then for lack of infantry support. Not any more.

Lucille Potter peered over the forward lip of the foxhole beside Mutt. "That's trouble," she said. He nodded. It was big trouble. If he ran, the tank's machine gun or the Lizard foot soldiers would pick him off. If he stayed, the tank would penetrate the position and then the Lizard infantry would get him.

Off to the right, somebody fired one of those new bazooka rockets at the Lizard tank. The rocket hit the tank right in the turret, but it didn't penetrate. "Damn fool," Mutt ground out. Doctrine said you were supposed to shoot a bazooka only at the rear or sides of a Lizard tank; the frontal armor on the aliens' machines was just too thick for you to kill one with a straight-on shot.

Being too eager cost the fellow who'd fired at the tank. It turned toward him and his buddies and opened up first with its machine gun and then its main armament. For good measure, the Lizard infantry moved in on the bazooka man, too—their job was to make sure nobody got a good shot at the armored fighting vehicle. By the time they were done, there probably wasn't enough of the American and his buddies left to bury.

Which meant they forgot about Mutt. For a second, he didn't think that would do him any good: if the line was overrun, he would be, too, in short order. Ever so cautiously, he raised his head again. There sat the tank, maybe a hundred feet away, ass end on to him, still pouring fire at a target more necessary to destroy than he was.

He ducked back down, turned to Lucille Potter. "Gimme that ether," he snapped.

"What? Why?" She took a protective grip on the black bag.

"The—stuff'll burn, won't it?" His pa's hard hand on his backside and across his face had taught him never to swear where a woman could hear, but he almost slipped that time. "Now gimme it!"

Lucille's eyes widened. She opened the bag, handed him the

glass jar. It was about half full of a clear, oily-looking liquid. He hefted it thoughtfully. Yeah, it would throw just fine. His bat had kept him from having a decent big-league career; nobody'd ever complained about his arm. He'd been a good man with a grenade in France, too.

It wasn't even as if he had to throw all of a sudden, as he would have with a runner breaking for second. He could take a few moments, think through what he was going to do, see every step of it in his mind before it actually happened.

Doing that took longer than the throw itself. He popped up as if exploding out of his crouch behind a batter, fired the jar for all he was worth, and ducked back down again. Nobody who wasn't looking right at him would have known he'd appeared.

"Did you hit it?" Lucille demanded.

"Miss Lucille, I tell you for a fact, I didn't stay up long enough to find out. I tried to smash it off the back of the turret so it'd drip down into that nice, hot engine compartment." Mutt's shoulder twinged; he hadn't put that much into a snap throw in years. It had felt straight, but you never could tell. A little long, a little short, and he might as well not have bothered.

Then he heard hoarse yells from the Americans in other scattered foxholes. That encouraged him to take another cautious peek. When he did, he yelled himself, in sheer delight. Flames danced all over the engine compartment and were licking up the back of the turret. As he watched, an escape hatch popped open and a Lizard jumped onto the ground.

Mutt ducked down for his tommy gun. "Miss Lucille, that there is one Lizard tank that's out stealing."

She pounded him on the back as any other soldier would have. He wouldn't have tried to kiss another soldier, though. She let him do it, but she didn't do much in the way of kissing back. He didn't worry about that; he popped up out of the foxhole and started blazing away at the fleeing Lizard tank crew and the foot soldiers, who were much less terrifying without armor to back them up.

The Lizards fell back. The tank kept burning. A Sherman would have brewed up a hell of a lot faster than it did, but eventually its ammunition and its fuel tank went up in a spectacular blast.

Mutt felt as if he'd been hit over the head with a sledge-hammer. "Lord!" he exclaimed. "You couldn't make a fancier explosion in the movies."

"No, probably not," Lucille Potter agreed, "nor one that did more for us. We'll hold Randolph a while longer now, I expect. That was a wonderful throw; I've never seen a better one. You must have been a very fine baseball player."

"You don't make the majors unless you're pretty fair," he said, shrugging. "You don't stick there unless you're better'n that, and I wasn't." He brushed a hand across the front of his shirt, as if he'd been a pitcher shaking off a sign rather than a catcher; baseball wasn't what he wanted to talk about at the moment. After a couple of tentative coughs, he said, "Miss Lucille, I hope you don't think I was too forward there."

"When you kissed me, you mean? I didn't mind," she said, but not in a way that encouraged him to try it again; by her tone, once had been okay but twice wouldn't be. He kicked at the churned-up dirt inside the foxhole. Lucille added, "I'm not interested, Mutt, not that way. It's not you—you're a good man. But I'm just not."

"Okay," he said; he was too old to let his pecker do his thinking for him. But that didn't mean he'd forgotten he had one. He pushed up his helmet so he could scratch his head above one ear. "If you like me, why—" He broke off there. If she didn't want to talk about it, that was her business.

For the first time since he'd met her, he found her at a loss for words. She frowned, obviously not caring for that herself. Slowly, she said, "Mutt, it's not something I can easily explain, or care to. I—"

Easily or not, she didn't get the chance to explain. Following a cry of "Miss Lucille!" a soldier from another squad in the platoon came scrambling over to the foxhole and gasped out, "Miss Lucille, we've got two men down, one hit in the shoulder, the other in the chest. Peters—the guy with the chest wound—he's in bad shape."

"I'm coming," she said briskly, and climbed out of the hole she'd shared with Mutt. As she hurried away, he scratched his head again.

Even in these times, David Goldfarb had expected things to be handled with more ceremony. The Prime Minister, after all,

did not visit the Bruntingthorpe Research and Development Test Flying Aerodrome every day.

But there was no line of RAF men in blue serge standing to attention for Winston Churchill to inspect, no flyby of a squadron of Pioneers or Meteors to impress him with what Fred Hipple and his team had accomplished in jet propulsion. In fact, up until an hour before Churchill got to Bruntingthorpe, no one knew he was coming.

Group Captain Hipple brought the news back from the administrative section's Nissen hut. It produced a brief, startled silence from his subordinates, who were laboring mightily to pull secrets from the wreckage of the Lizard fighter-bomber that had been brought down not far from the aerodrome.

Typically, Flight Officer Basil Roundbush was first to break that silence: "Generous of him to give us notice enough to make sure our flies are closed."

"I can't tell you how delighted I am to be confident yours is, dear boy," Hipple returned. Roundbush covered his face with his hands, acknowledging the hit. The group captain might have been shorter than his subordinates, but gave away nothing in wit. He continued, "I gather no one knew until moments ago: quite a lot of security laid on, for reasons which should be plain enough."

"Wouldn't do for the Lizards to pay us a visit just now, would it, sir?" Goldfarb said.

"Yes, that would prove—embarrassing," Hipple said, an understatement Roundbush might have coveted.

And so, just as Goldfarb had, the Prime Minister came down from Leicester by bicycle, pedaling along on an elderly model like a grandfather out for a constitutional. He dismounted outside the meteorology hut, where Hipple and his team still labored after the latest Lizard bombing raid. When Goldfarb saw the round pink face and the familiar cigar through the window, he gulped. He'd never expected to meet the leader of the British Empire.

Wing Commander Julian Peary's reaction was more prosaic. In the big deep voice that went so oddly with his slight physique, he said, "I do hope he's not damaged any of the beets."

It was only half a joke. Like everyone else at Bruntingthorpe—like everyone else in Britain, or so it seemed—Hipple's team cultivated a garden. The British Isles held more

people than they could easily feed, and shipments from America were down, not so much because the Lizards bombed them (they still took much less notice of ships than of air or rail or road transport) as because the Yanks, beset at home, had little to spare.

So, gardens. Beets, potatoes, peas, beans, turnips, parsnips, cabbages, maize . . . whatever the climate would permit, people grew—and sometimes guarded with cricket bats, savage dogs, or shotguns against two-legged thieves too big to be frightened by scarecrows.

Everyone did come to attention when the Prime Minister, accompanied by a bodyguard who looked as if he never smiled, walked into the Nissen hut. "As you were, gentlemen, please," Churchill said. "After all, officially I am not here, but speaking over the BBC in London. Because I am in the habit of speaking live, I can occasionally use the subterfuge of sound recordings to let myself be in two places at once." He let out a conspiratorial chuckle. "I hope you won't give me away."

Automatically, Goldfarb shook his head. Hearing Churchill's voice without the static and distortion of a wireless set was to him even more intimate than seeing the Prime Minister in the tubby flesh rather than through photographs: pictures captured his image more accurately than the airwaves did his voice.

Churchill strode over to Fred Hipple, who was standing beside a wooden table on which lay pieces of the turbine from the crashed Lizard fighter's jet engine. Pointing to them, the Prime Minister asked, "How long before we shall be able to duplicate that engine, Group Captain?"

"Duplicate it, sir?" Hipple said. "It won't be soon; the Lizards are far ahead of us in control mechanisms for the engine, in machining techniques, and in the materials they employ: they do things with titanium and ceramics we've never dreamt of, much less attempted. But in determining how and why they make things as they do, we learn how to do better ourselves."

"I see," Churchill said thoughtfully. "So even though you have the book in front of you"—he pointed to the disassembled chunks of turbine again—"you cannot simply read off what is on its pages, but must decode it as if it were written in a cipher."

"That's a good analogy, sir," Hipple said. "The facts of the engine are relatively straightforward, even if we can't yet produce one identical to it ourselves. When it comes to the radar

from the same downed aircraft, I fear we are still missing a great many code groups, so to speak."

"So I have been given to understand," Churchill said, "although I do not fully grasp where the difficulty lies."

"Let me take you over to Radarman Goldfarb, then, sir," Hipple said. "He joined the team to help emplace a radar set in production Meteors, and has labored valiantly to unlock the secrets of the Lizard unit that fell into our hands."

As the group captain brought the Prime Minister over to his workbench, Goldfarb thought, not for the first time, that Fred Hipple was a good man to work for. A lot of superior officers would have done all the explaining to the brass themselves, and pretended their subordinates didn't exist. But Hipple introduced Goldfarb to Churchill, then stood back and let him speak for himself.

He didn't find it easy at first. When he stammered, the Prime Minister shifted the subject away from radar: "Goldfarb," he said musingly. "Was I not told you are the lad with a family connection to Mr. Russie, the former Lizard spokesman from Poland?"

"Yes, that's true, sir," Goldfarb answered. "We're cousins. When my father came to England before the Great War, he urged his sister and her husband to come with him, and he kept urging them to get out until the second war started in '39. They wouldn't listen to him, though. Moishe Russie is their son."

"So your family kept up the connection, then?"

"Till the war cut us off, yes, sir. After that, I didn't know what had happened to any of my relatives until Moishe began speaking on the wireless." He didn't tell Churchill most of his kinsfolk had died in the ghetto; the Prime Minister presumably knew that already. Besides, Goldfarb couldn't think about their fate without filling up with a terrible anger that made him wish England were still at war with the Nazis rather than the Lizards.

Churchill said, "I shan't forget this link. It may yet prove useful for us." Before Goldfarb could work up the nerve to ask him how, he swung back to radar: "Suppose you explain to me how and why this set is so different from ours, and so baffling."

"I'll try, sir," Goldfarb said. "One of our radars, like a wireless set, depends on valves—vacuum tubes, the Americans

would say—for its operation. The Lizards don't use valves. Instead, they have these things." He pointed to the boards with little lumps and silvery spiderwebs of metal set across them.

"And so?" Churchill said. "Why should a mere substitution pose a problem?"

"Because we don't know how the bloody things work," Goldfarb blurted. Wishing the ground would open up and swallow him, he tried to make amends: "That is, we have no theory to explain how these little lumps of silicon—which is what they are, sir—can perform the function of valves. And, because they're nothing like what we're used to, we're having to find out what each one does by cut and try, so to speak: we run power into it and see what happens. We don't know how much power to use, either."

Churchill fortunately took his strong language in stride. "And what have you learnt from your experiments?"

"That the Lizards know more about radar than we do, sir," Goldfarb answered. "That's the long and short of it, I'm afraid. We can't begin to make parts to match these: a chemical engineer with whom I've spoken says our best silicon isn't pure enough. And some of the little lumps, when you look at them under a microscope, are so finely etched that we can't imagine how, let alone why, it's been done."

"How and why are for those with the luxury of time, which we have not got," Churchill said. "We need to know what the device does, whether we can match it, and how to make it less useful to the foe."

"Yes, sir," Goldfarb said admiringly. Churchill was no boffin, but he had a firm grip on priorities. No one yet fully understood the theory of the magnetron, or how and why the narrow channels connecting its eight outer holes to the larger central one exponentially boosted the strength of the signal. That the device operated so, however, was undeniable fact, and had given the RAF a great lead over German radar—although not, worse luck, over what the Lizards used.

Group Captain Hipple said, "What *have* we learnt which is exploitable, Goldfarb?"

"Sorry, sir; I should have realized at once that was what the Prime Minister needed to know. We can copy the design of the Lizards' magnetron; that, at least, we recognize. It gives a signal of shorter wavelength and hence more precise direction than any we've made ourselves. And the nose dish that re-

ceives returning pulses is a very fine bit of engineering which shouldn't be impossible to incorporate into later marks of the Meteor."

"Very good, Radarman Goldfarb," Churchill said. "I shan't keep you from your work any longer. With the aid of men like you and your comrades in this hut, we shall triumph over this adversity as we have over all others. And you, Radarman, you may yet have a role to play even more important than your work here."

The Prime Minister looked uncommonly cherubic. Three years in the RAF had taught Goldfarb that rankers who wore that expression had more up their sleeves than their arms. They'd also taught him he couldn't do anything about it, so he said what he had to say: "I'll be happy to serve in any way I can, sir."

Churchill nodded genially, then went back to Hipple and his colleagues for more talk about jet engines. After another few minutes, he put his hat back on, tipped it to Hipple, and left the Nissen hut.

Basil Roundbush grinned at Goldfarb. "I say, old man, after Winnie makes you an MP, do remember the little people who knew you before you grew rich and famous."

"An MP?" Goldfarb shook his head in mock dismay. "Lord, I hope that's not what he had in mind. He said he had something important instead of this."

That sally met with general approval. One of the meteorologists said, "Good job you didn't tell him you're a Labour supporter, Goldfarb."

"It doesn't matter, not now." Goldfarb had backed Labour, yes, as offering more to the working man than the Tories could (and, as was true of a lot of Jewish immigrants and their progeny, his own politics had a slant to the left). But he also knew no one but Churchill could have rallied Britain against Hitler, and no one else could have kept her in the fight against the Lizards.

Thinking of the Nazis and the Lizards together made Goldfarb think of the invasion so many had feared in 1940. The Germans hadn't been able to bring it off, not least because radar kept them from driving the RAF from the skies. If the Lizards came, no one could offer any such guarantee of success. Ironically, the Germans holding northern France served as England's shield against invasion by the aliens.

But the shield was not perfect. The Lizards had control of the air when they chose to use it. They could leapfrog over northern France and the Channel both. Just because they hadn't done it didn't mean they wouldn't or couldn't.

Goldfarb snorted. The only thing he could do about that was try to make British radar more effective, which would in turn make the Lizards pay more if they decided to invade. It wasn't as much as he'd have wanted to do in an ideal world, but it was more than most people could say, so he supposed it would do.

And he'd not only met Winston Churchill, but talked business with him! That wasn't something everyone could say. He couldn't write home to his family that the Prime Minister had been here—the censors would never pass it—but he could tell them if he ever got down to London. He'd almost given up on the notion of leave.

Fred Hipple said, "Churchill's full of good ideas. The only difficulty is, he's also full of bad ones, and sometimes telling the one from the other's not easy till after the fact."

"What he said about tackling the Lizards' radar circuitry was first-rate," Goldfarb said. "*What* is more important for us now than *how* or *why*; we can use what we learn without knowing why it works, just as some stupid clot can drive a motorcar without cluttering his head with the theory of internal combustion."

"Ah, but someone must understand the theory, or your stupid clot would have no motorcar to drive," Basil Roundbush said.

"That's true only to a limited degree," Hipple said. "Even now, theory takes you only so far in aircraft design; eventually, you just have to go out and see how the beast flies. That was much more the case during the Great War, when practically everything, from what the older engineers have told me, was cut and try. Yet the aircraft they manufactured did fly."

"Most of the time," Roundbush said darkly. "I'm bloody glad I never had to go up in them."

Goldfarb ignored that. Roundbush made wisecracks the same way other men fiddled with rosaries or cracked their knuckles or tugged at one particular lock of hair: it was a nervous tic, nothing more.

Clucking softly to himself, Goldfarb fixed a power source to one side of a Lizard circuit element and an ohmmeter to the

other. He'd measure voltage and amperage next: with these strange components, you couldn't tell what they were supposed to do to a current that ran through them except by experiment.

He turned on the power. The ohmmeter swung; the component did resist the current's flow. Goldfarb grunted in satisfaction. He'd thought it would: it looked like others that had. He noted down the reading, as well as where the circuit element sat on its board and what it looked like. Then he turned off the power and hooked up the voltage meter. One tiny piece at a time, he added to the jigsaw puzzle.

As Vyacheslav Molotov turned the knob that led him into the antechamber in front of Stalin's night office, he felt and suppressed a familiar nervousness. Elsewhere in the Soviet Union, his word went unchallenged. In negotiating with the capitalist states that hated the Soviet revolution, even in discussions with the Lizards, he was the unyielding representative of his nation. He knew he had a reputation for being inflexible, and did everything he could to play it up.

Not here, though. Anyone who was unyielding and inflexible with Stalin would soon know the stiffness of death. Then Molotov had no more time for such reflections, for Stalin's orderly—oh, the fellow had a fancy title, but that was what he was—nodded to him and said, "Go on in. He expects you, Vyacheslav Mikhailovich."

Molotov nodded and entered Stalin's sanctum. This was not where the General Secretary of the Communist Party of the Soviet Union was photographed with diplomats or soldiers. He had a fancy office upstairs for that. He worked here, at hours that suited him. It was one-thirty in the morning. Stalin would be at it for at least another couple of hours. Those who dealt with him had to adjust themselves accordingly.

Stalin looked up from the desk with the gooseneck lamp. "Good morning, Vyacheslav Mikhailovich," he said with his throaty Georgian accent. His voice held no irony; morning it was, as far as he was concerned.

"Good morning, Iosef Vissarionovich," Molotov replied. Whatever his feelings about the matter were, he had schooled himself not to reveal them. He found that important at any time, doubly so around the ruler of the Soviet Union.

Stalin waved Molotov to a chair, then stood up himself. Though well-proportioned, he was short, and did not like other

men looming over him. What he did not like did not occur. He filled his pipe from a leather tobacco pouch, lit a match, and got the pipe going.

The harsh smell of *makhorka*, cheap Russian tobacco, made Molotov's nose twitch in spite of himself. Under the iron-gray mustache, Stalin's lip curled. "I know it's vile, but it's all I can find these days. What shipping we get has no room aboard for luxuries."

That said as much as anything about the plight in which mankind found itself. When the leader of one of the three greatest nations on the planet could not get decent tobacco even for himself, the Lizards were the ones with the upper hand. Well, if he understood what was in Stalin's mind, this meeting was to be about how to tilt the balance back the other way.

Stalin sucked in more smoke, paced back and forth. At length he said, "So the Americans and Germans are pressing ahead with their programs to make bombs of this explosive metal?"

"So I have been given to understand, Iosef Vissarionovich," Molotov answered. "I am also told by our intelligence services that they had these programs in place before the Lizards began their invasion of the Earth."

"We also had such a program in place," Stalin answered placidly.

That relieved Molotov, who had heard of no such program. He wondered how far along Soviet scientists had been compared to those in the decadent capitalist and fascist countries. Faith in the strength of Marxist-Leninist precepts made him hope they might have been ahead; concern over how far the Soviet Union had had to come since the revolution made him fear they might have been behind. With hope and fear so commingled, he dared not ask Stalin which was the true state of affairs.

Stalin went on, "We now have an advantage over both the United States and the Hitlerites: in that raid against the Lizards last fall, we obtained a considerable supply of the explosive metal, as you know. I had hoped the German taking the metal back to the Hitlerites would be waylaid in Poland, and his share lost." Stalin looked unhappy.

So did Molotov, who said, "This much I did know, and how

he had to give up half his share, though not all, to the Polish Jews, who then passed it on to the Americans."

"Yes," Stalin said. "Hitler is a fool, do you know that?"

"You have said it many times, Iosef Vissarionovich," Molotov answered. That was true, but it had not kept Stalin from making his nonaggression pact with Germany in 1939, or from living up to it for almost the next two years, or from being so confident Hitler would also live up to it that he'd ignored warnings of an impending Nazi attack, ignored them so completely that the Soviet state had almost crashed in ruins because of it. Since Molotov had supported Stalin in those choices, he could hardly bring them up now (if he hadn't supported him then, he would be in no position to bring them up now).

Stalin drew on his pipe again. His cheeks, pitted from a boyhood bout of smallpox, twitched with distaste. "Not even from so close as Turkey can I get decent tobacco. But do you know why I say Hitler is a fool?"

"For wantonly attacking the peace-loving people of the Soviet Union, who had done nothing to deserve it." Molotov gave the obvious answer, and a true one, but it left him unhappy. Stalin was looking for something else.

Sure enough, he shook his head. But, to Molotov's relief, he was only amused, not angry. "That is not what was in my mind, Vyacheslav Mikhailovich. I say he was a fool because, when his scientists discovered the uranium atom could be split, they published their findings for all the world to see." Stalin chuckled rheumily. "Had we made that finding here . . . Can you imagine such an article appearing in the *Proceedings* of the *Akademia Nauk*, the Soviet Academy of Sciences?"

"Hardly," Molotov said, and he chuckled, too. He was normally the most mirthless of men, but when Stalin laughed, you laughed with him. Besides, this was the sort of thing he did find funny. Stalin was dead right here—Soviet secrecy would have kept such an important secret from leaking out where prying eyes could fasten on it.

"I will tell you something else that will amuse you," Stalin said. "It takes a certain amount of explosive metal to explode, our scientists tell me. Below this amount, it will not go off no matter what you do. Do you understand? Oh, it is a lovely joke." Stalin laughed again.

Molotov also laughed, but uncertainly. This time, he did not see the joke.

Stalin must have sensed that; his uncanny skill at scenting weakness in his subordinates was not least among the talents that had kept him in power for twenty years. Still in that jovial mood, he said, "Never fear, Vyacheslav Mikhailovich; I shall explain. I would far sooner the Germans and Americans had no explosive metal, but because the Polish Jews divided it between them, neither has enough for a bomb. Now do you see?"

"No," Molotov confessed, but he reversed course a moment later: "Wait. Yes, perhaps I do. Do you mean that we, with an undivided share, have enough to make one of these bombs for ourselves?"

"That is exactly what I mean," Stalin said. "See, you are a clever fellow after all. The Germans and the Americans will still have to do all the research they would have required anyhow, but we—we shall soon be ready to fight the Lizards fire against fire, so to speak."

Just contemplating that felt good to Molotov. Like Stalin, like everyone, he had lived in dread of the day when Moscow, like Berlin and Washington, might suddenly cease to exist. To be able to retaliate in kind against the Lizards brought a glow of anticipation to his sallow features.

But his joy was not undiluted. He said, "Iosef Vissarionovich, we shall have the one bomb, with no immediate prospect for producing more, is that right? Once we have used the weapon in our hands, what is to keep the Lizards from dropping a great many such weapons on us?"

Stalin scowled. He did not care for anyone going against anything he said, even in the slightest way. Nevertheless, he thought seriously before he answered; Molotov's question was to the point. At last he said, "First of all, our scientists will go on working to produce explosive metal for us. They will be strongly encouraged to succeed."

Stalin's smile reminded Molotov of that of a lion resting against a zebra carcass from which it had just finished feeding. Molotov had no trouble visualizing the sort of encouragement the Soviet nuclear physicists would get: *dachas*, cars, women if they wanted them, for success . . . and the *gulag* or a bullet in the back of the neck if they failed. Probably a couple of them would be purged just to focus the minds of the others on

what they were doing. Stalin's methods were ugly, but they got results.

"How long before the physicists can do this for us?" Molotov said.

"They babble about three or four years, as if this were not an emergency," Stalin said dismissively. "I have given them eighteen months. They shall do as the Party requires of them, or else suffer the consequences."

Molotov chose his words with care: "It might be better if they did not undergo the supreme penalty, Iosef Vissarionovich. Men of their technical training would be difficult to replace adequately."

"Yes, yes." Stalin sounded impatient, always a danger sign. "But they are the servants of the peasants and workers of the Soviet Union, not their masters; we must not let them get ideas above their station, or the virus of the bourgeoisie will infect us once again."

"No, that cannot be permitted," Molotov agreed. "Let us say that they do all they have promised. How do we protect the Soviet Union in the time between our using the bomb we have made from the Lizards' explosive metal and that in which we begin to manufacture it for ourselves?"

"For one thing, we do not use that one bomb immediately," Stalin answered. "We *cannot* use it immediately, for it is not yet made. But even if it were, I would wait to pick the proper moment. And besides, Vyacheslav Mikhailovich"—Stalin looked smug—"how will the Lizards be certain we have only the one bomb? Once we use it, they shall have to assume we can do it again, not so?"

"Unless they assume we used their explosive metal for the first one," Molotov said.

He wished he'd kept his mouth shut. Stalin didn't shout or bluster at him; that he would have withstood with ease. Instead, the General Secretary fixed him with a glare as cold and dark and silent as midwinter at Murmansk. That was Stalin's sign of ultimate displeasure; he ordered generals and commissars shot with just such an expression.

Here, though, Molotov's point was too manifestly true for Stalin to ignore. The glare softened, as winter's grip did at last even in Murmansk. Stalin said, "This is another good argument for carefully choosing the time and place we use the bomb. But you also must remember, if we face defeat without

it, we shall surely use it against the invaders no matter what they do to us in return. They are more dangerous than the Germans, and must be fought with whatever means come to hand."

"True enough," Molotov said. The Soviet Union had 190,000,000 people; throw twenty or thirty million on the fire, or even more, and it remained a going concern. Just getting rid of the *kulaks* and bringing in collectivized agriculture had killed millions through deliberate famine. If more deaths were what building socialism in the USSR required, more deaths there would be.

"I am glad you agreed, Vyacheslav Mikhailovich," Stalin said silkily. Under the silk lay jagged steel; had Molotov persisted in disagreeing, something most disagreeable would have happened to him.

. The Foreign Commissar of the Soviet Union was fearless before the leaders of the decadent capitalist states; he had even confronted Atvar, who led the Lizards. Before Stalin, Molotov quailed. Stalin genuinely terrified him, as he did every other Soviet citizen. Back in revolutionary days, the little mustachioed Georgian had not been so much, but since, oh, but since . . .

Nevertheless, Molotov owed allegiance not just to Stalin, but to the Soviet Union as a whole. If he was to serve the USSR properly, he needed information. Getting it without angering his master was the trick. Carefully, he said, "The Lizards have taken a heavy toll on our bombing planes. Will we be able to deliver the bomb once we have it?"

"I am told the device will be too heavy and bulky to fit in any of our bombers," Stalin said. Molotov admired the courage of the man who had told—had had to tell—that to Stalin. But the Soviet leader did not seem nearly so angry as Molotov would have guessed. Instead, his face assumed an expression of genial deviousness that made Molotov want to make sure he still had his wallet and watch. He went on, "If we can dispose of Trotsky in Mexico City, I expect we can find a way to put a bomb where we want it."

"No doubt you are right, Iosef Vissarionovich," Molotov said. Trotsky had thought he was safe enough to keep plotting against the Soviet Union, but several inches of tempered steel in his brain proved that a delusion.

"No doubt I am," Stalin agreed complacently. As undisputed master of the Soviet Union, he had developed ways not altogether different from those of other undisputed masters. Molotov had once or twice thought of saying as much, but it remained just that—a thought.

He did ask, "How soon can the Germans and Americans begin producing their own explosive metal?" The Americans didn't much worry him; they were far away and had worries closer to home. The Germans . . . Hitler had talked about using the new bombs against the Lizards in Poland. The Soviet Union was an older enemy, and almost as close.

"We are working to learn this. I expect we shall be informed well in advance, whatever the answer proves to be," Stalin answered, complacent still. Soviet espionage in capitalist countries continued to function well; many there devoted themselves to furthering the cause of the socialist revolution.

Molotov cast about for other questions he might safely ask. Before he could come up with any, Stalin bent over the papers on his desk, a sure sign of dismissal. "Thank you for your time, Iosef Vissarionovich," Molotov said as he stood to go.

Stalin grunted. His politeness was minimal, but then, so was Molotov's with anyone but him. When Molotov closed the door behind him, he permitted himself the luxury of a small sigh. He'd survived another audience.

For getting his consignment of uranium or whatever it was safely from Boston to Denver, Leslie Groves had been promoted to brigadier general. He hadn't yet bothered replacing his eagles with stars; he had more important things to worry about. His pay was accumulating at the new rate, not that that meant much, what with prices going straight through the roof.

At the moment what galled him worse than inflation was the lack of gratitude he was getting from the Metallurgical Laboratory scientists. Enrico Fermi looked at him with sorrowful Mediterranean eyes and said, "Valuable as this sample may be, it does not constitute a critical mass."

"I'm sorry, that's not a term I know," Groves said. He knew nuclear energy could be released, but nobody had done much publishing on matters nuclear since Hahn and Strassmann split the uranium atom, and, to complicate things further, the Met Lab crew had developed a jargon all their own.

"It means you have not brought us enough with which to make a bomb," Leo Szilard said bluntly. He and the other physicists round the table glared at Groves as if he were deliberately holding back another fifty kilos of priceless metal.

Since he wasn't, he glared, too. "My escort and I risked our lives across a couple of thousand miles to get that package to you," he growled. "If you're telling me we wasted our time, smiling when you say it isn't going to help." Even relatively lean as the journey had left him, he was the biggest man at the conference table, and used to using his physical presence to get what he wanted.

"No, no, this is not what we mean," Fermi said quickly. "You could not have known exactly what you had, and we could not, either, until you delivered it."

"We did not even know *that* you had it until you delivered it," Szilard said. "Security—pah!" He muttered something under his breath in what might have been Magyar. Whatever it was, it sounded pungent. Groves had seen his dossier. His politics had some radical leanings, but he was too brilliant for that to count against him.

Fermi added, "The material you brought will be invaluable in research, and in combining with what we eventually produce ourselves. But by itself, it is not sufficient."

"All right, you'll have to do here what you were going to do at Chicago," Groves said. "How's that coming?" He turned to the one man from the Met Lab crew he'd met before. "Dr. Larssen, what is the status of getting the project up and running again here in Denver?"

"We were building the graphite pile under Stagg Field at the University of Chicago," Jens Larssen answered. "Now we're reassembling it under the football stadium here. The work goes—well enough." He shrugged.

Groves gave Larssen a searching once-over. He didn't seem to have the driving energy he'd shown in White Sulphur Springs, West Virginia, the summer before. Then, he'd passionately urged the federal government-in-hiding to do all it could to hold Chicago against the Lizards. But the Met Lab had had to move even though Chicago was held, and now—well, it just didn't seem as if Larssen gave a damn. That kind of attitude wouldn't do, not when the work at hand was so urgent.

The meeting with the physicists went on for another half

hour, over lesser but still vital issues like keeping electricity coming into Denver and into the University of Denver in particular so the men could do their jobs. People in the United States had taken electricity for granted until the Lizards came. Now, over too much of the country, it was a vanished luxury. But if it vanished in Denver, the Met Lab would have to find somewhere else to go, and Groves didn't think the country—or the world—could afford the delay.

Unlike nuclear physics, electricity was something with which, by God, he was intimately familiar. "We'll keep it going for you," he promised, and hoped he could make good on the vow. If the Lizards got the idea humans were experimenting with nuclear energy here, they'd have something to say about the matter. Keeping them from finding out, then, was going to be a sizable part of keeping the lights on.

When the meeting broke up, Groves fell into step with Larssen and ignored the physicist's efforts to break away. "We need to talk, Dr. Larssen," he said.

"No we don't, Colonel—sorry, *General*—Groves," Larssen said, loading the title with all the scorn he could. "The Army's already done enough to screw up my life, thanks very much. I don't need any more help from you." He turned his back and started to stamp off.

Groves shot out a big, meaty hand and caught him by the arm. From the way Larssen whirled around, Groves thought he was going to swing on him. Decking a physicist wasn't part of his own job description, but if that was what it took, that was what he'd do.

Maybe Larssen saw that in his eyes, for he didn't throw the punch. Groves said, "Look, your life is your business. But when it makes you have trouble with your job, well, your particular job is too important to let that happen. So what's eating you, and how come you think it's the Army's fault?"

"You want to know? You really want to know?" Larssen didn't wait for an answer from Groves, but plowed ahead: "Well, why the hell shouldn't I tell you? Somebody else will if I don't. After I saw you last year, I managed to get all the way to western Indiana on my own. That's when I ran into General Patton, who wouldn't let me send my wife a message so she'd know I was alive and okay."

"Security—" Groves began.

"Yeah, security. So I couldn't get her a message then, and by the time I got to Chicago, it was too late—the Met Lab team had already taken off. And I couldn't get a message to Barbara after that—security again. So she figured I was dead. What was she supposed to think?"

"Oh," Groves said. "I'm sorry. That must have been a shock when she came into Denver. But I'll bet you had quite a reunion."

"It was great," Larssen said, his voice deadly cold. "She thought I was dead, so she fell for this corporal who rides herd on Lizard POWs. She married him up in Wyoming. I was already in Denver, but Colonel Hexham, God bless him, still wouldn't let me write. Security one more time. Now she's gonna have the guy's baby. So as far as I'm concerned, General Groves, sir, the U.S. Army can go fuck itself. And if you don't like it, throw me in the brig."

Groves opened his mouth, closed it again. He'd been through Chugwater just after that wedding in Wyoming. He'd known something was eating Larssen, but not what. No wonder the poor bastard was in a blue funk. Mahatma Gandhi wouldn't have stayed cool, calm, and collected with this landing on him.

"Maybe she'll come back to you," he said at last. It sounded lame, even in his own ears.

Larssen laughed scornfully. "Doesn't look that way. She's still going to bed with Sam stinking Yeager, that's for sure. Women!" He clapped a hand to his forehead. "You can't live without 'em and they won't live with you."

Groves hadn't seen his own wife in months, either, or sent her a note or anything else. He didn't worry about her running around, though; he just worried about her being all right. Maybe that just meant he was older and more settled than Larssen and his wife. Maybe it meant his marriage was in better shape. Or maybe (unsettling thought) it meant he didn't know what to worry about.

He fell back on his own training: "Dr. Larssen, you cannot let it get you down to the point where it affects your work. You cannot. More than just you and your wife depends on what you do here, more even than your country. I am not exaggerating when I say the fate of humanity rests on your shoulders."

"I know that," Larssen said. "But it's hard to give a damn about the fate of humanity when the one human being who really matters to you goes and does something like this."

There Groves could not argue with him, nor did he try. He said, "You're not the only one in that boat. It happens all the time—maybe more in war than in peace, because things are more broken up nowadays—but all the time. You have to pick up the pieces and keep going."

"You think I don't know that?" Larssen said. "I tell myself the same thing twenty times a day. But it's damned hard when I keep seeing her there with that other guy. It hurts too much to stand."

Groves thought about shipping out the other guy—Yeager, Larssen had said his name was. With the war on, keeping a physicist happy counted for more than the feelings of a Lizard liaison man. But even if he did that, he had no guarantee it would bring Barbara back into Jens' arms, not if she was carrying Yeager's baby.

And she and Yeager wouldn't have got married if they hadn't thought Larssen was dead. They'd tried to make things right, the best way they knew how. It hadn't worked, but they hadn't had all the data they needed, and humans couldn't be engineered like electrons, anyhow.

Just the same, Groves wished he could order Barbara to go to bed with Jens for the good of the country. It would have made things a lot simpler. But, while a medieval baron might have gotten away with an order like that, a twentieth-century woman would spit in his eye if he tried it. That was what freedom was about. He believed in freedom . . . no matter how inconvenient it was at the moment.

"Professor Larssen, you've got yourself a mess," he said heavily.

"Yeah. Now tell me one I haven't heard."

When Larssen broke away this time, Groves didn't try to stop him. He just stood and watched till the physicist turned a corner and disappeared. Then he shook his head. "That's trouble, waiting to happen," he muttered, and started slowly down the hall himself.

Atvar turned one eye turret to the left side of the audience chamber, the other to the right. The assembled shiplords stared

back at him. He tried to gauge their temper. They'd been struggling for close to two years, almost one of Tosev 3's slow revolutions around its star, to bring the miserable world into the Empire. By all they'd known when they left from Home, the conquest should have been over in a matter of days—which only proved they hadn't known much.

"My fellow males, let us consider the status of our enterprise," he said.

"It shall be done, Exalted Fleetlord," the shiplords chorused in a show of the perfect obedience the Race so esteemed. No virtue was more fundamental than obedience. So Atvar had been taught since he came from his egg; so he'd believed till he came to Tosev 3.

He still believed it, but not as he had back on Home. Tosev 3 corroded every assumption the Race made about how life should be lived. The only thing the Big Uglies knew about obedience was that they weren't very good at it. They'd even overthrown and murdered emperors: to Atvar, whose ruling dynasty had held the throne for tens of thousands of years, a crime almost incomprehensibly heinous.

He said, "We do continue to make progress in our campaigns. Our counterattacks south of the Tosevite city known as Chicago on the smaller continental mass have pushed back the enemy, and—"

Straha, shiplord of the *206th Emperor Yower*, raised a hand. Atvar wished he could ignore the male. Unfortunately, Straha was next most senior shiplord after Kirel, who commanded the bannership itself. Even more unfortunately, from Atvar's point of view, Straha headed a loud and vocal faction of males whose principal amusement seemed to be carping about the way the war against the Tosevites was going.

Having been (reluctantly) recognized, Straha said, "May it please the exalted fleetlord, I would respectfully note that the campaign continues to have obvious shortcomings. I hope I shall not try his patience if I elucidate?"

"Proceed," Atvar said. *Maybe,* he thought hopefully, *Straha will say something really unforgivable and give me the excuse I've been looking for to sack him.* It hadn't happened yet, worse luck.

Straha stood a little straighter, the better to display his elaborate, punctiliously applied body paint. He had his own agenda, Atvar knew: if he could persuade enough males that the

fleetlord was botching his leadership of the war, he might become fleetlord himself. It would be irregular, but everything about the conquest—the attempted conquest—of Tosev 3 was irregular. If Straha succeeded where Atvar had failed, the Emperor would turn his eye turrets away from the irregularity.

The fractious shiplord said, "First and most important is the increased punishment our armor is taking at the hands of the Big Uglies. Loss rates are up significantly from last year's fighting to this. Such a toll cannot continue indefinitely."

There Atvar, try as he would, could not disagree with Straha. He made his voice sharp, though, as he answered, "I cannot produce landcruisers out of thin air, nor can the Big Uglies under our control manufacture any that meet our needs. Meanwhile, those out of our control continue to improve their models, and to introduce new weapons such as antilandcruiser rockets. Thus our losses are higher of late."

"The Tosevites out of our control always seem capable of more than those we have conquered," Straha said acidly.

With an effort, the fleetlord ignored the sarcasm and replied to the literal sense of Straha's words: "This is not surprising, Shiplord. The most technologically advanced regions of this inhomogeneous planet are precisely the ones most capable of extended resistance and, I suppose, of innovation."

He spoke the last word with a certain amount of distaste. In the Empire, innovation came seldom, and its effects were tightly controlled. On Tosev 3, it ran wild, fueled by the endless squabbling among the Big Uglies' tiny empires. Atvar thought such quick change surely malignant for the long-term health of a civilization, but the Tosevites cared nothing for the long term. And in the short term, quick change made them more dangerous, not less.

"Let that be as you say, Exalted Fleetlord," Straha answered. Atvar gave him a suspicious look; he'd yielded too easily. Sure enough, he went on, "Some of our losses, however, may be better explained by causes other than Tosevite technical progress. I speak in reference to the continued and growing use among our fighting males of the herb termed ginger."

"I concede the problem, Shiplord," Atvar said. He could hardly do otherwise, what with some of the after-action reports he'd seen from the landcruiser combats in France. Had things gone as planned, the Race would have been pushing into

Deutschland. Instead, they'd taken a pounding almost as costly as the one that had held them out of Chicago, and without the excuse of winter.

Atvar continued, "Surely, though, you cannot hold me responsible for the effects of an unanticipated alien herb. We are making every effort to diminish its consequences on our operations. If you have any concrete suggestions in that regard, I would gratefully receive them."

He'd hoped that would shut Straha up. It didn't; nothing seemed to. But it did make the shiplord change the subject: "Exalted Fleetlord, what have we learned of the Big Uglies' efforts to produce their own nuclear weapons?"

Where Straha had been playing to his own faction before, now he seized the attention of all the assembled males. If the Tosevites got their clawless hands on nuclear weapons, the campaign stopped being a war of conquest and turned into a war of survival. And what would the onrushing colonization fleet do if, between them, the Big Uglies and the Race rendered Tosev 3 uninhabitable?

Hating Straha, Atvar answered, "Though they did steal nuclear material from us, we have found no sign that they can yet produce a weapon with it." The fleetlord had expected that question to arise, if not from Straha, then from someone else. He touched a recessed button on the podium. A holograph of one of the Race's power plants appeared. Seeing the familiar egg-shaped protective dome over the reactor made him long bitterly for Home. Forcing down the emotion, he went on, "We have also detected no indications of any structures like this one, which would be required for them to utilize their own radioactive materials."

Most of the shiplords relaxed when they heard that. Even Straha said, "So they won't be able to use nuclear weapons against us for the next few years, eh? Well, there's something, anyhow." If that wasn't praise, it wasn't carping criticism, either. Atvar gratefully accepted it.

Loyal, steadfast Kirel raised a hand. Atvar was delighted to recognize him. Then Kirel said, "Excuse me, Exalted Fleetlord, but the Big Uglies are good at camouflage. And besides, some of their primitive structures look very little like those of ours which perform equivalent functions. Are we truly as certain as we would like to be that their nuclear weapons programs are

not progressing under our very snouts, to emerge as unexpectedly as some of their other weapons?"

Aside from the difficulty of proving a negative, Atvar had no answer prepared for that. The meeting did not dissolve on the note for which he'd hoped.

☆ X ☆

Teerts was coming to look forward to mealtimes. For one thing, the Nipponese had been feeding him better lately, with many more bits of meat and fish mixed in with the rice that made up the greater part of his diet. For another, they'd also taken to spicing his food instead of leaving it bland and boring; his tongue tingled pleasantly when he ate now. The spices weren't the same as the ones cooks back on Home would have used, but they livened up meals in a similar way.

And for a third, food these days gave him a lift that carried him altogether out of the depression that had gripped him since his killercraft went down near Harbin. For a while after he ate, he felt bright and strong and ever so wise. The feeling never lasted as long as he wished it would, but having it even for a little while was welcome.

The Nipponese seemed to notice his changed attitude, too. They'd developed the habit of interrogating him right after he ate. He didn't mind. Food made him seem so omniscient that he dealt with their questions with effortless ease.

He heard a squeak and a rattle down the hall: the food cart. He sprang to his feet, waited eagerly by the bars of his cell for the cart to arrive. One guard unlocked the cell. Another stood watch with a knife-tipped rifle. The fellow who actually served the food handed Teerts his bowl.

"Thank you, superior sir," he said in Nipponese, bowing as he did so. The guard locked the cell door again. The cart clattered away.

Out of necessity, Teerts had become adept with the little paired sticks the Nipponese used to manipulate food. He brought a chunk of fish to his mouth, twisted his tongue

around it. It didn't taste the way it had for a good many meals. It wasn't bad, though. *They've changed the herbs they're using,* he thought, and gulped it down.

He got to the bottom of the bowl in a hurry; although the Nipponese were feeding him better than they had, he wasn't any great threat to get fat. As he ran his tongue over his hard outer mouthparts to clean them, he waited for the wonderful feeling of well-being that had come to accompany each meal.

He didn't get it, not this time. He'd been more than unusually gloomy when the feeling passed away after a meal. Now, failing to find it at all, he felt desperate, betrayed; the iron bars of his cell seemed to be closing in around him. He paced restlessly back and forth, his tailstump jerking like a metronome.

He hadn't realized how much he'd depended on that mealtime burst of euphoria till it was denied him. He opened his mouth, displaying his full set of small, sharp teeth. If Major Okamoto came by, he'd gnaw a chunk off him. *That* would give him a good feeling, by the Emperor!

Not much later, Major Okamoto did come down the hallway. He stopped in front of Teerts' cell. The captured killercraft pilot's dreams of vengeance turned to fear at the sight of the Big Ugly, as they always did.

"Good day," Okamoto said in the language of the Race. He'd become quite fluent, much more so than Teerts was in Nipponese. "How are you feeling today?"

"Superior sir, I am not so well as I would like," Teerts answered; among the Race, that question was taken literally.

Okamoto's rubbery face twisted into what Teerts had come to recognize as an expression of amusement. That worried the male; Okamoto's amusement often came at his expense. But the Big Ugly's words were mild enough: "I may know what is troubling you, and may even have a medicine to cure your trouble."

"*Honto?*—Really?" Teerts asked suspiciously: From all he'd seen of what the Big Uglies called medicine, he'd sooner have taken his chances on being sick.

"*Hai, honto,*" Okamoto answered, also falling back into Nipponese. From a pocket of his uniform, he pulled out a small waxed-paper bag. He poured a little of the brown powder it held into the palm of his hand, then held the hand out to Teerts through the bars. "Here, put your tongue on this."

Teerts sniffed first. The powder had a pungent, spicy odor

that seemed familiar, though he could not place it at once. He reflected that the Tosevites could kill him any time they chose; they did not need to put on an elaborate charade if they wanted him dead. Therefore he flicked out his tongue and licked up the powder.

As soon as he tasted it, he knew what it was: the flavor that had been missing from his latest bowl of food. A moment later, he realized the Nipponese must have been feeding it to him in tiny doses till now. He didn't just feel good; he felt as if the sacred Emperor were some sort of lowly cousin of his. Ruling the Race would have been too small a job for him; keeping track of all the planets in all the galaxies seemed about right.

Through the omnipotence that blazed in him, he saw Okamoto's face contort again. "You like that, *neh*?" the Big Ugly asked, all but the last word in Teerts' tongue.

"Yes," Teerts said, as if from very far away. He wished Okamoto were very far away, so he would not pester him at this transcendent moment.

But the interrogator and interpreter did not pester him. The Big Ugly just leaned back against the bars of the empty cell across from Teerts' and waited. For a while, Teerts ignored him as being beneath notice, let alone contempt. The glorious feeling from the powder he'd licked up, though, didn't last as long as he'd hoped it would. And when it was gone . . .

When it was gone, Teerts crashed into depths deeper than the heights he had scaled. The weight of all the worlds he'd so blithely imagined he could oversee came down on his narrow shoulders and crushed him. Now he ignored Okamoto because the Big Ugly was outside his sphere of intensely personal misery. Nothing the Nipponese did to him could be worse than what his own body and brain were doing. He huddled in a corner of the cell and wished he could die.

Okamoto's voice pursued him: "Not so good? Want another taste?" The Big Ugly held out his broad, fleshy hand, a small mound of powder in the middle of the palm.

Even before his conscious mind willed him to action, Teerts was on his feet and bounding toward the bars between which that hand so temptingly protruded. But before his tongue could touch that precious powder, Okamoto jerked the hand back. Teerts almost slammed his muzzle against the cold, unyielding

iron that caged him. Careless of his own safety, he cursed Okamoto as vilely as he knew how.

The Tosevite threw back his head and let out several of the loud barking noises his kind used for laughter. "So you want more ginger, do you? I thought you might. We have learned males of the Race are—how do you say it?—very fond of this herb."

Ginger. Now Teerts had a name for what he craved. For some reason, that only made him crave it more. His fury collapsed into depression once again. Instead of hissing at Okamoto, he pleaded with him: "Give it to me, I beg. How can you hold it away from me if you know how badly I need it?"

Okamoto laughed again. "One who lets himself be captured does not deserve to have anything *given* to him." When it came to prisoners of war, the Nipponese knew only scorn. Okamoto went on, "Maybe, though, just maybe, you can *earn* more ginger for yourself. Do you understand?"

Teerts understood too miserably well. The trap's teeth were sharp, sharp. His captors had given him a taste for ginger in his food, withheld it, shown him exactly what he craved, and now were withholding it again. They expected that would make him submit. They were, he admitted to himself, dead right. Hating the cringing whine he heard in his own voice, he said, "What do you want me to do, superior sir?"

"More exact answers to the questions we have been putting to you on explosive metals might make us more pleased with you," Okamoto said.

Teerts knew that was a lie. Because he'd let himself be taken prisoner, the Nipponese would never be happy with him, no matter what he did. But they might find him more useful; he'd already seen how his treatment varied with their perception of his value. If he satisfied them, they would give him ginger. The thought tolled in his head like the reverberations from a big bass drum.

Despite it, he had to say, "I have already given you the best and truest answers I can."

"So you claim now," Okamoto answered. "We shall see how you reply when you want ginger more than you can imagine now. Maybe then you will remember better than you do today."

The teeth of the trap were not only sharp, they were jagged as well. The Nipponese didn't just want Teerts to be their pris-

oner; they wanted him to be their slave. Slavery had vanished
from the culture of the Race long before Home was unified,
but the Rabotevs (or was it the Hallessi?—Teerts had always
dozed through history lessons) practiced it whenever their
world, whichever it was, came into the Empire. They returned
the concept, if not the institution, to the notice of the Race.
Teerts feared it wasn't just a concept on Tosev 3.

He also feared that if he went without ginger, he would go
mad. The craving ate at him like acid dripping on his scaly
skin. "Please, let me taste it now," he begged.

Some of his Nipponese captors had been wantonly cruel,
and exulted in their cruelty in the exact proportion that they
enjoyed power over his helplessness. They would have refused, merely to experience the pleasure they took from watching him suffer. Okamoto, to give him his limited due, did not
daub on that pattern of body paint. Having shown Teerts he
was indeed trapped, the Big Ugly let him sample the bait once
more.

The feeling of power and wisdom flooded through Teerts
again. While he reached that ecstatic, exalted peak, he did his
best to come up with a way to escape the prison where the
Nipponese held him. For an all but omnipotent genius, it
should have been easy.

But no brilliant ideas came. Maybe the ginger did sharpen
his analytical faculty a little: he swiftly concluded the feeling
of brilliance it gave him was just that, a feeling, and nothing
more. Had the powder not been coursing through his veins, he
would have been bitterly disappointed. As things were, he
noted the problem, then dismissed it.

Tosevites were impetuous, hot-blooded, always *doing things*.
The Race's virtues were study, patience, careful planning. So
Teerts had been indoctrinated, and little he had seen inclined
him to doubt what his killercraft squadron's briefing officers
had said. But now, out in the hallway, Okamoto stood quietly
and waited as patiently as any male of the Race.

And Teerts? As the joy from the ginger ebbed in him, leaving only a memory of sensation, Teerts became a veritable par-
ody of a Big Ugly, grabbing at the bars of his cell, shouting
curses, reaching uselessly for Okamoto in a foredoomed effort
to get more ginger onto his tongue: in short, he acted blindly,
without the slightest concern for consequences. He should have

been ashamed of himself. He *was* ashamed of himself—but not enough to stop.

Okamoto waited until his blustering had died away, swallowed in the crushing depression that followed ginger euphoria. Then, at just the right instant, the Nipponese said, "Tell me everything you know about the process that transforms element 92 to element 94."

"The special word for this in our language is 'transmutes,' " Teerts said. "It takes place in several steps. First—" He wondered how much Okamoto would make him talk before he got another taste.

Bobby Fiore threw an easy peg to the young Chinese man who stood waiting to catch the ball. The fellow actually did catch it, too; it slapped into the leather glove (a duplicate of Fiore's) he wore, and he covered it with his bare hand.

"Good job!" Fiore said, using tone and expression and dumb show to get across what he still had trouble saying in Chinese. "Now throw it back." Again, gesture showed what he wanted.

The Chinese, whose name was Lo, threw high. Fiore sprang and caught the ball. He landed lightly, ready to throw again himself: after so many years on so many infields, he could probably do that in his sleep. Drop a ball anywhere near him and he'd be on it like a cat.

"Don't throw like a girl," he told Lo; this once, it was just as well that his pupil didn't understand exactly what he had to say. He demonstrated, exaggerating the from-the-elbow style the Chinese had used and shaking his head violently to show it wasn't the best way to do the job. Then he showed the full-arm motion American kids picked up on farmyards, parks, and vacant lots.

Lo didn't seem to think one better than the other. Instead of using his handmade, expensive baseball to prove the point, Bobby Fiore bent down to get an egg-sized rock. He and Lo were not far from the razor-wire fence around the Lizards' camp. He turned and threw the rock as far as he could into the green fields beyond the perimeter.

He found another rock, tossed it underhand to Lo. "Let's see you top that, throwing like you do," he said. Again, gestures eked out meaning. Lo nodded and let fly, grunting with effort. His rock flew barely half as far as Fiore's had. He looked at

the American, nodded thoughtfully, and tried the full-arm motion. Fiore clapped his hands. "That's the idea!"

The truth was, he couldn't antagonize a cash customer. He and Liu Han still put on their baseball show, but it didn't pull in as much as it had when it was new. A few Chinese had been interested enough to pay to learn more, so he was teaching them to hit and catch and throw. Had the camp had enough open space, they could have put on a real game.

He didn't care to kowtow to Chinamen, but he'd grown used to the little luxuries spare cash allowed him to buy. And it wasn't as if he was selling something they had to have. If he got 'em mad at him, they'd just leave. So he did his best to stay on good behavior.

"Come on, try it with the ball," he said, and tossed it to Lo. The Chinese threw it back, still not too straight but with a better motion. "That's the way to do it!" Fiore said, clapping his hands in encouragement.

After several more throws that showed he was starting to get the idea, Lo picked up another rock and flung it out over the razor wire into the field. Throwing with his whole arm, he made it go a good deal farther than he'd managed before, but still not as far as Fiore had flung it. The ballplayer puffed out his chest, thinking no Chink was going to get the better of him.

Maybe Lo thought the same thing, for he bowed to Fiore and spoke several sharp sentences. Almost in spite of himself, Fiore was starting to understand Chinese. He didn't follow all of this, but got the idea that Lo was praising his arm and wanted to bring by some friends who would also be interested in the way he threw.

"Yeah, sure, that'd be fine," Fiore answered in English, and then did his best to turn it into Chinese. Evidently Lo got the idea, because he bowed again and nodded, then gave the glove back to Fiore and went on his way.

Well enough pleased with how the afternoon had gone, Fiore headed back toward the house he shared with Liu Han. He started whistling "Begin the Beguine" to himself as he walked along, but had to cut it out when the Chinese he walked past stared at him. As far as he was concerned, Chinese music sounded as if it were made by stepping on cats' tails—out-of-tune cats, at that. The locals returned the sentiment when he made melodies he liked. Since there were lots of them and one of him, he shut up.

When he opened the door to the hut the Lizards had given him and Liu Han, his nostrils twitched appreciatively. Something tasty was cooking, even if the vegetables that went with it would be strange and underdone for his taste. "Smells good," he said, and added the Lizards' emphatic cough.

Liu Han looked up from the pan in which she was cooking. It was, to Fiore's way of thinking, a funny kind of pan, being shaped like the wide, conical hats a lot of Chinese wore. It had a funny name, too: she called it a *walk*. Whenever he heard that, he pictured the pan tossing away its bat and trotting down to first base.

Liu Han tilted the *walk* on its stand so he could see the bite-sized pieces of chicken in it. "Cooked with five spices," she said. He nodded, smiling. He didn't know what all five spices were, but they made for mighty tasty cooking.

After supper, he gave her the trade dollars Lo had paid him for learning the art of throwing straight. "He has other people he may want me to teach, too," he said. "If they all pay as well as he did, that should keep us in groceries a good long while."

He said it first in English, then added Chinese and Lizard words till he was sure she'd got the idea. When she talked to him, she used a Chinese frame padded with English and Lizard. As time passed, they gained more and more words in common.

She said, "If they pay silver like this Lo, I be fat even without baby." She was starting to show now, her belly pressing against the cotton tunic that had been loose.

"Babe, you still look good to me," he said, which made her smile. He got the idea she was surprised he kept wanting her even though she was pregnant. He hadn't been sure he would, either, but the growing mound of her belly didn't bother him. It meant he couldn't just climb on top all the time, but doing it other ways was broadening his horizons.

Thinking about it made him want to do it. One nice thing about the way Liu Han cooked was that it didn't leave him feeling as if he'd swallowed an anvil, the way pasta did sometimes. If you got too full, you had trouble staying interested in other things. As it was . . .

Before he could get up and head for the blankets on the *kang*, somebody knocked on the door. He made a sour face. Liu Han giggled; she must have known what was on his mind.

"Whoever it is, I'll get rid of him in a hurry," he said, climbing to his feet.

But when he opened the door, there stood Lo with several other men behind him. *Business,* Fiore thought. He waved them in. Business counted, too, and Liu Han would still be there after they'd gone. Now she'd be hostess and interpreter. She offered the newcomers tea. Fiore still missed his coffee, thick with cream and sugar, but tea, he'd decided, would do in a pinch.

The last of the newcomers shut the door behind him. Lo and his friends—six men in all—crowded the hut. They sat quietly and seemed polite, but the longer Fiore looked at them, the more he wished he hadn't let them all in at once. They were all young and on the hard side and, with their silence, more disciplined than the usually voluble Chinese of the camp. He carefully didn't glance over to the corner where he'd leaned his bat against the wall, but he didn't let them get between him and it.

He knew about shakedowns. His uncle Giuseppe, a baker, had paid protection money for a while for the privilege of going to work every day without getting his arms broken. He wasn't going to let that happen to him, not from a bunch of Chinamen. They could do their stuff on him tonight, but he'd have the Lizards on them tomorrow.

Then he realized the only one whose name he knew was Lo, and even Lo was only half a name. The rest—would he recognize them again? Maybe. Maybe not.

He grabbed the bull by the horns, asking, "What can I do for you guys? You're interested in learning to throw the right way, yeah?" He made a proper, full-arm throwing motion without any ball.

"We are interested in throwing, yes," Lo answered through Liu Han. Then he asked a question of his own: "Are you and your woman lackeys and running dogs of the little scaly devils or just their prisoners?"

Bobby Fiore and Liu Han looked at each other. Though he had been thinking of siccing the Lizards on these guys if they turned out to be hoodlums, that question had only one possible answer. "Prisoners," he said, and mimed holding his hands up to the bars of a cell.

Lo smiled. So did two or three of his buddies. The others just sat, still and watchful. Lo said, "If you are prisoners, you

must want to help the oppressed peasants and workers strike a blow for freedom."

Liu Han's translation wasn't anywhere near as smooth as that. Fiore cocked his head to one side anyway. Traveling through small and medium-sized towns in an America staggered by the Depression, he'd heard plenty of guys standing on crates at street corners who talked like that. He pointed a finger at Lo. "You're a Red, that's what you are—a Communist, a Bolshevik."

Liu Han didn't recognize any of the English (or Russian). She stared and spread her hands, at a loss to interpret. But one of the terms made sense to Lo. He nodded soberly to Bobby Fiore, as if to say he was smarter than the Chinese had figured. Then he spoke to Liu Han, letting her know what was going on.

She didn't gasp as if she'd just seen a rat scurry across the floor, the way a lot of American women would have. She just nodded and tried to explain to Fiore, then fell silent when she realized he already understood. "They not bad," she told him. "They fight Japanese, more than Kuomintang does."

"Okay," he said. "The Reds were on our side before the Lizards came, sure. And everybody wants to give *them* a good swift kick. But what do these guys want with me?"

Lo didn't answer, not with words. Instead, he nudged one of his comrades. The young man reached under his tunic and pulled out a grenade. He didn't say anything, either. He just let it sit in the palm of his hand.

Bobby didn't need more than a heartbeat before the light went on in his head. He started to laugh. "So you want me to do your pitching for you, huh?" he said, not caring that neither Lo nor Liu Han understood what he was talking about. "I wish Sam Yeager was here. You think my arm's hot stuff, you oughta see his."

Lo politely waited till he was done before speaking. Liu Han hesitantly translated: "They want you—" She forgot the English for *throw*, but made a gesture to show what she meant. Fiore nodded. Then she pointed at the grenade.

"Yeah, I already worked that out," Fiore said. He'd worked out some other things, too: if he said no, for instance, he and Liu Han were liable to end up wearing whatever Chinamen used for concrete overshoes. This wasn't just a shakedown. If he said no, he was a big danger to these people. From every-

thing he'd ever heard, Bolsheviks didn't let people who were dangerous to them keep walking and breathing.

And besides, he didn't want to say no. He wished he could have chucked some grenades at the Lizards back in Cairo, Illinois, after they caught him the first time. That would have kept him out of this whole mess. Even though he did care for Liu Han, he would have given a lot to be back in the good old U.S. of A.

Since he couldn't have that, giving the little scaly bastards a hard time here on the other side of the world would have to do. "So what do you want me to blow up?" he asked Lo.

Maybe the Red hadn't expected such enthusiastic cooperation. He talked in low tones with his friends before he turned back to Liu Han. She sounded worried as she told Fiore, "They want you to go with them. No say where."

He wondered if he ought to insist that Lo tell Liu Han where he'd be. After a second's doubt, he decided that would be stupid. If she didn't know, she couldn't tell anybody, especially the Lizards . . . and, if she didn't know, the Reds would have less reason to come after her to shut her up in case things went wrong.

He got to his feet. "Let's go take care of it," he said to Lo.

He felt edgy, almost bouncy, as he walked, as if Mutt Daniels (and he wondered what had happened to old Mutt) had flashed him the sign to steal home on the next pitch. Well, why not? He wasn't just trying to steal home. He was going into combat.

Sooner or later, he was sure, he would have volunteered for the Army. But even then, he would have trained for months before he got the chance to see action. Now—it was as if he'd got his rifle and headed up to the front line one right after the other. No wonder he felt all loosey-goosey.

He blew Liu Han a kiss. Lo and his fellow Bolsheviks snickered and said things that were probably rude to one another: Chinese men weren't in the habit of showing they gave a damn about their women. *Well, to hell with them, too,* he thought. Liu Han managed a return smile, but he could see she was frightened about this whole business.

Night in the prison camp was darker than anything Fiore had known back in the States, even in the panicky blackouts that had followed Pearl Harbor. Few of the huts had any windows, and few of what windows there were had lights showing

through them. If the moon was up in the sky, a thick layer of clouds made sure nobody could see it. Though that made Fiore stumble along, he didn't bellyache, not even to himself: darkness would give the Lizards a harder time spotting him. That he liked.

The Chinese picked their way through the black as if they had headlights. A couple of times, Bobby Fiore heard people getting out of their way in a hurry. A large group of disciplined men traveling confidently was something few wanted to mess with. He liked that, too.

Before long, he had no idea where in the camp Lo was taking him. *It all looks alike to me,* he thought, and stifled a nervous giggle. He didn't know if the Bolsheviks were walking him around in circles to get him lost or if it just worked out that way, but lost he undoubtedly was.

Lo opened the door of a shabby little hut, gestured for his companions and Fiore to go in. The inside of the hut was darker than the alley had been. That didn't stop Lo. He shoved aside a heavy wooden chest—by all appearances, the only furniture in the place—and pulled up a square piece of board underneath it. He and two of his friends dropped down into the tunnel the board concealed.

One of the remaining Reds nudged Fiore and pointed to the round mouth of the tunnel. He went into it with all the eagerness of a man walking to the electric chair. As he had when he left the hut he shared with Liu Han, he learned new lessons about how dark darkness could be. As far as his eyes were concerned, he'd just gone blind. But with Chinese ahead and Chinese pushing him on from behind, he could have no doubt about which direction to go.

The tunnel wasn't tall enough for him to stand upright, or even to crouch. He had to crawl along on hands and knees, and even then the top of his head kept bumping on the roof and showering clods of dirt down onto his neck. The air in the tunnel smelled like moist earth, dank and musty, and felt dead, as if nobody had any business breathing down here.

He had no idea how long he crawled, either in time or distance. It seemed forever, either way. He imagined the tunnel was sloping up several times, but each one proved to be just that: imaginary. Without eyes to help it, his sense of balance played tricks on him.

At last, though, he smelled fresh air. He hurried forward,

and now found himself going unmistakably upward as well. He scrambled out and lay gasping in relief in a hollow in a field. After the tunnel, that seemed a wonderful luxury. It also seemed almost bright as day. The other three Chinese Reds came out of the hole just as eagerly as he had. That made him feel better.

Lo cautiously raised his head. He turned to Bobby Fiore, pointed. Fiore raised his head, too. Off in the distance sat a Lizard guard station on the camp perimeter. Fiore mimed lobbing a grenade in that direction. Lo smiled, his teeth startlingly white in the darkness. Then he reached out and thumped Fiore on the shoulder, as if to say, *You're okay, Mac*.

He whispered something to one of the other young men, who handed Bobby Fiore a grenade. He felt for the pin, found it. Lo held up fingers close to his face—one, two, three. Then he, too, mimed throwing. "Yeah, I know I gotta get rid of it," Fiore said laconically.

The fellow who'd given him the grenade proved to have three more, which he also passed on. Fiore took them, but less enthusiastically each time. He figured he could throw one, maybe two, and get away in the confusion, but anything after that and he'd be asking to get blown to pieces.

But the Reds weren't asking him to do anything they weren't game for themselves. Some of them pulled out pistols from the waistbands of their trousers; Lo and one other fellow had submachine guns instead—not tommy guns like gangsters, but stubbier, lighter weapons of a make Fiore didn't recognize. He wondered if they were Russian. Any which way, he was glad he hadn't tried using that baseball bat back in his hut.

Lo started crawling through the field—beans were growing in it, Fiore discovered—toward the Lizard outpost. The other raiders and Fiore trailed after him. The reek of night soil (as poetic a way of saying shit as he'd ever heard) filled his nostrils; the Chinese used it for fertilizer.

The Lizards obviously weren't expecting trouble from the outside. The humans easily got within fifty yards of their perimeter. Lo looked a question to Bobby Fiore: was this close enough? He nodded. Lo nodded back and thumped him on the shoulder again. For a Chinaman and a Communist, Lo was all right.

The raiders slithered out into a rough skirmish line. Lo stayed close by Fiore. He gave his comrades maybe a minute

and a half to find firing positions, then pointed first to Fiore and then to the guard station.

I get to open the show, huh? It was an honor Fiore could have done without, but nobody'd asked his opinion. He yanked the pin out of one of the grenades, hurled it as if he'd just taken a relay in short right and was trying to nail a runner at the plate. Then he flung himself flat on the stinking ground.

Bang! The blast was oddly disappointing; he'd expected more. But it did what it was supposed to do: it got the Lizards' attention. Fiore heard hissing shouts, saw motion in and around the guard post.

That was what the Chinese had been waiting for. Their guns opened up with a roar quite satisfyingly loud. Lo went through a whole magazine in what seemed no more than a heartbeat; his submachine gun spat a flame bright and searingly yellow as the sun. He rammed in another clip and started shooting again.

Did the hisses turn to screams? Did Lizards fall, pierced by bullets? Fiore didn't know for sure. He jumped up and threw another grenade. Its boom added to the cacophony all around.

For somebody who'd never seen action till that moment, he'd gauged it pretty well. No sooner had he hit the dirt again than the Lizards woke up. Searchlights came on. If the muzzle flash from Lo's submachine gun had been sun-bright, they were like looking at the naked face of God. And the machine guns they opened up with reminded Fiore of God, too, or at least of His wrath. Bobby even wished he were back in the tunnel.

Off to his left, one of the Chinese raiders started screaming and wouldn't stop. Off to his right, fire from the second submachine gun cut off in the middle of a burst and didn't start up again. Just over his head, bullets clipped off the tops of growing bean plants like a harvester from hell.

Lo kept right on shooting, which made him either brave or out of his ever-loving mind. Two searchlights swung toward him, which meant that for a moment none was pointing at Bobby Fiore. He threw his third grenade, got down, and started rolling away from where he had been. The location didn't seem healthy any more.

Lo's weapon fell silent. Fiore didn't know whether he was dead or also moving. He kept rolling himself until he fetched up against a long obstruction: a dead Chinese, pistol still in

hand. Fiore took it and scuttled away from the Lizard guns. He'd done all the fighting he intended to do today.

He put all the distance he could between himself and that terrible fire. Bullets lashed the plants all around him, kicking up dirt that spattered his hands, his feet, his neck. Somehow, none of the bullets hit him. If Lizard infantry came out after him, he knew he was dead. But the aliens relied on firepower instead, and however awesome it was, it wasn't perfect—not quite. The last Chinaman stopped shooting and started shrieking.

Alternating Hail Marys with under-his-breath mutters of "Where the fuck's that tunnel?" Fiore slithered back toward where he thought it was. After a while, he realized he must have gone too far. At the same instant, he also realized he couldn't possibly go back, not if he wanted to keep on breathing.

"If I can't get back into camp, that means I better get my ass outta here," he mumbled. He crawled and scuttled as fast as he could. No searchlights picked him up as he dodged between rows of beans. Then he tumbled into a muddy ditch or tiny creekbed in the poorly tended field that providentially ran diagonally away from the Lizard guard post. He hoped the Chinese Reds had done some damage there, but was whatever they'd done worth six lives?

He didn't know. He was damned sure it wasn't worth seven, though.

After an eternity that might have lasted fifteen minutes, the beans on either side of the ditch gave way to bushes and saplings. About then, a helicopter came rattling over the field and raked it with fire. Dust and pulverized bean plants flew into the sky. The noise was like the end of the world. Bobby Fiore's teeth chattered in terror. The same sort of flying gunships had strafed his train and the fields around it back in Illinois.

After a while, the gunship flew away. It hadn't lashed the place where Fiore lay trembling. That still didn't mean he was safe. The farther out of there he got, the better off he'd be. He made himself move even though he shook. He didn't feel as if he were in a tight baseball game any more. Combat against the Lizards was more like the fly taking on the swatter.

He was altogether alone and on his own. He counted up his assets: he had one grenade, a pistol with an uncertain number

of cartridges, and a tiny smattering of Chinese. It didn't seem like enough.

"Mild bloody climate," George Bagnall muttered, stamping snow from his boots and brushing it from his shoulders. "Sod Jerome bloody Jones."

"Not so bad in here," Ken Embry answered. "Shut the door. You're letting in the bloody spring."

"Right." Bagnall slammed the door with a satisfying crash. He promptly started to sweat, and divested himself of fur cap and leather-and-fur flying suit. As far as he could tell, the Soviet Union in general and Pskov in particular had only two temperatures, too cold and too hot. The wood-burning stove in the corner of the house he and Embry had been assigned was more than capable of keeping it warm: too much more than capable. But none of the windows opened (the notion seemed alien to the Russian mind), and if you let the fire go out, you were facing chilblains again within the hour.

"Want some tea?" Embry asked, pointing to a dented samovar that added its quotient of warmth to the close, tropical air.

"Real tea, by God?" Bagnall demanded eagerly.

"Not likely," the pilot answered with a sneer. "Same sort of leaves and roots and muck the Bolshies are drinking these days. No milk, either, and no cups, same as always." The Russians drank tea—and their ersatz, too—from glasses, and used sugar but no milk. Considering that at the moment there was no milk in Pskov, save from nursing mothers and a few officers' closely guarded cows and goats, the Englishmen had had to get used to it that way, too. Bagnall consoled himself by thinking he was less likely to catch tuberculosis without milk in his tea; the Reds didn't fret over attestation.

He poured himself a glass of the murky brown brew, stirred in sugar (plenty of beets around Pskov), and tasted. "I've had worse," he admitted. "Where'd you come by it?"

"Bought it from a *babushka*," Embry answered. "God knows where she got it—probably grew the herbs herself, then fixed them up to sell. Not what you'd call perfect communism, but then not much here seems to be."

"No, hardly," Bagnall agreed. "I wonder if it has to do with the Germans' having been here most of a year before the Lizards arrived."

"I have my doubts," Embry said. "From all I've seen, my

guess is that the Russians did what they had to do for the collective farm and the factory and then turned around and did all they could for themselves."

"Mm—you're likely right." Even after some weeks in Pskov, Bagnall did not know what to make of the Russians. He admired their courage and resilience. About everything else he had doubts. Had Englishmen so tamely submitted to those above them, no one would ever have questioned the divine right of kings. Only their resilience had let the Russians survive the string of incompetents and tyrants who ruled them.

"And what is the news of the day?" Embry asked.

"I was just thinking I find Russians difficult to fathom," Bagnall said, "but in one regard they are perfectly comprehensible: they still hate the Germans. And, I assure you, the sentiment is most generously returned."

Ken Embry rolled his eyes. "Oh, God, what now?"

"Here, wait, let me get some more of this. It isn't tea, but it isn't too bad, either." Bagnall poured his glass full, sipped, and went on, "One of the things we shall have to do, on the unlikely assumption the ground ever unthaws, is build miles upon miles of antitank ditches. Let me merely state that where to site these ditches, the personnel to excavate them, and the troops to defend them once dug are matters which remain in dispute."

"Do you care to give me the particulars?" Embry asked, with an expression that said he wasn't particularly eager to hear them but felt he should. Bagnall understood that expression; he suspected his own matched it.

He said, "General Chill is willing to have his *Wehrmacht* lads do some of the digging, but feels the rest should fall on the shoulders of what he terms the 'otherwise useless population.' Typical German tact there, what?"

"I am certain his Soviet colleagues received that in the spirit in which it was intended," Embry said.

"No doubt," Bagnall said dryly. "They were also particularly pleased with his proposal that Russian soldiers and partisans be those particularly concerned with stopping the Lizards' tanks once they traverse said ditches."

"I can see that they would be. How generous of the distinguished German officer to offer his Soviet allies the opportunity to commit suicide under such distinguished circumstances."

"If you stick that tongue any farther into your cheek, you're

liable to bite it off," Bagnall said. As long as he'd known Embry, he and the pilot had dueled to see which of them could wield the twin scalpels of irony and understatement more effectively. He feared Embry had just taken the lead on points.

The pilot asked, "And why has General Chill been so extraordinarily gracious?"

"His justification is that the Nazis, with their heavier weapons, would be better used as a reserve to meet any possible Lizard breakthroughs."

"Oh," Embry said in a slightly different tone.

"Just what I thought," Bagnall answered. The rationale made just enough military sense to force one to wonder whether Chill's plan shouldn't be carried out as proposed. The flight engineer added, "Germans are bloody good at coming up with plausible reasons for things that are to their advantage."

"To their short-term advantage," Embry amended. "Setting the Russians up to be massacred will not endear Chill to them."

Bagnall snorted. "Somehow I doubt that will cause him to lose any great quantity of sleep. He wants to keep his own forces intact first."

"He also wants to hold Pskov," Embry said. "He won't do that without the Russians' help—nor will they, without his. A lovely muddle, wouldn't you say?"

"If you want my opinion, it would be even lovelier if viewed from a distance—say from a London pub—than when we're caught in the middle of it."

"Something to that," Embry sighed. "Real springtime ... leaves ... flowers ... birds ... a pint pot of best bitter ... perhaps even Scotch."

The pain of longing pierced Bagnall like a stiletto. He feared he'd never see England or its loveliness again. As for Scotch ... well, the spirit the Russians brewed from potatoes would warm a man, or send him to sleep if he drank enough of it, but it didn't taste like anything. He'd also heard that drinking neutral spirits kept you from feeling the effects the next morning. He shook his head. He'd shot that theory right behind the ear more often than he cared to remember.

Embry said, "Speaking of getting stuck in the middle, is there more talk of turning us into infantrymen again?"

Bagnall didn't blame him for sounding anxious; their one foray against the Lizard outpost south of Pskov had been

plenty to put the flight engineer off the life of a foot soldier forever. The choice, unfortunately, did not rest with him. He said, "They didn't say anything about that when I was in the *Krom*. But then, they might not have wanted to, either."

"For fear we'd bugger off, you mean?" Embry said. Bagnall nodded. The pilot went on, "Nothing I'd like better. Only— where would we go?"

It was a good question. The short answer, unfortunately for both of them, was *nowhere*, not with the woods full of partisan bands, German patrols, and just plain bandits. Next to some of them, the prospect of facing the Lizards seemed less disastrous. The Lizards wouldn't do anything worse than killing you. Bagnall said, "You don't really believe those stories about the cannibals in the forest, do you?"

"Let's just say it's something I'd sooner not find out by experiment."

"Too right there."

Before Bagnall could go on, someone knocked at the door. The plaintive voice that came through the thick boards was London-accented: "Can you let me in? I'm fair frozen."

"Radarman Jones!" Bagnall threw the door wide. Jerome Jones came in. Bagnall quickly shut the door after him, and waved him over to the samovar. "Drink some of that. It's fairly good."

"Where's the beautiful Tatiana?" Ken Embry asked Jones as he poured himself a glass of herb tea. Embry sounded jealous. Bagnall didn't blame him. Somehow Jones had managed to connect with a Russian sniper who was even more decorative than she was deadly.

"She's off trying to kill things, I suppose," the radarman answered. He sipped the tea, made a face. "Maybe not bad, but it could be better."

"Being all alone, then, you deigned to honor us with a visit, eh?" Bagnall said.

"Oh, bloody hell," Jones muttered, then hastily added, "sir." His position in Pskov was, to put it mildly, irregular. While Bagnall and Embry were both officers and he very much from the other ranks, he had the specialization in which the Russians—and the Nazis—were interested.

Ken Embry said, "It's all right, Jones. We know they treat you like a field marshal everywhere else in town. Decent of

you to remember your military manners around low cannon-fodder types like ourselves."

The radarman winced. Even Bagnall, used to such sarcastic sallies, had trouble being sure how much was intended as wit and how much fired with intent to wound. A spell as an infantryman in an attack that got crushed was enough to jaundice anyone's outlook.

Giving the pilot the benefit of the doubt, Bagnall said, "Don't let him faze you, Jones. Our mission was to get you here, and that we've done. What came afterwards, the Lanc getting bombed—well, *nichevo*."

"There's a useful word, eh, sir?" Jones said, anxious to change the subject. "Can't be helped, nothing to be done about it—that the Russians pack it all into one word says a lot about them, I think."

"Yes, and not all of it good, either," Embry said, evidently willing to drop his bitterness. "These people have spent their entire history being stepped on. Tsars, commissars, what have you—it'd be a miracle indeed if that didn't show in the language."

"Shall we put Mr. Jones' knowledge of Russian to more practical use?" Bagnall said. Without waiting for a reply from Embry, he asked the radarman, "What do you hear, going up and down in the city?"

"The name is Jones, sir, as you noted, not Job," Jones replied with a grin which rapidly slipped. "People are hungry, people are battered. They don't love the Germans or the Bolsheviks. If they thought the Lizards would feed them and leave them alone otherwise, a lot would just as soon see them as top dogs."

"If I'd stayed safe at home in England, I'd have trouble imagining that," Bagnall said. Of course, flying bomber missions first against the Germans and then against the Lizards had been anything but safe, but Jones and Embry both nodded, understanding what he meant. He went on, "After the Jews rose for the Lizards and against the Nazis, I thought they were the blackest traitors in the history of the world—until their story started coming out. If a tenth part of what they say is true, Germany has more blood on her hands than a thousand years of Hitler's *Reich* can wash away."

"And they and we are allies," Embry said heavily.

"And they and we are allies, yes," Bagnall agreed. "And so

are they and the Russians, and so are we and the Russians, and Stalin, by all that's said, matches Hitler for butchery any day of the week, even if he's not so showy about it."

"It's a rum old world," Embry said.

Not far away, somebody fired a rifle in the street. Somebody else fired another one, with a report that sounded different: one weapon was German, the other Soviet. Another handful of shots followed, then silence. Bagnall waited tensely, wondering if the shooting would start up again. That would be all anyone needed—war inside Pskov between alleged allies to accompany war outside against foes. But silence held for a couple of minutes.

Then the shooting started again, worse than ever—one of those new German machine guns, the ones with the terrifyingly high cyclic rate that made them sound even more dreadful than they really were, added to the chaos. Several Russian submachine guns gave answer. Through the raucous racket of gunfire came hoarse screams. Bagnall couldn't tell if they were Russian or German.

"Oh, bloody hell," Jerome Jones said.

Embry took hold of one end of a chest of drawers and started pushing it toward the front door, saying, "Best we put up something of a barricade, wouldn't you say?"

Bagnall didn't say anything, but did put his back into helping the pilot manhandle the heavy wooden chest into place. Then he picked up a chair and, grunting, set it on top of the low chest. Together, he and Embry leaned a table against the window by the doorway.

"Jones, you have your pistol with you?" Bagnall asked, then answered himself: "Yes, I see you do. Good." He went into the bedroom and returned with his Mauser, Ken Embry's, and as much ammunition as they had left from the raid on the Lizard base. "I hope we shan't have to use these, but—"

"Quite," Embry said. He glanced over at Jones. "No offense, old man, but I'd sooner Tatiana were here than you. She'd be likelier to keep us safe."

"No offense taken, sir," the radarman answered. "I'd sooner Tatiana were here, too. Given any choice at all, I'd sooner be back in Dover, or better yet, London."

Since Bagnall had had almost the same thought not long before, he could only nod. Embry went into the bedroom. He came back with their pair of coal-scuttle helmets. "I don't

know whether we ought to put these on. They'll keep out splinters or glancing bullets, but they'll also make the Russians take us for Jerries, which might prove less than ideal under the circumstances."

A random bullet smashed through the wooden front wall, just missed Jones and Bagnall, and buried itself in plaster next to the samovar. "I'll wear a helmet," Bagnall said. "The Russians may ask questions about who we are and whose side we're on, but their ammunition doesn't."

He heard the pop of a mortar and, a moment later, the much louder bang as its bomb went off. He found cover behind another chair and aimed his rifle at the doorway. "The Lizards may not need to take Pskov," he said. "Seems to me more as if the Russians and Germans want to give it to them."

A tracked Lizard troop carrier rattled down the wet dirt road, splattering mud in all directions. Some of it splashed Mordechai Anielewicz as he trudged along on the soft shoulder. The Lizards in the tracked carrier took no special notice of him: to them, he was just another gun-toting Big Ugly on the move.

His lips skinned back from his teeth in a humorless smile. The motion set his whole face itching. Moishe Russie, when he fled the Lizards, had been able to get rid of his beard in one fell swoop. Growing one took longer and, as far as Anielewicz was concerned, was a lot less comfortable.

Also uncomfortable was the *Gewehr 98* slung across his back. He valued the rifle all the same: he'd promised himself Zolraag and his minions would not take him alive, and it was the means by which he could keep that promise. He'd also had the sense to take German marching boots a size too large when the time came to disappear from Warsaw. His feet had swollen in them, yes, but he could still take them off and put them on without trouble.

He'd sent Russie west to Lodz. Now that it was his turn to escape the Lizards, he was walking south and east, into the part of Poland the Russians had occupied in 1939 before the Germans ran them out less than two years later. His chuckle sounded anything but mirthful. "Sooner or later, the people who used to work with the Lizards are going to be scattered all over the countryside," he said, and waved his arms to show

what he meant. The motion startled a magpie, which flew away, chattering angrily.

He sympathized with the bird. Till he'd moved suddenly, it had taken him as harmless. He'd thought the same about the Lizards, or at least that they were a better bargain than the Nazis. For the Jews of Poland, he still thought them a better bargain than the Nazis; had they not come, Poland would have been *Judenfrei*—without Jews—by now.

But he was coming to see that the world was a wider place than Poland. The Lizards might not be out to exterminate mankind, as the Nazis aimed to exterminate Polish Jewry, but they intended to do to humanity as the Germans had done to the Poles themselves: turn them into hewers of wood and drawers of water forever. Anielewicz couldn't stomach that.

A Pole came up the road, heading toward Warsaw with a wheelbarrow full of turnips. The wheel of the wheelbarrow got stuck in a patch the Lizards' troop carrier had chewed to slime. Anielewicz helped the Pole free it from the clinging ooze. It was quite a fight; the wheelbarrow seemed to think it ought to be a submarine.

Finally, though, the two men wrestled it up onto firmer ground. "God and the Black Virgin of Czestochowa, that was tough," the Pole said, shedding his tweed cap so he could wipe his forehead with a frayed sleeve. "Thank you, friend."

"Any time," Anielewicz answered. Back before the war, he'd been much more fluent in Polish than Yiddish. He'd thought himself secular then, not so much denying his Judaism as ignoring it, until the Nazis showed him it couldn't be ignored. "Those are good fat turnips you've got there."

"Take a couple for yourself. You hadn't been here, I might have lost the whole load," the fellow said. His grin showed a couple of missing front teeth. "Besides, you've got a rifle. How am I supposed to stop you?"

"I don't steal," Anielewicz answered. *Not now I don't, anyway. I'm not starving at the moment. When the Nazis ran the Warsaw ghetto, though . . .*

The Pole's grin got wider. "*Armija Krajowa* fighter, are you?" It was a reasonable guess; Anielewicz's looks were more Polish than Jewish, too. Without waiting for an answer, the man went on, "Better I should give you the turnips than sell 'em to the damned Yids in Warsaw, anyhow, eh?"

He had no way of knowing how close he came to dying in

the middle of the muddy road without ever learning why. Mordechai Anielewicz took a tight grip on his temper; it wasn't as if he hadn't known plenty of Poles were anti-Semites—and a murder here was liable to make it easier for pursuers to trace him. So he just said, "They're still hungry in there. I expect you'll get a good price."

"Hungry? Why should the Jews be hungry? They've got their mouths pressed to the Lizards' backsides, and they eat their—" The Pole spat into the roadway in lieu of finishing, but left no doubt about what he'd meant.

Again Anielewicz forced himself to coolness. If the Pole thought he was a countryman rather than a Jew on the dodge, his presence here would attract no notice. So he told himself. But oh, the temptation—

"Here, wait," The turnip seller undid a Polish Army canteen from his belt, yanked out the cork which had replaced the proper stopper. "Have a belt of this to help you on your way."

This was vodka, obviously homemade and strong enough to scar the lining of Anielewicz's throat as it went down. After a small nip, he handed the canteen back to the Pole. "Thank you," he said, wheezing a little.

"Any time, pal." The Pole tilted his head back for a couple of long swallows. "Ahh! Jesus, that's good. Us Catholics got to hang together. Ain't nobody gonna do it for us, am I right? Not the damned Jews, not the godless Russians, not the stinking Germans, and sure as hell not the Lizards. Am I right?"

Anielewicz made himself nod. The worst thing was that the Pole *was* right, at least from his parochial perspective. No one would give his people any special help, so they'd have to help themselves. But if every people helped itself at the expense of its neighbors, how would any people—or all the peoples together—withstand the Lizards?

With a wave, Anielewicz headed down the road, leaving the Pole to trundle his turnips on toward Warsaw. The Jewish fighting leader (*Jewish refugee,* he corrected himself—someone new would head the fighters now) wondered what the peddler would have done, knowing he was a Jew. Probably nothing much, since he had a gun and the Pole didn't, but he didn't think he would have got the turnips, let alone the belt of vodka.

A Lizard jet flew by, high overhead. Its vapor trail caught Anielewicz's eye before he heard the thin, attenuated bellow of

its engines. It probably carried a load of destruction. He hoped someone would shoot it down . . . after it had dropped the load of destruction on a Nazi's head.

The road ran through fields of barley, potatoes, and beets. Peasants and their animals plowed those fields as they had every spring for the past thousand years. No tractors snorted or chuffed alongside the horses and mules—gasoline was next to impossible to come by. That had been true under the Germans and was even truer under the Lizards.

Overall, though, the aliens' rule lay lightly on the land. After that armored troop carrier splattered past him, Anielewicz didn't see another Lizard vehicle for the rest of the day. The Lizards garrisoned Warsaw and other towns like Lublin (to which Anielewicz intended to give a wide berth, for just that reason), but used the threat of their power rather than the power itself to hold down the countryside.

"I wonder how many Lizards there are altogether, not just in Poland, but all over the world," he mused aloud. Few enough so that they were stretched thin trying to hold it down and run it, that seemed clear.

He wondered how humanity could best exploit such a weakness. That musing quickly turned to one more practical: he wondered what he was going to do about supper and a place to sleep. Sure, he had hard bread and cheese in his pack to go with the turnips, but none of that was inspiring fare. Similarly, he could roll himself in a blanket on the ground, but he didn't want to unless he had to.

The problem soon solved itself: a farmer coming in from the fields waved to him and called, "Are you hungry, friend? Always happy to feed an *Armija Krajowa* man. Besides, I killed a pig yesterday, and I've got more meat than my family can eat. Join us, if you care to."

Anielewicz hadn't touched pork since the ghetto walls came down, but to decline such a feast would only have made the farmer suspicious. "Thank you very much," he said. "You're sure it's no trouble?"

"Not a bit. Come in, wash up, sit and rest your feet."

The farmhouse stood between two thatch-roofed outbuildings. The farmer shooed some chickens away from the woodpile and into a henhouse in one of those outbuildings, then slammed the door on them. At the fellow's urging, Anielewicz clumped up the wooden stairs and into the foyer.

A big brass basin there served for a sink. He washed his hands and face, dried them on a linen towel hung on a nail above the basin. The farmer courteously waited for him to use the water first, then cleaned himself off. After that, introductions were in order: the farmer gave his own name as Wladyslaw Sawatski; his wife was Emilia (a pleasant-looking woman who wore a kerchief over her hair), his teenage son Jozef, and his daughters Maria and Ewa (one older than Jozef, one younger).

Anielewicz said he was Janusz Borwicz, giving himself a good Polish name to go with his Polish looks. Everyone made much of him. He got the seat at the head of the table in the parlor, he got a mug of apple brandy big enough to make three people *shikker*, and he got the family's undivided attention. He gave them all the Warsaw gossip he had, especially the part pertaining to the Polish majority.

"Did you fight the Germans when the Lizards came?" Jozef Sawatski asked. He and his father—and both his sisters, too—leaned forward at that.

They wanted war stories, Mordechai realized. Well, he could give them some. "Yes, as a matter of fact, I did," he said truthfully. Again, he edited the tales to disguise his Jewishness.

Wladyslaw Sawatski, who had a brandy mug the size of Anielewicz's, slammed it down on the table with a roar of approval. "Well done, by God!" he exclaimed. "If we'd fought like that in '39, we wouldn't have needed these—creatures—to get the Nazis off our backs."

Anielewicz doubted that. Sandwiched between Germany and Russia, Poland was going to get walloped every so often. Before he could come up with a polite way to disagree with his host, Emilia Sawatski turned to her daughters and said, "Why don't you go and bring in the food now?" Alone in the family, she hadn't cared about tales of conflict.

In came supper, mountains of it: boiled potatoes, boiled *kielbasa* sausage, big pork steaks, headcheese, fresh-baked bread. Warsaw might be hungry, but the countryside seemed to be doing pretty well for itself.

As Maria, the older girl, plopped a length of sausage onto Anielewicz's plate, she gave him a sidelong glance, then spoke in silky tones to her father. "You're not going to send a hero like Janusz out onto the road after supper, are you, Papa? He'll sleep here tonight, won't he?"

She wants to go to bed with me, Anielewicz realized with some alarm. That alarm had nothing to do with Maria's person: she was eighteen or nineteen, and quite pretty in a wide-faced, blue-eyed way. Anielewicz didn't particularly worry about angering her father, either. But if he took off his trousers for her, he wouldn't be able to hide being a Jew.

Wladyslaw Sawatski looked from Maria to Mordechai and back again. The glance was full of understanding: whatever else he might be, Sawatski was no fool. He said, "I was going to let him rest in the barn, Maria, but as you say, he is a hero, and too good for straw. He can sleep on the sofa in the front room there."

He pointed to show Anielewicz where that was. Mordechai was not surprised to discover it lay right outside the doorway to a bedroom that would surely be Wladyslaw's. You'd have to be crazy to try to screw there.

He said, "Thank you, sir. That will be excellent." Sawatski might figure he was lying, but he meant every word of it. Maria had to nod—after all, her father had given her just what she'd said she wanted. Anielewicz hadn't expected to find rabbinic wisdom in a Polish farmer, but there it was.

The meat on his plate smelled delicious. Then Ewa Sawatski asked, "Don't you want any butter on your potatoes?"

He stared at her. Mixing meat and dairy products in the same meal—? Then he remembered the meat was pork. If he was eating pork, how could another violation of dietary law matter? "Thank you," he said, and took some butter.

Wladyslaw filled his mug when it got empty. The farmer gave himself a refill, too. His cheeks were red as if he'd rouged them, but that was all the brandy did to him. Mordechai's head was starting to swim, but he didn't think he could decline the drink. Poles poured it down till they couldn't see, didn't they?

The women went into the kitchen to clean up. Wladyslaw sent Jozef off to bed, saying, "We have plenty of work tomorrow." But he still lingered at the table, politely ready to talk as long as Anielewicz felt like it.

That wasn't long. When Mordechai yawned and couldn't stop, Sawatski got him a pillow and a blanket and settled him on the sofa. It was hard and lumpy, but he'd slept on worse in the ghetto and during the fighting afterwards. No sooner had he taken off his boots and stretched himself out at full length

than he was asleep. If Maria sneaked out bent on seduction in the night, he didn't wake up for her.

Breakfast the next morning was an enormous bowl of oatmeal flavored with butter and coarse salt. Emilia Sawatski waved away Mordechai's thanks and wouldn't even take the turnips he tried to give her. "We have enough here, and you may need them in your travel," she said. "God keep you as you go."

Wladyslaw walked out to the road with Anielewicz. He too said, "God keep you," then added quietly, "Friend Janusz, you do a good job of pretending to be a Pole rather than a Jew, but not always good enough. You're awkward when you cross yourself, for instance"—in a single swift motion, the farmer showed how it should be done—"and you don't always do it at quite the right time. At another man's house, you might put yourself in danger."

Mordechai stared at him. Finally, he managed, "You knew, yet you took me in anyway?"

"You looked like a man who needed taking in." Sawatski slapped Anielewicz on the back. "Now go on. I hope you stay safe to wherever you're headed."

He asked no questions about that; Anielewicz noticed so much. Still dazed (no man, and especially no young man, cares to be shown he is not as clever as he thought he was), he started down the road away from Warsaw. He'd had so much bitter experience with anti-Semitic Poles that he'd come to think the whole nation hated its Jews. Being reminded that wasn't so made him feel good all the rest of the day.

☆ XI ☆

Ussmak hated the barracks at Besançon. Because they'd been made for Big Uglies, they were by his standards dark and dank and cold. But even if they'd been a section of Home miraculously transplanted to Tosev 3, he would not have been happy in them, not now. To him, they stank of failure.

Landcruisers, after all, were supposed to go forward, pounding the enemy into submission and paving the way for new advances. Instead, after the debacle against the Deutsche, his crew and the others who survived were pulled back here so officers could investigate what had gone wrong.

Hessef and Tvenkel had only two concerns: to keep the investigators from learning they had a ginger habit, and to do as much tasting as they could. Those concerns were in Ussmak's mind, too, but not as intensely; he'd done a better job of coming to terms with ginger than his commander or gunner.

But if the investigating officers didn't figure out ginger had played a big part in the landcruisers' lackluster performance, what was their report good for? *Wastepaper,* Ussmak thought.

A new male with a sack full of gear came into the barracks. His toeclaws clicked on the hard tile floor. Ussmak idly turned one eye turret toward the fellow, but gave him both eyes when he'd read his body paint. "By the Emperor, you're a driver, too."

The newcomer cast down his eyes. So did Ussmak. The new male said, "Good to see someone who shares my specialization." He tossed his stuff onto a vacant cot. "What are you called, friend?"

"Ussmak. And you?"

301

"Drefsab." The new driver swiveled both eye turrets. "What a dismal, ugly hole this is."

"Too right," Ussmak said. "Even for the Big Uglies who used to live here, it was nothing to boast about. For properly civilized males—" He let that hang. "Where did they transfer you from?"

"I've been serving in the far east of this continent, against the Chinese and Nipponese," Drefsab answered.

"You must have come out of your eggshell lucky," Ussmak said enviously. "That's easy duty, from all I've heard."

"The Chinese don't have much in the way of landcruisers at all," Drefsab agreed. "The Nipponese have some, but they aren't very tough. Hit them and they're guaranteed to brew up—one-shot firestarters, we call them." The new male let his mouth fall open at the joke.

Ussmak laughed, too, but said, "Don't get overconfident here or you'll pay for it. I was in the SSSR just after the invasion, and the Soviets, while their landcruisers weren't too bad, didn't have the faintest idea how to use them. Then I got hurt, and then I came here. I didn't believe what the males told me about the Deutsche, but I've been in action against them now, and it's true."

"I listen," Drefsab said. "Tell me more."

"Their new landcruisers have guns heavy enough to hurt us with a side or rear deck shot, and front armor thick enough to turn a glancing shot from one of our guns. You can forget about the one-shot firestarter business here. And they use their machines well: reverse slopes, ambushes, any trick you can think of and too many you've never imagined in your worst nightmares."

Drefsab looked thoughtful. "As bad as that? I've heard of some of the things you're talking about, but I figured half of that, maybe more, was males shooting off steam to haze the new fellow."

"Listen, my friend, we were rolling north from here not long ago when we got our eye turrets handed to us." Ussmak told Drefsab about the push that had started for Belfort and ended up back here at the Besançon barracks.

"We were held—by Big Uglies?" The new driver sounded as if he couldn't believe it. Ussmak didn't blame him. When the Race tried to go somewhere on Tosev 3, it generally got

there. In lower tones, Drefsab went on, "What happened? Were all the landcruisers tongue-deep in the ginger jar?"

Although Drefsab had spoken quietly, Ussmak scanned the barracks before he answered. No one was paying any particular attention. Good. Almost whispering, Ussmak said, "As a matter of fact, that might have had something to do with it. Have you been assigned to a landcruiser crew yet?"

"No," Drefsab said.

"I'll give you a few names to try to stay away from, then."

"Thank you, superior sir." By their paint, Drefsab and Ussmak were of virtually identical rank, but Drefsab honored him not only for the favor but also because of his longer service at this post. Now the new male glanced around the barracks. He too whispered: "Not that I have anything against a taste now and again, you understand—but not in combat, by the Emperor."

After he'd raised his eyes from the ritual gesture of respect for the sovereign, Ussmak said cautiously, "No, that's not so bad." It was what he tried to do himself. But if Drefsab had asked him for a taste, he would have denied keeping any ginger. He had no reason to trust the other male.

Instead, though, Drefsab produced a tiny glass vial from one of the pockets of his equipment bag. "Want some of the herb?" he murmured. "We're not in combat now."

Ussmak's suspicions flickered and blew out. When Drefsab poured a little ginger into his hand, Ussmak bent his head down and flicked it off the scales with his tongue. The new driver tasted, too. They sat companionably together, enjoying the surge of pleasure the powdered herb gave them.

"Very fine," Ussmak said. "It makes me want to go out and kill all the Deutsche I can find—or maybe Hessef instead." He had to explain that: "Hessef is *my* landcruiser commander. If ginger truly made you as smart as it makes you think you are, Hessef would be the greatest genius the Race ever produced. Barracks, battle, it's all the same to him: a good enough time for a taste. And Tvenkel the gunner tastes enough to make him shoot before he takes proper aim. I've seen him do it."

"That doesn't strike me as smart, not if the Deutsche are as good as you make them out to be," Drefsab said.

"They are," Ussmak answered. "When we got to this miserable iceball of a planet, we had equipment and training simulations. The Deutsche had experience in real combat, and their

equipment keeps getting better, while ours doesn't. Let them choose the terms of the fight and they can be a handful."

Drefsab made the vial disappear. "You don't taste before you're going into action?"

"I try not to." Ussmak moved his eye turrets in a way that said he was ashamed of his own weakness. "When the hunger for ginger comes on a male—but you know about that."

"Yes, I know about that," Drefsab agreed soberly. "The way I look on it is this: a male can yield himself up to the herb and let it be all he lives for, or he can taste the herb as it suits him and go on with the rest of his life as best he can. That's the road I try to follow, and if it has some bumps and rocky places in it—well, what road on Tosev 3 doesn't?"

Ussmak stared at him in admiration. Here was a philosophy for a ginger taster—no, after hearing such words, he needed to be honest with himself: a ginger addict—who nonetheless tried to remember he was a male of the Race, obedient to orders, attentive to duty. He said to Drefsab, "Superior sir, I envy you your wisdom."

Drefsab made a gesture of dismissal. "Wisdom? For all I know, I may well be fooling myself, and now you. Whatever it is, the price I paid to win it is much too high. Better by far the herb had never set its claws in me."

"I don't know," Ussmak said. "After I've tasted, I feel as if ginger were the only worthwhile thing this miserable world produces."

"*After* I've tasted, so do I," Drefsab said. "But before, or when I need a taste badly and there's none to be had . . . times like those, Ussmak, I'm certain ginger is worst for the Race, not best."

Times like those, Ussmak had the same feeling. He'd heard stories that some males, if they got desperate enough for ginger, traded pieces of the Race's military hardware for the herb. He'd never done anything like that himself, but he understood the temptation.

Before he found a safe way to tell that to Drefsab (some things you didn't say directly even to a male who'd given you a taste of ginger, not until you were positive you could trust him with your life as well as with the herb), he heard a brief, shrill whistle in the air, followed by a loud *crummp!* The glass from a couple of windows in the barracks blew inward in a shower of tinkling shards.

Ussmak sprang to his feet. As he did so, a loudspeaker blared, "Mortars incoming from forest patch grid 27-Red. Pursuit in force—"

Ussmak didn't wait to hear any more, not with a good taste of ginger running through him. "Come on," he shouted to Drefsab. "Out to the landcruiser park."

Another mortar bomb hit in the yard in front of the barracks. His words punctuated by the blast, Drefsab said, "But I've been assigned to no crew."

"So what? Some commander and gunner won't want to wait for their own driver." Ussmak was as sure of that as of his own name. Ginger ran rampant through the base at Besançon; some commander or other would be feeling more intrepid than patient.

The two males ran side by side down the stairs to the yard. Ussmak almost stumbled; the risers were built for Big Uglies, not the smaller Race. Then he almost stumbled again, this time because a blast from a mortar bomb nearly hurled him off his feet. Fragments whistled by; he knew only luck kept them from carving him into jagged, bloody bits.

Off to one side of the barracks, guns opened up, flinging blast and sharp-edged bits of hot brass back at the Tosevites who were hurling them at the Race's bastion in Besançon. With luck, artillery would take care of the raiders before landcruisers had to go in after them.

When no more mortar bombs fell for a little while, Ussmak hoped that had happened. But then the bombs started coming in again. The Big Uglies didn't have antiartillery radar, but they'd learned they had to shift their guns to keep the Race from pounding them to bits. That was the trouble with the Big Uglies: they learned too fast.

Hessef and Tvenkel came dashing up from wherever the investigation team had been questioning them. "Come on!" they shouted together. Ussmak scrambled into his landcruiser the instant he got to it; unless a mortar bomb landed on top of the turret or in the engine compartment, it was the safest place he could be.

The familiar vibration of the big hydrogen-burning engine starting up made him feel this was the purpose for which he'd been hatched. He noted with sober pride that his was the third landcruiser to move out of its revetment. Sometimes the ener-

getic aggression ginger brought wasn't such a bad thing after all.

With the intercom button taped to one hearing diaphragm, he listened to Hessef telling Tvenkel, "Quick, another taste. I want to be all razor wire when we go after those Deutsche or Français or whoever's trifling with us."

"Here you go, superior sir," the gunner answered. "And wouldn't the egg-addled snoops who were just grilling us pitch a fit if they knew what we were doing now?"

"Who cares about them?" Hessef said. "They're probably hiding under their desks or else wishing they were back *in* those addled eggs." Silence followed—likely the silence of the two males laughing together.

Ussmak laughed, too, a little. What the other crewmales said was true, but that didn't mean he was happy about their going into action with heads full of ginger, even if he was doing the same thing himself. *It's not my fault*, he thought virtuously. *I didn't know the Big Uglies would sneak a mortar into range.*

Square 27-Red was northeast of the fortress, and east of the river that wound through Besançon. Following the two landcruiser crews that had managed to get moving ahead of him, Ussmak roared down the hill on which the fortress sat and toward the nearest bridge. Big Uglies stared at the landcruisers as they went by. Ussmak was sure they wished one of those mortar bombs had blown him to bits.

Sometimes when he rumbled through town, he drove unbuttoned and noticed the fancy wrought-iron grillwork that decorated so many of the local buildings. Not today; today action was liable to be immediate, so he had only his vision slits and periscopes to peer through. The streets, even the big ones, were none too wide for landcruisers. He had to drive carefully to keep from mashing a pedestrian or two and making the Français love the Race even less than they did already.

He felt the explosion ahead as much as he heard it; for a moment, he thought it was an earthquake. Then gouts of flame shot from the lead landcruiser, which lay on its side. He slammed on the brakes as hard as he could. The murdered landcruiser's ammunition load began cooking off, adding fireworks to the funeral pyre. Ussmak shivered in horror. *If I'd been just a clawtip faster out of the revetment, I'd have driven over that bomb in the street*, he thought. The Big Uglies must

have figured out just how the Race would respond to a mortar attack and set their ambush accordingly.

"Reverse!" Hessef yelled into Ussmak's hearing diaphragm. "Get out of here!" The order was sensible, and Ussmak obeyed it. But the commander of the landcruiser behind him didn't have reflexes as fast as Hessef's (maybe they weren't ginger-enhanced). With a loud crunch, the rear of Ussmak's machine slammed into the front of that one. A moment later, the landcruiser in front of Ussmak backed into him.

Had the terrorists who planted the explosive under the road stayed around, they might have had a field day attacking stuck landcruisers with firebombs. Perhaps they hadn't realized how well their plan would work: the multiple accident of which Ussmak found himself a part was far from the only one in the line of landcruisers. The machines, fortunately, were tough, and suffered little damage.

The same could not be said about the Big Uglies who'd been standing anywhere near where the bomb went off. Ussmak watched other Tosevites carry away broken, bleeding bodies. They were only aliens, and aliens who hated him at that, but Ussmak wanted to turn his eye turrets away from them anyhow. They reminded him how easily he could have been broken and bleeding and dead.

With patience, which the Race did have in full measure, the snarls unkinked and the landcruisers chose the next best route out of Besançon. This time a special antiexplosives unit preceded the lead machine. Near the bridge over the River Doubs, everybody halted: the unit found another bomb buried under a new patch of pavement.

Even though air conditioning kept the interior of the landcruiser's fighting compartment comfortably warm, Ussmak shivered. The Big Uglies had known what the males of the Race would do, and done their best to hurt them not just once but twice—and their best had been pretty good.

Eventually, the landcruisers did reach square 27-Red. By then, of course, the raiders and their mortar were long gone.

Back at the barracks that evening, Ussmak said to Drefsab, "They made idiots of us today."

"Not altogether," Drefsab said. Ussmak waggled one eye turret slightly in a gesture of curiosity. The other male amplified: "We did a good job of making idiots of ourselves." With that Ussmak could not disagree. It was, however, an opinion to

be shared only among those of inconsequential rank—or so he thought.

But he was wrong. Three days later, inspectors of a sort altogether different from the first lot descended on Besançon. Most of the males whom Ussmak knew to be ginger tasters (and especially ginger tasters who'd let their habits get the better of them) disappeared from the base: Hessef and Tvenkel among them.

Drefsab wasn't seen at Besançon any more after that, either. Ussmak wondered at the connection; before long, wonder hardened into near certainty. He knew more than a little relief that the inspectors hadn't swept him up along with his crewmales.

If I ever see Drefsab again, I'll have to thank him, he thought.

"Jesus Christ, Jäger, you're still alive?" The big, deep voice boomed through the German encampment.

Heinrich Jäger looked up from the pot of extremely ersatz coffee he was brewing over a tiny cookfire. He jumped to his feet. "Skorzeny!" He shook his head in bemusement. "And *you* wonder that *I'm* alive, after the madcap stunts you've pulled off?" He hurried over to shake the SS man's hand.

Otto Skorzeny said, "Pooh. Yes, my stunts, if that's what you want to call them, are maybe more dangerous than what you do for a living, but I spend weeks between them planning. You're in action all the time, and going up against Lizard panzers isn't a child's game, either." He glanced at Jäger's collar tabs. "And a colonel, too. You've stayed up with me." His rank badges these days also had three pips.

Jäger said, "That's your fault. That madman raid on the Lizards in the Ukraine—" He shuddered. He hadn't had a tank wrapped around him like an armored skin then.

"Ah, but you brought home the bacon, or half the rashers, anyhow," Skorzeny said. "For that, you deserve everything you got."

"Then you should be a colonel-general by now," Jäger retorted. Skorzeny grinned; the jagged scar that ran from the corner of his mouth toward his left ear pulled up with the motion of his cheek. Jäger went on, "Here, do you have a cup? Drink some coffee with me. It's vile, but it's hot."

Skorzeny pulled the tin cup from his mess kit. As he held it

out, he clicked his heels with mocking formality. *"Danke sehr, Herr Oberst!"*

"Thank me after you've tasted it," Jäger said. The advice proved good; Skorzeny's scar made the face he pulled seem only more hideous. Jäger chuckled under his breath—wherever he'd seen Skorzeny, in Moscow, in the Ukraine, and now here, the man hadn't cared a fig for military discipline. And now here—Jäger's gaze sharpened. "What *does* bring you here, *Standartenführer* Skorzeny?" He used the formal SS title with less irony than he would have aimed at any other soldier of Hitler's elite.

"I am going to get into Besançon," Skorzeny announced, as if entering the Lizard-held city were as easy as a stroll around the block.

"Are you?" Jäger said noncommittally. Then he brightened. "Did you have anything to do with that bomb last week? I hear it took out one of their panzers, maybe two."

"Petty sabotage has its place, but I do not engage in it." Skorzeny grinned again, this time like a predator. "My sabotage is on the grand scale. I aim to buy something of value which one of our little scaly friends is interested in selling. I have the payment here." He reached over his shoulder, patted his knapsack.

Jäger jabbed: "They trust you to carry gold without disappearing?"

"O ye of little faith." Skorzeny sipped the not-quite-coffee again. "That is without a doubt the worst muck I have ever drunk in my life. No, the Lizards care nothing for gold. I have a kilo and a half of ginger in there, Jäger."

"Ginger?" Jäger scratched his head. "I don't understand."

"Think of it as morphine, if you like, then, or perhaps cocaine," Skorzeny said. "Once the Lizards get a taste for it, they'll do anything to get more, and *anything* includes, in this case, one of the rangefinders that make their panzers so deadly accurate."

"Better than what we have in the Panther?" Jäger set an affectionate hand on the road wheel of the brush-covered machine parked by the fire. "It's a big step up from what they put into my old Panzer III."

"Get ready for a bigger step, old son," Skorzeny said. "I don't know all the details, but I do know it's a whole new principle."

"Can we use it if you get it?" Jäger asked. "Some of the things the Lizards use seem good only for driving our own scientists mad." He thought of his own brief and unhappy stay with the physicists who were trying to turn the explosive metal he and Skorzeny had stolen into a bomb.

If Skorzeny had that same thought, he didn't show it. "I don't worry about such things. That's not my job, no more than setting foreign policy for the *Reich*. My job is getting the toys so other people can play with them."

"That is a sensible way for a soldier to look at the world." After a couple of seconds, Jäger wished he hadn't said that. He'd believed it wholeheartedly until he found out how the SS went about massacring Jews: someone had given them that job, and they went ahead and did it without worrying about anything else. He changed the subject: "All right, you're going into Besançon to get this fancy new rangefinder. How do you expect me to help? We're still close to eighty kilometers north of it, and if I roll out my panzers for an attack, they'll all be scrap metal before I get a quarter of the way there. Or have you arranged for your Lizard who likes ginger so well to sell you all their rangefinders instead of just one?"

"That would be nice, wouldn't it?" Skorzeny slugged back the rest of his coffee, made a horrible face. "This *Dreck* is even worse after it cools down. Damn, Jäger, you disappoint me. I expected you to run me right down the Grande Rue in Besançon and on to the citadel, cannon blazing."

"Good luck," Jäger blurted before he realized the other man was joking.

"How's this, then?" Skorzeny said, chuckling still. "Suppose you lay on an attack—a few panzers, artillery, infantry, whatever you can afford to expend and seem convincingly aggressive without hurting your defense too much—on the eastern half of the front. I want you to draw as much attention as you can away from the western section, where I, a simple peasant, shall pedal my bicycle—you do have a bicycle around here for me to pedal, don't you?—into Lizard-held territory and on down to Besançon. I have a way to get word to you when I shall require a similar diversion to aid my return."

Jäger thought about the men and equipment he would lose in a pair of diversionary assaults. "The rangefinder is as good as all that?" he asked.

"So I've been told." Skorzeny gave him a fishy stare.

"Would you prefer formal written orders, Colonel? I assure you, that can be arranged. I'd hoped to rely more on our previous acquaintance."

"No, I don't need formal orders," Jäger said, sighing. "I shall do as you say, of course. I only hope this rangefinder is worth the blood it will cost."

"I hope the same thing. But we won't find out unless I get the gadget, will we?"

"No." Jäger sighed again. "When do you want us to put in the diversionary attack, *Herr Standartenführer*?"

"Do what you need to do, *Herr Oberst*," Skorzeny answered. "I don't want you to go out there and get slaughtered because you hadn't shifted enough artillery and armor. Will three days give you enough time to prepare?"

"I suppose so. The front is narrow, and units won't have far to travel." Jäger also knew, but could not mention, that the more men and machines he fed into the assault, the more would be expended. War assumed expending soldiers. The trick was to keep from expending them on things that weren't worth the price.

He moved men, panzers, and artillery mostly by night, to keep the Lizards from noticing what he was up to. He didn't completely fool them; their artillery picked up on the eastern sector of the front, and an air strike incinerated a couple of trucks towing 88mm antitank guns caught out in the open. But most of the shift went through without a hitch.

At 0500 on the morning of the appointed day, with dawn staining the eastern sky, artillery began flinging shells at the Lizards' positions near the Château de Belvoir. Rifle-carrying men in field gray loped forward. Jäger, standing up in the cupola as a good panzer commander should, braced himself as his Panther rumbled ahead.

The Lizards' advance positions, being lightly held, were soon overrun, though not before one of the aliens turned a Panzer IV to Jäger's right to a funeral pyre with a rocket. He didn't see any enemy panzers, for which he thanked God; intelligence said they'd pulled back toward Besançon after the rough time he'd given them in their latest attack.

But even without armor, the Lizards were a handful. Jäger hadn't pushed forward more than a couple of kilometers before a helicopter rose into the sky and peppered his force with rockets and machine-gun fire. Another panzer, this one a Tiger,

brewed up. He winced—not only a powerful new machine, but also a veteran crew, gone forever. A lot of foot soldiers were down, too.

He got in sight of the main Lizard position outside the Château de Belvoir, lobbed a couple of high-explosive shells at the château itself (not without an inward pang at destroying old monuments; he'd thought of archaeology as a career until World War I sucked him into the army for good), and, having taken enough casualties to provide the diversion Skorzeny wanted, withdrew to lick his wounds and wait to be called on to sacrifice again.

"I hope the Lizards don't follow us home," Klaus Meinecke said as the Panther made its way back to the start line. "If they do, they're liable to catch us with our pants down around our ankles."

"Too true," Jäger said; the gunner had found an uncomfortably vivid way to put words to his own fears.

Maybe the Lizards suspected the Germans of trying to lure them into a trap. Whatever their reasons, they didn't pursue. Jäger gratefully seized the time they gave him to rebuild his defensive position. After that, he went back to watchful waiting, all the while wondering how Skorzeny was going to get word to him that he needed more strong young men thrown into the fire.

A week after the diversionary attack, a Frenchman in a tweed jacket, a dirty white shirt, and baggy black wool trousers came up to him, sketched a salute, and said, in bad German, "Our friend with the"—his finger traced a scar on his left cheek—"he needs the help you promise. Tomorrow morning, he say, is the good time. You understand?"

"Oui, monsieur. Merci," Jäger answered. The Frenchman's thin, intelligent face did not yield to a smile, but one eyebrow rose. He accepted a chunk of black bread, offering in exchange a swig of red wine from the flask on his belt. Then, without another word, he vanished back into the woods.

Jäger got on the field telephone to the nearest *Luftwaffe* base. "Can you give me air support?" he asked. "When their damned helicopter gunships show up, I lose panzers I can't spare."

"When I go after those gunships, I lose aircraft I can't spare," the *Luftwaffe* man retorted, "and aircraft are just as vital to the defense of the *Reich* as panzers. *Guten Tag*." The

phone line went dead. Jäger concluded he was not going to get his air support.

He didn't. The attack went on nonetheless. It even had a moment of triumph, when Meinecke incinerated a Lizard infantry fighting vehicle with a well-placed round from the Panther's long 75mm gun. But, on the whole, the Germans suffered worse than they had in the first diversionary assault. That had put the Lizards' wind up, and they were ready and waiting this time. Maybe that meant they'd pulled some troops from the western section of their line. Jäger hoped so; it would mean he was doing what he was supposed to.

When he'd soaked up enough casualties and damage to make the Lizards believe (with luck) he'd really tried to accomplish something, he retreated once more. No sooner had he returned to the jumping-off point than a runner came panting up and said, "Sir, there's a Lizard panzer advancing on our front line about five kilometers west of here."

"A Lizard panzer?" Jäger said. The messenger nodded. Jäger frowned. That wasn't as bad as it might have been, but even one Lizard panzer made a formidable foe. *Poor Skorzeny,* he thought: *they must have caught on to his scheme this time.* Then anger surged through him at having to mount diversionary attacks in support of a plan that hadn't been likely to succeed anyhow.

"Sir, that's not all," the messenger said.

"What else, then?" Jäger asked.

"The panzer has a white flag flying from above the driver's station, sir," the fellow answered, with the air of a man reporting something he doesn't expect to be believed. "I saw it with my own eyes."

"This I must see with *my* own eyes," Jäger said. He hopped into a little *Volkswagen* light army car, waved the messenger in beside him as a guide, and headed west. He hoped he had enough petrol to get where he was going. The light army car's engine put out less than twenty-five horsepower and didn't use much petrol, but the *Wehrmacht* had little to spare, either.

As Jäger drove, a suspicion began to form in the back of his mind. He shook his head. *No,* he told himself. *Impossible. Not even Skorzeny could—*

But Skorzeny had. When Jäger and the messenger pulled up in front of the Lizard panzer, the driver's hatch came open and

the SS man squeezed out, wriggling and twisting like a circus elephant inching through a narrow doorway.

Jäger gave him a formal military salute. That didn't seem good enough, so he also took off his cap, which made Skorzeny grin his frightening grin. "I give up," Jäger said. "How the devil did you manage *this*?" Just standing in front of the Lizard panzer was frightening to a man who'd faced its like in battle. Its smooth lines and beautifully sloped armor made every German panzer save possibly the Panther seem not merely archaic but ugly to boot. Staring down the barrel of its big main armament was like looking into a tunnel of death.

Before answering, Skorzeny writhed and twisted; Jäger heard his back and shoulders crunch. "Better," he said. "By God, I felt like a tinned sardine cooped up in there, except they don't have to bend sardines to get 'em into the tin. How did I get it? I tell you, Jäger, I didn't think I was going to get anything in Besançon. The Lizards just cleaned out every ginger-*fresser* they could catch."

"I gather they didn't catch them all," Jäger said, pointing to the panzer.

"Nobody ever does." Skorzeny grinned again. "I made contact with one they'd missed. When I showed him all the ginger I had, he said, 'You just want a rangefinder? I'd give you a whole panzer for that.' So I took him up on it."

"But how did you get it out of the city?" Jäger asked plaintively.

"There were only two dicey bits," Skorzeny said with an airy wave. "First was getting me into the vehicle park. We did that in dead of night. Second was seeing if I'd fit into the driver's compartment. I do, but just barely. After that, I up and drove it away. It steers on the same principles as our machines, but it's a lot easier to drive: the steering is power assisted and the gearbox shifts automatically."

"Didn't any of them challenge you?" Jäger said.

"Why should they? If you were a Lizard, you'd never think a human could take off in one of your panzers, now would you?"

"God in heaven, no," Jäger answered honestly. "You'd have to be out of your mind even to dream such a thing."

"Just what I thought," Skorzeny agreed. "And just what the Lizards thought, too, evidently. Since they weren't looking for me to try any such thing, I was able to bring it off right under

their snouts. You couldn't pay me enough to try it twice, though. Next time, they'll be watching and—" He made a chopping motion with his right hand.

Jäger still couldn't believe the axe hadn't fallen during this first mad escapade. He nervously glanced up at the sky. If a Lizard plane spotted them now, gunships and fighter-bombers would be on the way here in bare minutes to destroy their own panzer.

As if picking the thought from his head, Skorzeny said, "I'd better move along. I need to get this beast under cover as quick as I can, then arrange to ship it back to Germany so the lads with the high foreheads and the thick glasses can figure out what makes it tick."

"Can you wait long enough for me to look inside?" Without waiting for an answer, Jäger scrambled up onto the upper deck of the fighting compartment and stuck his head through the driver's hatch. He envied the Lizards the compactness their smaller body size allowed; Skorzeny must have been bent almost double in there.

The driver's controls and instruments were a curious mix of the familiar and the strange. The wheel, the foot pedals (though there was no clutch), and the shift lever might have come from a German panzer. But the driver's instrument panel, with screens and dials full of unfamiliar curlicues that had to be Lizard letters and numbers, looked complicated enough to have belonged in the cockpit of a Focke-Wulf 190.

In spite of that, the space wasn't cluttered: very much on the contrary. *Refined* was the word that crossed Jäger's mind as he contemplated the layout. In any German panzer—any human panzer—not everything was exactly where it would most efficiently belong. Sometimes you couldn't see a dial without moving your head, or reach for your submachine gun without banging your wrist against a projecting piece of metal. None of that here—all such tiny flaws had been designed out of the area. He wondered how long the Lizards had been making little progressive changes to get everything both perfect and perfectly finished. A long time, he suspected.

He climbed up onto the top of the turret, undogged the commander's cupola. Ignoring Skorzeny's impatient growl, he slithered down into the turret. This was where he belonged in a panzer, where he could most easily judge what was similar and what was different about the way the Lizards did things.

Again, he noticed refinement. No sharp edges, no outthrust chunks of metal anywhere. You could, if you were Lizard-sized, move around without fear of banging your head. Then he noticed the turret had no loader's seat, just as there'd been no hull gunner's position in the Lizard panzer's forward compartment. Did the gunner or commander have to load shells, then? He couldn't believe it. That would badly slow the panzer's rate of fire, and he knew from bitter experience the Lizards could shoot quicker than their German counterparts.

Some of the gadgetry that filled the turret without crowding it had to be an automatic loader, then. He wondered how it worked. No time to wonder, not now, except to hope German engineers could copy it. The gunner's station, like the driver's instrument panel, was a lot more complex than he was used to. He wondered how the Lizard who sat there could figure out what he needed to do in time to do it. Pilots managed, so maybe the gunner could, too. No—again from experience, certainly the gunner could, too.

Skorzeny's voice, peremptory now, came down through the open cupola: "Get your arse out of there, Jäger. I'm going to drive this beast away right now."

Regretfully—he hadn't seen all he wanted—Jäger slithered out and dropped down to the ground. The SS man climbed up onto the deck of the Lizard panzer and got back into the forward compartment. He was thicker through the waist than Jäger and had a devil of a time squeezing in, but he managed.

Back when the *Wehrmacht* first ran into the Russian T-34, there'd been talk of building an exact copy. In the end, the Germans didn't do that, although the Panther incorporated a lot of the T-34's best features. *If the Reich copied this Lizard panzer,* Jäger thought, *they'd have to train ten-year-olds to crew it.* Nobody else really fit.

Skorzeny started up the motor. It was amazingly quiet, and didn't belch clouds of stinking fumes—refinement again. Jäger wondered what it used for fuel. Skorzeny put it in gear and drove off. Jäger stared after him, shaking his head. The man was an arrogant bastard, but he accomplished things nobody in his right mind would dream of trying, let alone pulling off.

Atvar glowered at the male who stood stiffly in front of his desk. "You did not clean out that clutch of ginger-lickers as thoroughly as you should have," he said.

"The exalted fleetlord is correct," Drefsab replied tonelessly. "He may of course punish me as he sees fit."

Some of Atvar's anger evaporated. Drefsab had himself been trapped in ginger addiction; that he worked at all against his corrupted colleagues gave the fleetlord a weapon he would otherwise have had to do without. Nevertheless, he snapped, "A landcruiser disappearing! I never would have thought it possible."

"Which is probably just how it happened, Exalted Fleetlord," Drefsab said: "No one else thought it was possible, either, and so no one took the precautions that would have kept it from happening."

"That Big Ugly with the scar again," Atvar said. "They all look alike, but that male's disfigurement makes him stand out. He has given us nothing but grief—the landcruiser now, and spiriting Mussolini away from right under our muzzles . . . and I have some reason to believe he was involved in the raid where the Big Uglies hijacked our scattered nuclear material."

"Skorzeny." Drefsab turned the sibilants at the beginning and middle of the name into long hisses.

"That is what Deutsch propaganda called him after the Mussolini fiasco, yes," Atvar said. "In spite of your unfortunate taste for ginger, Drefsab, you remain, I believe, the most effective operative I have available to me."

"The exalted fleetlord is gracious enough to overestimate my capacities," Drefsab murmured.

"I had better not be overestimating them," Atvar said. "My orders for you are simple: I want you to rid Tosev 3 of this Skorzeny, by whatever means become necessary. Losing him will hurt the Deutsche more than losing a hundred landcruisers. And the Deutsche, along with the British and the Americans, are the most troublesome and ingeniously obstreperous Big Uglies there are, which, considering the nature of the Big Uglies, is saying a great deal. He must be eliminated, and you are the male to do it."

Drefsab saluted. "Exalted Fleetlord, it shall be done."

After several months' living and travel in places mostly without electricity, Sam Yeager had all but forgotten how wonderful having the stuff could be. The reasons weren't always the obvious ones, either. Keeping food fresh was great, sure. So was having light at night, even if you did need blackout

curtains so the Lizards wouldn't spot it. But he hadn't realized how much he missed the movies till he got to see one again.

Part of the feeling sprang from the company he kept. Having Barbara on the plush seat beside him, her hand warm in his, would have put a warm glow on anything this side of going to the dentist (not a major concern for Yeager anyhow, not with his store-bought teeth). Later, his hand would probably drop to her thigh. In the dim cavern of the movie theater, nobody was likely to notice, or to care if he did notice.

But part of what Sam got from the movies had nothing to do with Barbara. For a couple of hours, he could forget how miserable the world outside this haven on Sixteenth Street looked and pretend what happened on the screen was what mattered.

"Funny," he whispered to Barbara as they waited for the projectionist to start the newsreel: "I can get out of myself with a good story in a magazine or a book, but watching a show is more special somehow."

"Reading lets me get away from things, too," she answered, "but a lot of people can't escape that way. I feel sorry for them, but I know it's true. The other thing is, when you're reading, you're by yourself. Here you're with lots of other people looking for the same release you're after. It makes a difference."

"I found what I was after," Sam said, and squeezed her hand. She turned to smile at him. Before she could say anything, the lights dimmed and the big screen at the front of the theater came to sparkling life.

The newsreel wasn't the smoothly professional production it would have been before the Lizards came. Yeager didn't know whether the aliens held Hollywood itself, but the distribution system for new films coming out of California had completely broken down.

What the moviegoers got instead was a U.S. Army production, probably put together right here in Denver. Some of the bits had sound added; some used cards with words on them, something Sam remembered from silent film days but had thought to be gone for good.

EASTERN FRANCE, one of those cards announced. The camera panned slowly, lovingly, across burned-out Lizard tanks. A tough-looking fellow in German uniform walked among the wreckage.

People cheered wildly. Barbara murmured, "Has everyone forgotten the Nazis were our worst enemies a year ago?"

"Yes," Yeager whispered back. He had no love for the Nazis, but if they were hurting the Lizards, more power to 'em. He hadn't loved the Russian Reds last year, either, but he'd been damn glad they were in the fight against Hitler.

Another card flashed: MOSCOW. There stood Stalin, shaking hands with a factory worker in a cloth cap. Behind them, a row of almost-completed airplanes stretched as far as the eye—or the camera—could see. Yet another card said, THE SOVIET UNION STAYS IN THE FIGHT. More cheers echoed through the movie theater.

The next segment had sound; a fellow with a flat midwestern accent said, "Outside of Bloomington, the Lizards banged their snouts into tough American resistance as they tried to push north toward Chicago again." Another picture of a wrecked Lizard tank was followed by shots of tired-looking but happy GIs around a campfire.

Yeager almost bounced out of his chair. "There's Mutt, by God!" he told Barbara. "My old manager, I mean. Jesus, I wonder how he lived through all the fighting. He's got sergeant's stripes, too—did you see?"

"I wouldn't have recognized him, Sam. He wasn't *my* manager," she answered, which made him feel foolish. She added, "I'm glad he's all right."

"Boy, so am I," he said, "I've played for some real hard cases in my day, but he was one of the other kind, the good ones. He—" People to either side and behind made shushing noises. Yeager subsided, abashed.

The newsreel cut to a card that said, SOMEWHERE IN THE U.S.A. "Ladies and gentlemen, the President of the United States!" the announcer said.

In the black-and-white film, Franklin D. Roosevelt sat behind a desk in what looked like a hotel room. The drapes were drawn behind him, perhaps merely to give him a backdrop, perhaps to keep the Lizards from figuring out where he was by what the camera showed out the window.

Roosevelt was in his shirtsleeves, his collar unbuttoned and his tie loose. He looked tired and worn, but kept the cigarette holder at a jaunty angle in his mouth. He still had cigarettes, Yeager noted without resentment: FDR was working hard enough to be entitled to them.

The President took the holder from his mouth, stubbed out the cigarette instead of letting it smolder to add a picturesque plume of smoke to the scene. He leaned toward the microphone in front of him. "My friends," he said (and Yeager felt Roosevelt was speaking straight to him), "the fight goes on."

Applause rippled through the theater, then quickly faded so people could listen to what the President had to say. Even his first half-dozen words gave Sam fresh hope. FDR had always had that gift. He hadn't always made things better, but he'd always made people feel they *would* get better, which was half the battle by itself—it made people go to work to improve their own lot instead of moaning about how dreadful everything was.

Roosevelt said, "The enemy is on our soil and in the air above our homes. These creatures from another world believe they can frighten us into surrender by raining destruction down on our heads. As our gallant British allies did with the Germans in 1940, we shall prove them wrong.

"Every day we have more new weapons to hurl against the Lizards. Every day they have less with which to resist. Those of you who still live free, everything you do to help the war effort helps ensure that your children, and your children's children, will grow up in freedom, too. And to those of you in occupied territory who may see this, I say: do not collaborate with the enemy in any way. Do not work in his factories, do not grow crops for him, do nothing you can possibly avoid. Without human beings to be his slaves, sooner or later he will be helpless.

"For we have hurt him, in America, in Europe, and in Asia as well. He is not superhuman, he is merely inhuman. Our united nations—now all the nations on this planet—will surely triumph in the end. Thank you and God bless you."

The next news segment showed ways to conserve scrap metal. It had a soundtrack, but Yeager didn't pay much attention to it. He didn't think anyone else did, either. Just hearing FDR's voice was a tonic. Roosevelt made you think everything would turn out okay, one way or another.

The newsreel ended with a burst of patriotic music. Sam sighed; now he'd have "The Stars and Stripes Forever" noisily going around in his head for the next several days. It happened every time he heard the song.

"Here comes the real movie," somebody near him said as

the opening credits for *You're in the Army Now* filled the screen. Yeager had seen it four or five times since it came out in 1941. New movies just weren't getting out these days, and even if they did, they often couldn't have been shown, because electricity was lost in so many places.

When he'd seen the antics of Phil Silvers and Jimmy Durante and the horrified reactions of their superior officers before, they'd left him limp with laughter. Now that he was in the Army himself, they didn't seem so funny any more. Soldiers like that would have endangered their buddies. He wanted to give both comics a swift kick in the rear.

Beside him, though, Barbara laughed at the capers they cut. Sam tried to enjoy the escape with her. The musical numbers helped: they reminded him this was Hollywood, not anything real. Getting angry at the actors for doing what was in the script didn't do him any good. Once he'd figured that out, he was able to lean back and enjoy the movie again.

The house lights came up. Barbara let out a long sigh, as if she didn't feel like coming back to the real world. Given its complications, Yeager didn't much blame her. But the world was there, and you had to deal with it whether you wanted to or not.

"Come on," he said. "Let's pick up our bikes and head back to the university."

Barbara sighed again, then yawned. "I suppose so. When we get back there, I think I want to lie down for a while. I'm so tired all the time these days." She managed a wan smile. "I've heard this is what being expecting is supposed to do to you, and boy, it sure does."

"We'll take it nice and easy on the way back," said Yeager, who was still inclined to treat Barbara as if she were made of cut glass and liable to break if jostled. "You rest, and I'll go round up Ullhass and Ristin."

"Okay, Sam."

Outside the theater, a herd of bicycles covered the sidewalk and the street by the curb. Keeping an eye on them, in lieu of a sheepdog, was a large, burly fellow with a .45 on his hip. With no gas available for private cars, bikes had become the way of choice to get around, and stealing them as big a problem as horse theft in Denver's younger days. As many people packed a gun now as they had in the old days, too; an unarmed guard wouldn't have done much good.

Most of Denver was laid out on a north-south, east-west grid. The downtown area, though, nestled into the angle of the Platte River and Cherry Creek, turned that grid at a forty-five-degree angle. Yeager and Barbara pedaled southeast down Sixteenth Street to Broadway, one of the main north-south thoroughfares.

The Pioneer Monument at the corner of Broadway and Colfax caught Sam's eye. Around the fountain were three reclining bronzes: a prospector, a hunter, and a pioneer mother. At the top of the monument stood a mounted scout.

On him Yeager turned a critical gaze. "I've seen statues that looked realer," he remarked, pointing.

"He does look more like an oversized mantelpiece ornament than a pioneer, doesn't he?" Barbara said. They both laughed.

They turned left onto Colfax. Bicycles, people on foot, horse- and mule-drawn wagons, and quite a few folks riding horses made traffic, if anything, dicier than it had been when cars and trucks dominated. Then everything had moved more or less at the same speed. Now the ponderous wagons were almost like ambulatory roadblocks, but you went around them at your peril, too, because a lot of them were big enough to hide what was alongside till too late.

The gilded dome of the three-story granite State Capitol on Colfax dominated the city skyline. On the west lawn of the capitol building stood a Union soldier in bronze, flanked by two Civil War brass cannon.

Yeager pointed to the statue. He said, "Going up against the Lizards, sometimes I felt the way he would if he had to fight today's Germans or Japs with his muzzle-loader and those guns."

"There's an unpleasant thought," Barbara said. They pedaled along; on the east lawn of the capitol stood an Indian, also in bronze. She nodded to that statue. "I suppose he felt the same way when he had to fight the white man's guns with nothing better than a bow and arrow."

"Yeah, he probably did at that," said Sam, who'd never thought to look at it from the Indian's perspective. "He got guns of his own, though, and he hit us some pretty good licks, too—at least, I wouldn't have wanted to be in General Custer's boots."

"You're right." But instead of cheering up, Barbara looked glum. "Even though the Indians hit us some good licks, they

lost—look at the United States now, or the way it was before
the Lizards came, anyway. Does that mean we'll lose to the
Lizards, even if we do hurt them in the fight?"

"I don't know." Sam chewed on that for the next block or
so. "Not necessarily," he said at last. "The Indians never did
figure out how to make their own guns and gunpowder; they
always had to get 'em from white men." He looked around to
make sure nobody was paying undue attention to their conversation before he went on, "But we're well on our way to making bombs to match the ones the Lizards have."

"That's true." Barbara did cheer up, but only for a moment.
She said, "I wonder if there'll be anything left of the world by
the time we're done fighting the Lizards."

The science-fiction pulps had printed plenty of stories about
worlds ruined one way or another, but Sam hadn't really
thought about living (or more likely dying) in one. Slowly, he
said, "If the choice is wrecking the Earth or living under the
Lizards, I'd vote for wrecking it. From what Ullhass and Ristin
say, the Race has kept two other sets of aliens under their
thumbs for thousands of years. I wouldn't wish that on anybody."

"No, neither would I," Barbara said. "But we sure do remind me of a couple of little kids quarreling over a toy: 'If I
can't have it, you can't either!'—and *smash!* If we end up
smashing a whole world . . . but what else can we do?"

"I don't know," Yeager answered. He did his best to think
about something else. The end of the world wasn't something
he wanted to talk about with the woman he loved.

They turned right off Colfax onto University Boulevard.
Traffic there was thinner and moved faster than it had in the
center of town. Yeager looked around, enjoying the scenery.
He'd been up at altitude now, in Wyoming and Colorado, that
he could pedal along as readily as he had at sea level.

Just past Exposition Avenue, he saw a couple of cyclists
speeding north up University: a skinny blond fellow in civvies
followed closely by a burly man in uniform with a Springfield
on his back. The skinny guy saw Sam and Barbara, too. He
scowled as he whizzed by.

"Oh, dear," Barbara said. "That was Jens." She shook her
head back and forth, hard enough to make her bike wobble.
"He hates me now, I think." Her voice had tears in it.

"He's a fool if he does," Sam said. "You had to choose

somebody, honey. I wouldn't have hated you if you'd gone back to him. I just thank God every day that you decided to pick me." That she had still surprised and delighted him.

"I'm going to have your baby, Sam," she said. "That changes everything. If it weren't for the baby—oh, I don't know what I'd do. But with things the way they are, I didn't see that I had any other choice."

They rode along in silence for a while. *If I hadn't knocked her up, she'd have gone back to Larssen,* Sam thought. It made sense to him: she'd known Jens a lot longer, and he was, on paper, more her type. She was a brain and, while Yeager didn't think of himself as stupid, he knew damn well he'd never make an intellectual.

Not quite out of the blue, Barbara said, "Both of you always treated me well—till now. If I'd chosen Jens, I don't think you'd act the way he is."

"I just said that," he answered. "The thing of it is, I've had enough things go wrong in my life that I've sort of learned to roll with the punches. That one would have been a Joe Louis right, but I would've gotten back on my feet and gone on the best I could." He paused again; speaking ill of Larssen was liable to make Barbara spring to his defense. Picking his words carefully, he went on, "I'm not sure Jens ever had anything really tough happen to him before."

"I think you're right," Barbara said. "That's very perceptive of you. Even all his grandparents are still alive, or they were before the Lizards came—now, who can say? But he sailed through college, sailed through his graduate work, and had a job waiting for him at Berkeley when he finished. Then he got recruited for the Metallurgical Laboratory—"

"—which was every physicist's dream," Yeager finished for her. "Yeah." Not a lot of people had jobs waiting for them when they finished school, not in the Depression they didn't. So Larssen's family had all been healthy, too? And he'd found this wonderful girl. Maybe he'd started getting the idea he was fireproof. "Nobody's fireproof," Yeager muttered with the conviction of a man who'd had to hustle for work every spring training since he turned eighteen.

"What did you say, honey?" Barbara asked.

The casual endearment warmed him. He said, "I was just thinking things go wrong for everybody sooner or later."

" 'Count no man lucky before the end,' " Barbara said. It

sounded like a quotation, but Yeager didn't know where it was from. She continued, "I don't think Jens has ever had to deal with anything like this before, and I don't think he's dealing with it very well." Again Sam heard unshed tears. "I wish he were."

"I know, hon. I do, too. It would make everything a lot easier." But Sam didn't expect things would always be easy. He was, as he'd said, ready to ride them out when they got tough. And if Jens Larssen wasn't, that was his lookout.

Yeager carried his bicycle upstairs to the apartment he and Barbara had taken across the street from the University of Denver campus. Then he went down and carried hers up, too.

"I'm going to go take my little hissing chums off Smitty's hands," he said. "Have to see what he'll want from me later on for baby-sitting them so I could get free for my Saturday matinee with you."

Barbara glanced at the electric clock on the mantel. It showed a quarter to four. So did Sam's watch; he was having to get reused to the idea of clocks that kept good time. She said, "It'll still be afternoon for a little while longer, won't it?"

As he took her in his arms, Yeager wondered if she just needed reassurance after the brief, wordless, but unpleasant encounter with Jens Larssen. If she did, he was ready to give it. If you couldn't do that, you didn't have much business being a husband, as far as he was concerned.

Liu Han felt like a trapped animal with the little scaly devils staring at her from all sides. "No, superior sirs, I don't know where Bobby Fiore went that night," she said in a mixture of the little devils' language and Chinese. "These men wanted him to teach them to throw, and he went with them to do that. He didn't come back."

One of the scaly devils showed her a photograph. It was not a plain black-and-white image; she'd seen those before, and even the color pictures the foreign devils printed in some of their fancy magazines. But this photograph was of the sort the little scaly devils made: not only more real than any human could match, but also with the depth the scaly devils put into their moving pictures. It made her feel as if she could reach in and touch the man it showed.

"Have you seen this male before?" the scaly devil holding the picture demanded in vile but understandable Chinese.

"I—may have, superior sir," Liu Han said, gulping. Just because she felt she could reach into the picture didn't mean she wanted to. The man it showed was obviously dead, lying in a bean field with his blood and brains splashing the plants and ground around his head. He had a neat hole just above his left eye.

"What do you mean, you may have?" another scaly devil shouted. "Either you have or you have not. We think you have. Now answer me!"

"Please, superior sir," Liu Han said desperately. "People dead look different from people alive. I cannot be certain. I am sorry, superior sir." She was sorry Lo—for the dead man in the picture was undoubtedly he—had ever wanted Bobby Fiore to show him how to throw. She was even sorrier he and his henchmen had come to the hut and taken Bobby Fiore away.

But she was not going to tell the little scaly devils anything she didn't have to. She knew they were dangerous, yes, and they had her in their power. But she also had a very healthy respect—fear was not too strong a word—for the Communists. If she spilled her guts to the little devils, she knew she would pay: maybe not right now, but before too long.

The scaly devil holding the picture let his mouth hang open: he was laughing at her. "To you, maybe. To us, all Big Uglies look alike, alive or dead." He translated the joke into his own language for the benefit of his comrades. They laughed, too.

But the little devil who had shouted at Liu Han said, "This is no joke. These bandits injured males of the Race. Only through the mercy of the watchful Emperor"—he cast down his eyes, as did the other little devils—"was no one killed."

No one killed? Liu Han thought. *What of Lo and his friends?* She was reminded of signs the European devils were said to have put up in their parks in Shanghai: No Dogs or Chinese Allowed. To the little scaly devils, all human beings might as well have been dogs.

"We should give her the drug that makes her tell the truth," the scaly devil with the picture said. "Then we will find out what she really knows."

Liu Han shivered. She was ready to believe the scaly devils had such a drug. They were devils, after all, with powers effectively unlimited. If they gave it to her, they would find out she hadn't told them everything, and then . . . then they would do something horrible to her. She didn't care to think about that.

But then Ttomalss spoke up. The—what had Bobby Fiore named his calling?—the psychologist, that was it, said, "No, Ssamraff, for two reasons. No first because the drug is not as effective as we believed it would be when we first made it. And no second because this female Big Ugly has a hatchling growing inside her."

Most of that was in Chinese, so Liu Han could follow it. Ssamraff replied in the same language: "Who cares what she has growing inside her?"

"This growth is disgusting, yes, but it is part of a research study," Ttomalss insisted. "Having the Big Ugly male who sired it disappear is bad enough. But drugs could do to Big Ugly hatchlings what they sometimes do to our own as they grow in the egg before the female lays it. We do not want this hatchling to emerge defective if we can avoid it. Therefore I say no to this drug."

"And I say we need to learn who is trying to foully murder males of the Race," Ssamraff retorted. "This, to me, is more important." But he spoke weakly; his body paint was less ornate than Ttomalss', which, Liu Han had gathered, meant he was of lower rank.

The little devils had made her give her body to strange men in their experiments. They had watched her pregnancy with the same interest she would have given to a farrowing sow, and no more. Now, though, because she was pregnant, they wouldn't give her the drug that might have made her betray Lo and the other Reds. *About time I got some good out of being only an animal to them,* she thought.

Ssamraff said, "If we cannot drug the female, how can we properly question her, then?" He swung his turreted eyes toward Liu Han. She still had trouble reading the scaly devils' expressions, but if that wasn't a venomous stare, she'd never seen one. "I am sure she is telling less than she knows."

"No, superior sir," Liu Han protested, and then stopped in some confusion: not only Ssamraff, but all the devils were staring at her. She realized he'd spoken in his tongue—as had she when she answered.

"You know more of our words than I thought," Ttomalss said in Chinese.

Liu Han gratefully returned to the same language: "I am very sorry, superior sir, but I did not realize I was not supposed to learn."

"I did not say that," the psychologist answered. "But because you know, we have to be more careful with what we say around you."

"Because she knows, we should be trying to find out what she knows," Ssamraff insisted. "This male she was mating with had something to do with the attack on our guard station. I think she is lying when she says she knows nothing of these other males we killed. They are dead, and the one she mates with is missing. Is this not a connection that hisses to be explored?"

"We are exploring it," Ttomalss answered. "But, as I said, we shall not use drugs."

Ssamraff turned one eye turret toward Liu Han to see how she would react as he spoke in his own language: "What about pain, then? The Big Uglies are very good at using pain when they have questions to ask. Maybe this once we should imitate them."

A lump of ice formed in Liu Han's belly. The Communists and the Kuomintang—to say nothing of local bandit chiefs—routinely used torture. She had no reason to doubt the little scaly devils would be devilishly good at it.

But Ttomalss said, "No, not while the hatchling grows inside her. I told you, you may not disturb the conditions under which this experiment is being conducted."

This time, even the little devil who'd shouted at Liu Han supported Ttomalss: "Using pain to force our will even on a Big Ugly is—" Liu Han didn't understand the last word he used, but Ssamraff sputtered in indignation almost laughably obvious, so it must have been one he didn't care for.

When he could speak instead of sputtering, he said, "I shall protest this interference with an important military investigation."

"Go ahead," Ttomalss said. "And I shall protest your interference with an important scientific investigation. You have no sense of the long term, Ssamraff. We are going to rule the Big Uglies for the next hundred thousand years. We need to learn how they work. Don't you see you are making that harder?"

"If we don't root out the ones who keep shooting at us, we may never rule them at all," Ssamraff said.

To Liu Han's way of thinking, he had a point, but the other little scaly devils recoiled as if he'd just said something much worse than suggesting that they torture her to find out what she

knew of Lo and the Communists. Ttomalss said, "Will you add that to your report? I hope you do; it will show you up as the shortsighted male you are. I shall certainly make a note of your statement when I file my own protest. You were rash to be so foolish in front of a witness." His eye turrets swung toward the little devil who'd yelled at Liu Han.

Ssamraff looked at that little devil, too. He must not have liked what he saw, for he said, "I shall make no protest in this matter. By the Emperor I pledge it." He flicked his glance down at the floor for a moment.

So did the other little scaly devils. Then Ttomalss said, "I knew you were a male of sense, Ssamraff. No one wants to have a charge of shortsightedness down on his record, not if he hopes to improve the design of his body paint."

"That is so," Ssamraff admitted. "But this I also tell you: to view in the long term on Tosev 3 is also dangerous. The Big Uglies change too fast to make projections reliable—or else we would have conquered them long since." He turned and skittered out of Liu Han's hut. Had he been a man instead of a scaly devil, she thought he would have stomped away.

Ttomalss and the devil who'd shouted at her both laughed as if he'd been funny. Liu Han didn't see the joke.

crewd Lo and the Lizardskis. Promise them-oh-Will you do
this to your race? I hope you do. If you don't, there you go, just
don't expect much warmth. I still probably make a note of how
responsive I rate my own. Just for sure. You await you to learn
people in traffic of a moment." The sun throws within together the
sky dusky, who'd stand of a-up-life.
Stopping he had a ...."If you ...roof. He takes and have
Brimwin in his ...a...the more about ...the more...in the
latter. Try his ...it's very nearby... He thacked, he stared
down at the shiny town together.
Suddenly the oft-rating was all ovit. "Don't mention, one
time will more a sense of effect. Sgot it? No, who wants to

Sometimes, in the Warsaw ghetto, Moishe Russie had developed a feeling that something was wrong, that trouble (*worse* trouble, he amended to himself: just being in the ghetto was *tsuris* aplenty) would land on him if he didn't do something right away. He'd learned to act on that feeling. He was still alive, so he supposed following it had done him some good. Now, here in Lodz, he had it again.

It wasn't the usual fears he'd known, not the heart-clutching spasm of alarm he'd had, for instance, when he'd seen his face on the wall in the Balut Market square with warnings that he raped and murdered little girls. *You'd have to be* meshuggeh, he thought, *not to be frightened over something like that.*

But what he felt now was different, smaller—just a tickling at the back of his neck and the skin over his spine that something wasn't quite right somewhere. The first day it was there, he tried to make believe he didn't notice it. The second day, he knew it was there, but he didn't tell Rivka. *I could be wrong,* he thought.

The third day—or rather the evening, after Reuven had gone to bed—he said out of the blue, "I think we should move someplace else."

Rivka looked up from the sock she was darning. "Why?" she asked. "What's wrong here?"

"I don't know," he admitted. "Maybe nothing. But maybe something, too."

"If you were a woman, they'd call that the vapors," Rivka said. But instead of laughing at him as she had every right to do, she grew serious. "Someplace else where? A different flat in Lodz? A different town? A different country?"

"I'd say a different planet, but the Lizards seem to be using the others, too." Now he laughed, but it wasn't funny.

"*Nu*, if you think we should go, we'll go," Rivka said. "Better we should move and not need to than need to and not move. Why don't you start looking for a new flat tomorrow, if you think that will be good enough."

"I just don't know," he said. "I wish I could tune the feeling like a wireless set, but it doesn't work that way."

"No, it doesn't," she agreed gravely. "What do you want to do? Do you want to go to Zgierz, for instance? That's not far, but it would probably mean leaving things behind. Still, we've left enough things behind by now that a few more won't matter. So long as the three of us are together, nothing else counts. If the war has taught us anything, that's it."

"You're right." Russie got up from his battered chair, walked over to the bare light bulb by which Rivka sat. He let his hand rest on her shoulder. "But we shouldn't need a war to remind us of that."

She set down the sock and put her hand on top of his. "We don't, not really. But it has shown us we don't need things to get by in the world, just people we love."

"A good thing, too, because we don't have many things." Moishe stopped, afraid his attempt at a joke had wounded his wife. Not only had they left things behind, they'd left people as well: a little daughter, other loved ones dead in the ghetto. And unlike things, you could not get a new set of people.

If she noticed the catch in Moishe's voice, Rivka gave no sign. She stayed resolutely practical, saying, "You never did answer me. Do you want to get out of Lodz, or shall we stay here?"

"The towns around here, most of them are *Judenfrei*," he said. "We'd stick out. We don't look Polish. We can't look Polish, I don't think." He sighed. "Litzmannstadt"—the name the Germans gave Lodz—"would have been *Judenfrei*, too, if the Lizards hadn't come."

"All right, we'll stay here, then," Rivka said, accepting his oblique answer.

He didn't know if he was doing the right thing. Maybe they would be wiser to flee far from Lodz, even if that meant taking to the road to go to the eastern parts of Lizard-held Poland where the Nazis had not had time to rout out all the Jews. But

he couldn't make himself flee like that for what might have been, as Rivka said, a case of the vapors.

To make himself feel he was doing something, he said, "I'll start looking for a new flat tomorrow over by Mostowski Street." That was about as far from where they were as one could go and remain in the Lodz ghetto.

"All right," Rivka said again. She picked up the sock and put another few stitches in it. After a moment, though, she added meditatively, "We'll have to keep on shopping in the Balut Market square, though."

"That's true." Moishe started to pace back and forth. To go? To stay? He still couldn't make up his mind.

"It will be all right," Rivka said. "God has protected us for this long; would He abandon us now?"

That argument would have been more persuasive, Moishe thought, *before 1939.* Since then, how many of His people had God allowed to die? Moishe didn't say that to his wife; he didn't even care to think it himself. His own faith was shakier these days than he wished it were, and he didn't want to be guilty of troubling hers.

Instead, he yawned and said, "Let's go to bed."

Rivka put down the sock again. She hesitated, then said, "Do you want me to look for the flat? The fewer people who see you, the smaller the risk we run."

Moishe knew that was true. Nonetheless, his pride revolted at hiding behind Rivka every day—and he had no evidence whatever to back up his hunch. So he said, "It shouldn't be a problem. I'll be only a moment crossing the Balut, and I don't look like my poster picture anyhow, not clean-shaven."

Rivka gave him her best dubious look, but didn't say anything. He reckoned that a victory.

And, indeed, no one paid him any mind as he crossed the market square and turned east into the heart of the ghetto. The shabby brick buildings cast the narrow streets into shadow. Though the Lizards had driven the Germans out of Lodz nearly a year before, the atmosphere of the hellishly crowded ghetto still clung to the place, maybe more strongly than in Warsaw.

Maybe it's the smell, Russie thought. It was a smell of despair and stale cabbage and unwashed bodies and more garbage and sewage than the trash collectors and sewers could handle. Not all the people the Nazis had crammed into Lodz

had been able to go home. Some had no homes, not after the Germans had fought Poles and Russians, and the Lizards fought the Germans. Some, carried into the ghetto in cattle cars from Germany and Austria, had homes outside Lizard-held territory. Even now, the ghetto was a desperately crowded place.

Posters of Chaim Rumkowski shouted at people from every blank wall surface. As far as Moishe could tell, people weren't doing much in the way of listening. In all those teeming streets, he saw only a couple of persons glance up at the posters, and one of those, an old woman, shook her head and laughed after she did. Somehow that made Russie feel a little better about mankind.

His own poster still appeared here and there, too, now beginning to fray and tatter a bit. No one looked up at that any more, either, to his relief.

When he got to Mostowski Street, he started poking his nose into blocks of flats and asking if they had any rooms to let. At first he thought he would have no choice but to stay where he was or else leave town. But at the fourth building he visited, the fellow who ran the place said, "You are a lucky man, my friend, do you know that? I just had a family move out not an hour ago."

"Why?" Moishe asked in a challenging voice. "Were you charging them a thousand zlotys a day, or did the cockroaches and rats make alliance and drive them out? It's probably a pigsty you're going to show me."

From one Jew to another, that hit hard a couple of ways. The landlord, or manager, or whatever he was, clapped a hand to his forehead in a theatrical display of injured innocence. "A pigsty? I should kick you out of here on your *tokhus* to talk like that. One look at this flat and you'll be down on your knees begging to rent."

"I don't get down on my knees for God and I should do it for you? You should live so long," Moishe said. "Besides, you still haven't said what ridiculous price you want."

"You shouldn't even see it, with a mouth like yours." But the landlord was already walking back toward the stairway, Moishe at his heels. "Besides, such a deadbeat couldn't pay four hundred zlotys a month."

"If he lived in Lodz, King Solomon couldn't pay four hundred zlotys a month, you *ganef*." Moishe stopped. "I'm sorry

I wasted my time. Good day." He didn't leave. "A hundred fifty I might manage."

The landlord had one foot on the stairs. He didn't put the other one with it. "I might manage to starve, if I didn't have better sense than to listen to an obvious *shlemiel* like you. I would be giving this lovely flat away at 350 zlotys."

"Then give it away, but not to me. I have better ways to spend my money, thank you very much. A hundred seventy-five would be too much, let alone twice that."

"Definitely a *shlemiel*, and you think I'm one, too." But the landlord started climbing the stairs, and Moishe climbed with him. The stairwell reeked of stale piss. Moishe didn't know a stairwell in the ghetto that didn't.

By the time they got to the flat, they were only a hundred zlotys apart. There they stuck, because Moishe refused to haggle any further until he saw what he might be renting. The landlord chose a key from the fat ring on his belt, opened the door with a flourish. Moishe stuck in his head. The place was cut from the same mold as the one he was living in: a main room, with a kitchen to one side and a bedroom to the other. It was a little smaller than his present flat, but not enough to matter. "The electricity works?" he asked.

The manager pulled the chain that hung down from the ceiling lamp in the living room. The light came on. "The electricity works," he said unnecessarily.

Moishe went into the kitchen. Water ran when he turned the faucet handle. "How is the plumbing?"

"*Verkakte,*" the landlord answered, which made Russie suspect he might have some honesty lurking in him. "But for Lodz, for now, it's not bad. Two seventy-five is about as low as I can go, pal."

"It's not that bad," Moishe said grudgingly. "If I let my little boy go hungry, I might make two twenty-five."

"You give me two twenty-five and my little boy will starve. Shall we split the difference? Two fifty?"

"Two forty," Moishe said.

"Two forty-five."

"Done."

"And you call me a *ganef*." The landlord shook his head. "*Gottenyu,* you're the toughest haggler I've run into in a while. If I told you how much more money I was getting out

of the last people in here, you'd cry for me. So when are you and your family coming in?"

"We could start bringing our things in today," Moishe answered. "It's not that we have a lot to move, believe me."

"This I do believe," the landlord said. "The Germans stole, the Poles stole, people stole from each other—and the ones who didn't had to burn their furniture to cook food or keep from freezing to death last winter or the one before or the one before that. So fetch in whatever you've got, *nu*? But before one stick of it goes in there, you put your first month's rent right here." He held out his hand, palm up.

"You'll have it," Moishe promised, "Mister, uh—"

"Stefan Berkowicz. And you are who, so I can tell my wife the name of the man who cheated me?"

"Emmanuel Lajfuner," Russie answered without hesitation, inventing an easily memorable name so he wouldn't forget it before he got home. He and Berkowicz parted on good terms.

When he described the haggle to Rivka, he proudly repeated the landlord's praise for his skill and tenacity. She shrugged and said, "If he's like most landlords, he says that to all the people who take a flat in his building, just to make them feel good. But you could have done worse; you have, often enough."

Praise with that faint damn left Moishe feeling vaguely punctured. He let Rivka go downstairs and hire a pushcart in which to haul their belongings. Then it was just carrying things down to the cart till it was full, manhandling it over to the new building, and lugging them up to the flat (Berkowicz got his zlotys first). Except for the bedraggled sofa, there wasn't anything one man couldn't handle by himself.

Two small sets of dishes and pans, moved in different loads; some rickety chairs; a pile of clothes, not very clean, not very fine; a few toys; a handful of books Moishe had picked up now here, now there; a mattress, some blankets; and a wooden frame. *Not much to make up a life,* Moishe thought. But while he was alive, he could hope to gain more.

"It will do," Rivka said when she first set foot in the new flat. Having expected worse sarcasm than that, Moishe grinned in foolish relief. Rivka stalked into the bedroom, prowled the tiny kitchen. She came back nodding in acceptance if not approval. "Yes, it will do."

Without talking about it, they arranged such furniture as

they owned in about the same places it had occupied in the flat they were leaving. Moishe looked around the new place. Yes, that helped give it the feeling of home.

"Almost done," he said late that afternoon. He was sweaty and filthy and as tired as he'd ever been, but one of the good things (one of the few good things) about moving was that you could see you were making progress.

"What's left?" Rivka asked. "I thought this was just about everything."

"Just about. But there's still one more stool, and a couple of old blankets that went up on the high shelf when spring finally got here, and that sack of canned goods we hid under them for whenever, God forbid, we might be really hungry again." As Moishe knew only too well, he was imperfectly organized. But he had a catchall memory which helped make up for that: he might not put papers, say, in the pile where they were supposed to go, but he never forgot where he *had* put them. So now he knew exactly what had been moved and what still remained in the old flat.

"If it weren't for the food, I'd tell you not to bother," Rivka said. "But you're right—we've been hungry too much. I never want to have to go through that again. Come back as fast as you can."

"I will," Moishe promised. Straightening his cap, he trudged down the stairs. His arms and shoulders twinged aching protest as he picked up the handles of the pushcart. Ignoring the aches as best he could, he made his slow way through the crowded streets and back to the old flat.

He was just pulling the sack of cans down from the shelf in the bedroom when someone rapped on the open front door. He muttered under his breath and put the sack back as quietly as he could, so the cans didn't clank together—letting people know you had food squirreled away invited it to disappear. He wondered whether it would be one of his neighbors coming to say good-bye or the landlord with a prospective tenant for the flat.

He'd be polite to whoever it was and send him on his way. Then he'd be able to get on his own way. Fixing a polite smile on his face, he walked into the living room.

In the doorway stood two burly Order Service men, both still wearing the red-and-white armbands with black *Magen Davids* left over from the days of Nazi rule in the Lodz ghetto.

They carried stout truncheons. Behind them were two Lizards armed with weapons a great deal worse.

"You Moishe Russie?" the uglier Order Service ruffian asked. Without waiting for an answer, he raised his club. "You better come with us."

Flying over the Russian steppe, traveling across it by train, Ludmila Gorbunova had of course known how vast it was. But nothing had prepared her for walking over what seemed an improbably large chunk of it to get where she was going.

"I'll have to draw new boots when we get back to the airstrip," she told Nikifor Sholudenko.

His mobile features assumed what she had come to think of as an NKVD sneer. "So long as you are in a position to draw them, all will be well. Even if you are in a position to draw them with none to be had, all will be well enough."

She nodded; Sholudenko was undoubtedly right. Then one of her legs sank almost knee-deep into a patch of ooze she hadn't noticed. It was almost like going into quicksand. She had to work her way out a little at a time. When, slimy and dripping, she was on the move again, she muttered, "Too bad nobody would be able to issue me a new pair of feet."

Sholudenko pointed to water glinting from behind an apple orchard. "That looks like a pond. Do you want to clean off?"

"All right," Ludmila said. Since she'd flipped her U-2, the time when they returned to the airstrip, formerly so urgent, had taken on an atmosphere of *nichevo*. When she and Sholudenko weren't sure of the day on which they'd arrive, an hour or two one way or the other ceased to mean anything.

They walked over to the orchard, which did lie in front of a pond. Ludmila yanked off her filthy boot. The water was bitterly cold, but the mud came off her foot and leg. She'd coated both feet with a thick layer of goose grease she'd begged from a *babushka*. If you were going to get wet, as anyone who traveled during the *rasputitsa* surely would, the grease helped keep rot from starting between your toes.

She washed the boot inside and out, using a scrap of cloth from inside her pack to dry it as well as she could. Then she splashed more water on her face: she knew how dirty she was, and had in full measure the Russian love of personal cleanliness. "I wish this were a proper steam bath," she said. "Without the heat first, I don't want to take a cold plunge."

"No, that would be asking for pneumonia," Sholudenko agreed. "Can't take the risk, not out in the field."

He spoke like a soldier, not like someone who'd surely enjoyed a comfortable billet in a town until the Nazis invaded the SSSR, and maybe till the Lizards came. Ludmila had to admit he performed the same way: he marched and camped capably and without complaint. She'd viewed the secret police as birds were supposed to view snakes—as hunters almost fascinating in their deadliness and power, men whose attention it was far better never to attract. But as the days went by, Sholudenko seemed more and more just another man to her. She didn't know how far she could trust that.

He knelt by the side of the pond and splashed his face, too. While he washed, Ludmila stood watch. What with Lizards and collaborators and bandits who robbed indiscriminately, not a kilometer of Ukrainian territory was liable to be safe.

As if to drive that point home, a column of half a dozen Lizard tanks rolled up the road the pilot and NKVD man had just left. "I'm glad they didn't see us carrying firearms," Ludmila said.

"Yes, that could have proved embarrassing," Sholudenko said. "For some reason, they've developed the habit of firing machine-gun bursts first and asking questions later. A wasteful way to conduct interrogations, not that they asked my opinion of it."

The casual way he talked about such things made the hair prickle up on Ludmila's arms, as if she were a wild animal fluffing out its fur to make itself look bigger and fiercer. She wondered what sort of interrogations he'd conducted. Once or twice she'd almost asked him things like that, but at the last minute she always held back. Even though he was NKVD, he seemed decent enough. If she knew what he'd done instead of having to guess, she might not be able to stomach him any more.

He said, "I wouldn't mind following those tanks to find out where they're going . . . if I could keep up with them, and if I had a radio to get the information to someone who could use it." He wiped his face with his sleeve and grinned wryly. "And I might as well wish for buried treasure while I'm about it, eh?"

"As a matter of fact, yes," Ludmila said, which made Sholudenko laugh. She went on, "Those tanks may not be going

anywhere. If they hit some really thick mud, they'll bog down. I saw that happen more than once last fall."

"Yes, I've seen the same thing," he agreed. "Doesn't do to count on it, though. They've swallowed up too much of the *rodina* without bogging down."

Ludmila nodded. *Strange,* she thought, *that an NKVD man should talk about the* rodina. From the day the Germans invaded, the Soviet government had started trotting out all the ancient symbols of Holy Mother Russia. After the Revolution, the Bolsheviks had scorned such symbols as reminders of the decadent, nationalistic past—until they needed them, to rally the Soviet people against the Nazis. Stalin had even made his peace with the Patriarch of Moscow, although the government remained resolutely atheist.

Sholudenko said, "I think we can get moving again. I don't hear the tanks any more."

"No, nor I," Ludmila said after cocking her head and listening carefully. "But you have to be careful: their machines aren't as noisy as ours, and could be lying in wait."

"I assure you, Senior Lieutenant Gorbunova, I have discovered this for myself," Sholudenko said with sarcastic formality. Ludmila chewed on her lower lip. She had that coming—the NKVD man, having to serve on the ground, had earned the unlucky privilege of becoming intimately acquainted with Lizard hardware at ranges closer than she cared to think about. He went on, "It is, even so, a lesson which bears repeating: this I do not deny."

Mollified by the half apology (which was, by that one half, more than she'd ever imagined getting from the NKVD), Ludmila slid the boot back onto her foot. She and Sholudenko left the grove together and headed back toward the road. One glance was plenty to keep them walking on the verge; the column of Lizard tanks had chewed the roadbed to slimy pulp worse than the patch into which Ludmila had stumbled before. This muck, though, went on for kilometers.

Tramping along by the road wasn't easy, either. The ground was still squashy and slippery, and the year's new weeds and bushes, growing frantically now that warm weather and long stretches of sunlight were here at last, reached out with branches and shoots to try to trip up the travelers.

So it seemed to Ludmila, at any rate, after she picked herself up for the fourth time in a couple of hours. She snarled out

something so full of guttural hatred that Sholudenko clapped his hands and said, "I've never had a *kulak* call me worse than you just gave that burdock. It certainly had it coming, I must say."

Ludmila's face turned incandescent. By Sholudenko's snicker, the blush was quite visible, too. What would her mother have said if she heard her cursing like—like . . . she couldn't think of any comparison dreadful enough. Going on two years in the Red Air Force had so coarsened her that she wondered if she would be fit for anything decent when peace returned.

When she said that aloud, Sholudenko waved his arms to encompass the entire scene around them. Then he pointed at the deep ruts, already filling with water, the treads the Lizard tanks had carved in the road. "First worry if peace will ever return," he said. "After that you can concern yourself with trifles."

"You're right," she said. "From where we stand, this war is liable to go on forever."

"History is always a struggle—such is the nature of the dialectic," the NKVD man said: standard Marxist doctrine. All at once, though, he turned human again: "I wouldn't mind if the struggle were a little less overt."

Ludmila pointed ahead. "There's a village. With luck, we'll be able to lay up for a while. With a lot of luck, we'll even find some food."

As they drew closer, Ludmila saw the village looked deserted. Some of the cottages had been burned; others showed bare spots in their thatches, as if they were balding old men. A dog's skeleton, beginning to fall apart into separate bones, lay in the middle of the street.

That was the last thing Ludmila noticed before a shot rang out and kicked up mud a couple of meters in front of her. Her reflexes were good—she was down on her belly and yanking her own pistol out of the holster before she had time for conscious thought.

Another shot—she still didn't see the flash. Her head swiveled as if on a pivot. Where was cover? Where was Sholudenko? He'd hit the dirt as fast as she had. She rolled through muck toward a wooden fence. It wasn't much in the way of shelter, but it was a lot better than nothing.

"Who's shooting at us? And why?" she called to Sholudenko.

"The devil's uncle may know, but I don't," the NKVD man answered. He crouched behind a well, whose stones warded him better than the fence shielded Ludmila. He raised his voice: "Hold fire! We're friends!"

"Liar!" The shout was punctuated by a burst of submachine-gun fire from another cottage. Bullets sparked off the stone facing of the well. Whoever was in there yelled, "You can't fool us. You're from Tolokonnikov's faction, come to run us out."

"I don't have the slightest idea who Tolokonnikov is, you maniac," Sholudenko said. All he got for an answer was another shout of "Liar!" and a fresh hail of bullets from that submachine gun. Whomever the anti-Tolokonnikovites did favor, he gave them plenty of ammunition.

Ludmila spied the flame the weapon spat. She was seventy or eighty meters away, very long range for a pistol, but she squeezed off a couple of shots anyway, to take the heat off Sholudenko. Then, quick as she could, she rolled away. The relentless submachine gun chewed up the place where she'd been.

The NKVD man fired, too, and was rewarded by a scream and sudden silence from the submachine gun. *Don't get up,* Ludmila willed at him, suspecting a trap. He didn't. Sure enough, in a couple of minutes the gunner opened up again.

By then, Ludmila had found a boulder behind which to shelter. From that more secure position, she called, "Who is this Tolokonnikov, and what do you have against him?" If the people who didn't like him acted this way, her guess was that he probably had something going for him.

She got no coherent answer out of the anti-Tolokonnikovites, only another magazine's worth of bullets from the submachine gun and a yell of, "Shut up, you treacherous bitch!" Deadly as shell fragments, rock splinters knocked free by the gunfire flew just above her head.

She wondered how long the stalemate could go on. The answer she came up with was glum: *indefinitely.* There wasn't enough cover for either side to have much hope of moving to outflank the other. She and Sholudenko couldn't very well retreat, either. That left sitting tight, shooting every so often, and hoping you got lucky.

Then the equation suddenly grew another variable. Somebody showed himself for a moment: just long enough to chuck

a grenade through the window from which the fellow with the submachine gun had been firing. A moment after it went off, he jumped in the window himself. Ludmila heard a rifle shot, then silence.

The grenade chucker came out by way of the window, too, and vanished from her sight. "Whose side is *he* on?" she called to Sholudenko.

"I keep telling you, ask the devil's uncle," he answered. "Maybe Tolokonnikov's, maybe his own, maybe even ours, though I wouldn't bet my life on that."

The anti-Tolokonnikovite with the pistol, the one who'd fired first, took a fatal moment too long to realize his comrade had been disposed of. Ludmila wasn't sure what was happening because she couldn't see, but she heard another grenade, a rifle shot, a pistol shot, and then two rifle shots closer together. After that came silence all the more deafening because of the clamor that had gone before.

"Now what?" Ludmila asked.

"I think we wait some more," Sholudenko answered. "After they got cute when I fired at them, I don't fancy taking any more chances, thank you very much."

The highly charged silence persisted. At last, from out of the village, came a cautious call: *"Ludmila, bist du da?"*

She shook her head. "Someone here knows you?" Sholudenko asked quietly. "Someone *German* here knows you?" That was not a good thing to admit to an NKVD man, but she did not see she had much choice.

"Georg, is that you?" she asked, also in German. If Sholudenko spoke it, well and good. If he didn't, she'd already become an object of suspicion in his eyes, and so had little more to lose.

"Ja," he answered, still not showing himself. "Tell me the name of the general who commands our base, so I can be sure it is truly you."

"Tovarishch Feofan Karpov is a colonel, as you know perfectly well," she said. "He is also certain to be furious with you for leaving the base without his leave, as I guess you did—you're the best mechanic he has."

"I begin to see," Sholudenko said—so he did understand German, then. "Is he your, ah, special friend?"

"No," Ludmila answered angrily. "But he wishes he were, which sometimes makes him a nuisance." Then, as if she

were reading the NKVD man's mind, she added hastily, "Don't harm him for that. He is an excellent mechanic, and has given the Red Air Force good service even if he is a fascist."

"This I will hear," Sholudenko said. "Had you been sentimental—" He let the sentence hang, but Ludmila had no trouble completing it for herself.

Through the front window of the hut where Schultz had disposed of the second anti-Tolokonnikovite, Ludmila spied something move. She couldn't quite tell what it was. A few seconds later Georg Schultz came out, still holding an old rag on the end of a stick. Ludmila realized that was what she'd seen. Had anyone fired at it, Schultz would have sat tight. *Yes, he's been through combat once or twice, hasn't he?* she thought with reluctant admiration.

Schultz certainly looked like a veteran. He wore his usual mixture of Russian and German gear, though the Nazi helmet on his head gave his nonuniform uniform a Germanic cast. Stuffed into his belt, along with a couple of potato-masher grenades, was a pistol. He held a Soviet PPSh-41 submachine gun, and had slung his rifle over his back.

The panzer gunner's teeth showed in a grin that seemed all the whiter because of the beard surrounding it—a beard that did nothing to hinder his piratical aspect. "Who's your *Kamerad*?" he asked Ludmila.

Sholudenko answered for himself, giving his name and patronymic but not announcing he was NKVD (Ludmila would have been astonished had he admitted it). He went on in German: "So what's this? Did you desert your post to seek the fair maiden here? Your colonel will not be happy with you."

Shultz shrugged. "Fuck him. It's not my army, or even my air force, if you know what I mean. And when I get back with her"—he jerked a thumb at Ludmila—"old man Karpov'll be glad enough to see both of us that he won't bellyache all that much. You should have heard him—'My best pilot gone. Whatever shall I do?' " He raised his voice to a falsetto nothing like the colonel's but comically effective all the same.

"How did you know where to look for me?" Ludmila asked.

"I can follow a compass bearing, and I figured you were smart enough to be doing the same if you were able." Schultz sounded affronted. Then his face cleared. "You mean, how did

I find out which bearing to follow?" He set a finger alongside his nose. "Believe me, there are ways."

Ludmila glanced over at Sholudenko, who was undoubtedly taking all that in. But the NKVD man just asked, "How far from the airstrip are we?"

"Eighty, ninety kilometers, something like that." Schultz looked from him to Ludmila and back again before asking her, "Who is this fellow?"

"The man I was supposed to meet. Instead of bringing back the information he had, I find I'm bringing him, too."

By way of reply, Schultz just grunted. Ludmila felt like laughing at him. If he'd found her alone on the steppe, as he'd probably figured he would, he'd have had several days to try to seduce her or, failing that, just to rape her. Now he had to be wondering if she'd slept with Sholudenko.

None of your business, Nazi, she thought. With the first smile of genuine amusement she'd worn since she flipped her aircraft, she said, "Shall we be off, comrades?" The rest of the trek back to the airstrip was liable to be interesting.

Along with the rest of the physicists, Jens Larssen watched tensely as Enrico Fermi manipulated the levers that raised the cadmium control rods from the heart of the rebuilt atomic pile under the University of Denver football stadium.

"If we have the design correct, this time the *k*-factor will be greater than one," Fermi said quietly. "We will have our self-sustaining chain reaction."

Beside him, Leslie Groves grunted. "We should have reached this point months ago. We would have, if the damned Lizards hadn't come."

"This is true, General," Fermi said, though Groves still wore colonel's eagles. "But from now on work will be much faster, partly because of the radioactives we have stolen from the Lizards and partly because they have shown us that what we seek is possible."

Larssen thought about Prometheus stealing fire from the gods and bringing it down to mankind. He thought about what happened to Prometheus afterwards too: chained to a rock somewhere, with an eagle gnawing his liver forever. He suspected a lot of his colleagues had had that image at one time or another.

Unlike most of them, of course, he didn't need the Met Lab

to have a feel for the myth of Prometheus. Every time he saw Barbara hand in hand with that Sam Yeager, the eagle took another peck at his liver.

The project was an anodyne of sorts, though the pain never left him, not entirely. He watched the instruments, listened to the growing chatter and then the steady roar of the Geiger counter as it let the world know about the growing cloud of neutrons down in the heart of the pile. "Any second now," he breathed, more than half to himself.

Fermi drew out the rods another couple of centimeters. He too glanced at the dials, worked his slide rule, scrawled a quick calculation on a scrap of paper. "Gentlemen, I make the k-factor here to be 1.0005. This pile produces more free neutrons than it consumes."

A few of the physicists clapped their hands. More just nodded soberly. This was what the numbers predicted. All the same, it remained a solemn moment. Arthur Compton said, "The Italian navigator has discovered the New World."

"Gentlemen, this means you can now produce the explosive metal we need to make bombs like the ones the Lizards use?" Groves said.

"It means we are a long step closer," Fermi said. With that, he lowered the control rods back into the pile. Needles swung to the left on the instrument board beside him; the rhythm of the Geiger counter's clicks slowed. Fermi let out a small sigh of relief. "And, it seems, we can control the intensity of the reaction. This is also of some considerable importance."

Most of the scientists smiled; Leo Szilard laughed out loud. Larssen had the urge to yank the cadmium rods all the way out of the pile and leave them out until the uranium spat radiation all over the stadium, all over the university, all over Denver. He fought it down, as he had other lethal, but less spectacular, impulses over the past weeks.

"What do we do next?" Groves demanded. "What exactly do we have to accomplish to turn what we've got here into a bomb?" The big man was not a nuclear physicist, but he had more determination than any four Nobel Prize winners Jens could think of. If anybody could drive the project to success by sheer force of will, Groves was probably the one.

Leo Szilard, on the other hand, had his own sort of practicality. "There is in my office a bottle of good whiskey," he remarked. "What we do next, I say, is to have a drink."

The motion passed by acclamation. Jens trooped over to the science building with everyone else. It was good whiskey; it filled his mouth with the taste of smoke and left a smooth, warm trail down to his stomach. The only thing it couldn't do was make him feel good, which was why people had started distilling whiskey in the first place.

Szilard raised the bottle. A couple of fingers' worth, coppery bright like a new penny, still sloshed there. Jens held out his glass (actually, a hundred-milliliter Erlenmeyer flask he devoutly hoped had never held anything radioactive) for a refill.

"You have earned it," Szilard said, pouring. "All that work on the pile—"

Jens knocked back the second shot. It hit hard, reminding him he hadn't had any lunch. It also reminded him he didn't have any business celebrating; no matter how well his work was doing, his life was strictly from nowhere.

"Good booze," said one of the engineers who'd worked under him. "Now we all oughtta go out and get laid."

Larssen set the flask on a bookshelf and slithered out of the crowded office. His eyes filled with tears which he knew came out of the whiskey bottle but which humiliated him all the same. A week before, he'd picked up a floozy in Denver. He'd been drunk then, not two drinks tiddly but plastered. He wasn't able to get it up. The girl had been kind about it, which only made things worse. He wondered when he'd have the nerve to try that again. Failure once was bad enough. Failure twice? Why go on living?

With that cheerful thought echoing in his head, he went downstairs to reclaim his bicycle. Oscar the guard stood by the newly built wooden bike rack to make sure none of the machines walked with Jesus. He nodded when he saw Jens. "Back to BOQ, sir?" he asked.

"Yeah," Jens said through clenched teeth. He hated his Army cot, he hated the base, he hated having to go to the base and sleep on the cot, and he hated Colonel Hexham with a deep and abiding loathing that matured like a fine burgundy as the days went by. He wished he could have used Hexham as a control rod in the nuclear pile. If only the man had had a neutron capture cross-section like cadmium's . . .

And then, to make his day complete, Barbara came strolling up the walk toward the apartment she and Sam Yeager were using. Sometimes she just ignored him; that his own behavior

might have had something to do with that hadn't crossed his mind. But Barbara wasn't the sort to be rude in public. She nodded to him and slowed down a little.

He walked over to her. Oscar was good at sticking with him—all the physicists had bodyguards these days—but knew better than to follow real close this time. A small voice inside Jens warned him he'd only end up bruising himself, but two nips of Szilard's good hooch made him selectively deaf. "Hello, dear," he said.

"Hello," Barbara answered—the lack of a return endearment set a fire under his temper. "How are you today?"

"About the same as usual," he said: "not so good. I want you back."

"Jens, we've been over this a hundred times," she said, her voice tired. "It wouldn't work. Even if it might have right after I got to Denver, it wouldn't any more. It's too late."

"What the devil is that supposed to mean?" he demanded.

Her eyes narrowed; she took half a step back from him. Instead of answering, she said, "You've been drinking."

He didn't explain that they were drinks of triumph. "What if I have?" he said. "You going to tell me Mr. Sam Walk-on-Water Yeager never takes a drink?"

He knew the words were a mistake as soon as he said them. That, of course, did him no good. Barbara's face froze. "Goodbye," she said. "I'll see you some other time." She started walking again.

He reached out and grabbed her arm. "Barbara, you've got to listen to me—"

"Let me go!" she said angrily. She tried to twist away. He held on.

As if by malign magic, Oscar appeared. He stepped between Jens and Barbara. "Sir, the lady asked you to let go," he said, quietly as usual, and detached Larssen's hand from Barbara's forearm. He wasn't what you'd call gentle, but Jens got the feeling he could have been a lot rougher if he felt like it.

Sober, he never would have swung on Oscar. With two whiskeys in him, he didn't give a damn any more. He'd seen some action himself, by God—and, by God, Barbara was his *wife* . . . wasn't she?

Oscar knocked his fist aside and hit him in the pit of the stomach. Jens folded up like a fan, trying to breathe and not having much luck, trying not to puke and doing a little better

with that. Even as he went down on his knees, he was pretty sure Oscar had pulled that punch, too; with arms like those, Oscar could have ruptured his spleen if he really got annoyed.

"Are you all right, ma'am?" Oscar asked Barbara.

"Yes," she said, and then, a moment later, "Thank you. This has been hell on everybody, and on Jens especially. I know that, and I'm sorry, but I've done what I have to do." Only then did her voice change: "You didn't hurt him, did you?"

"No, ma'am, not like you mean. He'll be okay in a minute or two. Why don't you go on back to your place?" Jens kept his eyes on the pavement in front of him, but he couldn't help listening to Barbara's receding—rapidly receding—footsteps. Oscar hauled him to his feet with the same emotionless strength he'd shown before. "Let me dust you off, sir," he said, and started to do just that.

Jens knocked his hands away. "Fuck you," he gasped with all the air he had in him. He didn't care if he turned blue and died after that, and what with the way he still couldn't breathe, he thought he just might.

"Yes, sir," Oscar said, tonelessly still. Just then, Jens' motor finally turned over, and he managed a long, wonderful mouthful of air. Oscar nodded in approval. "There you go, sir. Not too bad. When you get on that bike, I'll ride with you to BOQ, and tomorrow you can see about getting yourself a new guard."

"Won't be soon enough," Jens said, louder now that his lungs were following orders again.

"If you'll forgive me, sir, I feel the same way," Oscar replied.

Snarling, Jens stalked back to his bicycle, Oscar right on his heels. Jens rocketed away from the university. Oscar stuck with him; he'd already found out he couldn't shake the guard. He wasn't really trying—he was just doing his best to get rid of his own rage.

Gravel kicked up under his wheels as he banked his weight to the side for the right turn from University to Alameda and on to Lowry Field. Of all the places in the world, Lowry Field BOQ was the last one he wanted to go. But where else was he supposed to sleep tonight?

For a moment, he didn't care about that, either. As the air base approached, all he wanted to do was keep on going, past the BOQ, past the endlessly cratered, endlessly repaired run-

ways, past everything—keep on going to somewhere better than this stinking place, this stinking life.

You keep on going the direction you're headed in, you'll end up in Lizard country, an interior voice reminded him. That was enough, for now, to make him swing the bike up toward BOQ like a good little boy.

But even as he and Oscar parked their bicycles side by side, he was looking east again.

"Come on, you mis'able lugs—get movin',"' Mutt Daniels growled. Rain ran off his helmet and down the back of his neck. *That never would've happened with an old limey-style tin hat,* he thought resentfully. The anger put an extra snap in his voice as he added, "We ain't on the newsreels today."

"We ain't south o' Bloomington no more, neither," Dracula Szabo put in.

"You are painfully correct, Private Szabo," Lucille Potter said in her precise, schoolmarmish voice. She pointed ahead to the complex of low, stout buildings just coming into view through the curtains of rain. "That looks to be Pontiac State Penitentiary up there."

When they got a little closer, Szabo grunted. "Looks like somebody kicked the sh—uh, the tar out of it, too."

"Us 'n' the Lizards must have done fought over this stretch of ground last year," Mutt said. The penitentiary complex looked like any fortified area that had been a battleground a few times, which is to say, not a whole lot of it was left standing. A bullet-pocked wall here, half a building a hundred yards over that way, another wall somewhere else—the rest was rubble.

Bloomington lay thirty-five bloody miles behind Mutt now. Most of it was rubble, too, now that the Lizards had run the Army out again. That made three times the town had changed hands in the past year. *Even if the Lizards went home and the war ended tomorrow,* Mutt thought, *the U.S.A. would be years pulling itself back up on its pins.* He'd never imagined his own country turning into something that looked like the worst he'd seen in France in 1918.

He did his best not to think about that. A sergeant, like a manager, had to keep his mind on what was happening now— you could lose the trees for the forest if you weren't careful.

Officers got paid to worry about forests. Mutt said, "Any place better'n this we can camp?"

From behind him, somebody said, "It's got good protection, Sarge."

"I know it does, from the ground, anyway," Daniels said. "But if the Lizards bomb us, we're sittin' ducks."

"There's a park—Riverview Park, I think the name of it is," Lucille Potter said. "I've been there once or twice. The Vermilion River winds around three sides of it. Plenty of trees there, and benches, and an auditorium, too, if anything is left of it. It's not far."

"You know how to get there from here?" Mutt asked. When Lucille nodded, he said, "Okay, Riverview Park it is." He raised his voice: "Hey, Freddie, look alive up there. Miss Lucille's comin' up on point with you. She knows where a decent place for us to lay our bodies down is at." *I hope,* he added to himself.

He'd seen a lot of parks in Illinois, and knew what to expect: rolling grass, plenty of trees, places where you could start a fire for a cookout, probably a place to rent a fishing boat, too, since the park was on a river. The grass would be hay length now, most likely; he didn't figure anybody would have mowed it since the Lizards came.

Lucille Potter found Riverview Park without any trouble. Whether it was worth finding was another question. Once, in one of those crazy magazines Sam Yeager used to read, Mutt had seen a picture of the craters of the moon. Add in mud and the occasional tree that hadn't been blown to pieces and you'd have a pretty good idea of what the park was like.

Daniels wondered if enough trees still stood to offer his squad decent cover from Lizard air attack. The rain wouldn't stop the scaly sons of bitches; he'd already seen that. They weren't a whole lot less accurate in bad weather than in good, either. He didn't know how they managed that. He just wished to the dripping heavens that they weren't able to do it.

From up ahead Freddie Laplace called, "There's bones stickin' up outta the ground."

"Yeah? So what?" Mutt answered. "This here place been fought over two-three times, in case you didn't notice."

"I know that, Sarge," Laplace answered in an injured voice. "Thing of it is, some of 'em look like they're Lizard bones." He sounded half intrigued, half sick.

"What's that?" Lucille Potter said sharply. "Let me see those, Frederick."

Mutt went over to have a look at what Freddie had found, too. Lizard bones were the most interesting thing Riverview Park had to offer, as far as he was concerned. If he didn't take a gander at them, he'd have to get out his entrenching tool and start digging himself a hole in the torn-up mud.

Squelch, squelch, squelch. His boots threatened to come off at every step. The rain kept pattering down. Mutt sighed. Too damn bad you couldn't call a war on account of rain. Or on second thought, maybe not. On the ground if not in the air, the storm probably slowed down the Lizards worse than it did the Americans. "'Course, we were slower to start with," he muttered under his breath.

Freddie Laplace, a skinny little guy with a highly developed sense of self-preservation, pointed down into a shell hole that was rapidly turning into a pond. Sure enough, white bones stuck out of the dirt. "Those never came from no human bein', Sarge," Freddie said.

"You're right," Lucille Potter answered. "Those never came from any creature on Earth."

"Just look like arm bones to me," Mutt said. "Yeah, they got claws 'stead of fingers, but so what?" He wrinkled his nose. "Still got some old meat on 'em, too." The rain banished the worst of the after-the-battle stench, but not all of it.

Lucille let out an impatient sniff. "Use your eyes, Mutt. You must know that people have two long bones in their forearms and one in their upper arms. See for yourself—with the Lizards it's just the opposite."

"Well, I'll be a—" The memory of his father's callused hand kept Mutt from saying what he'd be. Now that Lucille pointed it out, though, he saw she was right. His knowledge of anatomy came from no formal study, but from farming and from dealing with players who hurt themselves on the field—and with his own injuries, back when he was playing himself. Now that his attention was focused, he added, "I never seen any wrist bones like those, neither."

"They have to be different from ours," Lucille said. "A human wrist pivots the hand off two bones, these off only one. The muscle attachments would be very different, too, but we can't see much of them any more."

Freddie Laplace worked at the mud with his entrenching tool, not to dig in but to expose more of the dead Lizard's skeleton. In spite of the rain, the dead-meat stink grew bad enough to make Mutt cough. He'd already seen that Lizards bled red. Now he learned they had no more dignity in death than men slain the same way.

"Lord, I wonder what happens to 'em come Judgment Day?" he said, very much as if he were asking the Deity. He'd been raised a hardshell Baptist, and never bothered to question his childhood faith after he grew to manhood. But if God had made the Lizards at some time or other during Creation (and on which day would that have been?), would He resurrect them in the body come the Last Day? Mutt figured preachers somewhere were getting hot and bothered about that.

Freddie exposed some of the alien corpse's ribcage. "Ain't that peculiar?" he said. "More like latticework than a proper cage."

"How come you know so much about it?" Mutt asked him.

"My old man, he runs a butcher shop up in Bangor, Maine," Laplace answered. "There's one thing I seen a lot of, Sarge, it's bones."

Mutt nodded, conceding the point. Lucille Potter said, "That latticework arrangement is very strong—the English used it for the skeletons of their Blenheim and Wellington bombers."

"Is that a fact?" Daniels said. He was just making talk, though; if Miss Lucille said something was so, you could take it to the bank.

She asked Freddie, "Do you think you can dig out his skull for me?"

"I'll give it a try, ma'am," Laplace said, as if she'd asked him up to the blackboard for a tough multiplication problem he thought he could do. He started scraping away more mud with the folding shovel. Lucille Potter made little eager noises, as if he were digging up a brand-new Chevy (not that there were any brand-new Chevies) and enough gas to run it for a year.

Try and figure women, Mutt thought as he watched Lucille take a scalpel from her little case of instruments. A dead Lizard interested her ... but a live sergeant didn't.

Mutt sighed. He thought Lucille liked him well enough. He knew he liked her well enough, and then some. He knew she knew that, too; she could hardly have doubted it after the kiss he'd given her when he used her bottle of ether to take out the

Lizard tank. But the spark that jumped one way didn't come back the other.

He wondered if she'd left a sweetheart behind when she signed up as an Army nurse. He had his doubts about that; she had *maiden lady* written all over her. *Just my luck,* he thought.

He was not a man to spend a lot of time brooding over what he couldn't help. If he had been that sort of man, years of catching and then of managing would have changed him into a different sort: too many decisions to let any one reach earth-shaking proportions, even if it didn't work. If you couldn't understand that down in your guts, you were liable to end up like Willard Hershberger, the Reds' catcher who'd cut his throat in a New York hotel room after he called the pitch Mel Ott hit into the Polo Grounds stands for a ninth-inning game-winning homer.

And so Mutt went around to see that the rest of his squad was well dug in and that Dracula Szabo had picked a spot with a good field of fire for his BAR. Daniels didn't expect to be attacked here, but you never could tell.

"We got anything decent for chow tonight, Sarge?" Szabo asked.

"C-rations, I expect, and damn lucky to have those," Mutt answered. "Better'n what we ever saw in France; you can believe that." The only real thing Daniels had against the canned rations was that the supply boys had trouble getting enough of them into the field to keep him from being hungry more than he liked. With the Lizards controlling the air, logistics got real sticky.

Szabo had what Mutt thought of as a city slicker's face: controlled, knowing, often with an expression that seemed to say he'd be laughing at you if only you were worth laughing at. It was a face that ached for a slap. Whether it did or whether it didn't, though, Dracula had his uses. Now he reached under his poncho and showed Mutt three dead chickens. "Reckon we can do some better than C-rats," he said smugly, grinning like a fox who'd just raided the hen coop.

That was probably just what he was, too, Mutt thought. He said, "We ain't supposed to forage on our own people," but his heart wasn't in it. Roast chicken did go down better than canned stew.

"Aw, Sarge, they were just struttin' around, no people any-

where close," Szabo said, as innocently as if he were telling the truth. Maybe more innocently.

But he knew as well as Mutt that Mutt wasn't going to call him on it. "I'm right glad o' that," Daniels said. "You go, ah, findin' chickens where there is people around, you'll have Miss Lucille diggin' pellets outta your ass. Birdshot if you're lucky, buckshot if you ain't."

"Not while I'm luggin' a BAR," Szabo said with quiet assurance. "Didn't Miss Lucille say something about an auditorium somewhere in this park? If there's any roof at all, cooking these birds gets a lot easier."

Mutt looked around. Riverview Park was good-sized, and with the rain coming down in curtains he couldn't see anything that looked like a building. "I'll ask her where it's at," he said, and sloshed back to where she was playing mad scientist with the late, unlamented Lizard's remains.

"Look at this, Mutt," Lucille said when he came up. She used her scalpel to point enthusiastically at the Lizard's jaws. "Lots of little teeth, all pretty much the same, not specialized like ours."

"Yeah, I seen that when I captured a couple live ones not long after they invaded us," Mutt answered, averting his eyes; the skull had enough rotting meat still on it to threaten to kill his appetite.

"You captured Lizards, Sarge?" Freddie Laplace sounded impressed as all get-out. Lucille just took it in stride, the way she did most things. Mutt would have been happier had it been the other way around.

Nothing he could do about it, though. He asked her where the auditorium was; she pointed eastward. He slogged in that direction, hoping some of the place was still intact. Sure enough, he discovered that, although it had taken a shell hit that left one wall only a baby brickyard, the rest seemed sound enough.

In the rain, finding anything more than fifty yards away wasn't easy. Mud thin as bad diarrhea slopped over his boot tops and soaked his socks. He hoped he wouldn't come down with pneumonia or the grippe.

"Halt! Who goes?" Szabo's voice came out of the water, as if from behind a falls. Daniels couldn't see him at all. Dracula might be a chicken thief, but he made a pretty fair soldier.

"It's me," Mutt called. "Found that auditorium place. You

want to give me them birds, I'll cook 'em for you. I grew up on a farm; reckon I'll do a better job than you would anyways."

"Yeah, okay. Come on this way." Szabo stood up so Mutt could spot him. "Not gonna be any Lizards around for a while, though, Sarge—is it okay if I wander over there in an hour or so, and you'll make sure there's some dark meat left for me?"

"I think maybe we can do that," Daniels said. "You put somebody here on your weapon before you go wandering, though, you hear me? In case we do have trouble, we're gonna need all the firepower we can get our hands on."

"Don't you worry about that, Sarge," Szabo said. "Even roast chicken ain't worth gettin' my ass shot off for." He spoke with great conviction. From any other dogface in the squad, Daniels would have found that convincing. With Szabo, you never could tell.

He took the chickens back to the auditorium. Whoever had been there last, Americans or Lizards, had chopped up a lot of the folding wooden seats that faced the stage: more than they'd used for their fires. Taking advantage of the free lumber, Mutt built his blaze on the concrete floor where others had made theirs before him.

He pulled out his trusty Zippo. He wondered how long it would stay trusty. He had a package of flints in his shirt pocket, but the Zippo was burning kerosene these days, not lighter fluid, and he didn't know when he'd come across any more kerosene, either. For now, it still gave him a flame on the first try.

He quickly found out why the previous occupants of the auditorium had been so eager to use the seats for fuel: the varnish that made them shiny also made them catch fire with the greatest of ease. He went back out into the rain to throw away the chicken guts and to get some sticks on which to skewer the pieces of chicken he was going to cook.

His belly growled when the savory smell of roasting meat came through the smoke from the fire. His grandfathers would have done their cooking in the War Between the States the same way he was now, except they'd have used lucifer matches instead of the Zippo to get the fire going.

"Chow!" he yelled when he had a fair number of pieces finished. Men straggled in by ones and twos, ate quickly, and went back out into the rain. When Lucille Potter came in for

hers, Mutt asked jokingly, "You wash your hands before supper?"

"You'd best believe I did—and with soap, too." Being a nurse, Lucille was in dead earnest about cleanliness. "Did you wash yours before you cleaned these birds and cut them up?"

"Well, you might say so," Mutt answered; his hands had certainly been wet, anyhow. "Didn't use soap, though."

Had Lucille Potter's stare been any fishier, she'd have grown fins. Before she could say anything, Szabo strolled into the auditorium. "You save me a drumstick, Sarge?"

"Here's a whole leg, kid," Mutt said. The BAR man blissfully started gnawing away. Daniels took half a breast off the fire, waved it in the air to cool it down, and also began to eat. He had to pause a couple of times to spit out burnt bits of feather; he'd done a lousy job of plucking the chickens.

Then he paused again, this time with the hunk of white meat nowhere near his mouth. Through the splashing rain came deep-throated engine rumblings and the mucky grinding noise of caterpillar tracks working hard to propel their burden over bad ground. The chicken Mutt had already swallowed turned to a small lump of lead in his stomach.

"Tanks." The word came out as hardly more than a whisper, as if he didn't want to believe it himself. Then he bellowed it with all the fear and force he had in him: *"Tanks!"*

Dracula Szabo dropped the mostly bare drumstick and thigh and sprinted back toward his BAR. What good it would do against Lizard armor, Mutt couldn't imagine. He also didn't think the rain would give him another chance to take out a Lizard tank with a bottle of ether—even assuming Lucille had any more, which wasn't obvious.

He threw down his own piece of meat, grabbed his submachine gun, and peered out ever so cautiously through the gaping hole in the auditorium wall. The tanks were out there somewhere not far away, but he couldn't see them. They weren't firing; maybe they didn't know his squad was in the park.

"That's great," he muttered. "Gettin' trapped behind enemy lines is just what I had in mind."

"Enemy lines?" All his attention on the noises coming from the dripping gloom outside, Mutt hadn't noticed Lucille Potter coming up behind him. She went on, "Those are *our* tanks, Mutt. They're coming down from the north—either the Lizards

haven't taken out the bridges over the Vermilion or else we've repaired them—and they make a lot more racket than the machines the Lizards use."

Mutt listened again, this time without panic blinding his ears. After a two-beat pause he used around Lucille to replace a useful seven-letter word, he said, "You're right. Lord, I was ready to start shooting at my own side."

"Some of the men are still liable to do that," Lucille said.

"Yeah." Mutt stepped outside, shouted into the rain: "Hold your fire! American tanks comin' south. Hold fire!"

One of the grunting, snorting machines rumbled by close enough for the commander to hear that cry. To Mutt, he was just a vague shape sticking up from the top of the turret. He called back in unmistakable New England accents, "We're friendly all right, buddy. We're usin' the rain to move up without the Lizards spotting us—give the little scaly sons of bitches a surprise if they come after you guys."

"Sounds right good, pal," Daniels answered, waving. The tank—he could tell it was a Sherman; the turret was too big for a Lee—rattled on toward the south edge of Riverview Park. In a way, Mutt envied the crew for having inches of hardened steel between them and the foe. In another way, he was happy enough to be just an infantryman. The Lizards didn't particularly notice him. Tanks, though, drew their special fire. They had some fancy can openers, too.

The tank commander had to know that better than Mutt did. He kept heading south anyhow. Mutt wondered how many times he'd been in action, and if this one would be the last. With a wave to the departing tank that was half salute, he went back into the ruined auditorium to finish his chicken.

✫ XIII ✫

Vyacheslav Molotov jounced along toward the farm outside Moscow in a *panje* wagon, as if he were a peasant with a couple of sacks of radishes he hadn't been able to sell. From the way the NKVD man driving the wagon behaved, Molotov might have been a sack of radishes himself. The Soviet foreign commissar didn't mind. He was rarely in the mood for idle chitchat, with today no exception to the rule.

All around him, the land burgeoned with Russian spring. The sun rose early now, and set late, and everything that had lain dormant through winter flourished in the long hours of daylight. Fresh green grass pushed up through and hid last year's growth, now gray-brown and dead. The willows and birches by the Moscow River wore new bright leafy coats. Concealed by those new leaves, birds chirped and warbled. Molotov did not know which bird went with which song. He could barely tell a titmouse from a toucan, not that you were likely to find a toucan in a Russian treetop even in springtime.

Ducks stuck their behinds in the air as they tipped up for food in the river. The driver looked at them and murmured, "I wish I had a shotgun." Molotov saw reply as unnecessary; the driver would likely have said the same thing had he been alone in the wagon.

Molotov wished not for a shotgun but a car. Yes, gasoline was in short supply, with almost all of it earmarked for the front. But as the number two man in the Soviet Union behind Stalin, he could have arranged for a limousine had he wanted one. The Lizards, however, were more likely to shoot up motor vehicles than horse-drawn wagons. Molotov played it safe.

When the driver pulled off the road and onto a meandering

path, Molotov thought the fellow had lost his way. The farm ahead looked like an archetypical *kolkhoz*, maybe a little smaller than most of its ilk. Chickens ran around clucking and pecking, fat pigs wallowed in mud. In the fields, men walked behind mules. The only buildings were row houses for the *kolkhozniks* and barns for the animals.

Then one of the men, dressed like any farmer in boots, baggy trousers, collarless tunic, and cloth cap, opened the door to a barn and went inside. Before he closed it after himself, the foreign commissar saw that the inside was brightly lit by electric light. Even before the Germans and the Lizards came, that would have been unusual for a *kolkhoz*. Now it was inconceivable.

His smile came broader and more fulsome than most who knew him would have imagined his face could form. "A splendid job of *maskirovka*," he said enthusiastically. "Whoever designed and implemented the deception plan, he deserves to be promoted."

"Comrade Foreign Commissar, I am given to understand the responsible parties have been recognized," the driver said. He looked like a peasant—he looked like a drunk—but he talked like an educated man. Maskirovka *again*, Molotov thought. He knew intellectually he would not have a drunken peasant taking him to arguably the most important place in the Soviet Union, but the man played his role well.

Molotov pointed to the barn. "That is where they do their research?"

"Comrade, all I know is that that is where I was told to deliver you," the driver answered. "What they do in there I could not tell you, and I do not want to know."

He pulled back on the reins. The horse drawing the high-wheeled *panje* wagon obediently stopped. Molotov, who was not a large man (even if he was taller than Stalin), scrambled down without grace but also without falling. As he headed for the barn door, the driver took a flask from his hip pocket and swigged from it. Maybe he was an educated drunk.

The barn door looked like a barn door. After that, though, the *maskirovka* failed: the air that came out of the barn did not smell as it should. Molotov supposed that didn't matter; if the Lizards got close enough to go sniffing around, the Soviet Union was likely to be finished, anyhow.

He opened the door, closed it behind him as quickly as the

fellow who looked like a farmer had done. Inside, the wooden building was uncompromisingly clean and uncompromisingly scientific. Even the "farmer's" costume, when seen close up, was spotless.

The fellow hurried up to Molotov. "Comrade Foreign Commissar, I am delighted to see you here," he said, extending a hand. He was a broad-shouldered man of about forty, with a chin beard and alert eyes in a tired face. "I am Igor Ivanovich Kurchatov, director of the explosive metal project." He brushed back a lock of hair that drooped (*Hitlerlike,* Molotov thought irrelevantly) onto his forehead.

"I have questions on two fronts, Igor Ivanovich," Molotov said. "First, how soon will you finish the bomb built from the captured Lizard explosive metal? And second, how soon will this facility begin producing more of this metal for us to use?"

Kurchatov's eyes widened slightly. "You come straight to the point."

"Time-wasting formalities are for the bourgeoisie," Molotov replied. "Tell me what I need to know so I can report it to Comrade Stalin."

Stalin, of course, received regular reports from the project. Beria had been here to see how things went, too. But Molotov, along with being foreign commissar, also served as deputy chairman to Stalin on the State Committee on Defense. Kurchatov licked his lips before he answered; he was well aware of that. He said, "In the first area, we have made great progress. We are almost ready to begin fabricating the components for the bomb."

"That is good news," Molotov agreed.

"Yes, Comrade," Kurchatov said. "Since we have the explosive metal in place, it becomes a straightforward engineering matter of putting two masses of it, neither explosive alone, together so they exceed what is called the critical mass, the amount required for an explosion."

"I see," Molotov said, though he really didn't. If something was explosive, it seemed to him, the only difference between a little and a lot should have been the size of the boom. But all the Soviet physicists and other academicians insisted this strange metal did not work that way. If they achieved the results they claimed, he supposed that would prove them right. He asked, "And how have you decided to join the pieces together?"

"The simplest way we could think of was to shape one into a cylinder with a hole through the center and the other into a smaller cylinder that would fit precisely into the hole. An explosive charge will propel it into the proper position. We shall take great care that it does not go awry."

"Such care is well-advised, Comrade Director," Molotov said. But although he kept his voice icy, he intuitively liked the design Kurchatov had described. It had a Russian simplicity to it: slam the one into the other and *bang!* Molotov knew his own people well enough to know also that they had more trouble keeping complicated plans on track than did, say, the Germans; Russians had a way of substituting brute force for sophistication. They'd held the Nazis outside Moscow and Leningrad that way. Now they were on the edge of striking a mighty blow against the Lizards, more deadly invaders still.

A mighty blow . . . "After we use up our stock of explosive metal, we have no more—is that correct?" Molotov asked.

"Yes, Comrade Foreign Commissar." Kurchatov licked his lips and went no further.

Molotov frowned. He had been afraid this would happen. The academicians had a habit of promising Stalin the moon, whether they could deliver or not. *Maybe the horse will learn to sing,* he thought, an echo from some ancient history read in his student days. He shook his head, banishing the memory. The here and now was what counted.

He knew the dilemma the scientists faced. If they told Stalin they could not give him something he wanted, they'd head for the *gulag* . . . unless they got a bullet in the back of the neck instead. But if, after promising, they failed to come through, the same applied again.

And the Soviet Union desperately needed a continuous supply of explosive metal. In that Molotov agreed with Stalin. (He tried to remember the last time he had disagreed with Stalin. He couldn't. It was too long ago.) He said, "What are the difficulties in production, Igor Ivanovich, and how are you working to overcome them?"

As if on cue, another man in farmer's clothes came up. Kurchatov said, "Comrade Foreign Commissar, let me present to you Georgi Aleksandrovich Flerov, who recently discovered the spontaneous fission of the uranium nucleus and who is in charge of the team investigating these difficulties."

Flerov was younger than Kurchatov; even in the clothes of

a peasant, he looked like a scholar. He also looked nervous. Because he was in charge, he was responsible for what his team did—and for what it didn't do.

"Comrade Foreign Commissar, the answer to your first question, or to the first part of it, is simple," he said, trying to hold his rather light voice steady. "The chief difficulty in production is that we do not yet know how to produce. Our techniques in nuclear research are several years behind those of the capitalists and fascists, and we are having to learn what they already know."

Molotov gave him a baleful stare. "Comrade Stalin will not be pleased to hear this."

Kurchatov blanched. So did Flerov, but he said, "If Comrade Stalin chooses to liquidate this team, no one in the Soviet Union will be able to produce these explosives for him. Everyone with that expertise who is still alive is here. We are what the *rodina* has, for better or worse."

Molotov was not used to defiance, even frightened, deferential defiance. He harshened his voice as he replied, "We were promised full-scale production of explosive metal within eighteen months. If the team assembled here cannot accomplish this—"

"The Germans are not likely to have that within eighteen months, Comrade Foreign Commissar," Flerov said. "Neither are the Americans, though the breakdown in travel has left us less well-informed about their doings."

Has played hob with espionage, you mean, Molotov thought: Flerov had a little diplomat in him after all. That, however, was a side issue. Molotov said, "If you cannot produce as promised, we will remove you and bring in those who can."

"Good luck to you and good-bye to the *rodina*," Flerov said. "You may find charlatans who tell you worse lies than we could ever imagine. You will not find capable physicists—and if you dispose of us, you may never see uranium or plutonium produced in the Soviet Union."

He was not bluffing. Molotov had watched too many men trying to lie for their lives; he knew nonsense and bluff when he heard them. He didn't hear them from Flerov. Rounding on Kurchatov, he said, "You direct this project. Why have you not kept us informed about your trouble in holding to the schedule?"

"Comrade Foreign Commissar, we are ahead of schedule in preparing the first bomb," Kurchatov said. "That ought to count in our favor, even if the other half of the project is going more slowly than we thought it would. We can rock the Lizards back on their heels with one explosion."

"Igor Ivanovich—" Flerov began urgently.

Molotov raised a hand to cut him off. He glared at Kurchatov. "You may be an excellent physicist, Comrade, but you are politically naive. If we rock the Lizards with one explosion, with how many will they rock us?"

Under the harsh electric lights, Kurchatov's face went an ugly yellowish-gray. Flerov said, "Comrade Foreign Commissar, this has been a matter of only theoretical discussion."

"You need to make it one of the theses of your dialectic," Molotov said. He was convinced Stalin had the right of that: the Lizards would hit back hard at any nation that used the explosive metal against them.

"We shall do as you say," Kurchatov said.

"See that you do," Molotov answered. "Meanwhile, the Soviet Union—to say nothing of all mankind—requires a supply of explosive metal. You cannot make it within eighteen months, you say. How long, then?" Molotov was not large, nor physically imposing. But when he spoke with the authority of the Soviet Union in his voice, he might have been a giant.

Kurchatov and Flerov looked at each other. "If things go well, four years," Flerov said.

"If things go very well, three and a half," Kurchatov said. The younger man gave him a dubious look, but finally spread his hands, conceding the point.

Three and a half years? More likely four? Molotov felt as if he'd been kicked in the belly. The Soviet Union would have its one weapon, which it could hardly use for fear of bringing hideous retaliation down on its head? And the Germans and the Americans—and, for all he knew, maybe the English and the Japanese, too—ahead in the race to make bombs of their own?

"How am I to tell this to Comrade Stalin?" he asked. The question hung in the air. Not only would the scientists incur Stalin's wrath for being too optimistic, but it might fall on Molotov as well, as the bearer of bad news.

If the academicians were as irreplaceable as they thought, the odds were good that Stalin wouldn't do anything to them.

Over the years, Molotov had done his best to make himself indispensable to Stalin, but indispensable wasn't the same as irreplaceable, and he knew it.

He asked, "Can I tell the General Secretary you will succeed within two and a half to three years?" If he could arrange to present a small disappointment rather than a big one, he might yet deflect Stalin's anger.

"Comrade Foreign Commissar, you can of course tell the Great Stalin whatever you please, but that will not be the truth," Kurchatov said. "When the time passes and we do not succeed, you will have to explain why."

"If the Lizards give us so much time for research and engineering," Flerov added; he looked to be enjoying Molotov's discomfiture.

"If the Lizards overrun this place, Comrades, I assure you that you will have no more joy from it than I," Molotov said stonily. Had the Germans defeated the Soviet Union, Molotov would have gone up against a wall (with a blindfold if he was lucky), but nuclear physicists might have been useful enough to save their skins by turning their coats. The Lizards, however, would not want human beings to know atoms existed, let alone that they could be split. Driving that home, Molotov added, "And if the Lizards overrun this place, it will be in large measure because you and your team have failed to give the workers and people of the Soviet Union the weapons they need to carry on the fight."

"We are doing everything men can do," Flerov protested. "There are too many things we simply do not know."

Now he was the one who sounded uncertain, querulous. That was how Molotov wanted it. He snapped, "You had better learn, then."

Softly, Igor Kurchatov said, "It is easier to give orders to generals, Comrade Foreign Commissar, than to nature. She reveals her secrets at a pace she chooses."

"She has revealed altogether too many of them to the Lizards," Molotov said. "If they can find them, so can you." He turned his back to show the interview was over. He thought he'd recovered well from the shocking news the academicians had given him. How well he would recover after he gave Stalin that news was, unfortunately, another question.

* * *

The peddler smiled in appreciation as David Goldfarb handed him a silver one-mark piece with Kaiser Wilhelm's mustachioed image stamped on it. "That's good money, friend," he said. Along with the baked apple on a stick that Goldfarb had bought, he gave back a fistful of copper and pot-metal coins by way of change. His expression turned sly. "You have money that good, it doesn't matter how funny your Yiddish sounds."

"Geh kak afen yam," Goldfarb said genially, doing his best to hide the sudden pounding of his heart. "Where I come from, everybody talks like me."

"What a miserable, ignorant place that must be," the peddler retorted. "At first, I thought you had a nice Warsaw accent. The more I listen to you, though, the more I figure you're from Chelm."

Goldfarb snorted. The legendary town was full of *shlemiels.* What he really spoke, of course, was Yiddish with a Warsaw accent corrupted by living his whole life in England. He hadn't thought it was corrupted till the British sub dropped him on the flat, muddy coast of Poland. Now, comparing the way he spoke to the Yiddish of people who used it every day of their lives, he counted himself lucky that they understood him at all.

As an excuse not to say where he really did come from, he bit into the apple. Hot, sweet juice flooded into his mouth. "Mmm," he said, a wordless, happy sound.

"It would be really good if I could get some cinnamon," the peddler said. "But there's none to be had, not for love nor money."

"Good anyhow," Goldfarb mumbled, his full mouth muffling whatever odd accent the King's English gave him. With a nod to the peddler, he walked south down the dirt track toward Lodz. He was, he thought, just a couple of hours away. He hoped that wouldn't be too late. From what he'd heard just before he sailed from England, his cousin Moishe was in jail somewhere in Lodz. He wondered how he was supposed to get Moishe out.

With a noncom's fatalism, he put that out of his mind. He'd worry about it when the time came. First he had to get to Lodz. He'd already discovered that a couple of years of fighting the war electronically had left his wind a shadow of what it was supposed to be. His physical-training sergeant would not have approved.

"Something to be said for not laying about puffing on fags all day long—it'd be even shorter if I'd had more to smoke," he said in low-voiced English. "All the same, I miss 'em."

He looked around. Just a glimpse of the endless flat farmland of the Polish plain had been plenty to tell him all he needed to know about that country's unhappy history. Besides the shelter of the English Channel, the United Kingdom had mountains in the west and north in which to take refuge: witness the survival of Welsh and Scots Gaelic over the centuries.

Poland, now—all the Poles had was the Germans on one side and the Russians on the other, and nothing whatever to keep either one of them out except their own courage. And when the Germans outweighed them three to one and the Russians two or three times as badly as that, even suicidal courage too often wasn't enough.

No wonder they give their Jews a hard time, he thought with a sudden burst of insight: *they're sure they can beat the Jews.* After losing so many wars to their neighbors, having in their midst people they could trounce had to feel sweet. That didn't make him love the people who had driven his parents from Poland, but it did help him understand them.

Goldfarb looked around again. Almost everywhere in England, he'd been able to see hills on the horizon. Here, it went on forever. The endless flat terrain made him feel insignificant and at the same time conspicuous, as if he were a fly crawling across a big china platter.

The green of Polish fields was different from what he'd known in England, too: duller somehow. Maybe it was the light, maybe the soil; whatever it was, he'd noticed it almost at once.

He'd noticed the workers in those fields, too. Englishmen who labored on the land were farmers. The Poles were inarguably peasants. He had trouble defining the difference but, as with the colors of the fields, it was unmistakable. Maybe part of it lay in the way the Polish farmers went about their work. By the standards Goldfarb was used to, they might as well have been moving in slow motion. Their attitude seemed to say that how hard they worked didn't matter—they weren't going to realize much from their labors, anyway.

A noise in the sky, like an angry cockchafer . . . Goldfarb had heard that noise more times than he cared to remember, and his reaction to it was instinctive: he threw himself

flat. Hugging the ground, a flight of German bombers roared by, heading east.

Ju-88s, Goldfarb thought, identifying them by sound and shape as automatically as he would have told his father from an uncle. He was used to praying for fighters and antiaircraft guns to blow German bombers out of the sky. Now he found himself wishing them luck. That felt strange, wrong; the world had taken a lot of strange turns since the Lizards came.

He got to his feet and peered south. Smoke smudged the horizon there, the first mark he'd seen. *That ought to be Lodz,* he thought. A little farther and he could start doing the job the British high command had, in their wisdom, decided he was right for.

Cloth cap, black jacket and wool trousers—they all shouted *I am a Jew!* He wondered why Hitler had bothered adding yellow stars to the getup; they struck him as hardly necessary. Even his underwear was different from what he'd worn in England, and chafed him in strange places.

He had to look like a Jew. He spoke Yiddish, but his Polish was fragmentary and mostly foul. In England, even before he went into uniform, he'd dressed and sounded like everyone else. Here in Poland, he felt isolated from a large majority of the people around him. "Get used to it," he muttered. "Most places, Jews *don't* fit in."

An ornate brass signpost said, LODZ, 5KM. Fastened above it was an angular wooden sign with angular black letters on a white background: LITZMANNSTADT, 5KM. Just seeing that sign pointing like an arrow at the heart of Lodz set Goldfarb's teeth on edge. Typical German arrogance, to slap a new name on the town once they'd conquered it.

He wondered if the Lizards called it something altogether different.

A little more than an hour brought him into the outskirts of Lodz. He'd been told the town had fallen to the Nazis almost undamaged. It wasn't undamaged now. The briefings he'd read on the submarine said the Germans had put up a hell of a scrap before the Lizards drove them out of town, and that they'd lobbed occasional rockets or flying bombs (the briefings weren't very clear about which) at it ever since.

Most of the people in the outer part of the city were Poles. If any German settlers remained from Lodz's brief spell as Litzmannstadt, they were lying low. Sneers from the Poles

were bad enough. He didn't know what he would have done with Germans gaping at him. All at once, he regretted hoping the German bombers had a good mission. Then he got angry at himself for that regret. The Germans might not be much in the way of human beings, but against the Lizards they and England were on the same side.

He walked on down Lagiewnicka Street toward the ghetto. The wall the Nazis had built was still partly intact, although in the street itself it had been knocked down to allow traffic once more. As soon as he set foot on the Jewish side, he decided that while the Germans and England might be on the same side, the Germans and he would never be.

The smell and the crowding hit him twin sledgehammer blows. He'd lived his whole life with plumbing that worked. He'd never reckoned that a *mitzvah*, a blessing, but it was. The brown reek of sewage (or rather, slops), garbage, and unwashed humanity made him wish he could turn off his nose.

And the crowd! He'd heard men who'd been in India and China talk of ant heaps of people, but he hadn't understood what that meant. The streets were jammed with men, women, children, carts, wagons—a good-sized city was boiled down into a few square blocks, like bouillon made into a cube. People bought, sold, argued, pushed past one another, got in each other's way, so that block after block of ghetto street felt like the most crowded pub where Goldfarb had ever had a pint.

The people—the Jews—were dirty, skinny, many of them sickly-looking. After tramping down from the Polish coast, Goldfarb was none too clean himself, but whenever he saw someone eyeing him, he feared the flesh on his bones made him conspicuous.

And this misery, he realized, remained after the Nazis were the better part of a year out of Lodz. The Jews now were fed better and treated like human beings. What the ghetto had been like under German rule was—not unimaginable, for he imagined it all too vividly, but horrifying in a way he'd never imagined till now.

"Thank you, Father, for getting out when you did," he said.

For a couple of blocks he simply let himself be washed along like a fish in a swift-flowing stream. Then he began moving against the current in a direction of his own choosing.

Posters of Mordechai Chaim Rumkowski seemed to follow him wherever he went. Some were tattered and faded, some as

new and bright as if they'd been put up yesterday, which they probably had. Rumkowski stared down at Goldfarb from a variety of poses, but always looked stern and commanding.

Goldfarb shook his head; the briefing papers had had considerable to say about Rumkowski and his regime in Lodz, but not much of that was good. In sum, he amounted to a pocket Jewish Hitler. *Just what we need,* Goldfarb thought.

A couple of times, he passed Order Service men with their armbands and truncheons. He noticed them not only for those, but also because they looked uncommonly well-fed. *A pocket Jewish SS, too. Wonderful.* Goldfarb kept his head down and did his best to pretend he was invisible.

But he had to look up from time to time to tell where he was going; studying a street map of Lodz didn't do enough to let him make his way through the town itself. Luckily, being one mote in a swirling crowd kept him from drawing special notice. After three wrong turns—about half as many as he'd expected—he walked into a block of flats on Mostowski Street and started climbing stairs.

He knocked on what he hoped was the right door. A woman a couple of years older than he was—she would have been pretty if she hadn't been so thin—opened it and stared at his unfamiliar face with fear-widened eyes. "Who are you?" she demanded.

Goldfarb got the idea something unpleasant would happen to him if he gave the wrong answer. He said, "I'm supposed to tell you even Job didn't suffer forever."

"And I'm supposed to tell you it must have seemed that way to him." The woman's whole body relaxed. "Come in. You must be Moishe's cousin from England."

"That's right," he said. She closed the door behind him. He went on, "And you're Rivka? Where's your son?"

"He's out playing. In the crowds on the street, the risk is small, and besides, someone has an eye on him."

"Good." Goldfarb looked around. The flat was tiny, but so bare that it seemed larger. He shook his head in sympathy. "You must be sick to death of moving."

Rivka Russie smiled for the first time, tiredly. "You have no idea. Reuven and I have moved three times since Moishe didn't come back to the flat we'd just taken." She shook her head. "He thought someone had known who he was. We must have been just too late getting out of the other place. If it

hadn't been for the underground, I don't know what we would have done. Got caught, I suppose."

"They got word to England, too," Goldfarb said, "and orders eventually got to me." He wondered if they would have, had Churchill not spent a while talking with him at Bruntingthorpe. "I'm supposed to help get Moishe out of here and take him—and you and the boy—back to England with me. If I can."

"Can you do that?" Rivka asked eagerly.

"*Gott vayss*—God knows," he said. That won a startled laugh from her. He went on, "I'm no commando or hero or anything like that. I'll work with your people and I'll do the best I can, that's all."

"A better answer than I expected." Her voice was judicious.

"Is he still in Lodz?" Goldfarb asked. "That's the last information I had, but it's not necessarily good any more."

"As far as we know, yes. The Lizards aren't in a lot of hurry about dealing with him. That doesn't make sense to me, when he did such a good job of embarrassing them."

"They're more sure than quick," Goldfarb said, remembering pages from the briefing book. "Very methodical, but not swift. What sort of charge do they have him up on?"

"Disobedience," Rivka said. "From everything he ever said while he was on better terms with them, they couldn't accuse him of anything much worse."

That fit in with what Goldfarb had read, too. The Lizards seemed rank-, class-, and duty-conscious to a degree that made the English and even the Japanese look like wild-eyed, bomb-throwing anarchists. In that kind of society, disobedience had to be as heinous a sin as blasphemy in the Middle Ages.

"Still here in Lodz," Goldfarb mused. "That's good, I suppose. The Lizards' main Polish headquarters is in Warsaw. Getting him out of there would be a lot tougher." He grinned wryly. "Besides, I don't fancy walking all that way east, not when I've just come here from the coast the same way."

"Would you like some tea?" Rivka asked. A moment later, she added another, more indignant question: "What's so funny?"

"Nothing, really," Goldfarb said, though he was still chuckling. "It's only that any woman in my family would have asked exactly the same question."

"I *am* a woman in your family," Rivka said quietly.

"That's true. You are." They eyed each other across the gulf of lifetimes spent in very different lands. Goldfarb's parents had escaped the ghetto; to him, this place was something medieval returned to malignant life, and Rivka in her long black dress almost as much a part of the past come again. He wondered how he seemed to her: exotic stranger from a land rich and peaceful compared to Poland, in spite of everything Hitler and the Lizards had done to England, or just an *apikoros*, someone who'd abandoned most of his Judaism to get along in the wider world? He didn't know how to ask, or even if it was his business.

"Do you want that cup of tea?" Rivka asked again. "It's not real tea, I'm afraid, only chopped-up herbs and leaves."

"Same sort of muck we've been drinking at home," Goldfarb said. "Yes, I'd like some, if it's not too much trouble."

Rivka Russie made the "tea" on an electric hot plate. She served it to him in a glass with sugar but no milk. That was how his parents drank it, but he'd come to prefer the way most Englishmen took theirs. Asking for milk here, though, didn't seem likely to produce anything but embarrassment. Cautiously, he sipped.

He raised an eyebrow. "Not bad at all. Better than most of what I've had lately, as a matter of fact." To prove he meant it, he quickly drained the glass. Then he said, "So you're still in touch with the underground?"

"Yes," Rivka answered. "If it weren't for them, the Order Service men would have taken Reuven and me along with Moishe by now."

"Can you let me know how to get hold of them? If nothing else, I'll need somewhere to sleep while I'm looking things over." *Can't very well stay in a flat with my cousin's wife, not when he's in gaol.*

"It's not as hard as you might think." Amusement shone in Rivka's eyes. "Go across the hall to flat number twenty-four. Knock on the door—twice, then once."

He'd used a password to identify himself to her. Now he had to trot out a secret knock? He'd always thought that sort of thing more the province of sensational novels than sober fact, but he was learning better in a hurry. If you wanted to keep going when every man's hand was raised against you, you had to figure out ways to keep from being noticed.

He went across the hall, found the battered door with a tar-

nished brass 24 on it. *Knock, knock . . . knock.* He waited. The
door opened. The big man standing in it said, *"Nu?"*

"Nu, the lady across the way sent me here," Goldfarb replied. With his shaggy beard and soldier's cap over civilian
clothes, the big man looked like a bandit chief. He also looked
like someone it would be wiser not to annoy. Goldfarb was
glad he'd had the right code to introduce himself to Rivka
Russie; without it, this fellow likely would have descended
on him like a falling building. He'd been right to have his
wind up.

But now the man grinned (showing bad teeth) and stuck out
his hand. "So you're Russie's English cousin, are you? You
can call me Leon."

"Right." The fellow had a blacksmith's grip, Goldfarb discovered. He also noted that while the local Jew had said he
could call him Leon, that didn't mean it was his name: another
precaution out of the books, and probably as necessary as the
rest.

"Don't stand there—come in," Leon said. "Never can tell
who's liable to be looking down the hall." He closed the door
behind Goldfarb. "Take your pack off if you like—it looks
heavy."

"Thanks." Goldfarb did. The apartment was, if anything,
barer than Rivka's. Only mattresses on the floor said people
lived, or at least slept, here. He said, "Moishe's still in Lodz?"
Leon, he figured, would know more surely than Rivka had.

The big man nodded. "He's in Prison One on Franciszkanska Street—the Nazis called it Franzstrasse, just like they
called Lodz Litzmannstadt. We call it Franzstrasse ourselves,
sometimes, because there's a big sign with that name right
across from the prison that nobody's ever bothered taking
down."

"Prison One, eh?" Goldfarb said. "How many are there?"

"Plenty," Leon answered. "Along with being good at killing
people, the Nazis were good at putting them away, too."

"Do you know where in the prison he's locked up?"
Goldfarb asked. "For that matter, do you have plans for the
building?"

"Who do you think turned it into a prison? The Germans
should have dirtied their hands doing the work themselves?"
Leon said. "Oh yes, we have the plans. And we know where
your cousin is, too. The Lizards don't let Jews anywhere near

him—they're learning—but they haven't learned yet that some Poles are on our side, too."

"This whole business must make you *meshuggeh* sometimes," Goldfarb said. "The Lizards are better to Jews here than the Nazis ever were, but they're bad for everybody else, so sometimes you find yourself working with the Germans. And the Poles don't like Jews, either, but I guess they don't like the Lizards any better."

"It's a mess, all right," Leon agreed. "I'm just glad I don't have to do much in the way of figuring out. You wanted plans, I'll show you plans." He went over to a cabinet, yanked out a roll of paper, and brought it over to Goldfarb. When Goldfarb opened it, he saw they weren't just plans but Germanically meticulous engineering drawings. Leon pointed. "They have machine guns on the roof, here and here. We'll have to do something about those."

"Yes," Goldfarb said in a small voice. "A machine gun we don't do something about would put rather a hole in our scheme, wouldn't it?"

That might have been Leon's first taste of British understatement; he grunted laughter. "Put a hole in us, you mean—probably lots of holes. But let's say we can take out the machine guns—"

"Because if we don't, we can't go on anyhow," Goldfarb broke in.

"Exactly," Leon said. "So let's say we do. You're supposed to be bringing some presents with you. Have you got them?"

By way of answer, Goldfarb opened the battered Polish Army pack that had come from an exile in England. No one had paid any attention to it since he'd landed here. Close to half the people on the road wore one like it, and a lot of those who didn't had corresponding German or Russian gear instead.

Leon looked inside. His long exhalation puffed out his mustache. "They don't look like much," he said dubiously.

"They're bloody hell to load, but they'll do the job if I can't get close enough to use them. I've practiced with them. Believe me, they will," Goldfarb said.

"And what's all this mess?" Leon pointed into the pack, which held, along with the bombs he'd already disparaged, a motley assortment of metal tubes, levers, and a spring that might have come from the suspension of a lorry.

"The mechanism for shooting them," Goldfarb answered.

"They built one in sections especially for me, lucky chap that I am, so the business end wouldn't keep sticking out the top of my pack. The whole bloody thing together is called a PIAT— Projector, Infantry, Antitank." The last four words were necessarily in English.

Leon, luckily, understood "tank." He shook his head anyhow. "No tanks"—he said *panzers*—"at the jail."

"There'd better not be," Goldfarb said. "But a bomb that will make a hole in the side of a tank will make a big hole in the side of a building."

He got the impression that that was the first thing he'd said which impressed Leon, even a little. The man from the underground (Goldfarb suppressed a picture of Leon coming up from a London tube station) plucked at his beard. "Maybe you have something there. How far will it shoot?"

"A couple of hundred yards—uh, meters." *Watch that,* Goldfarb told himself. *You can give yourself away if you don't think metric.*

"Should be far enough." Leon's sardonic smile said he'd caught the slip, too. "Do you want to look over the prison before you try cracking it?"

"I'd better. I'm supposed to know what I'm doing before I do it, right?"

"It helps, yes." Leon studied him. "You've seen some action, I think."

"In the air, yes. Not on the ground, not like you mean. On the ground, I've just been strafed like everybody else."

"Yes, I know about that, too," Leon said. "But even in the air—that'll do. You won't panic when things start going crazy. Why don't you leave your hardware here? We don't want to bring it around to the prison till it's time to use it."

"Makes sense to me, as long as you're sure nobody's going to steal it while we're gone."

Leon showed teeth in something that was not a smile. "Anyone who steals from us . . . he's very sorry and he never, ever does it again. This happens once or twice and people start to get the idea."

That probably meant just what Goldfarb thought it did. He didn't want to know for sure. Goldfarb left the pack on the floor and walked out of the flat after Leon.

Franciszkanska Street was about ten minutes away. Again crowds and sights and smells buffeted Goldfarb. Again he re-

minded himself that this was how things were long after the Nazis had been driven away.

He stuck to Leon like a pair of socks; even though he'd memorized the local map, he didn't want to do much navigating on his own. Leon presently remarked, "We'll just walk by, casual as you please. Nobody will think anything about us looking as long as we don't stop and stare. The first rule is not to make yourself conspicuous."

Goldfarb looked, turning his head as if to carry on a conversation with Leon. At first glance, the prison was a tough nut to crack: two machine guns on the roof, barred windows, razor wire around the perimeter. At second glance, he said quietly, "It's too close to everything else and it doesn't have enough guards."

"They didn't send a blind man over," Leon said, beaming. "Right both times. That gives us our chance."

"And what do we do to take it?" Goldfarb asked as they left Prison One behind.

"For now, *you* don't do anything," Leon said. "You sit tight and wait for the right time. Me, I have to go see some people and find out what I need to do to incite myself a riot."

Bobby Fiore paced along a dirt track somewhere in China. His comrades said they weren't far from Shanghai. That meant little to him, because he couldn't have put Shanghai on the map to keep himself out of the electric chair. His guess was that it wasn't too far from the ocean: the air had the vaguely salty tang he'd known when he played in places like Washington State and Louisiana, anyhow.

The weight of the pistol on his hip was comforting, like an old friend. His baggy tunic hid the little gun. He'd acquired a new straw hat. If you ignored his nose and the five o'clock shadow on his cheeks, he made a pretty fair imitation peasant.

He still didn't know what to make of the rest of the band. Some of the men who trudged along in the loose column were Chinese Reds like Lo and the rest of the gang who had gotten him into this mess in the first place. They too looked like peasants, which was fair enough, because he gathered most of them were.

But the others . . . He glanced over at the fellow nearest him, who carried a rifle and wore a ragged khaki uniform.

"Hey, Yosh!" he called, and mimed pivoting at second base to turn a double play.

Yoshi Fukuoka grinned, exposing a couple of gold teeth. He dropped the rifle and went into a first baseman's stretch, scissoring himself into a split and reaching out with an imaginary mitt to snag the equally imaginary ball. "Out!" he yelled, the word perfectly comprehensible to Fiore, who lifted a clenched fist in the air, thumb pointing up.

The Reds looked from one of them to the other. They didn't get it. To them, Fukuoka was an eastern devil and Fiore a foreign devil, and the only reason they were tagging along with the Japs was that they all hated the Lizards worse than they hated each other.

Fiore hadn't even counted on that much. When he stumbled into the Japanese camp—and when he figured out the soldiers there were Japs and not Chinamen, which took him a while—he wished he could find himself a priest for last rites, because roasting over a slow fire was the best he'd expected from them. They'd bombed Pearl Harbor, they'd butchered Liu Han's husband—what was he supposed to expect?

The Japs had taken a little while to figure out he was an American, too. Their Chinese—the only language they had in common with him—was almost as bad as his, and a good-sized honker and round eyes had counted for less at first than his outfit. When they did realize what he was, they'd seemed more alarmed than hostile.

"Doolittle?" Fukuoka had asked, flying bombers over the ground with his hand.

Even though he thought he'd get killed in the next couple of minutes, that had sent Bobby into laughter which, looking back on it, was probably close to hysterical. He knew a lot of the men from Jimmy Doolittle's raid on Tokyo had landed in China, but getting mistaken for one by a jittery Jap was too much.

"I ain't no bomber pilot," he'd said in English. "I'm just a second baseman, and a lousy one, to boot."

He hadn't expected that to mean a thing to his interrogator, but the Jap's eyes had widened as much as they could. "Second base?" he'd echoed, pointing at Fiore. *"Beisoboru?"*

When Fiore still didn't get it, Fukuoka had gone into an unmistakable hitting stance. The light went on in Fiore's head.

"Baseball!" he yelled. "Son of a bitch, I don't believe it. You play ball, too?"

It hadn't been enough for him to win friends and influence people right off, but it had kept him from getting shot or bayoneted or suffering any of the other interesting things that could have happened to him. His questioning stayed questions, not torture. When, haltingly, he explained how he'd been part of the attack on the prison camp guard station, that got him promoted from prisoner to fellow fighter.

"You want kill . . . ?" One of the Japs had said a word in his own language. When he saw Fiore didn't get it, he'd amended it to, "Little scaly devils?"

"Yeah!" Bobby had said savagely. The Japanese might not have known English, but they understood that just fine.

And so he'd started marching with them. That still drove him crazy. They were the enemy, they'd kicked the U.S.A. in the balls at Pearl Harbor, jumped on the Philippines and Singapore and Burma and eight zillion little islands God knows where in the Pacific, and here he was eating rice out of the same bowl with them. It felt like treason. He had uneasy visions of standing trial for treason if he ever got back to the States. But the Japs hated Lizards more than they hated Americans, and, he'd discovered, he hated Lizards worse than he hated Japs. He'd stayed.

The Reds had joined the band a couple of days after he did. They and the Japs hadn't seemed to have any trouble getting along. That puzzled Bobby—they'd been shooting at each other right up to the day the Lizards came, and probably for a while afterwards, too.

The leader of the Red detachment was a man of about his own age named Nieh Ho-T'ing. Fiore spent more time talking with the Chinese than he did with any of the Japs except Fukuoka the ballplayer; he had more words in common with them. When he asked why they didn't have any trouble making common cause with their recent foes, Nieh had looked at him as if he were a moron and replied, "The enemy of my enemy is a friend."

It seemed as simple as that to the Japs, too. They were looking for fighters, they knew the Reds could fight, and that was all she wrote. If they thought about anything else, they sure didn't show it.

Shanghai was in Lizard hands. The closer the band got to it,

the more Bobby began to jitter. "What do we do if we see a Lizard tank?" he demanded of Nieh.

The Chinese officer shrugged, which infuriated Fiore. "Run," he answered placidly. "If we cannot run, we fight. If we must, we die. We hope to hurt the enemy as they kill us."

"Thanks a hell of a lot," Fiore muttered in English. He had no doubt Nieh Ho-T'ing meant just what he said, too. He had that do-or-die look Fiore had sometimes seen in the eyes of starting pitchers before a big game. It hadn't always meant victory, but it generally did mean a hell of an effort.

The Japs had that look, too. In his dreadful Chinese, Fukuoka told stories about pilots who'd flown their bombers right at landed Lizard spaceships, accepting the loss of their own lives as long as they could hurt the foe, too. Fiore shivered. Martyrs were all very well in church, but disconcerting when encountered in real life. He couldn't decide whether they were insanely brave or just plain insane.

They came to a road sign that said SHANGHAI 50 KM along with its incomprehensible Chinese chicken scratches. At last the band split into little groups of men to make their advance less obvious.

Bobby Fiore didn't know much about Shanghai, or care. He felt like a man who'd just got out of jail. In essence, he *was* a man who'd just got out of jail. After a year or so trapped first in Cairo, Illinois, then on the Lizard spaceship, and then in the Chinese prison camp, just being on his own and moving from place to place again felt wonderful.

He'd been a nomad for fifteen years, riding trains and buses across the United States from one rickety minor-league park, one middle-sized town, to the next, every April to September. He'd done his share of winter barnstorming, too. He wasn't used to being cooped up in one place for weeks and months at a time.

He wondered how Liu Han was doing, and hoped the Lizards weren't giving her too hard a time because he'd gone grenade-chucking with Lo the Red. He shook his head. She was a sweet gal, no doubt about that—and he wondered what a kid who was half dago, half chink would look like. He rubbed his nose, laughing a little. He would have bet money the schnoz got passed on.

But no going back, not unless he wanted to stick his head in the noose. He wasn't a man to go back, anyhow. He looked

ahead, toward whatever came next: the next series, the next train ride, the next broad. Liu Han had been fun—she'd been more than fun; that much he admitted to himself—but she was history. And history, somebody said, was bunk.

Peasants in their garden plots and rice paddies looked up when the armed band passed, then went back to work. They'd seen armed bands before: Chinese, Japanese, Lizards. As long as nobody shot at them, they worked. In the end, the armed bands couldn't do without them, not unless the people—and Lizards—wanted to quit eating.

Up ahead on the road, something stirred. Its approach was rapid, purposeful, mechanical—which meant it belonged to the Lizards. Bobby Fiore gulped. Seeing Lizards coming reminded him he wasn't marching along from place to place here. He'd signed up to fight, and the bill was about to come due.

The Japs ahead started jumping off the road, looking for cover. That suddenly struck Bobby as a real good idea. He remembered the little streambed that had cut across the field outside the prison camp. Better an idea should strike him than whatever the Lizards fired his way. He got behind a big bush by the side of the road. A moment later he wished he'd gone into a ditch instead, but by then it was too late to move.

He willed a thought at the Japs: *don't start shooting.* Attack right now would be suicidal—rifles against armor just didn't work. Through the thick, leafy branches of the bush, he couldn't see just what kind of armor it was, but the little band of fighters didn't have the tools to take on any kind.

Closer and closer the Lizard vehicles came, moving with the near silence that characterized the breed. Bobby pulled out his pistol, which all at once seemed a miserable little weapon indeed. Instead of squeezing the trigger, he squeezed off a couple of Hail Marys.

Somebody fired. "Oh, shit," Bobby said, in the same reverent tone he'd used a moment before to address the Mother of God. Now he could tell what the fighters were up against: not tanks, but what he thought the U.S. Army called half-tracks— soldier-haulers with machine guns of their own. Maybe a Lizard had been dumb enough to ride with his head sticking out so a Jap could try to blow it off.

Fiore didn't think that showed the kind of brains which would have taken the Jap very far on "The $64,000 Question." Take a potshot at armor and the armor would chew you up—

which it proceeded to do. The half-tracks stopped and began hosing down the area with their automatic weapons. The bush behind which Bobby was hiding suffered herbicide as bullets amputated the top two-thirds. Flat on his belly behind it, Fiore didn't get hit.

He had his pistol out and his surviving grenade alongside him, but he couldn't make himself use the weapons. That would only have brought more fire down on him—and he wanted to live. He had trouble understanding how anybody in combat ever fired at anybody else. You could get killed like that.

The Japanese soldiers didn't seem to worry about it. They kept on blazing away at the Lizards' vehicles—those of them who hadn't got killed in the curtain of lead the half-tracks laid down, anyway. Bobby had no idea how much damage the Japs were doing, but he was pretty damn sure it wouldn't be enough.

It wasn't. Along with keeping up the machine-gun fire, the half-tracks lowered their rear doors. A couple of squads of Lizards skittered out, their personal automatic weapons blazing. They weren't just going to hurt the people who'd shot at them, they were going to wipe 'em off the face of the earth.

"Oh, shit," Fiore said again, even more sincerely than he had before. If the Lizards caught him here with a pistol and a grenade, he was dead, no two ways about it. He didn't want to be dead, not even a little bit. He shoved the evidence under the chopped-off part of the bush and rolled backwards till he fell with a splash into a rice paddy.

He crouched down there as low as he could, huddling in the mud and doing his best to make like a farmer. Some of the real farmers were still in the knee-deep water. One or two weren't going to get out again; red stains spread around their bodies. Others, sensible chaps, ran for their lives.

The Japs didn't run, or Fiore didn't see any who did. They held their ground and fought till they were all dead. The Lizards' superior firepower smashed them like a shoe coming down on a cockroach.

Then the shooting tapered off. Fiore fervently hoped that meant the Lizards would get back into their half-tracks and go away. Instead, some of them came prowling his way, making sure they hadn't missed anybody.

One of them pointed his rifle right at Bobby Fiore. "Who

you?" he demanded in lousy Chinese. He was standing no more than a foot and a half from the weapons Bobby had stashed. Bobby was dreadfully aware he hadn't stashed them all that well, either. The Lizard repeated. "Who you?"

"Name is, uh, Nieh Ho-T'ing," Fiore said, stealing a handle from the Red officer. "Just farmer. Like rice?" He pointed to the plants peeping out of the water all around him, hoping the Lizard wouldn't notice how bad his own Chinese was.

He might not have fooled another human being, with his accent, his nose, his eyes, and the stubble on his cheeks, but the Lizard wasn't trained to pick up the differences between one flavor of Big Uglies and the next. He just hissed something in his own language, then switched back to Chinese: "You know these bad shooters?"

"No," Fiore said, half bowed so he looked down into the murky water and didn't show much of his face. "They eastern devils, I think. Me good Chinese man."

The Lizard hissed again, then went off to ask questions of somebody else. Bobby Fiore didn't move until all the males got back into the half-tracks and rolled away.

"Jesus," he said when they were gone. "I lived through it." He scrambled up out of the rice paddy and reclaimed the weapons he'd stashed. He'd started to feel naked without a pistol, even if it wasn't any good against armor—and having a grenade around made you warm and comfortable, too.

He wasn't the only one scuttling for guns, either. The Japs were all communing with their ancestors, but most of the Chinese Reds had played possum the same way he had. Now they came splashing from the paddies and grabbed their rifles and pistols and submachine guns.

They searched the corpses of the Japanese, too, but added little to what they already had. Nieh Ho-T'ing made a sour face as he walked over to Fiore. "Scaly devils are good soldiers," he said disappointedly. "They don't leave guns around for just anybody to pick up. Too bad."

"Yeah, too bad," Fiore echoed. Water dripped from his pants and formed little puddles and streams by his feet. Whenever he moved, the wet cotton made *shlup-shlup* noises right out of an animated cartoon.

Nieh nodded to him. "You did well. Unlike these imperialists"—he pointed to a couple of dead Japs not far away—"you understand that in guerrilla war the fighter is but one fish in a

vast school of peasants. When danger too great to oppose confronts him, he disappears into the school. He does not call attention to himself."

Fiore didn't understand all of that, but he got the gist. "Look like farmer, they not shoot me," he said.

"That's what I was talking about," Nieh answered impatiently. Bobby Fiore gave an absentminded emphatic cough to show he understood. Nieh had started to go off; his soaked pants went *shlup-shlup*, too. He spun back around, spraying small drops of water as he did so. "You speak the language of the little scaly devils?" he demanded.

"A bit." Bobby held his hands close together to show how small a bit it was. "Speak more Chinese." *And if that wouldn't make my mama fall over in a faint, what would?* he thought, and then, *She's gonna have a half-Chinese grandkid, even if she doesn't know it. That oughta do the job.*

Nieh Ho-T'ing didn't care about grandkids. "You speak some, though?" he persisted. "And you understand more than you speak?"

"Yeah, I guess so," Fiore said in English. Feeling himself flush, he did his best to turn it into Chinese.

Nieh nodded—he got the idea. He patted Bobby on the back. "Oh, yes, we will gladly take you to Shanghai. You will be very useful there. We do not have many who can follow what the little devils say."

"Good," Bobby answered, smiling to show how happy he was. And he was happy, too—the Reds could just as easily have shot him and left him here by the side of the road to make sure he didn't make a nuisance of himself later on. But since he made a good tool, they'd keep him around and use him. Just like Lo, Nieh Ho-T'ing hadn't asked how he felt about any of that. He had the feeling the Reds weren't good at asking—they just took.

He started to laugh. Nieh gave him a curious look. He waved the Red away: it wasn't a joke he knew how to translate into Chinese. But of all the things he'd never expected, getting shanghaied to Shanghai was right up at the top of the list.

"Exalted Fleetlord, here is a report that will please you," the shiplord Kirel said as he summoned a new document onto the screen.

Atvar read intently for a little while, then stopped and stared

at Kirel. "Major release of radioactivity in Deutschland?" he said. "This is supposed to *please* me? It means the Big Uglies there are a short step away from a nuclear bomb."

"But they do not know how to take that next step," Kirel replied. "If you please, Exalted Fleetlord, examine the analysis."

Atvar did as his subordinate asked. As he read, his mouth fell open in a great chortle of glee. "Idiots, fools, maniacs! They achieved a self-sustaining pile *without proper damping*?"

"From the radiation that has been—is being—released, they seem to have done just that," Kirel answered, also gleefully. "And it's melted down on them, and contaminated the whole area, and, with any luck at all, killed off a whole great slew of their best scientists."

"If these are their best—" Atvar's hiss was full of amazement. "They've done almost as much damage to themselves as we did to them when we dropped the nuclear bomb on Berlin."

"No doubt you are right, Exalted Fleetlord," Kirel said. "One of the main characteristics of the Tosevites is their tendency to leap headlong into any new technology which comes within their capabilities. Where we would study consequences first, they simply charge ahead. Because of that, no doubt, they went in the flick of an eye turret from spear-flinging savages to—"

"Industrialized savages," Atvar put in.

"Exactly so," Kirel agreed. "This time, though, in leaping they fell and smashed their snouts. Not all ventures into new technology come without risks."

"Something went right," Atvar said happily. "Ever since we came to Tosev 3, we've been nibbled to pieces here: two killercraft lost in one place, five landcruisers in another, deceitful diplomacy from the Big Uglies, the allies we've made among them who betrayed us—"

"That male in Poland who embarrassed us by recanting his friendship is back in our claws," Kirel said.

"So he is. I'd forgotten that," Atvar said. "We'll have to determine the most expedient means of punishing him, too: find some way to remind the Tosevites who have joined us that they would do well to remember who gives them their meat. No hurry there. He is not going anyplace save by our leave."

"No indeed, Exalted Fleetlord," Kirel said. "We also need to consider the effect of stepping up our pressure on Deutschland

in light of their failure with the atomic pile. We may find them discouraged and demoralized. Computer models suggest as much, at any rate."

"Let me see." Atvar punched up detail maps of the north-western section of Tosev 3's main continental mass. He hissed as he checked them. "The guerrillas in Italia give us as much trouble as armies elsewhere . . . and though the local king and his males loudly swear they are loyal to us, they do cooperate with the rebels. Our drives in eastern France have bogged down again—not surprising, when half the local landcruiser crews cared more about tasting ginger than fighting. We're still reorganizing there. But from the east—something might be done."

"I have taken the liberty of analyzing the forces we have available as well as those with which the Deutsche could oppose us," Kirel said. "I believe we are in a position to make significant gains there, and perhaps, if all goes well, to come close to knocking the Deutsche out of the fight against us."

"That would be excellent," Atvar said. "Forcing them into submission would improve our logistics against both Britain and the SSSR—and they are dangerous in their own right. Their missiles, their jet planes, their new landcruisers are all variables I would like to see removed from the equation."

"They are dangerous in more ways than that, Exalted Fleetlord," Kirel said quietly. "More even than the emperor-slayers in the SSSR, they have industrialized murder. Eliminating them might also eliminate that idea from the planet."

Atvar remembered the images and reports from the camp called Treblinka, and from the bigger one, just going into operation when the Race overran it, called Auschwitz. The Race had never invented any places like those. Neither had the Hallessi or the Rabotevs. So many things about Tosev 3 were unique; that was one piece of uniqueness he wished to the tip of his tailstump that the Big Uglies had not come up with.

He said, "When we are through here, the Tosevites will not be able to do that to one another. And we will have no need to do it to them, for they will be our subjects. In obedience to the will of the Emperor, this *shall* be done."

Along with Atvar, Kirel cast down his eyes. "So it shall. I hope two things, Exalted Fleetlord: that the other Big Uglies working toward nuclear weapons make the same error as the

Deutsche, and that the disaster permanently ended the Deutsch nuclear program. Given their viciousness, I would not want to see them of all Tosevites armed with atomic bombs."

"Nor I," Atvar said.

☆ **XIV** ☆

Heinrich Jäger gave his interrogator a dirty look. "I have told you over and over, Major, I don't know one damned thing about nuclear physics and I wasn't within a good many kilometers of Haigerloch when whatever happened there happened. How you expect to get any information out of me under those circumstances is a mystery."

The *Gestapo* man said, "What happened at Haigerloch is a mystery, Colonel Jäger. We are interviewing everyone at all involved with that project in an effort to learn what went wrong. And you will not deny that you were involved." He pointed to the German Cross in gold that Jäger wore.

Jäger had donned the garishly ugly medal when he was summoned to Berchtesgaden, to remind people like this needle-nosed snoop that the *Führer* had given it to him with his own hands: anyone who dared think him a traitor had better think again. Now he wished he'd left the miserable thing in its case.

He said, "I could better serve the *Reich* if I were returned to my combat unit. Professor Heisenberg was of the same opinion, and endorsed my application for transfer from Haigerloch months before this incident."

"Professor Heisenberg is dead," the *Gestapo* man said in a flat voice. Jäger winced; nobody had told him that before. Seeing the wince, the man on the safe side of the desk nodded. "You begin to understand the magnitude of the—problem now, perhaps?"

"Perhaps I do," Jäger answered; unless he missed his guess, the interrogator had been on the point of saying something like "disaster," but choked it back just in time. The fellow had a

386

point. If Heisenberg was dead, the bomb program *was* a disaster.

"If you do understand, why are you not cooperating with us?" the *Gestapo* man demanded.

The brief sympathy Jäger had felt for him melted away like a panzer battalion under heavy Russian attack in the middle of winter. "Do you speak German?" he demanded. "I don't know anything. How am I supposed to tell you something I don't know?"

The secret policeman took that in stride. Jäger wondered what sort of interrogations he'd carried out, how many desperate denials, true and untrue, he'd heard. In a way, innocence might have been worse than guilt. If you were guilty, at least you had something to reveal at last, to make things stop. If you were innocent, they'd just keep coming after you.

Because he was a *Wehrmacht* colonel with his share and more of tin plate on his chest, Jäger didn't face the full battery of techniques the *Gestapo* might have lavished on a Soviet officer, say, or a Jew. He had some notion of what those techniques were, and counted himself lucky not to make their intimate acquaintance.

"Very well, Colonel Jäger," the *Gestapo* major said with a sigh; maybe he regretted not being able to use such forceful persuasion on someone from his own side, or maybe he just didn't think he was as good an interrogator without it. "You may go, although you are not yet dismissed back to your unit. We may have more questions for you as we make progress on other related investigations."

"Thank you so much." Jäger rose from his chair. He feared irony was lost on the *Gestapo* man, who looked to prefer the bludgeon to the rapier, but made the effort nonetheless. *The bludgeon is for Russians,* he thought.

Waiting in the antechamber to the interrogation room—as if the *Gestapo* man inside were a dentist rather than a thug—sat Professor Kurt Diebner, leafing through a *Signals* old enough to show only Germany's human foes. He nodded to Jäger. "So they have vacuumed you up, too, Colonel?"

"So they have." He looked curiously at Diebner. "I would not have expected you—" He paused, unable to think of a tactful way to go on.

The physicist didn't bother with tact. "To be among the living? Only the luck of the draw, which does make a man

thoughtful. Heisenberg chose to take the pile over critical when I was away visiting my sister. Maybe not all luck, after all—he might not have wanted me around to share in his moment of fame."

Jäger suspected Diebner was right. Heisenberg had shown nothing but scorn for him at Haigerloch, though to the panzer colonel's admittedly limited perspective, Diebner was accomplishing as much as anyone else and more than most people. Jäger said, "The Lizards must have ways to keep things from going wrong when they make explosive metal."

Diebner ran a hand through his thinning, slicked-back hair. "They have also been doing it rather longer than we have, Colonel. Haste was our undoing. You know the phrase *festina lente*?"

"Make haste slowly." In his *Gymnasium* days, Jäger had done his share of Latin.

"Just so. It's generally good advice, but not advice we can afford at this stage of the war. We must have those bombs to fight the Lizards. The hope was that, if the reaction got out of hand, throwing a lump of cadmium metal into the heavy water of the pile would bring it back under control. This evidently proved too optimistic. And also, if I remember the engineering drawings correctly, there was no plug to drain the heavy water out of the pile and so shut down the reaction that way. Most unfortunate."

"Especially to everyone who was working on the pile at the time," Jäger said. "If you know all this, Dr. Diebner, and you've told it to the authorities, why are they still questioning everyone else, too?"

"First, I suppose, to confirm what I say—and I do not know everything that led up to the disaster, because I was out of town. And also, more likely than not, to find someone on whom to lay the blame."

That made sense to Jäger; after all, he'd been trying to escape being that someone. The *Wehrmacht* played games with assigning responsibility for maneuvers that didn't work, too. Another old saying crossed his mind: "Victory has a hundred fathers, but defeat is an orphan." That wasn't true any more; these days, the powers that be launched a paternity suit to pin a failure on somebody. The results weren't always just, but he suspected they weren't supposed to be.

The *Gestapo* major came out, probably to find out why

Diebner hadn't gone in. He scowled to discover two of his subjects talking with each other. Jäger felt guilty, then angry at the secret policeman for intimidating him. He stomped out of the waiting room—and almost bumped into a big man who was just coming in. "Skorzeny!" he exclaimed.

"So they dragged you into the net, too, did they?" the scar-faced SS colonel said. "They're going to rake me over the coals even though, as far as I know, I've never been within a hundred kilometers of the little pissant town where the screw-up happened. Some major's supposed to grill me in five minutes."

"He's running late," Jäger said. "He just got done with me and started in on one of the physicists. Want to go someplace and drink some *schnapps*? Nothing much else to do around here."

Skorzeny slapped him on the back. "First good idea I've heard since they hauled me back here, by God! Let's go—even if the *schnapps* they're making these days tastes like it's cooked from potato peelings, it'll put fire in your belly. And I was hoping I'd run into you, as a matter of fact. I'm working on a scheme where you just might fit in very nicely."

"Really?" Jäger raised an eyebrow. "How generous of the SS to look kindly on a poor but honest *Wehrmacht* man—"

"Oh, can the shit," Skorzeny said. "You happen to know things that would be useful to me. Now let's go get those drinks you were talking about. After I ply you with liquor, I'll try seducing you." He leered at Jäger.

"Ahh, you only want me for my body," the panzer man said.

"No, it's your mind I crave," Skorzeny insisted.

Laughing, the two men found a tavern down the street from *Gestapo* headquarters. The fellow behind the bar wore uniform, as did just about everyone in Berchtesgaden these days. "Even the whores here are all kitted out with field-gray panties," Skorzeny grumbled as he and Jäger took a table in the dimly lit cave. He raised his snifter in salute, knocked back his *schnapps*, and made a horrible face. "God, that's vile."

Jäger also took a healthy nip. "It is, isn't it?" But warmth did spread out from his belly. "It's got the old antifreeze in it, though, no doubt about that." He leaned forward. "Before you jump on me, I'm going to pick your brain: what sort of good-ies are they fishing out of that tank you stole? I want to pre-

tend I'm still a panzer man, you see, not a physicist or a bandit like you."

Skorzeny chuckled. "Flattery gets you nowhere. But I'll talk—why the hell not? Half of it I don't understand. Half of it nobody understands, which is part of the problem: the Lizards build machines that are smarter than the people we have trying to figure out what they do. But there'll be new ammunition coming down the line by and by, and new armor, too—layers of steel and ceramic bonded together the devil's uncle only knows how."

"You served on the Russian front, all right," Jäger said. "New ammunition, new armor—that's not bad. One day I may even get to use them. Probably not one day soon, though, eh?" Skorzeny did not deny it. Jäger sighed, finished his shot, went back to the bar for another round, and returned to the table. Skorzeny pounced on the fresh drink like a tiger. Jäger sat down, then asked, "So what is this scheme you have that involves me?"

"Ah, that. You were going to be an archaeologist before the first war sucked you into the Army, right?"

"You've been poking through my records," Jäger said without much malice. He drank more *schnapps*. It didn't seem so bad now—maybe the first shot had stunned his taste buds. "What the devil does archaeology have to do with the price of potatoes?"

"You know the Lizards have Italy," Skorzeny said. "They're not as happy there as they used to be, and the Italians aren't so happy with them, either. I had a little something to do with that, getting Mussolini out of the old castle where they'd tucked him away for safekeeping." He looked smug. He'd earned the right, too.

"You're planning to go down there again, and you want me along?" the panzer colonel asked. "I'd stick out like a sore thumb—not just my looks, mind you, but I don't speak much Italian."

But Skorzeny shook his massive head. "Not Italy. The Lizards are messing about on the eastern shore of the Adriatic, over in Croatia. I have trouble stomaching Ante Pavelic, but he's an ally, and we don't want the Lizards getting a toehold over there. You follow so far?"

"The strategy, yes." Jäger didn't say that he marveled at an SS man's having trouble stomaching anything. Word had trick-

led through the *Wehrmacht* that the Croat allies, puppets, whatever you wanted to call them, took their fascism—to say nothing of their blood feuds—very seriously indeed. Maybe Skorzeny's admission was proof of that. Jäger went on, "I still don't see what it has to do with me, though."

Skorzeny looked like a fisherman trying out a new lure. "Suppose I were to tell you—and I can, because it's true—the main Lizard base in Croatia is just outside Split. What would that mean to you?"

"Diocletian's palace," Jäger answered without a moment's hesitation. "I even visited there once, on holiday eight or ten years ago. Hell of an impressive building, even after better than sixteen hundred years."

"I know you visited; the report you wrote probably went into the operational planning for Operation *Strafgericht*. *Strafgericht* indeed; we punished the Yugoslavs properly for ducking out of their alliance with us. But that's by the way. What counts is that you know the area, and not just from that visit but from study as well. That's why I say you could be very useful to me."

"You're not planning on blowing up the palace, are you?" Jäger asked with sudden anxiety. Monuments suffered in wartime; that couldn't be helped. He'd seen enough Russian churches in flames during *Barbarossa*, but a Russian church didn't carry the same weight for him as a Roman Emperor's palace.

"I will if I have to," Skorzeny said. "I understand what you're saying, Jäger, but if you're going to let that kind of attitude hold you back, then I've made a mistake and you're the wrong fellow for the job."

"I may be anyhow. I've got a regiment waiting for me south of Belfort, remember."

"You're a good panzer man, Jäger, but you're not a genius panzer man," Skorzeny said. "The regiment will do well enough under someone else. For me, though, your special knowledge would truly come in handy. Do I tempt you, or not?"

Jäger rubbed his chin. He had no doubt Skorzeny could cut through the chain of command and get him reassigned: he'd pulled off enough coups for the brass to listen to him. The question was, did he want to go on fighting the same old war himself or try something new?

"Buy me another *schnapps*," he said to Skorzeny.

The SS colonel grinned. "You want me to get you drunk first, so you can say you didn't know what I was doing when I had my way with you? All right, Jäger, I'll play." He strode to the bar.

Lieutenant General Kurt Chill turned a sardonic eye on his Soviet opposite numbers—or maybe, George Bagnall thought, it was just the effect the torches that blazed in the Pskov *Krom* created. But no, the general's German was sardonic, too: "I trust, gentlemen, we can create a united front for the defense of Pleskau? This would have been desirable before, but cooperation has unfortunately proved limited."

The two Russian partisan leaders, Nikolai Vasiliev and Aleksandr German, stirred in their seats. Aleksandr German spoke Yiddish as well as Russian, and so followed Chill's words well enough. He said, "Call our city by its proper name, not the one you Nazis hung on it. Cooperation? Ha! You at least had that much courtesy before."

Bagnall, whose German was imperfect, frowned as he tried to keep track of the Jewish partisan leader's Yiddish. Vasiliev had no Yiddish or German; he had to wait until an interpreter finished murmuring in his ear. Then he boomed *"Da!"* and followed it up with a spate of incomprehensible Russian.

The interpreter performed his office: "Brigadier Vasiliev also rejects the use of the term 'united front.' It is properly applied to unions of progressive organizations, not associations with reactionary causes."

Beside Bagnall, Jerome Jones whistled under his breath. "He shaded that translation. 'Fascist jackals' is really what Vasiliev called the Nazis."

"Why does this not surprise me?" Bagnall whispered back. "If you want to know what I think, that they've come back to calling each other names instead of trying to kill each other is progress."

"Something to that," Jones said.

He started to add more, but Chill was speaking again: "If we do not join together now, whatever the name of that union may be, what we call this city will matter no more. The Lizards will give it their own name."

"And how do we stop that?" As usual, German got his comment in a beat ahead of Vasiliev.

The Russian partisan leader amplified what his comrade had said: "Yes, how do we dare put our men on the same firing line as yours without fearing they'll be shot in the back?"

"The same way I dare put *Wehrmacht* men into line alongside yours," Chill said: "by remembering the enemy is worse. As for being shot in the back, how many Red Army units went into action with NKVD men behind them to make sure they were properly heroic?"

"Not our partisans," German said. Then he fell silent, and Vasiliev had nothing to add, from which Bagnall inferred General Chill had scored a point.

Chill folded his arms across his chest. "Does either of you gentlemen propose to take overall command of the defenses of Pleskau—excuse me, Pskov?"

Aleksandr German and Vasiliev looked at each other. Neither seemed overjoyed at the prospect of doing as Chill had suggested. In their *valenki*, Bagnall wouldn't have been overjoyed, either. Conducting hit-and-run raids from the forest wasn't the same as fighting a stand-up campaign. The partisans knew well how to make nuisances of themselves. They also had to be uneasily aware that partisan warfare hadn't kept the Germans from Pskov or driven them out of it.

Finally, Vasiliev said, *"Nyet."* He went on through his interpreter. "You are best suited to lead the defense, provided you do it so that you are defending the town and the people and the Soviet fighters in the area as well as your own Nazis."

"If I defend the area, I defend all of it, or as much as I can with the men and resources I have available," Chill answered. "This also means that if I give an order to one of your units, I expect it to be obeyed."

"Certainly," Vasiliev answered, "so long as the unit's commander and political commissar judge the order to be in the best interest of the cause as a whole, not just to the advantage of you Germans."

"That is not good enough," Chill replied coldly. "They must take the overall well-being as their governing assumption, and obey whether they see the need or not. One of the reasons for having an overall commander is to have a man in a position where he can see things his subordinates do not."

"Nyet," Vasiliev said again. Aleksandr German echoed him.

"Oh, bugger, here we go again," Bagnall whispered to Jerome Jones. The radarman nodded. Bagnall went on, "We've

got to do something, before we go through another round of the idiocy that had the Bolshies and Nazis blazing away at each other a few weeks ago. I don't know about you, but I don't fancy getting stuck between them again."

"Nor I," Jones whispered back. "If that's what the ground-pounders call war, thank God for the RAF, is all I have to say."

"You get no arguments from me," Bagnall said. "Remember, I'd already found that out. You weren't along for the raid on the Lizard base south of here." *They thought you were too valuable to risk,* he thought without much rancor. *Ken and poor dead Alf and I, we were expendable, but not you—you know your radars too well.*

As if thinking along similar lines, Jones answered, "I tried to come along. The bloody Russians wouldn't let me."

"Did you? I didn't know that." Bagnall's opinion of Jones went up a peg. To volunteer to get shot at when you didn't have to took something special.

As most Englishmen would, Jones brushed that aside. "It doesn't matter, anyway. We have to worry about now, as you said." He got up and said loudly, *"Tovarishchi!"* Even Bagnall knew that one—it meant *Comrades!* Jones went on, in Russian and then in German, "If we want to hand Pskov to the Lizards on a silver platter, we can go on just as we are now."

"Yes? And so?" Kurt Chill asked. "What is your solution? Shall we all place ourselves under *your* command?" His smile was hard and bright and sharp, like a shark's.

Jones turned pale and sat down in a hurry. "I've got a picture of that, I do, bloody generals kowtowing to a radarman. Not flipping likely."

"Why not?" Bagnall got to his feet. He had only German, and not all he wanted of that, but he gave it his best shot: "The Red Army doesn't trust the *Wehrmacht*, and the *Wehrmacht* doesn't trust the Red Army. But have we English done anything to make either side distrust us? Let General Chill command. If Russian units don't like what he proposes, let them complain to us. If we think the orders are fair, let them obey as if the commands came from Stalin. Is that a fair arrangement?"

Silence followed, save for the murmur of Vasiliev's interpreter as he translated Bagnall's words. After a few seconds, Chill said, "In general, weakening command is a bad idea. A

commander needs all the authority over his troops he can get. But in these special circumstances—"

"The Englishmen would have to decide quickly," Aleksandr German said. "If they cannot make up their minds, orders may become irrelevant before they give their answer."

"That would be part of the packet," Bagnall agreed.

"The Englishmen would also have to remember that we are all allies together here against the Lizards, and that England is not specially aligned with the Russians against the *Reich*," Lieutenant General Chill said. "Decisions which fail to show this evenhandedness would make the arrangement unworkable in short order—and we would start shooting at each other again."

"Yes, yes," Bagnall said impatiently. "If I didn't think we could do that, I wouldn't have advanced the idea. I might also say I'm not the only one in this room who has had trouble remembering we are all allies together and that plans should show us much."

Chill glared at him, but so did German and Vasiliev. Jerome Jones whispered, "You did well there, not to single out either side. This way each of them can pretend to be sure you're talking about the other chap. Downright byzantine of you, in fact."

"Is that a compliment?" Bagnall asked.

"I meant it for one," the radarman answered.

Chill spoke to the Russian partisan leaders. "Is this agreeable to you, gentlemen? Shall we let the Englishmen arbitrate between us?"

"He rides that 'gentlemen' hard," Jones murmured. "Throws it right in the face of the comrades—just to irk 'em, unless I miss my guess. Gentlemen don't fit into the dictatorship of the proletariat."

Bagnall listened with but half an ear. He was watching the two men who'd headed the "forest republic" before the Lizards arrived. They didn't look happy as they muttered back and forth. Bagnall didn't care whether they were happy. He just hoped they could live with the arrangement.

Finally, grudgingly, Nikolai Vasiliev turned to General Chill and spoke a single sentence of Russian. The translator turned it into German: "Better the English than you."

"On that, if you reverse roles, we agree completely," Chill said. He turned to Bagnall, gave him an ironic bow. "Congratulations. You and your British colleagues have just become a

three-man board of field marshals. Shall I order your batons and have a tailor sew red stripes to your trouser seams?"

"That won't be necessary," Bagnall said. "What I need is assurance from you and from your Soviet counterparts that you'll abide by whatever decisions we end up making. Without that, we might as well not start down this road."

The German general gave him a long look, then slowly nodded. "You do have some understanding of the difficulties with which you are involving yourself. I wondered if this was so. Very well, let it be as you say. By my oath as a soldier and officer of the *Wehrmacht* and the German *Reich*, I swear that I shall accept without question your decision on cases brought before you for arbitration."

"What about you?" Bagnall asked the two Soviet brigadiers.

Aleksandr German and Vasiliev seemed imperfectly delighted once more, but German said, "If in a dispute you rule against us, we shall accept your decision as if it came from the Great Stalin himself. This I swear."

"*Da,*" Vasiliev added after the interpreter had translated for him. "Stalin." He spoke the Soviet leader's name like a religious man invoking the Deity—or perhaps a powerful demon.

Kurt Chill said, "Enjoy the responsibility, my English friends." He sent Bagnall and Jones a stiff-armed salute, then strode out of the meeting chamber in the *Krom*.

Bagnall felt the responsibility, too, as if the air had suddenly turned hard and heavy above his shoulders. He said, "Ken won't be pleased with us for getting him into this when he wasn't even at the meeting."

"That's what he gets for not coming," Jones replied.

"Mm—maybe so." Bagnall looked sidelong at the radarman. "Do you suppose the Germans will want you to give up the fair Tatiana, so as to have no reason to be biased toward the Soviet side?"

"They'd better not," Jones said, "or I'll bloody well have reason to be biased against them. The one good thing in this whole pestilential town—if anyone tries separating me from her, he'll have a row on his hands, that I tell you."

"What?" Bagnall raised an eyebrow. "You're not enamored of spring in Pskov? You spoke so glowingly of it, I recall, when we were flying here in the Lanc."

"Bugger spring in Pskov, too," Jones retorted, and stomped off.

In fact, spring in Pskov was pretty enough. The Velikaya River, ice-free at last, boomed over the rapids as it neared Lake Pskov. Gray boulders, tinted with pink, stood out on steep hillsides against the dark green of the all-surrounding woods. Grass grew tall on the streets of deserted villages around the city.

The sky was a deep, luminous blue, with only a few puffy little white clouds slowly drifting across it from west to east. Along with those clouds, Bagnall saw three parallel lines of white, as straight as if drawn with a ruler. *Condensation trails from Lizard jets,* he thought, and his delight in the beauty of the day vanished. The Lizards might not be moving yet, but they were watching.

Mordechai Anielewicz looked up from the beet field at the sound of jet engines. Off to the north he saw three small silvery darts heading west. *They'll be landing at Warsaw,* he thought with the automatic accuracy of one who'd been spotting Lizard planes for as long as there had been Lizard planes to spot—and German planes before that. *Wonder what they've been up to.*

Whoever headed the Jewish fighters these days would have someone at the airport fluent enough at the Lizards' speech to answer that for him. So would General Bor-Komorowski of the Polish Home Army. Anielewicz missed getting information like that, being connected to a wider world. He hadn't realized his horizons would contract so dramatically when he left Warsaw for Leczna.

Contract they had. The town had had several radios, but without electricity, what good were they? Poland's big cities had electricity, but nobody'd bothered repairing the lines out to all the country towns. Leczna probably hadn't had electricity at all until after the First World War. Now that it was gone again, people just did without.

Anielewicz went back to work. He pulled out a weed, made sure he had the whole root, then moved ahead about half a meter and did it again. *An odd task,* he thought: *mindless and exacting at the same time.* You wondered where the hours had gone when you knocked off at the end of the day.

A couple of rows over, a Pole looked up from his weeding and said, "Hey you, Jew! What does the creature that says he's governor of Warsaw call himself again?"

The fellow spoke quite without malice, using Anielewicz's religion to identify him, not particularly to scorn him. That he might feel scorned anyhow never entered the Pole's mind. Because he knew that, Anielewicz didn't feel scorned, or at least not badly. "Zolraag," he answered, carefully pronouncing the two distinct *a* sounds.

"Zolraag," the Pole echoed, less clearly. He took off his cap, scratched his head. "Is he as little as all the others like him? It hardly seems natural."

"All the males I've ever seen are about the same size," Mordechai answered. The Pole scratched his head again. Anielewicz had worked with the Lizards almost every day; he knew them as well as any man could. Here in Leczna, Lizards were hardly more than a rumor. The locals might have seen them when they ran the Nazis out of town, or when they went to Lublin to buy and sell. Other than that, the aliens were a mystery here.

"They are as nasty as people say?" the Pole asked.

How was he supposed to answer that? Slowly, he said, "They aren't as vicious as the Germans, and they aren't as smart, either—or maybe it's just that they don't understand people any better than we understand them, and that makes them seem dumber than they are. But they can do more with machines than the Germans ever dreamed of, and that makes them dangerous."

"You reason like a priest," the farmworker said. It wasn't quite a compliment, for he went on, "Ask a simple question and you get back, 'Well, sort of this but sort of that, too, because of these things. And on the other hand—' " He snorted. "I just wanted a yes or a no."

"But some questions don't have simple yes-or-no answers," Anielewicz said. Though he'd been a secular man, his ancestry had generations of Talmudic scholars in it—and just being a Jew was plenty to teach you things were rarely as simple as they looked at first glance.

The Pole didn't believe that; Anielewicz could see as much. The fellow took a flask of vodka off his hip, swigged, and offered it to Anielewicz. Mordechai took a nip. Vodka helped you get through the day.

After a while, the Pole said, "So what did you do to get yourself run out of Warsaw and show up in a little town like this?"

"I shot the last man who asked me a question like that," Anielewicz replied, deadpan.

The farmworker stared at him, then let out a hoarse guffaw. "Oh, you're a funny one, you are. We got to watch you every minute, hey?" He leered at Mordechai. "Some of the girls are watching you already, you know that?"

Anielewicz grunted. He did know that. He didn't quite know what to do about it. As leader of the Jewish fighters, he hadn't had time for women, and they might have endangered security. Now he was just an exile. His training in underground work insisted he still ought to hold himself aloof. But he was a man in his mid-twenties, and emphatically not a monk.

Grinning, the Pole said, "You go out to the backhouses at night, you have to be careful not to look toward the haystacks or under the wagons. Never can tell when you're liable to see something you're not supposed to."

"Is that a fact?" Mordechai said, though he knew it was. The Poles were not only less straitlaced than the Jews who lived among them, they also used vodka or brandy to give themselves an excuse for acting that way. Anielewicz added, "I don't see how anyone is up to doing anything except sleep after a day in the fields."

"You think this is work, wait till harvest comes," the Pole said, which made Anielewicz groan. The local laughed, then went on more soberly: "All the old-timers, the ones left alive, they're sneering at us, on account of we're having to make do without tractors and such, so I shouldn't give you a hard time, friend. You pull your weight, and every pair of hands we can find is welcome. We want to keep ourselves fed through winter, we better work now." He stooped, tore out a weed, moved ahead.

He probably didn't care what happened two kilometers outside Leczna, but he'd put his finger on a worldwide truth there. With so much farm machinery out of commission or out of fuel, people everywhere were having to do all they could just to stay alive. That meant they were able to do less to fight the Lizards, too.

Anielewicz wondered if the aliens had planned it that way. Maybe not; some of the things Zolraag had said suggested they hadn't expected people to *have* machines, let alone readapt to doing without them. But if the Lizards reduced all of mankind to nothing more than peasants grubbing a bare living from the

soil, would people ever be able to get free of them? He shook his head like a horse bedeviled by gnats. He couldn't see it.

Then rational thought went away for a while as the ancient rhythm of the fields took over. The next time he looked up from the furrows, the sun hung low in the west, sinking into the mist that rose from the flat, moist land as it cooled with approaching evening.

"Where does the time go?" he said, startled.

He'd spoken more to himself than to anyone else, but the Polish farmworker was still close enough to hear him. The Pole laughed, loud and long. "Got away from you, did it? That happens sometimes. You wonder what the devil you've been doing all day, till you look back and see what you've done."

Mordechai looked back. Sure enough, he'd done a lot. He was an educated man, a city man. No matter how necessary farmwork was, he'd been sure it would drive him mad with boredom. He didn't know whether to be relieved or alarmed that that hadn't happened. Relief seemed natural, but if someone like him could sink down to the level of a farmer with no thought past his fields, what did that say about the rest of humanity? If the Lizards pressed the yoke of serfdom down on their necks, would they wear it?

He shook his head again. If he was going to start thinking, he would have preferred to start with something more cheerful. The mist rose; the sun sank until he could stare straight at its blood-red disk without hurting his eyes. The Pole said, "Hell with it. We're not going to get any more done today. Let's go back to town."

"All right by me." Anielewicz's back protested when he stood up straight. If aches bothered the Pole, he didn't show it. He'd worked on a farm all his life, not just for a couple of weeks.

Leczna was an ordinary Polish town, bigger than a village, not nearly big enough to be called a city. It was small enough for people to know one another, and for Mordechai to stand out as a stranger. People still greeted him in a friendly enough way, Jews and Poles alike. The two groups seemed to get on pretty well—better than in most places in Poland, anyhow.

Maybe the friendly greetings came because he was staying with the Ussishkins. Judah Ussishkin had been doctoring Jews and gentiles alike for more than thirty years; his wife Sarah, a midwife herself, must have delivered half the population of the

town. If the Ussishkins vouched for you, you were good as gold in Leczna.

Most of the Jews lived in the southeastern part of town. As was fitting for one who worked with both halves of the populace, Dr. Ussishkin had his house at the edge of the Jewish district. His next-door neighbors on one side, in fact, were Poles. Roman Klopotowski waved to Anielewicz as he came down the street toward the doctor's house. So did Klopotowski's daughter Zofia.

Mordechai waved back, which made Zofia's face light up. She was a pretty blond girl—no, woman; she had to be past twenty. Anielewicz wondered why she hadn't married. Whatever the reason, she'd plainly set her sights on him.

He didn't know what to do about that (he knew what he wanted to do, but wasn't nearly so sure it was a good idea). For the moment, he did nothing but walk up the steps onto the front porch of Dr. Ussishkin's house and, after wiping his feet, on into the parlor.

"Good evening, my guest," Judah Ussishkin said with a dip of his head that was almost a bow. He was a broad-shouldered man of about sixty, with a curly gray beard, sharp dark eyes behind steel-rimmed spectacles, and an old-fashioned courtliness that brought with it a whiff of the vanished days of the Russian Empire.

"Good evening," Mordechai answered, nodding in return. He'd grown up in a more hurried age, and could not match the doctor's manners. He might even have resented them had they not been so obviously genuine rather than affectation. "How was your day?"

"Well enough, thank you for asking, although it would have been better still had I had more medicines with which to work."

"We would all be better off if we had more of everything," Mordechai said.

The doctor raised a forefinger. "There I must disagree with you, my young friend: of troubles we have more than a sufficiency." Anielewicz laughed ruefully and nodded, yielding the point.

Sarah Ussishkin came out of the kitchen and interrupted: "Of potatoes we also have a sufficiency, at least for now. Potato soup is waiting, whenever you *tzaddiks* decide you'd rather eat than philosophize." Her smile belied the scolding

tone in her voice. She'd probably been a beauty when she was young; she remained a handsome woman despite gray hair, the beginning of a stoop, and a face that had seen too many sorrows and not enough joys. She moved with a dancer's grace, making her long black skirt swirl about her at every step.

The potato soup steamed in its pot and in three bowls on the table by the stove. Judah Ussishkin murmured a blessing before he picked up his spoon. Out of politeness to him, Anielewicz waited till he was done, though he'd lost that habit and his stomach was growling like an angry wolf.

The soup was thick not only with grated potatoes but also with chopped onion. Chicken fat added rich flavor and sat in little golden globules on the surface of the soup. Mordechai pointed to them. "I always used to call those 'eyes' when I was a little boy."

"Did you?" Sarah laughed. "How funny. Our Aaron and Benjamin said just the same thing." The laughter did not last long. One of the Ussishkins' sons had been a young rabbi in Warsaw, the other a student there. No word had come from them since the Lizards drove out the Nazis and the closed ghetto ended. The odds were mournfully good that meant they were both dead.

Mordechai's soup bowl emptied with amazing speed. Sarah Ussishkin filled it again, and he emptied it the second time almost as fast as the first. "You have a healthy appetite," Judah said approvingly.

"If a man works like a horse, he needs to eat like a horse, too," Anielewicz replied. The Germans hadn't cared about that; they'd worked the Jews like elephants and fed them like ants. But the work they'd got out of the Jews was just a sidelight; they'd been more interested in getting rid of them.

Supper was just ending when someone pounded on the front door. "Sarah, come quick!" a frightened male voice bawled in Yiddish. "Hannah's pains are close together."

Sarah Ussishkin made a wry face as she got up from her chair. "It could be worse, I suppose," she said. "That usually happens in the middle of a meal." The pounding and shouting went on. She raised her voice: "Leave us our door in one piece, Isaac. I'm coming." The racket stopped. Sarah turned to her husband for a moment. "I'll probably see you tomorrow sometime."

"Very likely," he agreed. "God forbid you should have to

call me sooner, for that could only mean something badly wrong. I have chloroform, a little, but when it is gone, it is gone forever."

"This is Hannah's third," Sarah said reassuringly. "The first two were so simple I could have stayed here for them." Isaac started banging on the door again. "I'm coming," she told him again, this time following words with action.

"She's right about that," Judah told Anielewicz after his wife had gone. "Hannah has hips like—" Having caught himself about to be ungallant, he shook his head in self-reproach. As if to make amends, he changed the subject. "Would you care for a game of chess?"

"Why not? You'll teach me something." Before the war, Anielewicz had fancied himself as a chess player. But either his game had gone to pot after close to four years of neglect or Judah Ussishkin could have played in tournaments, because he'd managed only one draw and no wins in half a dozen or so games against the doctor.

Tonight proved no exception. Down a knight, his castled king's position not well enough protected to withstand the attack he saw coming, Mordechai tipped the king over, signifying surrender. "You might have gotten out of that," Ussishkin said.

"Not against you," Mordechai answered. "I know better. Do you want to try another game? I can do better than that."

"Your turn for white," Judah said. As they rearranged the pieces on the board, he added, "Not everyone would keep coming back after a string of losses."

"I'm learning from you," Anielewicz said. "And maybe my game is coming back a little. When I'm playing as well as I can, I might be able to put you to some trouble, anyhow." He pushed his queen's pawn to open.

They were in the middle of a hard-fought game with no great advantage for either side—Mordechai was proud of avoiding a trap a few moves before—when more pounding on the door made them both jump. Isaac shouted, "Doctor, Sarah wants you to come. Right away, she says."

"*Oy,*" Judah said, cultivated manner for once forgotten. He pushed back his chair and stood up. "The game will have to keep, I'm afraid." He moved a pawn. "Think about that while I'm gone." He snatched up his bag and hurried out to the anxious Isaac.

Anielewicz studied the board. The pawn move didn't look particularly menacing. Maybe Judah was trying to make him think too much . . . or maybe he really was missing something. He looked at the board again, shrugged, and started to get ready to go to sleep.

He hadn't even pulled his shirt off over his head when the thrum of aircraft engines overhead made him freeze. They were human-made planes; he'd heard and hated that heavy drone for most of a month on end in 1939, when the *Luftwaffe* systematically pounded a Warsaw that could hardly defend itself. These aircraft, though, were coming out of the east. *Red Air Force?* Anielewicz wondered; the Russians had flown occasional bombing raids after Hitler invaded them. *Or are the Nazis still in business over there, too?* He knew German ground forces had kept fighting inside the Soviet Union even after the Lizards came; was the *Luftwaffe* still a going concern, too?

He went outside. If the bombers unloaded on Leczna, that was the worst place to be, but he didn't think the little town was anybody's primary target—and it had been a while since humans tried an air raid on Lizard-held territory.

Several other people stood in the street, too, their heads craning this way and that as they tried to spot the planes. Cloud cover was thick; there wasn't anything to see. The pilots probably hoped the bad weather would help shield them. Then, off to the south, a streak of fire rose into the sky, and another and another. "Lizard rockets," somebody close by said in Polish—Zofia Klopotowski.

The rockets vanished into the clouds. A moment later, an enormous explosion rattled windows. "A whole plane, bombs and all," Anielewicz said sadly.

A streak of fire came out of the clouds—falling, not rising. "He's not going to make it," Zofia said, her tone echoing Mordechai's. Sure enough, the stricken bomber smashed into the ground a few kilometers south of Leczna. Another peal of man-made thunder split the air.

The rest of the planes in the flight droned on toward their goal. Had Anielewicz been up there and watched his comrades hacked from the sky, he would have reversed course and run for home. It might not have done him any good. More missiles rose. More aircraft blew up in midair or tumbled in ruins to the ground. Those that survived kept stubbornly heading west.

As the engines faded out of hearing, most people headed for their homes. A few lingered. Zofia said, "I wonder if I should be glad the Lizards are shooting down the Russians or Germans or whoever was in those planes. We live better now than we did under the Reds or the Nazis."

Mordechai stared at her. "But they're making slaves of us," he exclaimed.

"So were the Reds and the Nazis," she replied. "And you Jews were quick enough to hop in bed with the Lizards when they pushed this way."

Her choice of language made him cough, but he said, "The Nazis weren't just making slaves of us, they were killing us in carload lots. We had nothing to lose—and we didn't see at the start that the Lizards wanted only servants, not partners. They want to do to the whole world what the Germans and Russians did to Poland. That's not right, is it?"

"Maybe not," Zofia said. "But if the Lizards lose and the Germans and Russians come back here, Poland still won't be free, and we'll all be worse off."

Anielewicz thought about the revenge Stalin or Hitler would exact against people who had supported—the dictators would say "collaborated with"—the Lizards. He shuddered. Still, he answered, "But if the Lizards win, there won't be any free people at all left on Earth, not here, not in England, not in America—and they'll be able to do whatever they want with the whole world, not just with one country."

Zofia looked thoughtful, or Mordechai thought she did—the night was too dark for him to be sure. She said, "That's true. I have trouble worrying about anything outside Leczna. This is the only place I've ever known. But you, you've been lots of places, and you can hold the world in your mind." She sounded wistful, or perhaps even jealous.

He wanted to laugh. He'd done some traveling in Poland, but hardly enough to make him a cosmopolitan. In an important way, though, she was right: books and school had taken his mind places his body had never gone, and left him with a wider view of things than she had. And having a pretty girl look up to him, for whatever reason, was a long way from the worst thing that had ever happened.

He glanced around and realized with some surprise that he and Zofia were the last two people left on the street. Everyone else was snug inside, and probably snug in bed, too. He waited

for Zofia to notice the lull in their talk, say good night, and go back to her father's house. When she didn't, but kept standing quietly by him, he reached out and, quite in the spirit of experiment, let his hand rest on her shoulder.

She didn't shrug him off. She stepped closer, so that his arm went around her. "I wondered how long that would take you," she said with a small laugh.

Miffed, he almost said something sharp, but luckily had a better idea: he bent his face down to hers. Her lips were upturned and waiting. For some time, neither of them said anything. Then he whispered, "Where can we go?"

"The doctor didn't take his car, did he?" she whispered back. Ussishkin owned an ancient Fiat, one of the handful of automobiles in town. She answered her own question: "No, of course he didn't. No one has any petrol these days. So it's right in back of his house. If we're quiet."

The Fiat's back door squeaked alarmingly when Anielewicz opened it for Zofia, who let out an almost soundless giggle. He slid in beside her. They were cramped, but managed to loosen and eventually pull off each other's clothes all the same. His hand strayed down from her breasts to her thighs and the warm, moist softness between them.

She gripped him, too. When she did, she paused a moment in surprise, then giggled again, deep down in her throat. "That's right," she said, as if reminding herself. "You're a Jew. It's different."

He hadn't really thought he was her first, but the remark jolted him a little just the same. He made a wordless questioning noise.

"My fiancé—his name was Czeslaw—went to fight the Germans," she said. "He never came back."

"Oh. I'm sorry." He wished he'd ignored her. Hoping he hadn't ruined the mood, he kissed her again. Evidently he hadn't; she sighed and lay back as well as she could on the narrow seat of the car. He poised himself above her. "Zofia," he said as they joined. She wrapped her arms around his back.

When he paid attention to anything but her again, he saw the old Fiat's windows, which Ussishkin kept closed against pests, had steamed up. That made him laugh. "What is it?" Zofia asked. Her voice came slightly muffled; she was pulling her blouse back on over her head. He explained. She said, "Well, what would you expect?"

He dressed, too, as fast as he could. Getting back into clothes in the backseat was even more awkward than escaping from them had been, but he managed. He opened the car door and slid out, Zofia right behind him. They stood for a couple of seconds, looking at each other. As people do in such circumstances, Mordechai wondered where that first coupling would end up taking them. He said, "You'd better get back to your house. Your father will wonder where you've been." Actually, he was afraid Roman Klopotowski might know where she'd been, but he didn't want to say that.

She stood on tiptoe so she could kiss him on the cheek. "That's for caring enough about me to worry what my father will think," she said. Then she kissed him again, open-mouthed. "And that's for the rest."

He squeezed her. "If I weren't so tired from working in the fields—"

She burst out laughing, so loud he twitched in alarm. "Men are such braggarts. It's all right. We'll find other times."

That meant he'd pleased her. He felt several centimeters taller. "I hope we do."

"Of course you hope we do. Men always hope that," Zofia said without much anger. She laughed again. "I don't know why you Jews go to so much trouble and hurt to make yourselves different. Once it's in there, it's the same either way."

"Is it? Well, I can't help that," Anielewicz said. "I am sorry about your Czeslaw. Too many people, Poles and Jews, haven't come back from the war."

"I know." She shook her head. "That's God's truth, it certainly is. It's been a long time—three and a half years, more. I'm entitled to live my own life." She spoke defiantly, as if Mordechai were going to disagree with her.

But he said, "Of course you are. And now you had better go home."

"All right. I'll see you soon." She hurried away.

Anielewicz went back into the Ussishkins' house. They came in a few minutes later, tired but smiling. Judah said, "We got a good baby, a boy, and Hannah I think will be all right, too. I didn't have to do a cesarean, for which I thank God—no real chance for asepsis here, try as I will."

"That's all good news," Anielewicz said.

"It is indeed." The doctor looked at him. "But what are you doing still awake? You've been studying the chessboard, unless

I miss my guess. I have noticed you don't like to lose, however polite you may be. So what are you going to do?"

The chess game hadn't crossed Mordechai's mind once since the sound of airplane engines made him go outside. Now he walked back over to the board. Thanks to the pawn move Ussishkin had crowed about, he couldn't attack with his queen as he'd planned. He shifted the piece to a square farther back along the diagonal than he'd intended.

Fast as a striking snake, Judah Ussishkin moved a knight. It neatly forked the queen and one of Mordechai's rooks. He stared in dismay. Here was another game he wasn't going to win—and Ussishkin was right, he hated to lose.

All at once, though, it didn't seem to matter so much. All right, so he'd lose at chess one more time. He'd played a different game tonight, and won it.

Leslie Groves looked down the table at the scientists from the Metallurgical Laboratory. "The fate of the United States—and probably the world—depends on your answer to this question: how do we turn the theoretical physics of a working atomic pile into practical engineering? We have to industrialize the process as fast as we can."

"A certain amount of caution is indicated," Arthur Compton said. "By what we've been told, they're paying in Germany for rushing ahead with no thought for consequences."

"That was an engineering flaw we've already uncovered, wasn't it?" Groves said.

"A flaw? You might say so." Enrico Fermi made a fine Latin gesture of contempt. "When their pile went critical, they had no way to shut it down again—and so the reaction continued, out of control. For all I know, it continues still; no one can get close enough to find out for certain. It cost the Germans many able men, whatever we may think of them politically."

"Heisenberg," someone said softly. An almost invisible pall of gloom seemed to descend on the table. Many of the assembled physicists had known the dead German; you couldn't be a nuclear physicist without knowing his work.

"I am not about to let a foreign accident slow down our own program," Groves said, "especially when it's an accident we won't have. What were they doing, throwing pieces of cad-

mium metal into the heavy water of their pile to try to slow it down? We've designed better than that."

"In this particular regard, yes," Leo Szilard said. "But who can say what other problems may be lurking in the metaphysical undergrowth?"

Groves gave the Hungarian scientist an unfriendly look. However brilliant he was, he was always finding ways things could go wrong. Maybe he was so imaginative, he saw flaws no one else would. Or maybe he just liked to borrow trouble.

Whichever it was, Groves didn't intend to put up with it. He growled, "If we never tried anything new, we wouldn't have to worry about anything going wrong. Of course, if we'd had that attitude all along, the Lizards would have conquered us about twenty minutes after they landed here, because we'd all have been living in villages and sacrificing goats whenever we had a thunderstorm. So we will go ahead and see what the problems are. Objections?"

No one had any. Groves nodded, satisfied. The physicists were a bunch of prima donnas such as he'd never had to deal with in the Army, but no matter how high in the clouds their heads were, they had their hearts in the right place.

He said, "Okay, back to square one. What do we have to do to turn our experimental pile here into a bomb factory?"

"Get out of Denver," Jens Larssen muttered. Groves glowered at him; he'd had enough of Larssen's surly attitude.

Then, to his surprise, he noticed several other physicists were nodding. Groves did his best to smooth out his features. "Why?" he asked, as mildly as he could.

Larssen looked around; maybe he didn't want the floor. But he'd opened his mouth, and so he had it. He reached into a shirt pocket, as if digging for a pack of cigarettes. Not coming up with one, he said, "Why? The most important reason is, we don't have the water we'll need."

"Like any other energy source, a nuclear pile also generates heat," Fermi amplified. "Running water makes an effective coolant. Whether we can divert enough water here from other uses is an open question."

Groves said, "How much are we going to need? The Mississippi? The Lizards are holding most of it these days, I'm afraid."

He'd intended that for sarcasm. Fermi didn't take it as such. He said, "That being so, the Columbia is probably best for our

purposes. It is swift-flowing, with a large volume of water, and the Lizards are not strong in the Northwest."

"You want this operation to move again, after we've just gotten set up here?" Groves demanded. "You want to pack everything up into wagons and haul it over the *Rockies*?" What he wanted to do was start heaving nuclear physicists out the window, Nobel laureates first.

"A move like the move we made from Chicago, no, that would not be necessary," Fermi said. "We can keep this facility intact, continue to use it for research. But production, as you call it, would be better placed elsewhere."

Heads bobbed up and down, all along the table. Groves sighed. He'd been given the power to bind and loose on this project, but he'd expected to wield it against bureaucrats and soldiers; he hadn't imagined the scientists he was supposed to ride herd on would complicate his life so. He said, "If you're springing this on me now, you probably have a site all picked out."

That's what he would have done, anyhow. But then, he was a hardheaded engineer. The ivory-tower boys didn't always think the way he did. This time, though, Fermi nodded. "From what we can tell by long-distance research, the town of Hanford, Washington, seems quite suitable, but we shall have to send someone to take a look at this place to make certain it meets our needs."

Larssen stuck his hand in the air. "I'll go." A couple of other men also volunteered.

Groves pretended not to see them. "Dr. Larssen, I think I may take you up on that. You have experience traveling through a war zone by yourself, and—" He let the rest hang.

Larssen didn't. "—and it'd be best for everybody if I got out of here for a while, you were going to say. Now tell me one I hadn't heard." He ran a hand through his shock of thick blond hair. "I've got a question for you. Will the Lizard POWs stay with the research end or go to the production site?"

"Not my call." Groves turned to Fermi. "Professor?"

"I think perhaps they may be more useful to us here," Fermi said slowly.

"That's kind of what I thought, too," Larssen said. "Okay, now I know." He didn't need to draw anybody a picture. If the Lizards—and Sam Yeager, and Barbara Larssen-turned-

Yeager—stayed here, Jens would likely end up at Hanford for good, assuming the place panned out.

That set off an alarm bell in Groves' mind. "We will need a scrupulously accurate report on Hanford's suitability, Dr. Larssen."

"You'll get one," Jens promised. "I won't talk it up just so I can move there, if that's what you're worried about."

"Okay." Groves thought for a minute, then said, "We ought to send a GI with you, too. That would help make sure you got back here in one piece."

Larssen's eyes grew hard and cold. "You try sending anybody from the Army with me, General, and I won't go. The Army's already done me enough bad turns—I don't need any more. I'll be there all by my lonesome, and I'll get back, too. You don't like that, put somebody else on the road."

Groves glared. Larssen glared right back. Groves ran into the limits of his power to command. If he told Larssen to shut up and do as he was told, the physicist was liable to go on strike again and end up in the brig instead of Hanford. And even if he did leave Denver with a soldier tagging along, what would his report be worth when he got back? He'd already proved he could survive on his own. Groves muttered under his breath. Sometimes you had to throw in your hand; no help for it. "Have it your way, then," he growled. Larssen looked disgustingly smug.

Leo Szilard stuck a forefinger in the air. Groves nodded his way, glad of the chance to forget Larssen for a moment. Szilard said, "Building a pile is a large work of engineering. How do we keep the Lizards from spotting it and knocking it to pieces? Hanford now, I would say as a statement of high probability, has no such large works."

"We have to make it look as if we're building something else, something innocuous," Groves said after a little thought. "Just what, I don't know. We can work on that while Dr. Larssen is traveling. We'll involve the Army Corps of Engineers, too; we won't need to depend on our own ingenuity."

"If I were a Lizard," Szilard said, "I would knock down any large building humans began, on general principles. The aliens must know we are trying to devise nuclear weapons."

Groves shook his head again, not in contradiction but in annoyance. He had no doubt Szilard was right; if he'd been a Lizard himself, he'd have done the same thing. "Hiding an

atomic pile in the middle of a city isn't the world's greatest idea, either," he said. "We've done it here because we had no choice, and also because this was an experiment. If something goes wrong with a big pile, we'll have ourselves a mess just like the one the Germans got. How many people would it kill?"

"A good many—you are right about that," Szilard said. "That is why we settled on the Hanford site. But we also do have to consider whether working out in the open would come to the enemy's attention. Winning the war must come first. Before we go to work, we must weigh the risks to city folk against those to the project as a whole from starting up a pile out in the open, so to speak."

Enrico Fermi sighed. "Leo, you presented this view at the meeting where we decided what we would advise General Groves. The vote went against you, nor was it close. Why do you bring up the matter now?"

"Because, whether in the end he accepts it or not, he needs to be aware of it," Szilard answered. Behind glasses, his eyes twinkled. *And to raise a little hell,* Groves guessed.

He said, "We'll need Dr. Larssen's report on the area. I suspect we'll also need to do some serious thinking about how we'll camouflage the pile if we do build there." His smile challenged the eggheads. "Since we have so many brilliant minds here, I'm sure that will be no trouble at all."

A couple of innocents beamed; perhaps their sarcasm detectors were out of commission for the duration. A couple of people with short fuses—Jens Larssen was one—glared at him. Several people looked thoughtful: if he set them a problem, they'd start working on it. He approved of that attitude; it was what he would have done himself.

"Gentlemen, I think that's enough for today," he said.

Major Okamoto seemed out of place in a laboratory, Teerts thought. What the Big Uglies called a lab wasn't impressive to a male of the Race: the equipment was primitive and chaotically arranged, and there wasn't a computer anywhere. One of the Nipponese who wore a white coat manipulated a curious device whose middle moved in and out as if it were a musical instrument.

"Superior sir, what is that thing?" Teerts asked Okamoto, pointing.

"What thing?" Okamoto looked as if he wanted to be interrogating, not interpreting and answering questions. "Oh, that. That's a slide rule. It's faster than calculating by hand."

"Slide rule," Teerts repeated, to fix the term in his memory. "How does it work?"

Okamoto started to answer, then turned and spoke in rapidfire Nipponese to the Big Ugly who was wielding the curious artifact. The scientist spoke directly to Teerts: "It adds and subtracts logarithms—you understand this word?"

"No, superior sir," Teerts admitted. Explanations followed, with considerable backing and filling. Eventually Teerts got the idea. It was, he supposed, clever in an archaic way. "How accurate is this slide rule?" he asked.

"Three significant figures," the Nipponese answered.

Teerts was appalled. The Big Uglies hoped to do serious scientific research and engineering with accuracy to only one part in a thousand? That gave him a whole new reason to hope their effort to harness nuclear energy failed. He didn't want to be anywhere close if it succeeded: it was liable to succeed altogether too well, and blow a big piece of Tokyo into radioactive slag.

The Nipponese added, "For finer calculations, we go back to pen and paper, but pen and paper are slow. Do you understand?"

"Yes, superior sir." Teerts revised his opinion of the Big Uglies' abilities—slightly. Because they had no electronic aids, they did what they could to calculate more quickly. If that meant they lost some accuracy, they were willing to make the trade.

The Race didn't work that way. If they came to a place where they needed two different qualities and had to lose some of one to get some of the other, they generally waited instead, until in the slow passage of time their arts improved to the point where the trade was no longer necessary. Because of that slow, careful evolution, the Race's technology was extremely reliable.

What the Big Uglies called technology was anything but. Not only didn't they seem to believe in fail-safes, he sometimes wondered if they believed in safety at all. Much of Tokyo, which was not a small city even by the standards of the Race, looked to be built from wood and paper. He marveled that it hadn't burnt down a hundred times. Traffic was even

more horrifying than it had been in Harbin, and if a vehicle ran into another one, or over a male who was also using the street, too bad. Along with inaccuracy, the Big Uglies accepted a lot of carnage as the price they had to pay for getting things done.

That thought put Teerts in mind of something he thought he'd heard a couple of the Nipponese scientists discussing. He turned to Major Okamoto. "Excuse me, superior sir, may I ask another question?"

"Ask," Okamoto said with the air of an important male granting a most unimportant underling a boon beyond his station. Despite so many differences between them, in some ways the Race and Big Uglies weren't that far apart.

"Thank you for your generosity, superior sir." Teerts played the inferior role to the hilt, as if he were addressing the fleetlord rather than a rather tubby Tosevite whom he devoutly wished dead. "Did this humble one correctly hear that some other Tosevites also experimenting with explosive metal suffered a mishap?"

Again Okamoto and the scientist held a quick colloquy. The latter said, "Why not tell him? If he is ever in a position to escape, the war will be so badly lost that that will be the least of our worries."

"Very well." Okamoto gave his attention back to Teerts. "Yes, this did happen. The Germans had an atomic pile—what is the phrase?—reach critical mass and get out of control."

Teerts let out a horrified hiss. The Big Uglies didn't just accept risk, they pursued it with insane zeal. "How did this happen?" he asked.

"I am not certain the details are known, especially since the accident killed some of their scientists," Okamoto said. "But those who still live are pressing ahead. We shall not make the mistakes they did. The Americans have succeeded in running a pile without immediately joining their ancestors, and they are sharing some of their methods with us."

"Oh." Teerts wished he had some ginger to chase away the lump of ice that formed in his belly. When the Race came to Tosev 3, the patchwork of tiny empires that dotted the planet's surface had been a matter for jokes. It wasn't funny any more. Back on Home, only one line of experiment at a time would have been pursued. Here, all the competing little empires worked separately. Disunion usually was weakness, but could also prove strength, as now.

Yoshio Nishina came into the room. His alarmingly mobile lips—or so they seemed to Teerts—pulled back so that he showed what was for a Big Ugly a lot of teeth. Teerts had learned that meant he was happy. He spoke with the other scientist and with Major Okamoto. Teerts did his best to follow, but found himself left behind.

Okamoto eventually noticed he'd got lost. "We have had a new success," the interpreter said. "We have bombarded uranium with neutrons and produced the element plutonium. Production is still very slow, but plutonium will be easier to separate from uranium-238 than uranium-235 is."

"Hai," Nishina echoed emphatically. "We prepared uranium hexafluoride gas to use to separate the two isotopes of uranium from each other, but it is so corrosive that we are having an impossible time working with it. But separating plutonium from uranium is a straightforward chemical process."

Major Okamoto had to translate some of that, too. He and Teerts used a mixture of terms from Nipponese and the language of the Race to talk about matters nuclear. Teerts took for granted a whole range of facts the Big Uglies were just uncovering, but though he knew *that* things could be done, he often had no idea as to *how.* There they were ahead of him.

Nishina added, "Once we accumulate enough plutonium, we shall surely be able to assemble a bomb in short order. Then we will meet your people on even terms."

Teerts bowed, which he found a useful way of responding without saying anything. The Nipponese didn't seem to have any idea how destructive nuclear weapons really were. Maybe it was because they'd never had any dropped on them. As he had a dozen times before, Teerts tried to get across to them that nuclear combat wasn't anything to anticipate with relish.

They wouldn't listen, any more than they had those other dozen times. They thought he was just trying to slow down their research (which he was, and which, he knew, compromised his position). Okamoto said, "My country was backward until less than a hundred years ago. We saw then that we had to learn the ways of the Tosevite empires that knew more than we did, or else become their slaves."

Less than two hundred of our years, Teerts thought. Two hundred of his years before, the Race had been just about where it was now, leisurely contemplating the conquest of

Tosev 3. Best wait till all was perfectly ready. What difference could a few years make, one way or the other?

They'd found out.

Okamoto went on, "Less than fifty years ago, our soldiers and sailors beat the Russians, one of the empires that had been far ahead of us. Less than two years ago, our airplanes and ships smashed those of the United States, which had been probably the strongest empire on Tosev 3. By then we were better than they. Do you see where I am leading with this?"

"No, superior sir," Teerts said, though he feared he did.

Major Okamoto drove the point home with what Teerts had come to think of as customary Tosevite brutality: "We do not let anyone keep a lead on us in technology. We will catch up with you, too, and teach you to learn better than to attack us without warning."

Nishina and the other scientist nodded emphatically at that. In the abstract, Teerts didn't suppose he could blame them. Had other starfarers attacked Home, he would have done everything he could to defend it. But war with nuclear weapons was anything but abstract—and if the Nipponese did build and use one, the Race would surely respond in kind, most likely on the biggest city Nippon had. *Right on top of my head, in other words.*

"This is not your concern," Okamoto said when he worried about it out loud. "We will punish them for the wounds they have inflicted on us. Past that, all I need say is that dying for the Emperor is an honor."

He meant the Nipponese emperor, whose line was said to run back more than two thousand years and to be astonishingly ancient on account of that. Teerts was tempted to bitter laughter. Dying for *the* Emperor was an honor, too, but he didn't want to do it any time soon, especially not at the hands of the Race.

Nishina turned toward him. "Let's go back to what we were discussing last week: the best arrangement for the uranium in a pile. I have the Americans' report. I want to know how the Race does the same thing. You are likely to have more efficient procedures."

I should hope so, Teerts thought. "How *do* the Americans do it, superior sir?" he asked as innocently as he could, hoping to get some idea of the Big Uglies' technical prowess.

But the Nipponese, though technically backward, were old

in games of deceit. "You tell us how you do it," Okamoto said. "We do the comparing. The rest is none of your business, and you would be sorry if you made it so."

Teerts bowed once more. That was how the Nipponese apologized. "Yes, superior sir," he said, and told what he knew. Anything was preferable to giving Okamoto the excuse to start acting like an interrogator again.

In games of chance: "You can do as you like," Ottomon said.
"So long as you're paying. The rest is none of your business, but
you would be easier if you made it so."

Back bowed one more. That was how the Mavrosts and
Ottoman "Young or nice," he said, and said what R? I say
something will probably to giving Ottoman he swear to earn
asing him an interfering

☆ XV ☆

Ristin let his mouth hang open, showing off his pointy little
teeth and Lizardy tongue: he was laughing at Sam Yeager.
"You have what?" he said in pretty fluent if accented English.
"Seven days in a week? Twelve inches in a foot? Three feet in
a mile?"

"A yard," Sam corrected.

"I thought something with grass growing in it was a yard,"
Ristin said. "But never mind. How do you remember all these
things? How do you keep from going mad trying to remember?"

"All what you're used to," Yeager said, a little uncomfortably: he remembered trying to turn pecks into bushels into tons
in school. That was one of the reasons he'd signed a minor-
league contract first chance he got—except for banking and his
batting average, he'd never worried about math since. He went
on, "Most places except the United States use the metric system, where everything is ten of this and ten of that." If he
hadn't read science fiction, he wouldn't have known about the
metric system, either.

"Even time?" Ristin asked. "No sixty seconds make a minute or an hour or whatever it is, and twenty-four minutes or
hours make a day?" He sputtered like a derisive steam engine,
then tacked on an emphatic cough to show he really meant it.

"Well, no," Sam admitted. "All that stuff stays the same all
over the world. It's—tradition, that's what it is." He smiled
happily—the Lizards lived and died by tradition.

But Ristin wasn't buying it, not this time. He said, "In our
ancient days, before we were—what is the word? civilized?—
yes, civilized, we had traditions like that, traditions that did

418

harm, not good. We made them work for us or we got rid of them. This was a hundred thousand years ago. We do not miss these bad traditions."

"A hundred thousand years ago," Yeager echoed. He'd gotten the idea that Lizard years weren't as long as the ones people used, but even so . . . "A hundred thousand years ago—fifty thousand years ago, too, come to that— people were just cavemen. Savages, I mean. Nobody knew how to read and write, nobody knew how to grow their own food. Hell, nobody knew anything to speak of."

Ristin's eye turrets moved just a little. Most people wouldn't even have noticed, but Sam had spent more time around Lizards than just about anybody. He knew the alien was thinking something he didn't want to say. He could even make a pretty fair guess about what it was: "As far as you're concerned, we still don't know anything to speak of."

Ristin jerked as if Sam had stuck him with a pin. "How did you know that?"

"A little bird told me," Yeager said, grinning.

"Tell it to the Marines," Ristin retorted. He didn't quite understand what a Marine was, but he had the phrase down pat and used it at the right times. Sam wanted to bust out laughing every time he heard it.

"Shall we go outside?" he asked. "It's a nice day."

"No, it's not. It's cold. It's always cold on this miserable iceball of a world." Ristin relented. "It's not as cold as it was, though. You are right about that." He gave an exaggerated shiver to show how cold it had been. "If you say we must go out, it shall be done."

"I didn't say we had to," Yeager answered. "I just asked if you wanted to."

"Not very much," Ristin said. "Before I was a soldier, I was a male of the city. The—what do you call them?—wide open spaces are not for me. I saw enough of them on the long, long way from Chicago to this place to last me forever."

Sam was amused to hear his own turns of phrase coming out of the mouth of a creature born under the light of another star. It made him feel as if, in some small way, he'd affected the course of history. He said, "Have it your own way, then, even though I don't call some grass on the University of Denver the wide open spaces. Maybe it's just as well; Ullhass

ought to be back in a few minutes, and then I can take both you guys back to your rooms."

"They do not need you to be there any more to translate?" Ristin asked.

"That's what they say." Yeager shrugged. "Professor Fermi hasn't called me this session, so I guess maybe he doesn't. Both of you speak English pretty well now."

"If you are not needed for this, will they take you away from us?" Ristin showed his teeth. "You want me and Ullhass to forget how we speak English? Then they still need you. We do not want you to go. You have been good to us since you catch us all this time ago. We think then that you people hurt us, kill us. You showed us different. We want you to stay."

"Don't worry about me. I'll be okay," Yeager said. A year before, he'd have found absurd the notion that anything a turret-eyed creature with a hissing accent said could touch him. Touched he was, though, and sometimes he had to remind himself how alien Ristin really was. He went on, "I've been a bench warmer before. It's not the end of the world."

"It may be." From sympathetic, Ristin turned serious. "If you humans do build an atomic bomb, it may be. You will use it, and we will use it, and little will be left when all is done."

"We weren't the first ones to use them," Yeager said. "What about Washington and Berlin?"

"Warning shots," Ristin said. "We could choose to use them in a way that did little harm"—he ignored the choked noise that escaped from Sam's throat—"because we had them and you did not. If they turn into just another weapon of war, the planet will be badly hurt."

"But if we don't use them, the Race is probably going to conquer us," Yeager said.

Now Ristin made a noise that reminded Sam of a water heater in desperate need of replacement. "This is—how do you say two things that cannot be true at the same time but are anyhow?"

"A paradox?" Sam suggested after some thought; it wasn't a word he hauled out every day.

"If that is what you say. Paradox," Ristin repeated. "You may lose the war without these bombs, but you may lose it, too, because of them. Is this a paradox?"

"I guess so." Yeager gave the Lizard a hard look. "But if

you think things are like that, how come you and Ullhass have been so much help to the Met Lab?"

"At first, we did not think you Big Uglies could know enough to make a bomb anyhow, so no harm done," Ristin said. Sam knew he was worried, because he didn't often slip and use the Lizard slang name for human beings. He went on, "Soon we found how wrong we were. You know enough and more, and were mostly using us to check the answers you had already. Again, because of this not much harm could come, so we went along."

"Oh," Yeager said. "Nice to know we surprised you."

Ristin's mouth opened and he wagged his head slightly: he was laughing at himself. "This whole planet has been a surprise, and not a good one. From the first time people started shooting at us with rifles and cannon, we knew everything we had believed about Tosev 3 was wrong."

Somebody rapped on the door of the office where Yeager and Ristin were talking. "That'll be Ullhass," Yeager said.

But when the door opened, Barbara came through it. "You are not Ullhass," Ristin said in accusing tones. He let his mouth hang open again to show he'd made a joke.

"You know what?" Sam said. "I'm darn glad she isn't. Hi, hon." He gave her a hug and a peck of a kiss. "I didn't think they were going to let you off work till later."

"One thing about English majors: we do learn how to type," Barbara said. "As long as we don't run out of ribbons, I'll have plenty to do. Or until the baby comes—whichever happens first. They ought to give me a couple of days off for that."

"They'd better," Yeager said, and added the emphatic cough. He laughed at himself. To Ristin, he said, "That's what I get for hanging around with the likes of you."

"What, a civilized language?" Ristin said, laughing his kind of laugh once more. He turned *civilized* into a long hiss.

Despite his accent, he gave as good as he got. Yeager didn't fire back at him. Instead, he asked Barbara, "Why did they let you go early?"

"I turned green, I guess," she answered. "I don't know why they call it morning sickness. It gets me any old time of day it feels like."

"You look okay now," he said.

"I got rid of what ailed me," Barbara said bleakly. "I'm just

glad the plumbing works. If it didn't, somebody—probably me—would have a mess to clean up."

"You're supposed to be eating for two, not throwing up what one has," Sam said.

"If you know a secret way to make lunch stay down, I wish you'd tell me what it is," Barbara answered, now with a snap in her voice. "Everybody says this is supposed to go away after I get further along. I hope to heaven that's true."

Another knock, this one on the frame of the open door. "Here you go, Corporal," said a kid in dungarees with a pistol holster on his belt. "I've brought your pet Lizard back for you." Ullhass walked in and exchanged sibilant greetings with Ristin. The kid, who except for the pistol looked like a college freshman, nodded to Yeager, gave Barbara a quick once-over and obviously decided she was too old for him, nodded again, and trotted off down the hall.

"I am not a pet. I am a male of the Race," Ullhass said with considerable dignity.

Yeager soothed him: "I know, pal. But haven't you noticed that people don't always say exactly what they mean?"

"Yes, I have seen this," Ullhass said. "Because I am a prisoner, I will not tell you what I think of it."

"If you ask me, you just did," Yeager answered. "You were very polite about it, though. Now come on, boys; I'll take you home."

Home for the Lizards was an office converted into an apartment. *Maybe cell block was a better word for it,* Yeager thought: at least, he'd never seen any apartments with stout iron bars across the windows and an armed guard waiting outside the door. But Ristin and Ullhass liked it. Nobody bothered them in there, and the steam radiator let them heat the room to the bake-oven level they enjoyed.

Once they were safely ensconced, Yeager walked Barbara out onto the lawn. Unlike Ristin, she didn't complain it was too cold. All she said was, "I wish I had some cigarettes. Maybe they'd keep me from wanting to toss my cookies."

"Now that you haven't smoked in a while, they'd probably just make you sicker." Sam slipped an arm around Barbara's waist, which was still deliciously slim. "As long as you are off early, you want to go back to the place and . . . ?" He let his voice trail away, but squeezed her a little.

Her answering smile was wan. "I'd love to go back to the

place, but if you don't mind, all I want to do is lie down, maybe take a nap. I'm tired all the time, and my stomach isn't what you call happy right now, either. Is it okay?" She sounded anxious.

"Yeah, it's okay," Yeager answered. "Fifteen years ago, I probably would have fussed and sulked, but I'm a grown-up now. I can wait till tomorrow." *My dick doesn't think for me the way it used to,* he thought, but that wasn't something he could say to a new-wed wife.

Barbara let her hand rest on his. "Thanks, hon."

"First time I ever got thanked for getting old," he said.

She made a face at him. "You can't have it both ways. Are you a grown-up and saying it's okay because it really is, or are you just getting old and saying it's okay because you're all feeble and tired?"

"Ooh." He mimed a wound. When she wanted to, she could get him chasing his tail like nobody's business. He didn't think of himself as dumb (but then, who does?), but he hadn't had formal training in logic and in fencing with words. Trading barbs with ballplayers in his dugout and the ones on the other side of the field wasn't the same thing.

Barbara let out a loud, theatrical groan as she got to the top of the stairs. "That's going to be even less fun when I'm further along," she said. "Maybe we should have looked for a place on the ground floor. Too late to worry about it now, I suppose."

She groaned again, this time with pleasure, when she flopped onto the sofa in the front room. "Wouldn't you be more comfortable on the bed?" Yeager asked.

"Actually, no. I can put my feet up this way." The overstuffed sofa had equally overstuffed arms, so maybe that really was comfortable. Sam shrugged. If Barbara was happy, he was happy, too.

Somebody knocked on the door. "Who's that?" Sam and Barbara said in the same breath. *Why doesn't he go away?* lay beneath the words.

Whoever it was didn't go away, but kept on knocking. Yeager strode over and threw open the door, intending to give a pushy Fuller Brush man a piece of his mind. But it wasn't a Fuller Brush man, it was Jens Larssen. He looked at Sam like a man finding a cockroach in his salad. "I want to talk to my wife," he said.

"She's not your wife any more. We've been through this," Yeager said tiredly, but his hands bunched into fists at his sides. "What do you want to say to her?"

"It's none of your damn business," Jens said, which almost started the fight then and there. But before Yeager quite decided to knock his block off, he added, "But I came to tell her good-bye."

"Where are you going, Jens?" In her stocking feet, Barbara came up behind Sam so quietly that he hadn't heard her.

"Washington State," Larssen answered. "I shouldn't even tell you that much, but I figured you ought to know, in case I don't come back."

"That sounds as if I shouldn't ask when you're going," Barbara said, and Larssen nodded to show she was right. Coolly, she told him, "Good luck, Jens."

He turned red. Because he was so fair, the process was easy to watch. He said, "For all you care, I could be going off to desert to the Lizards."

"I don't think you'd do that," she said, but Larssen was right: she didn't sound as if she much cared. Yeager had all he could do to keep from breaking into a happy grin. Barbara went on, "I told you good luck and I meant it. I don't know what more you want that I can give you."

"You know good and well what I want," Jens said, and Yeager gathered himself again. If Larssen wanted that fight bad enough, he'd get it.

"That I can't give you, I said," Barbara answered.

Jens Larssen glared at her, at Sam, at her again, as if he couldn't decide which of them he wanted to belt more. With a snarl of curses, some in English, others in throaty Norwegian, he stomped off. His furious footfalls thundered on the stairs. He slammed the front door of the apartment building hard enough to rattle windows.

"I wish that hadn't happened," Barbara said. "I wish—oh, what difference does it make what I wish now? If he's going away for a while, that may be the best thing that could happen. We'll get some peace and quiet, and maybe by the time he gets back he'll have figured out he can't do anything about this."

"God, I hope so," Yeager said. "What he's put you through ever since we got here isn't right." He'd been riding the roller coaster himself, but he kept quiet about that. Barbara was the one who'd had the tough time, because she'd been in love with

Jens—*right up to the minute she found out he was still alive,*
Sam thought. Since then, since she'd chosen to stay Barbara
Yeager instead of going back to being Barbara Larssen, Jens
had done his best to act about as unlovable as a human being
could.

Barbara's sigh showed a weariness that had nothing to do
with her being pregnant. "Very strange to think that a year ago
he and I were happy together. I don't think he's the same person any more. He never used to be bitter—but then, he never
used to have much to be bitter about, either. I guess you can't
really tell about someone till you see him when the chips are
down."

"You're probably right." Sam had seen that playing ball—
some guys wanted to be out there with the game on the line,
while others hoped they wouldn't come up or be on the mound
or have the ball hit to them in that kind of spot.

Musingly, Barbara went on, "I suppose that's one of the reasons people write so much about love and war: they're the situations that put the most strain on a person's character, so you
can see it at its best and at its worst."

"Makes sense." Yeager hadn't thought about it in those
terms, but it did make sense to him. He'd seen enough war
close up to know it was more terrifying than exciting, but it remained endlessly interesting to read about. He'd never thought
about why until now. "You put things in a whole new light for
me," he said admiringly.

She looked at him, then reached out and took his hands in
hers. "You've put some things in a new light for me, too, Sam," she murmured.

He felt ten feet tall the rest of the day, and didn't give Jens
Larssen another thought.

"Superior sir, I greet you and welcome you to our fine base
here," Ussmak said to the new landcruiser commander. *My latest,* he thought, and wondered how many more he'd go
through before Tosev 3 was conquered—if it ever was.

That gloomy reflection was a far cry from the spirit of unity
with which he—and all landcruiser males—had gone into this
campaign. Then, they'd thought crews would stay together
through the whole war. They'd trained on that assumption, so
that a male without his crew was an object of pity, both to his
comrades and to himself.

Things hadn't quite worked that way. Ussmak had had two commanders and a gunner killed on him, and another commander and gunner swept away in the wild hunt for ginger lickers. He studied this new male and wondered how long *he'd* last.

The fellow seemed promising enough. He was good-looking and alert, and his neatly applied body paint argued that he didn't have his tongue in a ginger jar (though you never could tell; Ussmak was fastidious about his own paint just to keep his superiors from getting—justifiably—suspicious).

"Landcruiser Driver Ussmak, I am Landcruiser Commander Nejas; you are assigned to my crew," the male said. "Skoob, our gunner, will be along shortly; he must be completing reporting formalities. Both of us will draw heavily on your knowledge, as you have more combat experience than we do."

"I shall help you in any way I can, superior sir," Ussmak said, as he had to. He did his best to sound fulsome, but was not rejoicing inside. He'd hoped he'd get crewed with veterans, but no such luck. As delicately as he could, he added, "The Deutsche are not opponents to take lightly."

"So I am given to understand," Nejas said. "I am also given to understand that this garrison has problems beyond the Deutsche, however. Is it true that the Big Uglies actually spirited a landcruiser out of the vehicle park here?"

"I fear it is, superior sir." Ussmak was embarrassed about that himself, though he'd had nothing to do with it. It showed Drefsab hadn't managed to sweep out all the ginger tasters, and it showed some of them didn't care for anything on Tosev 3 past where their next taste was coming from.

"Disgraceful," Nejas said. "We must have order aboard our own ship before we can hope to put down the Tosevites."

Another male came into the barracks and swiveled his eye turrets every which way, taking the measure of the place. By the time he was through, he looked dismayed. Ussmak understood that; he'd felt the same way the first time he'd inspected his new housing. From everything he'd heard, even the Big Uglies lived better than this these days.

The newcomer might have been Nejas' broodbrother. They both had the same perfect body paint, the same alert stance, and, somehow, the same air of trusting innocence about them, as if they'd just come out of cold sleep and didn't know anything about the way the war against the Big Uglies was (or

rather wasn't) going, about what ginger had done to the landcruiser crews at Besançon, or about any of the many other unpleasant surprises Tosev 3 had given the Race. Ussmak didn't know whether to envy or pity them.

Nejas said, "Driver Ussmak, here is Skoob, the gunner of our landcruiser crew."

Ussmak closely studied Skoob's body paint. It said the other male's rank was about the same as his. Nejas' neutral introduction said the same thing. Ussmak had the feeling he was vastly superior in combat experience: what Nejas had said told him as much, at any rate. On the other hand, Skoob looked to have been together with Nejas for a long time. Ussmak said, "I greet you, superior sir."

Skoob took the deference as nothing less than his due, which irked Ussmak. "I greet you, driver," he said. "May we brew up many Tosevite landcruisers together."

"May it be so." Ussmak wished he had a taste of ginger; better that than the taste of condescension he got from Skoob. But, because his life would depend in no small measure on how well the gunner did his job, he went on politely, "The other half of the bargain involves keeping the Big Uglies from brewing us up."

"Shouldn't be that difficult," Nejas said. "I've studied the technical specifications for all the Tosevites' landcruisers, even the latest ones from the Deutsche. They've improved, yes, but we still handily outclass them."

"Superior sir, in theory there's no doubt you're right," Ussmak said. "The only trouble is—may I speak frankly?"

"Please do," Nejas said, Skoob echoing him a moment later. From that, they were an established crewpair. *I was wise to defer to Skoob after all, even if he is arrogant,* Ussmak thought.

Still, he hoped their willingness to listen meant something. "The trouble with the Big Uglies is, they don't fight the way we'd expect, or the way our simulations prepared us to meet. They're masters at setting ambushes, at using terrain to mask what they're up to, at using feints and minefields to channel our moves into the direction they want, and their intelligence is superb."

"Ours should be better," Skoob said. "We have reconnaissance satellites in place, after all, to see how they move."

"How they move, yes, but not always what the moves mean," Ussmak said. "They're very good at concealing that—

until they hurt us. And we may have satellites, but they have every Big Ugly between here and their positions to let them know where we're going. This isn't like the SSSR, where a lot of the Tosevites preferred us to either the Deutsche or the Russkis. These Big Uglies don't want us, and they wish we'd all disappear."

Nejas' tongue flicked out and then in again, as if at a bad taste. "Helicopter gunships should take the edge off their tactics."

"Superior sir, they're of less use here than they were in the SSSR," Ussmak said. "For one thing, the countryside gives the Deutsche good cover—I said that before. And for another, they've learned to bring antiaircraft artillery well forward. They've hurt our gunships badly enough that the males in charge of them have grown reluctant to commit them to battle except in emergency, and sometimes then, too."

"What good are they to us if they cannot be used?" Skoob asked angrily.

"A good question," Ussmak admitted. "But what good are they to us if they get blown out of the air before they damage the Big Uglies' landcruisers?"

"You are saying we face defeat?" Nejas' voice was silky with danger. Ussmak guessed part of his mission was keeping an eye turret turned for defeatists as well as ginger tasters.

"Superior sir, no, I am not saying that," the driver replied. "I am saying we need to be more wary than we thought we would against the Tosevites."

"More wary, possibly," Nejas said with the air of a male making a concession to another who was inferior mentally as well as in rank. "But, when faced in accord with sound tactical doctrine, I have no doubt the Big Uglies will fall."

Ussmak had had no doubts, either, not until he had a couple of landcruisers wrecked while he was in them. "Superior sir, I say only that the Tosevites are more devious than our tactical doctrine allows for." He held up a hand to keep Nejas from interrupting, then told the story of the mortar attack on the Race's local base and the land mine waiting for the armor as it hurried toward the bridge that would let it get at the raiders.

Nejas did break in: "I have heard of this incident. My impression is that males with their heads in the ginger vial were in large measure responsible for our losing an armored fighting

vehicle. They charged straight ahead without considering possible risks."

"Superior sir, that's true," Ussmak said, recalling just how true it was. "But it's not the point I was trying to make. Had they gone more cautiously, they would have taken an alternate route . . . under which the Big Uglies also had a bomb waiting. We are devious by doctrine and training; they seem to be devious straight from hatchlinghood. They play a deeper game than we do."

That got through, to Skoob if not to Nejas. The gunner said, "How do we protect ourselves against this Tosevite deviousness, then?"

"If I had the whole answer to that, I'd be fleetlord, not a landcruiser driver," Ussmak said, which made both his new crewmales laugh. He went on, "The one thing I will say is that, if a move against the Big Uglies looks easy and obvious, you'll probably find it has claws attached. And the first thing you think of after the obvious move may well be wrong, too. And so may the second one."

"I have it," Skoob said. "The thing to do is post our landcruisers in a circle in the middle of a large, open field—and then make sure the Big Uglies aren't digging under them."

Ussmak let his mouth drop open at that: good to see one of the new males could crack wise, anyhow. Nejas remained serious. Letting his eyes roam around the barracks once more, he said, "This is such a gloomy place, I'd hardly mind getting out of it to fight in a landcruiser. I expect I'd be more comfortable in one than I will here. Does it have anything in its favor?"

"The plumbing is excellent," Ussmak said. Through the newcomers' hisses of surprise, he explained, "The Big Uglies have messier body wastes than we do, so they need more in the way of plumbing. And this whole planet is so wet, they use water more for washing and such than we would dare back on Home. Standing under a decently warm spray is invigorating, even if it does play hob with your body paint."

"Let me at it," Skoob said. "We were on duty down south of here, somewhere in the landmass unit the Tosevites call Africa. It was warm enough there, but the water was in the streams or falling from the sky in sheets; the local Big Uglies didn't know anything about putting it in pipes."

Nejas also made enthusiastic noises. Ussmak said, "Here,

throw your gear on these beds"—they had been Hessef's and Tvenkel's—"and I'll show you what we have."

All three males were luxuriating in the showers when the unit commander, a male named Kassnass, stuck his head into the chamber and said, "All out. We have an operations meeting coming up."

Feeling unjustly deprived, to say nothing of damp, Ussmak and his crewmates listened to Kassnass set forth the newest plan for a push toward Belfort. To the driver, it seemed more of the same. Nejas and Skoob, however, listened as if entranced. From what Ussmak had heard, they wouldn't have faced serious opposition in this Africa place, which was almost as backward technologically as the Race had thought all of Tosev 3 to be. Things were different here.

The unit commander turned one eye turret from the holograms on which the positions of the Deutsche and the Race were marked to the males assembled before him. "A lot of you are new here," he said. "We've had troubles with this garrison, but, by the Emperor"—he and the landcruiser crews cast down their eye turrets—"we've cleaned up most of that now. Our veterans know how devious the Deutsche can be. You newcomers, follow where they lead and stay cautious. If something looks too good to be true, it probably is."

"That's so," Ussmak whispered to Nejas and Skoob. Neither of them responded; he hoped they'd pay more attention to Kassnass than they did to him.

Kassnass went on, "Don't let them lure you into rugged country or the woods; you're vulnerable if you get separated from the other landcruisers in the unit, because then the Big Uglies will concentrate fire on you from several directions at once. Remember, they can afford to lose five or six or ten landcruisers for every one of ours they take out, and they know it, too. We have speed and firepower and armor on our side; they have numbers, trickery, and fanatical courage. We have to use our advantages and minimize theirs."

They're the enemy and they're only Big Uglies, so of course we call their courage fanatical, Ussmak thought. *Saying they're just doing their best to stay alive like anybody else would give them too much credit for sense.*

The males trooped out to the revetments that protected the landcruisers, Ussmak guiding his new commander and gunner. The earth was scored with hits from Tosevite mortars; bomb

fragment scars pocked the sides of buildings. Nejas and Skoob rapidly swiveled their eye turrets. Ussmak guessed they hadn't seen resistance like this from the Big Uglies.

Once in place in the driver's position, he stopped worrying about what they'd seen and what they hadn't. He had a vial of ginger stashed in the landcruiser's fuse box, but he didn't open it up and taste, not now. He wanted to be clear and rational, not berserk, if he saw action unexpectedly soon.

Helicopter gunships took off with whickering roars audible even through the landcruiser's thick armor. They'd reach the target area well before the ground vehicles did. With luck, they'd soften up the Deutsche and not take too much damage themselves. Ussmak knew somebody reckoned the mission important; as he'd told his crewmates, helicopters had grown too scarce and precious to hazard lightly.

Through the streets of Besançon, past the busy-looking buildings with their filigrees of iron railings and balconies. Engineers preceded the landcruisers, to make sure no more explosive surprises awaited. All the same, Ussmak drove buttoned up and regarded every Big Ugly he saw through his vision slits as a potential—no, even a likely—spy. The Deutsche would know they were coming even before the helicopters arrived.

Ussmak breathed easier when his landcruiser rumbled over the bridge across the Doubs and headed for open country. He was also taking the measure of Nejas as a landcruiser commander. The new male might not have seen much action, but he seemed crisp and decisive. Ussmak approved. He hadn't felt part of a proper landcruiser crew since a sniper killed Votal, his first commander. He hadn't realized how much he missed the feeling till he saw some chance of getting it back.

Somewhere off in the trees, a machine gun opened up with harassing fire. A couple of bullets pinged off the landcruiser. Nejas said, "Take no notice of him. He can't hurt us, anyway." Ussmak hissed in delight. He'd seen males with heads abuzz with ginger badly delay a mission by trying to hunt out Tosevite nuisances.

The column rolled north and east. Reports came back that the helicopters had struck hard at the Tosevite landcruisers. Ussmak hoped the reports were right. Knowing the Big Uglies could hurt him put combat in a new light.

A flash, a streak of fire barely seen, a crash that made the landcruiser ring like a bell. "Turret rotate from zero to twenty-

five," Nejas called—urgently, but without the panic or rage or excessive excitement a ginger taster would have used. "Machine-gun fire into those bushes."

"It shall be done, superior sir," Skoob replied. The turret swung through a quarter of a circle, from northeast to northwest. The machine gun yammered. "No way to tell whether I got him, superior sir, but he won't shoot another rocket at one of our landcruisers for a while, I hope."

"Let us hope not," Nejas said. "We're lucky that one hit us on the turret and not in the side of the hull, where the armor is thinner. Briefings say the results can be most unpleasant."

"Briefings don't know the half of it, superior sir," Ussmak said. Vivid inside his head were flames and explosions and unremitting fear, fear that had come flooding back at that impact against the turret and now receded only slowly.

The landcruiser column rolled on. Every now and again, bullets from the bushes struck sparks off armor plate, but the column did not slow. Ussmak kept driving buttoned up. He felt half blind, but didn't care to have one of those rounds clip off the top of his head.

"Why don't they keep those pests from harassing us?" Nejas asked after yet another band of Tosevites sprayed the column with gunfire. "This is *our* territory; if we can't keep raiders from slipping in, we might as well not have conquered it."

"Superior sir, the trouble is that almost all the Tosevites hereabouts favor the raiders and shelter them, and we have an impossible time trying to figure out who really lives in the farms and villages and who doesn't. Identity cards help, but they aren't enough. This is their planet, after all; they know it better than we can hope to."

"It was simpler down in Africa," the landcruiser commander said mournfully. "The Big Uglies there had no weapons that could hurt a landcruiser, and did what they were told once we made a few examples of those who disobeyed."

"We tried that here, too, I've heard," Ussmak said. "This was before I arrived. The trouble was, the Big Uglies had been making examples of one another yet fighting just the same. They ignored the examples we made, the same way they'd ignored their own."

"Mad," Skoob said. Ussmak didn't contradict him.

The landcruisers began passing old battlefields, some still showing the scars of fires set by shot-up landcruisers. The

hulks of destroyed Deutsch armored fighting vehicles still sprawled in death. Some of them were the angular little machines Ussmak had encountered on the plains of the SSSR, but others were the big new ones that could endanger a landcruiser of the Race if well-handled—and the Deutsche handled them well.

Nejas said, "Those are impressive-looking hulks, aren't they? Even holograms don't do them justice. When I first saw one, I wondered why our males hadn't salvaged it; I needed a moment to realize the Big Uglies had made it. I apologize for wondering about some of the things you said, Ussmak. Now I believe you."

Ussmak didn't answer, but felt a burst of pleasure more subtle than the jolt he got from ginger, and perhaps more satisfying as well. It had been too long since a superior acknowledged that the Race's obligations ran down as well as up. His last pair of landcruiser commanders had taken him for granted, as if he were just a component of the machine he drove. Not even being a ginger buddy with Hessef had changed that. No wonder he'd felt isolated, alone, hardly part of the Race at all. Now . . . it was almost as if he'd come out of the eggshell anew.

Smoke rose from the woods up ahead. An artillery shell burst off to one side of the road: the helicopters hadn't routed the Deutsche, then. Ussmak had hoped he'd be going in to mop up. He hadn't really believed it, but he'd hoped.

A cannon belched fire and smoke from behind some bushes. *Wham!* Ussmak felt as if he'd been kicked in the muzzle. But the landcruiser's heavy glacis plate kept the Tosevite shell from penetrating. Without being ordered, Ussmak swung the vehicle in the direction from which the round had come. "I almost fouled my seat," he said. "If the Big Uglies had waited till we passed and shot at the side of our hull—"

Nejas took the time to give him one word: "Yes." Then the landcruiser commander snapped an order to Skoob: "Gunner!" A moment later another single-word command followed: "Sabot!"

Skoob put the automatic loader through its paces. A round of armor-piercing discarding sabot ammunition clattered into the breech of the gun, which closed with a solid thunk. "Up!" the gunner reported.

"Landcruiser, front!" Nejas said, noting the target for Skoob.

"Identified," Skoob answered: he had it in his thermal sight. "Fire!"

"On the way," Skoob said. The report of the landcruiser cannon was less than thunderous inside the hull, but the massive vehicle rocked back from the recoil and a sheet of flame billowed across Ussmak's vision slits. Again the driver knew pleasure almost as intense as ginger gave: this was how a crew was supposed to work together. He hadn't known anything like it since Votal got killed. He'd forgotten how satisfying it could be.

And, just as ginger brought a burst of ecstasy as it shot from the tongue to the brain, so teamwork also had its reward: fire and black smoke boiled up behind the bushes as the Deutsch landcruiser that had tried to impede the progress of the Race paid the price for its temerity. The turret machine gun chattered, mowing down the Big Uglies who'd bailed out of their wrecked vehicle.

"Ahead, driver," Nejas said.

"It shall be done, superior sir," Ussmak said. Along with part of the column of landcruisers, he pushed the machine forward down the road past the ambush the Big Uglies had hoped to set. The rest of the Race's armor went after the Deutsche who'd tried to waylay them. The fight was savage, but didn't last long. When they weren't caught by surprise in disadvantageous positions, the Race's landcruisers remained far superior to those of the foe. They methodically pounded the Deutsche till no more Deutsche were left to pound, then rejoined the rear of the advancing column.

"These Big Uglies are better than any Tosevites I've seen before," Nejas said, "but they don't seem to be anything we can't handle."

Ussmak wondered about that. Had his previous crew, their wits cooked on ginger and their tactics and even their commands full of drug-induced sloppiness, really been so inept? He had trouble believing it, but here was an ambush that would have thrown them into fits, brushed away like any minor annoyance.

On the highway, black smoke rose from burning trucks that formed a barricade across the paved surface. The landcruisers in front of Ussmak's peeled off to the grassy verge to the left to bypass the obstacle. Ussmak was about to swing his handle-

bar controller to follow them when dirt fountained up under one and it slewed sideways to a stop.

He hit the brakes, hard. "Mines!" he shouted.

Concealed Deutsch landcruisers and guns opened up on the crippled vehicle. No armor could take that pounding for long. Blue flames spurted from the engine compartment as a hydrogen line began to burn. Then the landcruiser went up in a ball of fire.

Big Ugly males with satchel charges burst from cover to attack the vehicles that had stopped. Machine guns cut down most of them, but a couple managed to fling the explosives either under the rear of a turret or through an open cupola hatch. The roars from those explosions shook Ussmak even inside his armored eggshell.

"Driver, I apologize," Nejas said. But then, a moment later, he was all business again: "Gunner ... Sabot!" The cannon spoke, and killed a Big Ugly landcruiser. Nejas gave his attention back to Ussmak. "Driver, there's a narrow space of ground on the right between the road and the trees. Take it—if we can get by, we'll put ourselves in the Tosevites' rear."

"Superior sir, that space is probably mined, too," Ussmak said.

"I know," Nejas answered calmly. "The gain we win by passing is worth the risk. Steer as close to the burning vehicles as you can without making our own paint catch fire."

"It shall be done." Ussmak tramped down hard on the accelerator. The sooner the passage was over, the sooner his scales would stop itching with anticipation of the blast that would put his landcruiser out of commission. With a hiss of relief loud as an air brake, he was through and back on the road again. Big Uglies turned a machine gun on his landcruiser. He let his mouth fall open in scornful laughter: that wouldn't do them any good. Nor did it; from the turret, the coaxial machine gun scythed down the Tosevites.

"Keep advancing," Nejas said urgently. "We have more landcruisers behind us, and mechanized infantry combat vehicles as well. If we can deploy in the Big Uglies' rear, we ruin their whole position."

Ussmak stepped on it again. The landcruiser bounded ahead. Speed, sometimes, was as important a weapon as a cannon. He spied a Deutsch landcruiser barreling through the undergrowth,

trying to find a place from which to block the onslaught of the Race's armor.

"Gunner! . . . Sabot!" Nejas shouted—he'd seen it, too. But before Skoob could acknowledge the order and crank the round into the cannon, a streak of fire off to one side took the Big Ugly vehicle in the engine compartment. Red and yellow flames shot up from it, setting the bushes afire.

"Superior, sir, I think the infantry's dismounted from their carriers," Ussmak said. "That was an antilandcruiser rocket."

"You're right," Nejas said, and then, "Steer right, away from the road." Ussmak obeyed, and caught sight of another Tosevite landcruiser. Nejas gave orders to Skoob, the cannon barked, the landcruiser jerked with the recoil . . . and the Deutsch machine brewed up.

Before long, Ussmak saw something he hadn't seen much of since the early days on the endless plains of the SSSR: Big Uglies coming out of their overrun hiding places with arms raised in token of surrender. He hissed in wonder. Just for a moment, the sense of inevitable triumph he'd felt then—before the Race really understood how the Big Uglies could fight—came flooding back. He doubted anything was inevitable any more, but the way to Belfort and, with luck, beyond lay open.

When the landcruiser finally stopped for the evening, he thought, he'd have a taste of ginger to celebrate. Just a small one, of course.

Mutt Daniels tasted the rich black earth just outside Danforth, Illinois. He knew soil; he'd grown up as a dirt farmer, after all. If he hadn't had a talent for baseball, he'd have spent his life eastbound behind the west end of a mule. This was soil as good as he'd ever come across; no wonder the corn grew here in great green waves.

All the same, he wished he weren't making its acquaintance under these circumstances. He tasted it because he lay flat on his belly between the rows, his face jammed into the dirt so he wouldn't get a shell splinter in the eye. With the coming of spring, the Lizards were driving hard. He didn't know how the Army would hold them out of Chicago this time. "Gotta try, though," he muttered, and tasted dirt again.

More shells came in. They lifted Mutt up, slammed him back to the ground like a wrestler putting on a show in a tank

town. Unlike a wrestler, they didn't pull any punches—he'd be black and blue all over.

"Medic!" somebody shouted, not far away. The tone wasn't anguish; surprise was more like it. That meant one of two things: either the wound wasn't bad or the fellow who'd got it didn't realize how bad it was. Mutt had seen that before, men perfectly calm and rational with their guts hanging out and blood soaking into the dark dirt and making it blacker than it already was.

"Medic!" The cry came again, rawer this time. Mutt crawled toward it, tommy gun at the ready; no telling what the tall corn might hide.

But only Lucille Potter crouched by Freddie Laplace when Daniels reached him. She was gently getting him to take his bloodstained hands off his calf. "Oh . . . goodness, Freddie," Mutt said, inhibited in his choice of language by Lucille's presence. He hurt not only for Laplace but for the squad; the little guy was—had been—far and away their best point man.

"Give me a hand, Mutt, if you please," Lucille Potter said. The place where the shell fragment had gone in was a small, neat hole. The exit wound—Mutt gulped. He'd seen worse, but this one wasn't pretty. It looked as if somebody had dug into the back of Laplace's leg with a sharp-edged serving spoon and taken out enough meat to feed a man a pretty good dinner. Lucille was already cutting away the trouser leg so she could work on the wound.

"Careful with that scissors," Laplace said. "You don't want to slice me any worse than I am already." Mutt nodded to himself; if that was what Freddie was worrying about, he didn't know how bad he'd been hit.

"I'll be careful," Lucille answered gently. "We're going to have to get you back to an aid station after Mutt and I bandage you up."

"Sorry, Sarge," Laplace said, still eerily composed. "I don't think I can walk that far."

"Don't worry about it, kid." Mutt was wondering whether Laplace would keep that leg, not about his walking on it. "We'll get you there. You just want to hold still now while Miss Lucille patches you up."

"I'll try, Sarge. It—hurts." Freddie was doing his best to be a good Scout, but it didn't sound easy any more. After a while, the numbness that often came with a wound wore off, and then

you started to realize what had happened to you. That wasn't any fun at all.

Lucille dusted the wound with sulfa powder, then folded the skin over it as best she could. "Too big and ragged to sew up," she murmured to Mutt. "Just lucky it didn't smash the bones up, too. He may walk on it again one of these days." She packed gauze into the hole and put more gauze and tape over it. Then she pointed back toward one of the windmills outside of Danforth. It had a big new Red Cross banner hanging from it. "Let's get him over there."

"Right you are." Mutt stooped with Lucille Potter and got Laplace upright, with one of his arms draped over each of their shoulders. They hauled him along toward the windmill. "Musta been Dutch settled around these parts," Mutt mused. "Not many other folks use those things."

"That's true, but I couldn't tell you for certain," Lucille said. "We're too far upstate for me to know much about the people hereabouts."

"You know more'n I do," Daniels said. Freddie Laplace didn't stick his two cents' worth in. He hung limply in the grasp of the pair who carried him, his head down on his chest. If he was out, it probably counted as a mercy.

"Oh, God, another one," an unshaven medic with a grimy Red Cross armband said when they hauled Freddie into the makeshift aid station in the room at the bottom of the windmill. "We just got Captain Maczek in here—he took one in the chest."

"Shit," Lucille Potter said crisply, which was exactly what Mutt was thinking. The word made his jaw drop just the same.

The medic stared at her, too. She stared back until he lowered his eyes and took charge of Laplace, saying, "We'll patch him up the best way we know how. Looks like you did good emergency work on him." He knuckled his eyes, yawned enormously. "Jesus, I'm tired. Other thing we've got to worry about is getting out of here in case we're overrun. We've been falling back a lot lately."

Mutt almost gave him a hot answer—anybody who bitched about the job the Army was doing could go to hell as far as he was concerned. But the medic had a real worry there, because they probably would have to retreat farther. And medic wasn't exactly a cushy job, either; the Lizards honored the Red

Cross most of the time, but not always—and even if they meant to honor it, their weapons weren't perfect, either.

So, sighing, he tramped away from the windmill and back toward his squad. Lucille Potter followed him. She said, "With the captain down, Mutt, they're liable to give you a platoon and turn you into a lieutenant."

"Yeah, maybe," he said. "If they don't reckon I'm too old." He thought he could do the job; if he'd run a ballclub, he could handle a platoon. But how many guys in their fifties suddenly sprouted bars on their shoulders?

"If this were peacetime, you're right—they would," Lucille said. "But the way things are now, I don't think they'll worry about it—they can't afford to."

"Maybe," Mutt said. "I'll believe it when I see it, though. And the way things are now, like you said, I ain't gonna worry about it one way or the other. The Lizards can shoot me just as well for bein' a lieutenant as for bein' a sergeant."

"You have the proper attitude," Lucille said approvingly.

A compliment from her made Mutt scuff his worn-out Army boot over the ground like a damn schoolkid. "One thing bein' a manager'll teach you, Miss Lucille," he said, "and that's that some things, you can't do nothin' about, if you know what I mean. You don't learn that pretty darn quick, you go crazy."

"Control what you can, know what you can't, and don't worry about it." Lucille nodded. "It's a good way to live."

Before Mutt could answer, a burst of firing came from the front line. "That's Lizard small arms," he said, breaking into a trot and then into a run. "I better get back there." He was afraid they'd need Lucille's talents, too, but he didn't say that, any more than he would have told a pitcher he had a no-hitter going. You didn't want to put the jinx on.

Running through the corn made his heart pound in his throat, partly from exertion and partly for fear he'd blunder in among the Lizards and get himself shot before he even knew they were there. But the sound of the gunfire and a pretty good sense of direction brought him back to the right place. He flopped down in the sweet-smelling dirt, scraped out a bare minimum of a foxhole with his entrenching tool, and started firing short bursts from his tommy gun toward the racket from the Lizards' automatics. Not for the first time, he wished he had a weapon like theirs. As he'd said to Lucille Potter, though, some things you couldn't do anything about.

The Lizards were pushing hard; firing started to come from both flanks as well as straight ahead. "We gotta fall back," Mutt yelled, hating the words. "Dracula, you 'n' me'll stay here to cover the rest. When they're clear, we back up, too."

"Right, Sarge." To show he had the idea, Dracula Szabo squeezed off a burst from his BAR.

When you advanced, if you were smart, you split into groups, one group firing while the other one moved. You had to be even smarter to carry out that fire-and-move routine while you gave ground. What you wanted to do at a time like that was run like hell. It was the worst thing you could do, but you always had a devil of a time making your body believe it.

The guys in Daniels' squad were veterans; they knew what they had to do. As soon as they found decent positions, they hunkered down and started firing again. "Back!" Mutt shouted to Szabo. Shooting as they went, they retreated through the rest of the squad. The Lizards kept pressing. Another couple of rounds of fire-and-fall-back brought the Americans into the town of Danforth.

It had held three or four hundred people before the fighting started; if the locals had any brains, they'd abandoned their trim white and green houses a while ago. A lot of the houses weren't so trim any more, not after artillery and air strikes. The sour odor of old smoke hung in the air.

Mutt pounded on a front door. When nobody answered, he kicked it open and ran inside. One of the windows gave him a good field of fire to the south, the direction from which the Lizards were coming. He crouched down behind it and got ready to give them a warm welcome.

"Mind if I join you?" Lucille Potter's question made him jump and start to point his gun toward the doorway, but he stopped in a hurry and waved her in.

Freight-train noises overhead and a series of loud bursts a few hundred yards south of town made Mutt whoop with delight. "About time our artillery got off the dime," he said. "Feed the Lizards a taste of what they give us."

Before long, northbound roars and whistles balanced those coming from out of the north. "They're awfully quick with counterbattery fire," Lucille said. "Awfully accurate, too."

"Yeah, I know," Daniels said. "But—heck, come to that, all their equipment is better'n ours—artillery and planes and tanks and even the rifles their dogfaces carry. Whenever they want to

bad enough, they can move us out of the way. But it's like they don't want to all the time."

"Unless I miss my guess, they're stretched thin," Lucille Potter answered. "They aren't just fighting in Illinois or fighting against the United States; they're trying to take over the whole world. And the world is a big place. Trying to hold it all down can't be easy for them."

"Lord, I hope it's not." Grateful for talk to help get him through the lull without worrying about what would happen when it stopped, Mutt gave her an admiring glance. "Miss Lucille, you got a good way of lookin' at things." He hesitated, then added, "Matter of fact, you look right good yourself."

"Mutt . . ." Lucille hesitated, too. Finally, with exasperation in her voice, she said, "Is this really the right time or place to be talking about things like that?"

"Far as I can see, you don't think there's ever any right time or place," Mutt said, also with some annoyance. "I ain't no caveman, Miss Lucille, I just—"

The lull ended at that moment: some of the Lizard artillery, instead of going after its American opposite number, started coming in on Danforth. The rising whistle of shells warned Mutt they were going to hit just about on top of him. He threw himself flat even before Lucille yelled "Get down!" and also jammed her face into the floorboards.

The barrage put Daniels in mind of France in 1918. The windows of the house, those that weren't broken already, blew in, scattering broken glass all over the room. A glittering shard dug into the floor and stuck like a spear, maybe six inches from Mutt's nose. He stared at it, cross-eyed.

The shells kept falling, till the blast of each was lost in the collective din. Bricks fell from the chimney and crashed on the roof. Shell fragments punched through the walls of the house as if they were made of cardboard. In spite of his helmet, Mutt felt naked. You could take only so many heavy shellings before something in you started to crack. You didn't want it to happen, but it did. Once you got your quota, you weren't worth a whole lot.

As the pounding went on, Mutt began to think he wasn't far from his own limit. Trying not to go to pieces in front of Lucille Potter helped him ride it out. He glanced away from the broken chunk of glass toward her. She was flattened out

just like him, and didn't look to be having any easier time of it than he was.

Later, he was never sure which one of them rolled toward the other. Whichever it was, they clung to each other tight as they could. In spite of what they'd been talking about when the barrage hit, there was nothing in the least sexual about the embrace—it was more on the order of drowning men grabbing at spars. Mutt had hung on to doughboys the same way when the *Boches* gave American trenches a going-over in the last war.

Because he was a veteran of 1918, he got to his feet in a hurry when the curtain of Lizard shells moved from the southern edge of Danforth, where he was, to the middle and northern parts of town. He knew about walking barrages, and knew soldiers often walked right behind them.

Danforth looked as if it had gone through the meat grinder and then been overcooked since the last time he'd looked out the window. Now most of the houses were in ruins, the ground cratered, and smoke and dust rising everywhere. And through the smoke, sure enough, came the skittering shapes of Lizard infantry.

He aimed and sprayed a long burst through them, fighting to hold the tommy gun's muzzle down. The Lizards went over like tenpins. He wasn't sure how many—if any—he'd hit and how many were just ducking for cover.

Off to one side, the BAR opened up. "Might have known Dracula was too sneaky to kill," Mutt said to nobody in particular. If the Lizards had any brains, they'd try a rush-and-support advance to flush him and Szabo out in the open. He aimed to throw a monkey wrench into that scheme. From a different window, he fired at the bunch he thought would be moving. He caught a couple of them on their feet. They went down, scrambling for cover.

"In the two-reelers, this is about the time the U.S. Cavalry gallops over the horizon," Lucille Potter said as the Lizards started shooting back.

"Right about now, Miss Lucille, I'd be glad to see 'em, and that's a fact," Mutt said. Dracula's BAR was stuttering away, and he had his tommy gun (though he didn't have as many clips as he would have liked), but only a couple of rifles had opened up with them. Rifles didn't add a whole lot as far as firepower went, but they covered places the automatic weapons

couldn't reach and denied the Lizards the cover they'd need to flank out Mutt and Szabo.

And then, just as if it had been a two-reeler, the cavalry did come riding to the rescue. A platoon of Shermans rumbled through the streets of Danforth, a couple of them so fresh off the assembly line that only dust, not paint, covered the bright metal of their armor. Machine guns blazing and cannon firing high explosive, they bore down on the Lizard infantry.

The Lizards didn't have armor with them; they'd been more cautious about committing tanks to action since the Americans started using bazookas. They did have antitank rockets of their own, though, and quickly turned two Shermans into blazing wrecks. Then the tanks shelled the rocketeers, and after that they had the fight pretty much their own way. Most of the Lizards died in place. A few tried to flee and were cut down. A couple came out with their hands up; they'd learned the Americans didn't do anything dreadful to prisoners.

Mutt let out the catamount screech his grandfathers had called the Rebel yell. The house in which he and Lucille Potter sheltered was pretty well ventilated, but the yell echoed in it just the same. He turned around and hugged her. This time he meant business; he kissed her hard and his hands cupped her backside.

As she had when he'd taken out the Lizard tank with her bottle of ether, she let him kiss her but she didn't do anything in the way of kissing back. "What's the matter with you?" he growled. "Don't you like me?"

"I like you fine, Mutt," she answered calmly. "I think you know it, too. You're a good man. But that doesn't mean I want to sleep with you—or with anybody else, if that's what you're wondering."

Over the years, Mutt had done a fair number of things he'd enjoyed at the time but wasn't proud of afterwards. Forcing a woman who said—and obviously meant—she wasn't interested wasn't any of them, though. Frustrated almost past words, he said, "Well, why the . . . dickens not? You're a fine-lookin' lady, it ain't like you don't have any juice in you—"

"That's so," she said, and then looked as if she regretted agreeing.

"By Jesus," Mutt murmured. In a lifetime knocking around the United States, he'd seen and heard about a lot of things nobody who stayed on a Mississippi farm ever dreamt of. "Don't

tell me you're one o' them—what do they call 'em?—lizzies, is that right?"

"It's close enough, anyhow." Lucille's face shut up as tight as a poker player's—especially one who was raising on a busted flush. Poker-faced still, she said, "Okay, Mutt, what if I am?"

She hadn't said she was, not quite, but she didn't deny it, either, only waited to see what he'd say next. He didn't know what the hell to say. He'd run across a few queers in his time, but to find out somebody he liked not just because he wanted to lay her but on account of who she was—and he couldn't be fooled on something like that, not when they'd been living in each other's pockets through months of grinding combat—was one of these creatures almost as alien as a Lizard . . . that was a jolt, no doubt about it.

"I dunno," he said at last. "Reckon I'll keep my mouth shut. Last thing I want to do is cost us a medic as good as you are."

She startled him immensely by leaning forward and kissing him on the cheek. An instant later, she looked contrite. "I'm sorry, Mutt. I don't want to play games with you. But that's one of the kindest things anybody ever said about me. If I'm good at what I do, why should the rest matter?"

Words like *unnatural* and *perverted* flashed across his mind. But he'd had plenty of chances to see that Lucille was good people—somebody you could trust your life to, in the most literal sense of the words.

"I dunno," he repeated, "but it does, somehow." Just then, the Lizards started shelling the front part of Danforth again, probably sowing their little artillery-carried mines to keep the Shermans from pushing farther south anytime soon. Mutt had never imagined he could be relieved to take cover from a bombardment, but right at that moment he was.

Liu Han hated going out to the market. People looked hard at her and muttered behind her back. Nobody had ever done anything to her—the little scaly devils were powerful protectors—but the fear was always there.

Little devils paced through the prison camp marketplace, too. They were smaller than people, but nobody got too close to them; wherever they went, they took open space with them. It was, more often than not, the only open space in the crowded market.

The baby in her belly gave her a kick. Even the loose cotton tunic she wore couldn't disguise her pregnancy any longer. She didn't know what to feel about Bobby Fiore: sadness that he was gone and worry about whether he was all right mingled with shame over the way the scaly devils had forced them together and a different sort of shame at conceiving by a foreign devil.

She let the market din wash over her and take her away from herself. "Cucumbers!"—a fellow pulled a couple of them from a wicker basket tied round his middle. They were long and twisty like snakes. A few feet away another man cried the virtues of his snake meat. "Cabbages!" "Fine purple horseradish!"

"Pork!" The man selling disjointed pieces of pig carcass wore shorts and an open jacket. His shiny brown belly showed through, and looked remarkably like one of the bigger cuts of meat he had on display.

Liu Han hesitated between his stall and the one next to it, which displayed not only chickens but fans made from chicken feathers glued to brightly painted horn frames. "Make up your mind, foolish woman!" somebody screeched at her. She hardly minded; that, at least, was an impersonal insult.

She went up to the man who sold chickens. Before she could say anything, he quietly told her, "Take your business somewhere else. I don't want any money from the running dogs of the imperialist scaly devils."

A Communist, she thought dully. Then anger flared in her. "What if I tell the scaly devils who and what you are?" she snapped.

"You're not the dowager empress, to put me in fear with a word," he retorted. "If you do that, I will find out about it and disappear before they can take me—or if I don't, my family will be looked after. But you—you've been a quiet running dog so far. But if you begin to sing as if you were in the Peking opera, I promise you'll be sorry for it. Now go."

Liu Han went, a stone in her heart. Even buying pork at a good price from the fellow in the stupid jacket didn't ease her spirit. Nor did the cries of the merchants who hawked amber or slippers with upturned toes or tortoiseshell or lace or beaded embroidery or fancy shawls or any of a hundred other different things. The little scaly devils were generous to her: why not, when they wanted to learn from her how a healthy woman

gave birth? For the first time in her life, she could have most of the things she wanted. Contrary to what she'd always believed, that didn't make her happy.

A little boy in rags flashed by. "Running dog!" he squealed at Liu Han, and vanished into the crowd before she got a good look at his face. His mocking laughter was all she could report to the scaly devils, assuming she was foolish enough to bother.

The baby kicked her again. How was he supposed to grow up when everyone down to street urchins scorned his mother so? The easy tears of pregnancy filled her eyes, spilled down her cheeks.

She started back toward the house she'd shared with Bobby Fiore. Though it was a house finer than the one she'd had back in her own village, it seemed as empty as the gleaming metal chamber in which the little scaly devils had imprisoned her on their plane that never came down. The resemblance didn't end there, either. Like that metal chamber, it wasn't a home in any proper sense of the word, but a cage where the little devils kept her while they studied her.

Suddenly she had had all the study she could stand. Maybe no scaly devils waited back at the house right now to take photographs of her and touch her in intimate places and ask her questions that were none of their business and talk among themselves with their hisses and pops and squeaks as if she had no more mind of her own than the *kang* that kept her warm at night. But so what? If they weren't there now, they would be later today or tomorrow or the day after that.

Back in her village, the Kuomintang was strong; even thinking about being a Communist was dangerous, though Communist armies had done more than most in fighting the Japanese. Bobby Fiore hadn't had any use for the Reds, either, but he'd willingly gone with them to take a poke at the scaly devils. She hoped he still lived; even if he was a foreign devil, he was a good man—better to get along with than her Chinese husband had been.

If the Communists had fought the Japanese, if Bobby Fiore had gone with them to raid the little devils . . . they were likely to be doing more against the devils than anyone else. "I owe them too much to let them do whatever they want with me forever," Liu Han muttered.

Instead of going on to her house, she turned around and went back to the stall of the fellow who sold chickens and

chicken-feather fans. He was haggling with a skinny man over the price of a couple of chicken feet. When the skinny man sullenly paid his price and went away, he gave Liu Han an unfriendly look. "What are you doing here? I thought I told you to go away."

"You did," she said, "and I will, if that's what you really want. But if you and your friends"—she did not name them out loud—"are interested in knowing more about the little scaly devils who come to my hut, you'll ask me to stay."

The poultry seller's expression did not change. "You'll have to earn our trust, show you're telling the truth," he said, his voice still hostile. But he did not yell for Liu Han to leave.

"I can do that," she said. "I will."

"Maybe we'll talk, then," he said, and smiled for the first time.

☆ **XVI** ☆

Moishe Russie paced back and forth in his cell. It could have been worse; he could have been in a Nazi prison. They would have had special fun with him because he was a Jew. To the Lizards, he was just another prisoner, to be kept on ice like a bream until they figured out exactly what they wanted to do with him—or to him.

He supposed he should thank God they weren't often in a hurry. They'd interrogated him after he was caught. On the whole, he'd spoken freely. He didn't know many names, so he couldn't incriminate most of the people who'd helped him—and he figured they were smart enough not to stay in any one place too long, either.

The Lizards hadn't bothered questioning him lately. They just held him, fed him (at least as much as he'd been eating while he was free), and left him to fight boredom as best he could. They didn't put prisoners in the cells to either side of his or across from it. Even if they had, neither the Lizard guards nor their Polish and Jewish flunkies allowed much chatter.

The Lizard guards ignored him as long as he didn't cause trouble. The Poles and Jews who served them still thought he was a child molester and a murderer. "I hope they cut your balls off one at a time before they hang you," a Pole said. He'd given up answering back. They didn't believe him, anyhow.

Some blankets, a bucket of water and a tin cup, another bucket for slops—such were his worldly goods. He wished he had a book. He didn't care what it was; he would have devoured a manual on procedures for inspecting light bulbs. As

things were, he stood, he sat, he paced, he yawned. He yawned a lot.

A Polish guard stopped in front of the cell. He shifted the club he carried from right hand to left so he could take a key out of his pocket. "On your feet, you," he growled. "They got more questions for you, or maybe they're just gonna chop you up to see how you got to be the kind of filthy thing you are."

As Russie got up, he remembered there were worse things than boredom. Interrogation was one of them, not so much for what the Lizards did as for the never-ending terror of what they might do.

Crash! Something hit the side of the prison like a bomb. At first, as he staggered and clapped hands to ears, Moishe thought that was just what it was, that the Germans had landed one of their rockets right in the middle of Lodz.

Then another crash came, hard on the heels of the first. It flung the Pole headlong against the bars of Russie's cell. The guard went down, stunned and bleeding from the nose. The key flew from his hand. In a spy story, Moishe thought, it would have had the consideration to land in his cell so he could grab it and escape. Instead, it bounced down the hall, impossibly far out of reach.

Still another crash—this one knocked Russie off his feet and showed daylight through a hole in the far wall. As he curled up into a frightened ball, he wondered what the devil was going on. The Nazis couldn't have fired three rocket bombs so fast . . . could they? Or was it artillery? How could they have brought artillery through Lizard-held territory to shell Lodz?

His ears rang, but not so much that he couldn't hear the nasty chatter of gunfire. A Lizard ran down the hall, carrying one of his kind's wicked little automatic rifles. He fired out through the hole the shells had made in the wall. Whoever was outside returned fire. The Lizard reeled back, red, red blood spurting from several wounds.

Someone—a human—burst in through the hole. Another Lizard came running up. The man cut him down; he had a submachine gun that at close range was as lethal as anything the aliens used. More men rushed in behind the first. One of them shouted, "Russie!"

"Here!" Moishe yelled. He uncoiled and scrambled to his feet, hope suddenly overpowering fright.

The fellow who'd called his name spoke in oddly accented

Yiddish: "Stand back, cousin. I'm going to blow the lock off your door."

Spy stories came in handy after all. Russie pointed to the floor of the corridor. "No need. There's the key. This *mamzer*"—he pointed to the unconscious Pole—"was about to take me away for more questions."

"*Oy.* Wouldn't that have been a balls-up?" The last wasn't in Yiddish; Moishe wasn't sure what language it was in. He had precious little time to wonder; the man grabbed the key, turned it in the lock. He yanked the door open. "Come on. Let's get out of here."

Moishe needed no further urging. Alarms were clanging somewhere, off in the distance; power here seemed to be out. As he ran toward the hole in the outer wall, he asked, "Who are you, anyway?"

"I'm a cousin of yours from England. David Goldfarb's my name. Now cut the talk, will you?"

Moishe obediently cut the talk. Bullets started flying again; he ran even harder than he had before. Behind him, somebody screamed. The medical student part of him wanted to go back and help. The rest made him keep running—out through the hole, out through the open space around the prison, out through a gap in the razor wire, out through the screaming, gaping people in the street.

"There are machine guns on the roof," he gasped. "Why aren't they shooting at us?"

"Snipers," his cousin answered. "Good ones. Shut up. Keep running. We aren't out of this mess yet."

Russie kept running. Then, abruptly, his companions, those who survived, threw away their weapons as they rounded a corner. When they rounded another corner, they stopped running. David Goldfarb grinned. "Now we're just ordinary people—you see?"

"I see," Moishe answered—and, once it was pointed out to him, he did.

"It won't last," said one of the gunmen who'd been with Goldfarb. "They'll turn this town inside out looking for us. Somebody kills a Lizard, they get nasty about that." His teeth showed white through tangled brown beard.

"Which means it's a good idea to get away from the net before they go fishing," Goldfarb said. "Cousin Moishe, we're going to take you back to England."

"Without Rivka and Reuven, I won't go." As soon as the words were out of his mouth, Russie realized how selfish and boorish they sounded. These men had risked their lives to save him; their comrades had died. Who was he to set conditions on what they did? But he didn't apologize, because however selfish what he'd said sounded, he also realized he'd meant it.

He waited for Goldfarb to scream at him, and for the other man—who looked tough enough for anything, no matter how desperate—to pound him senseless and then do whatever he chose. Instead they just kept walking along, easygoing, as if he'd made a remark about the weather. Goldfarb said, "That's taken care of. They'll be waiting for us along the way."

"That's—wonderful," Moishe said dazedly. Too much was happening too fast for him to take it all in. He let his cousin and the other fighter lead him through the streets of Lodz while he tried to adjust to the heady joys of freedom. It made him giddy, as if he'd gulped down a couple of shots of plum brandy on an empty stomach.

A tattered poster with his face on it peered down from a wall. He rubbed his chin. The Lizards hadn't let him use a razor, so his beard was coming back. It wasn't as long as he'd worn it before, but pretty soon he'd look like his pictures again.

"Don't worry about it," Goldfarb said when he fretted out loud. "Once we get you out of town, we'll take care of things like that."

"How will you get me out?" Moishe asked.

"Don't worry about it," Goldfarb repeated.

His nameless friend laughed and said, "Asking a Jew not to worry is like asking the sun not to rise. You can ask all you like, but that doesn't mean you'll get what you ask for." That was apt enough to make Moishe laugh, too.

Before long, they walked into a block of flats. Lodz was already beginning to boil around them. The sound of explosions and gunfire carried a long way; rumor rippled out from around the prison almost as fast as the racket. The two women who went into the building just behind Moishe and his companions were already wondering who had escaped. *If only they knew*, he thought dizzily.

They climbed stairs. The fellow without a name rapped on a door—one, two, one again. "Spy stuff," David Goldfarb mut-

tered. The other fellow poked him in the ribs with an elbow, hard enough to make him give back a pace.

The door opened. "Come in, come in." The skinny little bald man who greeted them looked like a tailor, but tailors did not commonly carry submachine guns. He looked them over, lowered the weapon. "Just you three? Where are the rest?"

"Just us," Goldfarb answered. "A couple scattered off to the other hidey-holes, a couple others won't be going anywhere any more. About what we figured." The casual way he said that chilled Russie. His cousin went on, "We're not hanging around here, either, you know. You have what we need?"

"You need to ask?" With a scornful sniff the bald little man pointed to bundles on the couch. "There—change your clothes."

"Clothes are only part of it," Goldfarb's tough-looking friend said. "The rest is taken care of, too?"

"The rest is taken care of." The bald fellow sniffed again, this time angrily. "We wouldn't be good for much if it weren't, would we?"

"Who knows what we're good for?" the nameless fighter answered, but he shrugged off his shabby wool jacket and started unbuttoning his shirt. Moishe had no jacket to shrug off. He shed with a long sigh of relief the clothes he'd been wearing since he was captured. Their replacements didn't fit as well, but so what? They were clean.

"Good thing the Lizards haven't figured out prison uniforms; they'd have made it harder for us to do a vanishing act with you," Goldfarb said as he, too, changed. His Yiddish was plenty fluent, but full of odd turns of phrase he didn't seem to notice, as if he was using it to express ideas that came first in English. He probably was.

"You're staying here, right, Shmuel?" asked the nondescript little Jew who kept the flat. The nameless fighter, now nameless no more, nodded. So did the little fellow, who turned to Moishe and Goldfarb. He handed each of them a thin rectangle of some shiny stuff, about the size of a playing card. Moishe looked at his. A picture that vaguely resembled him looked back from it. The card gave details of a life he'd never led. The bald little man said, "Don't pull these out unless you have to. With luck, you'll be away before they do a proper job of cordoning off the city."

"And without luck, we'll buy a plot," Goldfarb said, holding

up his own card. "This bloke looks more like Goebbels than he does like me."

"Best we could do," the bald Jew said with a shrug. "That's why you don't want to wave it around unless somebody asks for it. But if somebody does, he probably won't look at it; he'll feed it into a Lizard machine—and it shows you've been authorized for the past two weeks to leave Lodz on a buying trip." He clucked mournfully. "Cost us plenty to pay off a Pole who works for the Lizards to make these for us, and he'd only take the best."

"Gold?" Russie asked.

"Worse," the fellow answered. "Tobacco. Gold at least stays in circulation. Tobacco, you smoke it and it's gone."

"Tobacco." Goldfarb sounded even more mournful than the bald Jew had. "What I wouldn't give for a fag. It's been a bloody long time."

Russie didn't care one way or the other about tobacco. He'd never got the habit, and his medical studies made him pretty sure it wasn't good for you. But it did show how far the underground had gone to rescue him. That warmed him, especially since some people thought him a traitor for broadcasting for the Lizards. He said, "Thank you more than I know how to tell you. I—"

Shmuel cut him off: "Listen, you'd better get out of here. You want to thank us, broadcast from England."

"He's right," David Goldfarb said. "Come on, cousin. Standing around chattering doesn't up the chances of our living to collect an old-age pension—not that we're in serious danger of it at any rate, things being as they are."

Out of the flat, out of the block of flats, they went. As they walked north, they listened to rumors swirl around them: "All the prisoners free—" "The Nazis did it. My aunt saw a man in a German helmet—" "Half the Lizards in Lodz killed, I heard. My wife's brother says—"

"By tomorrow, they'll be saying the Lizards dropped an atomic bomb on this place," Goldfarb remarked dryly.

"Did you hear what he said?" someone going the other way exclaimed. "They used an atomic bomb to blow up the prison." Russie and Goldfarb looked at each other, shook their heads, and started to laugh.

Less than an hour had gone by since the first blast (*piat,* Goldfarb called it, which sounded more Polish than either Yid-

dish or English) hit the prison, but the streets heading out of the ghetto already had checkpoints on them; the Lizards and their human henchmen, Order Service thugs and Polish bullies, had wasted not a moment. Some people took one look and decided they didn't need to leave after all; others queued up to show they had the right.

Moishe started to get into a line that led up to a couple of Poles. Goldfarb pulled him out of it. "No, no," he said loudly. "Come on over here. This line is much shorter."

Of course that line was much shorter: at its head stood three Lizards. Nobody in his right mind wanted to trust his fate to them when human beings were around. Humans might be thugs, but at least they were your own kind of thugs. But Moishe couldn't drag Goldfarb back from the line he'd chosen without making a scene, and he didn't dare do that. Convinced his cousin was leading them to their doom, he took his place in the queue that led up to the aliens.

Sure enough, the wait to get to them was short. A Lizard turned one eye turret toward Russie, the other toward Goldfarb. "You is?" he asked in bad Yiddish. He repeated the question in worse Polish.

"Adam Zilverstajn," Goldfarb answered at once, using the name on his new, forged identity card.

"Felix Kirshbojm," Moishe said more hesitantly.

He waited for alarms to go off, for guns to be pointed and maybe fired. But the Lizard just stuck out his hand and said, "Card." Again, Goldfarb promptly surrendered his. Again, Moishe paused almost long enough to draw suspicion to himself before he handed his over.

The Lizard fed Goldfarb's card into a slot on a square metal box that sat on a table next to him. The box gulped it down as if alive. While still collaborating with the Lizards, Russie had seen enough of their astonishing gadgetry to wonder if perhaps that wasn't so. It spat out Goldfarb's phony card. The Lizard looked at a display—*like a miniature movie screen,* Moishe thought—it held in its hand. "You go on business? You be back—seven days?" it said as it returned the card to Moishe's cousin.

"That's right," Goldfarb agreed.

Then Russie's card went into the machine. He almost broke and ran as the Lizard turned an eye turret toward the handheld display; he was sure words like *traitor* and *escapee* showed up

there. But evidently they didn't, for the Lizard waited till the card came out again, then said, "You go business seven days, too?"

"Yes," Moishe said, remembering not to tack "superior sir" onto the end.

"You both go seven days," the Lizard said. "You go—how to say— together?"

"Yes," Moishe repeated. He wondered if the Lizards were looking for people traveling in groups. But the guard just handed him his card and got ready to receive the next set of people passing through the checkpoint.

David Goldfarb indulged in the luxury of a long, heartfelt "Whew!" as soon as they'd walked a couple of hundred meters past the guard and out of the ghetto.

Whew! did not seem enough to Moishe. *"Gottenyu,"* he said, and then added, "I thought you'd killed us both when you pulled me into that line with the Lizards."

"Oh, that." Now Goldfarb looked jaunty. "No, I knew just what I was doing there."

"You could have fooled me!"

"No, seriously—look at it. If we go through a line with Poles or those Order Service would-be Nazi *shmucks*, they're liable to look at the pictures on the cards—and if they do that, we're dead. No matter what the machine tells them, they'll see we don't really look like the pictures on the cards, or not enough, anyhow. But the Lizards can't tell you from Hedy Lamarr without the machine to do it for them. That's why I wanted them to check us."

Moishe thought it over and found himself nodding. "Cousin," he said admiringly, "you've got *chutzpah.*"

"Never get anywhere with the girls if I didn't," Goldfarb said, grinning. "You ought to see a chap I served with named Jerome Jones—he had crust enough to make a pie, he did."

Watching the way his cousin smiled put Moishe in mind of his mother. But Goldfarb also had an alienness about him that went deeper than the curious expressions peppering his Yiddish. He wasn't automatically wary the way Polish Jews were. "So that's what growing up really free does for you," Moishe murmured.

"What did you say?"

"Never mind. Where will we pick up Rivka and Reuven?" Russie wondered if Goldfarb had lied to him about them just

to get him moving. The man had the gall for it, no two ways about that.

But Goldfarb just asked, "Are you sure you want to find out? Suppose the Lizards catch you but kill me? The less you know, the less they can squeeze out of you."

"They aren't as good at squeezing as you'd think," Moishe said. "They didn't come close to getting everything I know out of me." Nevertheless, he didn't push the question. Mordechai Anielewicz's Jewish fighters had had that don't-ask-if-you-don't-need-to-know rule, too. Which meant . . . "You were—you are—a soldier."

Goldfarb nodded. "RAF, actually, but yes. And you were going to be a doctor, before the Nazis came. My father used to beat me over the head with that; all I ever wanted to do was fiddle around with the insides of radios and such. Made me a valuable piece of goods when the war came, though: they put me into radar training straightaway, and I kept an eye on the Jerries all through the Blitz."

Russie didn't follow all of that; a couple of key words were in English, of which he knew next to nothing. He was content just to walk along for a while, savoring his freedom and daring to think about staying free a while longer. If his accomplished cousin was from the British military, maybe a submarine like the one Anielewicz had sometimes summoned lay waiting off the Polish coast. He started to ask about that, then changed his mind. If he didn't need to know, what was the point in trying to learn?

Goldfarb hurried up Krawiecka Street. He looked nervously to the right and left as he did. Finally, he said, "The sooner we're out of Lodz, the better I'll like it. Outside the ghetto, a Jew really sticks out around here, doesn't he?"

"Well, of course," Moishe answered. Then he realized it wasn't *of course*, not to his cousin. Years of living in the ghetto and before that in a Poland that didn't know how to deal with its three million Jews had made him so used to being the suspected and despised outsider that he took it for granted. Being reminded things weren't like that all over the world came as a distinct shock. "Must be nice, seeming like everyone else," he said wistfully.

"You mean, instead of getting slammed down just for being a Jew?" David Goldfarb said. Russie nodded. His cousin went on, "It is, I suppose. There's a good deal of small stuff left to

fret over: people have a way of taking for granted that you're cheap or not very brave or what have you. But next to what I've seen here, what my folks left—blimey!" That wasn't Yiddish, either, but Moishe had no trouble figuring out what it meant.

If the submarine came, if it whisked him and his family off to England—would he be able to deal with so much freedom? Learning a new language as a grown man wouldn't come easy for him. Thinking thus, for a moment he was almost paralyzed with dread at the prospect of abandoning everything familiar, no matter how unpleasant it could be.

Then he and Goldfarb strode past a couple of Polish housewives chattering on a front porch. The two pretty women stopped talking and stared at them as if they expected the plague to break out in their wake. They kept on staring until the men had gone a block farther down the road.

Moishe sighed. "No, maybe I won't be sorry to get out of here after all."

"I know what you mean," his cousin answered. "Everyone here keeps thinking we're about to make off with the good silver. I shan't be sorry to see the last of that myself. If all goes well, we should have you and yours back in England in a couple of weeks. How does that strike you?"

"The word that comes to mind is *mechaieh*," Moishe said. His cousin grinned and clapped him on the back.

"Hurry up!" Ludmila Gorbunova shouted. "If I don't get the ammunition into my machine gun, how am I supposed to shoot it at the Lizards?"

"Patience, patience," Georg Schultz answered as he checked the belts that fed the guns. "If your weapon jams when you're taking it into action, you might as well not have it. Do things right at first and you won't be sorry later."

Nikifor Sholudenko paused before he passed Schultz another belt. "The Soviet Union is not your country," he observed. "To you it means little if Sukhinichi falls. To us it means Moscow is in danger, just as it was from your fascists in 1941."

"Screw Moscow," Schultz answered, sending the NKVD man a glance redolent of dislike. "If Sukhinichi falls, it probably means I get shot. You think that doesn't matter to me, you're crazy."

"Enough, you two," Ludmila said. She'd been saying that

ever since the German and the security man met. She'd kept them from trying to kill each other on the tramp back to the village where they'd shot it out with the anti-Tolokonnikovites (she still didn't know who Tolokonnikov was or what sort of faction he led), and sometimes kept them from sniping at each other with words for as long as half an hour.

"You be careful up there," Schultz told her, in the not-to-be-denied tones of a field marshal giving orders—or a man who wanted to go to bed with her. She knew which only too well. Wanting to go to bed with her was the only thing on which he and Sholudenko agreed. The air base had needed a political officer when Sholudenko got there, but that wasn't the only reason Sholudenko had arranged to stay on here, even if it was the official one.

In a way, climbing into the cockpit of her new U-2 was a relief. She didn't have to argue with the Lizards or cajole them along; all they wanted to do was kill her. Avoiding that was a lot simpler than the passes from Schultz and Sholudenko she kept ducking.

Schultz spun the prop. He'd been right about one thing—Colonel Karpov had been so glad to have his mechanical talents back that he'd overlooked the little matter of going off without bothering to get permission first. That Schultz had actually returned with Ludmila hadn't hurt there, either.

The *Kukuruznik*'s little five-cylinder radial buzzed into life. It had a note slightly different from the one she'd grown used to, but Schultz insisted that was nothing to worry about. On engines, if not many other places, Ludmila trusted his word.

She released the brake, gave the biplane full throttle, and bounced across the still-muddy steppe till she was airborne. She stayed at treetop height as she flew south and west toward the front. One rule the Red Air Force had learned: the higher you flew against the Lizards, the less likely you were to come back.

The front south of Sukhinichi was not far away, and got closer all the time whether she was in the air or not. With the coming of good weather, the Lizards were on the move again, pushing through German remnants and Soviet troops alike as they advanced on Moscow. By crackling shortwave Stalin had ordered, *"Ni shagu nazad!*—Not one step back!" Giving the order and being strong enough to make sure it was obeyed were not the same thing, worse luck.

The Red Army had brought up all the artillery it could to try to stem the Lizard tide. Ludmila flew past bare-chested young men in khaki trousers serving their guns for all they were worth. When a cannon, or sometimes a whole battery, discharged close by, the blast made the U-2 tremble in the air like a falling leaf caught by a gust of wind. The gun crews waved at her plane, not because they knew she was a woman, but for joy at seeing anything human-built in the air.

Tanks rumbled along the dirt roads. Some of them spewed smoke to help mask their positions. Ludmila hoped that would do some good; going up against Lizard armor was worse than facing the Germans. The Nazis had had better tactics but worse tanks. The Lizards' tanks were better than the T-34s and KV-1s that were the pride of Soviet armored forces, and their tactics weren't bad, either.

A curtain of dust thrown up from shell hits marked the front. Ludmila took a deep breath as she drew near; every second she spent in and around that curtain or on the other side was a second in which she was hideously more likely to die than at any other time. Her bowels clenched and loosened, her bladder felt very full though it wasn't. She noticed none of that, not consciously.

What she did notice was the Soviet line beginning to go to pieces. Along with the dust, smoke from burning tanks filled the air and made her cough and choke when she flew through plumes of it. She didn't see many tanks right at the front to try to halt the Lizards' advance. Most either hunkered down where they were or pulled back toward Sukhinichi.

Ludmila shook her head. That wasn't going to hold things together; it would probably end up costing the vital railway center, too. The Germans had had surprisingly few tanks, but they'd massed them and used them aggressively against Soviet troops. She'd thought the Red Army had grasped the principle. It didn't seem that way, not from what she was seeing here.

Without armor to support them, the Russian infantrymen who huddled in their trenches had to take whatever the Lizards dished out without much hope of hitting back. She wondered how long they would stay and fight, even with NKVD men with submachine guns back of the line to discourage them from doing anything else.

As the soldiers at the guns had, some of the infantry waved as she flew over them. She wondered if the young peasants

and workers down below appreciated the irony of her sallying forth against the Lizards in an aircraft that had seemed obsolete even against the Nazis. She doubted it. All they saw was a plane with red stars on the fuselage and wings. That was enough to give them hope.

Then she was on the other side of the line, the side the Lizards controlled. The ground below her resembled nothing so much as the craters of the moon she'd once examined in a science text: the aliens were advancing through territory that had already been fought over. If that bothered them, they didn't show it.

Pop, pop! A couple of bullets tore through the doped fabric that covered the U-2's wings. Ludmila grunted in dismay. The only thing that would protect her was the aircraft's speed, and the *Kukuruznik* wasn't very fast . . .

Off to one side a couple of kilometers, she glimpsed the fierce tadpole shape of a Lizard helicopter gunship. She heeled the U-2 away from it and dove even closer to the deck. The gunship could fly rings around her and blow her out of the sky, and painful experience had taught that the machine guns she carried wouldn't do anything more than scratch its paint.

Luck stayed with her: the helicopter continued on up toward the front without spying her. And her turn brought her straight toward a convoy of lorries—some Lizard-made, others captured from the Red Army or the Nazis—also moving up with troops and supplies. She never would have spotted them if she hadn't had to evade the gunship.

With a joyful whoop, she thumbed the firing button. The *Kukuruznik* jerked a little as its twin machine guns began to hammer away. Orange lines of tracers showed she was scoring hits. A German-made lorry suddenly became a ball of flame. Ludmila whooped louder.

Lizards bailed out of vehicles and started shooting at her. She got out of there as fast as she could.

After a good strafing run like that, she could have flown back to her base and truthfully reported success. But, like most good combat pilots, she lusted for more. She buzzed on, deeper into Lizard-held territory.

Back of the line, fire came her way less often. The Lizards seemed less alert, or maybe just hadn't counted on many human planes getting through. She wished she were flying a Pe-2 bomber with a couple of thousand kilos of high explosive

rather than a wheezing trainer that had had a brace of machine guns strapped onto it. But then, the Lizards shot down Pe-2s with effortless ease.

She spied more lorries—human-made ones, stopped to fuel up. She raked them with machine-gun fire, and felt a mix of terror and crazy exhilaration when flames shot so high that she had to pull up sharply to keep from flying straight through them.

The machine guns had performed without a jam. They usually did, so she didn't know how much Georg Schultz's relentless perfectionism had to do with that, but it couldn't have hurt. She swung the U-2 back toward the north; she was low on fuel and she'd used a lot of ammunition. She was willing to bet Schultz had spent the time she was flying methodically filling belts with bullets.

Coming back, she was fired on not only by the Lizards but also by jittery Soviet troops convinced anything in the air, especially if it flew over them from the other side of the line, had to be dangerous. But the *Kukuruznik*, not least because it was so simple, was a rugged machine: unless you hit the engine or the pilot or were lucky enough to snap a control wire with a bullet, you wouldn't hurt it much.

Ludmila flew over advancing Lizard tanks. They were across a small river whose line the Soviets had been holding when she'd gone out on her attack run an hour or so before. She bit her lip. It was as she'd feared: in spite of everything the Red Army could do, in spite of her own pinprick successes inside Lizard-held territory, the local position was deteriorating. Sukhinichi would fall, and after that only Kaluga stood between the Lizards and Moscow.

The U-2 bounced to a stop. A couple of groundcrew men lugged jerricans of petrol toward the airplane, squelching through mud that was still pretty thick. Behind them came Georg Schultz, ammunition belts draped across his chest so that he resembled nothing so much as a Cossack bandit. He took a chunk of black bread from a pocket of the German infantry blouse he still wore, held it out to Ludmila. *"Khleb,"* he said, one Russian word he'd mastered.

"Spasebo," she answered, and took a bite. Right in back of Schultz slogged Nikifor Sholudenko. Maybe he didn't want the German spending even a moment alone with her because they were rivals, or maybe just because he was NKVD. Either way,

Ludmila was glad to see him: he was someone to whom she could report, which meant she wouldn't have to hunt up Colonel Karpov.

Or could she? The air base looked like an anthill somebody had kicked, with people running every which way to no apparent purpose. Before she could ask any questions, Schultz spread his arms wide and exclaimed, "*Bolshoye drap*—big skedaddle." That was, ironically, the same term the Russians had used to describe the flight of bureaucrats from Moscow when it looked as if the Germans would capture the capital in October 1941. Ludmila wondered if Schultz was using it with malice aforethought.

That, however, mattered relatively little. "Skedaddle?" Ludmila said in dismay. "We're pulling out of here?"

"We are indeed," Nikifor Sholudenko said. "Orders are to shorten, consolidate, and strengthen the defensive front." He didn't bother to add that that was a euphemism for *retreat*, just as *severe fighting* meant *a battle we're losing*. Ludmila knew that as well as he did. So, very likely, did Georg Schultz.

Ludmila said, "May I fly another mission before we pull back? I stung them the last time; they hardly had any air defenses set up."

"Who can defend against one of these things?" Schultz said in German, setting an affectionate hand on the U-2's cloth-covered fuselage. "They peep in through the keyhole when you're taking a leak."

Sholudenko snorted at that, but to Ludmila he shook his head. "Colonel Karpov's orders are that we leave now. They came in just after you took off; if you hadn't been airborne, we probably would have already cleared out."

"Where are we going?" Ludmila asked.

The NKVD man pulled out a scrap of paper, glanced down at it. "They're setting up a new base at Collective Farm 139, bearing 43, distance fifty-two kilometers."

Ludmila translated distance and bearing into a dot on the map. "That's right outside Kaluga," she said unhappily.

"Just west of it, as a matter of fact," Sholudenko agreed. "We're going to fight the Lizards house by house and street by street in Sukhinichi to delay them while we prepare new positions between Sukhinichi and Kaluga. Then, at need, we will fight house by house in Kaluga. I hope the need does not arise."

He stopped there; not even an NKVD man, answerable to no one at the air base but himself and perhaps, for something particularly heinous, Colonel Karpov, wanted to say too much. But Ludmila had no trouble reading between the lines. He didn't expect whatever makeshift line the Red Army would set up north of Sukhinichi to hold the Lizards. He didn't expect to hold them at Kaluga, either, not by the sound of what he said. And between Kaluga and Moscow lay only plains and forest—no more cities in which to slow down and maul the invaders.

"We're in trouble," Georg Schultz said in German. Ludmila wondered at his naïveté in speaking so freely: the Nazis might not have the NKVD, but they certainly did have the *Gestapo*. Didn't Schultz know you weren't supposed to open your mouth where people you couldn't trust were listening?

Sholudenko gave him an odd look. "The Soviet Union is in trouble," he conceded. "No more so than Germany, however, and no more so than any of the rest of the world."

Before Schultz could answer, Colonel Karpov came running up the airstrip, shouting, "Get out! Get out! Lizard armor has broken through west of Sukhinichi, and they're heading this way. We have maybe an hour to get clear—maybe not, too. Get out!"

Wearily, Ludmila climbed back into the little *Kukuruznik*. Groundcrew men turned the plane into the wind; Georg Schultz spun the two-bladed wooden prop. The engine, reliable even if puny, caught at once. The biplane rattled down the runway and hopped into the air. Ludmila swung it northeast, toward Collective Farm 139.

Schultz, Sholudenko, and Karpov stood on the ground waving to her. She waved back, wondering if she would ever see them again. Suddenly, instead of being the one who flew dangerous combat missions, she was the one who could escape the oncoming Lizards. If they were only an hour away, they had a good chance of overrunning the humans trying to escape from the air base.

She checked her airspeed indicator and her watch. At the U-2's piddling turn of speed, Collective Farm 139 was about half an hour away. She hoped she'd be able to spot the new base, and then hoped she wouldn't: if the *maskirovka* was bad, the Lizards would notice it.

Of course, if the *maskirovka* was good, she'd fly around and

around and probably have to set down in the wrong place because she was running out of fuel. Airspeed indicator, watch, and compass were not the most sophisticated navigational instruments around, but they were what she had.

A Lizard warplane shot by, far overhead. The howl of its jet engines put her in mind of wolves deep in the forest baying at the moon. She patted the fabric sides of her U-2. It was also an effective combat aircraft, no matter how puny and absurd alongside the jet. It had seemed puny and absurd alongside an Me-109, too.

She was still flying along when the Lizard plane came shrieking back on the reciprocal to its former course. She wasn't even done shifting bases, and it had already finished its mission of destruction.

Speed. The word tolled in Ludmila's mind, a mournful bell. The Lizards had more of it at their disposal than people did: their tanks rolled faster, their planes flew faster. Because of that, they held the initiative, at least while the weather was good. Fighting them was like fighting the Germans, only worse. Nobody ever won a war by reacting to what the other fellow did.

A bullet cracked past her head, rudely slaughtering that line of thought. She shook her fist at the ground, not that it would do any good. The stupid *muzhik* down there was no doubt convinced that anything so clever as an airplane had to belong to the enemy. Had Stalin had the chance to continue peacefully building socialism in the Soviet Union, such ignorance might have become a thing of the past in a generation's time. As it was . . .

A peasant working in a newly sown field of barley took off his jacket and waved it as she buzzed over him. The jacket had a red lining. Ludmila started to fly on by, then exclaimed, "*Bozhemoi*, I'm an idiot!" The Red Air Force wouldn't send up a flare, literally or figuratively, to let her know exactly where the new base was. If they did, the Lizards would make sure said base didn't last long. She could credit good navigation—or more likely good luck—for finding her target at all.

She wheeled the *Kukuruznik* through the sky. As she bled off speed and what little altitude she had, she spotted marks that cut across plowed furrows. They told her where planes

were landing and taking off. She brought the U-2 around one more time, landed it in more or less the same place.

As if by magic, men appeared where she had been willing to swear only grain grew. They sprinted toward the biplane, bawling, "Out! Out! Out!"

Ludmila scrambled out. As her booted feet dug into the still-muddy ground, she began, "Senior Lieutenant Gorbunova reporting as—"

"Tell us all that shit later," said one of the fellows who was hauling the U-2 away toward concealment, though of what sort Ludmila couldn't imagine. He turned to a comrade. "Tolya, get her under cover, too."

Tolya needed a shave and smelled as if he hadn't seen soap and water in a long time. Ludmila didn't hold it against him; she was probably just as rank, but didn't notice it on herself any longer. "Come on, Comrade Pilot," Tolya said. If he noticed she was a woman, or cared, he didn't let on.

Some of his friends unrolled a broad stretch of matting that so cunningly mimicked the surrounding ground, she hadn't even noticed it (she was glad she hadn't tried taxiing across it). It covered a trench wide and deep enough to swallow an airplane. As soon as the *Kukuruznik* vanished into the trench, the mats went back on.

Tolya led Ludmila toward some battered buildings perhaps half a kilometer away. "We don't have to do anything special for people," he explained, "not with the stuff for the *kolkhozniki* still standing."

"I've flown from bases where people lived underground, too," Ludmila said.

"We didn't have much digging time here," her guide said, "and machines come first."

Somebody unrolled another strip of matting and ducked under it carrying a lighted torch. "Is he starting a fire down there?" Ludmila asked. Tolya nodded. "Why?" she said.

"More *maskirovka*," he answered. "We found out the Lizards like to paste things that are warm. We don't know how they spot them, but they do. If we give them some they can't really hurt—"

"They waste munitions." Ludmila nodded. "*Ochen khorosho*—very good."

Even though they were alone in the middle of a field, Tolya looked around and lowered his voice before he spoke again:

"Comrade Pilot, you've flown over the front south of Sukhinichi? How did it look to you?"

It was coming to pieces, Ludmila thought. But she didn't want to say that, not to someone she didn't know or trust: who knew what he might be under his baggy, peasant-style tunic and trousers? Yet she didn't want to lie to him, either. Carefully, she replied, "Let me put it this way: I'm glad you don't have much in the way of heavy, permanent installations here."

"Huh?" Tolya's brow furrowed. Then he grunted. "Oh. I see. We may have to move in a hurry, is that it?"

Ludmila didn't answer; she just kept walking toward what was left of the collective farm's buildings. Beside her, Tolya grunted again and asked no more questions; he'd understood her not-answer exactly as she meant it.

Alone on a bicycle with a pack on his back and a rifle slung over his shoulder: Jens Larssen had spent a lot of time and covered a lot of miles that way. Ever since his Plymouth gave up the ghost back in Ohio, he'd gone to Chicago and then all around Denver on two wheels rather than four.

This, though, was different. For one thing, he'd been on flat ground in the Midwest, not slogging his way up through a gap in the Continental Divide. More important, back then he'd had a goal: he'd been riding toward the Met Lab and toward Barbara. Now he was running away, and he knew it.

"Hanford," he said under his breath. As far as he could tell, they all just wanted an excuse to get him out of their hair. "You'd think I was a goddamn albatross or something."

All right, so he'd made it real clear he wasn't happy about his wife shacking up with this Yeager bum. The way everybody acted, it was his fault, not hers. She'd run out on him, and she got the sympathy when he tried to put some sense into her thick head.

"It just isn't right," he muttered. "She bailed out, and I'm the one who's stuck in the plane wreck." He knew his work had suffered since the Met Lab crew got to Denver. That was another reason everybody was glad to get him out of town, on a bike if not on a rail. But how was he supposed to keep his eyes on calculations or oscilloscope readings if they were really seeing Barbara naked and laughing, her legs wrapped around that stinking corporal as he bucked above her?

He reached back over his right shoulder with his left hand

to touch the hard, upthrust barrel of the Springfield. He'd thought about lying in wait for Yeager, ending those terrible visions for good. But he had enough sense left to realize he'd probably get caught and, even if he didn't, blowing Yeager's head off, however delightful that might be, wouldn't bring Barbara back to him.

"It's a good thing I'm not stupid," he told the asphalt of US 40 under his wheels. "I'd be in a whole heap of trouble if I were."

He looked back over his shoulder. He was thirty miles out of Denver now, and had gained a couple of thousand feet; he could see not only the city, but the plain beyond it that sloped almost imperceptibly downward toward the Mississippi a long way away. Down in the flatlands, the Lizards held sway. If he hadn't gone away from the city heading west, he might have left heading east.

Looked at rationally, that made as little sense as ambushing Sam Yeager, and Jens knew it. Knowing and caring were two different critters. Instead of just getting his own back from Yeager, selling out the Met Lab project gave him vengeance wholesale rather than retail, paying back all at once everybody who'd done him wrong. The idea had a horrid fascination to it, the way the sharp edge of a broken tooth irresistibly lures the tongue. *Feel*, it seems to say. *This isn't the way it should be, but feel it anyhow.*

Pushing the bike along at 7,500 feet took more out of him than making it go through the flat farming country of Indiana. He stopped every so often for a blow, and just to admire the scenery ahead. Now the Rockies loomed in every direction except right behind him. In the clear, thin air, the snowcapped peaks and the deep green cloak of pine forest below them looked close enough to reach out and touch. The sky was a deep, deep blue, with a texture to it he'd never known before.

But for the sound of his own slightly winded breathing and the rustle of bushes in the breeze, everything was quiet: no buzz and wheeze of cars, no growling rumble of trucks. Jens had passed a patient convoy of horse-drawn wagons four or five miles back, and another coming into Denver just as he was leaving, but that was about it. He knew the Lizard-induced dearth of traffic meant the war effort was going to hell, but it sure worked wonders for the tourist business.

"Except there's no tourist business any more, either," he

said. The habit of talking to himself when he was alone on his bike had come back in a hurry.

He swung his feet back up onto the pedals, got rolling again. In a couple of minutes, he came up to a sign: IDAHO SPRINGS, 2 MILES. That made him lift one hand from the handlebars to scratch his head. "Idaho Springs?" he muttered. "This was still Colorado, last I looked."

A few hundred yards ahead another sign said, HOT SPRINGS BATHING, 50¢. VAPOR CAVES, ONLY $1. That explained the springs, but left him still wondering how a chunk of Idaho had shifted south and east.

The town might have had a thousand people before the Lizards came. It straggled along a narrow canyon. A lot of the houses looked deserted, and the doors to several shops hung open. Jens had seen a lot of towns like that. But if people had fled from everyplace, where had they all gone? His reluctant conclusion was that a lot of them were dead.

Not everybody was gone from Idaho Springs. A bald man in black overalls came out of a dry-goods store and waved to Larssen. He waved back, slowed to a stop. "Where you from, mister?" the local asked. "Where you goin'?"

Jens thought about replying that it was none of Nosy Parker's business, but his eye happened to catch a bit of motion in a second-story window that the breeze couldn't have caused: a curtain shifted slightly, perhaps from a rifle barrel stirring behind it. The folk of Idaho Springs were ready to take care of themselves.

And so, instead of getting smart, Jens said carefully, "I'm out of Denver, heading west on Army business. I can show you a letter of authorization, if you'd like." The letter wasn't signed by Groves; the detested Colonel Hexham's John Hancock was on it instead. Larssen had been tempted to wipe his backside with it; now he was glad he'd refrained.

Black Overalls shook his head. "Nah, you don't need to bother. If you was one of them bad guys, don't reckon you'd be so eager to show it off." The upstairs curtain twitched again as the not-quite-unseen watcher drew back. The bald guy went on, "Anything we can do for you here?"

Jens' stomach rumbled. He said, "I wouldn't turn down some food—or even a drink, if you folks have some hooch you can spare. If you don't, don't put yourselves out on ac-

count of me," he added hastily; in these times of scarcity, people got mighty touchy about sharing things like liquor.

But the fellow in black overalls just grinned. "We can spare a bit, I expect. We'd always stock up for the folks who'd come to visit the springs, you know, and there ain't been many o' them lately. You just want to ride on up ahead for another long block to the First Street Cafe. Tell Mary there Harvey says it's okay to get you fed."

"Thanks, uh, Harvey." Jens started the bicycle rolling again. His back itched as he rode past the window where he'd seen the curtain move, but nothing at all stirred there now. If he'd satisfied Harvey, he must have satisfied the local hired gun, too.

The Idaho Springs city hall was an adobe building with a couple of big millstones in the yard in front of it. A sign identified them as coming from an old Mexican *arastra*, a mule-powered gadget that ground ore as an ordinary mill ground grain. Colorado had more history than Jens had thought about.

The First Street Cafe, by contrast, looked like a bank. It had its name spelled out in gold Old English letters across a plate glass window. Jens stopped in front of it, let down the kickstand on his bike. He didn't think bike rustlers would be as big a worry here as they were in Denver. All the same, he resolved not to eat with his back to the street.

He opened the door to the café. A bell jingled above his head. As his eyes adjusted to the gloom inside, he saw the place was empty. That amazed him, because a wonderful smell filled the air. From the room in back, a woman's voice called, "That you, Jack?"

"Uh, no," Jens said. "I'm a stranger here. Harvey was kind enough to say I could beg a meal from you, if you're Mary."

Brief silence fell, then, "Yeah, I'm Mary. Just a second, pal; I'll be right with you." He heard footsteps back there, then she came out behind the counter and looked him over, hands on hips. Voice slightly mocking, she went on, "So Harvey says I'm supposed to feed you, huh? You're skinny enough you could do with some feeding, that's for sure. Chicken stew do you? It had better—it's what I've got."

"Chicken stew would be swell, thank you." That was what was making the wonderful smell, Jens realized.

"Okay. Comin' right up. You can sit anywhere; we ain't

what you'd call crowded." With a laugh, Mary turned and disappeared again.

Jens chose a table that let him keep an eye on his bicycle. Plates clattered and silverware jingled in the back room; Mary softly sang something to herself that, if he recognized the tune, was a scandalous ditty he'd last heard at the Lowry Field BOQ.

From a lot of women, such lyrics would have scandalized him. Somehow they seemed to suit this Mary. On thirty seconds' acquaintance, she reminded him of Sal, the brassy waitress with whom, among many others, the Lizards had cooped him up in a church in Fiat, Indiana. Her hair was midnight-black instead of Sal's peroxided yellow, and they didn't look like each other, either, but he thought he saw in Mary a lot of the same take-it-or-leave-it toughness Sal had shown.

He still wished he'd laid Sal—especially considering the way everything else had turned out. It could have happened, but he'd figured Barbara was waiting for him, so he'd stayed good. *Shows how much I know,* he thought bitterly.

"Here you go, pal." Mary set knife and fork and a plate in front of him: falling-off-the-bone chicken in thick gravy, with dumplings and carrots. The smell alone was enough to put ten pounds on him.

He tasted. The taste was better than the smell. He hadn't thought it could be. He made a wordless, full-mouth noise of bliss.

"Glad you like it," Mary said, sounding amused. A moment later she added, "Listen, it's about dinnertime, and like I said, we ain't exactly packed. You mind if I bring out a plate and join you?"

"Please," he said. "Why should I mind? This is your place and your terrific food—" He thought he was going to say more, but took another bite instead.

"Be right with you, then." She went back to get some stew of her own. Jens twisted his head to watch the way she walked. *Like a woman,* he thought: *what a surprise.* Her long gray wool skirt didn't show much of her legs, but she had nice ankles. He wondered if she was older or younger than he. Close, either way.

She came back with not only a plate, but two glass beer mugs filled with a deep amber fluid. "You look like you could use one of these," she said as she sat down across the table

from him. "Just homebrew, but it's not bad. Joe Simpson who makes it, he used to work down at the Coors brewery in Golden, so he knows what he's doin'."

Jens gulped at the beer. It wasn't Coors—he'd drunk that in Denver—but it was a long way from bad. "Oh, Lord," he said ecstatically. "Will you marry me?"

She paused with a forkful of dumpling halfway to her mouth, gave him a long, appraising stare. He felt himself turning red; he'd just meant it for a joke. But maybe Mary liked what she saw. With a slightly wintry smile, she answered, "I dunno, but I'll tell you this right now—it's the best damn offer I had today, and that's a fact. Hell, if you was to tempt me with a cigarette, who knows what I might up and do?"

"I wish I could," he said, regretfully for two different reasons. "I haven't seen one in months."

"Yeah, me neither." She let out a long, mournful sigh. "Don't even know why I bothered to ask. If you had smokes, I'd've smelled 'em on you minute you walked in." She took another bite, then said, "Mind if I ask you what your name is?"

He told her, and discovered in turn that her last name was Cooley. *Black Irish,* he thought. That fit; her eyes were very, very blue and her skin even fairer than his, transparent white rather than pink.

She might not have been able to smell tobacco smoke on him, but he was sure she could smell sweat—getting the bike here from Denver had been work, no two ways about it. It didn't worry him the way it would have a year before. He could smell her, too, and it was amazing how fast you got used to bodies that weren't as clean as they might have been. If most everybody needed a bath, things evened out.

He finished the stew, scraped up gravy with his fork until the plate was damn near clean again. He didn't want to up and leave; he felt full and happy and more nearly homey than he had since he'd found out he didn't really have a home any more. To give himself an excuse to stay a while longer, he pointed to the mug and said, "Could I have another one of those, please? That one hit the spot, but it didn't quite fill it up."

"Sure thing, pal. I'll get me one, too." She headed for the back room again. This time, Jens thought she might have no-

ticed him eyeing her as she walked, but if she had, she didn't let on. She soon came back with the beer.

"Thanks," he said as she sat down once more. The scritch of the chair legs on the bricks of the café floor was almost the only sound. Jens asked, "How do you keep this place open with no customers?"

"What do you mean, no customers? You're here, aren't you?" Her face was full of impudent amusement. "But yeah, it's pretty quiet at dinnertime. Supper, now, folks come for supper. And I reckon the Army would shoot me if I closed up shop; I feed a lot of their people goin' in and out of Denver. But then, you said you're one of them, right?"

"Yeah." Jens took another pull at his beer. He eyed her over the top of the mug. "Bet you have to keep a shotgun by the till to keep some of the Army guys from getting too friendly."

Mary laughed. "Spilling something hot on 'em mostly does the trick." She drank, too. " 'Course, the other thing is, there's passes and then there's passes."

Was that an invitation? It sure sounded like one. Jens hesitated, not least because the memory of his ignominious failure with that chippie back in Denver still stung. If he couldn't get it up twice running, what was he supposed to do? Ride his bike off a cliff? He'd have plenty of chances, pedaling along US 40 through the mountains. Sometimes, though, leading with your chin was also a test of manhood. He stretched out his foot under the table. As if by accident, the side of his leg brushed against hers.

If she'd pulled away, he would have risen from the table feeling foolish, paid whatever she asked for the stew and the beer, and headed west. As it was, she stretched, too, slowly and languorously. He wondered if that sinuous motion came naturally or if she'd seen it in the movies and practiced. Either way, it made his heart thump like a drum.

He got up, walked around the table, and went down on one knee beside her. It was a position in which he could have proposed, although he had propositioning more in mind. He got the idea, though, that she didn't want a lot of talk.

When he leaned forward and kissed her, she grabbed his head and pulled him to her hard enough to mash his lips against her teeth. He broke away for a moment, partly to breathe and partly to let his mouth glide to her earlobe and

then down the smooth side of her neck. She arched her back like a cat and sighed deep in her throat.

His hand slid under her skirt. Her legs parted for him. He was gently rubbing at the crotch of her cotton panties when he remembered that plate-glass window. Idaho Springs wasn't much of a town, but anybody walking by could see in. Hell, anybody walking by could *walk* in. "Is there someplace we can go?" he asked hoarsely.

That seemed to remind her of the big window, too. "Come on back to the kitchen with me," she said. He didn't want to take his hand away, but she couldn't stand up unless he did.

She paused only a moment, to scoop up an old Army blanket from behind the counter on which the cash register sat. The stove in the kitchen, a coal-burner burning wood these days, made the place hot, but Jens didn't care. He was plenty hot himself.

He unbuttoned the buttons that ran down the back of Mary's white blouse and unhooked her brassiere. Her breasts filled his hands. He squeezed, not too hard. She shivered in his arms. He fumbled at the button that held her skirt closed, undid it, and yanked down the zipper beneath. The skirt made a puddle on the floor. She stepped out of it, kicked off her shoes, and pulled down her panties. Her pubic hair was startlingly dark against her pale, pale skin.

She spread the blanket on the floor while he tried not to tear his clothes getting out of them in excess haste. Everything would be all right this time—he was sure of it.

Everything was better than all right. She moaned and gasped and called his name and squeezed him with those wonderful contractions of the inner muscles so he exploded in the same instant she did. "Lord!" he said, more an exclamation of sincere respect than a prayer.

She smiled up at him, her face—probably like his—still a little slack with pleasure. "That was good," she said. "And you're a gentleman, you know that?"

"How do you mean?" he asked absently, not quite listening: he was hoping he'd rise again.

But she answered: "You keep your weight on your elbows." That made him not only laugh but also slip and stop being a gentleman, at least by her standards. She squawked and wiggled, and he slid out of her. When he sat back on his knees,

she reached for her discarded clothes, so she hadn't been interested in a second round, anyhow.

Jens dressed even faster than he'd undressed. Where before he'd thought of nothing but getting his ashes hauled, now he recalled how much a stranger he was here, and what could happen to strangers when they fooled around with small-town women.

Another question formed in the back of his mind: did Mary expect to get paid? If he asked and the answer was no, he'd mortally offend her. If he didn't ask and the answer was yes, he'd offend her a different way, one that might end up with his having a discussion he didn't want with the gunman behind that curtained window.

After a few seconds' thought, he found a compromise that pleased him. "What do I owe you for lunch and everything?" he asked. If she wanted to interpret *and everything* to mean a couple of beers, fine. If she thought it meant more than that, well, okay, too.

"Paper money?" Mary asked. Jens nodded. She said, "Thirty bucks ought to cover it."

Given the way prices had gone crazy since the Lizards came, that wasn't out of line for good chicken stew and two mugs of beer. Jens felt a surge of pride that she hadn't been a pro. He dug in his pocket for a roll that would have astonished him in prewar days, peeled off two twenties, and gave them to her. "I'll get your change," she said, and started for the cash register.

"Don't be silly," he told her.

She smiled. "I said you were a gentleman."

"Listen, Mary, when I come back from where I'm going—" he began, with the sentimentality satiation and a bit of beer can bring.

She cut him off. "If I ever see you again, tell me whatever you're going to tell me. Till then, I'm not gonna worry about it. The war's made everybody a little bit crazy."

"Isn't that the truth?" he said, and thought about Barbara for the first time since he decided to try playing footsie with Mary. *Take that, bitch,* he said to himself. Aloud, to Mary, he went on, "Thanks for everything—and I mean for everything. I'd better be heading out now."

She sighed. "I know. Nobody ever stays in Idaho Springs—except me." She took a couple of quick steps forward, pecked

him on the cheek, and moved back again before he could grab her. "Wherever it is you're going to, you be careful, hear me?"

"I will." Suddenly he wanted to stay in Idaho Springs, a town he'd never heard of until he started planning the trip for Hanford. *Amazing what a roll in the hay can do,* he thought. But discipline held, aided by doubts whether Mary wanted anything more from him than that one roll, either.

The doorbell jingled again as he walked out of the First Street Cafe. He climbed onto his bicycle. "Giddyap," he muttered as he started to pedal. The world wasn't such a bad old place after all.

He held that view even though he needed a solid day to get to the top of Berthoud Pass, which wasn't much more than twenty miles beyond Idaho Springs. He spent the night in the mining hamlet of Empire, then tackled the run to the pass the next morning. He didn't think he'd ever worked so hard in this life. He'd gained a thousand feet between Idaho Springs and Empire, and picked up another three thousand in the thirteen miles between Empire and the top of the pass. Not only was he going up an ever-steeper grade, he was doing it in air that got thinner and thinner. Berthoud Pass topped out at better than eleven thousand feet: 11,315, said a sign that announced the Continental Divide.

"Whew." Jens paused for a well-earned rest. He was covered with sweat and his heart was beating harder than it had when he'd come atop Mary Cooley, a day before and most of a mile lower. Denver had taken some getting used to. He wondered if anybody this side of an Andean Indian could hope to get used to the thin air of Berthoud Pass.

And yet signs on side roads pointed the way to ski resorts. People actually came up here for fun. He shook his head. "Me, I'm just glad it's downhill from here on out," he said, swigging from one of the canteens he'd filled back at Bards Creek in Empire. The kind folk there had also given him chunks of roast chicken to take along. He gnawed on a drumstick as he tried without much luck to catch his breath.

He thought he'd sweated out every drop of water in him, but emptying the canteen proved him wrong. He went off behind a boulder—not that anybody would have seen him if he'd taken a leak right out in the middle of US 40—and unzipped his fly.

The second he started to whiz, he hissed in sudden and un-

expected pain; somebody might as well have lighted a match and stuck it up his joint. And along with the urine came thick yellow pus. "What the hell is that?" he burst out, and then, a moment later, as realization struck, "Jesus Christ, I've got the fucking clap!"

And where he'd got it was painfully obvious, in the most literal sense of the word. Not from the palm of his own hand, that was for goddamn sure. Somebody who'd lie down with one stranger passing through Idaho Springs . . . he wondered how many strangers she'd lain down with. One of them had left her a present, and she'd been generous enough to give it to him.

"That's great," he said. "That's just wonderful." Here he'd been on the point of rejoining the human race, and this had to happen. What he'd hoped would be his ticket out of the black gloom that had seized him ever since Barbara started laying that miserable ballplayer now turned out to be just another kick in the nuts—again, literally.

He thought about turning the bicycle around and heading back toward Idaho Springs. *Give that tramp a Springfield thank-you,* he thought. It would be an easy ride, too—all downhill. *Down that grade, I could do twenty miles in twenty minutes.* He knew he was exaggerating, but not by that much.

In the end, he shook his head. He didn't quite have cold-blooded murder in him. Revenge was something else. As far as he was concerned, the whole human race had given him a screwing that made the dose he'd got from Mary Cooley look like a pat on the back by comparison.

Well, not quite like a pat on the back. As he climbed back onto the bicycle and started down the western slope of the Rockies, he was already dreading the next time he'd have to piss. Back before the war, sulfa had started knocking gonorrhea for a loop. If any doctor so much as had the stuff these days, he'd be saving it for matters more urgent than a case of VD.

"Hanford," Jens muttered. His breath smoked as the word escaped his lips; even now, the snow didn't lie that far above Berthoud Pass. He pedaled harder to get warm again.

He'd go on to Hanford. He'd see what there was to see. He'd head back for Denver and make his report. He wondered how much good it would do, or whether General Leslie hot-shot Groves would pay the least bit of attention to it if he

didn't like what he said. None of the Met Lab people paid any attention to him these days. They were probably too busy laughing at him behind his back—and they'd laugh even harder when he came home with a drippy faucet. So would Barbara.

He wondered why he was wasting so much effort on sons of bitches—and one proper bitch—who wouldn't appreciate what he did if he went out and built a bomb singlehanded. But he'd said he'd go and he'd said he'd come back, and duty still counted for a lot with him.

"Hell, hadn't been for duty, I'd still be married—yes, sir, I sure would," he said. They'd asked him to take word about the Met Lab from Chicago to the government-in-hiding in West Virginia, and he'd gone and done it. But getting back hadn't been so easy—and nobody'd bothered to ask his wife to keep her legs closed while he was gone.

So he'd do what he'd promised. He hadn't made any promises about afterwards, though. He might take it into his head to ride east out of Denver after all.

He picked up speed and he rolled downhill. The thin air that blew against his face was spicy with the smell of the pines from the Arapaho National Forest all around.

"Or who knows?" he said. "I might even run into some Lizards on the way to Hanford. They'd listen to me, I bet. What do you think?" The breeze didn't answer.

☆ **XVII** ☆

Atvar stood on sand, looking out to sea. "This is a most re-spectable climate," the fleetlord said. "Decently warm, de-cently dry—" The wind blew bits of grit into his eyes. They bothered him not in the least; his nictitating membranes flicked them out of the way without conscious thought on his part.

Kirel came crunching up beside him. "Even this northern Africa is not truly Home, though, Exalted Fleetlord," he said. "It grows beastly cold at night—and winter here, by the re-ports, is almost as hideous as anywhere else on Tosev 3."

"Not winter now." For a moment, Atvar turned an eye turret toward the star the Race called Tosev. As always, its light struck him as too harsh, too white, not quite like the mellow sunshine of Home. "I thought I would come down to the plan-et's surface to see it at its best, not its worst."

"It is well-suited to us here," Kirel admitted. "Reports say the Tosevites from Europe there"—he pointed north across the blue, blue water—"who were fighting here when we arrived, spent most of their time complaining about how hot and dry this part of their planet was. Even the natives don't care for the area during summer."

"I have long since given up trying to fathom the Big Uglies' tastes," Atvar said. "I would call them revoltingly ignorant, ex-cept that, were they only a little more ignorant, our conquest would have been accomplished some time ago."

"With the return of good—well, bearable—weather to the lands of our principal foes, the optimism I felt at the outset of our campaign here begins to return as well," Kirel said. "We've gained against the Deutsche from both east and west; we're driving toward the capital of the SSSR, this Moskva be-

ing an important rail and transport center along with an administrative site; we continue to consolidate our hold on China despite bandits behind our lines; and the Americans fall back on the lesser continental land mass."

"All true," Atvar agreed, more happily than he'd spoken of the military situation on Tosev 3 for some time. "I begin to hope the colonists may yet find a pacified world awaiting their settlement. During the past winter in this hemisphere, I wouldn't have put much credit in that."

"Nor I, Exalted Fleetlord. But if our munitions hold out, I think we can successfully complete the conquest and settle down to administering rather than fighting."

Atvar wished the shiplord hadn't added that qualifying phrase. Munitions were a continuing problem. Provident as usual, the Race had given the conquest fleet far more supplies and weapons systems than it had expected the warriors to need against the animal-riding, sword-swinging savages the probes had shown inhabiting Tosev 3.

The only trouble was that, while Atvar still reckoned the Big Uglies savages, these days they made landcruisers, fired automatic weapons, and were beginning to fly jet aircraft and launch missiles. What would have been lavish supplies against primitives had to be carefully rationed to keep from running out before the Tosevites did. Atvar knew such care slowed the war effort, but he lacked the munitions to shut down all the Big Uglies' industrial areas and keep them shut down.

"It does make things harder," Kirel said when Atvar spoke of his concern. "Still, I count us ahead of the game in that we've not had to use nuclear weapons to any great degree. Wrecking the planet for the colonists would not leave our names in good odor in the annals of the Race."

Would not leave Atvar's name in good odor, was what he meant, though he was too polite to say so. The fleetlord won the glory—if any glory was to be won. If not, he won the blame. Atvar didn't intend to win any blame.

"Some males—Straha, for instance," he observed, "would destroy Tosev 3 in order to conquer it. They might as well be Big Uglies themselves, for all the care they give to the future."

"Truth in your words, Exalted Fleetlord," Kirel said; he didn't care for Straha, either. But he was also a thoroughgoing and conscientious officer, so he added, "In truth, though,

sometimes the Tosevites are exasperating enough to make me wonder if we shouldn't exterminate them to keep them from troubling us later. Take this latest trouble with—what was that Big Ugly's name?—Moishe Russie."

"Oh yes—that." Atvar stuck out his tongue, as at a bad smell. "I thought it had to be one of Skorzeny's exploits till intelligence reminded me Russie belonged to one of the groups the Deutsche were busy slaughtering until we came to Tosev 3. Computer analysis makes it unlikely they would have tried to rescue one of their foes, and I must say I agree with the machines here."

"As do I," Kirel said with a hissing sigh. "But don't you think dismissing Zolraag as governor of the province was a trifle harsh? Other than when dealing with Russie and matters concerning him, his record was good enough."

"What he's cost us in those matters outweighs the rest," Atvar said. "He petitioned for a reconsideration; I denied it. We hold too much of Tosev 3 only because the locals submit to us out of fear. If we are made to look like idiots, we shall no longer be objects of fear, and we shall have to divert forces from serious fighting to hold down areas now quiet. No, Zolraag deserved sacking, and sacking he got."

Kirel cast his eyes to the ground in obedience to the fleetlord's will. Another male came up to him and Atvar, one whose rather drab body paint made him seem out of place in such august company. "I greet you, Exalted Fleetlord, Superb Shiplord," he said. His words were perfectly correct, his voice held the proper deference, and yet Atvar doubted his sincerity even so.

"I greet you, Drefsab," the fleetlord returned, swinging one eye turret toward the intelligence operative. Drefsab's motions were quick and jerky. With another male, that might have betrayed a ginger habit, but Drefsab had moved that way even before he became addicted to the Tosevite herb; he had a Big Ugly's restlessness trapped in a body that belonged to the Race. Atvar said, "I presume you have come to report on the progress of your project in—what is the name of that Emperorless land?"

"*Nezavisna Drzava Hrvatska*—the Independent State of Croatia," Drefsab answered. His clawed fingers twitched restlessly, a sure sign of disgust. "Do you know, Exalted Fleetlord,

there are times when the Big Uglies are as easy to manipulate as hatchlings still wet from the juices of their eggs?"

"I wish there were more such times," Kirel observed.

"So do we all," Atvar said. "How have you managed to manipulate the—Croats?—then?"

"They're subordinates of the Deutsche, of course," Drefsab said. "The Deutsche gained their support by giving them weapons and a free hand against their local enemies, which essentially means anyone who lives nearby and is not a Croat. All I had to do was promise more and better weapons and an even freer hand, and all at once they became most cooperative."

Atvar felt faintly sick. The guidelines on conquering Tosev 3 he'd brought from Home, tomes composed thousands of years before, after the Race subjected first the Rabotevs and then the Hallessi, suggested playing local groups against one another. That sounded clean and logical. The reality, at least on Tosev 3, was apt to be sordid and soaked in blood.

Drefsab went on, "When measured against Tosev 3 as a whole—as opposed to Tosev 3 as a hole, which the Emperor surely knows it is—the Independent State of Croatia is of no importance whatever, being barely visible to the naked eye. But its position gives it importance to the Deutsche, who do not want us gaining influence there at their expense. And we have deliberately kept our effort there on a small scale, confining it to the coastal city of Split."

"If you can damage the Deutsche in this Croatia place, why make only a small effort?" Kirel asked. "They are among the most dangerous of the Tosevites."

"To us, though, Superb Shiplord, Croatia has no great significance," Drefsab said. "And, in any case, I am seeking to elicit a specific response from the Deutsche. I don't want them flooding the area with males; the terrain inland is mountainous and very bad for both armor and aircraft. I want them to bring in their own specialists in sabotage and destruction, and then I want to trap and destroy those specialists."

"This is the lure you have prepared for Skorzeny," Atvar exclaimed.

"Exalted Fleetlord, it is," Drefsab agreed. "As you pointed out, he has embarrassed the Race too many times. Soon he will do so no more."

"Eliminating Skorzeny will go a long way toward getting rid

of a weakness you just finished discussing, Exalted Fleetlord," Kirel said excitedly. "Big Uglies around the world will have new reason to fear us once we take him out of play."

"Exactly so." Atvar turned his eye turrets back toward Drefsab. "How fares your other battle?"

"The one against the Tosevite herb, you mean?" Drefsab let out a long hiss. "I still taste now and again; that far, the addiction keeps its hold. I continue to struggle not to let it master all my thoughts. It has my body, but I work to keep my mind as free as I can."

"Another lonely battle, and a brave one," Atvar said. "So many yield both to ginger."

"As free as I can, I said," Drefsab answered. Dropping his eyes in deference, he went on, "Emperor knows the craving never leaves, not altogether. Under the worst circumstances, who knows what I might do for a taste? For that very reason, I attempt to avoid placing myself in those circumstances."

Atvar and Kirel also looked down at the yellow-brown sand. When the fleetlord raised his eyes once more, he said, "Your discipline in the face of this adversity does you great credit. Because of it, I am all the more certain you will succeed in eliminating that menace, Skorzeny."

"Exalted Fleetlord, it shall be done," Drefsab said.

Vyacheslav Molotov peered between the backs of Stalin and his generals to study the map pinned down on the table in front of them. From the way things looked, Soviet forces were effectively pinned down, too.

"Comrade General Secretary, if Moscow is to be held, we need more men, more armor, more aircraft, and above all more time to place our assets in proper position," Marshal Georgi Zhukov said. "Absent these, I do not see how we are to prevail."

Few men dared speak so boldly to Stalin; Zhukov had won the right by his successes first in Mongolia against the Japanese, then defending Moscow from the Germans, and finally in holding the Lizards at bay through the winter just past. Stalin sucked on his pipe. It was empty; not even he could get tobacco these days. He said, "Georgi Konstantinovich, you saved this city once. Can you not do it again?"

"Then I had fresh troops from Siberia, and the fascists were

at the end of their tether," Zhukov answered. "Neither applies here. Without some special miracle, we shall be defeated—and the dialectic does not allow for miracles."

Stalin grunted. Like so many revolutionaries, especially Georgian ones, he'd had seminary training. Now he said, "The dialectic may not allow for miracles, Comrade Marshal, but nevertheless I think I may be able to furnish you with one."

Zhukov scratched his head. He was a blocky, round-faced man, much more typically Russian in looks than the slender Molotov. "What sort of miracle do you have in mind?" he asked.

Molotov had wondered the same thing, but all at once he knew. Fear coursed through him. "Iosef Vissarionovich, we have discussed the reasons for not using this weapon," he said urgently. "As far as I can see, they remain valid."

That was as close as he'd come in years to criticizing Stalin. The general secretary whirled around in surprise, the pipe jumping in his mouth. "If the choice is between going down to defeat after using every weapon we have and yielding tamely without making every effort to hit back at the enemy, I prefer the former."

Zhukov didn't say anything. Ivan Koniev asked, "What weapon is this? If we have a weapon that will let us hurt the Lizards, I say we use it—and to the devil's grandmother with the consequences."

After Zhukov, Koniev was the best general Stalin had. If he didn't know about the explosive-metal bomb project, the secrecy was even more extraordinary than Molotov had imagined. He asked Stalin, "May we speak freely of this weapon?"

The pipe waggled again. "The time has come when we *must* speak freely of this weapon," Stalin answered. He turned to Koniev. "We have, Ivan Stepanovich, a bomb of the sort the Lizards used on Berlin and Washington. If they break through at Kaluga and advance on Moscow, I propose to use it against them."

With his crooked front teeth, Koniev looked even more like a middle-aged peasant than Zhukov did. *"Bozhemoi,"* he said softly. "If we have such—you are right, Comrade General Secretary: if we have such bombs, we should use them against the foe."

"We have *one* such bomb," Molotov said, "and no prospect

of getting more for some time. No one knows how many of these bombs the Lizards have—but we may be about to find out by experiment."

"Oh," Koniev said, and then again, in a whisper, *"Bozhe-moi."* Glancing nervously at Stalin, he went on, "This is a choice we must face with great seriousness. One of these bombs, by report, can devastate a city as thoroughly as several weeks of unchallenged bombardment by an ordinary air force."

Now the pipe worked angrily in Stalin's mouth. Before he could speak, Molotov said, "These reports are true, Comrade General. I have seen photographs of both Washington and Berlin. The melted stump of the Washington Monument—" He did not go on, both from the remembered horror of the photographs and for fear of further antagonizing Stalin. But he was too afraid of what would happen if explosive-metal bombs began to be used freely to keep silent.

Stalin paced back and forth. He did not put down the incipient rebellion at once, which was unusual. *Maybe,* Molotov thought, *he has doubts, too.* Stalin nodded to Zhukov. "How say you, Georgi Konstantinovich?"

Zhukov and Stalin were the same sort of military team as Molotov and Stalin were a political team: Stalin the guiding will, the other man the instrument that shaped the will to practical ends. Zhukov licked his lips; plainly he was of two minds, too. At last he said, "Comrade General Secretary, if we do not use this weapon, I see nothing that will keep us from being overrun. We may be able to continue partisan warfare against the Lizards, but not much more. How can what they do to us after we use the weapon be worse than what they will do to us if we do not use it?"

"Have you *seen* the pictures of Berlin?" Molotov demanded. By then, he was certain, he had raised Stalin's wrath, but he was too upset even to be frightened. That was most unusual; he would have to examine the feeling later. No time now.

Zhukov nodded. "Comrade Foreign Commissar, I have. They are terrible. But have you seen pictures of Kiev after first the fascists and then the Lizards went through it? They are just as bad. This bomb is a more efficient means of destruction, but destruction will take place with it or without it."

As always, Molotov held his features immobile. Behind that unsmiling mask, his heart sank. It sank still further when Gen-

eral Koniev asked, "How do we deliver this bomb? Can we drop it from an airplane? If we can do that, can we have some hope of putting an airplane where we most need it without the Lizards' shooting it down?"

"Before we examine ways and means, we still need to consider whether we should take this course." Molotov's impassive voice concealed the desperation that grew inside him.

Stalin pretended he had not spoken and answered Koniev instead: "Comrade, the bomb is too bulky to fit into any of our bombers, and, as you say, the Lizards shoot them down too readily to make them a good way to deliver it anyhow. But planes are for taking bombs to an enemy who is far away. If the enemy is instead coming to you—" He let the sentence hang.

Molotov scratched his head, not sure where Stalin was going with that. It must have made sense to Zhukov and Koniev, though; they both chuckled. Zhukov finished the phrase for Stalin: "—you put the bomb where he will be, and wait."

"Just so," Stalin said happily. "In fact, we shall encourage him to concentrate in the sector where we shall place the bomb, to make sure we do him as much damage as we can." Now it made sense to Molotov, too, but it didn't make him any happier.

Koniev said, "Two risks here. The first is that the weapon will be discovered; past *maskirovka*, I don't see what we can do about that. The second is that a weapon left behind won't go off when we want it to. How do we make sure that does not happen?"

"We have multiple devices to set it off," Stalin answered. "One is by radio signal, one is with a battery, and one is with a clockwork manufactured by German prisoners in our employ." He spoke utterly without irony; Molotov had no doubt those prisoners were no longer among the living. "They did not know to what device the clockwork would be affixed, of course. But it has been tested repeatedly; it is most reliable."

"Just as well, considering the use to which it will be put." But Koniev nodded. "You are right, Comrade General Secretary: however vile the fascists may be, they make excellent mechanical devices. This clockwork or one of the other means you noted should definitely be able to set off the bomb at a time of our choosing."

"So the engineers and scientists have assured me," Stalin

said with a slight purr in his voice that told what would happen if the engineers and scientists were wrong. Molotov would not have wanted to be in the shoes of the men who labored on that *kolkhoz* outside of Moscow.

He pushed forward between Zhukov and Koniev. Both officers looked at him in surprise; he was usually a good deal less assertive at military conferences, which he attended mostly so he would know how developments on the battlefield affected the foreign policy of the Soviet Union. He studied the map. Red units represented Soviet forces, green the Lizards, and occasional pockets of blue German troops that still fought on in the land they had invaded almost two years before.

Even to his unsoldierly eye, the situation looked grim. The makeshift line patched together between Sukhinichi and Kaluga wasn't going to hold. He could see that already; not enough Red Army forces were in place to hold back the advancing Lizard armor. And once the line was pierced, it was fall back or get cut off from your comrades and surrounded. Nazi panzers had done that to Soviet troops again and again in the desperate summer and fall of 1941.

Nonetheless, he stabbed a hesitant finger out toward Kaluga. "Cannot we stop them here?" he asked. "Any effort, it seems to me, would be better than using the explosive metal bomb and facing whatever retaliation the Lizards may choose to inflict."

"Even Kaluga is too close to Moscow, far too close," Stalin said. "From airstrips behind the city, they can smash us to pieces." But he glanced at Zhukov before he went on, "If they don't come past Kaluga, we shall not deploy the bomb."

"That is an excellent decision, Iosef Vissarionovich," Molotov said fulsomely. Zhukov and Koniev both nodded. Molotov felt sweat under the armpits of his white cotton shirt. He wondered if the Tsar's courtiers had had to tread so carefully in guiding their sovereign toward a sensible course. He doubted it—not since the days of Peter the Great, anyhow, or maybe Ivan the Terrible.

When Stalin spoke again, his voice held some of the steel that had given Iosef Dzhugashvili his revolutionary sobriquet: "If the Lizards advance past Kaluga, however, the bomb will be used against them."

Molotov looked to Koniev and Zhukov for support. He

found none. The marshal and the general were both nodding, perhaps without enthusiasm but without hesitation, either. Molotov made his own head go up and down. *Useless to argue with Stalin,* he told himself. *Useless to antagonize him.* He kept on nodding, though in his heart winter's chill had returned to oust the bright spring day.

Heinrich Jäger glanced up at the sun before he raised the binoculars to his eyes. In the afternoon, the Lizards down in Split might have been able to spot reflections from the lenses. The hill-fortress of Klis in which he sheltered sat only a few kilometers inland from the city on the Adriatic coast.

The Zeiss optics brought Split leaping almost within arm's length. Sixteen hundred years after it was built, Diocletian's palace still dominated Jäger's view of the city. *Fortress is a better word,* he thought. Actually, it was in essence a Roman legionary camp transformed into stone: a rough rectangle with sides of 150 to 200 meters, each one pierced by a single, central gate. Three of the four towers at the corners of the rectangle were still standing.

Jäger lowered the binoculars. "Not a place I'd care to try attacking, even nowadays, without heavy artillery on my side," he said.

Beside him, Otto Skorzeny grunted. "I can see why you went into armor, Jäger: you have no head for the subtleties."

"What's that Hungarian curse?—a horse's cock up your arse?" Jäger said. Both men laughed. Jäger peered through the binoculars again. Even they couldn't make the Lizard sentries on the walls of the palace and in positions around it seem much more than little moving antlike specks. They were well-sited, no doubt about that; in set-piece situations, the Lizards were quite competent.

Skorzeny chuckled again. "I wonder if our scaly friends down there know that we have better plans of their strongpoint than they do."

"They wouldn't have picked it if they did," Jäger answered. The plans hadn't come out of the archives of the German General Staff, but from the *Zeitschrift für sudosteuropäischen Archäologie.* Skorzeny found that vastly amusing, and called Jäger *"Herr Doktor Professor"* every chance he got. But even Skorzeny had to admit that the quality of the plans couldn't have been better had military engineers drafted them.

"I think you're right," the SS man said. "To them it's just the strongest building in town, so naturally it's where they moved in."

"Yes." Jäger wondered if the Lizards had a concept of archaeology. Word filtering out of intelligence said they were conservative by nature (which he'd already discovered from fighting against them) and that they'd had their own culture as a going concern since the days when people were barbarians if not downright (and barely upright) savages. That made Jäger think they wouldn't reckon any building a mere millennium and a half old worth studying as a monument of antiquity.

"So, what are you going to do about getting those cursed creatures out of there?" Marko Petrovic asked in fluent if accented German. The Croatian captain's khaki uniform contrasted with the field gray the Germans wore. Even though Petrovic wore a uniform, being around him made Jäger nervous—he seemed more bandit chief than officer. His thick black beard only added to the effect. It did not, however, completely conceal facial scars that made the one seaming Skorzeny's cheek a mere scratch by comparison.

Skorzeny turned to the Croat and said, "Patience, my friend. We want to do the job properly, not just quickly."

Petrovic scowled. His beard and scars made that scowl fearsome, but the look in his eye chilled Jäger more. To Petrovic, it wasn't just a military problem; he took it personally. That would make him a bold fighter, but a heedless one: Jäger performed the evaluation as automatically as he breathed.

"What's the complication?" the Croat demanded. "We're in easy shelling range of the place now. We move in some artillery, open up, and—"

The idea of shelling a building that had stood since the start of the fourth century sickened Jäger, but that wasn't why he shook his head. "Artillery wouldn't root them all out, Captain, and it would give them an excuse to expand their perimeter to take in these hills. They're staying in town; I'd just as soon keep them down there as long as they're willing to sit quietly."

"You would not be bleating 'patience' if Split were a town in the *Reich*," Petrovic said.

He had a point; Hitler waxed apoplectic over German territory lost. Jäger was not about to admit that, though. He said, "We have a chance to drive them out, not just annoy them. I aim to make certain we don't waste it."

Petrovic glowered—like a lot of the locals, he had a face that was made for glowering: long and bony, with heavy eyebrows and deep-set eyes—but subsided. Skorzeny swatted him on the back and said, "Don't you worry. We'll fix those miserable creatures for you." He sounded breezy and altogether confident.

If he convinced Petrovic, the Croat captain did a good job of hiding it. He said, "You Germans think you can do everything. You'd better be right this time, or—" He didn't say *or what*, but walked off shaking his head.

Jäger was glad he'd gone. "Some of these Croats are scary bastards," he said in a low voice. Skorzeny nodded, and anyone who worried him enough for him to admit it was a very rugged customer indeed. Jäger went on, "We'd better get the Lizards out of there, because if we don't, Ante Pavelic and the *Ustashi* will be just as happy in bed with them as with us, as long as the Lizards let them go on killing Serbs and Jews and Bosnians and—"

"—all their other neighbors," Skorzeny finished for him. He didn't acknowledge that the Germans had done the same thing on a bigger scale all through the east. He couldn't have been ignorant of that; he just deliberately didn't think about it. Jäger had seen that with other German officers. He'd been the same way himself, until he saw too much for him to ignore. To him, a lot of his colleagues seemed willfully blind.

Skorzeny pulled a flask off his belt, unstoppered it, took a healthy belt, and passed it to Jäger. It was vodka, made from potatoes that had died happy. Jäger drank, too. *"Zhiveli,"* he said, one of the few words of Serbo-Croatian he'd picked up.

Skorzeny laughed. "That probably means something like 'here's hoping your sheep is a virgin,' " he said, which made Jäger cough and choke. The SS man had another swig, then stowed the flask again. He glanced around with a skilled imitation of casual uninterest to make sure nobody but Jäger was in earshot, then murmured, "I picked up something interesting in town yesterday."

"Ah?" Jäger said.

The SS colonel nodded. "You remember when I went into Besançon, I had the devil's own time finding any Lizards to do business with, because one of their high mucky-mucks had gone through there and cleaned out a whole raft of the chaps who'd gotten themselves hooked on ginger?"

"I remember your saying so, yes," Jäger answered. "It didn't seem to stop you." He also remembered his own amazement and then awe as the bulky Skorzeny writhed his way out of a Lizard panzer several sizes too small for him.

"That's my job, not getting stopped," Skorzeny said with a smug grin that twisted the scar on his cheek. "Turns out the name of that mucky-muck was Drefsab, or something like that. Half the Lizards in Besançon thought he was wonderful for doing such a good job of clearing out the ginger lickers; the other half hated him for doing such a good job."

"What about it?" Jäger said, then paused. "Wait a minute, let me guess—this Dref-whoever is down there in Split now?"

"You're clever, you know that?" The SS man eyed him half in annoyance at having his surprise spoiled, half in admiration. "I wasn't stupid to bring you along here, either. That's it exactly, Jäger: the very same Lizard."

"Coincidence?"

"Anything is possible." Skorzeny's tone said he didn't believe it for a minute. "But by what he did back in France, he's got to be one of their top troubleshooters. And there aren't any ginger lickers down there. The locals would be selling to them if there were, and the ten kilos I brought with me is gathering dust here in Klis. And if it's not about ginger, what's he doing down there?"

"Dickering with the Croats?"

Skorzeny rubbed his chin. "That makes more sense than anything I've come up with. The Lizards need to do some dickering, not just to get their toehold here but also because the Italians were occupying Split until they surrendered to the Lizards. Then the Croats threw 'em out. The scaly boys might be making a deal for Italy as well as for themselves. But it's like a song that's a little out of tune—it doesn't seem quite right to me somehow."

Jäger was indignant at having his brainchild criticized. "Why not?"

"What this Drefsab did in Besançon, that was police work, security work—call it whatever you like. But would you send a *Gestapo* man to negotiate a treaty?"

Now Jäger looked around to make certain neither Captain Petrovic nor any of his merry men could overhear. "If I were negotiating with Ante Pavelic and his Croatian thugs, I just might."

Skorzeny threw back his head and bellowed laughter. A couple of riflemen in the khaki of the Independent State of Croatia glanced over to see what was so funny. Wheezing still, Skorzeny said, "Wicked man! I've told you before, you were wasted in panzers."

"You've told me lots of things. That doesn't make them true," Jäger said, which made the SS man give him a shot in the ribs with an elbow. He elbowed back, more to remind Skorzeny he couldn't be pushed around than because he felt like fighting. Jäger gave away centimeters, kilograms, and nasty attitude in any scrap with him; he didn't think Skorzeny knew what *quit* meant, either.

"Here, dig out those plans again," Skorzeny said. "I think I know what I want to do, but I'm not quite sure yet." Jäger obediently dug. Skorzeny bent over the drawings, clucking like a mother hen. "I like these underground galleries. We can do things with them."

The halls to which he pointed lay below the southern part of Diocletian's palace. "There used to be upper halls above them, too, with the same plan, but those are long gone," Jäger said.

"Then screw them." Skorzeny didn't care about archaeology, just military potential. "What I want to know is, what's in these galleries?"

"Back in Roman days, they used to be storerooms," Jäger said. "I'm not so sure what's in there now. We need to talk to our good and loyal Croatian allies." He was proud of himself; that came out without a hint of irony.

"Yes, indeed," Skorzeny said, accepting the advice in the spirit in which it was given. "What I'm thinking is, maybe we can dig a tunnel from outside the wall into one of those galleries—"

"Always making sure we don't happen to tunnel into the Lizards' barracks."

"That would make things more complicated." Skorzeny chuckled. "But if we can do that, we have our good and loyal allies make a nice, loud, showy attack on the walls, draw any Lizard who happens to be underground up to the top . . . and then we bring in some of our lads through the tunnel and up, and—what was that? The horse's cock up the arse?"

"Yes," Jäger said. "I like that." Then, like a proper devil's advocate, he started picking holes in the plan: "Moving men and weapons into the city and into the place that houses the

tunnel or at least somewhere close by it isn't going to be easy. And we'll need a lot of men. That's a big palace down there, big enough for a church and a baptistry and a museum to fit inside, plus God knows what all else. The Lizards will have packed a lot of fighters into it."

"I'm not worried about the Lizards," Skorzeny said. "If these Croats decide to hop into bed with them, though, that'll nail our hides to the wall. We have to keep that from happening, no matter what; I don't give a damn what we have to give Pavelic to keep him on our side."

"Free rein would probably do it, and he has that already, pretty much," Jäger said with distaste. The Independent State of Croatia seemed to have only one plan for staying independent: hammering all its neighbors enough to make sure nobody close by got strong enough to take revenge.

If Skorzeny felt the same revulsion Jäger did, he didn't show it. He said, "We can promise him more chunks of the coast that the Italians are still occupying. He'll like that—it'll give him fresh traitors to get rid of." He spoke without sarcasm; he might have been talking about the best way to sweeten the deal for a secondhand car.

Jäger couldn't be so cold-blooded. Very softly, he said, "That *Schweinhund* Pavelic runs a filthy regime."

"You bet he does, but he's our *Schweinhund*, and we want to make sure he stays that way," Skorzeny answered, just as quietly. "If it does, every one of these Lizards, that Drefsab included, is ours, too." He brought a fist down onto his knee. "That *will* happen."

Compared to yielding to the Lizards, making deals with Ante Pavelic seemed worthwhile. Compared to anything else, Jäger found it most repugnant. And yet, before the Lizards came, Pavelic had been a loyal and enthusiastic supporter of the German *Reich*. Jäger wondered what that said about Germany. *Nothing good,* he thought.

Shanghai amazed Bobby Fiore. Much of the town was pure Chinese, and reminded him of a large-scale, rowdier version of the prison camp where he'd lived with Liu Han. So far, so good; he'd expected as much. What he hadn't expected was the long streets packed full of European-style buildings from the 1920s. It was as if part of Paris, say, had been picked up, carried halfway round the world, and dropped down smack in

the middle of China. As far as Fiore was concerned, it didn't fit.

The other thing that amazed him was how much damage the city had taken. You walked around, you knew they'd been in a war here. The Japs had bombed the place to hell and gone, and then burned it when they took it in 1937; he still remembered the news photo of the naked little burned Chinese boy sitting up and crying in the ruins. When he first saw it, he'd been ready to go to war with Japan right then. But he'd cooled down, and so had everybody else. Then Pearl Harbor came along and said he'd been right the first time.

When the Lizards took Shanghai away from the Japs, they hadn't exactly given it a peck on the cheek, either. Whole blocks were leveled, and human bones still lay here and there. The Chinese weren't what you'd call eager to bury Japanese remains. Their attitude was more on the order of *let 'em rot.*

In spite of everything, though, the town, especially the Chinese part of it, kept right on humming. The Lizards made their headquarters in some of the Western-style buildings; the rest remained ruins. In the Chinese districts, things were going up faster than you could shake a stick at them.

But since the Lizards mostly stayed in the International Settlement, Bobby Fiore mostly stayed there, too. The job he'd taken on for the Reds was to keep on looking as much like a Chinaman as he could, to keep his ears open, and to report to Nieh Ho-T'ing anything interesting he heard. The Red officer had promised he'd get to go along when the guerrillas tried a raid based on what he'd learned.

So far, that hadn't happened. "And I'm not gonna worry about it, neither," Fiore muttered under his breath. "Yeah, I wouldn't mind nailing a few of those scaly bastards, but I didn't hire out to be no hero."

He walked across the Garden Bridge over Soochow Creek from the Bund to the Hongkew district to the north. Soochow Creek itself was filled with junks and other small Chinese boats whose names Fiore didn't know: from all he'd heard, people were born and raised and grew up and died on those boats. Some of them made their living fishing on the creek; others worked on land but didn't have anyplace else to stay.

The Hongkew district, in spite of its Chinese name, was part of the International Settlement. The Lizards had an observation post, and probably a machine-gun nest, in the clock tower of

the Head Post Office, which lay along Soochow Creek between Broadway and North Szechuen Road.

Bobby Fiore was tempted to duck into the Temple of the Queen of Heaven just a few yards north of the Garden Bridge, even though the Chinese didn't mean the Virgin. In the temple's inner court were the images of the gods Lin Tsiang Ching, who was supposed to see everything within a thousand *li* of Shanghai, and Ching Tsiang Ching, who was supposed to hear everything within the same distance.

Fiore glanced up toward heaven. "They're just patron saints, kind of," he murmured to the Catholic God he assumed to be glancing down at him. The heavens remained mute. He walked past the Temple of the Queen of Heaven this time, though he'd gone in before.

Streets and sidewalks were crowded. No cars and trucks were running except Lizard models and human-made ones taken over by the Lizards, but people, rickshaws, pedicabs, and draft animals took up the slack. Beggars staked out squares of sidewalk; some of them chalked on the paving stones messages of woe Fiore couldn't read. They reminded him of the poor out-of-work bastards who'd hawked apples on streetcorners when the Depression was at its worst.

If the streets had been crowded, the Hongkew marketplace, at the corner of Boone and Woosung Roads, was jammed. Fishermen from Soochow Creek, farmers, butchers—all cried their wares at something just over the top of their lungs. If the market in the prison camp where he'd stayed with Liu Han was Fan's Field in Decatur, this place had to be Yankee Stadium.

Not only locals shopped here, either. Lizards made their skittering, herky-jerky progress from one stall to another. They could simply have taken whatever they wanted; from what Nieh Ho-T'ing had said, they'd done that at first.

"Now they pay," he'd said. "They learn that if they give nothing to get something, it is not in the market square the next time they want it."

Sure enough, a Lizard bought a live, kicking lobster and paid the stall keeper in Chinese silver dollars, which, for reasons Fiore could not fathom, were also called Mex dollars. The Lizard's companion said to him, "These are tasty creatures. Go on, Ianxx, buy several more. We can cook them for the commandant's midday reception tomorrow."

"It shall be done, superior sir," said the lobster buyer, presumably Ianxx. He went back to bargaining with the fisherman.

Fiore bent his head down and did his best to look Chinese. The brim of his conical straw hat covered his nose and too-round eyes; he wore drab, dark cottons that reminded him of pajamas, just like most other people. The Lizards should have no reason to notice his skin wasn't exactly the right color.

They didn't. They went off with their purchases, holding them carefully to avoid the lobsters' flailing claws. Bobby Fiore followed them back across the Garden Bridge. The Lizards paid no attention to him; as far as they were concerned, he was just another Big Ugly.

Now which commandant were you talking about? he asked them silently. They went through the Public Garden near the south edge of the Garden Bridge, and then on to the British Consulate. Fiore skinned back his teeth in a fierce grin; that was where the Lizard commandant for all Shanghai had his headquarters.

Not all of the International Settlement was posh buildings full of foreigners—or rather, now, full of Lizards. In an alley off Foochow Road, jammed in between other equally unpretentious erections, was a dilapidated place called the Sweetheart; the door had the name in English and what he presumed to be its equivalent in Chinese characters. When Fiore went inside, he was greeted by a blast of scratchy jazz from a phonograph and by the multilingual chatter of the working girls in the front lounge.

He snorted laughter. Nieh Ho-T'ing was one smart cookie. The Reds had a reputation for being bluenoses. Who would have figured one of their big wheels would set up shop in a whorehouse?

As far as Bobby knew, Nieh didn't go to bed with any of the girls. He didn't mind if Fiore enjoyed himself, though, and some of the Russians, girls whose parents had been on the losing side of the Revolution and had to get out one step ahead of Lenin's bully boys, were simply gorgeous. He wondered what they thought of being in cahoots with a Red now. He hadn't tried finding out; he'd learned to keep his mouth shut when he wasn't sure about the person he was talking to.

He opened the door to the lounge. The jazz got louder. The

chatter, on the other hand, suddenly stopped. Then the girls recognized him and started gabbing again.

He looked around like a kid in a candy store. Russians, Eurasians, Chinese, Koreans, some in European-style lingerie, others in clinging dresses of Chinese silk slit up to here and sometimes down to there, too ... just being a fly on the wall at the Sweetheart was almost as good as getting laid at some of the dismal sporting houses he'd been to back in the States.

"Is Uncle Wu around?" he asked; that was the name Nieh Ho-T'ing used hereabouts. Another wonderful thing about the Sweetheart was that he could speak English. Almost all the girls understood it, and two or three of them were about as fluent as he was.

One of the Russians, a blonde in a silk dress slit up to here and then a couple of inches farther, pointed to the stairway and said, "*Da,* Bobby, he is in his room now."

"Thanks, Shura." Bobby made himself look away from the display of creamy thigh and head for the stairs.

Up on the second floor, he made sure he knocked on the third door on the left. If he'd picked the wrong one by mistake, he might have interrupted somebody who didn't want to be interrupted. Too many people in Shanghai carried guns to make that a good idea.

As a matter of fact, when Nieh Ho-T'ing opened the door, he was holding a submachine gun himself. He relaxed when he saw Fiore—or relaxed as far as he ever did, which wasn't much. "Come in," he said, and closed the door behind Fiore. "What do you have for me?"

Bobby hated shifting from English to his halting Chinese, but he knew Nieh Ho-T'ing would burst a blood vessel if he suggested using one of the hookers to interpret. The Red officer waved him to a chair. On either wall, multitudes of mirrored images of him also sat down: this was a room in a brothel, sure enough.

He told Nieh Ho-T'ing what he'd heard in the Hongkew market. Nieh listened, asked questions, and finally nodded. "Luncheon tomorrow for their commandant in the British Consulate, you say?" he mused when Fiore was done. "Maybe we can make it a livelier occasion than the little scaly devils expect, eh?"

"Yeah," Bobby Fiore said; one of his frustrations in speak-

ing Chinese was that he couldn't qualify anything. He had to go thumbs-up or thumbs-down, with nothing in the middle.

Nieh Ho-T'ing smiled, not altogether pleasantly. He said, "I was wise to use you and not liquidate you out in the country-side. You have brought information I can employ, and which I could not have had without you."

"That's nice," Fiore said with an uneasy answering smile. *Liquidate* wasn't a Chinese word he'd figured he'd pick up in ordinary conversation, but Nieh used it a lot. The Reds were in deadly earnest about what they did. You weren't with them, you'd better have your life insurance paid up.

The really crazy part of it was, whenever Nieh Ho-T'ing didn't make like a revolutionary or a Mafia soldier, he was as nice a guy as you'd ever want to meet. It was as if he put all the murderous stuff in a box and took it out whenever he needed it, but when he wasn't using it, you wouldn't guess it was there.

Now his smile was broad and happy, as if such things as liq-uidation had never crossed his mind. He said, "I'm going to do you a favor in return for the one you did me. I am sure you will take it in the intended spirit."

"Yeah? What kind of favor?" Fiore asked suspiciously. Fa-vors always sounded good. Sometimes they were, as when Nieh had said it was okay for him to fool around with the girls downstairs. But sometimes . . .

This was one of *those* times. Still beaming, Nieh said, "I am going to keep the promise I made you: you will be part of our raiding team."

"Uh, thank you." That was the best Fiore could do in Chi-nese. If he'd been speaking English, it would have come out, *Oh boy, thanks a lot.*

If Nieh Ho-Ting noticed the irony and lack of enthusiasm, he didn't show it. "Aiding in the fight against the imperialist devils from another world is surely the duty of every human being. Those who do not join in the struggle are the devils' running dogs, and we know the fate of running dogs, eh?"

"Uh, yeah, sure," Bobby Fiore muttered. Talk about stuck between a rock and a hard place! If he came along for the ride, the Lizards would shoot him. If he didn't, the Chinese Reds would take care of the job. Either way, he could forget about finding out how the latest serial over at the Nanking on Ave-nue Edward VII was going to end.

Musingly, Nieh Ho-T'ing said, "Your pistol is not a good enough weapon for this work. We will make certain you have a submachine gun." He held up a hand. "No, don't thank me. It is for the mission as much as for yourself."

Bobby hadn't planned on thanking him. He wished he were back in the Lizard prison camp with Liu Han, and that he'd never, ever tried to teach that Chinaman named Lo how not to throw like a girl.

With a slight curl to his lip—he really was a bluenose at heart—Nieh said, "Why don't you go downstairs and amuse yourself for a time, if you have nothing better to do? I need to find out if we can do what needs doing on such short notice, and the best way to do it if we can."

Fiore didn't need any more urging to go downstairs. If he was going off to get shot at (he carefully didn't think of it as *to get shot*) tomorrow, he'd have fun tonight. Not much later, he ended up back in one of those mirrored rooms with Shura the White Russian blonde. By any objective standard, she was prettier and better in the sack than Liu Han had been, so he wondered why he didn't feel as happy as he might have when he went back to the room where he slept.

The only thing he could think of was that he'd cared about Liu Han and she about him, but Shura was just going through the motions, even if she played the mattress the way Billy Herman played second base. "Goddamn," he muttered sleepily. "I guess it was love." Next thing he knew, the sun was up.

He went down to breakfast like a condemned man heading off for his last meal. Even eyeing the girls couldn't snap him out of his funk. He was finishing his cup of tea when Nieh Ho-T'ing stuck his head into the kitchen and waved to him. "Come here. We have things to talk about."

Bobby came. Nieh handed Fiore a rattan suitcase. It was heavy. When Fiore opened it, he found a Russian submachine gun, several magazines of ammunition, and four potato-masher grenades.

"You will not go in with us," Nieh said. "You loiter across from the front entrance to the British Consulate. When the time comes—you will know, I assure you—kill the guards there if you can and help any human beings who come out through those doors."

"Okay," Fiore said in English when he was sure he understood what Nieh wanted from him. The Red nodded; he got

that. Fiore switched to his lousy Chinese: "How will you get in the consulate? How will you bring more guns in?"

"I should not tell you—security." But Nieh Ho-T'ing looked too pleased with himself to keep his mouth shut altogether. He went on, "This much I will say: the consulate will have some new human cooks and waiters today, and they will be bringing in ducks to go with the lobsters for the commandant's feast."

He clammed up again—if Bobby couldn't work it out from there, that was his tough luck. But he could, and started to laugh when he thought about how those ducks would be stuffed. No wonder Nieh looked so smug! "Good luck," Fiore said. He stuck out his hand, but yanked it back; Chinamen didn't go in for handshakes.

Nieh Ho-T'ing surprised him, though, by reaching out and taking his hand. "My Soviet comrades have this custom; I know what it means," he said, then looked at his watch. "Take your place at noon. The banquet is supposed to begin at half past the hour, and will not last long."

"Okay," Fiore said. If he'd been in a town where he spoke the language, he would have thought about taking it on the lam with the arsenal. Getting the Reds mad at him, though, seemed a worse bet than taking his chances on the Lizards.

He had plenty of time for another screw before he took off. Shura came back upstairs with him willingly enough. Afterwards, she blinked when he gave her an extra couple of dollars Mex; he was usually as cheap as he could get away with. "You rob a bank, Bobby?" she asked.

"Two of 'em, babe," he said, deadpan, as he started to dress. She blinked again, then decided it was a joke and laughed.

Suitcase in hand, he headed for the Bund. He knew Nieh Ho-T'ing and his buddies were taking the real risk; if the Lizards inside the British Consulate were on their toes, the scheme was dead in the water.

He got to Number 33, the Bund, just as clocks were striking twelve. Nieh would be pleased with him; when he said noon, he meant on the dot. Now Bobby had to hang around and look inconspicuous till the fireworks started. He bought a bowl of watery soup from a passing vendor, then had an inspiration and bought the bowl itself. He sat down on the pavement with it beside him and made like a beggar.

Every once in a while, somebody tossed a copper in the

bowl, or even some silver. Bobby kept track—when the shooting started, he had just over a dollar, Mex.

The British Consulate was a large, imposing building. Not even its stonework, though, could muffle the rattle of automatic weapons fire. The Lizard guards at the main entrance whirled around and stared, as if unsure what to do next and unable to believe the ears they didn't have.

Fiore didn't give them much of a chance to think it over. As soon as he heard guns, he opened the suitcase, yanked out a grenade, unscrewed the metal cap at the bottom, pulled the porcelain bead inside to work the friction igniter, and let fly as if he were making a throw to the plate.

Had there been a runner, he would have been out. The grenade landed right in the middle of the four Lizards. When it went off a second later, people who had been exclaiming over the shots inside the consulate started screaming and running instead.

The only trouble was, it didn't knock out all the Lizards. A couple of them started shooting, even if they didn't know just where it had come from. The screams along the Bund turned into shrieks. Fiore dove behind a solid bench of wood and iron; he opened up with the submachine gun. He hoped he didn't hit anybody on the street, but he wasn't going to lose any sleep if he did—those Lizards had to go down. And down they went.

More shots from inside the British Consulate, then those entry doors burst open. Nieh and half a dozen other Chinamen, some wearing cooks' clothes, the rest looking like penguins in fancy waiter getup (though waiters didn't commonly tote automatic weapons), sprinted down the steps and then down the street.

Lizards opened up on them from the roof and from second-story windows. The fleeing humans started spinning and dropping and kicking, like flies swatted not quite hard enough to die right away. "You just talked about the bastards at the door, goddammit," Bobby muttered, as if Nieh Ho-T'ing were close enough to hear. "You didn't say nothin' about the rest of 'em."

He raised the submachine gun and blazed away at the Lizards till his magazine ran dry. He grabbed another one, slammed it into the weapon, and had just started shooting again when a burst of three bullets stitched across his chest.

The submachine gun fell out of his hands. He tried to reach for it, found he couldn't. He didn't hurt. Then he did. Then he didn't, ever again.

Brigadier General Leslie Groves strode across the campus of the University of Denver with his head down, as if he were a bull looking to trample anyone who got in his way. That hard-charging attitude had been instinctive in him until one day he noticed and deliberately cultivated it. Thanks in no small part to that, not a whole lot of people got in his way these days.

"Physicists," he snorted under his breath, again bullishly. The trouble with them was, they were so lost in their own rarefied world a lot of the time that they didn't always feel the pressure he put on them, let alone yield to it.

He didn't note anything out of the ordinary about the day until he walked into the Science building and discovered he didn't recognize any of the soldiers crowding the downstairs lobby. That made him frown; Sam Yeager and the rest of the dogfaces with the Met Lab crew were as familiar to him as his shoelaces.

He looked around for the highest-ranking officer he could find. "Why have we been invaded, Major?" he asked.

The fellow with the gold oak leaves on his shoulders saluted. "If you'd be so kind as to come with me, General—" he said in the polite phrases lower-ranking officers use to give their superiors orders.

Groves was so kind as to come with him until he figured out where he was going, which didn't take long. "Major, if I need an escort to find my own office, I'm the wrong man to head this project," he growled. The major didn't answer; he just kept walking. Groves fumed but followed. Sure enough, they were heading for his office. In front of it stood a couple of men who looked as tough and alert as soldiers but wore medium-snappy civilian suits. A light went on in Groves' head. He turned to the major and asked, "Secret Service?"

"Yes, sir."

One of the T-men, after checking Groves' face against a little photo he held in the palm of his hand, nodded to the other. The second one opened the door and said, "General Groves is here, sir."

"Well, he'd better come in, then, hadn't he?" an infinitely

familiar voice replied from within. "It being his office, after all."

"Why the devil didn't I get any warning President Roosevelt was coming to Denver?" Groves hissed to the major.

"Security," the other officer whispered back. "We have to assume the Lizards monitor everything we broadcast, and we've lost couriers, too. The less we say, the safer FDR is. Now go on in; he's been waiting for you."

Groves went in. He'd met Roosevelt before, and knew the President wasn't as vibrant in person as he appeared in the newsreels: being cooped up in a wheelchair would do that to you. But since the last time he'd seen FDR, a year earlier at White Sulphur Springs, the change was shocking. Roosevelt's flesh seemed to have fallen in on his bones; he might have aged a decade or more in that year. He looked like a man worn to death's door.

For all that, though, his grip was still strong when he reached out to shake General Groves' hand after the engineer had saluted. "You've lost weight, General," he observed, amusement in his eyes—his body might be falling to pieces around it, but his mind was still sharp.

"Yes, sir," Groves answered. Roosevelt had lost weight, too, but he wasn't about to remark on it.

"Sit down, sit down." The President waved him to the swivel chair behind his desk. Groves obediently sat. Roosevelt turned the wheelchair to face him. Even his hands had lost flesh; the skin hung loose on them. He sighed and said, "I wish to God I had a cigarette, but that's neither here nor there—certainly not here, worse luck." FDR sighed again. "Do you know, General, when Einstein sent me that letter of his back in '39, I had the feeling all his talk of nuclear weapons and bombs that could blow up the world was likely to be so much moonshine, but I couldn't take the chance of being wrong. And, it turns out, I was right—and how I wish I hadn't been!"

"Yes, sir," Groves repeated, but then added, "If you hadn't been right, though, sir, we'd have been in no position to resist the Lizards and to copy what they've done."

"That's true, but it's not what I meant," Roosevelt said. "I wish I'd been right, and that all the talk about nuclear weapons and atomic power and who knows what *were* so much moon-

shine. Then all I'd have to worry about would be beating Hitler and Hirohito, and the Lizards would be back on the second planet of the star Tau Ceti where they belong, and people wouldn't meet them for another million years, if we ever did."

"Is that where they're from?" Groves asked with interest. "I'll have to have our liaison man put the question to the Lizard POWs we have here."

FDR made a gesture of indifference. "As you like, and if you have the time; otherwise don't trouble yourself about it. These Lizards are an astonishing intelligence resource, aren't they?"

"Yes, sir," Groves said enthusiastically. "The ones we have here have been extremely cooperative."

"Not just them, General. With what we're learning from systematic interrogation of all our captives, we'll leap forward by decades, maybe centuries." Roosevelt's expression, which had brightened, turned cloudy again. "If we win the war, that is—which is what I came to talk about. What I want to know is, how soon will we have nuclear weapons of our own to use against the Lizards?" He leaned forward in his chair, intently awaiting Groves' reply.

Groves nodded; he'd expected the question. "Sir, I am told we can have one nuclear bomb fairly soon. England supplied us with enough plutonium that we need to manufacture only a few more kilograms of our own to have enough for a bomb. Within a year, the scientists here tell me."

"That's not soon enough." Roosevelt made a sour face. "It may do, but every day they shave off it will bring the country one day closer to being saved. How long for more after the first?"

Now it was Groves' turn to look unhappy. "You understand, sir, that we have to come up with all the explosive material for them on our own. The pile—that's what they call it—the Met Lab staff has built here isn't ideally designed for that, although we are improving it as we gain experience. And one of our physicists is scouting a site where we can build a pile that will give us larger amounts of plutonium." He wondered how Jens Larssen was doing.

"I know about Hanford," Roosevelt said impatiently. "I don't need the technical details, General—that's why *you're* here. But I do need to know how long I have to wait for my

weaponry so I can make sure there's still a country left when I get it."

"I understand," Groves said. "If all goes well—if the pile goes up on schedule and works as advertised, and if the Lizards don't overrun Hanford or wherever we put it—you should have more bombs starting about six months after the first one: by the end of 1944, more or less."

"Not soon enough," Roosevelt repeated. "Still, we're better off than the rest. The Germans might have been right there with us, but you've no doubt heard about the mistakes they made with their pile. The British are relying on us; we're passing information to the Japanese, who are well behind us; and the Russians—I don't know about the Russians."

Groves' opinion of Soviet scientific prowess was not high. Then he remembered the Russians had got some plutonium from that raid on the Lizards, too. "A wild card," he said.

"That's right." Roosevelt nodded emphatically. His famous jaw still had granite in it, no matter how badly the rest of his features had weathered. "I've been in touch with Stalin. He's worried—the Lizards are pushing hard against Moscow. If it falls, who can say whether the Russians will keep on listening to their government, and if they don't, we've lost a big piece of the war."

"Yes, sir," Groves said. Although he was as security-conscious as a man in his position had to be, he also had a well-honed curiosity—and how often did you get to pick the brain of the President of the United States? "How bad is it over in the Soviet Union, sir?"

"It's not good," FDR said. "Stalin told me that if I had any men to spare, he'd leave them under their own officers, leave them under my direct personal command if that was wanted, as long as they went over there and fought the Lizards."

Groves' lips puckered into a soundless whistle. That was a cry of pain if ever he'd heard one. "He's not just worried, sir, he's desperate. What did you tell him?"

"I answered no, of course," Roosevelt said. "We have a few small differences with the Lizards on our own soil at the moment." The high-pitched laugh so familiar from the radio and the newsreel screen filled the office. As it had so often in the past, it lifted Groves' spirits—but only for a moment. The danger facing—filling—the United States was too great to be

laughed off. The President continued, "For instance, the Lizards are pushing hard against Chicago, too. They have us cut in half along the Mississippi almost as badly as the North did with the South during the Civil War, to say nothing of the other areas they've carved out of the country. It hinders us every way you can think of, militarily and economically both."

"Believe me, sir, I understand that," Groves said, remembering how he'd had to bring the plutonium to Denver by way of Canada. "What can we do about it, though?"

"Fight 'em," Roosevelt answered. "If they're going to beat us, they'll have to *beat* us, no other way. From what we hear from prisoners we've captured, they've taken over two other whole worlds before they attacked us, and they've ruled them for thousands of years. If we lose, General, if we lay down and give up, it's for keeps. That's why I came to talk about the atomic bomb: if I have any weapon I can use against those dastardly creatures, I want to know about it."

"I'm sorry I can't give you better news, sir."

"So am I." Roosevelt hunched his shoulders and let out another long sigh. His shirt and jacket both seemed a couple of sizes too big. The burden of the war was killing him; Groves realized with a jolt that that was literally true. He wondered where Vice President Henry Wallace was and what sort of shape he was in.

He couldn't say that to the President. What he did say was, "The trick will be to get through the time between using the one bomb we can make fairly quickly and the rest, which will take longer."

"Yes indeed," FDR said. "I'd hoped that would be a shorter gap. As it is, we'll have to be very careful picking the time when we use the first one. You're right that we would be very vulnerable to whatever atomic response the Lizards make."

Groves had seen pictures of the slag heap the Lizards had made of Washington, D.C. He heard men who'd seen it talk about the incongruous beauty of the tall cloud of dust and hot gas that had sprouted over the city like a gigantic, poisonous toadstool. He imagined such toadstools springing into being above other cities across the United States, across the world. A bit of Latin from his prep-school days came back to haunt him: *they make a desert and they call it peace.*

When he murmured that aloud, the President nodded and

said, "Exactly so. And in a curious way, that may turn out to be one of our greatest strengths. Our Lizard prisoners insist to a man—well, to a Lizard—that they don't want to use their atomic weapons here on a large scale. They say it would do too much damage to the planet: they want to control Earth and settle colonists on it, not just smash us by any means that come to hand."

"Whereas, we can do anything we have to, to get rid of them," Groves said. "Yes, sir, I see what you mean. Odd that we should have fewer constraints on our strategy than they do when they have the more powerful weapons."

"That's just what I mean," Roosevelt agreed. "If we— humanity, that is—can say, 'If we don't get to keep our world, you won't use it, either,' that will give our scaly friends something new and interesting to think about. Their colonization fleet will be here in a generation's time, and I gather it can't be conveniently recalled. If the Lizards lay Earth to waste, the colonists are like somebody invited to a party at a house that's just burnt to the ground: all dressed up with no place to go."

"And no one to pass them a hose to put out the fire, either," Groves observed.

That won a chuckle from FDR. "Nice to know you were paying attention when I made my Lend-Lease speech."

Any military man who didn't pay attention to what his commander-in-chief said was an idiot, as far as Groves was concerned. He replied, "The question is how far we can push that line of reasoning, sir. If the Lizards are faced with the prospect of either losing the war or hurting us as badly as we hurt them, which will they choose?"

"I don't know," Roosevelt said, which made Groves respect his honesty. "I tell you this, though, General: compared to the problems we have right now, I shouldn't mind facing that one at all. I want you and your crew here to exert every effort possible to producing that first atomic bomb and then as many more as fast as you can. If we go down, I'd sooner go down with guns blazing than with our hands in the air."

"Yes, sir, so would I," Groves said. "We'll do everything we can, sir."

"I'm sure you will, General." Roosevelt turned his wheelchair and rolled toward the door. He got to it and opened it before Groves could come around the desk to do the job for him. That made the old jaunty look come back to his haggard fea-

tures, just for a moment. He liked to preserve as much independence as his circumstances allowed.

And in that, Groves thought, he was a good representative for the whole planet.

☆ **XVIII** ☆

Mordechai Anielewicz had never imagined he would be relieved that the Lizards had set up a rocket battery right outside
Leczna, but he was. That gave him an excuse to stay indoors,
which meant he didn't have to see Zofia Klopotowski for a
while.

"It's not that I don't like her, you understand," he told Dr.
Judah Ussishkin over the chessboard one night.

"No, it wouldn't be that, would it?" Ussishkin's voice was
dry. He moved a knight. "She's fond of you, too."

Anielewicz's face flamed as he studied the move. Zofia
would have been more fond of him in direct proportion to any
increased stamina he showed. He'd never imagined an affair
with a woman who was more lecherous than he was; up till
now, he'd always had to do the persuading. But Zofia would
drop anything to get between the sheets—or under a wagon, or
into the backseat of Dr. Ussishkin's moribund Fiat.

Trying to keep his mind on the game, Mordechai pushed a
pawn one square ahead. That kept the knight from taking a position in which, with one more move, it could fork his queen
and a rook.

A beatific smile wreathed Ussishkin's tired face. "Ah, my
boy, you are learning," he said. "Your defense has made good
progress since we began to play. Soon, now, you will learn to
put together an effective attack, and then you will be a player
to be reckoned with."

"Coming from you, Doctor, that's a compliment." Anielewicz wanted to be a player to be reckoned with, and he wanted
to mount an effective attack. He hadn't got to be head of the
Jewish fighters in Lizard-occupied Poland by sitting back and

waiting for things to happen; his instinct was to try to make them happen. Against Ussishkin, he hadn't been able to, not yet.

He did his best; the midgame might have seen a machine gun rake the chessboard, so fast and furious did pieces fall. But when the exchanges were done, he found himself down a bishop and a pawn and facing another losing position. He tipped over his king.

"You make me work harder all the time," Ussishkin said. "I got some plum brandy for stitching up a farmer's cut hand yesterday. Will you take a glass with me?"

"Yes, thank you, but don't ask me for another game of chess afterwards," Mordechai said. "If I can't beat you sober, I'm sure I can't beat you *shikker.*"

Ussishkin smiled as he poured. "Chess and brandy do not mix." The brandy came from a bottle that had once, by its label, held vodka. People still had vodka these days, but it was homemade. For that matter, the plum brandy had to be homemade, too. Ussishkin lifted his glass in salute. *"L'chaym."*

"L'chaym." Anielewicz drank. The raw brandy charred all the way down; sweat sprang out on his face. "Phew! If that were any stronger, you wouldn't need gasoline for your automobile."

"Ah, but if I got it running, think how disappointed you and Zofia would be," Ussishkin said. Mordechai blushed again. In the candlelight, the doctor didn't notice, or pretended he didn't. He turned serious. "I know telling a young man to be careful is more often than not a waste of time, but I will try with you. Do be careful. If you make her pregnant, her father will not be pleased, which means the rest of the Poles here will not be pleased, either. We and they have gotten on as well as could be expected, all things considered. I would not like that to change."

"No, neither would I," Mordechai said. For one thing, Leczna held a good many more Poles than Jews; strife would not be to the minority's advantage. For another, strife among the locals was liable to draw the Lizards' unwelcome attention to the town. They already had more interest than Anielewicz liked, for they drew their food locally. He preferred staying in obscurity.

"You seem sensible, for one so young." Ussishkin sipped his

brandy again. He didn't cough or flush or give any other sign he wasn't drinking water. An aspiring engineer till the war, Anielewicz guessed he'd had his gullet plated with stainless steel. The doctor went on, "You should also remember—if she does conceive, the child would be raised a Catholic. And she might try to insist on your marrying her. I doubt"—now Ussishkin coughed, not from the plum brandy but to show he did more than doubt—"she would convert. Would you?"

"No." Mordechai answered without hesitation. Before the Germans invaded, he hadn't been pious; he'd lived in the secular world, not that of the *shtetl* and the *yeshiva*. But the Nazis didn't care whether you were secular or not. They wanted to be rid of you any which way. More and more, he'd decided that if he was a Jew, he'd *be* a Jew. Turning Christian was not an option.

"Marriages of mixed religion are sometimes happy, but more often battlegrounds," Ussishkin observed.

Mordechai didn't want to marry Zofia Klopotowski. He wouldn't have wanted to marry her if she were Jewish. He did, however, want to keep on making love with her, if not quite as often as she had in mind. If he did, she'd probably catch sooner or later, which would lead to the unpleasant consequences the doctor had outlined. He knocked back the rest of his brandy, wheezed, and said, "Life is never simple."

"There I cannot argue with you. Death is simple; I have seen so much death these past few years that it seems very simple to me." Ussishkin exhaled, a long, gusty breath that made candle flames flutter. Then he poured fresh plum brandy into his glass. "And if I start talking like a philosopher instead of a tired doctor, I must need to be more sober or more drunk." He sipped. "You see my choice."

"Oh, yes." Mordechai put an edge of irony in his voice. He wondered how many years had rolled past since Judah Ussishkin last got truly drunk. *Probably more than I've been alive,* he thought.

Far off in the distance, he heard airplane engines, at first like gnats with deep voices but rapidly swelling to full-throated roars. Then roars, these harsh and abrupt, rose from the rocket battery the Lizards had stationed out beyond the beet fields.

Ussishkin's face grew sad. "More death tonight, this time in the air."

"Yes." Anielewicz wondered how many German or Russian planes, how many young Germans or Russians, were falling out of the sky. Almost as many as the Lizards had shot at—their rockets were ungodly accurate. Flying a mission knowing you were likely to run into such took courage. Even if you were a Nazi, it took courage.

Somewhere not far away, a thunderclap announced a bomber's return to earth. Dr. Ussishkin gulped down the second glass of brandy, then got himself a third. Anielewicz raised an eyebrow; maybe he did mean to get drunk. The physician said, "A pity the Lizards can slay with impunity."

"Not with impunity. We—" Anielewicz shut up. One glass of brandy had led him to say one word too many. He didn't know how much Ussishkin knew about his role as Jewish fighting leader; he'd carefully refrained from asking the doctor, for fear of giving away more than he learned. But Ussishkin had to be aware he was part of the resistance, for Anielewicz was not the first man who'd taken refuge here.

In a musing voice, as if speculating about an obscure and much disputed biblical text, Ussishkin said, "I wonder if anything could be done about those rockets without endangering the townsfolk."

"Something could probably be done," Anielewicz said; he'd studied the site with professional interest while the Lizards prepared it. "What would happen to the town afterwards is a different question."

"The Lizards are not the hostage takers the Nazis were," Ussishkin said, still musingly.

"I have the feeling they knew war only from books before they got here," Mordechai answered. "A lot of the filthy stuff, no matter how well it works, doesn't get into that kind of book." He glanced sharply over at Ussishkin. "Or are you saying *I* should do something about that rocket installation?"

The doctor hesitated; he knew they were treading dangerous ground. At last he said, "I thought you might perhaps have some experience in such things. Was I wrong?"

"Yes—and no," Anielewicz said. Sometimes you had to know when to drop your cover, too. "Playing games with the Lizards here is a lot different from what it's like in a place like Warsaw. A lot more buildings to hide among there—a lot more people to hide among, too. Here their rocket launchers and ev-

erything they use for them are set up right out in the open—hard to get at without being spotted."

"I don't suppose the razor-wire circles around them make matters any easier, either," Ussishkin murmured.

"They certainly don't." Anielewicz thought about going off in the night and trying to pot a few Lizards from long range with his Mauser. But the Lizards had gadgets that let them see in the dark the way cats wished they could. Even without those gadgets, sniping wouldn't really hurt the effectiveness of the battery: the Lizards would just replace whatever males he managed to wound or kill.

Then, all of a sudden, he laughed out loud. "And what amuses you?" Judah Ussishkin asked. "Somehow I doubt it's razor wire."

"No, not razor wire," Anielewicz admitted. "But I think I know how to get through it." He explained. It didn't take long.

By the time he was done, Ussishkin's eyes were wide and staring. "This will work?" he demanded.

"They had enough trouble with it in Warsaw," Mordechai said. "I don't know just what it will do here, but it ought to do *something*."

"You're still lying low, aren't you?" Ussishkin said, then answered his own question: "Yes, of course you are. And even if you weren't, I'd be a better choice to approach Tadeusz Sobieski, anyhow. He's known me all his life; when he was born, my Sarah delivered him. I'll talk with him first thing in the morning. We'll see if he can be as generous to the Lizards as you have in mind."

With that, Anielewicz had to be content. He stayed inside Dr. Ussishkin's house. Sarah wouldn't let him help with the cooking or cleaning, so he read books and studied the chessboard. Every day, a horse-drawn wagon rattled down the street, carrying supplies from Sobieski the grocer to the Lizards at their rocket battery.

For several days, nothing happened. Then one bright, sunny afternoon, a time when neither the *Luftwaffe* nor the Red Air Force would be insane enough to put planes in the air over Poland, the battery launched all its rockets, one after another, *roar! roar! roar!* into the sky.

Farmworkers came running in from the fields. Mordechai felt like hugging himself with glee as he listened to scraps of

their excited conversation: "The things have gone crazy!" "Shot off their rockets, then started shooting at each other!" "Never seen fireworks like them in all my born days!"

Dr. Ussishkin came into the house a few minutes later. "You were right, it seems," he said to Anielewicz. "This was the day Tadeusz laced all the supplies with as much ginger as he had. They do have a strong reaction to the stuff, don't they?"

"It's more than a drunk for them; more like a drug," Mordechai answered. "It makes them fast and nervous—hairtrigger, I guess you might say. Somebody must have imagined he heard engines or thought he saw something in one of their instruments, and that would have been plenty to touch them off."

"I wonder what they'll do now," Ussishkin said. "Not the ones who went berserk out there today, but the higherranking ones who ordered the battery placed where it was."

They didn't have long to wait for their answer. At least one of the Lizards must have survived and radioed Lublin, for inside the hour several Lizard lorries from the urban center rolled through the streets of Leczna. When they left the next day, they took the rocket launchers with them. If the battery went up again, it went up somewhere else.

With the Lizards out of the neighborhood, Anielewicz had no more excuse for staying indoors all the time. Zofia Klopotowski waylaid him and dragged him into the bushes, or as near as made no difference. After his spell of celibacy, he kept up with her for a while, but then his ardor began to flag.

Just as he'd never imagined he'd have been relieved to see the Lizards erect their rocket battery in his own back yard, so to speak, he found equally surprising his halfhearted wish that they'd come back.

A disheveled soldier shouted frantically in Russian. When George Bagnall didn't understand fast enough to suit him, he started to point his submachine gun at the grounded aviator.

By then, Bagnall had had a bellyful of frantic Russians. He'd even had a bellyful of frantic Germans, a species that did not exist in stereotype but proved quite common under the stress of combat. He got to his feet, knocked the gun barrel aside with a contemptuous swipe, and growled, "Why don't you shove that thing up your arse—or would you rather I did it for you?"

He spoke in English, but the tone got across. So did his manner. The Red Army man stopped treating him like a servant and started treating him like an officer. The old saw about the Hun being either at your throat or at your feet seemed to apply even more to Russians than it did to Germans. If you gave in to them, they rode roughshod over you, but if you showed a little bulge, they figured you had to be the boss and started tugging at their forelocks.

Bagnall turned to Jerome Jones. "What's this bloody goon babbling about? I have more Russian than I did when we got stuck here—not hard, that, since I had none—but I can't make head nor tail of it when he goes on so blinking fast."

"I'll see if I can find out, sir," Jones answered. The radarman had spoken a little Russian before he landed in Pskov; after several months—*and no doubt a good deal of intimate practice with the fair Tatiana,* Bagnall thought enviously—he was pretty fluent. He said something to the Russian soldier, who shouted and pointed to the map on the wall.

"The usual?" Bagnall asked.

"The usual," Jones agreed tiredly: "wanting to know if his unit should conform to General Chill's orders and pull back from the second line to the third one." He switched back to Russian, calmed down the soldier, and sent him on his way. "They'll obey, even if he is a Nazi. They probably should have obeyed two hours ago, before Ivan there came looking for us, but, God willing, they won't have taken too many extra casualties for being stubborn."

Bagnall sighed. "When I proposed this scheme, I thought we'd get only the serious business." He made a face. "I was young and naive—I admit it."

"You'd damned well better," said Ken Embry, who was pouring himself a glass of herb-and-root tea from a battered samovar on the opposite side of the gloomy room in the Pskov *Krom*. "You must have thought being tsar came with the *droit de seigneur* attached."

"Only for Jones here," Bagnall retorted, which made the radarman stammer and cough. "At the time, I remember thinking two things. First was to keep the Nazis and Bolshies from bashing each other so the Lizards wouldn't have themselves a walkover here."

"We've managed that, for the moment, anyhow," Embry

said. "If the Lizards committed more tanks to this front, we'd have a dry time of it, but they seem to have decided they need them elsewhere. They get no complaints from me on that score, I assure you."

"Nor from me," Bagnall said. "They're quite enough trouble as is."

"There's fighting on the outskirts of Kaluga, the wireless reports," Jerome Jones said. "That's not far southwest of Moscow, and there's damn all between it and Red Square. Doesn't sound what you'd call good."

"No, that's bad," Embry agreed. "Makes me glad so many of the fighters here are partisans—locals—and not regular-army types recruited from God knows where. If you're fighting for your own particular home, you're less likely to want to pack it in if Moscow falls."

"I hadn't thought of that, but I dare say you're right," Bagnall answered, "even if it is a most unsocialist thing to say."

"What, that you're gladder to fight for your own property? Well, I'm a Tory from a long line of Tories, and I don't feel the slightest bit guilty about it," Embry said. "All right, George, you didn't want the Russians and the Jerries to go at each other. What was the other notion in what passes for your mind as to why we needed this particular headache?"

"After that raid on the Lizards' outpost, I had a serious disinclination toward infantry combat, if you must know," Bagnall said. "What of you?"

"Well, I must admit that, given the choice between another stint of it and ending up in the kip with that barmaid in Dover we all knew, I'd be likely to choose Sylvia," Embry said judiciously. "I do believe, however, that we perform a useful function here. If we didn't, I'd feel worse about not shouldering my trusty rifle and going out to do or die for Holy Mother Russia."

"Oh, quite," Bagnall agreed. "Keeping the Germans and the Soviets from each other's throats isn't the least contribution we could make to the war effort in Pskov."

Lizard planes roared low overhead. Antiaircraft guns, mostly German, threw shells into the air at them, adding to the racket that pierced the *Krom's* thick stone walls. None of the antiaircraft guns was stationed very close to Pskov's old citadel. The

ack-ack wasn't good enough to keep the Lizards from hitting just about anything they wanted to hit, and drew their notice to whatever it tried to protect. Bagnall approved of not having their notice drawn to the *Krom*: being buried under tons of rock was not the way of shuffling off this mortal coil he had in mind.

Lieutenant General Kurt Chill stalked into the room, followed by Brigadier Aleksandr German, one of the chiefs of what had been the partisan Forest Republic until the Lizards came. Both men looked furious. They had even more basic reasons than most in Pskov for disliking and distrusting each other: it wasn't just *Wehrmacht* against Red Army with them, it was Nazi against Jew.

"Well, gentlemen, what seems to be the bone of contention now?" Bagnall asked, as if the disagreements in Pskov were over the teams to pick for a football pool rather than moves that would get men killed. Sometimes that detached tone helped calm the excited men who came for arbitration.

And sometimes it didn't. Aleksandr German shouted, "This Hitlerite maniac won't give me the support I need. If he doesn't send some men, a lot of the left is going to come apart. And does he care? Not even a little bit. As long as he can keep *his* precious troops intact, who cares what happens to the front?"

Bagnall could barely follow the partisan brigadier's fast, guttural Yiddish. It was close enough to German for Chill to have no trouble understanding it, though. He snapped, "The man is a fool. He wants me to commit elements of the 122nd Antitank Battalion to an area where no panzers are opposing his forces. If I send the battalion piecemeal into fights which are not its proper province, none of it will be left when it is most desperately needed, as it will be."

"You've got those damned 88s," Aleksandr German said. "They aren't just antitank guns, and we're getting chewed up because we don't have any artillery to answer the Lizards."

"'Let's look at the situation map," Bagnall said.

"We've had to fall back here and here," Aleksandr German said, pointing. "If they force a crossing of this stream, we're in trouble, because they can nip in toward the center and start rolling up the line. We're holding there for now, but God knows how long we can keep doing it without some help— which *Herr* General Chill won't give us."

Chill pointed at the map, too. "You have Russian units here you can draw on for reinforcements."

"I have bodies, God knows," Aleksandr German said, and then was seized by a coughing fit as he realized he'd twice invoked a deity he wasn't supposed to believe in. He wiped his mouth on a sleeve and went on, "Bodies won't do the job by themselves, though. I need to break up the Lizards' concentrations back of their lines."

"It's a wasteful use of antitank troops," Chill said.

"I've been wasting Russians—why should your pampered pets be any different?" Aleksandr German retorted.

"They are specialists, and irreplaceable," the *Wehrmacht* man replied. "If we expend them here, they will not be available when and where their unique training and equipment are truly essential."

Aleksandr German slammed a fist against the map. "They are essential now, in the place where I requested them," he shouted. "If we don't use them there, we won't have a later for you to trot them out with all your fancy talk about right timing and right equipment. Look at the mess my men are in."

Chill looked, then shook his head with a disdainful expression on his face.

"Maybe you should reconsider," Bagnall told him.

The German general fixed him with a baleful stare. "I knew this piece of dumbheadedness was doomed to fail the moment it was suggested," he said. "It is nothing more than a smokescreen to get good German troops thrown into the fire to save the Anglo-Russian alliance."

"Oh, balls," Bagnall said in English. Chill understood him; his face got even chillier. Aleksandr German didn't, but he got the tone. The RAF man went on, in German again, "Not half an hour ago, I sent a Russian off confirming your—or some German's, anyhow—order to fall back. I'm trying to do the best job I can, given my look at the map."

"Perhaps you left your spectacles behind when you left London," Chill suggested acidly.

"Maybe I did, but I don't think so." Bagnall turned to Aleksandr German. "Brigadier, I know there aren't many tanks on your section of the front; if the Lizards had a lot of tanks, they'd be here by now, and we'd all be dead, not bickering. But are they using those troop carriers with the turret-mounted guns?"

"Yes, we have seen a good many of them," the partisan leader answered at once.

"There!" Bagnall said to Kurt Chill. "Are those troop carriers a good enough target for your antitank lads? You'd have to be lucky to take out a Lizard tank with an 88, but you can do all sorts of lovely things to a troop carrier with one."

"This is so." Chill rounded on Aleksandr German. "Why did you not say light armor was part of the threat you were facing? Had I known, I would have released units from the battalion at once."

"Who can tell what will make up a fascist's mind?" Aleksandr German answered. "If you're going to send men, you'd better go and do it." They left the map room together, arguing now about how many men and guns and where they needed to go rather than whether to send any at all.

Bagnall indulged in the luxury of a long, heartfelt "Whew!" Jerome Jones walked over and patted him on the back.

"Nicely done," Ken Embry said. "We are earning our keep here after all, seems to me." He got himself a glass of hot, brownish muck from the samovar, then let one eyelid droop in an unmistakable wink. "D'you suppose Comrade Brigadier German has really seen a whole fleet of armored troop carriers, or even so many as one?"

Jones gaped; his head swung from Embry to Bagnall and back again. Bagnall said, "I haven't the foggiest notion, truth to tell. But he picked up his cue in a hurry, didn't he? If armor rumbles into the neighborhood, even a literal-minded Jerry can hardly quarrel with rolling out the antitank guns, now can he?"

"Doesn't look as though he can, at any rate," Embry said. "I would have to say that hand goes to the heroic partisan." He raised his glass in salute.

"Comrade German is one very sharp chap," Bagnall said. "How good he is as a soldier or a leader of men I'm still not certain, but he misses very little."

"You threw out that line sure it was a lie and expecting him to snap at it anyhow," Jones said, almost in accusation.

"Haven't you ever done the like, with a barmaid for instance?" Bagnall asked, and was amused to watch the radarman turn red. "My notion was that if he said no, we'd be no worse off than we were already: Chill was going to balk, and we have nothing save whatever he uses as a sense of honor to

get him to keep the promise he made to accept our decision. Giving him a reason he could swallow for doing what we wanted looked to be a good idea."

"And next time, with luck, he'll be likelier to go along," Embry said. "Unless, of course, his men get wiped out and the position overrun, which is a risk in this business."

"If that happens, it will announce itself," Bagnall said, "most likely by artillery shells starting to land on Pskov." He pointed to the map. "We can't lose much more ground without coming into range of their guns."

"Nothing to do now but wait," Jones said. "Feels like being back at Dover, waiting for the Jerries to fly over and show up on the radar screen: it's a cricket match with the other side at bat, and you have to respond to what their batsman does."

Hours passed. A *babushka* brought in bowls of borscht, thick beet soup with a dollop of sour cream floating on top. Bagnall mechanically spooned it up till the bowl was empty. He'd never fancied either beets or sour cream, but he fancied going hungry even less. *Fuel*, he told himself. *Nasty-tasting fuel, but you need to top off your tanks.*

Evening came late to Pskov these days: the town didn't have the white nights of Leningrad to the north and east, but twilight lingered long. The western sky was still a bright salmon-pink when Tatiana came into the map room. Just the sight of her roused all the Englishmen, who were fighting yawns: even in the shapeless blouse and baggy trousers of a Red Army soldier, she seemed much too decorative to have a rifle with a telescopic sight slung over her back.

Jerome Jones greeted her in Russian. She nodded to him, but astonished Bagnall by walking up to him and kissing him to a point just short of asphyxiation. Her clothes might have concealed her shape, but she felt all woman in his arms.

"My God!" he exclaimed in delighted amazement. "What's that in aid of?"

"I'll ask," Jones said, much less enthusiastically. He started speaking Russian again; Tatiana replied volubly. He translated. "She says she's thanking you for getting the Nazi mother-molester—her words—to move his guns forward. They hit a munitions store when they shelled the rear area, and took out several troop carriers at the front lines."

"They really were there," Embry broke in.

Tatiana went on right through him. After a moment, Jones followed her: "She says she had a good day sniping, too, thanks to the confusion the guns sowed among them, and she thanks you for that, too."

"Looks as though we've held, at least for the time being," Embry said.

Bagnall nodded, but he kept glancing over at Tatiana. She was watching him, too, as if through that rifle sight. Her gaze was smoky as the fires Pskov used for heating and cooking. It warmed Bagnall and chilled him at the same time. He could tell she wanted to sleep with him, but the only reason he could see for it was that he'd helped her do a better job of killing.

The old saw about the female of the species being more deadly than the male floated through his mind. He'd heard it a dozen times over the years, but never expected to run across its exemplification. He didn't meet Tatiana's gaze again. No matter how pretty she was, as far as he was concerned, Jerome Jones was welcome to her.

Crack! Sam Yeager took an automatic step back. Then he realized the line drive was hit in front of him. He dashed in, dove. The ball stuck in his glove. His right hand closed over it to make sure it didn't pop out. He rolled over on the grass, held up his glove to show he had the ball.

The fellow who'd smacked the drive flipped away his bat in disgust. Yeager's teammates and, from behind the backstop, Barbara yelled and clapped. "Nice catch, Sam!" "Great play!" "You're a regular Hoover out there."

He threw the ball back to the PFC who was playing short, wondering what all the fuss was about. If you couldn't make that play, you weren't a ballplayer, not by the standards he set for himself. Of course, by those standards he was probably the only ballplayer at the Sunday afternoon pickup game. He might not have ever come close to the big leagues, but even a Class B outfielder looked like Joe DiMaggio here.

After an error on a routine ground ball, a strikeout ended the inning. Yeager tossed his glove to the ground outside the foul line and trotted in to the chicken-wire cage that served for a dugout. He was due to lead off the bottom of the sixth.

He'd walked his first time up and swung at a bad ball the second, hitting a little bleeder that had been an easy out. The

pitcher for the other side had a pretty strong arm, but he also thought he was Bob Feller—or maybe getting Yeager the last time had made him cocky. After wasting a curve down and away, he tried to bust Sam in on the fists with a fastball.

It wasn't fast enough or far enough in. Sam's eyes lit up as soon as he pulled the trigger. *Thwack!* When you hit the ball dead square, your hands hardly know it's met the bat—but the rest of you does, and so does everybody else. The pitcher wheeled through one of those ungainly pirouettes pitchers turn to follow the flight of a long ball.

The ball would have been out of Fan's Field or any other park in the Three-I League, but the field they were playing on didn't have fences. The left fielder and center fielder both chased after the drive. Sam ran like hell. He scored standing up. His teammates pounded him on the back and slapped him on the butt.

Behind the backstop, Barbara bounced up and down. Beside her, Ullhass and Ristin hissed excitedly. They weren't about to try going anywhere, not with so many soldiers around.

Yeager sat down on the park bench in the dugout. "Whew!" he said, panting. "I'm getting too old to work that hard." Somebody found a threadbare towel and fanned him with it, as if he were between rounds in a fight with Joe Louis. "I'm not dead yet," he exclaimed, and made a grab for it.

He got another hit his next time up, a line single to center, stole second, and went to third when the catcher's throw flew over the shortstop's head. The next batter picked him up with a ground single between the drawn-in shortstop and third baseman; that was the last run in a 7–3 win.

"You beat them almost singlehanded," Barbara said when he came around the wire fence to join her and the Lizard POWs.

"I like to play," he answered. Lowering his voice, he added, "And this isn't near as tough a game as I'm used to."

"You certainly made it look easy," she said.

"Make the plays and it does look easy, like anything else," he said. "Mess them up and you make people think nobody could ever play it right. God knows I've done that often enough, too—otherwise I wouldn't have been in the bush leagues all those years."

"How can you hit a round ball with a round stick and have it go so far?" Ristin asked. "It seems impossible."

"It's a bat, not a stick," Yeager answered. "As to how you hit it, it takes practice." He'd let the Lizards swing at easy tosses a few times. They choked way up on the bat; they were only about the size of ten-year-olds. Even so, they had trouble making contact.

"Come on," somebody called. "Picnic's starting."

It wasn't a proper picnic, to Yeager's way of thinking: no fire for wieners, just sandwiches and some beer. But the MPs and air raid wardens would have come down on them like a ton of bricks—if Lizard bombers hadn't already used the point of flame as a target for some of their explosive goodies.

The sandwiches were tasty: ham and roast beef on home-baked bread. And the Coors brewery was close enough to Denver that even horse-drawn wagons brought enough into town to keep people happy. The beer wasn't as cold as Sam would have liked, but he'd grown up in the days before iceboxes were universal, and falling back to those days wasn't too hard for him.

The breeze kicked up as the sun went down. Yeager wouldn't have minded a fire then, not at all: Denver nights got chilly in a hurry. Ullhass and Ristin felt it worse than he did; they put on the heavy wool sweaters they'd had knotted around their skinny, scaly waists. The sky got dark in a hurry, too, once the sun slipped behind the Rockies. Stars glittered brightly in the midnight-blue bowl of the heavens.

The ballplayers were used to having the Lizard POWs around. One of them pointed up to the points of light in the sky and asked, "Hey, Ristin, which one of those do you come from?"

"It is behind Tosev—your star for this world," Ristin answered. "You cannot see it now."

"The Lizards come from the second planet of Tau Ceti," Yeager said. "They've got their hooks on the second planet of Epsilon Eridani and the first planet of Epsilon Indi. We were next on the list."

"Those are the names of stars?" said the fellow who'd asked Ristin where he was from. "I've never heard of any of 'em."

"I hadn't, either, not till the Lizards came," Sam answered. "I grew up on a farm, too—I thought I knew stars like the back of my hand. I knew the Dippers and Orion and the Dogs and the zodiac and things like that, but there's a lot more sky

than I ever figured on. And Epsilon Indi's like the Southern Cross—too far south to see from here."

"So what're these places like?" the man asked.

"Tosev is hotter and brighter than the sun—the sun of Home, I mean," Ristin said. "Rabotev—what you call Epsilon Eridani"—he hissed the name—"is like our sun, but Halless, Epsilon Indi"—another hiss—"is cooler and more orange. Next to any of the worlds the Race rules, Tosev 3 is cold and wet and not very comfortable." He gave a theatrical shiver.

"The sun's a type-G star, a yellow one," Yeager added. "So is Tau Ceti, but it's at the cool end of the G range and the sun's at the warm end. Epsilon Eridani's at the warm end of the K range, which is the next one over from G, and Epsilon Indi's a little fellow at the cool end of that range."

"How much of this stuff did you know before you started riding herd on the Lizards there?" somebody asked slyly.

"Some; not all," Yeager said. "If I hadn't known some, I would have been lost—but then, if I hadn't known some, I wouldn't have gotten the job in the first place." He added, "I've learned a heck of a lot since then, too." He would have made that stronger if Barbara hadn't been sitting on the grass beside him.

She reached out and squeezed his hand. "I'm proud of how much you know," she said. He grinned like a fool. Till Barbara, he'd never known a woman who gave a damn how smart he was—and precious few men, either. If a ballplayer read books on the train or the bus, he got tagged "Professor," and it wasn't the sort of nickname you wanted to have.

He climbed to his feet. "Come on, Ullhass, Ristin—time to take you back to your nice heated room." The adjective got the Lizards moving in a hurry, as it usually did. Sam chuckled under his breath. He'd always figured white men knew more than Indians, because Columbus had found America and the Indians hadn't discovered Europe. By that standard, the Lizards knew more than people: Sam might have flown to far planets in his mind, but the Lizards had come here for real. All the same, though, the gap wasn't so wide that he couldn't manipulate them.

"So long, Sam." "See you in the morning." "Way to play today, Slugger." The ballplayers said their good-byes. The pitcher off whom he'd homered and singled added, "I'll get

you next time—or maybe we'll be on the same side and I won't have to worry about it."

"They like you," Barbara remarked as they picked their way across the dark University of Denver campus with Ristin and Ullhass.

Keeping an eye on them made his answer come slower than it would have otherwise: "Why shouldn't they like me? I'm a regular guy; I get along with people pretty well."

Now Barbara walked along silently for a while. At last she said, "When I would go out with Jens, it was always as if we were on the outside looking in, not part of the crowd. This is different. I like it."

"Okay, good," he said. "I like it, too." Every time she compared him favorably to her former husband, he swelled with pride. He laughed a little. Maybe she was using that the same way he used the promise of heat with the Lizards.

"What's funny?" Barbara asked.

"Nothing's funny. I'm happy, that's all." He slipped an arm around her waist. "Crazy thing to say in the middle of a war, isn't it? But it's true."

He got Ristin and Ullhass settled in their secured quarters, then headed back to the apartment with Barbara. They were just coming to East Evans Street when a flight of Lizard planes roared over downtown Denver to the north. Along with the roar of their engines and the flat *crummp!* of exploding bombs came the roar of all the antiaircraft guns in town. Inside half a minute, the sky turned into a Fourth of July extravaganza, with tracers and bursting shells and wildly wigwagging searchlights doing duty for skyrockets and pinwheels and Roman candles.

Shrapnel pattered down like hail. "We better not stand here watching like a couple of dummies," Sam said. "That stuff's no good when it lands on your head." Holding Barbara's hand, he led her across the street and into the apartment building. He felt safer with a tile roof over him and solid brick walls all around.

The antiaircraft guns kept hammering for fifteen or twenty minutes, which had to be long after the Lizards' planes were gone. Behind blackout curtains, Sam and Barbara got ready for bed. When she turned out the light, the bedroom was dark as the legendary coal cellar at midnight.

Sam slid toward her under the cover. Even through his pajamas and the cotton nightgown she wore, the feel of her in his arms was worth all the gold in Fort Knox, and another five bucks besides. "Yeah, happy."

"So am I." Barbara giggled. "By the way he's poking me there, you're not just happy."

She wasn't shy about it, or upset, either. That was the good half of her having been married before: she was used to the way men worked. But Yeager shook his head. "Nah, *he's* horny, but I'm not really," he answered. "I'd sooner just hold you for a while and then go to sleep."

She squeezed him tight enough to bring the air out in a surprised *oof.* "That's a very sweet thing to say."

"It's a very *tired* thing to say," he answered, which made her poke him in the ribs. "If I were ten years younger—aah, phooey, if I were ten years younger, you wouldn't want anything to do with me."

"You're right," she said. "But I like you fine the way you are. You really have learned an amazing amount about the Lizards in a very short time." As if to prove her own point, she added an emphatic cough.

"Mm, I suppose so," he said. "Not as much as I want to, though, not just for the sake of the war but because I'm curious, too. And there's one thing I don't begin to have a clue about."

"What's that?"

"How to get rid of them," Yeager said. Barbara nodded against his chest. He fell asleep with her still in his arms.

Ussmak gunned the landcruiser toward the next Tosevite town ahead: Mulhouse, its name was. After so long going up and down the road between Besançon and Belfort, pushing past Belfort made him feel he was exploring new territory. He spoke that conceit aloud: "We might as well be part of the band of Sherran—you know, the first male to march all the way around Home."

"We studied Sherran just out of hatchlinghood, driver," Nejas said. "How long ago did he live? A hundred fifty thousand years, something like that—long before the Emperors unified Home under their benevolent rule."

Ussmak cast down his eye turrets, but only for a perfunctory

instant. No matter how important formalities were to the life of the Race, not getting killed counted for even more. And the more built-up the area got, the more danger the landcruiser faced and the smaller the chance he had to react to it.

A cloth whipped in the breeze above a half-burnt building: not the red, white, and blue stripes of France, but a white circle on a red background, with a twisty black symbol on the white. The Big Uglies used such flapping rags to tell one of their tiny empires from the next. Ussmak felt a certain amount of pride that the forces of the Race had at last penetrated into Deutschland.

Bullets rattled off the landcruiser's flank and turret. The cupola up top closed with a clang. Ussmak hissed in relief: for the first time in a long while, he had himself a landcruiser commander whom he would have minded seeing dead.

"Driver halt," Nejas ordered, and Ussmak obediently pressed on the brake pedal. "Gunner, turret bearing 030. That building with the banner above it, two rounds high explosive. The machine gun is in there somewhere."

"Two rounds high explosive," Skoob echoed. "It shall be done, superior sir."

The landcruiser's main armament spoke once, twice. Inside the hull, shielded by steel and ceramic, the reports were not especially loud, but the heavy armored fighting vehicle rocked back on its tracks after each one. Through his vision slits, Ussmak watched the building, already in ruins, fly to pieces; the flag on the makeshift staff was wiped away as if it had never existed.

"Forward, driver," Nejas said in tones of satisfaction.

"Forward, superior sir," Ussmak acknowledged, and stepped on the accelerator. No sooner had the landcruiser begun to roll, though, than more bullets pattered off its side and rear deck.

"Shall I give them another couple of rounds, superior sir?" Skoob asked.

"No, the infantry will dig them out soon enough," the landcruiser commander said. "Small-arms ammunition is still in good supply, but we're low on shells, and we'll need high-explosive as well as armor-piercing if we have to fight inside Mulhouse." He didn't sound happy at the prospect. Ussmak didn't blame him: landcruisers were made for quick, slashing attacks to cut off and trap large bodies of the enemy, not to get

bogged down battling for a city one street at a time. But taking cities with infantry alone used up males at an alarming rate, even with air strikes. Armor had to help.

A cloud of dust rose not far in front of the landcruiser; dirt and asphalt rose in a graceful fountain, then pattered down again, some of it onto Ussmak's vision slits. He hit the cleaner button to clear them. Inside the landcruiser, he needed to worry about only a lucky hit from artillery—and if a round did pierce the vehicle, he'd probably be dead before he knew it.

Night was falling when they approached the built-up area Ussmak had seen ahead. Nejas said, "We have orders to halt outside of town. This shall be done, of course." Again the commander sounded less than pleased. As if trying to convince himself, he went on, "However good our night-vision equipment may be, our commanders do not care to go in amongst the Big Uglies' buildings in darkness. This is no doubt a wise precaution."

Ussmak wondered. If you lost momentum, sometimes you had trouble getting it back again. He said, "Superior sir, just this once I wish our commanders would stick their tongues in the ginger jar." Maybe he'd have a taste himself after everything was secured for the night. Nejas had searched the landcruiser for his little vial, but he'd never found it.

The commander said, "Just this once, maybe they should. I never thought I would hear myself say that, driver, but you may well be right."

Several landcruisers bivouacked together, under the cover of some broad, leafy trees. Not for the first time, Ussmak marveled at the spectacular profusion of plants on Tosev 3—far more varieties than Home enjoyed, or Rabotev 2, or Halless 1. He wondered if all the water on this world had something to do with that: it was the most obvious difference between the planets of the Empire and the Big Uglies' homeworld.

Even with infantry sentries all around, Nejas ordered his crewmales to stay in the landcruiser till they'd finished eating. Then he and Skoob took their blankets and went under the big armored hull to sleep, which gave them almost as much protection from the alert Deutsch snipers as staying inside the turret would have. Ussmak's seat flattened out enough to let him stay inside the forward hull section through the night.

That night should have passed peacefully, but it didn't. He jerked awake in alarm when the turret hatches clanged open.

Fearing Big Ugly raiders, he grabbed for his personal weapon and crawled back through the hull to poke his head up through the bottom of the turret ring.

The silhouette above him unmistakably belonged to a male of the Race. "What's going on?" Ussmak said indignantly. "I could have shot you as easy as not."

"Don't speak to me of shooting." Nejas sounded furious. "For a tenth of a day's pay, I'd turn the main armament of this landcruiser on what are lyingly called our supply services."

"Give the order, superior sir," Skoob said. The gunner had to be even more irate than his commander. "You wouldn't need to pay me to make me obey. I'd do it for free, and gladly. No supply service would be better than the mishatched one we have in place—or no worse, anyhow, for as best I can tell, we have no supply service in place."

"We expended a couple of rounds of high explosive against that machine-gun nest yesterday, if you'll recall?" Nejas said. "And we used the usual amount of armor-piercing fin-stabilized discarding sabot rounds, too—you may have noticed we've been fighting lately." He sounded as sardonic as Dref-sab, the most cynical male Ussmak had ever met.

The driver caught the drift of the way things were going. "We didn't get resupplied?" he asked.

"We got resupplied," Skoob said. Again echoing his commander, he went on sarcastically, "In their infinite wisdom and generosity, the fleetlords of the supply service have deigned to dole out to us five magnificent new rounds, one of which is actually high explosive."

"Aii." Ussmak let out a hiss of pain. "They've shorted us before, but never anywhere near so badly. If they do that for another two or three days, we won't have any ammunition left."

"It's all right," Skoob said. "Before long, they'll stop issuing hydrogen, too, so we won't be going anywhere anyhow."

That alarmed Ussmak all over again. Nejas said, "It's not quite so bad. To make hydrogen, all they need is water and energy. If Tosev 3 has too much of anything, it's water, and energy is cheap. But ammunition needs precision manufacture, too, and the Big Uglies who can do precision manufacture, or most of them, anyhow, aren't on our side. So we're short on landcruiser shells. They made it sound very logical when they explained it."

"Superior sir, I don't care about logic like that," the gunner retorted. "I have a logic of my own: if I don't get rounds for my gun, and if the Race doesn't take over some of the places here that can turn out our rounds, we'll lose—but how can we take them if we don't have the ammunition to do it?"

"Believe me, I wasn't supporting what the supply service males said, just setting it forth," Nejas said. "As far as I'm concerned, they all come out of addled eggs. If we don't have the ammunition to do the job now, it's just going to be tougher later."

The gunner grunted. "Right you are, superior sir. Let's get what they gave us stowed—the Emperor knows we'll need it tomorrow, even if the supply service hasn't a clue." One after another, the five new rounds clunked into place in the racks.

"Go back to sleep, driver," Nejas said when the job was done. "That's what we're going to do, anyhow."

Ussmak did his best to go back to sleep, but found himself worrying instead. Skoob's circular logic set his own head spinning. If the Race didn't have the munitions to overcome the Big Uglies, how were they supposed to conquer Tosev 3? For that matter, how were they supposed to conquer Mulhouse? They could fight their way into the town, but what were they supposed to do when they had no more shells and supply services had none to bring forward?

Get killed, that's what, Ussmak thought. He'd come too close to getting killed already, he'd seen too many males die around him, to contemplate that with equanimity. He wiggled and twisted on the lowered seat, trying to find a position where he wouldn't have to think. The manufacturers of the seat seemed to have overlooked that important design feature.

When sleep would not come no matter how he tried to lure it, he sat up and ever so cautiously took his vial of ginger from its hiding place. Even though he was alone in the landcruiser, he let his eye turrets swivel in all directions to make sure no one was watching him. Only then did his tongue flick out to taste the precious powder.

Instantly, his worries about how the advance into Deutschland would continue fell away. Of course the Race would do whatever was required. Ussmak could see, could all but reach out and touch, the best and easiest way to smash the Big Uglies once and for all. He wished Nejas and Skoob were in here with him. His wisdom would amaze them.

But somehow, try as he would, he couldn't make the image glittering in his ginger-filled mind turn from mere image into concrete words and plans. That was the herb's frustration: what it showed you seemed real until you tried to make it so. Then it proved as evanescent as the steam of his breath on a chilly Tosevite morning.

"Maybe if I have another taste, everything will come clear," Ussmak said. He reached for the vial again. Even before his hand closed on it, his tongue flicked out in anticipation.

Liu Han hated the little scaly devils' photographs, whether they moved or stood still. Oh, they were marvelous in their way, full of lifelike color and able to be viewed from more than one perspective, almost as if they were life itself magically captured.

But they had seldom shown her anything she wanted to see. When the little devils held her prisoner on the airplane that never came down, they'd made moving pictures of the congress they'd forced her to have with men she hadn't wanted. Then, after Bobby Fiore put a child in her, they'd terrified her with images of a black woman dying in childbirth. And now . . .

She stared down at the still photograph the scaly devil named Ttomalss had just handed her. A man lay on his back on the paved sidewalk of some city. His face looked peaceful, but he rested in a great glistening pool of blood and a submachine gun lay beside him.

"This is the Big Ugly male named Bobby Fiore?" Ttomalss asked in fair Chinese.

"Yes, superior sir," Liu Han said in a small voice. "Where is this picture from? May I ask?"

"From the city called Shanghai. You know this city?"

"Yes, I know this city—I know of it, I should say, because I have never been there. I have never been close to it." Liu Han wanted to make that as plain as she could. If Bobby Fiore had been killed fighting against the scaly devils, as certainly looked likely, she didn't want Ttomalss to suspect she was involved. Of that she was innocent.

The little devil turned one eye turret toward the photograph, the other toward her. She always found that disconcerting. He said, "This male of yours met these evil males who fight us

while he was in this camp. He met with them here, in this house. We have proof of this, and you do not ever say it is a lie. If he is with the Big Ugly bandits, maybe you are with these bandits, too?" In spite of the interrogative cough, his words sounded much more like a threat.

"No, superior sir." Liu Han used the other cough, the emphatic one. She would have been more emphatic still had she not been feeding the Communists information for weeks. Fear clogged her throat. To the little scaly devils, she was hardly more than an animal. Moreover, she was a woman, and women always ended up with the raw end of any deal.

"I think you are telling me lies." Ttomalss used the emphatic cough, too.

Liu Han burst into tears. Part of that was strategy as calculating as any general's. Tears bothered the little scaly devils even more than they bothered men: the little devils never cried. Seeing water from a person's eyes affected them much as seeing smoke coming out of someone's ears would have affected her. It distracted them and kept them from pushing as hard as they would have otherwise.

But if she forced the timing of the tears, at bottom they were real enough. Without the scaly devils, she never would have had anything to do with Bobby Fiore; he'd been just another of the men with whom they'd paired her. But he'd been as good to her as circumstances allowed—and he was the father of the child that kicked in her belly even now. Seeing him dead in a great puddle of his own blood was like a blow to the face.

And she wept for herself. Just before the little scaly devils came down from the sky, the Japanese had bombed her village and killed her husband and son. Now Bobby Fiore was gone, too. Everyone she cared about seemed to die.

She hugged herself; her forearms went around the swell of her abdomen. The baby kicked again. What would the little devils do with it once it came out into the world? Fear filled her again.

Ttomalss said, "Stop this disgusting dripping and answer what I say. I think you are lying, I tell you. I think you know much more of these bandits than you admit . . . Is that the right word, admit? Good. I think you hide this from us. We do not put up with these lies forever, I promise. Maybe not for long at all."

"Do you know what I think?" Liu Han said. "I think you have night soil where your wits should be. How am I supposed to be a bandit? I am in this camp. You put me here. You put all the people in here. If there are bandits among them, whose fault is that? Not mine, I tell you."

She managed to startle Ttomalss enough to make him turn both eye turrets toward her. "There are bandits in this camp; I admit that. When we set it up, we did not know how many foolish and dangerous factions you Big Uglies had, so we did not weed you carefully before we planted you here. But just because the bandits are here does not mean a properly obedient person will have anything to do with them."

The phrase he used had the literal meaning of *properly respectful to one's elders*. Hearing a little devil speak of filial piety was almost enough to send Liu Han from tears to hysterical laughter. But she sensed she'd made him retreat; he spoke to her now more as equal to equal, not in the badgering way he'd used before.

She pressed her tiny advantage: "Besides, how could I have anything to do with bandits? You watch me all the time. The only place I ever go is to the market. What can I do there?"

"The bandits came here," Ttomalss said. "This male"—he held up the photo of Bobby Fiore's corpse—"went with them. You knew it, and you said nothing to us. You are not to be trusted."

"I did not know where Bobby Fiore went, or why," she returned. "I never saw him again after that—till now." She started to cry again.

"I told you not to do that," the little devil said peevishly.

"I can't—help it," Liu Han said. "You show me a horrible picture that says my man is dead, you say I did all sorts of dreadful things"—*most of which I did*—"and now you want me not to cry? Too much!"

Ttomalss threw his hands in the air, much as Liu Han's husband had when he'd given up arguing with her. She hardly mourned him and her boy any more; her life had taken too many other hammer blows since they died. The scaly devil said, "Enough! Maybe you are telling the truth. Our drug to learn this works imperfectly, and I noted that we do not want to give it to you for fear of harming the hatchling growing inside you. You Big Uglies are revolting in so many different

ways, and we have to learn about all of them if we are to rule you properly."

"Yes, superior sir." Being bold came anything but easy for Liu Han, however useful she found it. She always breathed a silent sigh of relief when she returned to the submissive behavior that had been drilled into her since childhood.

The scaly devil said, "You will be closely watched. If you have any sense, you will act in a way that shows you remember this." He stalked out of Liu Han's dwelling. Had he been a man, he would have slammed the door behind him. Since he was a scaly devil, he left it open. Liu Han had learned that meant he thought anyone on the street was welcome to come in.

She poured herself a cup of tea from the battered brass pot that simmered above a charcoal brazier. Sipping it helped relax her—but not enough. She walked over and closed the door, but that didn't make her feel any more secure. She was as much the little devils' captive here as she had been in the metal cell on the airplane that never came down.

She wanted to scream and curse and tell Ttomalss exactly what she thought of him, but made herself hold back. Screaming and cursing would make her a scandal among her neighbors, and being the little scaly devils' creature made her scandal enough already. Besides, they might be taking talking cinema pictures of her, as they had to her shame up in that metal cell. If she cursed them, they could find out about it.

The baby moved inside her, not a kick this time but a slow, oceanic roll followed by a quick flutter. Again her arms went protectively round her belly. If she kept on obeying the little devils, what would the baby's fate be?

And if she didn't obey them, what would its fate be then? She didn't think the Communists would disappear even if the scaly devils conquered all of China (*all of the world,* she added to herself, something that never would have occurred to her before she spent time with Bobby Fiore). They'd kept right on fighting the Japanese; they would count on the people to hide them from the little devils. And they were very good at revenge.

In the end, fear wasn't what made her go out of her house and walk slowly toward the prison camp marketplace. Fury was: fury with the little scaly devils for turning her life upside

down, for treating her like a beast rather than a human being, for showing her, without the slightest worry over what she might feel to see him dead, the picture of the man she'd come to love—all they wanted from her was to confirm the body did belong to Bobby Fiore.

"Bean sprouts!" "Candles!" "Fine tea here!" "Carved jade!" "Peas in their pods!" "Sandals and straw hats!" "You can't beat my tasty ducks!" "Fine silk parasols—keep your pretty skin white!" "Pork sits sweet in your belly!"

The hubbub of the market square surrounded Liu Han. Along with vendors shouting the virtues of their wares, customers shouted scorn in the age-old struggle to get a better price. The din was dreadful. Liu Han could hardly hear herself think.

Ttomalss had warned her she would be closely watched. She believed that; the little scaly devils didn't understand people well enough to lie convincingly. But just because they watched her and listened to her, could they understand anything she said in this racket? She couldn't understand people who were yelling right beside her, and the little devils had trouble following even the most plain-spoken Chinese. She could probably say most of what she wanted without their being any the wiser.

She went slowly through the market, stopping now here, now there to haggle and gossip. Even had she been foolish enough to go straight to her contact in the marketplace, the Communists would have trained her to know better. As things were, she spent a lot of time loudly complaining about the little devils to a cadaverous-looking man who sold herbal medicines—and who worked for the Kuomintang. If the scaly devils landed on him, they'd be doing the Communists a favor.

Eventually, in the course of her wanderings, she reached the poultry dealer who had his stand next to the big-bellied pork merchant with the open vest. As she looked over the cut-up chunks of duck and chicken, she remarked, as if it were something that mattered little to her, "The little devils showed me a picture of Bobby Fiore today. They do not say so, but they put an end to him."

"I am sorry to hear this, but we know the ghost Life-Is-Transcendent has been seeking him." The poultry seller also spoke obliquely; that prancing ghost was a precursor of the god of death.

"He was in a city," Liu Han said.

"May he have aided the rise of the proletarian movement," the poultry seller answered. He paused, then asked very quietly, "Was the city Shanghai?"

"What if it was?" Liu Han was indifferent. To her, one city was just like another. She'd never lived in a place that had more people than this prison.

"If it was," the fellow went on, "a heavy blow against oppression and for the liberty of the oppressed peasants and workers of the world was struck there not long ago. In his passing, the foreign devil may well have shown himself to be a hero of the Chinese people."

Liu Han nodded. Since the scaly devils had the photo of Bobby Fiore dead, she'd figured they were likely the ones who had shot him—and the likeliest reason they had for shooting him was his being part of a Red raiding team. He wouldn't have thought of himself as a hero of the Chinese people: she was sure of that. Though living with her had rubbed some of the rough edges off him, at heart he remained a foreign devil.

She didn't much care that he had died a hero, either. She would rather have had him back at her hut, foreign and difficult but alive. She would rather have had many things that hadn't happened.

The poultry seller said, "What other interesting gossip have you heard?" The kind of gossip he found interesting had to do with the little scaly devils.

"What do you want for these chicken backs here?" she asked, not responding right away. He named a price. She shrieked at him. He yelled back. She attacked his gouging with a fury that astonished her. Then, after a moment, she realized she'd found a safe way to vent her sorrow for Bobby Fiore.

For whatever reasons he had, the poultry seller got caught up in the squabble, too. "I tell you, foolish woman, you are too stingy to deserve to live," he shouted, waving his arms.

"And I tell you, the little scaly devils are on especial watch for your kind, so you had better take care!" Liu Han waved her arms, too. At the same time, she watched the poultry seller's face to make sure he understood *your kind* to mean Communists, not thieving merchants. He nodded. He followed that perfectly well. She wondered how long he'd been a conspirator, looking for double meanings everywhere and finding them, too.

She hadn't been a conspirator long, but she'd managed to

put a double meaning across. Even if the little devils were listening to and understanding every word she said, they wouldn't have grasped the second message she'd given the poultry seller. She was learning the ways of conspiracy herself.

☆ **XIX** ☆

London was packed with soldiers and RAF men, sailors and government workers. Everyone looked worn and hungry and shabby. The Germans and then the Lizards had given the city a fearful pounding from the air. Bombs and fires had cut broad swaths of devastation through it. The phrase on everyone's lips was, "It's not the place it used to be."

All the same, it struck Moishe Russie as a close approximation to the earthly paradise. No one turned to scowl at him as he hurried west down Oxford Street toward Number 200. In Warsaw and Lodz, gentiles had made him feel he still wore the yellow Star of David on his chest even after the Lizards drove away the Nazis. The Lizards weren't hunting him here, either. There were no Lizards here. He didn't miss them.

And what the English reckoned privation looked like abundance to him. People ate mostly bread and potatoes, turnips and beets, and everything was rationed, but nobody starved. Nobody was close to starving. His son Reuven even got a weekly ration of milk: not a lot but, from what he remembered of his nutrition textbooks, enough.

They'd apologized for the modest Soho flat in which they'd set up his family, but it would have made three of the ones he'd had in Lodz. He hadn't seen so much furniture in years: they weren't burning it for fuel here. He even had hot water from a tap whenever he wanted it.

A guard in a tin hat in front of the BBC Overseas Services building nodded as he showed his pass and went in. Waiting inside, sipping a cup of ersatz tea quite as dreadful as anything available in Poland, stood Nathan Jacobi. "Good to see you, Mr. Russie," he said in English, and then fell back into Yid-

dish: "And now, shall we go and give the Lizards' little stumpy tails a good yank?"

"That would be a pleasure," Moishe said sincerely. He pulled his script from a coat pocket. "This is the latest draft, with all the censors' notes included. I'm ready to record it for broadcast."

"Jolly good," Jacobi said, again in English. Like David Goldfarb, he flipped back and forth between languages at will, sometimes hardly seeming to realize he was doing so. Unlike Goldfarb's, his Yiddish was not only fluent but elegant and un-accented; he spoke like an educated Warsaw Jew. Russie wondered if his English was as polished.

Jacobi led the way to a recording studio. But for a couple of glass squares so the engineers could watch the proceedings, the walls were covered with sound-deadening tiles, each punched with its own square grid of holes. On the table sat a microphone with a BBC plaque screwed onto its side. A bare electric bulb threw harsh light down onto the table and the chairs in front of it.

The arrangements were as up-to-date as human technology could produce. Moishe wished they impressed him more than they did. They were certainly finer than anything the Polish wireless services had had in 1939. But that was not the standard by which Russie judged them. In the first months after the Lizards took Warsaw, he'd broadcast anti-Nazi statements for them. Compared to their equipment, the BBC gear looked angular, bulky, and not very efficient, rather like an early wind-up gramophone with trumpet speaker set alongside a modern phonograph.

He sighed as he sat down on one of the hard-backed wooden chairs and set his script in front of him. The censors' stamps—a triangular one that said PASSED FOR SECURITY and a rectangle that read PASSED FOR CONTENT—obscured a couple of words. He bent down to peer at them and make sure he could read them without hesitation; even though the talk was being recorded for later broadcast, he wanted to be as smooth as he could.

He glanced over to the engineer in the next room. When the man suddenly shot out a finger toward him, he began to talk: "Good day, people of Earth. This is Moishe Russie speaking to you from London in free England. That I am here shows the

Lizards lie when they say they are invincible and their victory inevitable. They are very strong; no one could deny that. But they are not supermen"—he'd had to borrow *Übermenschen* from the German to put that across—"and they can be beaten.

"I do not intend to say anything about how I came from Poland to London, for fear of closing that way for others who may come after me. But I will say that I was rescued from a Lizard prison in Lodz, that Englishmen and local Jews took part in the rescue, and they defeated both the Lizards and their human henchmen.

"Too many men, women, and children live in parts of the world under Lizard occupation. I understand that, if you are to survive, you must to some degree go on about your daily work. But I urge you from the bottom of my heart to cooperate with the enemy as little as you can and to sabotage his efforts wherever you can. Those who serve as their prison guards and police, those who seek work in their factories to make munitions that will be used against their fellow human beings—they are traitors to mankind. When victory comes, collaborators will be remembered . . . and punished. If you see the chance, move against them now."

He had his talk nicely timed—he'd practiced it with Rivka back in the flat. He was just reaching his summing-up when the engineer held up one finger to show he had a minute left, and came to the end as the fellow drew his index finger across his throat. The engineer grinned and gave him a two-finger V for victory.

Then it was Nathan Jacobi's turn. He read an English translation (similarly stamped with censors' marks) of what Russie had just said in Yiddish, the better to reach as large an audience as possible. His timing was as impeccable as Moishe's had been. This time the engineer signaled his approval with an upraised thumb.

"I think that went very well," Jacobi said. "With any luck at all, it should leave the Lizards quite nicely browned off."

"I hope so," Moishe said. He got up and stretched. Wireless broadcasting was not physically demanding, but it left him worn all the same. Getting out of the studio always came as a relief.

Jacobi held the door open for him. They went out together. Waiting in the hallway stood a tall, thin, tweedy Englishman

with a long, craggy face and dark hair combed high in a pompadour. He nodded to Jacobi. They spoke together in English. Jacobi turned to Moishe and switched to Yiddish: "I'd like to introduce you to Eric Blair. He's talks producer of the Indian Section, and he goes in after us."

Russie stuck out his hand and said, "Tell him I'm pleased to meet him."

Blair shook hands with him, then spoke in English again. Jacobi translated: "He says he's even more pleased to meet you: you've escaped from two different sets of tyrants, and honestly described the evils of both." He added, "Blair is a very fine fellow, hates tyrants of all stripes. He fought against the fascists in Spain—almost got killed there—but he couldn't stomach what the Communists were doing on the Republican side. An honest man."

"We need more honest men," Moishe said.

Jacobi translated that for Blair. The Englishman smiled, but suffered a coughing fit before he could answer. Moishe had heard those wet coughs in Warsaw more times than he cared to remember. *Tuberculosis,* the medical student in him said. Blair mastered the coughs, then spoke apologetically to Jacobi.

"He says he's glad he did that out here rather than in the studio while he was recording," Jacobi said. Moishe nodded; he understood and admired the workmanlike, professional attitude. You worked as hard as you could for as long as you could, and if you fell in the traces you had to hope someone else would carry on.

Blair pulled his script from a waistcoat pocket and went into the studio. Jacobi said, "I'll see you later, Moishe. I'm afraid I have a mountain of forms to fill out. Perhaps we should put up stacks of paper in place of barrage balloons. They'd be rather better at keeping the Lizards away, I think."

He headed away to his upstairs office. Moishe went outside. He decided not to head back to his flat right away, but walked west down Oxford Street toward Hyde Park. People—mostly women, often with small children in tow—bustled in and out of Selfridge's. He'd been in the great department store once or twice himself. Even with wartime shortages, it held more goods and more different kinds of goods than were likely to be left in all of Poland. He wondered if the British knew how lucky they were.

The great marble arch where Oxford Street, Park Lane, and Bayswater Road came together marked the northeast corner of Hyde Park. Across Park Lane from the arch was the Speakers' Corner, where men and women climbed up on crates or chairs or whatever they had handy and harangued whoever would hear. He tried to imagine such a thing in Warsaw, whether under Poles, Nazis, or Lizards. The only thing he could picture was the public executions that would follow unbridled public speech. Maybe England had earned its luck after all.

Only a handful of people listened to—or heckled—the speakers. The rest of the park was almost as crowded with people tending their gardens. Every bit of open space in London grew potatoes, wheat, maize, beets, beans, peas, cabbages. German submarines had put Britain under siege; the coming of the Lizards brought little relief. They weren't as hard on shipping, but America and the rest of the world had less to send these days.

The island wasn't having an easy time trying to feed itself. Perhaps in the long run it couldn't, not if it wanted to keep on turning out war goods, too. But if the English knew they were beaten, they didn't let on.

All through the park, trenches, some bare, some with corrugated tin roofs, were scattered among the garden plots. Like Warsaw, London had learned the value of air raid shelters no matter how makeshift. Moishe had dived into one of them himself when the sirens began to wail a few days before. The old woman sprawled in the dirt a few feet away had nodded politely, as if they were meeting over tea. They'd stayed in there till the all-clear sounded, then dusted themselves off and gone on about their business.

Moishe turned and retraced his steps down Oxford Street. He explored with caution; wandering a couple of blocks away from the streets he'd already learned had got him lost more than once. And he was always looking the wrong way, forgetting traffic moved on the left side of the street, not the right. Had more motorcars been on the road, he probably would have been hit by now.

He turned right onto Regent Street, then left onto Beak. A group of men was going into a restaurant there—the Barcelona, he saw as he drew closer. He recognized the tall, thin figure of Eric Blair in the party; the India Section man must have finished his talk and headed off for lunch.

Beak Street led Russie to Lexington and from it to Broadwick Street, on which sat his block of flats. As with much of the Soho district, it held more foreigners than Englishmen: Spaniards, Indians, Chinese, Greeks—and now a family of ghetto Jews.

He turned the key in the lock, opened the door. The rich odor of cooking soup greeted him like a friend from home. He shrugged out of his jacket; the electric fire here kept the flat comfortably warm. Not sleeping under mounds of blankets and overcoats was another reward of coming to England.

Rivka walked out of the kitchen to greet him. She wore a white blouse and a blue pleated skirt that reached halfway from the floor to her knees. Moishe thought it shockingly immodest, but all the skirts and dresses she'd been given when she got to England were of the same length.

"You look like an Englishwoman," he told her.

She cocked her head to one side, giving that a woman's consideration. After a moment, she shook her head. "I *dress* like an Englishwoman," she said, with the same precision a *yeshiva* student might have used to dissect a subtle Talmudic point. "But they're even pinker and blonder than the Poles, I think." She flicked an imaginary bit of lint from her own dark curls.

He yielded: "Well, maybe so. They all seem so heavy, too." He wondered whether that perception was real or just a product of so many years of looking at people who were slowly— sometimes not so slowly—starving to death. The latter, he suspected. "That soup smells good." In his own mind, food had grown ever so much more important than it seemed before the war.

"Even with ration books, there's such a lot to buy here," Rivka answered. The pantry already bulged with tins and jars and with sacks of flour and potatoes. Rivka didn't take food for granted these days, either.

"Where's Reuven?" Moishe asked.

"Across the hall, playing with the Stephanopoulos twins." Rivka made a wry face. "They haven't a word in common, but they all like to throw things and yell, so they're friends."

"I suppose that's good." Moishe did wonder, though. In Poland, the Nazis—and the Poles, too—had cared too much that Jews were different from them. No one here seemed to care at all. In its own way, that was disconcerting, too.

As if to ease his mind over something he hadn't even mentioned, Rivka said, "David's mother telephoned this morning while you were at the studio. We had a good chat."

"That is good," he said. Working phones were another thing he was having to get used to all over again.

"They want us over for supper tomorrow night," Rivka said. "We can take the underground; she gave me directions on how to do it." She sounded excited, as if she were going on safari. Moishe suddenly got the feeling she was adapting to the new city, the new country, faster than he was.

Teerts felt bright, alert, and happy when Major Okamoto led him into the laboratory. He knew he felt that way because the Nipponese had laced his rice and raw fish with ginger—the spicy taste still lay hot on his tongue—but he didn't care. No matter what created it, the feeling was welcome. Until it wore off, he would feel like a male of the Race, a killercraft pilot, not a prisoner almost as much beneath contempt as the slops bucket in his cell.

Yoshio Nishina came round a corner. Teerts bowed in Nipponese politeness; no matter how much the ginger exhilarated him, he was not so foolish as to forget altogether where he was. "*Konichiwa*, superior sir," he said, mixing his own language and Nipponese.

"Good day to you as well, Teerts," replied the leader of the Nipponese nuclear weapons research team. "We have something new for you to evaluate today."

He spoke slowly, not just to help Teerts understand but also, the male thought, because of some internal hesitation. "What is it, superior sir?" Teerts asked. The warm buzz of ginger spinning inside his head made him not want to care, but experience with the Nipponese made him wary in spite of the herb to which they'd addicted him.

Now Nishina spoke quickly, to Okamoto rather than directly to Teerts. The Nipponese officer translated: "We need you to examine the setup of the uranium hexafluoride diffusion system we are establishing."

Teerts was a little puzzled. That was simple enough for him to have understood it in Nipponese. These days, Okamoto mainly reserved his translations for more complicated matters of physics. But pondering the ways of Big Uglies, even with

a head full of ginger, seemed pointless. Teerts bowed again and said, "It shall be done, superior sir. Show me these drawings I am to evaluate."

He sometimes wondered how the Big Uglies managed to build anything more complicated than a hut. Without computers that let them change plans with ease and view proposed objects from any angle, they had developed what seemed like a series of clumsy makeshifts to portray three-dimensional objects on two-dimensional paper. Some of them were like single views of computer graphics. Others, weirdly, showed top, front, and side views and expected the individual doing the viewing to combine them in his mind and visualize what the object was supposed to look like. Not used to the convention, Teerts had endless trouble with it.

Now, Major Okamoto bared his teeth in the Tosevite gesture of amiability. When the scientists smiled at Teerts, they were generally sincere. He did not trust Okamoto as far. Sometimes the interpreter seemed amiable, but sometimes he made sport with his prisoner. Teerts was getting better at reading Tosevite expressions; Okamoto's smile did not strike him as pleasant.

The major said, "Dr. Nishina is not speaking of drawings. We have erected this facility and begun processing the gas with it. We want you to examine it, not pictures of it."

Teerts was appalled, for a whole queue of reasons. "I thought you were concentrating on production of element 94—plutonium, you call it. That's what you said before."

"We have decided to produce both explosive metals," Okamoto answered. "The plutonium project at the moment goes well, but more slowly than expected. We have tried to speed up the uranium hexafluoride project to compensate, but there are difficulties with it. You will evaluate and suggest ways to fix the problems."

"You don't expect me to go inside this plant of yours, do you?" Teerts said. "You want me to check it from the outside."

"Whichever is necessary," Okamoto answered.

"But one reason you have so much trouble with uranium hexafluoride is that it's corrosive by nature," Teerts exclaimed in dismay, his voice turning into a guttural hiss of fright. "If I go in there, I may not come out. And I do not want to breathe either uranium or fluorine, you know."

"You are a prisoner. What you want is of no importance to

me," Okamoto said. "You can obey or you can face the consequences."

Ginger lent Teerts spirit he couldn't have summoned without it. "I am not a physicist," he shouted, loud enough for the stolid guard who accompanied Okamoto to unsling his rifle for the first time in many days. "I am not an engineer, not a chemist, either. I am a pilot. If you want a pilot's view of what is wrong with your plant, fine. I do not think it will help you much, though."

"You are a male of the Race." Major Okamoto fixed Teerts with a glare from the narrow eyes in that flat, muzzleless face: never had he looked more alien, or more alarming. "By your own boasting, your people have controlled atoms for thousands of years. Of course you will know more about them than we do."

"Honto," Nishina said: "That is true." He went on in Nipponese, slowly, so Teerts could understand: "I was speaking with someone from the Army, telling him what the atomic explosive would be like. He said to me, 'If you want an explosive, why not just use an explosive?' *Bakatare*—idiot!"

Teerts was of the opinion that most Big Uglies were idiots, and that most of the ones who weren't idiots were savage and vindictive instead. Expressing that opinion struck him as impolitic. He said, "You Tosevites have controlled fire for thousands of years. If someone sent one of you to inspect a factory that makes steel, how much would your report be worth to him?"

He used Nipponese for as much of that as he could, and spoke the rest in his own language. Okamoto interpreted for Nishina. Then, much to Teerts' delight, the two of them got into a shouting match. The physicist believed Teerts, the major thought he was lying. Finally, grudgingly, Okamoto yielded: "If you don't think he can be trusted to be accurate, or if you think he truly is too ignorant to be reliable, I must accept your judgment. But I tell you that with proper persuasion he could give us what we need to know."

"Superior sir, may I speak?" Teerts asked; he'd understood that well enough to respond to it. The surge of pleasure and nerve the ginger had brought was seeping away, leaving him more weary and glum than he would have been had he never set tongue on the stuff.

Okamoto gave him another baleful stare. "Speak." His voice held a clear warning that if Teerts' words were not very much to the point, he would regret it.

"Superior sir, I just wish to ask you this: have I not cooperated with you since the day I was captured? I have told everything I know about aircraft to the males of your Army and Navy, and I have told everything I know—much more than I thought I knew—to these males here, whom your Professor Nishina leads"—he bowed to the physicist—"even though they are trying to build weapons to harm the Race."

Okamoto bared his broad, flat teeth. To Teerts, they were unimpressive, being neither very sharp nor very numerous. He did, however, recognize the Big Ugly's ugly grimace as a threat gesture. Mastering himself, Okamoto answered, "You have cooperated, yes, but you are a prisoner, so you had better cooperate. We have given you better treatment since you showed yourself useful, too: more comfort, more food—"

"Ginger," Teerts added. He wasn't sure whether he was agreeing with Okamoto or contradicting him. The herb made him feel wonderful while he tasted it, but the Big Uglies weren't giving it to him for his benefit: they wanted to use it to warp him to their will. He didn't think they had, so far—but how could he be sure?

"Ginger, *hai*," Okamoto said. "Suppose I tell you that, after you go look at this uranium hexafluoride setup, we will give you not just ginger powder with your rice and fish, but pickled ginger root, as much as you can eat? You'd go then, *neh?*"

As much ginger as he could eat . . . did Tosev 3 hold that much ginger? The craving rose up and grabbed Teerts, like a hand around his throat. He needed all his will to say, "Superior sir, what good is ginger to me if I am not alive to taste it?"

Okamoto scowled again. He turned back to Nishina. "If he is not going to inspect the facility, do you have any more use for him today?" The physicist shook his head. To Teerts, Okamoto said, "Come along, then. I will take you back to your cell."

Teerts followed Okamoto out of the laboratory. The guard followed them both. Even through the melancholy he felt after ginger's exaltation left him, Teerts felt something akin to triumph.

That triumph faded as he went out onto the streets of Tokyo.

Even more than he had in Harbin, he felt himself a mote among the vast swarms of Big Uglies in those streets. He'd been alone in Harbin, yes, but the Race was advancing on the mainland city; had things gone well, he could have been reunited with his own kith at any time. But things had not gone well.

Here in Tokyo, even the illusion of rescue was denied him. Sea protected the islands at the heart of the Tosevite empire of Nippon from immediate invasion by the Race. He was irremediably and permanently at the mercy of the Big Uglies. They stared at him as he walked down the street; hatred seemed to rise from them in almost visible waves, like heat from red-glowing iron. For once, he was glad to be between Major Okamoto and the guard.

Tokyo struck him as a curious mixture. Some of the buildings were of stone and glass, others—more and more outside the central city—of wood and what looked like thick paper. The two styles seemed incompatible, as if they'd hatched from different eggs. He wondered how and why they coexisted here.

Air-raid sirens began to wail. As if by magic, the streets emptied. Okamoto led Teerts into a packed shelter in the basement of one of the stone-and-glass buildings. Outside, antiaircraft guns started pounding. Teerts hoped all the Race's pilots—males from his flight, perhaps—would return safely to their bases.

"Do you wonder why we hate you, when you do this to us?" Okamoto asked as the sharp, deep blasts of bombs contributed to the racket.

"No, superior sir," Teerts answered. He understood it well enough—and what it would do to him, sooner or later. His eye turrets swiveled this way and that. For the first time since he'd resigned himself to captivity, he began looking for ways to escape. He found none, but vowed to himself to keep looking.

Wearing His Majesty's uniform once more felt most welcome to David Goldfarb. The ribbon of the Military Medal, in the colors of the Union Jack, held a new place of pride just above his left breast pocket. He'd imagined the only way a radarman could win a ground combat medal was to have the Jerries or the Lizards invade England. Going to Poland as a commando hadn't been what he'd had in mind.

Bruntingthorpe had changed in the weeks he'd been away. More and more Pioneer and Meteor jet fighters sheltered in revetments. The place was becoming a working air base rather than an experimental station. But Fred Hipple's team for evaluating Lizard engines and radars still worked here—and, Goldfarb had not been surprised to discover on his return, still shared a Nissen hut with the meteorologists. The one they had occupied was replaced, but somebody else worked in it these days.

He traded greetings with his comrades as he went in and got ready to go to work. The stuff brewing in the pot above the spirit lamp wasn't exactly tea, but with plenty of honey it was drinkable. He poured himself a cup, adulterated it to taste, and went over to the Lizard radar unit.

It hadn't languished while he'd been performing deeds of derring-do and speaking Yiddish. Another radarman, an impossibly young-looking fellow named Leo Horton, had made a good deal of progress on it in the interim.

"Morning to you," Horton said in a nasal Devonshire accent.

"Morning," Goldfarb agreed. He sipped the not-quite-tea, hoping this morning's batch would carry a jolt. You couldn't gauge that in advance these days. Sometimes you could drink it by the gallon and do nothing but put your kidneys through their paces; sometimes half a cup would open your eyes wide as hangar doors. It all depended on what went into the witches' brew on any given day.

"I think I've made sense of some more of the circuitry," Horton said. He was frightfully clever, with a theoretical background in electronics and physics Goldfarb couldn't come close to matching. He also had a fine head for beer and, perhaps not least because he made them feel motherly, was cutting quite a swath through the barmaids up in Leicester. He reminded Goldfarb of an improved model of Jerome Jones, which was plenty to make him feel inadequate.

But business was business. "Good show," Goldfarb said. "Show me what you've got."

"You see this set of circuits here?" Horton pointed to an area of the disassembled radar not far from the magnetron. "I'm pretty sure it controls the strength of the signal."

"You know, I suspected that before I got drafted away from here," Goldfarb said. "I didn't have the chance to test it, though. What's your evidence?"

Horton opened a fat notebook with a cover almost the exact dark blue of his RAF uniform. "Here, look at these oscillo-scope readings when I shunt power through this lead here—" He pointed again to show which one he meant.

"I think you're right," Goldfarb said. "And look at the amplification." He whistled softly. "We wouldn't just be pro-moted—we'd be bloody knighted if we found out how the Liz-ards do this and we could fit it into our own sets."

"Too true, but good luck," Horton replied. "I can tell you what those circuits do, but I will be damned if I have the slightest notion of how they do it. If you took one of our Lancs and landed it at a Royal Flying Corps base in 1914—not that you could, because no runways then were anywhere near long enough—the mechanics then would stand a better chance of understanding the aircraft and all its systems than we do of making sense of—this." He jabbed a thumb at the Lizard radar.

"It's not quite so bad as that," Goldfarb said. "Group Cap-tain Hipple and his crew have made good progress with the engines."

"Oh, indeed. But he'd already figured out the basic princi-ples involved."

"We have the basic principles of radar," Goldfarb protested.

"But their radar is further ahead of ours than their jet en-gines are," Horton said. "It's just the quality of the metallurgy that drives the group captain mad. Here, the Lizards are using a whole different technology to achieve their results: no valves, everything so small the circuits only come clear under the mi-croscope. Figuring out *what* anything does is a triumph; figur-ing out *how* it does it is a wholly different question."

"Don't I know it," Goldfarb said ruefully. "There have been days—and plenty of 'em—when I'd sooner have kicked that bleeding radar out onto the rubbish pitch than worked on it."

"Ah, but you have managed to get away for a bit." Horton pointed to the Military Medal ribbon on Goldfarb's chest. "I wish I'd had the chance to try to earn one of those."

Remembering terror and flight, Goldfarb started to say he would have been just as glad not to have had the opportunity. But that wasn't really true. Getting his cousin Moishe and his family out of Poland had been worth doing; he knew only pride that he'd been able to help there.

The other thing he noted, with a small shock, was the edge

of genuine envy in Horton's voice. The new radarman's savvy had intimidated him ever since he got back to Bruntingthorpe. Finding out that Horton admired him was like a tonic. He remembered the gap that had existed back at Dover between those who went up to do battle in the air and those who stayed behind and fought their war with electrons and phosphors.

But Goldfarb had crossed to the far side of that gap. Even before he went to Poland, he'd gone aloft in a Lancaster to test the practicability of airborne radar sets. He'd taken Lizard fire then, too, but returned safely. Ground combat, though, was something else again. If one of those Lizard rockets had struck the Lanc, he never would have seen the alien who killed him. Ground combat was personal. He'd shot people and Lizards in Lodz and watched them fall. He still had nasty dreams about it.

Leo Horton was still waiting for an answer. Goldfarb said, "In the long run, what we do here will have more effect on how the war ends than anything anyone accomplishes gallivanting about with a bloody knife between his teeth."

"You go gallivanting about with a knife between your teeth and it'll turn bloody in short order, that's for certain," Horton said.

Flight Officer Basil Roundbush came in and poured himself a cup of ersatz tea. His broad, ruddy face lit up in a smile. "Not bad today, by Jove," he said.

"Probably does taste better after you run it through that soup strainer you've got on your upper lip," Goldfarb said.

"You're a cheeky bugger, you know that?" Roundbush took a step toward Goldfarb, as if in anger. Goldfarb needed a distinct effort of will to stand his ground; he gave away three or four inches and a couple of stone in weight. Not only that, Roundbush wore a virtual constellation of pot metal and bright ribbons on his chest. He'd flown Spitfires against the *Luftwaffe* in what then looked to be Britain's darkest hour.

"Just a joke, sir," Horton said hastily.

"You're new here," Roundbush said, his voice amused. "I know it's a joke, and what's more, Goldfarb there knows I know. Isn't that right, Goldfarb?" His expression defied the radarman to deny it.

"Yes, sir, I think so," Goldfarb answered, "although one can't be too certain with a man who grows such a vile caricature of a mustache."

Leo Horton looked alarmed. Roundbush threw back his head and roared laughter. "You *are* a cheeky bugger, and you skewered me as neatly there as if you were Errol Flynn in one of those Hollywood cinemas about pirates." He assumed a fencing stance and made cut-and-thrust motions that showed he had some idea of what he was about. He suddenly stopped and held up one finger. "I have it! Best way to rid ourselves of the Lizards would be to challenge them to a duel. Foil, epée, saber—makes no difference. Our champion against theirs, winner take all."

From one of the tables strewn with jet engine parts, Wing Commander Julian Peary called, "One of these days, Basil, you really should learn the difference between simplifying a problem and actually solving it."

"Yes, sir," Roundbush said, not at all respectfully. Then he turned wistful: "It would be nice, though, wouldn't it, to take them on in a contest where we might have the advantage."

"Something to that," Peary admitted.

Leo Horton bent over a scrap of paper, sketched rapidly. In a minute or two, he held up a creditable drawing of a Lizard wearing a long-snouted knight's helmet (complete with plume) and holding a broadsword. *Prepare to die, Earthling varlet,* the alien proclaimed in a cartoon-style speech bubble.

"That's not bad," Roundbush said. "We ought to post it on a board here."

"That's quite good," Goldfarb said. "You should think of doing portrait sketches for the girls."

Horton eyed him admiringly. "No flies on you. I've done that a few times. It works awfully well."

"Unfair competition, that's what I call it," Basil Roundbush grumped. "I shall write my MP and have him propose a bill classing it with all other forms of poaching."

As helpful as he'd been before, Peary said, "You couldn't poach an egg, and I wouldn't give long odds about your writing, either."

About then, Goldfarb noticed Fred Hipple standing in the doorway and listening to the back-and-forth. Roundbush saw the diminutive group captain at the same moment. Whatever hot reply he'd been about to make died in his throat with a gurgle. Hipple ran a forefinger along his thin brown mustache. "A band of brothers, one and all," he murmured as he came inside.

"Sir, if we can't rag one another, half the fun goes out of life," Roundbush said.

"For you, Basil, more than half, unless I'm sadly mistaken," Hipple said, which made the flight officer blush like a child. But Hipple's voice held no reproof; he went on, "So long as it doesn't interfere with the quality of our work, I see no reason for the badinage not to continue."

"Ah, capital," Roundbush said in relief. "That means I can include my distinguished gray-haired superior in that letter to my MP; perhaps I can arrange to have his tongue ruled a noxious substance and shipped out of the country, or at least possibly rabid and so subject to six months' quarantine."

Julian Peary was not about to let himself be upstaged: "If we inquire at all closely into what your tongue has been doing, Basil old boy, I dare say we'd find it needs more quarantine than a mere six months." Roundbush had turned pink at Hipple's gibe; now he went brick-red.

"Torpedoed at the waterline," Goldfarb whispered to Leo Horton. "He's sinking fast." The other radarman grinned and nodded.

Hipple turned to the two of them. Goldfarb was afraid he'd overheard, but he just said, "How are we coming at fitting a radar set into the Meteor fuselage, gentlemen?"

"As long as we don't fly with fuel tanks in there, we'll be fine, sir," Goldfarb answered, deadpan. Hipple gave him a fishy stare, then laughed—warily—and nodded. Goldfarb went on, "Horton, though, has made some exciting finds about which part of the circuitry controls signal amplitude."

He'd expected that to excite Hipple, who had been almost as eager to learn about radar as he had been to tinker with his beloved jet engines. But Hipple just asked, "Is it something we can apply immediately?"

"No, sir," Horton answered. "I know what they do, but not how they do it."

"Then we'll just have to leave it," Hipple said. "For now, we must be as utilitarian as possible."

Goldfarb and Horton exchanged glances. That didn't sound like the Fred Hipple they'd come to know. "What's up, sir?" Goldfarb asked. Roundbush and the other RAF officers who worked directly under the group captain also paid close attention.

But Hipple just said, "Time is not running in our favor at the moment," and buried his nose in an engineering drawing.

"Time for what?" Goldfarb asked Horton in a tiny voice. The other radarman shrugged. *One more thing to worry about,* Goldfarb thought, and went back to work.

Except for being illuminated only by sunlight, Dr. Hiram Sharp's office in Ogden didn't seem much different from any other Jens Larssen had visited. Dr. Sharp himself, a round little man with gold-rimmed glasses, looked at Jens over the tops of them and said, "Son, you've got the clap."

"I knew that, thanks," Jens said. Somehow he hadn't expected such forthrightness from a doctor in Mormon Utah. He supposed doctors saw everything, even here. After that hesitation, he went on, "Can you do anything about it?"

"Not much," Dr. Sharp answered, altogether too cheerfully for Jens' taste. "If I had sulfa, I could give you some of that and cure you like nobody's business. If I had acriflavine, I could squirt it up your pipe in a bulb syringe. You wouldn't like that for beans, but it would do you some good. But since I don't, no point fretting over it."

The mere thought of somebody squirting medicine up his pipe made Larssen want to cover his crotch with both hands. "Well, what do you have that will do me some good?" he demanded.

Dr. Sharp opened a drawer, pulled out several little foil-wrapped packets, and handed them to him. "Rubbers," he said, as if Jens couldn't figure that out for himself. "Keep you from passing it along for a while, anyway." He pulled out a fountain pen and a book full of ruled pages. "Where'd you get it? You know? Have to keep records, even with everything all gone to hell these days."

"A waitress named Mary, back in Idaho Springs, Colorado."

"Well, well." The doctor scribbled a note. "You do get around, don't you, son? You know this here waitress' last name?"

"It was, uh, Cooley, I think."

"You think? You got to know her pretty well some ways, though, didn't you?" Dr. Sharp whistled tunelessly between his teeth. "Okay, never mind that for now. You screw anybody else between there and here?"

"No." Jens looked down at the rubbers in his hand. Next time he did end up in the sack with a woman, he might use one . . . or he might not. After what the bitches had done to him, he figured he was entitled to get some of his own back.

"Just been a Boy Scout since you got your dose, have you?" Sharp said. "Bet you wish you were a Boy Scout when you got it, too."

"The thought had crossed my mind," Larssen said dryly. The doctor chuckled. Jens went on, "Truth is, I've been moving too much to spend time chasing skirt. I'm on government business."

"Who isn't, these days?" Dr. Sharp said. "Government's just about the last thing left that's working—and it isn't working what you'd call well. God only knows how we're supposed to hold an election for President next year, what with the Lizards holding down half the country and beating the tar out of the other half."

"I hadn't thought of that," Jens admitted. It was an interesting problem from a theoretical point of view: as a theoretical physicist, he could appreciate that. The only even remotely similar election would have been the one of 1864, and by then the North had pretty much won the Civil War; it wasn't invaded itself. "Maybe FDR has volunteered for the duration."

"Maybe he has," Sharp said. "Damned if I know who'd run against him, anyhow, or how he'd campaign if he did."

"Yeah," Jens said. "Look, Doc, if you don't have any medicine that'll help me, what am I supposed to do about what I've got?"

Dr. Sharp sighed. "Live with it as best you can. I don't know what else to tell you. The drugs we've been getting the past few years, they've let us take a real bite out of germs for the first time ever. I felt like I was really doing something worthwhile. And now I'm just an herb-and-root man again, same as my grandpa back before the turn of the century. Oh, I'm maybe a better surgeon than Gramps was, and I know about asepsis and he didn't, but that's about it. I'm sorry, son, but I don't have anything special to give you."

"I'm sorry, too," Larssen said. "Do you think I'm likely to find any other doctors who have the drugs you were talking about?" Even if the acriflavine treatment sounded worse than the disease it was supposed to help, at least it would be over pretty soon. You got gonorrhea for keeps.

"Nobody else here in Ogden, that's for damn sure," Dr. Sharp answered. "We share what we have, not that it's much. Your best bet would be some fellow in a little town who hasn't used up all his supplies and doesn't mind sharing them with strangers passing through. A lot of that kind, though, won't treat anybody but the people they live with. It's like we're going back to tribes instead of being one country any more."

Jens nodded. "I've seen that, too. I don't much like it, but I don't know what to do about it, either." Before the Lizards came, he'd taken for granted the notion of a country stretching from sea to shining sea. Now he saw it was an artificial construct, built on the unspoken agreement of citizens and on long freedom from internal strife. He wondered how many other things he'd taken for granted weren't as self-evident as they seemed to be.

Like Barbara always loving you, for instance, he thought.

Dr. Sharp stuck out a hand. "Sorry I couldn't help you more, son. No charge, not when I didn't do anything. Good luck to you."

"Thanks a bunch, Doc." Larssen picked up the rifle he'd propped in a corner of the office, slung it over his shoulder, and left without shaking hands. Sharp stared after him, but you didn't want to get huffy with somebody packing a gun.

Jens had chained his bicycle to a telephone pole outside the doctor's office. It was still there when he went out to get it. Looking up and down Washington Boulevard (which US 89 turned into when it ran through Ogden), he saw quite a few bikes parked with no chains at all. The Mormons were still a trusting people. His mouth twisted. He'd been trusting, too, and look where it had got him.

"In Ogden goddamn Utah, on my way to a job nobody else wants," he muttered. A fellow in overalls driving a horse-drawn wagon down the street gave him a reproachful stare. He glared back so fiercely that Mr. Overalls went back to minding his own business, which was a pretty good idea any way you looked at it.

A puff of breeze from the west brought the smell of the Great Salt Lake to his nostrils. Ogden lay in a narrow stretch of ground between the lake and the forest-covered Wasatch Mountains. Larssen had grown used to the tang of the sea in his grad school days out in Berkeley, but the Great Salt Lake's odor was a lot stronger, almost unpleasant.

He'd heard you floated there, that you couldn't sink even if you wanted to. *Wish I could throw Yeager in, and find out by experiment,* he thought. *And that waitress, too. I'd hold 'em under if they didn't drown on their own.*

He stowed the chain, swung up onto his bike, and started pedaling north up Washington. He rolled past City Hall Park and the three-story brick pile of the Broom Hotel, with its eighteen odd, bulging windows. Another three-story building, at the corner of Twenty-fourth Street, had the wooden statue of a horse atop it, complete with a tail that streamed in the breeze.

He had to stop there to let a convoy of wagons head west down Twenty-fourth. While he waited, he turned to a fellow on horseback and asked, "You live here?" When the man nodded, Jens went on, "What's the story of the horse?" He pointed to the statue.

"Oh, Nigger Boy?" the man said. "He was a local racehorse, and he'd beat critters you couldn't believe if you didn't see it. Now he's the best weather forecaster in town."

"Oh, yeah?" Jens said. "How's that?"

The local grinned. "If he's wet, you know it's raining; if he's covered with snow, you know it's been snowing. And if his tail's blowin' around like it is now, it's windy out."

"Walked into that one, didn't I?" Jens said, snorting. The last wagon of the convoy creaked by. He started rolling again, and soon passed Tabernacle Park. The Ogden Latter Day Saints Tabernacle was one of the biggest, fanciest buildings in town. He'd seen that elsewhere in Utah, too, the temples much more the focus of public life than the buildings dedicated to secular administration.

Separation of church and state was another of the things he'd taken for granted that didn't turn out to be as automatic as he'd thought. Here in Utah, he got the feeling they separated things to keep outsiders happy, without really buying into the notion that that was the right and proper way to operate.

He shrugged. It wasn't his problem. He had plenty of his own.

Just past the city cemetery, a concrete bridge took him over the Ogden River. By then, he was just about out of town. The scrubby country ahead didn't look any too appetizing. *No wonder the Mormons settled here,* he thought. *Who else would be crazy enough to want land like this?*

He lifted one hand to scratch his head. As far as he was concerned, what the Mormons believed was good only for a belly laugh. Even so, he'd never felt safer in all his travels than he did in Utah. Whether the doctrines were true or not, they turned out solid people.

Is that what the answer is? he wondered: *as long as you seriously believe in* something, *almost no matter what, you have a pretty good chance of ending up okay?* He didn't care for the idea. He'd dedicated his career to pulling objective truth out of the physical world. Theological mumbo-jumbo wasn't supposed to stack up against that kind of dedication.

But it did. Maybe the Mormons didn't know a thing about nuclear physics, but they seemed pretty much content with the lives they were living, which was a hell of a lot more than he could say himself.

Putting your faith in what some book told you, without any other evidence to show it was on the right track, struck him as something right out of the Middle Ages. Ever since the Renaissance, people had been looking for a better, freer way to live. *Jesus loves me/ This I know/ 'Cause the Bible/ Tells me so.* Jens' lip curled derisively. Sunday school pap, that's what it was.

And yet . . . When you looked at it the right way, accepting your religion could be oddly liberating. Instead of being free to make choices, you were free from making them: they'd already been made for you, and all you had to do was follow along.

"Yeah, that's what Hitler and Stalin peddle, too," Larssen said as he left Ogden behind. Thinking was what he did best; the idea of turning that part of him over to somebody else sent the heebie-jeebies running up and down his spine.

People looked up from whatever they were doing when he rode past. He didn't know how they did it, but they could tell he didn't belong here. Maybe somebody'd pinned a sign to him: I AM A GENTILE. He laughed, partly at himself, partly at Utah. Hell, even Jews were gentiles here.

Up ahead on US 89, a fellow was riding a buckboard that had probably been sitting in the barn since his grandfather's day. As Jens put his back into pedaling and whizzed past the gray mule drawing the buggy, the man called out to him: "You headin' up toward Idaho, stranger?"

Stranger. Yeah, they could tell, all right. Larssen almost kept going without answering, but the question hadn't sounded hostile or suspicious. He slowed down and said, "What if I am?"

"Just that you oughta be careful, is all," the man on the buckboard answered. "Them Lizard things, there's some of 'em up there, I hear tell."

"Are there?" Jens said. If he wanted to abdicate responsibility for his life, that would be the way to do it. He had enough reasons for thinking it wouldn't be such a bad thing, either. He owed so many people so much ... "Are there? Good." He turned on the heat, and left the fellow in the buggy staring after him.

The only way Mutt Daniels had ever wanted to see the south side of Chicago was to bring in a big-league team to play the White Sox at Comiskey Park. He'd learned, though, that what you wanted and what life handed you all too often weren't the same thing.

Take the gold bars he wore on his shoulders. He hadn't even changed shirts when he got 'em, because he had only one shirt. He'd just taken off the stripes with somebody's bayonet and put on lieutenant's insignia instead. People from his old squad still called him Sarge. He didn't care. He felt like a sergeant, and the platoon he was leading now had taken enough casualties that it had only two squads' worth of guys, anyway.

One nice thing about turning into an officer was that he got his orders with one less layer of manure on top, and that they gave him a bigger picture of what was going on. As now: Captain Sid Klein (who'd been Lieutenant Klein till Captain Maczek got hit) drew in the dirt between the ruins of what hadn't been fancy apartment buildings even before the Lizards came, saying, "It may not look that way, boys, but the brass says we've got these scaly bastards right where we want 'em."

"Yeah, an' we retreated through half of Illinois to get 'em here, too," Mutt said.

The captain was half his age; damn near everybody in the Army, seemed like, was half his age. Klein said, "You may think you're joking, but you're not. When it comes to maneuver, they got us licked. Their tanks and trucks are faster than ours, and they've got those goddamn helicopters to give it to us in the rear when we're bent over the wrong way. But that

doesn't count for much in city fighting. Here it's just slugging, block by block, body by body."

Mutt's opposite number for the company's first platoon was a skinny midwesterner named Chester Hicks. "Puts a lot of bodies underground," he observed.

"Lord, you can say that again," Daniels said. "I did some of that block-by-block stuff last fall, and it's ugly. Even for war, it's ugly."

Captain Klein nodded. "You bet it is. But the brass don't think the Lizards can afford that kind of slugging any more. When the Germans were blitzing across Russia in '41, they got their noses bloody when they went into the towns, not out on the plains. Maybe it'll be the same way here."

"And if it ain't, so what, 'cause the Lizards drove us back here anyways," Mutt said.

"You're right about that." Captain Klein sighed and ran a hand through his short, curly red hair. "We gotta do all we can, though. Go on back to your boys and give 'em the word."

Mutt's platoon was defending a couple of blocks of East 111th Street. Off to the west was the Gothic ornateness of the Morgan Park Military Academy. Daniels wondered if the cadets were in the line somewhere, the way the boys from the Virginia Military Institute had marched out and fought during the States War. He didn't see anybody who looked like a cadet, but he knew that didn't mean anything. It was a hell of a big fight.

To the east was an American strongpoint on the high ground of Pullman, and then, east of that, the marsh around Lake Calumet. If the Lizards dislodged his boys, he aimed to fall back to the east if he could. North of 111th Street stood the low, ornate buildings that housed the Pullman car shops. He'd fought through blocks of factories before. That was even worse than the trenches had been back in France, but Captain Klein was right about one thing: digging determined troops out of a warren like that would cost the Lizards plenty.

Some of the platoon's foxholes and bits of trench were on the south side of 111th, some on the north. Some were literally in the middle of the street; bombs and shells had torn big holes in the asphalt.

Dracula Szabo waved to Daniels as he came up the broken sidewalk. Szabo was wearing the chevrons Mutt had cut off his own sleeve; Mutt's old squad belonged to him now. Mutt was

sure the men would get on better than most: as long as there were supplies to scrounge, Dracula would figure out how to scrounge them.

Now he said, "Took ya long enough to get back, Sarge—uh, I mean, Lieutenant. You're lucky we still got more o' what I came up with."

"Not more fancy booze?" Mutt said. "I told you a dozen times, if it ain't beer or bourbon, I ain't interested—not real interested, anyways," he amended hastily.

"Better'n booze," Dracula said, and before Daniels could deny that anything was better than booze, he named something that was, or at least harder to come by: "I found somebody's stash o' cigarettes: ten bee-yoo-tee-full, lovely cartons of Pall Malls."

"Goddamn," Mutt said reverently. "How'd you manage that one?"

"C'mere an' I'll show ya." Proud of his exploit, Szabo led Daniels to one of the battered houses on the south side of 111th Street, then down into the basement. It was dark down there, and full of cobwebs. Mutt didn't like it worth a damn. Dracula seemed right at home; he might have been in a Transylvanian castle.

He started stomping on the floor. "It was somewhere right around here," he muttered, then grunted in satisfaction. "There. You hear that?"

"A hollow," Daniels said.

"You betcha," Szabo agreed. He flicked on his Zippo, lifted up the board, pointed. "Lined with lead, too, so it don't get wet in there." He reached in, pulled out a couple of cartons, and handed them to Mutt. "Here, these are the last ones."

The precious tobacco had disappeared into Daniels' pack by the time he went outside again. He didn't know whether Dracula was telling the truth, but if he tried putting the arm on him this time, he was liable never to see any more bounty.

"I want to jam a whole pack in my face all at once," he said, "but I figure the first drag'll be enough to do for me—or maybe do me in, I ain't had one in so long."

"Yeah, I know what you mean," Szabo said. "It's been a while even for me." Mutt gave him a sharp stare at that—had he been holding out on other finds?—but Szabo just gazed back, bland as a preacher. Mutt gave up.

Suddenly he grinned and headed off to a brick cottage a few

hundred yards north of the front lines. The house had a big red cross painted inside a whitewashed circle on the roof and a red cross flag flying on a tall pole above it to show the Lizards what it was.

Before Mutt got halfway there, the grin evaporated. "She don't even smoke," he muttered to himself. "She said as much." He stopped, kicking a stone in irresolution. Then he pressed on, even so. "I know what to do with 'em just the same."

Perhaps because of the warning tokens, the house that held the aid station and several around it were more or less intact, though cattle could have grazed on their lawns. Here and there, untended zinnias and roses bloomed brightly. A medic on the front steps of the aid station nodded to Daniels. "Morning, Lieutenant."

"Mornin'." Mutt went on up the stairs past the tired-looking medic and into the aid station. Things had been pretty quiet the past couple of days; the Lizards didn't seem any too enthusiastic about the street fighting they'd have to do to take Chicago. Only a handful of injured men sprawled on the cots and couches packed into every available inch of floor space.

Lucille Potter bent over one of those men, changing a wound dressing. The fellow sucked in his breath to keep from crying out. When he was able to drive some of the rawness from his voice, he said carefully, "That hurt some, ma'am."

"I know it did, Henry," she answered, "but we have to keep the wound as clean as we can if we don't want it to get infected." Like a lot of nurses, she used the royal *we* when talking to patients. She looked up and saw Daniels. "Hello, Mutt. What brings you here?"

"Got a present for you, Miss Lucille," Daniels said. Henry and a couple of the other guys in the aid station laughed. One of them managed a wheezing wolf whistle.

Lucille's face froze. The look she gave Mutt said, *You're going to have to stay after school, Charlie.* She figured he was trying to get her into the sack with whatever his present turned out to be. As a matter of fact, he was, but he was smart enough to figure out that sometimes the indirect approach was the only one that stood a chance—if any approach stood a chance, which wasn't nearly obvious.

He shrugged off his pack, reached into it, and pulled out one of the cigarette cartons. The wounded dogface who'd let out

the wolf whistle whistled again, a single low, awed note. Mutt tossed the pack underhanded to Lucille. "Here you go. Share these out with the guys who come through here and want 'em."

Flesh clung too close to the bony underpinnings of her face for it to soften much, but her eyes were warm as she surehandedly caught the carton of Pall Malls. "Thank you, Mutt; I'll do that," she said. "A lot of people will be glad you found those."

"Don't give me the credit for that," he said. "Dracula found 'em."

"I might have known," she answered, smiling now. "But you were the one who thought to bring them here, so I'll thank you for that."

"Me too, sir," Henry said. "Ain't seen a butt—uh, a cigarette—in a he—heck of a long time."

"Got that right," the whistler said. "Ma'am, can I have one now, please? I'll be a good boy all the way till Christmas if I can, I promise." He drew a bandaged hand over his chest in a crisscross pattern.

"Victor, you're impossible," Lucille said, but she couldn't keep from laughing. She opened the carton, then opened a pack. The wounded men sighed as she took out a cigarette for each of them. Mutt could smell the tobacco all the way across the room. Lucille went through her pockets. Her mouth twisted in annoyance. "Does anyone have a match?"

"I do." Mutt produced a box. "Good for startin' fires at night—and besides, you never can tell when you might come across somethin'."

He handed the matches to Lucille. She lit cigarettes for her patients. The aroma of fresh tobacco had made his nose sit up and take notice. Real tobacco smoke, harsh and sweet at the same time, was almost too much to bear.

"Give the lieutenant one, too, ma'am," Victor said. "Hadn't've been for him, none of us'd have any." The other wounded soldiers agreed loudly. A couple of them paused to cough in the middle of agreeing; after you hadn't smoked for a while, you lost the knack.

Lucille brought the pack over to him. He took out a cigarette, tapped it against the palm of his hand to tamp down the tobacco, and stuck it in his mouth. He started to reach for the

matches, too, but Lucille had already struck one. He bent down over it to get a light.

"Now this here's livin'," he said, sucking in a long, deep drag of smoke: "gettin' your cigarette lit for you by a beautiful woman."

The GIs whooped. Lucille sent him an I'll-get-you-later look. He ignored it, partly on general principles, partly because he was busy coughing himself—the smoke tasted great, but it felt like mustard gas in his lungs. Spit flooded into his mouth. He felt dizzy, light-headed, the same way he had when he first puffed on a corncob pipe back in the dying days of the last century.

"Cigarettes may be good for morale," Lucille said primly, "but they're extremely unhealthful."

"What with everything out there that can kill me quick or chop me up, I ain't gonna worry about somethin' that's liable to kill me slow," Mutt said. He took another drag. This one did what it was supposed to do; his body remembered all the smoke he'd put into it after all.

The wounded soldiers laughed again. Lucille sent him that narrow-eyed stare again; if they'd been by themselves, she would have tapped her foot on the ground, too. Then a smile slowly stole across her face. "There is something to that," she admitted.

Mutt beamed; any concessions he managed to get from her made him feel grand. He brought his right hand up to the rim of his helmet in a sketched salute. "I'm gonna get back to my platoon, Miss Lucille," he said. "Hope those cigarettes last you a good long time, on account of that'll mean not too many guys gettin' hurt."

"Thank you for your kindness, Mutt," she answered. The soldiers echoed her. He nodded and waved and went outside.

The cigarette was still hanging out of the corner of his mouth, but the medic taking a break on the front steps didn't notice till he caught the smell of smoke. When he did, his head came up as if he were a bird dog taking a scent. He stared in disbelieving envy as Mutt smoked the Pall Mall down to where the coal singed his lips, then stubbed out the tiny butt on the sidewalk.

Everything stayed pretty quiet as Mutt made his way back to his unit. Off in the distance somewhere, artillery rumbled like far-off thunder. A couple of plumes of smoke rose, one over

toward Lake Calumet, the other way off in the west. But for somebody who'd seen more close combat than he wanted to think about, that kind of stuff was hardly worth noticing.

When he got back, he discovered that a lot of his dogfaces had acquired cigarettes, too. Dracula Szabo was looking sleek and prosperous. Mutt suspected he hadn't given his chums smokes for free. Keeping your lieutenant happy was part of the cost of doing business, but the rest of the soldiers were the guys you did business with. As long as nobody in the platoon beefed to Mutt about being gouged, he was willing to look the other way.

He sent scouts out well south of 111th Street to make sure the Lizards wouldn't get away with pulling a fast one after darkness fell. He was sorting through ration cans to see what he'd have for supper when Lucille Potter came up.

Everyone in the platoon who saw her greeted her like an older sister or a favorite aunt or even a mom: she'd been "theirs" for a long time before the shortage of anybody who knew anything about patching up the wounded forced her out of the front line. "Got some smokes for the guys you're taking care of, Miss Lucille," Dracula said.

"That's been taken care of, Bela, thank you, though you're kind to offer." She turned to Mutt, raised one eyebrow. "The ones you brought came from your own supply?"

"Well, yeah, Miss Lucille." Mutt kicked at bits of broken concrete from what had been a sidewalk.

"That just makes it nicer of you," she said, and he felt he'd done his problem on the blackboard right. "To share what Dracula passed on to you in particular—I don't think that that many people would have done as much."

"Wasn't so much of a much," he said, though under dirt and stubble he knew he was turning red. He held out a can of beef stew to Lucille. "Care to stay for some supper?"

"All right." She pulled a can opener out of a pistol-style holster on her belt and made short work of the lid to the stew. She dug in with a spoon, then sighed. "Another cow that died of old age—and the potatoes and carrots with it."

Mutt opened an identical can. He sighed, too, after his first taste. "You're right about that, sure enough. But it does stick to your ribs. Better food than they gave us in France, I'll tell you that. The trick in France was getting the Frenchies to feed you. Then you ate good. They could make horse meat taste

like a T-bone." He didn't know what all he'd eaten Over
There, but he remembered it fondly.

Before Lucille answered, Lizard artillery opened up, off to
the east. Shells whistled in maybe half a mile away—not close
enough to make him dive for cover. He looked over to see if
they'd done any damage. At first he didn't notice anything
new, but then he saw that the ornate water tower that had towered over the Pullman car factory wasn't there any more.

Lucille saw that, too. She said, "I don't think there are many
people—civilian people, I mean—left in Chicago to feed us.
This was the second biggest city in the United States a year
ago. Now it might as well be a ghost town out West somewhere."

"Yeah, I been by some o' those, places like Arizona, Ne-
vada. Whatever they used to be for isn't around any more, and
they aren't, either. Chicago is—or was—about bringin' things
in and shippin' 'em out, or makin' 'em here and shippin' 'em
out. What with the Lizards, that isn't around any more, either,"
Mutt said.

As if to punctuate his words, more shells thumped in, these
a little closer than the ones before. "They're working over the
front line," Lucille Potter observed. "But, Mutt, those ghost
towns out West never had more than a few hundred people, a
few thousand at most. Chicago had more than three million.
Where is everybody?"

"A lot of 'em are dead," he answered bleakly, and she nodded. "A lot of 'em run off, either scared away by the fighting
or on account of their factories couldn't go on working because of the Lizards or 'cause nobody could get food to 'em
here. So one way or another, they ain't here no more."

"You're right," she said. "You have a sensible way of looking at things."

"Yeah?" Mutt glanced around. None of his men was real
close; they were all going about their own business. He lowered his voice even so: "I'm so all-fired sensible, how come I
got stuck on you?"

"Most likely just because we lived in each other's pockets
for too long." Lucille shook her head. "If things were different,
Mutt, it might have worked both ways. Even the way things
are, I sometimes wonder—" She stopped and looked unhappy,
plainly thinking she'd said too much.

Mutt unwrapped a chocolate bar. Like smoking, the simple

action gave him something to do with his hands while he thought. He broke the bar in half and gave Lucille a piece. Then, ever so cautiously, he said, "You mean you might be lookin' at—tryin' a man?" He wasn't sure how to phrase that to keep from offending her, but did his best.

Lucille's face was wary, but she nodded. "*Might* be looking at it is about right, Mutt. I'm closer to it, I think, than I've ever been in my life, but I'd be lying if I said I was ready yet. I hope you can understand that and be patient."

"Miss Lucille, you get as old as I am, some things you ain't in a hurry about like you was when you were younger. It's just that—" Mutt was going to say something about the uncertainty of war arguing against delay, but he never got the chance: the uncertainty of war came to him.

The hideous whistle in the air rose to a banshee shriek. His body realized the Lizard shells were aimed straight at him before his mind did. Without conscious thought, he flattened out just as they landed.

The cluster of explosions—three in all—left him stunned. They picked him up from the ground and threw him back down as if a professional wrestler had body-slammed him. The blast tore at his ears and at his insides; somebody might have been reaching in through his nose and trying to rip out his lungs. Shell fragments whistled and whined all around him.

More shells crashed home, these not quite so close. Through the ringing in his ears and the crazy hammering of his heart, Mutt heard somebody scream. Somebody else—was that Dracula's voice?—shouted, "Miss Lucille!"

Mutt dug his face out of the dirt. "Aw, heck," he said. "They tagged somebody."

Lucille Potter didn't answer. She didn't move. One of those shell fragments that missed Mutt had neatly clipped off the top of her head. He could see her brain in there. Blood ran down into her graying hair. Her eyes were wide and staring. She'd never known what hit her, anyhow.

"Miss Lucille?" Yeah, that was Dracula calling. "We need you over here."

Mutt didn't say anything. He looked at her body, at the ruined Chicago neighborhood that had just had a little more ruin rained onto it. Without intending to, he started to cry. He couldn't remember the last time he'd done that. The tears

rolled down his cheeks and made tiny damp spots on the chewed-up ground. Then they soaked in and were gone as if they'd never existed.

Just like Lucille, he thought, and cried even harder.

☆ **XX** ☆

"Assembled shiplords, I am pleased to report to you that progress in the conquest of Tosev 3, while slower than we hoped when we reached this planet, is nonetheless accelerating," Atvar told the throng of high-ranking males aboard the *127th Emperor Hetto*. After some time down on Tosev 3, being back on his bannership felt good.

"Some details would be appreciated," Shiplord Straha called out.

"I have assembled the shiplords here this day to give those details," Atvar said. He did not show Straha the dislike he felt. Straha was waiting for him to get into trouble, for the campaign to fail. If enough went wrong, the shiplords might turn Atvar out of power and set someone in his place. Straha wanted to be that someone.

Kirel had had such ambitions, too, but Kirel was a good male—he put the cause of the Race ahead of personal ambition. All Straha cared about was himself and the moment. For all the forethought and restraint he showed, he might as well have been a Big Ugly.

To Kirel, Atvar murmured, "The first situation map, please."

"It shall be done, Exalted Fleetlord," Kirel replied. He touched a button on the podium. A large hologram sprang into being behind the two males.

"This is the big northern land area of the main continental mass," Atvar said by way of explanation. "As you will see, we have smashed through the line of defense centered on the town of Kaluga which the SSSR threw up in a last desperate attempt to hold our forces away from their capital, Moskva."

"The fall of this capital will give me particular satisfaction,

568

and not just from the military and strategic perspective," Kirel said. "The regime currently ruling the SSSR came to power, assembled shiplords, as many of you know, after murdering their emperor."

Although most of the males in the hall did know that, a murmur of horror ran through it just the same. Impericide was not a crime the Race had imagined until the Big Uglies brought it to their notice.

"The military and strategic considerations are not to be taken lightly, either," Atvar said. "Moskva being not only an administrative but also a communications hub, its capture will go a long way toward taking the SSSR out of the war. That accomplished, we shall be able to devote more of our resources to the defeat of Deutschland, and shall be able to attack the Deutsche from improved positions."

He enjoyed the buzz of approval that rose from the shiplords; he had not heard that sound often enough while discussing Tosevite affairs. At his hand signal, Kirel pressed the button again and brought up another map.

Atvar said, "This is the island of Britain, which lies off the northwestern coast of Tosev 3's main continental mass. The British have also made themselves into unmitigated nuisances to us. Because the island was so small, we did not reckon it of major significance in our opening attacks. We made the same error with the island empire of Nippon, on the eastern edge of this same land mass. Air strikes have harmed both empires, but not enough. The males and matériel freed up after the defeat of the SSSR will allow us to mount full-scale invasions of all these pestilential islands."

"Permission to speak, Exalted Fleetlord?" Straha called.

"Speak," Atvar said. Straha hadn't asked for permission the last time. The list of successes and anticipated successes must have served notice to him that he wasn't likely to be fleetlord any time soon.

Straha said, "With the Deutsche still holding northern—'France' is the proper geographic designation, is it not?—can we invade this Britain with reasonable hope of success, even assuming the SSSR drops out of the fight against us?"

"Computer models show our probability of success as being higher than seventy percent under the circumstances you describe," Atvar answered. "With the SSSR still in the war and forcing us to continue to expend resources to suppress it,

chances for a successful invasion of Britain drop to slightly below fifty percent. Shall I send you a printout of the analysis, Shiplord?"

"If you please, Exalted Fleetlord."

That was the most politeness Atvar had heard from Straha in a long time. The fleetlord signaled Kirel for the next map. When it appeared, Atvar said, "This, as you see, illustrates our position in the northern part of the lesser continental mass, particularly in our fight against the empire, or rather not-empire, known as the United States. The major urban center called Chicago, which eluded us in our previous attack, has now been reached by our armies; its reduction is only a matter of time."

Kirel said, "With other major moves planned, Exalted Fleetlord, can we afford the drain on our resources a hard-fought city campaign would entail?"

"My judgment is that we can," Atvar answered. Kirel might be a good and loyal male, but he was also too cautious and conservative to suit the fleetlord. Straha, on the other hand, fairly bounced in his seat, so eager was he to mix it up with the Big Uglies. Yes, he might have been a Tosevite himself.

"If the fleetlord decrees it shall be done, then of course it shall be done," Kirel declared. Atvar knew he would have to go back into cold sleep if he wanted to live long enough to hear Straha make the same pledge.

The fleetlord signaled to Kirel once more, and a new map replaced the one of the northern portion of the lesser continental mass. This one was far more detailed: it showed the street plan of a seacoast town and enough of the hinterland to depict a tumbledown ruin on a hilltop not far away.

"I admit, assembled shiplords, that the situation portrayed here lacks the large-scale strategic importance of those I have previously outlined," Atvar said. "Nonetheless, I shall set it forth for you because it also illustrates, in a different way, the progress we are making against the Tosevites. Have security briefings brought the Big Ugly named Skorzeny to the attention of everyone gathered here at this time?"

"The Tosevite terrorist? Yes, Exalted Fleetlord," one of the males said. Atvar was comfortably certain some of them had paid no attention to their security briefings. Some of them never did. Well, no matter, not today. As far as Skorzeny was concerned, it would soon be no matter ever again.

Atvar resumed: "One of our operatives has set up an elab-

orate scheme in this town—it is known as Split—to lure the vassal state known as Croatia out of the empire of Deutschland and toward acceptance of the dominion of the Race. If this succeeds, well and good. But the effort has deliberately been kept to a small scale, to let the Deutsche get the notion they can check it by similarly modest means. We have now confirmed that Skorzeny is operating in the area. All that remains is for our skilled operative to close the trap on him. I expect that to be completed within days. Without this Skorzeny, the Big Uglies will not be able to cause us nearly so much trouble."

The assembled shiplords didn't quite burst into cheers, but they came close. Atvar basked in the warm glow of their approval as if he were lying on a sandbank under summer sunshine back on Home.

Heinrich Jäger mooched through the streets of Split. In old Yugoslav Army boots, baggy civilian pants, and faded gray Italian Army tunic, he fit in perfectly. Half the men in town wore a mixture of military and civilian garb. Even his craggy features belonged here; he could have been a Croat or a Serb as easily as a German. He ambled right past a couple of Lizard patrols. They didn't turn so much as an eye turret his way.

The tavern across the street from the south wall of Diocletian's palace had seen better days. It had once had a window in front, but the square of plywood nailed where the window had been was weathered almost gray; it had been up there a long time.

Jäger opened the door, slid inside, shut it behind him in a hurry. The fellow behind the bar was about fifty, going gray, with bushy eyebrows that grew together above his bony beak of a nose. Jäger hadn't learned much in the way of Serbo-Croatian, but he had a little Italian. In that language, he said, "Are you Barisha? I hear you've got some special brandy in stock."

The bartender looked him over. "We keep the special stuff in the back room," he said at last. "You want to come with me?"

"*Sì, grazie,*" Jäger said. A couple of old men sat at a table in the corner, drinking beer. They didn't look up when Jäger accompanied Barisha into that back room.

The back room was considerably bigger than the one in

front; it took up not only the rear of Barisha's tavern but also of the shuttered shops to either side. It needed to be large, for it was packed with poorly shaven men in a motley mixture of clothes. One of the tallest of them grinned at him, his teeth shining in the candlelight. "Thought you'd never get here," the fellow said in German.

"I'm here, Skorzeny," Jäger answered. "You can take that makeup off your cheek now, if you care to."

"I was just getting used to going without the scar, too," the SS man said. "Come here—I've saved one of the *Fallschirmjägergewehrs* for you." He held the weapon up over his head.

Jäger pushed his way through the crowd. Some of the men carried infantry rifles, others submachine guns. A few, like Skorzeny himself, had paratroop rifles—automatic weapons that fired a full-sized cartridge from a twenty-round box magazine. Jäger eagerly took the FG-42 and several full magazines from Skorzeny. "This is as good as anything the Lizards carry," he said.

"Better than what the Lizards carry," Skorzeny said. "More powerful cartridge."

Not inclined to argue the point, Jäger said, "When are we going to go down the hole?" He pointed to a black pit that, from the look of it, might have led straight down to hell. It didn't; it led to the underground galleries inside the wall to Diocletian's palace.

"Five minutes by my watch after Captain Petrovic and his merry boys start their attack on the palace," Skorzeny answered. "Five minutes," he repeated in Italian and Serbo-Croatian. Everybody nodded.

A couple of men came in after Jäger. Skorzeny passed them submachine guns. Sneaking the weapons into Split had been harder than getting the men in, but Skorzeny and his local contacts, whoever they were, had managed the job.

A thuttering roar filled the back room, followed by another and another. In Italian, somebody yelled, "Start watching the time," to Skorzeny.

He shook his big head. "That's not fighting. That's just some of the Lizards heading off in helicopters." He grinned again. "So much the better. That leaves fewer of them for us to deal with."

* * *

Even up front with the pilot and weapons officer, the helicopter was noisy. Drefsab didn't care to think about what it was like for the eight males back in the troop compartment. He waited until all three of his assault aircraft had taken off before he turned to the pilot and said, "On to the ruined castle at Klis. The Deutsche and the Croats there have been plotting against us long enough. This time we bag Skorzeny and all his henchmales."

"To the castle at Klis," the pilot repeated, as if he were hearing the order for the first time rather than something like the hundred and first. "It shall be done, superior sir."

The town of Split shrank as the helicopter gained height. Drefsab found it remarkably ugly: bricks and stucco and red tile roofs were nothing like the concrete and glass and stone of Home. The ruined castle, already growing larger in the distance as the pilot shoved the collective forward, struck him as even uglier.

"Why are you so hot to be rid of this particular Big Ugly, superior sir?" the pilot asked.

"Because he is the biggest nuisance on this entire nuisance of a planet," Drefsab answered. "He is responsible for more grief to the Race than any other three Big Ugly males I can think of." He didn't go into detail; the pilot had no need to know. But his sincerity was so obvious that the pilot turned one eye turret to look at him for a moment before returning full attention to the flight.

The ruined gray stone pile of Klis drew swiftly nearer. Drefsab waited for the Tosevites hiding within to open up with small-arms fire. Satellite and aerial reconnaissance both claimed they had no antiaircraft artillery in there. He hoped the males in recon knew whereof they spoke.

He wished he'd tasted ginger before he got into the helicopter. His body craved it. But he'd restrained himself. Ginger would take away his doubts, and against a foe as wily as Skorzeny he wanted them all in place.

"Shouldn't they be shooting at us by now?" the weapons officer asked. The castle of Klis seemed very quiet and peaceful, as if no raiders had lived in it for thousands of years. Drefsab hissed softly. Thousands of years ago, the castle probably hadn't even been built. Tosev 3 was a *new* world.

He answered the male's question: "You never can tell with Big Uglies. They may be lying low, hoping to make us think

they aren't really there. Or they may have some sort of ambush set."

"I'd like to see them try, superior sir," the weapons officer said. "It'd be a sorry-looking ambush after it bit down on us."

Drefsab liked his confidence. "Let's give the place a sandstorm of fire, to make sure we don't have any trouble getting our males on the ground."

"It shall be done." The weapons officer and the pilot spoke together. The pilot called on the radio to his opposite numbers in the other two helicopters. One of them dropped to the ground to unload its soldiers. The other, along with the helicopter in which Drefsab flew, popped up into the air and started pasting the castle of Klis with rockets and machine-gun bullets. No return fire came. As soon as the eight males had scuttled out of the landed helicopter, it rose into the air to join the barrage, while the second one descended to disgorge its soldiers.

Drefsab took a firm grip on his personal weapon. He intended to go down there with the fighting males, and to be certain Skorzeny was dead. There were whole little Tosevite empires that had caused the Race less trouble than that one Deutsch male. Stolen nuclear materials, Mussolini kidnapped to spew propaganda against the Race, a landcruiser lifted out from under everyone's snout at Besançon, and who could guess how many other crimes lay at his feet.

Males scrambled away from the second helicopter, opening up with their personal weapons to add to the fire that made whatever defenders huddled in Klis keep their heads down. The pilot started to lower Drefsab's helicopter to let off the males it carried, but before he could grab the collective, the radio speaker taped to his hearing diaphragm began to chatter.

"You'd better hear this, superior sir," he said, and touched the control that fed the incoming signal to the main speaker in the flight cabin.

Through engine noise and ordnance, a male's voice squawked, "Superior sir, the outwalls of our base are under attack by a motley crew of Big Uglies with rifles and other small arms. Their forcing a breach seems unlikely, but our defending males have taken some casualties." Some of the noise of firing, Drefsab realized, was coming out of the speaker.

"If the situation is not urgent, I shall continue neutralizing this target before I return," he answered. His mouth fell open

in a laugh of amusement and relief. So Skorzeny had chosen this moment to attack, had he? Well, he would pay for it. The fighting males he'd left here would be destroyed. The Race would keep a garrison in Klis from now on. Control in this area would expand at the expense of the Deutsche, and one Drefsab, ginger-tasting addict though he was, would rise in prestige and importance to the leaders of the Race's forces on Tosev 3.

"Shall I proceed as planned, superior sir?" the pilot asked.

"Yes," Drefsab said, and the helicopter lost altitude. Drefsab ran a battery check on the radio gear implanted in his helmet. If the main base needed to get in touch with him, he wanted to ensure that he wasn't cut off. That was the only special precaution he took against Skorzeny's attack.

Ever so gently, the helicopter's wheels touched ground. Drefsab clapped the helmet onto his head and hurried back into the fighting compartment to exit with the rest of the males.

When Jäger fought, he was usually closed up inside the thick steel shell of a panzer, which muffled the racket all around him. The tavern's wall didn't do nearly so good a job as that; the rifle and machine-gun fire from and at the wall of Diocletian's palace all sounded as if it were aimed right at him. The other soldiers and guerrillas in the back room of Barisha's tavern took no special notice, so he assumed they were used to this kind of din.

Through it, Skorzeny said, "Two minutes!" in German, Italian, and Serbo-Croatian. In German alone, he went on, "Do we have all the men with the automatic weapons closest to the hole?"

The question was rhetorical; he'd bullied people into place before the shooting outside started. With his FG-42, Jäger was one of the lucky few who would lead the way through the tunnel. Around the troops with automatic rifles clustered those who carried submachine guns; the men who bore ordinary bolt-action rifles would bring up the rear.

"One minute!" Skorzeny said, and then, what seemed to Jäger a year or two later, "Now!" He was the first one to plunge into the tunnel.

Jäger went in either fourth or fifth; in all the jostling, he wasn't sure which. The dim light behind him vanished, leaving

him surrounded by absolute black. The toe of his boot caught the heel of the man in front of him. He stumbled and almost fell. When he straightened up, his head bumped the low ceiling. Dirt showered down; some got inside his collar and slid down his back. He wished he had a helmet—for more reasons than keeping the dirt off. He also wondered how Skorzeny was faring in the tunnel—the SS man, who lacked only eight or ten centimeters of two meters, probably had to bend himself double to move at all.

Though the tunnel couldn't have been more than fifteen meters long, it seemed to go on forever. It was narrow as well as low-ceilinged; whenever his elbow bumped a wall, Jäger felt as if it were closing in on him. He was afraid someone would start screaming in the confining dark. Some people couldn't even stand being shut up in a panzer with the hatches dogged. The tunnel was a hundred times worse.

He realized he could see the silhouette of the soldier in front of him. A couple of paces later, he emerged in a dusty storeroom illuminated only by lights from other rooms, none of them especially close. All the same, after the tunnel it seemed almost noonday bright.

"Spread out, spread out," Skorzeny urged in a hissing whisper. "Give the men behind you room to get out." When the whole force had emerged, Skorzeny thumped Jäger on the back. "The colonel here, being an expert in archaeology, knows where the stairs are."

By now, the SS man—and several others among the raiders—had studied the underground maze enough to know it as well as Jäger, if not better. He appreciated the nod even so: it reminded the men that his word counted next after Skorzeny's. He said, "I just don't want to find a lot of Lizards down here. If we have to fight underground, we won't get up to the surface and sweep them off the walls."

"That's what Petrovic's diversion is for," Skorzeny said: "to flush all of them up to the top so they won't notice us till too late—for them."

Jäger knew that was what the diversion was for. He also knew diversions weren't always diverting enough to do what they were supposed to do. He kept quiet. They'd find out soon enough how well this one had worked.

Skorzeny turned his attention to the group as a whole. "My advice is simple: shoot first." He repeated the phrase in Italian

and Serbo-Croatian. The men he led just grinned—they'd figured that one out for themselves. Skorzeny grinned, too. "Come on, you lugs." As he'd been first into the tunnel, he was first out of the storeroom.

Jäger had never seen the underground maze of hallways and chambers in Diocletian's palace, not till now. But he moved through it confidently, counting off turns under his breath as he trotted along. A blast of heat came from one big room he passed: the Lizard barracks. If ever the raiders would be discovered down here, this was the place.

No shouts, no hisses, no gunfire. There ahead were the stone stairs. Skorzeny bounded up them three at a time. The rest of the men, Jäger still near the front of the pack, ran at his heels. The panzer colonel's stomach knotted. An eye turret turned at the wrong moment and the assault could still turn into a slaughter.

Trying to match the Lizards' swiveling eyes, his head twisted every which way as he reached the top of the stairs. The aliens were still banging away from the wall, but the bulk of the baptistry hid them from him—and him from them.

Skorzeny used hand signals to divide the raiders into two groups and to show no one had better argue against Jäger's leading one of them. He pointed right and then forward to show Jäger's group was to go around the baptistry, then led his own group to the left.

"Come on," Jäger hissed to his men. He trotted at their fore: if you wanted to impress anybody who'd already seen Skorzeny in action, you'd better lead from the front. Otherwise, your men wouldn't follow you for long.

He waved the group to a halt as they came to the corner of the baptistry. FG-42 at the ready, he stepped out into the narrow street that led north to the wall. As he did so, he heard Skorzeny's group start firing.

A Lizard a couple of hundred meters ahead whirled at that unexpected sound. It caught sight of Jäger. Before it could bring up its rifle, he cut it down. "Forward!" he shouted, and ran up the street. The pound of boots on cobblestones behind him said he'd brought his troops with him.

Personal weapon at the ready, Drefsab scrambled over a big gray stone and dropped down into the enclosed area of the castle of Klis. His feet scrunched on dry weeds. Several other

males were already there, scurrying around and nervously checking anything that could hide a Big Ugly.

Thus far, they'd found precisely nothing. Drefsab was disappointed—he wanted Skorzeny dead and proved dead. But sealing off this place and taking possession of it for the Race wasn't bad in and of itself, either. *High time to expand the foothold in Croatia beyond the town of Split,* he thought.

"They've *been* here," a male said, pointing to the litter scattered wherever it wasn't visible from Split. "Why aren't they here now?" He sounded indignant; to the Race, the world by rights should have been a neatly predictable place.

"They may have timed their attack in town to match ours here," Drefsab answered. "Their intelligence is revoltingly good." That didn't surprise him overmuch; only natural for beings of one kind to stick together against those of another, especially when the latter were trying to conquer them.

He badly wanted a taste of ginger. He'd all but promised the fleetlord that he'd bring back Skorzeny's head in a clear block of acrylic resin. Would Atvar be content if presented with a mere strategic gain rather than said head? Unless Skorzeny got himself killed and identified back in Split, it looked as if Drefsab would have to find out. Ginger wouldn't change that, but would keep him from having to think about it for a while.

Another male waved to him from a stone-lined hole in the ground. "Over here, superior sir," he said. "Looks like the Big Uglies that haunted this place made their home underground."

Drefsab shone an electric torch into the hole. Even without it, he would have been sure this was a Big Ugly den: the Tosevites' rank, meaty smell filled the scent receptors on his tongue. He played the torch back and forth, then let out a low hiss. "This place will hold a lot of Big Uglies."

"That's true, superior sir," the male agreed. "Where do you suppose they've all gone?"

"Some of them back to their villages, I suppose, and some into town to attack our walls," Drefsab answered. He stuck out his tongue. The words did not taste right. From all he'd learned of Skorzeny, such a simpleminded frontal assault seemed out of character.

"If you want us to set up camp in this pile of stones, superior sir, I hope you don't expect *us* to use that place down there." The soldier also stuck out his tongue, and waggled it in derision and disgust. "It stinks."

"That it does," Drefsab said. "And no, I promise you won't have to set up your sleeping gear down there—not until we fumigate, anyhow." His mouth and the other male's dropped open in a laugh.

The speaker built into his helmet suddenly screamed at him: "Superior sir! Superior sir! We're under attack not just from outside the wall but also from within! Somehow a large party of Big Uglies managed to get inside the walls without being noticed. We're taking heavy casualties. Need for assistance urgent in the extreme!"

Drefsab made a noise like a pressure cooker forgotten on top of a hot stove. "None of them slipped away to their villages," he said when coherent speech returned. The male beside him stared in confusion; he hadn't heard the desperate call. Drefsab went on, "They all went down into Split." No, Skorzeny wasn't simpleminded at all.

"Who? The Big Uglies?" the male asked, still trying to figure out what was going on.

Drefsab ignored him. He waved to the soldiers scattered over the castle of Klis. "Back to the helicopters!" he shouted. "Quick as you can!"

A virtue of the Race was obedience to superiors. The males neither hesitated nor asked questions. They ran toward the helicopters as fast as their legs would take them. Behind the armor-glass windscreens, the pilots waved frantically. They'd got the message, too, then.

Drefsab dashed up to the cockpit. "To the fortress!" he snarled. "Skorzeny will pay for this. Oh, how he will pay."

All the pilot said was, "It shall be done." He pulled up on the collective. The helicopter sprang into the air. It wheeled within its own diameter and darted back toward Split. Only then did the pilot say, "May I ask your plan, superior sir?"

"Use our firepower to blast the Big Uglies out of the fortress," Drefsab answered. "They may have smuggled in men and rifles; I refuse to believe they could carry antiaircraft weapons into Split without our noticing."

"No doubt you are right about that, superior sir," the weapons officer said with all proper deference. "But I see I must remind you that we expended most of our munitions in the bombardment of that empty castle. We have little left to use back at the city."

Drefsab stared at him in blank dismay. After a moment, he

said, "Keep going anyhow. I'll think of something." The ground blurred by under the helicopter. He didn't have much time.

Jäger had fought house to house, street to street, in towns and cities in the Ukraine. He'd hated it then. Even with a panzer wrapped around him, it was deadly dangerous work. Doing it in nothing but these ragged clothes struck him as clinically insane. "You'd never get me to join the infantry now," he muttered, sheltered in the doorway of a building near the wall. "I did that the last war."

Bullets sprayed past him, biting chips out of stone and brickwork. They stung when they hit; if you got one in the eye, it could blind you. The Lizards all had automatic weapons and, by the way they hosed fire around, they might have had all the ammunition in the world, too. Jäger was too aware that he didn't. The FG-42 was a wonderful weapon, but it went through magazines in a hurry.

Several men in front of him shot back at the Lizards. That was the signal for him and half a dozen fellows with him to leapfrog forward past them. Leaving the doorway was as hard as getting out of a trench and springing across no-man's-land had been in France a generation ago. But fire and move was how you fought as a foot soldier if you wanted any kind of chance of living to do it again.

He bounded along the cobblestones, bent over as if his belly griped him to make himself as small a target for the Lizards as he could. The men firing hadn't suppressed all the enemies ahead. Bullets struck sparks from the cobbles close by his feet and ricocheted away at crazy angles.

He'd had a new doorway in mind when he started his dash. He threw himself into it, panting as if he'd just run a marathon rather than a few meters. A moment later, another fellow squeezed in behind him. In Slavic-accented German, he asked, "Think any of the things are inside here?"

Jäger made a sour face. "We're getting up close to their position. It could be."

"I have grenade," the Croat said, pulling a German potato-masher model from his belt. He tried a thick wooden door. The knob turned in his hand. That was plenty to make Jäger suspicious, and the Croat as well. He unscrewed the grenade's pro-

tective cap, yanked the igniter, opened the door, chucked in the grenade, and slammed it again.

The blast made Jäger's head pound. Fragments rattled off the door. Jäger flung it open once more, sprayed a quick burst into the chamber to catch any Lizards the grenade had missed. Then he dove behind a massive oaken desk that had probably sat there since the days of the Austro-Hungarian empire.

The Croat ran to the next door in, fired a few rounds from his submachine gun, then peered around the corner. That was the right order in which to do things. He grunted. "I think we maybe are lucky."

"Better for us to shoot up the place and not need to than to need to and not do it," Jäger said. The Croat nodded. Taking no chances even so, Jäger crawled back to the outer doorway.

Just as he got there, a blast like a 500-kilo bomb went off to the north. When he ever so cautiously looked out of the doorway, he saw a great hole in the outwall to Diocletian's palace. The antiquarian in him lamented. The soldier rejoiced— Skorzeny's raiders had distracted the Lizards enough to let Petrovic's men lay the explosives next to the wall.

He sprang to his feet, stormed forward. The best time to advance was while the enemy was momentarily stunned. Now the Lizards would have a doubly hard time: they'd have to fight Skorzeny's men and keep Petrovic's followers from getting through the breach in the wall. This mad raid just might work.

Then a stuttering roar filled the sky. Jäger dove for the nearest cover he could find. The Lizard helicopters were coming back.

Split was in flames, with smoke mounting fast into the sky. Drefsab hissed in astonished disbelief—who could have imagined a town could go from peace to ruin in so short a time? "Oh, Skorzeny, how you will pay," he whispered.

Even as the helicopters reached the outskirts of Split, a big explosion sent a great cloud of dust leaping into the air. "They've blown up part of the wall," the pilot said in dismay, scanning the electronically amplified vision display. "How did they get all these munitions into town under our muzzles?"

"Some have probably been there all along—the Big Uglies were fighting among themselves when we got here, you know. As for the rest, they're good at it," Drefsab said bitterly. "We

didn't X-ray every bit of every single animal cart going in, and now we're paying the price. But if we did that everywhere, we wouldn't have enough males to do anything else. The fault here is mine; I accept it."

That made him feel virtuous. Otherwise, it did nothing to change matters. Split kept on burning. Radio calls for help kept pouring in. Every one of them reported some fresh Tosevite gain. "What do we do, superior sir?" the weapons officer asked, fixing Drefsab with worried eyes. "We have no rockets left, and our machine-gun ammunition is low."

Worries about conserving ammunition, Drefsab thought, *had cost the Race victories.* If they lost here, it wouldn't be on account of that. "If we don't expend what we have, our ground position in Split falls," he said. "Next to that, ammunition—or, come to that, three helicopters—counts for nothing. Maybe we can kill enough of the Big Uglies to make the rest break contact and give our males a chance. Let's go try."

"It shall be done, superior sir." Neither the pilot nor the weapons officer sounded enthusiastic. Drefsab couldn't blame them for that—even if the Big Uglies didn't have antiaircraft guns, the helicopters were still going into danger: if they'd armored all the wires and hydraulics heavily enough to protect them from rifle fire, the aircraft would have been too heavy to fly. But the pilot didn't hesitate. He radioed Drefsab's orders to his two comrades.

The three helicopters skimmed low over the rooftops of Split. They started taking fire long before they got to the rectangular stone wall the Race had used as a perimeter for its base. Some bullets went *spanng!* off armored sections; others punched through sheet metal in less vital spots.

Drefsab quickly realized the ground fire away from the fortress came from Big Uglies who just happened to have rifles and pistols. It turned into a storm of bullets when the aircraft approached the fighting zone. "Shall I return fire against the Tosevite males outside the walls, superior sir?" the weapons officer asked.

"No," Drefsab said. "The ones who got inside are even more important. If we have only limited ammunition, we'll use it at the point of decision."

Again, the pilot relayed Drefsab's will to the males flying the other two helicopters. All three machines hovered above the narrowing area inside the walls that the Race still held. The

machine guns roared. Drefsab felt a savage surge of satisfaction, almost as good as ginger, as Big Uglies twisted and fell under assault from the air.

"We'll get them out of there yet!" he cried.

Another doorway. This time, Jäger didn't think it would be cover enough. He kicked in the door and rolled inside, automatic rifle at the ready. No Lizard shot at him. He crawled toward a north-facing window.

Outside, death reigned. He'd hated the Lizards' helicopters when he was in a panzer. Their rockets smashed through armor as if it were pasteboard. Against infantry, their machine guns were similarly destructive.

The fire wasn't aimed. It didn't need to be. As he'd seen in France in the last war, machine guns put out so many bullets that if this one didn't get you, the next one would. Without luck amounting to divine intervention, anyone caught on the street without cover would be dead.

The helicopters' noses seemed to be spitting flame. Jäger squeezed off a burst at the nearest of them, then rolled away as fast as he could. He had no idea whether he'd damaged the helicopter, but he was sure as need be that the Lizards would have spotted his muzzle flashes.

Sure enough, bullets battered the wall. Some pierced the stones; others sent shards of glass from the broken window flying like shell fragments. Something bit Jäger in the leg. Blood began to soak into his trousers. It wasn't a flood. He cautiously tried putting weight on the leg. It held. He might not run as fast as usual for a while, but he could move around pretty well. He headed up to the second story of the building. When he got there, he planned on firing another burst at the helicopters. It would also let him deliver plunging fire against the Lizards at the base of the wall. He was still on the stairs when the firing from the helicopters died away: first one machine gun fell silent, then a second, then a third.

His first thought was to rush—or come as close as he could to rushing with a sliver of glass in his leg—back down and join the final attack that would sweep away the last of the Lizards. His second thought was that his first one was less than smart. The Lizards surely had imagination enough to stop shooting and see how many men they could fool into thinking they'd run out of ammunition.

He went up to the second floor after all. The helicopters still hung menacingly in the air, but they weren't shooting. Men on the ground— Skorzeny's forces and Petrovic's both—kept blazing away at them, though. Jäger fired, too. This time the Lizards didn't shoot back.

"Maybe you *are* out of ammo," he muttered to himself. Even so, he didn't hurry downstairs and rush out into the street. Maybe they *weren't* out of ammo, too.

Drefsab turned to the weapons officer in anger and dismay when the machine gun stopped firing. "Is that all of it?" he demanded.

"Not quite, superior sir, but almost all," the fellow answered. "I've reserved the last couple of hundred rounds. Whatever decision you make on how or if we use them, though, I suggest you make it quickly. We already have one male wounded back in the fighting compartment, and we can't stay under such intense fire indefinitely. The odds of any one bullet doing us significant damage are low, but we are encountering a great many bullets."

That was an understatement. The patter and clatter of incoming rounds all but deafened Drefsab. He said, "The area close to the wall is too built up to let us land and take aboard those of our males who still live." He added the interrogative cough to that, though it looked pretty plain to him. Maybe the pilot would tell him he was wrong.

But the pilot didn't. "We could fit the fuselages of our machines down there, superior sir, but the rotors—" He didn't finish the sentence, but Drefsab had no trouble finishing it for him. The pilot went on, "We do still have fuel enough to return to Italia, where the Race holds unchallenged control." He sounded hopeful.

"No," Drefsab said flatly. He reached into a pouch on his belt, took out a vial of ginger, and tasted. The pilot and weapons officer gaped at him. He didn't care. Atvar the fleetlord knew he was addicted, so what these low-grade officers thought mattered not at all to him. He said, "We shall not flee."

"But, superior sir—" The pilot broke off, perhaps because of drilled subordination, perhaps because he couldn't decide whether to protest Drefsab's tactics or the vial of ginger he still held so blatantly in his left hand.

Ginger certainty and ginger cunning rushed through Drefsab. "The Big Uglies can't have brought all that many males into the fortress," he said. "If we land behind them, where we took off, we can catch them between two fires, as they've done with our males down there."

Now the pilot had something concrete to which to object: "But, superior sir, we've twenty-three effectives at most; I don't know if anyone aboard the other helicopters is wounded."

"Thirty," Drefsab corrected, his voice cold. "Pilots and weapons officers have their personal weapons, and I have mine. If we can drive the Big Uglies from the fortress, we may be able to hold on here long enough for reinforcements to arrive."

The pilot was still staring. Drefsab deliberately looked away from him, daring him to protest further. To underline his contempt, he tasted again. Ginger filled him with the burning urge to *do something*, and with the confidence that if he just acted boldly, everything would turn out fine.

"Back to the landing area," he snapped.

"It shall be done, superior sir," the pilot said miserably. He relayed Drefsab's command to the other two helicopters.

When the helicopters darted away, Jäger hoped with all his heart they were fleeing. But, though the engine noise diminished, it didn't vanish.

"Where are they going?" he muttered suspiciously. He couldn't believe they would just up and fly away, not when they'd done such a job of working over the humans' positions moments before. He tried to think himself into the head of the Lizard commander—Drefsab, Skorzeny had said his name was. The exercise had proved useful over and over again in the Soviet Union. If you could figure out what the other fellow needed to do, you were halfway to keeping him from doing it.

All right, assume this Drefsab was no fool. He wouldn't be, not if he'd made the Lizards shape up in Besançon (Jäger wondered how his regiment was faring; the news out of France— and then out of Germany—hadn't been good) and been entrusted with swinging the Croats away from Germany.

What to do, then? Those big Lizard helicopters carried soldiers as well as munitions. What would Skorzeny do if he had some men he could put anywhere he wanted? The answer to

that formed of itself in Jäger's mind: he'd stick them up the enemy's rear. He'd done just that, here in Split.

Next question was, would Skorzeny figure that out for himself? He'd better.

Jäger couldn't get in touch with him by radio or field telephone. But Skorzeny was no fool, either. He'd think of something like that . . . Jäger told himself hopefully.

The panzer colonel wondered if he ought to head back toward the rear. Before he made up his mind, he decided to evaluate the position he already held. He moved toward the window, peered out from well back in the room so as not to make himself an obvious target for the Lizards by the wall.

He needed only a couple of seconds to realize he was in too good a place to abandon. He could see four or five Lizards no more than a hundred meters from him, and they didn't know he was there. He switched the FG-42 from automatic to single-shot, raised it, breathed out, and touched the trigger on the exhale. The automatic rifle bucked against his shoulder. One of the Lizards toppled over bonelessly.

Even single-shot, the weapon was a lot faster than a bolt-action rifle. All you had to do was pull the trigger again. He missed a shot at his second Lizard, but his next round was on the way before the creature could react to the one before. He didn't think he made a clean kill on that Lizard, but he was sure he'd hit it. Getting it out of the fight would definitely do.

Instinct made him move away from the window after that. Hardly had he done so when bullets came searching for him. He nodded to himself. If you pushed things too far, you paid for it.

Firing broke out off to the south, at first mostly Lizards' weapons, then men's answering back. Jäger nodded again. Drefsab was trying to retrieve the situation, all right. He might have been a nasty little alien from the black depths of unknown space, but he knew what fighting was all about.

Drefsab had been trained as an intelligence officer. When he got to Tosev 3, he'd never expected to meet combat face-to-face. His brief forays in a landcruiser at Besançon hadn't come close to preparing him for what infantry fighting—especially in the heart of a town—was like.

The helicopters had remained under fire all the way to the landing area from which they'd taken off what seemed like a

couple of years before. A male was hit exiting through the troop compartment door, and another couple as they skittered toward cover. The weapons officers had used up the last precious rounds in the helicopter machine guns trying to suppress the Big Ugly defenders.

Drefsab had never felt so naked as when sprinting across the cobblestones toward a pile of rubble. Not even ginger's bravado could make him believe he was invulnerable to the bullets cracking past him. But he reached the rubble without getting hit. He sprawled down behind it and started shooting back.

He didn't need long to realize only a couple of Tosevites were defending against the males of the Race. The soldiers' commander figured out the same thing at the same time. His orders crackled in the speaker inside Drefsab's helmet. Some of the males sprayed bullets at the Big Uglies to make them keep their heads down. Others moved to gain positions from which they could fire at the enemy from the side. Soon the Tosevites were down. The males of the Race ran forward.

They hadn't taken the Big Uglies as much by surprise as Drefsab had hoped. The trouble was, they were fighting in too small a space. An alert commander—and no one had ever faulted the Tosevites for that—could quickly pull some of his males from the fighting near the wall and send them to meet the new threat. And the males of the Race trapped against the wall had trouble exploiting that because of the danger from the Big Uglies in the buildings on the other side.

No sooner had that thought crossed Drefsab's mind than an explosion to the north made him sure another piece of the wall had just gone down. He hissed in dismay. His detachment couldn't hold the fortress by itself. If the males he was trying to rescue perished, Split would fall.

"Hurry!" he shouted. "We have to fight through the Tosevites and reach them."

Two of the helicopter pilots were already down. They'd joined the attack bravely enough, but they had even less notion of how to fight on the ground than Drefsab did. And so many bullets were in the air that the most skilled soldier, if he was unlucky, would fall as readily as anyone else.

Crouched in a doorway, Drefsab tasted again. He needed the spirit ginger brought him. If it drained away, he wouldn't be able to keep on fighting. So he told himself, at any rate.

One of the buildings ahead, or more than one, had caught fire. Smoke filled the narrow street. A determined male—especially one who was full to bursting with ginger—could take advantage of the cover. Drefsab thought there would be plenty of hiding places ahead. He burst out of the doorway, sprinted up the street.

He changed directions every few steps. No one would get a good shot at him if he could help it. The thick smoke made him gasp and cough; nictitating membranes slid across his eyes to protect them from the stinging stuff.

Through the smoke, he didn't see the Tosevite until they almost ran into each other. He hadn't heard him, either; the din of battle made sure of that. Even for a Big Ugly, this male was enormous. He could have made two of Drefsab.

Weapons were great equalizers, though. As Drefsab swung his toward the Tosevite, he noted that the fellow had a scar on his face, hidden not quite well enough by paint and powder. He started to shout, "Skorzeny!"

But Skorzeny had a weapon, too, a rifle of unfamiliar make. It spat a stream of fire like the automatic rifles of the Race. Something hit Drefsab a series of hammer blows. He felt only the first one or two.

Lizard jets screamed overhead. Thunderous blasts ripped across the area Diocletian's palace had enclosed. Huddled in a doorway, Jäger prayed the building wouldn't fall down on top of him. He didn't think much would be left of the palace by the time the bombers were done. Sixteen hundred years of history, blown to hell in an afternoon.

The jets unloaded their last bombs and flew away. Stunned, battered, but with no worse wounds than that chunk of glass in his leg, Jäger slowly got to his feet. He looked around at the smoking ruins of what had been a scenic little port. "It's ours," he said.

"And a good thing, too," somebody behind him answered. He whirled. That hurt, but his battle reflexes permitted nothing less. There stood Skorzeny. Sweat had made his makeup run, but his face was so covered with grime and soot that the scar wasn't easy to spot, anyhow. He went on, "If we'd bogged down there, they might have been able to fly in reinforcements to their soldiers here. That wouldn't have been much fun."

"Not even a little bit," Jäger said fervently. He looked

around at the wreckage—and the carnage. "They're tougher than I thought they were."

"They can fight." Skorzeny looked around. If the devastation bothered him, he didn't show it. "We found out the Russians were tougher than we thought, too, but we would have licked them in the end." Nothing seemed to get him down. Give him a military job, no matter how bizarre or impossible it seemed, and he'd go out and do it.

A Croat aimed his rifle at a Lizard prisoner. *"Halt!"* Jäger shouted as loud as he could—if the Croat understood any German, that would be it.

"Stop that!" Skorzeny echoed, even louder than Jäger. "What the bleeding hell do you think you're doing, you shitheaded syphilitic cretinous puddle of dog puke?"

The Croat understood German, all right. He swung his rifle away from the frightened, cringing Lizard—and halfway toward Skorzeny. "I get rid of this thing," he said. "Maybe I get rid of you first."

Most of the men on the battered streets, most of the men who had done the fighting in Split, were Croats, not Germans. A lot of them started drifting over toward Skorzeny and Jäger. They didn't quite aim their weapons at the German officers, but they had them ready. Among them was Captain Petrovic. He looked as ready to get rid of the Germans as any of his troops.

Jäger said, "Shooting Lizards is wasteful. They know so much that we don't. Better to keep them alive and squeeze it out of them."

The Croat with the rifle spat. "This I care for what they know. I know I enjoy killing this one, so I do it."

"If you kill that Lizard, I'll kill you," Skorzeny said, as casually as if he were sitting over coffee with the Croat. "If you try to kill me, I'll kill you. Colonel Jäger is right, and you damn well know it."

The Croat's scowl got blacker yet. He did not move his rifle another centimeter in Skorzeny's direction, though. Jäger gestured to the Lizard: a peremptory *come-here*. The Lizard skittered over to stand beside him.

"Good," Skorzeny said softly. He turned to Petrovic, raised his voice: "Order your men to round up the rest of the Lizards and bring them here. From what I've heard, we should have twenty or so who surrendered, plus about as many wounded. I

want them all there—immediately. They're as big a haul as this whole town."

"You want," Petrovic said coldly. "So what? This is the Independent State of Croatia, not Germany. I give orders here, not you. What do you do if I tell you no?"

"Shoot you," Skorzeny answered. "If you think I can't take you out along with your cheerful friend over there"—he jerked his chin at the Croat who had threatened the Lizard—"before your bully boys bring me down, you're welcome to find out if you're right."

Petrovic was no coward. Had he been a coward, he wouldn't have thrown himself into the middle of the fighting that had just ended. Skorzeny stood, almost at ease, waiting for him to do whatever he would do. Jäger did his best to match the SS man's show of confidence. Matching his gall was something else again.

After a long, long pause, Petrovic barked orders in Serbo-Croatian. One of his men shouted a protest. Petrovic screamed abuse at him. Jäger hadn't picked up much of the local language, but the invective sounded impressive as hell.

The Croats straggled away. A few minutes later, they started coming back with Lizard prisoners, first the males who had given up as the fighting ebbed and then, on makeshift litters, the crudely bandaged ones wounds had forced out of combat. Their sounds of pain were unpleasantly close to the ones men made.

"I wasn't sure you'd get away with that," Jäger murmured to Skorzeny.

"You have to make it personal," Skorzeny whispered back. "These bastards take *everything* personally. I just played their game with them, and I won." His smile was smug as he added one final word: "Again."

Georg Schultz said, "I figured I'd get into Moscow one way or another, but I never guessed what those ways would be—first you flew me in, and now I'm retreating into it."

"It isn't funny." Ludmila Gorbunova tore a chunk of black bread with her teeth. Someone handed her a glass of ersatz tea. She gulped it down. Someone else gave her a bowl of *shchi*. She gulped the cabbage soup, too. While she refueled herself, groundcrew men took care of her aircraft, pouring pet-

rol into it, loading on light bombs, and stowing the belts of machine-gun ammunition Schultz had filled.

"I never said it was funny," the German said. He looked worn unto death, his skin gray rather than fair, his hair and beard unkempt, grease on his face and tunic—no one had much chance to wash these days. Purple pouches lay under his eyes.

Ludmila was sure she was no more prepossessing. She couldn't remember the last time she'd had more than a couple of hours of sleep at a stretch. Even before the Kaluga line began to unravel, she'd been desperately overtaxed. Since then . . .

The cry was *buy time.* When the Germans neared Moscow in 1941, old men, boys, and tens of thousands of women had dug trenches and antitank obstacles to slow their progress. They were out again. How much good their barriers would do against the Lizards when stronger ones had already failed was questionable, but the Soviet capital would not fall without as much of a fight as the Soviet people could put up.

"Ready, Comrade Pilot," one of the groundcrew men shouted.

Ready or not, Ludmila put down the bowl of *shchi*—thin, watery stuff, without ham or salami, and without enough cabbage, too—and got up. She climbed wearily into the U-2 biplane. Georg Schultz said, "I hope you come back. I hope we're still here when you come back."

Nikifor Sholudenko walked up just in time to hear the panzer-gunner-turned-mechanic say that. The NKVD man bristled. "The penalty for defeatist talk is death," he said.

Schultz rounded on him. "What's the penalty for killing the only decent technician this base has?" he retorted. "You do that, you do more to make your side lose than I do by talking."

"This may be true," Sholudenko said, "but there is no fixed sentence for it." His hand fell to the Tokarev pistol he wore on his hip.

Ludmila knew each of them wanted the other dead. Loudly, she said, "Spin my prop, one of you. Save your war with each other until after we've held off the Lizards." *If we hold off the Lizards,* she added to herself. Had she said that aloud, she wondered whether Sholudenko would have come down on her for defeatism. Probably not. He didn't want to see her dead—only naked.

The NKVD man and the ex-*Wehrmacht* sergeant both sprang toward the front of the *Kukuruznik*. Schultz got there first. When he yanked at the prop, Sholudenko had to back away; walking into a spinning prop blade would kill you as surely as a pistol, and a lot more messily.

Buzz! The prop caught; the five-cylinder radial engine spat out acrid exhaust fumes. Ludmila released the brake. The U-2 bounded over the rough airstrip (not really a strip at all, just a stretch of field), picking up speed. Ludmila gave it more throttle, eased the stick back. The ugly little biplane clawed its way into the air.

Even in flight, the U-2 did not go from duckling to swan. Yet, as a mosquito will bite and escape where a horsefly gets noticed and swatted, *Kukuruzniks* came back from missions more often than any other Soviet planes.

Not much was left of Kaluga. Ludmila flew over the outskirts of the industrial town. The Germans had wrecked part of it when they took it in their drive on Moscow in fall 1941, and the Russians had wrecked more when they took it back later the same year. Whatever they'd left standing, the Lizards had knocked down over the last couple of weeks.

The front lay north of Kaluga these days. The Lizards had cleared a few of the north-south streets through the town so they could move supplies forward. Lorries, some of their manufacture, others captured from the Nazis or the Soviets (some of those Russian-made, others American) rolled along, as if no enemies were to be found for a thousand kilometers.

I may not be much of an enemy, but I'm the best the Soviet Union has here, Ludmila thought. She worked her flaps and rudder, heeled the U-2 over into an attack run on the lorry column she'd spotted.

No one in the column spotted her until she was close enough to open fire. "The mosquito stings!" she hollered, and whooped with glee as Lizards bailed out of the lorries and dove for cover.

Some of them didn't bail out—some shot back. Bullets snarled past the U-2. Ludmila kept boring in. She pulled the bomb-release handle. The aircraft suddenly got lighter and more maneuverable as weight and drag fell away.

She gunned it for every ruble it was worth, although, with the *Kukuruznik*, such things were better measured in kopecks. The biplane shook slightly as the bombs exploded behind it.

Ludmila looked back over her shoulder. Some of the lorries were burning merrily. Between them and the little bomb craters she'd made, the Lizards wouldn't be moving much forward on that route for a while.

Pity the U-2 could carry only light bombs. "I don't just want to block off one road for a while," Ludmila said, as if a witch might hear and grant her wish. "I want to keep the Lizards from using the whole city."

What she wanted and what she could do, sadly, were not one and the same. She flew over Kaluga at rooftop height—not that many of the gutted houses and factories still had roofs—shooting at whatever targets she saw. None was as good as that first line of lorries.

The Lizards shot back. After a while, they started shooting the instant she came into range, sometimes before she opened up herself. *Time to go,* she thought. The Lizards used many more radios than the Red Army did; they must have spread the word that she was buzzing around.

She got out of Kaluga as fast as she could, ducking down between ruined buildings to make herself as nearly unhittable as she could. It must have worked; she escaped with no more damage than a few bullet holes through the fabric covering of the U-2's wings and fuselage.

She flew off toward the west; the Lizards had to know the air base lay in that direction, and flying into the afternoon sun made her a harder target for gunners in Kaluga. But she zig-zagged around a half-burned grove of plum trees and then headed east and north toward the front. With not much standing between the Lizards and Moscow, she had to do all she could, however little that was, to stem the tide of their advance.

Wreckage littered the ground north of Kaluga, the all-too-familiar signs of a Soviet army in disintegration: shattered tanks and armored cars, trench lines reduced to craters by artillery, unburied corpses in khaki. Even zooming by at full throttle, she gagged at the stink of death and decay that filled her nostrils.

Far less Lizard wreckage was strewn about. The Lizards made a point of salvaging their damaged equipment, which accounted for some of the disparity. But most of it sprang from their losing a lot less than their opponents had. That had been a constant of the war since its earliest days.

Artillery boomed and flashed, off toward the east. The Lizards' guns outranged those of the Red Army, too; from north of Kaluga, they could all but reach Moscow. Ludmila flew toward the guns. If she could shoot up the crews, that would be a good part of a day's work.

Though retreating, the Red Army hadn't given up the fight. She heard screams in the air; a ragged pattern of explosions tore up a square kilometer of ground not far ahead of the *Kukuruznik*. "*Katyushas!*" she cried in high glee. The rockets were some of the best weapons the Soviets had. Unlike more conventional artillery, they were easily portable, and a flight of them not only did a lot of damage but also spread terror.

Some Lizards were just emerging from their hidey-holes after the *Katyusha* salvo when Ludmila flew by. She opened up with her machine gun. The Lizards dove back into cover. She hoped some of them weren't fast enough to reach it, but was gone before she could be sure.

As she approached the Lizards' artillery position, she got down below treetop height. Some of those gun stations had tank chassis with antiaircraft cannon mounted in place of big guns protecting them. If she spotted one of those, she'd sheer off. A hit or two from their shells would turn the U-2 to kindling. She deliberately thought about it in terms of the aircraft rather than herself.

Jinking, weaving, Ludmila came up on the Lizard guns. She didn't see any of the antiaircraft tanks, so she bored in. "*Za rodina!*—For the motherland!" she shouted as her thumb came down on the firing button.

Lizard gunners scattered before her, like cockroaches across a kitchen floor when someone comes in with a lamp. Unlike cockroaches, some of them snatched up personal weapons and shot back. Muzzle flashes might have looked pretty as fireflies, but they meant the Lizards were trying to kill her. More thrumming noises spoke of bullets making hits on the *Kukuruznik*, but the little biplane kept flying.

Ludmila glanced at her fuel gauge. She had a bit more than half a tank left. *Time to head for home,* she thought regretfully; she hadn't had such a good day shooting up the Lizards in a long time. But she also knew about stretching her luck. If she tried to go on until she found one more perfect target, she was only too likely to make one instead.

"There will be more tomorrow," she said, and then laughed

at herself. She wouldn't wait for tomorrow to go out again: as soon as she had more fuel, more bullets, more bombs, she'd be in the air again. They kept using you until they used you up. Then they found somebody else—if they could.

What happens when they run out of everybody? she wondered. The answer came back stark: *then we lose.* It hadn't happened yet, no matter how black things sometimes looked. But when the Germans drove on Moscow in 1941, they'd faced Russian winter and fresh troops from Siberia. Now it was the beginning of summer, and if the Red Army had any fresh troops left, Ludmila didn't know where they might come from.

"Which means the veterans like me will just have to carry the load a while longer," she said, adding after a moment, "if any veterans like me are left alive." There was Georg Schultz, but he didn't really count; he'd started the war on the wrong side. Colonel Karpov had been through the whole thing, but he was more a military administrator than a fighting soldier. Ludmila had nothing against that; Karpov ran his air base as well as a man could in the chaos of a losing war. But it removed him from her list, or what would have been her list had she had anyone to put on it.

She wondered how Heinrich Jäger was doing these days. He'd been in it from the start, even if he came from the wrong side, too. The memory of their brief time together in Germany the winter before seemed faded, unreal. What would she do if she ever saw him again? She shook her head. For one thing, it wasn't likely. For another, how could she know till it happened?

Down on the ground, a man in a khaki Red Army uniform waved his cap as she flew by. She was back over Soviet-held territory now, well away from the bulge northeast of Kaluga where the Lizards were forcing their way toward Moscow. They were concentrating their effort on that push, and had loaded the bulge with troops and weapons. Ludmila dared hope the air base would still be operating when she got back to it.

The U-2 bucked in the air, as if it had taken a hit from an antiaircraft gun. Then the aircraft steadied. Ludmila swore; were Red Army gunners shooting at her again? She checked the sketchy instrument panel. Everything looked fine, though

she had trouble reading some of the dials because of the black shadow her head and shoulders cast on them.

She accepted that for a moment. Then she remembered she was flying into the sun.

Even as she wheeled the *Kukuruznik* through a tight turn, that impossible shadow began to fade. She looked back to see what could have made it; her first guess was a Lizard bomb. The shock wave from a bomb might have made her think she was hit.

But while the flash from a bomb might have given her a momentary shadow, it could hardly have lasted long enough for her to notice it. She figured that out while her head turned ahead of the plane's motion to see what had happened.

Because she checked the near distance first, she didn't spot anything right away. Then she raised her eyes a little higher, and felt like the prize fool of all time. The fireball that had printed her shadow on the instrument panel was already dissipating, but not the enormous cloud of dust and wreckage it had raised.

"*Bozhemoi*—My God," she whispered. That growing cloud had to be at least twenty-five kilometers off to the east, maybe more. It towered thousands of meters into the air, glowing yellow and pink and salmon and colors for which she had no name. Its shape took her back to fall days before the war, when she and her family would hunt mushrooms in the woods outside Kiev.

"*Bozhemoi*," she said again, when what it had to be hit her like a kick in the stomach: one of the Lizards' explosive-metal bombs, the kind that had flattened Berlin and Washington, D.C. She moaned, back deep in her throat—were the Lizards sealing the *rodina*'s doom by raining such destruction on it?

The cloud climbed and climbed. Five thousand meters? Six? Eight? She couldn't begin to guess. She simply watched, stunned, flying the U-2 with hands and feet but without much conscious thought. Little by little, though, as her wits began to work once more, she noticed where the bomb had gone off: not ahead of the Lizards' lines, to clear the road to Moscow, but right at the front or a little behind it—at a spot where it would hurt the Lizards much more than the Soviet forces opposing them.

Had the Lizards dropped it in the wrong place? She hadn't thought they made mistakes like that. Or, somehow, had the

scientists of the Soviet Union devised an explosive-metal bomb of their own?

"Please, God, let it be so," she said, and didn't feel the least bit guilty about praying.

Reports flooded onto Atvar's desk: video of the nuclear explosion from a spy satellite, confirmation (as if he needed any) from those ground commanders lucky enough not to have been incinerated in the blast, sketchy preliminary lists of units that hadn't been so lucky.

Kirel came in. Atvar grudged him a brief glance from one eye turret, then went back to plowing through the reports. "Forgive me, Exalted Fleetlord," Kirel said, "but I have a formal written communication from Straha, shiplord of the *206th Emperor Yower.*"

"Give it to me," Atvar said. Males used formal written communication only when they wanted to get something down on the record.

The communication was to the point: it read, EXALTED FLEETLORD, NOW WHAT?

"You've looked at it?" Atvar asked Kirel.

"Yes, Exalted Fleetlord," the shiplord answered glumly.

"All right. Reply on the usual circuits—no need to imitate this."

"Yes, Exalted Fleetlord," Kirel repeated. "And the reply is?"

"Very simple—just three words: I don't know."

Continue the most exciting
journey through the past
in all of science fiction!

Harry Turtledove's

WORLDWAR: UPSETTING THE BALANCE

For a look at the third installment
in the WORLDWAR series
from the master of alternate history,
read on...

Mordechai Anielewicz huddled in a deep foxhole in the
middle of a thick clump of bushes. He hoped it would give him
good enough cover. The forest partisans must have miscalculated
how much their raids were annoying the Lizards, for the aliens
were doing their best to sweep them into oblivion.

Firing came from ahead of him and from both sides. He
knew that meant he ought to get up and move, but getting up
and moving struck him as the quickest and easiest way to get
himself killed. Sometimes sitting tight was the best thing you
could do.

The Lizards were worse in the woods than even an urban
Jew like him. He heard them skittering past his hole in the
ground. He clutched his Mauser. If the Lizards started poking
through the bushes that shielded him, he'd sell his life as dear as
he could. If they didn't, he had no intention of advertising his
existence. The essence of partisan warfare was getting away to
fight another day.

Time crawled by on leaden feet. He took a Wehrmacht-
issue canteen from his belt, sipped cautiously—he had less water
than he wanted, and didn't know how long it would have to
last. Going out to find more didn't strike him as a good idea, not
right now.

The bushes rustled. Sh'ma yisroayl, adonai elohaynu, adornai ekhod ran through his head: the first prayer a Jew learned, the last one that was supposed to cross his lips before he died. He didn't say it now; he might have been wrong. But, as silently as he could, he turned toward the direction of the rustling. He was afraid he'd have to pop up and start shooting; otherwise the Lizards could finish him off with grenades.

"Shmuel?" A bare thread of whisper, but an unmistakably human voice.

"Yes. Who's that?" The voice was too attenuated for him to recognize it, but he could make a good guess. "Jerzy?"

By way of reply, he got a laugh as discreet as the whisper had been. "You damn Jews are too damn smart, you know that?" the partisans' point man answered. "Come on, though. You can't hang around here. Sooner or later, they'll spot you. I did."

If Jerzy said staying around wasn't safe, it probably wasn't. Anielewicz scrambled up and out of his hidey-hole. "How'd you notice me, anyway?" he asked. "I didn't think anybody could."

"That's just how," the point man answered. "I looked around and I saw an excellent hiding place that didn't look like it had anyone it in. I asked myself, who would be clever enough to take advantage of that kind of place? Your name popped into my head, and so—"

"I suppose I should be flattered," Mordechai said. "You damn Poles are too damn smart, you know that?"

Jerzy stared at him, then laughed loud enough to alarm them both. "Let's get out of here," he said then, quietly once more. "We'll head east, in the direction they're coming from. Now that the main line of them is past, we shouldn't have any trouble slipping away. They're probably aiming to drive us against some other force they have waiting. That's how the Nazis hunted partisans, anyhow."

"We caught plenty of you Pole bastards, too," someone behind them said in German. They both whirled. Friedrich sneered at them. "Poles and Jews talk too fucking much."

"That's because we have Germans to talk about," Anielewicz retorted. He hated the arrogant way Friedrich stood there, feet planted on the ground as if he'd sprung from it, every line of his body proclaiming that he thought himself a lord of creation, just as if it had been the winter of 1941, with the Lizards nowhere to be seen and the Nazis bestriding Europe like a colossus and driving hard on Moscow.

The German glared at him. "You've got smart answers for everything, don't you?" he said. Anielewicz tensed. A couple of more words to Friedrich and somebody was liable to die right

there; he resolved he wouldn't be the one. But then the Nazi went on, "Well, that's just like a Jew. You're right about one thing—we'd better get out of here. Come on."

They headed east down a game track Mordechai never would have noticed for himself. Just as if they were raiding rather than running, Jerzy took the point and Friedrich the rear, leaving Anielewicz to move along in the middle, making enough noise to impersonate a large band of men.

Friedrich said, "This partisan business stinks." Then he laughed softly. "Course, I don't remember hunting you bastards was a whole lot of fun, either."

"Hunting us bastards," Mordechai corrected him. "Remember which side you're on now." Having someone along who'd been on both sides could be useful. Anielewicz had theoretical knowledge of how partisan hunters had operated. Friedrich had done it. If only he weren't Friedrich...

Up ahead a few meters, Jerzy let out a hiss. "Hold up," he said. "We're coming to a road."

Mordechai stopped. He didn't hear Friedrich behind him, so he assumed Friedrich stopped, too. He wouldn't have sworn to it, though; he hadn't heard Friedrich when they were moving, either.

Jerzy said, "Come on up. I don't see anything. We'll cross one at a time."

Anielewicz moved up to him as quietly as he could. Sure enough, Friedrich was right behind him. Jerzy peered cautiously from behind a birch, then sprinted across the rutted, muddy dirt road and dove into the brush there. Mordechai waited a few seconds to make sure nothing untoward happened, then made the same dash and dive himself. Somehow Jerzy had done it silently, but the plants he dove into rustled and crackled in the most alarming way. His pique at himself only got worse when Friedrich, who would have made two of him, also crossed without producing any noise.

Jerzy cast about for the game trail, found it, and headed east once more. He said, "We want to get as far away from the fighting as we can. I don't know, but—"

"You feel it too, eh?" Friedrich said. "Like somebody just walked over your grave? I don't know what it is, but I don't like it. What about you, Shmuel?"

"No, not this time," Anielewicz admitted. He didn't trust his own instincts, though, not here. In the ghetto, he'd had a fine-tuned sense of when trouble was coming. He didn't have a feel for the forest, and he knew it.

The Del Rey Internet Newsletter...

A monthly electronic publication, posted on the Internet, GEnie, CompuServe, BIX, various BBSs, and the Panix gopher (gopher.panix.com). It features hype-free descriptions of books that are new in the stores, a list of our upcoming books, special announcements, a signing/reading/convention-attendance schedule for Del Rey authors, "In Depth" essays in which professionals in the field (authors, artists, designers, sales people, etc.) talk about their jobs in science fiction, a question-and-answer section, behind-the-scenes looks at sf publishing, and more!

Online editorial presence: Many of the Del Rey editors are online, on the Internet, GEnie, CompuServe, America Online, and Delphi. There is a Del Rey topic on GEnie and a Del Rey folder on America Online.

Our official e-mail address for Del Rey Books is
delrey@randomhouse.com

Internet information source!

A lot of Del Rey material is available to the Internet on a gopher server: all back issues and the current issue of the Del Rey Internet Newsletter, a description of the DRIN and summaries of all the issues' contents, sample chapters of upcoming or current books (readable or downloadable for free), submission requirements, mail-order information, and much more. We will be adding more items of all sorts (mostly new DRINs and sample chapters) regularly. The address of the gopher is gopher.panix.com

Why? We at Del Rey realize that the networks are the medium of the future. That's where you'll find us promoting our books, socializing with others in the sf field, and—most importantly—making contact and sharing information with sf readers.

For more information, e-mail
delrey@randomhouse.com

Book(s) purchased:_____

_____

_____

I understand I may choose one free book for each Dell Romance book purchased (plus applicable postage and handling). Please send me the following:

(Write the number of copies of each title selected next to that title.)

☐ **MY ENEMY, MY LOVE**
Elaine Coffman
From an award-winning author comes this compelling historical novel that pits a spirited beauty against a hard-nosed gunslinger hired to forcibly bring her home to her father. But the gunslinger finds himself unable to resist his captive.

☐ **AVENGING ANGEL**
Lori Copeland
Jilted by her thieving fiancee, a woman rides west seeking revenge, only to wind up in the arms of her enemy's brother.

☐ **A WOMAN'S ESTATE**
Roberta Gellis
An American woman in the early 1800s finds herself ensnared in a web of family intrigue and dangerous passions when her English nobleman husband passes away.

☐ **THE RAVEN AND THE ROSE**
Virginia Henley
A fast-paced, sexy novel of the 15th century that tells a tale of royal intrigue, spirited love, and reckless abandon.

☐ **THE WINDFLOWER**
Laura London
She longed for a pirate's kisses. . . even though she was kidnapped in error and forced to sail the seas on his pirate ship, forever a prisoner of her own reckless desire.

☐ **TO LOVE AN EAGLE**
Joanne Redd
Winner of the 1987 *Romantic Times* Reviewer's Choice Award for Best Western Romance by a New Author.

☐ **SAVAGE HEAT**
Nan Ryan
The spoiled young daughter of a U.S. Army General is kidnapped by a Sioux chieftain out of revenge and is at first terrified, then infuriated, and finally hopelessly aroused by him.

☐ **BLIND CHANCE**
Meryl Sawyer
Every woman wants to be a star, but what happens when the one nude scene she'd performed in front of the cameras haunts her, turning her into an underground sex symbol?

☐ **DIAMOND FIRE**
Helen Mittermeyer
A gorgeous and stubborn young woman must choose between protecting the dangerous secrets of her past or trusting and loving a mysterious millionaire who has secrets of his own.

☐ **LOVERS AND LIARS**
Brenda Joyce
She loved him for love's sake, he seduced her for the sake of sweet revenge. This is a story set in Hollywood, where there are two types of people—lovers and liars.

☐ **MY WICKED ENCHANTRESS**
Meagan McKinney
Set in 18th-century Louisiana, this is the tempestous and sensuous story of an impoverished Scottish heiress and the handsome American plantation owner who saves her life, then uses her in a dangerous game of revenge.

☐ **EVERY TIME I LOVE YOU**
Heather Graham
A bestselling romance of a rebel Colonist and a beautiful Tory loyalist who reincarnate their fiery affair 200 years later through the lives of two lovers.

Dell

TOTAL NUMBER OF FREE BOOKS SELECTED _____ X $1.00
= $_____ (Amount Enclosed)

Dell has other great books in print by these authors. If you enjoy them, check your local book outlets for other titles.

FREE FROM DELL

with purchase plus postage and handling

Congratulations! You have just purchased one or more titles featured in Dell's Romance 1990 Promotion. Our goal is to provide you with quality reading and entertainment, so we are pleased to extend to you a limited offer to receive a selected Dell romance title(s) *free* (plus $1.00 postage and handling per title) for each romance title purchased. Please read and follow all instructions carefully to avoid delays in your order.

1) Fill in your name and address on the coupon printed below. No facsimiles or copies of the coupon allowed.

2) The Dell Romance books are the only books featured in Dell's Romance 1990 Promotion. Any other Dell titles are not eligible for this offer.

3) Enclose your original cash register receipt with the price of the book(s) circled plus $1.00 per book for postage and handling, payable in check or money order to: Dell Romance 1990 Offer. Please do not send cash in the mail.
Canadian customers: Enclose your original cash register receipt with the price of the book(s) circled plus $1.00 per book for postage and handling in U.S. funds.

4) This offer is only in effect until March 29, 1991. Free Dell Romance requests postmarked after March 22, 1991 will not be honored, but your check for postage and handling will be returned.

5) Please allow 6-8 weeks for processing. Void where taxed or prohibited.

Mail to: Dell Romance 1990 Offer
P.O. Box 2088
Young America, MN 55399-2088

NAME_____

ADDRESS_____

CITY_____STATE_____ZIP_____

BOOKS PURCHASED AT_____

AGE_____

(Continued)